"*A Shadow in Summer* is rich in well-dev[elop]ters. Although the first of a quartet follow[ing]stands on its own as one of the best fantasies in years."

—*The Denver Post*

"The second volume in Daniel Abraham's Long Price Quartet delivers a mix of subtle intrigue, illicit murder, and ill-fated romance, and further explores one of the most unique and engaging systems of magic in contemporary fantasy."

—Jacqueline Carey, bestselling
author of *Kushiel's Justice*

"*A Shadow in Summer* is a thoroughly engrossing debut novel from a major new fantasist. The world of the Khaiem, the andat, and the poets makes a fresh and original setting for a poignant, human tale of power, heartbreak, and betrayal that kept me reading from first page to last. Abraham's varied cast of characters are a lively and interesting bunch, and he tells their stories in an elegant style that reminded me by turns of Gene Wolfe, Jack Vance, and M. John Harrison, while still remaining very much his own. So when is the next volume coming out?"

—George R. R. Martin, #1 *New York Times*
bestselling author

"*A Betrayal in Winter* features Daniel Abraham's gift for complex, realistic characters in a setting that has none of the tinsel or derivative, secondhand feel of so much fantasy. This series is a major accomplishment; *A Betrayal in Winter* more than fulfills the promise of *A Shadow in Summer*, and I look forward eagerly to reading the next."

—S. M. Stirling, author of *The Sky People*

TURN THE PAGE FOR MORE RAVES.

"Compellingly plotted and elegantly written, *A Betrayal in Winter* is a very successful continuation of what promises to be a significant and original contribution to fantasy literature."

—*Scifi.com*

"Reader, be warned: If you open Daniel Abraham's *A Shadow in Summer*, he will lead you into a strange, seductive world of beatings and poets and betrayals, intrigues you do not fully understand, wars you cannot stop, and places you are not sure you want to go. Intricate, elegant, and almost hypnotically told, this tale of gods held captive will hold you captive, too."

—Connie Willis, multiple Hugo– and
Nebula Award–winning author

"*A Shadow in Summer* is one of the most elegant and engaging fantasies I've read in years, based on an intriguing, original premise. I eagerly await the remaining volumes in Daniel Abraham's Long Price Quartet."

—Jacqueline Carey, bestselling
author of *Kushiel's Dart*

"*A Betrayal in Winter* is a novel to inhabit, full of multifaceted characters whose public poses often belie their inner motivations, and full also of hope that men and women can be equal and that systems which degrade us can be changed."

—*BookPage*

"Most 'otherworldly' fantasy is anything but, yet here Abraham has created an evocative world and culture that seems very strange and alien, yet still somehow feels real. An impressive start."

—*Kirkus Reviews* on *A Shadow in Summer*

"While I'm tempted to compare Abraham's writing to the darkness and psychological subtlety of some notable postwar Brits or that of George R. R. Martin (who aptly provides one of the blurbs), that wouldn't quite capture the feel of this book. There's something genuinely *new* here, and it will be fascinating to see how the Quartet develops."

—*Locus* on *A Shadow in Summer*

"Abraham has an interesting set of distinctive characters, a good sense of plot, and a fresh take on several of the usual fantasy tropes. He's also willing to examine real-world issues a lot of popular fantasy doesn't look at—abortion and violence against women, for example. It'll be interesting to see where subsequent volumes of this series take us."

—*Asimov's Science Fiction* on *A Shadow in Summer*

"Abraham's debut is impressive. The world-building is solid and internally consistent, and it's incredibly interesting. The varied characters—from the malicious and ambitious Liat to the secretive Itani—are fascinating and original. Readers looking for something new and a little offbeat will enjoy this book."

—*RT Book Reviews*

"A very nice debut, and an enjoyable read that has me very keen on reading [*A Betrayal in Winter*]; as for *A Shadow in Summer*, I take a pose of admiration."

—*FantasyBookSpot.com*

"Daniel Abraham gets better with every book. *A Shadow in Summer* was among the strongest first novels of the last decade, and *A Betrayal in Winter* is a terrific second book."

—George R. R. Martin, #1 *New York Times* bestselling author

TURN THE PAGE FOR MORE RAVES.

"From the opening lines, *A Shadow in Summer* carries us into an exotic, fantastic, yet utterly convincing world. Bravo! Drawing heavily on Eastern cultures, the author has created a mannered society in which every tone and gesture possesses special meaning. The writing is extremely visual. The setting is neither Japan nor China, however. Together with the multidimensional characters and wealth of fascinating detail, this place exists only in the extraordinary imagination of Daniel Abraham. I look forward to the next book in the series."

—Morgan Llywelyn, #1 *New York Times*
bestselling author

"Abraham's debut novel presents a fantasy world of ruling nobles, poet mystics, elemental spirits, and elegantly ritualized customs. The author's fresh approach to world-building and his emergent storytelling talent make this a good addition to most fantasy collections."

—*Library Journal*

"*A Shadow in Summer* is an ambitious debut that shows author Daniel Abraham genuinely trying to do something new in fantasy. The story is not a traditional quest or military epic. There's nothing particularly medieval-looking about the setting. None of the genre's stock heroes or villains (or creatures) puts in an appearance, nor is the use of magic remotely conventional."

—*SFReviews.net*

"There is much to love in the Long Price Quartet. It is epic in scope but character-centered, with a setting both unique and utterly believable. The storytelling is smooth, careful, and—best of all—unpredictable."

—Patrick Rothfuss, bestselling
author of *The Name of the Wind*

"Gesture and posture convey as much information as spoken words in Abraham's impressive first novel, a fantasy set in a world where poets create and bind powerful shape-shifting creatures."
—*Publishers Weekly* on *A Shadow in Summer*

"*A Shadow in Summer* is an ambitious, intelligent, and assured debut that should satisfy both readers hungry for the satisfactions of traditional fantasy and readers hungry for something more."
—*Science Fiction Weekly*

"In addition to the creation of an architecturally perfect fantasy world filled with a fascinating, highly distinctive set of characters, Daniel Abraham has introduced into fantasy one brilliant, stunning new idea, a magic system in which the Word is made Flesh."
—Walter Jon Williams, *USA Today* bestselling author, on *A Shadow in Summer*

"Daniel Abraham is an up-and-comer to watch. In a world of bloated fantasy clones, his voice is fresh and startlingly new; not only is his world-building original, but the characters who inhabit the universe he's created are both strange and fully human. The prose is subtle yet muscular. I've been privileged to watch this series develop, and I'm very much looking forward to the rest of it."
—S. M. Stirling on *A Shadow in Summer*

"Daniel Abraham's spectacular debut begins as an intimate story about one man's involvement in an unsavory job but soon expands into a breathtakingly complex conspiracy that could topple empires and kill thousands. In a word: Brilliant!"
—*BarnesandNoble.com* on *A Shadow in Summer*,
Editor's Choice: Top Ten Novels of 2006

THE FIRST HALF OF
The Long Price Quartet

SHADOW
AND
BETRAYAL

A SHADOW IN SUMMER
AND
A BETRAYAL IN WINTER

DANIEL
ABRAHAM

ORB

A TOM DOHERTY ASSOCIATES BOOK ▪ NEW YORK

SHADOW AND BETRAYAL

This is an omnibus edition containing the novels
A Shadow in Summer copyright © 2006 by Daniel Abraham and
A Betrayal in Winter copyright © 2007 by Daniel Abraham.

Edited by James Frenkel

Maps by Jackie Aher

An Orb Book
Published by Tom Doherty Associates, LLC
175 Fifth Avenue
New York, NY 10010

www.tor-forge.com

Library of Congress Cataloging-in-Publication Data

Abraham, Daniel.
  [Novels. Selections]
  Shadow and betrayal / Daniel Abraham. — First edition.
    pages cm
  "A Tom Doherty Associates book."
  First work originally published: A shadow in summer. New
York, NY : Tor, 2006. (Long price quartet ; bk. 1). 2nd work
originally published: A betrayal in winter. New York, NY : Tor,
2007. (Long price quartet ; bk. 2)
  ISBN 978-0-7653-3164-9 (pbk.)
  1. Fantasy fiction, American. I. Abraham, Daniel. Shadow
in summer. II. Abraham, Daniel. Betrayal in winter. III. Title.
  PS3601.B677A6 2012
  813'.6—dc23

                                                    2011047981

First Edition: March 2012

Printed in the United States of America

0 9 8 7 6 5 4 3 2 1

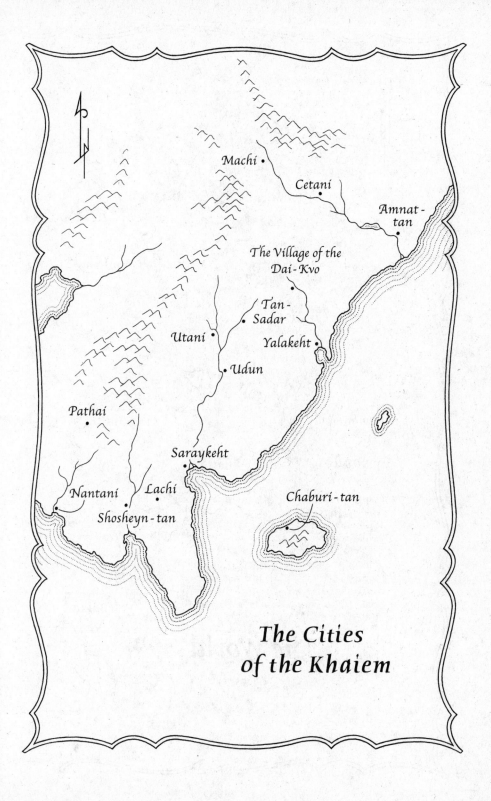

Machi •

Cetani •

Amnat-
tan •

The Village of the
Dai-Kvo

Tan-
Sadar •

Utani •

Yalakeht •

• Udun

Pathai
•

Saraykeht •

Nantani •   Lachi
         •   Chaburi-tan

Shosheyn-tan

The Cities
of the Khaiem

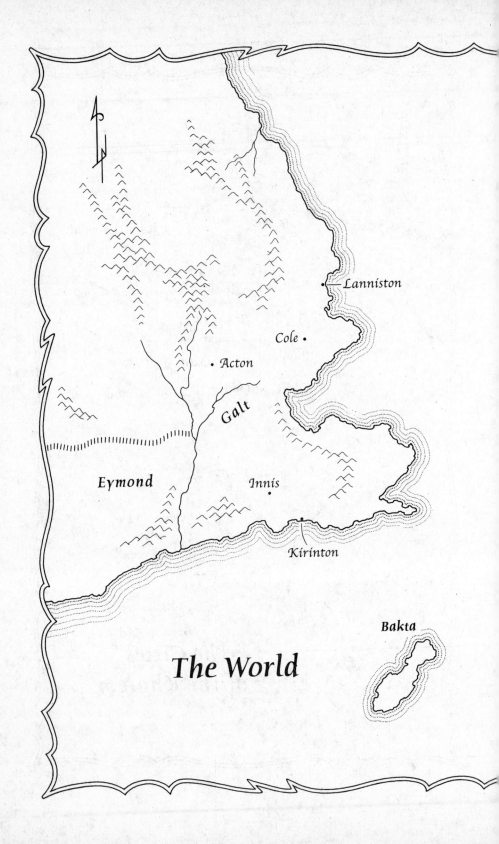

Lanniston

Cole

Acton

Galt

Eymond

Innis

Kirinton

Bakta

The World

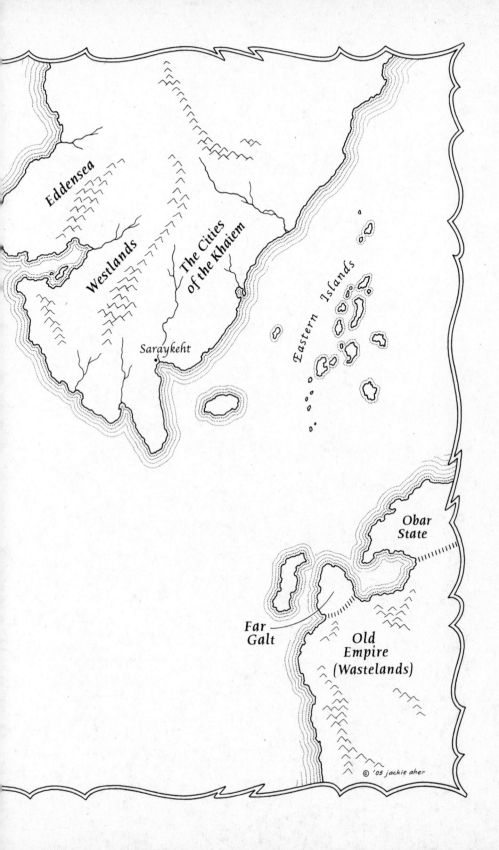

A SHADOW IN SUMMER

To Fred Saberhagen,
the first of my many teachers

ACKNOWLEDGMENTS

Romantic visions aside, writing is not something often done in isolation. I would like to thank everyone whose input made this book better than I could have done alone. Especially Walter Jon Williams, Melinda Snodgrass, Steve and Jan Stirling, Terry England, John Miller, Sally Gwylan, Yvonne Coats, Emily Mah, Sage Walker, Victor Milan, George R. R. Martin, and all the various members of the New Mexico Critical Mass Workshop.

Thanks are also due to Shawna McCarthy for her faith in the project, and Jim Frenkel for his hard work and kind attentions to a first-time novelist.

But I am especially grateful to Connie Willis, who gave me my first advice on the book, Tom Doherty, who gave me my last, and Katherine Abraham, without whom it wouldn't have been anywhere near as fun in between.

PROLOG

>+< Otah took the blow on the ear, the flesh opening under the rod. Tahi-kvo, Tahi the teacher, pulled the thin lacquered wood through the air with a fluttering sound like bird wings. Otah's discipline held. He did not shift or cry out. Tears welled in his eyes, but his hands remained in a pose of greeting.

"Again," Tahi-kvo barked. "And correctly!"

"We are honored by your presence, most high Dai-kvo," Otah said sweetly, as if it were the first time he had attempted the ritual phrase. The old man sitting before the fire considered him closely, then adopted a pose of acceptance. Tahi-kvo made a sound of satisfaction in the depths of his throat.

Otah bowed, holding still for three breaths and hoping that Tahi-kvo wouldn't strike him for trembling. The moment stretched, and Otah nearly let his eyes stray to his teacher. It was the old man with his ruined whisper who at last spoke the words that ended the ritual and released him.

"Go, disowned child, and attend to your studies."

Otah turned and walked humbly out of the room. Once he had pulled the thick wooden door closed behind him and walked down the chill hallway toward the common rooms, he gave himself permission to touch his new wound.

The other boys were quiet as he passed through the stone halls of the school, but several times their gazes held him and his new shame. Only the older boys in the black robes of Milah-kvo's disciples laughed at him. Otah took himself to the quarters where all the boys in his cohort slept. He removed the ceremonial gown, careful not to touch it with blood, and washed the wound in cold water. The stinging cream for cuts and scrapes was in an earthenware jar beside the water basin. He took two fingers and slathered the vinegar-smelling ointment onto the open flesh of his ear. Then, not for the first time since he had come to the school, he sat on his spare, hard bunk and wept.

"This boy," the Dai-kvo said as he took up the porcelain bowl of tea. Its heat was almost uncomfortable. "He holds some promise?"

"Some," Tahi allowed as he leaned the lacquered rod against the wall and took the seat beside his master.

"He seems familiar."

"Otah Machi. Sixth son of the Khai Machi."

"I recall his brothers. Also boys of some promise. What became of them?"

"They spent their years, took the brand, and were turned out. Most are. We have three hundred in the school now and forty in the black under Milah-kvo's care. Sons of the Khaiem or the ambitious families of the utkhaiem."

"So many? I see so few."

Tahi took a pose of agreement, the cant of his wrists giving it a nuance that might have been sorrow or apology.

"Not many are both strong enough and wise. And the stakes are high."

The Dai-kvo sipped his tea and considered the fire.

"I wonder," the old man said, "how many realize we are teaching them nothing."

"We teach them all. Letters, numbers. Any of them could take a trade after they leave the school."

"But nothing of use. Nothing of poetry. Nothing of the andat."

"If they realize that, most high, they're halfway to your door. And for the ones we turn away . . . It's better, most high."

"Is it?"

Tahi shrugged and looked into the fire. He looked older, the Dai-kvo thought, especially about the eyes. But he had met Tahi as a rude youth many years before. The age he saw there now, and the cruelty, were seeds he himself had cultivated.

"When they have failed, they take the brand and make their own fates," Tahi said.

"We take away their only hope of rejoining their families, of taking a place at the courts of the Khaiem. They have no family. They cannot control the andat," the Dai-kvo said. "We throw these boys away much as their fathers have. What becomes of them, I wonder?"

"Much the same as becomes of anyone, I imagine. The ones from low families of the utkhaiem are hardly worse off than when they came. The sons of the Khaiem . . . once they take the brand, they cannot inherit, and it saves them from being killed for their blood rights. That alone is a gift in its way."

It was true. Every generation saw the blood of the Khaiem spilled. It was the way of the Empire. And in times when all three of a Khai's acknowledged sons slaughtered one another, the high families of the utkhaiem unsheathed their knives, and cities were caught for a time in fits of violence from which the poets held themselves apart like priests at a dog fight. These boys in the school's care were exempt from those wars at only the price of everything they had known in their short lives. And yet . . .

"Disgrace is a thin gift," the Dai-kvo said.

Tahi, his old student who had once been a boy like these, sighed.

"It's what we can offer."

———

THE DAI-KVO LEFT IN THE MORNING JUST AFTER DAWN, STEPPING THROUGH THE great bronze doors that opened only for him. Otah stood in the ranks of his cohort, still holding a pose of farewell. Behind him, someone took the chance of scratching—Otah could hear the shifting sound of fingers against cloth. He didn't look back. Two of the oldest of Milah-kvo's black robes pulled the great doors closed.

In the dim winter light that filtered through high-set, thin windows, Otah could see the bustle of the black robes taking charge of the cohorts. The day's tasks varied. The morning might be spent working in the school—repairing walls or washing laundry or scraping ice from the garden walkways that no one seemed to travel besides the boys set to tend them. The evening would be spent in study. Numbers, letters, religion, history of the Old Empire, the Second Empire, the War, the cities of the Khaiem. And more often these last weeks, one of the two teachers would stand at the back of the room while one of the black robes lectured and questioned. Milah-kvo would sometimes interrupt and tell jokes or take the lecture himself, discussing things the black robes never spoke of. Tahi-kvo would only observe and punish. All of Otah's cohort bore the marks of the lacquered stick.

Riit-kvo, one of the oldest of the black robes, led Otah and his cohort to the cellars. For hours as the sun rose unseen, Otah swept dust from stones that seemed still cold from the last winter and then washed them with water and rags until his knuckles were raw. Then Riit-kvo called them to order, considered them, slapped one boy whose stance was not to his standards, and marched them to the dining hall. Otah looked neither forward nor back, but focused on the shoulders of the boy ahead of him.

The midday meal was cold meat, yesterday's bread, and a thin barley soup that Otah treasured because it was warm. Too soon, Riit called them to wash their bowls and knives and follow him. Otah found himself at the front of the line—an unenviable place—and so was the first to step into the cold listening room with its stone benches and thin windows that had never known glass. Tahi-kvo was waiting there for them.

None of them knew why the round-faced, scowling teacher had taken an interest in the cohort, though speculations were whispered in the dark of their barracks. The Dai-kvo had chosen one of them to go and study the secrets of the andat, to become one of the poets, gain power even higher than the Khaiem, and skip over the black robes of Milah-kvo entirely. Or one of their families had repented sending their child, however minor in the line of succession, to the school and was in negotiation to forgo the branding and take their disowned son back into the fold.

Otah had listened, but believed none of the stories. They were the fantasies of the frightened and the weak, and he knew that if he clung to one, it would shatter him. Dwelling in the misery of the school and hoping for nothing beyond survival was the only way to keep his soul from flying apart. He would endure his term and be turned out into the world. This was his third year at the school. He was twelve now, and near the halfway point of his time. And today was another evil to be borne as the day before and the day ahead. To think too far in the past or the future was dangerous. Only when he let his dreams loose did he think of learning the secrets of the andat, and that happened so rarely as to call itself never.

Riit-kvo, his eyes on the teacher at the back as much as on the students, began to declaim the parable of the Twin Dragons of Chaos. It was a story Otah knew, and he found his mind wandering. Through the stone arch of the window, Otah could see a crow hunched on a high branch. It reminded him of something he could not quite recall.

"Which of the gods tames the spirits of water?" Riit-kvo snapped. Otah pulled himself back to awareness and straightened his spine.

Riit-kvo pointed to a thick-set boy across the room.

"Oladac the Wanderer!" the boy said, taking a pose of gratitude to one's teacher.

"And why were the spirits who stood by and neither fought with the gods nor against them consigned to a lower hell than the servants of chaos?"

Again Riit-kvo pointed.

"Because they should have fought alongside the gods!" the boy shouted.

It was a wrong answer. Because they were cowards, Otah thought, and knew he was correct. Tahi's lacquered rod whirred and stuck the boy hard on the shoulder. Riit-kvo smirked and returned to his story.

After the class, there was another brief work detail for which Tahi-kvo did not join them. Then the evening meal, and then the end of another day. Otah was grateful to crawl into his bunk and pull the thin blanket up to his neck. In the winter, many of the boys slept in their robes against the cold, and Otah was among that number. Despite all this, he preferred the winter. During the warmer times, he would still wake some mornings having forgotten where he was, expecting to see the walls of his father's home, hear the voices of his older brothers—Biitrah, Danat, and Kaiin. Perhaps see his mother's smile. The rush of memory was worse than any blow of Tahi-kvo's rod, and he bent his will toward erasing the memories he had of his family. He was not loved or wanted in his home, and he understood that thinking too much about this truth would kill him.

As he drifted toward sleep, Riit-kvo's harsh voice murmuring the lesson of the spirits who refused to fight spun through his mind. They were cowards, consigned to the deepest and coldest hell.

When the question came, his eyes flew open. He sat up. The other boys were all in their cots. One, not far from him, was crying in his sleep. It was not an unusual sound. The words still burned in Otah's mind. The coward spirits, consigned to hell.

And what keeps them there? his quiet inner voice asked him. *Why do they remain in hell?*

He lay awake for hours, his mind racing.

THE TEACHERS' QUARTERS OPENED ON A COMMON ROOM. SHELVES LINED THE walls, filled with books and scrolls. A fire pit glowed with coals prepared for them by the most honored of Milah-kvo's black-robed boys. The wide gap of a window—glazed double to hold out the cold of winter, the heat of the summer—looked out over the roadway leading south to the high road. Tahi sat now, warming his feet at the fire and staring out into the cold plain beyond. Milah opened the door behind him and strode in.

"I expected you earlier," Tahi said.

Milah briefly took a pose of apology.

"Annat Ryota was complaining about the kitchen flue smoking again," he said.

Tahi grunted.

"Sit. The fire's warm."

"Fires often are," Milah agreed, his tone dry and mocking. Tahi managed a thin smile as his companion took a seat.

"What did he make of your boys?" Tahi asked.

"Much the same as last year. They have seen through the veil and now lead their brothers toward knowledge," Milah said, but his hands were in a pose of gentle mockery. "They are petty tyrants to a man. Any andat strong enough to be worth holding would eat them before their hearts beat twice."

"Pity."

"Hardly a surprise. And yours?"

Tahi chewed for a moment at his lower lip and leaned forward. He could feel Milah's gaze on him.

"Otah Machi disgraced himself," Tahi said. "But he accepted the punishment well. The Dai-kvo thinks he may have promise."

Milah shifted. When Tahi looked over, the teacher had taken a pose of query. Tahi considered the implicit question, then nodded.

"There have been some other signs," Tahi said. "I think you should put a watch over him. I hate to lose him to you, in a way."

"You like him."

Tahi took a pose of acknowledgement that held the nuance of a confession of failure.

"I may be cruel, old friend," Tahi said, dropping into the familiar, "but you're heartless."

The fair-haired teacher laughed, and Tahi couldn't help but join him. They sat silent then for a while, each in his own thoughts. Milah rose, shrugged off his thick woolen top robe. Beneath it he still wore the formal silks from his audience yesterday with the Dai-kvo. Tahi poured them both bowls of rice wine.

"It was good to see him again," Milah said sometime later. There was a melancholy note in his voice. Tahi took a pose of agreement, then sipped his wine.

"He looked so *old*," Tahi said.

OTAH'S PLAN, SUCH AS IT WAS, TOOK LITTLE PREPARATION, AND YET NEARLY THREE weeks passed between the moment he understood the parable of the spirits who stood aside and the night when he took action. That night, he waited until the others were asleep before he pushed off the thin blankets, put on every robe and legging he had, gathered his few things, and left his cohort for the last time.

The stone hallways were unlit, but he knew his way well enough that he had no need for light. He made his way to the kitchen. The pantry was unlocked—no one would steal food for fear of being found out and beaten. Otah scooped double handfuls of hard rolls and dried fruit into his satchel. There was no need for water. Snow still covered the ground, and Tahi-kvo had shown them how to melt snow with the heat of their own bodies walking without the cold penetrating to their hearts.

Once he was provisioned, his path led him to the great hall— moonlight from the high windows showing ghost-dim the great aisle where he had held a pose of obeisance every morning for the last three years. The doors, of course, were barred, and while he was strong enough to open them, the sounds might have woken someone. He took a pair of wide, netted snowshoes from the closet beside the great doors and went up the stairs to the listening room. There, the thin windows looked out on a world locked in winter. Otah's breath plumed already in the chill.

He threw the snowshoes and satchel out the window to the snow-cushioned ground below, then squeezed through and lowered himself from the outer stone sill until he hung by his fingertips. The fall was not so far.

He dusted the snow from his leggings, tied the snowshoes to his feet by their thick leather thongs, took up the bulging satchel and started off, walking south toward the high road.

The moon, near the top of its nightly arc, had moved the width of two thick-gloved hands toward the western horizon before Otah knew he was not alone. The footsteps that had kept perfect time with his own fell out of their pattern—as intentional a provocation as clearing a throat. Otah froze, then turned.

"Good evening, Otah Machi," Milah-kvo said, his tone casual. "A good night for a walk, eh? Cold though."

Otah did not speak, and Milah-kvo strode forward, his hand on his own satchel, his footsteps nearly silent. His breath was thick and white as a goose feather.

"Yes," the teacher said. "Cold, and far from your bed."

Otah took a pose of acknowledgement appropriate for a student to a teacher. It had no nuance of apology, and Otah hoped that Milah-kvo would not see his trembling, or if he did would ascribe it to the cold.

"Leaving before your term is complete, boy. You disgrace yourself."

Otah switched to a pose of thanks appropriate to the end of a lesson, but Milah-kvo waved the formality aside and sat in the snow, considering him with an interest that Otah found unnerving.

"Why do it?" Milah-kvo asked. "There's still hope of redeeming yourself. You might still be found worthy. So why run away? Are you so much a coward?"

Otah found his voice.

"It would be cowardice that kept me, Milah-kvo."

"How so?" The teacher's voice held nothing of judgment or testing. It was like a friend asking a question because he truly did not know the answer.

"There are no locks on hell," Otah said. It was the first time he had tried to express this to someone else, and it proved harder than he had expected. "If there aren't locks, then what can hold anyone there besides fear that leaving might be worse?"

"And you think the school is a kind of hell."

It was not a question, so Otah did not answer.

"If you keep to this path, you'll be the lowest of the low," Milah said. "A disgraced child without friend or ally. And without the brand to protect you, your older brothers may well track you down and kill you."

"Yes."

"Do you have someplace to go?"

"The high road leads to Pathai and Nantani."

"Where you know no one."

Otah took a pose of agreement.

"This doesn't frighten you?" the teacher asked.

"It is the decision I've made." He could see the amusement in Milah-kvo's face at his answer.

"Fair enough, but I think there's an alternative you haven't considered."

The teacher reached into his satchel and pulled out a small cloth bundle. He hefted it for a moment, considering, and dropped it on the snow between them. It was a black robe.

Otah took a pose of intellectual inquiry. It was a failure of vocabulary, but Milah-kvo took his meaning.

"Andat are powerful, Otah. Like small gods. And they don't love being held to a single form. They fight it, and since the forms they have are a reflection of the poets who bind them. . . . The world is full of willing victims—people who embrace the cruelty meted out against them. An andat formed from a mind like that would destroy the poet who bound it and escape. That you have chosen action is what the black robes mean."

"Then . . . the others . . . they all left the school too?"

Milah laughed. Even in the cold, it was a warm sound.

"No. No, you've all taken different paths. Ansha tried to wrestle Tahi-kvo's stick away from him. Ranit Kiru asked forbidden questions, took the punishment for them, and asked again until Tahi beat him asleep. He was too sore to wear any robe at all for weeks, but his bruises were black enough. But you've each *done* something. If you choose to take up the robe, that is. Leave it, and really, this is just a conversation. Interesting maybe, but trivial."

"And if I take it?"

"You will never be turned out of the school so long as you wear the black. You will help to teach the normal boys the lesson you've learned—to stand by your own strength."

Otah blinked, and something—some emotion he couldn't put a name to—bloomed in his breast. His flight from the school took on a new meaning. It was a badge of his strength, the proof of his courage.

"And the andat?"

"And the andat," Milah-kvo said. "You'll begin to learn of them in earnest. The Dai-kvo has never taken a student who wasn't first a black robe at the school."

Otah stooped, his fingers numb with cold, and picked up the robe. He met Milah-kvo's amused eyes and couldn't keep from grinning. Milah-kvo laughed, stood and put an arm around Otah's shoulder. It was the first kind act Otah could remember since he had come to the school.

"Come on, then. If we start now, we may get back to the school by break-fast."

Otah took a pose of enthusiastic agreement.

"And, while this once I think we can forgive it, don't make a habit of stealing from the kitchen. It upsets the cooks."

THE LETTER CAME SOME WEEKS LATER, AND MILAH WAS THE FIRST TO READ IT. Sitting in an upper room, his students abandoned for the moment, he read the careful script again and felt his face grow tight. When he had gone over it enough to know he could not have misunderstood, he tucked the folded paper into the sleeve of his robe and looked out the window. Winter was ending, and somehow the eternal renewal that was spring felt like an irony.

He heard Tahi enter, recognizing his old friend's footsteps.

"There was a courier," Tahi said. "Ansha said there was a courier from the Dai-kvo . . ."

Milah looked over his shoulder. His own feelings were echoed in Tahi's round face.

"From his attendant, actually."

"The Dai-kvo. Is he . . ."

"No," Milah said, fishing out the letter. "Not dead. Only dying."

Tahi took the proffered pages, but didn't look at them.

"Of what?"

"Time."

Tahi read the written words silently, then leaned against the wall with a sharp sigh.

"It . . . it isn't so bad as it could be," Tahi said.

"No. Not yet. He will see the school again. Twice, perhaps."

"He shouldn't come," Tahi snapped. "The visits are a formality. We know well enough which boys are ready. We can send them. He doesn't have to—"

Milah turned, interrupting him with a subtle pose that was a request for clarification and a mourning both. Tahi laughed bitterly and looked down.

"You're right," he said. "Still. I'd like the world better if we could carry a little of his weight for him. Even if it was only a short way."

Milah started to take a pose, but hesitated, stopped, only nodded.

"Otah Machi?" Tahi asked.

"Maybe. We might have to call him for Otah. Not yet, though. The robes have hardly been on him. The others are still learning to accept him as an equal. Once he's used to the power, then we'll see. I won't call the Dai-kvo until we're certain."

"He'll come next winter whether there's a boy ready or not."

"Perhaps. Or perhaps he'll die tonight. Or we will. No god made the world certain."

Tahi raised his hands in a pose of resignation.

IT WAS A WARM NIGHT IN LATE SPRING; THE SCENT OF GREEN SEEMED TO PERMEATE the world. Otah and his friends sprawled on the hillside east of the school. Milah-kvo sat with them, still talking, still telling stories though their lectures for the day were done. Stories of the andat.

"They are like . . . thoughts made real," Milah said, his hands moving in gestures which were not formal poses, but evoked a sense of wonder all the same. "Ideas tamed and given human shape. Take Water-Moving-Down. In the Old Empire, she was called Rain, then when Diit Amra recaptured her at the beginning of the War, they called her Seaward. But the thought, you see, was the same. And if you can hold that, you can stop rivers in their tracks. Or see that your crops get enough water, or flood your enemies. She was powerful."

"Could someone catch her again?" Ansha—no longer Ansha-kvo to Otah— asked.

Milah shook his head.

"I doubt it. She's been held and escaped too many times. I suppose some-one might find a new way to describe her, but . . . it's been tried."

There was a chill that even Otah felt at the words. Stories of the andat were like ghost tales, and the price a failed poet paid was always the gruesome ending of it.

"What was her price?" Nian Tomari asked, his voice hushed and eager.

"The last poet who made the attempt was a generation before me. They say that when he failed, his belly swelled like a pregnant woman's. When they cut him open, he was filled with ice and black seaweed."

The boys were quiet, imagining the scene—the poet's blood, the dark leaves, the pale ice. Dari slapped a gnat.

"Milah-kvo?" Otah said. "Why do the andat become more difficult to hold each time they escape?"

The teacher laughed.

"An excellent question, Otah. But one you'd have to ask of the Dai-kvo. It's more than you're ready to know."

Otah dropped into a pose of correction accepted, but in the back of his mind, the curiosity remained. The sun dipped below the horizon and a chill came into the air. Milah-kvo rose, and they followed him, wraith-children in their dark robes and twilight. Halfway back to the high stone buildings, Ansha started to run, and then Riit, and then Otah and then all of them, pounding up the slope to the great door, racing to be first or at least to not be last. When Milah arrived, they were red-faced and laughing.

"Otah," Enrath, an older, dark-faced boy from Tan-Sadar said. "You're taking the third cohort out tomorrow to turn the west gardens?"

"Yes," Otah said.

"Tahi-kvo wanted them finished and washed early. He's taking them for lessons after the meal."

"You could join the afternoon session with us," Milah suggested, overhearing.

Otah took a pose of gratitude as they entered the torch-lit great hall. One of Milah-kvo's lessons was infinitely better than a day spent leading one of the youngest cohorts through its chores.

"Do you know why worms travel in the ground?" Milah-kvo asked.

"Because they can't fly?" Ansha said, and laughed. A few other boys laughed with him.

"True enough," Milah-kvo said. "But they are good for the soil. They break it up so that the roots can dig deeper. So in a sense, Otah and the third cohort are doing worm work tomorrow."

"But worms do it by eating dirt and shitting it out," Enrath said. "Tahi-kvo said so."

"There is some difference in technique," Milah-kvo agreed dryly to the delight of them all, including Otah.

The black robes slept in smaller rooms, four to each, with a brazier in the center to keep it warm. The thaw had come, but the nights were still bitterly cold. Otah, as the youngest in his room, had the duty of tending the fire. In the dark of the mornings, Milah-kvo would come and wake them, knocking on their doors until all four voices within acknowledged him. They washed at communal tubs and ate at a long wooden table with Tahi-kvo at one end and Milah-kvo at the other. Otah still found himself uncomfortable about the round-faced teacher, however friendly his eyes had become.

After they had cleared their plates, the black robes divided; the larger half went to lead the cohorts through the day's duties, the smaller—rarely more than five or six—would go with Milah-kvo for a day's study. As Otah walked to the great hall, he was already planning the day ahead, anticipating handing the third cohort over to Tahi-kvo and joining the handful most favored by Milah-kvo.

In the great hall, the boys stood in their shivering ranks. The third cohort was one of the youngest—a dozen boys of perhaps eight years dressed in thin gray robes. Otah paced before them, searching for any improper stance or scratching.

"Today, we are turning the soil in the west gardens," Otah barked. Some of the smaller boys flinched. "Tahi-kvo demands the work be finished and that you be cleaned by midday. Follow!"

He marched them out to the gardens. Twice, he stopped to be sure they were in the proper order. When one—Navi Toyut, son of a high family of the utkhaiem in Yalakeht—was out of step, Otah slapped him smartly across the face. The boy corrected his gait.

The west gardens were brown and bare. Dry sticks—the winter corpses of last year's crop—lay strewn on the ground, the pale seedlings of weeds pushing up through them. Otah led them to the toolshed where the youngest boys brushed spider webs off the shovels and spades.

"Begin at the north end!" Otah shouted, and the cohort fell into place. The line was ragged, some boys taller than others and all unevenly spaced, leaving gaps in the line like missing milk teeth. Otah walked along, showing each boy where to stand and how to hold his shovel. When they were all in their places, Otah gave the sign to begin.

They set to, their thin arms working, but they were small and not strong. The smell of fresh earth rose, but only slowly. When Otah walked the turned soil behind them, his boots barely sank into it.

"Deeper!" he snapped. "Turn the soil, don't just scrape it. Worms could do better than this."

The cohort didn't speak, didn't look up, only leaned harder onto the dry, rough shafts of their spades. Otah shook his head and spat.

The sun had risen a hand and a half, and they had only completed two plots. As the day warmed, the boys shed their top robes, leaving them folded on the ground. There were still six plots to go. Otah paced behind the line, scowling. Time was running short.

"Tahi-kvo wants this done by midday!" Otah shouted. "If you disappoint him, I'll see all of you beaten."

They struggled to complete the task, but by the time they reached the end of the fourth plot, it was clear that it wouldn't happen. Otah gave stern orders that they should continue, then stalked off to find Tahi-kvo.

The teacher was overseeing a cohort that had been set to clean the kitchens. The lacquered rod whirred impatiently. Otah took a pose of apology before him.

"Tahi-kvo, the third cohort will not be able to turn the soil in the west gardens by midday. They are weak and stupid."

Tahi-kvo considered him, his expression unreadable. Otah felt his face growing warm with embarrassment. At last, Tahi-kvo took a formal pose of acceptance.

"It will wait for another day, then," he said. "When they have had their meal, take them back out and let them finish the task."

Otah took a pose of gratitude until Tahi-kvo turned his attention back to the cohort he was leading, then Otah turned and walked back out to the gardens. The third cohort had slacked in his absence, but began to work furiously as Otah came near. He stepped into the half-turned plot and stared at them.

"You have cost me an afternoon with Milah-kvo," Otah said, his voice low, but angry enough to carry. None of the boys would meet his gaze, guilty as dogs. He turned to the nearest boy—a thin boy with a spade in his hand. "You. Give me that."

The boy looked panicked, but held out the spade. Otah took it and thrust it down into the fresh soil. The blade sank only half way. Otah's shoulders curled in rage. The boy took a pose of apology, but Otah didn't acknowledge it.

"You're meant to turn the soil! Turn it! Are you too stupid to understand that?"

"Otah-kvo, I'm sorry. It's only—"

"If you can't do it like a man, you can do it as a worm. Get on your knees."

The boy's expression was uncomprehending.

"Get on your knees!" Otah shouted, leaning into the boy's face. Tears welled up in the boy's eyes, but he did as he was told. Otah picked up a clod of dirt and handed it to him. "Eat it."

The boy looked at the clod in his hand, then up at Otah. Then, weeping until his shoulders shook, he raised the dirt to his mouth and ate. The others in the cohort were standing in a circle, watching silently. The boy's mouth worked, mud on his lips.

"All of it!" Otah said.

The boy took another mouthful, then collapsed, sobbing, to the ground. Otah spat in disgust and turned to the others.

"Get to work!"

They scampered back to their places, small arms and legs working furiously with the vigor of fear. The mud-lipped boy sat weeping into his hands. Otah took the spade to him and pushed the blade into the ground at his side.

"Well?" Otah demanded quietly. "Is there something to wait for?"

The boy mumbled something Otah couldn't make out.

"What? If you're going to talk, make it so people can hear you."

"My hand," the boy forced through the sobs. "My hands hurt. I tried. I tried to dig deeper, but it hurt so much . . ."

He turned his palms up, and looking at the bleeding blisters was like leaning over a precipice; Otah felt suddenly dizzy. The boy looked up into his face, weeping, and the low keening was a sound Otah recognized though he had never heard it before; it was a sound he had longed to make for seasons of sleeping in the cold, hoping not to dream of his mother. It was the same tune he had heard in his old cohort, a child crying in his sleep.

The black robes suddenly felt awkward, and the memory of a thousand humiliations sang in Otah's mind the way a crystal glass might ring with the sound of singer's note.

He knelt beside the weeping boy, words rushing to his lips and then failing him. The others in the cohort stood silent.

"YOU SENT FOR ME?" TAHI ASKED. MILAH DIDN'T ANSWER, BUT GESTURED OUT THE window. Tahi came to stand by him and consider the spectacle below. In a half-turned plot of dirt, a black robe was cradling a crying child in his arms while the others in the cohort stood by, agape.

"How long has this been going on?" Tahi asked through a tight throat.

"They were like that when I noticed them. Before that, I don't know."

"Otah Machi?"

Milah only nodded.

"It has to stop."

"Yes. But I wanted you to see it."

In grim silence, the pair walked down the stairs, through the library, and out to the west gardens. The third cohort, seeing them come, pretended to work. All except Otah and the boy he held. They remained as they were.

"Otah!" Tahi barked. The black-robed boy looked up, eyes red and tear-filled.

"You're not well, Otah," Milah said gently. He drew Otah up. "You should come inside and rest."

Otah looked from one to the other, then hesitantly took a pose of submission and let Milah take his shoulder and guide him away. Tahi remained behind; Milah could hear his voice snapping at the third cohort like a whip.

Back in the quarters of the elite, Milah prepared a cup of strong tea for Otah and considered the situation. The others would hear of what had happened soon enough if they hadn't already. He wasn't sure whether that would make things better for the boy or worse. He wasn't even certain what he hoped. If it was what it appeared, it was the success he had dreaded. Before he acted, he had to be sure. He wouldn't call for the Dai-kvo if Otah weren't ready.

Otah, sitting slump-shouldered on his bunk, took the hot tea and sipped it dutifully. His eyes were dry now, and staring into the middle distance. Milah pulled a stool up beside him, and they sat for a long moment in silence before he spoke.

"You did that boy out there no favors today."

Otah lifted a hand in a pose of correction accepted.

"Comforting a boy like that . . . it doesn't make him stronger. I know it isn't easy being a teacher. It requires a hard sort of compassion to treat a child harshly, even when it is only for their own good in the end."

Otah nodded, but didn't look up. When he spoke, his voice was low.

"Has anyone ever been turned out from the black robes?"

"Expelled? No, no one. Why do you ask?"

"I've failed," Otah said, then paused. "I'm not strong enough to teach these lessons, Milah-kvo."

Milah looked down at his hands, thinking of his old master. Thinking of the cost that another journey to the school would exact from that old flesh. He couldn't keep the weight of the decision entirely out of his voice when he spoke.

"I am removing you from duty for a month's time," he said, "while we call for the Dai-kvo."

"OTAH," THE FAMILIAR VOICE WHISPERED. "WHAT DID YOU DO?"

Otah turned on his bunk. The brazier glowed, the coals giving off too little light to see by. Otah fixed his gaze on the embers.

"I made a mistake, Ansha," he said. It was the reply he'd given on the few occasions in the last days that someone had had the courage to ask.

"They say the Dai-kvo's coming. And out of season."

"It may have been a serious mistake."

It may be the first time that anyone has risen so far and failed so badly, Otah thought. The first time anyone so unsuited to the black robes had been given them. He remembered the cold, empty plain of snow he'd walked across the night Milah-kvo had promoted him. He could see now that his flight hadn't been a sign of strength after all—only a presentiment of failure.

"What did you *do*?" Ansha asked in the darkness.

Otah saw the boy's face again, saw the bloodied hand and the tears of humiliation running down the dirty cheeks. He had caused that pain, and he could not draw the line between the shame of having done it and the shame of being too weak to do it again. There was no way for him to explain that he couldn't lead the boys to strength because in his heart, he was still one of them.

"I wasn't worthy of my robe," he said.

Ansha didn't speak again, and soon Otah heard the low, deep breath of sleep. The others were all tired from their day's work. Otah had no reason to be tired after a day spent haunting the halls and rooms of the school with no duties and no purpose wearing the black robe only because he had no other robes of his own.

He waited in the darkness until even the embers deserted him and he was sure the others were deeply asleep. Then he rose, pulled on his robe, and walked quietly out into the corridor. It wasn't far to the chilly rooms where the younger cohorts slept. Otah walked among the sleeping forms. Their bodies were so small, and the blankets so thin. Otah had been in the black for so little time, and had forgotten so much.

The boy he was looking for was curled on a cot beside the great stone wall, his back to the room. Otah leaned over carefully and put a hand over the boy's mouth to stifle a cry if he made one. He woke silently, though, his eyes blinking open. Otah watched until he saw recognition bloom.

"Your hands are healing well?" Otah whispered.

The boy nodded.

"Good. Now stay quiet. We don't want to wake the others."

Otah drew his hand away, and the boy fell immediately into a pose of profound apology.

"Otah-kvo, I have dishonored you and the school. I . . ."

Otah gently folded the boy's fingers closed.

"You have nothing to blame yourself for," Otah said. "The mistake was mine. The price is mine."

"If I'd worked harder—"

"It would have gained you nothing," Otah said. "Nothing."

THE BRONZE DOORS BOOMED AND SWUNG OPEN. THE BOYS STOOD IN THEIR ranks holding poses of welcome as if they were so many statues. Otah, standing among the black robes, held his pose as well. He wondered what stories the cohorts of disowned children had been telling themselves about the visit: hopes of being returned to a lost family, or of being elevated to a poet. Dreams.

The old man walked in. He seemed less steady than Otah remembered him. After the ceremonial greetings, he blessed them all in his thick, ruined whisper. Then he and the teachers retired, and the black robes—all but Otah—took charge of the cohorts that they would lead for the day. Otah returned to his room and sat, sick at heart, waiting for the summons he knew was coming. It wasn't long.

"Otah," Tahi-kvo said from the doorway. "Get some tea for the Dai-kvo."

"But the ceremonial robe . . ."

"Not required. Just tea."

Otah rose into a pose of submission. The time had come.

THE DAI-KVO SAT SILENTLY, CONSIDERING THE FIRE IN THE GRATE. HIS HANDS, steepled before him, seemed smaller than Milah remembered them, the skin thinner and loose. His face showed the fatigue of his journey around the eyes and mouth, but when he caught Milah's gaze and took a pose part query, part challenge, Milah thought there was something else as well. A hunger, or hope.

"How are things back in the world?" Milah asked. "We don't hear much of the high cities here."

"Things are well enough," the Dai-kvo said. "And here? How are your boys?"

"Well enough, most high."

"Really? Some nights I find I wonder."

Milah took a pose inviting the Dai-kvo to elaborate, but to no effect. The ancient eyes had turned once more to the flames. Milah let his hands drop to his lap.

Tahi returned and took a pose of obedience and reverence before bending into his chair.

"The boy is coming," Tahi said.

The Dai-kvo took a pose of acknowledgement, but nothing more. Milah saw his own concern mirrored in Tahi. It seemed too long before the soft knock came at the door and Otah Machi entered, carrying a tray with three small bowls of tea. Stone-faced, the boy put the tray on the low table and took the ritual pose of greeting.

"I am honored by your presence, most high Dai-kvo," Otah said perfectly.

The old man's eyes were alive now, his gaze on Otah with a powerful interest. He nodded, but didn't commend the boy to his studies. Instead, he gestured to the empty seat that Milah usually took. The boy looked over, and Milah nodded. Otah sat, visibly sick with anxiety.

"Tell me," the Dai-kvo said, picking up a bowl of tea, "what do you know of the andat?"

The boy took a moment finding his voice, but when he did, there was no quavering in it.

"They are thoughts, most high. Translated by the poet into a form that includes volition."

The Dai-kvo sipped his tea, watching the boy. Waiting for him to say more. The silence pressed Otah to speak, but he appeared to have no more words. At last the Dai-kvo put down his cup.

"You know nothing more of them? How they are bound? What a poet must do to keep his work unlike that which has gone before? How one may pass a captured spirit from one generation to the next?"

"No, most high."

"And why not?" The Dai-kvo's voice was soft.

"Milah-kvo told us that more knowledge would be dangerous to us. We weren't ready for the deeper teachings."

"True," the Dai-kvo said. "True enough. You were only tested. Never taught."

Otah looked down. His face gray, he adopted a pose of contrition.

"I am sorry to have failed the school, most high. I know that I was to show them how to be strong, and I wanted to, but—"

"You have not failed, Otah. You have won through."

Otah's stance faltered, and his eyes filled with confusion. Milah coughed and, taking a pose that begged the Dai-kvo's permission, spoke.

"You recall our conversation in the snow the night I offered you the black? I said then that a weak-minded poet would be destroyed by the andat?"

Otah nodded.

"A cruel-hearted one would destroy the world," Milah said. "Strong and kind, Otah. It's a rare combination."

"We see it now less often than we once did," the Dai-kvo said. "Just as no boy has taken the black robes without a show of his strength of will, no one has put the black robe away without renouncing the cruelty that power brings. You have done both, Otah Machi. You've proven yourself worthy, and I would take you as my apprentice. Come back with me, boy, and I will teach you the secrets of the poets."

The boy looked as if he'd been clubbed. His face was bloodless, his hands still, but a slow comprehension shone in his eyes. The moment stretched until Tahi snapped.

"Well? You can say something, boy."

"What I did . . . the boy . . . I didn't *fail*?"

"That wasn't a failure. That was the moment of your highest honor."

A slow smile came to Otah's lips, but it was deathly cold. When he spoke, there was fury in his voice.

"Humiliating that boy was my moment of highest *honor*?"

Milah saw Tahi frown. He shook his head. This was between the boy and the Dai-kvo now.

"Comforting him was," the old man said.

"Comforting him for what *I* did."

"Yes. And yet how many of the other black-robed boys would have done the same? The school is built to embody these tests. It has been this way since the war that destroyed the Empire, and it has held the cities of the Khaiem together. There is a wisdom in it that runs very deep."

Slowly, Otah took a pose of gratitude to a teacher, but there was something odd about it—something in the cant of the wrists that spoke of an emotion Milah couldn't fathom.

"If that was honor, most high, then I truly understand."

"Do you?" the old man asked, and his voice sounded hopeful.

"Yes. I was your tool. It wasn't only me in that garden. *You* were there, too."

"What are you saying, boy?" Tahi snapped, but Otah went on as if he had not spoken.

"You say Tahi-kvo taught me strength and Milah-kvo compassion, but there are other lessons to be taken from them. As the school is of your design, I think it only right that you should know what I've learned at your hand."

The Dai-kvo looked confused, and his hands took some half-pose, but the boy didn't stop. His gaze was fastened on the old man, and he seemed fearless.

"Tahi-kvo showed me that my own judgement is my only guide and Milah-kvo that there is no value in a lesson half-learned. My judgement was to leave this place, and I was right. I should never have let myself be tempted back.

"And that, most high, is all I've ever learned here."

Otah rose and took a pose of departure.

"Otah!" Tahi barked. "Take your seat!"

The boy ignored him, turned, and walked out, closing the door behind him. Milah crossed his arms, staring at the door, unsure what to say or even think. In the grate, the ashes settled under their own weight.

"Milah," Tahi whispered.

Milah looked over, and Tahi gestured to the Dai-kvo. The old man sat, barely breathing. His hands were held in an attitude of profound regret.

1

As the stone towers of Machi dominated the cold cities of the north, so the seafront of Saraykeht dominated the summer cities in the south. The wharves stood out into the clear waters of the bay, ships from the other port cities of the Khaiem—Nantani, Yalakeht, Chaburi-Tan—docked there. Among them were also the low, shallow ships of the Westlands and the tall, deep sailing ships of the Galts so strung with canvas they seemed like a launderer's yard escaped to the sea. And along the seafront streets, vendors of all different cities and lands sold wares from tall, thin tables decked with brightly colored cloths and banners, each calling out to the passers-by over the cries of seagulls and the grumble of waves. A dozen languages, a hundred dialects, creoles, and pidgins danced in the hot, still air, and she knew them all.

Amat Kyaan, senior overseer for the Galtic House Wilsin, picked her way through the crowd with a cane despite the sureness of her steps. She savored the play of grammar and vocabulary crashing together like children playing sand tag. Knowing how to speak and what to say was her strength. It was the skill that had taken her from a desperate freelance scribe to here, wearing the colors of an honorable, if foreign, house and threading her way through the press of bodies and baled cotton to a meeting with her employer. There were ways from her rooms at the edge of the soft quarter to Marchat Wilsin's favorite bathhouse that wouldn't have braved the seafront. Still, whenever her mornings took her to the bathhouse, this was the way she picked. The seafront was, after all, the pride and symbol of her city.

She paused in the square at the mouth of the Nantan—the wide, gray-bricked street that marked the western edge of the warehouse quarter. The ancient bronze statue of Shian Sho, the last great emperor, stood looking out across the sea, as if in memory of his lost empire—rags and wastelands for eight generations now, except for the cities of the Khaiem where the unrest had never reached. Below him, young men labored, shirtless in the heat, hauling carts piled high with white, oily bales. Some laughed, some shouted, some worked with a dreadful seriousness. Some were free men taking advantage of the seasonal work. Others were indentured to houses or individual merchants. A few were slaves. And all of them were beautiful—even the fat and the awkward. Youth made them beautiful. The working of muscles under skin was more subtle and enticing than the finest robes of the Khaiem, maybe because it wasn't considered. How many of them, she wondered, would guess that their sex was on display to an old woman who only seemed to be resting for a moment on the way to a business meeting?

All of them, probably. Vain, lovely creatures. She sighed, lifted her cane, and moved on.

The sun had risen perhaps half the width of one hand when she reached her destination. The bathhouses were inland, clustered near the banks of the Qiit and the aqueducts. Marchat Wilsin preferred one of the smaller. Amat had been there often enough that the guards knew her by sight and took awkward poses of welcome as she entered. She often suspected Wilsin-cha of choosing this particular place because it let him forget his own inadequacies of language. She sketched a pose of welcome and passed inside.

Working for a foreign house had never been simple, and translating contracts and agreements was the least of it. The Galts were a clever people, aggressive and successful in war. They held lands as wide and fertile as the Empire had at its height; they could command the respect and fear of other nations. But the assumptions they made—that agreements could be enforced by blades, that threat of invasion or blockade might underscore a negotiation—failed in the cities of the Khaiem. They might send their troops to Eddensea or their ships to Bakta, but when called upon for subtlety, they floundered. Galt might conquer the rest of the world if it chose; it would still bow before the andat. Marchat Wilsin had lived long enough in Saraykeht to have accepted the bruise on his people's arrogance. Indulging his eccentricities, such as doing business in a bathhouse, was a small price.

The air inside was cooler, and ornate woodworked screens blocked the windows while still letting the occasional cedar-scented breeze through. Voices echoed off the hard floors and walls. Somewhere in the public rooms, a man was singing, the tones of his voice ringing like a bell. Amat went to the women's chamber, shrugged out of her robe and pulled off her sandals. The cool air felt good against her bare skin. She took a drink of chilled water from the large granite basin, and—naked as anyone else—walked through the public baths, filled with men and women shouting and splashing one another, to the private rooms at the back. To Marchat Wilsin's corner room, farthest from the sounds of voices and laughter.

"It's too hot in this pisshole of a city," Wilsin-cha growled as she entered the room. He lay half-submerged in the pool, the water lapping at his white, wooly chest. He had been a thinner man when she had first met him. His hair and beard had been dark. "It's like someone holding a hot towel over your face."

"Only in the summer," Amat said and she laid her cane beside the water and carefully slipped in. The ripples rocked the floating lacquer tray with its bowls of tea, but didn't spill it. "If it was any further north, you'd spend all winter complaining about how cold it was."

"It'd be a change of pace, at least."

He lifted a pink and wrinkled hand from the water and pushed the tray over toward her. The tea was fresh and seasoned with mint. The water was cool. Amat lay back against the tiled lip of the pool.

"So what's the news?" Marchat asked, bringing their morning ritual to a close.

Amat made her report. Things were going fairly well. The shipment of raw cotton from Eddensea was in and being unloaded. The contracts with the weavers were nearly complete, though there were some ambiguities of translation from Galtic into the Khaiate that still troubled her. And worse, the harvest of the northern fields was late.

"Will they be here in time to go in front of the andat?"

Amat took another sip of tea before answering.

"No."

Marchat cursed under his breath. "Eddensea can ship us a season's bales, but we can't get our own plants picked?"

"Apparently not."

"How short does it leave us?"

"Our space will be nine-tenths full."

Marchat scowled and stared at the air, seeing imagined numbers, reading the emptiness like a book. After a moment, he sighed.

"Is there any chance of speaking with the Khai on it? Renegotiating our terms?"

"None," Amat said.

Marchat made an impatient noise in the back of his throat.

"This is why I hate dealing with you people. In Eymond or Bakta, there'd be room to talk at least."

"Because you'd have soldiers sitting outside the wall," Amat said, dryly.

"Exactly. And then they'd find room to talk. See if one of the other houses is overstocked," he said.

"Chadhami is. But Tiyan and Yaanani are in competition for a contract with a Western lord. If one could move more swiftly than the other, it might seal the issue. We could charge them for the earlier session with the andat, and then take part of their space later when our crop comes in."

Marchat considered this. They negotiated the house's strategy for some time. Which little alliance to make, and how it could most profitably be broken later, should the need arise.

Amat knew more than she said, of course. That was her job—to hold everything about the company clear in her mind, present her employer with what he needed to know, and deal herself with the things beneath his notice.

The center of it all, of course, was the cotton trade. The complex web of relationships—weavers and dyers and sailmakers; shipping companies, farming houses, alum miners—that made Saraykeht one of the richest cities in the world. And, as with all the cities of the Khaiem, free from threat of war, unlike Galt and Eddensea and Bakta; the Westlands and the Eastern Islands. They were protected by their poets and the powers they wielded, and that protection allowed conferences like this one, allowed them to play the deadly serious game of trade and barter.

Once their decisions had been made and the details agreed upon, Amat arranged a time to bring the proposals by the compound. Doing business from a bathhouse was an affectation Wilsin-cha could only take so far, and dripping water on freshly-inked contracts was where she drew the line. She knew he understood that. As she rose, prepared to face the remainder of her day, he held up a hand to stop her.

"There's one other thing," he said. She lowered herself back into the water. "I need a bodyguard this evening just before the half candle. Nothing serious, just someone to help keep the dogs off."

Amat tilted her head. His voice was calm, its tone normal, but he wasn't meeting her eyes. She held up her hands in a pose of query.

"I have a meeting," he said, "in one of the low towns."

"Company business?" Amat asked, keeping her voice neutral.

He nodded.

"I see," she said. Then, after a moment, "I'll be at the compound at the half candle, then."

"No. Amat, I need some house thug to swat off animals and make bandits think twice. What's a woman with a cane going to do for me?"

"I'll bring a bodyguard with me."

"Just send him to me," Wilsin said with a final air. "I'll take care of it from there."

"As you see fit. And when did the company begin conducting trade without me?"

Marchat Wilsin grimaced and shook his head, muttering something to himself too low for her to catch. When he sighed, it sent a ripple that spilled some of the tea.

"It's a sensitive issue, Amat. That's all. It's something I'm taking care of myself. I'll give you all the details when I can, but . . ."

"But?"

"It's difficult. There are some details of the trade that . . . I'm going to have to keep quiet about."

"Why?"

"It's the sad trade," he said. "The girl's well enough along in the pregnancy that she's showing. And there are some facets to getting rid of the baby that I need to address discreetly."

Amat felt herself bristle, but kept her tone calm as she spoke.

"Ah. I see. Well, then. If you feel you can't trust my discretion, I suppose you'd best not talk to me of it at all. Perhaps I might recommend someone else to take my position."

He slapped the water impatiently. Amat crossed her arms. It was a bluff in the sense that they both knew the house would struggle badly without her, and that she would be worse off without her position in it—it wasn't a threat meant seriously. But she was the overseer of the house, and Amat didn't like being kept outside her own business. Marchat's pale face flushed red, but whether with annoyance or shame, she wasn't sure.

"Don't break my stones over this one, Amat. I don't like it any better than you do, but I can't play this one any differently than I am. There is a trade. I'll see to it. I'll petition the Khai Saraykeht for use of his andat. I'll see the girl's taken care of before and after, and I'll see that everyone who needs paying gets paid. I was in business before you signed on, you know. And I *am* your employer. You could assume I know what I'm doing."

"I was just going to say the same thing, pointed the other way. You've consulted me on your affairs for twenty years. If I haven't done something to earn your mistrust—"

"You haven't."

"Then why shut me out of this when you never have before?"

"If I could tell you that, I wouldn't have to shut you out of it," Marchat said. "Just take it that it's not my choice."

"Your uncle asked that I be left out? Or is it the client?"

"I need a bodyguard. At the half-candle."

Amat took a complex pose of agreement that also held a nuance of annoyance. He wouldn't catch the second meaning. Talking over his level was something she did when he'd upset her. She rose, and he scooped the lacquer tray closer and poured himself more tea.

"The client. Can you tell me who she is?" Amat asked.

"No. Thank you, Amat," Wilsin said.

In the women's chamber again, she dried herself and dressed. The street, when she stepped into it, seemed louder, more annoying, than when she went in. She turned toward the House Wilsin compound, to the north and uphill. She had to pause at a waterseller's stall, buy herself a drink, and rest in the shade to collect her thoughts. The sad trade—using the andat to end a pregnancy—wasn't the sort of business House Wilsin had undertaken before now, though other houses had acted as brokers in some instances. She wondered why the change in policy, and why the secrecy, and why Marchat Wilsin would have told her to arrange for the bodyguard if he hadn't wanted her, on some level, to find answers.

Maati held a pose of greeting, his heart in his throat. The pale-skinned man walked slowly around him, black eyes taking in every nuance of his stance. Maati's hands didn't tremble; he had trained for years, first at the school and then with the Dai-kvo. His body knew how to hide anxiety.

The man in poet's robes stopped, an expression half approval, half amusement on his face. Elegant fingers took a pose of greeting that was neither the warmest nor the least formal. With the reply made, Maati let his hands fall to his sides and stood. His first real thought, now that the shock of his teacher's sudden appearance was fading, was that he hadn't expected Heshai-kvo to be so young, or so beautiful.

"What is your name, boy?" the man asked. His voice was cool and hard.

"Maati Vaupathi," Maati said, crisply. "Once the tenth son of Nicha Vaupathi, and now the youngest of the poets."

"Ah. A westerner. It's still in your accent."

The teacher sat in the window seat, his arms folded, still openly considering Maati. The rooms, which had seemed sumptuous during the long worrisome days of Maati's waiting, seemed suddenly squalid with the black-haired man in them. A tin setting for a perfect gem. The soft cotton draperies that flowed from the ceiling, shifting in the hot breeze of late afternoon, seemed dirty beside the poet's skin. The man smiled, his expression not entirely kind. Maati took a pose of obeisance appropriate to a student before his teacher.

"I have come, Heshai-kvo, by the order of the Dai-kvo to learn from you, if you will have me as your pupil."

"Oh, stop that. Bowing and posing like we were dancers. Sit there. On the bed. I have some questions for you."

Maati did as he was told, tucking his legs beneath him in the formal way a student did in a lecture before the Dai-kvo. The man seemed to be amused by this, but said nothing about it.

"So. Maati. You came here . . . what? Six days ago?"

"Seven, Heshai-kvo."

"Seven. And yet no one came to meet you. No one came to collect you or show you the poet's house. It's a long time for a master to ignore his student, don't you think?"

It was exactly what Maati had thought, several times, but he didn't admit that now. Instead he took a pose accepting a lesson.

"I thought so at first. But as time passed, I saw that it was a kind of test, Heshai-kvo."

A tiny smile ghosted across the perfect lips, and Maati felt a rush of pleasure that he had guessed right. His new teacher motioned him to continue, and Maati sat up a degree straighter.

"I thought at first that it might be a test of my patience. To see whether I could be trusted not to hurry things when it wasn't my place. But later I decided that the real test was how I spent my time. Being patient and idle wouldn't teach me anything, and the Khai has the largest library in the summer cities."

"You spent your time in the library?"

Maati took a pose of confirmation, unsure what to make of the teacher's tone.

"These are the palaces of the Khai Saraykeht, Maati-kya," he said with sudden familiarity as he gestured out the window at the grounds, the palaces, the long flow of streets and red tile roofs that sprawled to the sea. "There are scores of utkhaiem and courtiers. I don't think a night passes here without a play being performed, or singers, or dancing. And you spent all your time with the scrolls?"

"I did spent one evening with a group of the utkhaiem. They were from the west . . . from Pathai. I lived there before I went to the school."

"And you thought they might have news of your family."

It wasn't an accusation, though it could have been. Maati pressed his lips thinner, embarrassed, and repeated the pose of confirmation. The smile it brought seemed sympathetic.

"And what did you learn in your productive, studious days with Saraykeht's books."

"I studied the history of the city, and its andat."

The elegant fingers made a motion that both approved and invited him to continue. The dark eyes held an interest that told Maati he had done well.

"I learned, for example, that the Dai-kvo—the last one—sent you here when Iana-kvo failed to hold Petals-Falling-Away after the old poet, Miat-kvo, died."

"And tell me, why do you think he did that?"

"Because Petals-Falling-Away had been used to speed cotton harvests for the previous fifty years," Maati said, pleased to know the answer. "It could make the plant . . . open, I guess. It made it easier to get the fibers. With the loss, the city needed another way to make the process—bringing in the raw cotton and turning it to cloth—better and faster than they could in Galt or the Westlands, or else the traders might go elsewhere, and the whole city would have to change. You had captured Removing-The-Part-That-Continues. Called Sterile in the North, or Seedless in the summer cities. With it, the merchant houses can contract with the Khai, and they won't have to comb the seeds out of the cotton. Even if it took twice as long to harvest, the cotton can still get to the spinners more quickly here than anywhere else. Now the other nations and cities actually send their raw cotton here. Then the weavers come here, because the raw cotton is here. And the dyers and the tailors because of the weavers. All the needle trades."

"Yes. And so Saraykeht holds its place, with only a few more pricked fingers and some blood on the cotton," the man said, taking a pose of confirmation with a softness to the wrists that confused Maati. "But then, blood's only blood, ne?"

The silence went on until Maati, uncomfortable, grasped for something to break it.

"You also rid the summer cities of rats and snakes."

The man came out of his reverie with something like a smile. When he spoke, his voice was amused and self-deprecating.

"Yes. At the price of drawing Galts and Westermen."

Maati took a pose of agreement less formal than before, and his teacher seemed not to mind. In fact, he seemed almost pleased.

"I also learned a lot about the particular needle trades," Maati said. "I wasn't sure how much you needed to know about what happens with the cotton once you're done with it. And sailing. I read a book about sailing."

"But you didn't actually go to the seafront, did you?"

"No."

The teacher took a pose of acceptance that wasn't approval or disapproval, but something of both.

"All this from one little test," he said. "But then, you came through the school very young, so you must have a talent for seeing tests. Tell me. How did you see through the Dai-kvo's little guessing games?"

"You . . . I'm sorry, Heshai-kvo. It's . . . you really want to know that?"

"It can be telling. Especially since you don't want to say. Do you?"

Maati took a pose of apology. He kept his eyes down while he spoke, but he didn't lie.

"When I got to the school—I was still among the younger cohorts—there was an older boy who said something to me. We'd been set to turn the soil in the gardens, and my hands were too soft. I couldn't do the work. And the black robe who was tending us—Otah-kvo, his name was—was very upset with me. But then, when I told him why I hadn't been able to do as he asked, he tried to comfort me. And he told me that if I had worked harder, it wouldn't have helped. That was just before he left the school."

"So? You mean someone told you? That hardly seems fair."

"He didn't though. He didn't *tell* me, exactly. He only said some things about the school. That it wasn't what it looked like. And the things he said made me start thinking. And then . . ."

"And once you knew to look, it wasn't hard to see. I understand."

"It wasn't quite like that."

"Do you ever wonder if you would have made it on your own? I mean if your Otah-kvo hadn't given the game away?"

Maati blushed. The secret he'd held for years with the Dai-kvo pried open in a single conversation. Heshai-kvo was a subtle man. He took a pose of acknowledgement. The teacher, however, was looking elsewhere, an expression passing over him that might have been annoyance or pain.

"Heshai-kvo?"

"I've just remembered something I'm to do. Walk with me."

Maati rose and followed. The palaces spread out, larger than the village that surrounded the Dai-kvo, each individual structure larger than the whole of the school. Together, they walked down the wide marble staircase, into a vaulted hall. The wide, bright air was touched by the scents of sandalwood and vanilla.

"Tell me, Maati. What do you think of slaves?"

The question was an odd one, and his first response—*I don't*—seemed too glib for the occasion. Instead, he took a pose requesting clarification as best he could while still walking more quickly than his usual pace.

"Permanent indenture. What's your opinion of it?"

"I don't know."

"Then think for a moment."

They passed through the hall and onto a wide, flower-strewn path that lead down and to the south. Gardens rich with exotic flowers and fountains spread out before them. Singing slaves, hidden from view by hedges or cloth screens, filled the air with wordless melodies. The sun blared heat like a trumpet, and the thick air made Maati feel almost as if he was swimming. It seemed they'd hardly started walking before Maati's inner robe was sticky with sweat. He found himself struggling to keep up.

As Maati considered the question, servants and utkhaiem passed, pausing to take poses of respect. His teacher took little notice of them or of the heat; where Maati's robes stuck, his flowed like water over stone and no sweat dampened his temples. Maati cleared his throat.

"People who have entered into permanent indenture have either chosen to do so, in return for the protection of the holders of their contracts, or lost their freedoms as punishment for some crime," Maati said, carefully keeping any judgement out of the statement.

"Is that what the Dai-kvo taught you?"

"No. It's just . . . it's just the way it is. I've always known that."

"And the third case? The andat?"

"I don't understand."

The teacher's dark eyebrows rose on the perfect skin of his forehead. His lips took the slightest of all possible smiles.

"The andat aren't criminals. Before they're bound, they have no thought, no will, no form. They're only ideas. How can an idea enter into a contract?"

"How can one refuse?" Maati countered.

"There are names, my boy, for men who take silence as consent."

They passed into the middle gardens. The low halls spread before them, and wider paths almost like streets. The temple rose off to their right, wide and high; its sloping lines reminded Maati of a seagull in flight. At one of the low halls, carts had gathered. Laborers milled around, speaking with one another. Maati caught a glimpse of a bale of cotton being carried in. With a thrill of excitement he realized what was happening. For the first time, he was going to see Heshai-kvo wield the power of the andat.

"Ah, well. Never mind," his teacher said, as if he had been waiting for some answer. "Only Maati? Later on, I'd like you to think about this conversation."

Maati took a pose appropriate to a student accepting an assignment. As they drew nearer, the laborers and merchants moved aside to make room for them. Members of the utkhaiem were also there in fine robes and expensive jewelry. Maati caught sight of an older woman in a robe the color of the sky at dawn—the personal attendant of the Khai Saraykeht.

"The Khai is here?" Maati asked, his voice smaller than he would have liked.

"He attends sometimes. It makes the merchants feel he's paying attention to them. Silly trick, but it seems to work."

Maati swallowed, half at the prospect of seeing the Khai, half at the indifference in his teacher's voice. They passed through the arches and into the shade of the low hall. Warehouse-large, the hall was filled with bale upon bale of raw cotton stacked to the high ceiling. The only space was a narrow gap at the very top, thinner than a bale, and another of perhaps a hand's width at the bottom where metal frames held the cotton off the floor. What little space remained was peopled by the representatives of the merchant houses whose laborers waited outside and, on a dais, the Khai Saraykeht—a man in his middle years, his hair shot with gray, his eyes heavy-lidded. His attendants stood around him, following commands so subtle they approached invisibility. Maati felt the weight of the silence as they entered. Then a murmur moved through the hall, voices too low to make out words or even sentiments. The Khai raised an eyebrow and took a pose of query with an almost inhuman grace.

At his side stood a thick-bodied man, his wide frog-like mouth gaping open in what might have been horror or astonishment. He also wore the robe of a poet. Maati felt his teacher's hand on his shoulder, solid, firm, and cold.

"Maati," the lovely, careful voice said so quietly that only the two of them could hear, "there's something you should know. I'm not Heshai-kvo."

Maati looked up. The dark eyes were on his, something like amusement in their depths.

"Wh-who are you, then?"

"A slave, my dear. The slave you hope to own."

Then the man who was not his teacher turned to the Khai Saraykeht and the spluttering, enraged poet. He took a pose of greeting more appropriate to acquaintances chanced upon at a teahouse than the two most powerful men of the city. Maati, his hands trembling, took a much more formal stance.

"What is this?" the poet—the frog-mouthed Heshai-kvo, he had to be—demanded.

"This?" the man said, turning and considering Maati as if he were a sculpture pointed out at a fair. "It seems to be a boy. Or perhaps a young man. Fifteen summers? Maybe sixteen? It's so hard to know what to call it at that age. I found it abandoned in the upper halls. Apparently it's been wandering around there for days. No one else seems to have any use for it. May I keep it?"

"Heshai," the Khai said. His voice was powerful. He seemed to speak in a conversational tone, but his voice carried like an actor's. The displeasure in the syllables stung.

"Oh," the man at Maati's side said. "Have I displeased? Well, master, you've no one to blame but yourself."

"Silence!" the poet snapped. Maati sensed as much as saw the man beside him go stiff. He chanced a glimpse at the perfect face. The features were fixed in pain, and slowly, as if fighting each movement, the elegant hands took forms of apology and self-surrender, the spine twisted into a pose of abject obeisance.

"I come to do your bidding, Khai Saraykeht," the man—no, the andat, Seedless—said, his voice honey and ashes. "Command me as you will."

The Khai took a pose of acknowledgement, its nuances barely civil. The frog-mouthed poet looked at Maati and gestured pointedly to his own side. Maati scurried to the dais. The andat moved more slowly, but followed.

"You should have waited," Heshai-kvo hissed. "This is a very busy time of year. I would have thought the Dai-kvo would teach you more patience."

Maati fell into a pose of abject apology.

"Heshai-kvo, I was misled. I thought that he . . . that it . . . I am shamed by my error."

"As you should be," the poet snapped. "Just arriving like this, unintroduced and—"

"Good and glorious Heshai," the Khai Saraykeht said, voice envenomed by sarcasm, "I understand that adding another pet to your collection must be trying. And indeed, I regret to interrupt, but . . ."

The Khai gestured grandly at the bales of cotton. His hands were perfect, and his motion the most elegant Maati had ever seen, smooth and controlled and eloquent.

Heshai-kvo briefly adopted a pose of regret, then turned to the beautiful man—Seedless, Sterile, andat. For a moment the two considered each other, some private, silent conversation passing between them. The andat curled his lip in something half sneer, half sorrow. Sweat dampened the teacher's back, and he began trembling as if with a great effort. Then the andat turned and raised his arms theatrically to the cotton.

A moment later, Maati heard a faint tick, like a single raindrop. And then more and more, until an invisible downpour filled the hall. From his position behind the Khai and the poet, he lowered himself looking under the raised platform on which the bales lay. The parquet floor was covered with small black dots skittering and jumping as they struck one another. Cotton seed.

"It is done," Heshai-kvo said, and Maati stood hurriedly.

The Khai clapped his hands and rose, his movement like a dancer's. His robes flowed through the air like something alive. For a moment Maati forgot himself and merely stood in awe.

A pair of servants pulled wide the great doors, and began a low wail, calling the merchants and their laborers to come and take what was theirs. The ut-khaiem took stations by the doors, prepared to collect the fees and taxes for each bale that left. The Khai stood on his dais, grave and beautiful, seeming more a ghost or god than Seedless, who more nearly was.

"You should have waited," Heshai-kvo said again over the voices of the laborers and the din of the merchants at their business. "This is a very bad start for your training. A *very* bad start."

Once again, Maati took a pose of regret, but the poet—his teacher, his new master—turned away, leaving the pose unanswered. Maati stood slowly, his face hot with a blush equally embarrassment and anger, his hands at his sides. At the edge of the dais, the andat sat, his bone-pale hands in his lap. He met Maati's gaze, shrugged, and took a pose of profound apology that might have been genuine or deeply insincere; Maati had no way to tell.

Before he could choose how to respond, Seedless smiled, lowered his hands and looked away.

Amat Kyaan sat at the second-floor window of her apartments, looking out over the city. The setting sun behind her reddened the walls of the soft quarter. Some comfort houses were already hanging out streamers and lamps, the glitter of the lights and the shimmering cloth competing with the glow of fireflies. A fruit seller rang her bell and sang her wares in a gentle melody. Amat Kyaan rubbed stinging salve into her knee and ankle, as she did every evening, to keep the pain at bay. It had been a long day, made longer by the nagging disquiet of her meeting with Marchat Wilsin. And even now, it wasn't finished. There was one more unpleasant task still to be done.

This would be her fifty-eighth summer in the world, and every one had been spent in Saraykeht. Her earliest memories were of her father spinning cured cotton into fine, tough thread, humming to himself as he worked. He was many years dead now, as was her mother. Her sister, Sikhet, had vanished into the comfort houses of the soft quarter when she was only sixteen. Amat Kyaan liked to think she caught glimpses of her still—older, wiser, safe. More likely it was her own desire that her sister be well. Her better mind knew it was only wishes. There had been too many years for the two of them not to have come upon each other.

She felt some nights that she had lived her life as an apology for letting her sister vanish into the soft world. And perhaps it had started that way: her decision to work for a trading house, her rise through the invisible levels of power and wealth, had been meant to balance her sister's assumed fall. But she was an older woman now, and everyone she might have apologized to was gone or dead. She had the status and the respect she needed to do as she pleased. She was no one's sister, no one's daughter, no one's wife or mother. By standing still, she had come almost loose from the world, and she found the solitude suited her.

A grass tick shuffled across her arm, preparing to tap her skin. She caught it, cracked it between her thumbnails, and flicked the corpse out into the street. There were more lanterns lit now, and the callers of different establishments were setting out singers and flute players to tempt men—and occasionally even women—to their doors. A patrol of eight frowning thugs swaggered down the streets, their robes the colors of the great comfort houses. It was too early for there to be many people drunk on the streets—the patrol walked and grimaced only to let the patrons coming in see that they were there.

There was no place safer than the Saraykeht soft quarter at night, and no place more dangerous. Here alone, she suspected, of all the cities of the Khaiem, no one would be attacked, no one raped, no one killed except perhaps the whores and showfighters who worked there. For their clients, every opportunity to twist a mind with strange herbs, to empty a pocket with dice and khit tiles, or to cheapen sex as barter would be made available in perfect safety. It was a beautiful, toxic dream, and she feared it as she loved it. It was a part of her city.

The soft, tentative knock at her door didn't startle her. She had been dreading it as much as expecting it. She turned, taking up her cane, and walked down the long, curved stair to the street level. The door was barred, not from fear, but to keep drunken laborers from mistaking hers for a comfort house. She lifted the bar and swung the door aside.

Liat Chokavi stood in the street, jaw tight, eyes cast down. She was a lovely little thing—brown eyes the color of milky tea and golden skin, smooth as an eggshell. If the girl's face was a little too round to be classically beautiful, her youth forgave her.

Amat Kyaan raised her left hand in a gesture that greeted her student. Liat adopted an answering pose of gratitude at being received, but the stance was undercut by the defensiveness of her body. Amat Kyaan suppressed a sigh and stood back, motioning the girl inside.

"I expected you earlier," she said as she closed the door.

Liat walked to the foot of the stair, but there paused and turned in a formal pose of apology.

"Honored teacher," she began, but Amat cut her off.

"Light the candles. I will be up in a moment."

Liat hesitated, but then turned and went up. Amat Kyaan could trace the girl's footsteps by the creaking of the timbers. She poured herself a cup of limed water, then went slowly up the stairs. The salve helped. Most days she woke able to convince herself that today there would be no trouble, and by nightfall her joints ached. Age was a coward and a thief, and she wasn't about to let it get the better of her. Still, as she took the steps to her workroom, she trusted as much of her weight to the cane as she could.

Liat sat on the raised cushion beside Amat Kyaan's oaken writing desk. Her legs were tucked up under her, her gaze on the floor. The lemon candles danced in a barely-felt breeze, the smoke driving away the worst of the flies. Amat sat at the window and arranged her robe as if she were preparing herself for work.

"Old Sanya must have had more objections than usual. He's normally quite prompt. Give the changes here, let's survey the damage, shall we?"

She held one hand out to the apprentice. A moment later, she lowered it.

"I misplaced the contracts," Liat said, her voice a tight whisper. "I apologize. It is entirely my fault."

Amat sipped her water. The lime made it taste cooler than it was.

"You *misplaced* the contracts?"

"Yes."

Amat let the silence hang. The girl didn't look up. A tear tracked down the round cheek.

"That isn't good," Amat said.

"Please don't send me back to Chaburi-Tan," the girl said. "My mother was so proud when I was accepted here and my father would—"

Amat raised a hand and the pleading stopped, Liat's gaze fixed on the floor. With a sigh, Amat pulled a bundle of papers from her sleeve and tossed them at Liat's knees.

At least the girl hadn't lied about it.

"One of the laborers found this between the bales from the Innis harvest," Amat said. "I gave him your week's wages as a reward."

Liat had the pages in her hands, and Amat watched the tension flow out of her, Liat's body collapsing on itself.

"Thank you," the girl said. Amat assumed she meant some god and not herself.

"I don't suppose I need to tell you what would have happened if these had come out? It would have destroyed every concession House Wilsin has had from Sanya's weavers in the last year."

"I know. I'm sorry. I really am."

"And do you have any idea how the contract might have fallen out of your sleeve? The warehouse seems an odd place to have lost them."

Liat blushed furiously and looked away. Amat knew that she had guessed correctly. It should have made her angry, but all she really felt was a kind of nostalgic sympathy. Liat was in the middle of her seventeenth summer, and some mistakes were easier to make at that age.

"Did you at least do something to make sure you aren't giving him a child?"

Liat's gaze flickered up at Amat and then away, fast as a mouse. The girl swallowed. Even the tips of her ears were crimson. She pretended to brush a fly off her leg.

"I got some teas from Chisen Wat," she said at last, and softly.

"Gods! Her? She's as likely to poison you by mistake. Go to Urrat on the Street of Beads. She's the one I always saw. You can tell her I sent you."

When Liat looked at her this time, the girl neither spoke nor looked away. She'd shocked her. And, as Amat felt the first rush of blood in her own cheeks, maybe she'd shocked herself a little, too. Amat took a pose of query.

"What? You think I was born before they invented sex? Go see Urrat. Maybe we can keep you from the worst parts of being young and stupid. Leaving contracts in your love nest. Which one was it, anyway? Still Itani Noyga?"

"Itani's my heartmate," Liat protested.

"Yes, yes. Of course."

He was a good-looking boy, Itani. Amat had seen him several times, mostly on occasions that involved prying her apprentice away from him and his cohort. He had a long face and broad shoulders, and was maybe a little too clever to be working as a laborer. He knew his letters and numbers. If he'd had more ambition, there might have been other work for a boy like that . . .

Amat frowned, her body taking a subtle tension even before the thought was fully in her mind. Itani Noyga, with his broad shoulders and strong legs. Certainly there was other work he could be put to. Driving away feral dogs, for example, and convincing roadside thugs to hunt for easier prey than Marchat Wilsin. Marchat wouldn't be keeping track of who each of his laborers were sharing pillows with.

And pillows were sometimes the best places to talk.

"Amat-cha? Are you all right?"

"Itani. Where is he now?"

"I don't know. Likely back at his quarters. Or maybe a teahouse."

"Do you think you could find him?"

Liat nodded. Amat gestured for a block of ink, and Liat rose, took one from the shelf and brought it to her desk. Amat took a length of paper and took a moment to calm herself before she began writing. The pen sounded as dry as a bird claw on pavement.

"There's an errand I want Itani for. Marchat Wilsin needs a bodyguard tonight. He's going to a meeting in one of the low towns at the half-candle, and he wants someone to walk with him. I don't know how long the meeting will last, but I can't assume it will be brief. I'll tell his overseer to release him from duty tomorrow."

She took another sheet of paper, scraped the pen across the ink and began a second letter. Liat, at her shoulder, read the words as she wrote them.

"This one, I want you to deliver to Rinat Lyanita after you find Itani," Amat said as she wrote. "If Itani doesn't know that he's to go, Rinat will do. I don't want Marchat waiting for someone who never arrives."

"Yes, Amat-cha, but . . ."

Amat blew on the ink to cure it. Liat's words failed, and she took no pose, but a single vertical line appeared between her brows. Amat tested the ink. It smudged only a little. Good enough for the task at hand. She folded both orders and sealed them with hard wax. There wasn't time to sew the seams.

"Ask it," Amat said. "And stop scowling. You'll give yourself a headache."

"The mistake was mine, Amat-cha. It isn't Itani's fault that I lost the contracts. Punishing him for my error is . . ."

"It isn't a punishment, Liat-kya," Amat said, using the familiar -kya to reassure her. "I just need him to do me this favor. And, when he comes back tomorrow, I want him to tell you all about the journey. What town he went to, who was there, how long the meeting went. Everything he can remember. Not to anyone else; just to you. And then you to me."

Liat took the papers and tucked them into her sleeve. The line was still between her brows. Amat wanted to reach over and smooth it out with her thumb, like it was a stray mark on paper. The girl was thinking too much. Perhaps this was a poor idea after all. Perhaps she should take the orders back.

But then she wouldn't discover what business Marchat Wilsin was doing without her.

"Can you do this for me, Liat-kya?"

"Of course, but . . . is something going on, Amat-cha?"

"Yes, but don't concern yourself with it. Just do as I ask, and I'll take care of the rest."

Liat took a pose of acceptance and leave-taking. Amat responded with thanks and dismissal appropriate for a supervisor to an apprentice. Liat went down the stairs, and Amat heard her close the door behind her as she went. Outside, the fireflies shone and vanished, brighter now as twilight dimmed the city. She watched the streets: the firekeeper at the corner with his banked kiln, the young men in groups heading west into the soft quarter, ready to trade lengths of silver and copper for pleasures that would be gone by morning. And there, among them, Liat Chokavi walking briskly to the east, toward the warehouses and laborers' quarters, the dyeworks and the weavers.

Amat watched until the girl vanished around a corner, passing beyond recall, then she went down and barred her door.

2

>+< The boundary arch on the low road east of Saraykeht was a short walk from the Wilsin compound. They reached it in about the time it took the crescent moon to shift the width of two of Marchat's thick fingers. Buildings and roads continued, splaying out into the high grasses and thick trees, but once they passed through the pale stone arch wide enough for three carts to pass through together and high as a tree, they had left the city.

"In Galt, there'd have been a wall," Marchat said.

The young man, Itani, took a pose of query.

"Around the city," Marchat said. "To protect it in time of war. We didn't have andat to aim at each other like your ancestors did. In Kirinton, where I was born, anytime you were bad, the Lord Watchman set you to repairing the wall."

"Can't have been pleasant," Itani agreed.

"What do they do in Saraykeht when a boy's caught stealing a pie?"

"I don't know."

"Never misbehaved as a child?"

Itani grinned. He had a strong smile.

"Rarely caught," Itani said. Marchat laughed.

They made an odd pair, he thought. Him, an old Galt with a walking staff as much to lean on as to swipe at dogs if the occasion arose, and this broad-backed, stone-armed young man in the rough canvas of a laborer. Not so odd, he hoped, as to attract attention.

"Noyga's your family name? Noyga. Yes. You work on Muhatia's crew, don't you?"

"He's a good man, Muhatia," Itani said.

"I hear he's a prick."

"That too," Itani agreed, in the same cheerful tone of voice. "A lot of the men don't like working with him. He's got a sharp tongue, and he hates running behind schedule."

"You don't mind him, though?"

Itani shrugged. It was another point in his favor. The boy disliked his overseer, that was clear, and yet here he was, alone with the head of the house and not willing to tell tales against him. It spoke well of him, and that was good for more than one reason. That he could trust Itani's discretion made his night one degree less awful.

"What else was different in Kirinton?" Itani asked, and as they walked, Marchat told him. Tales of the Galt of his childhood. The war with Eymond, the blackberry harvests, the midwinter bonfires when people brought their sins to be burned. The boy listened carefully, appreciatively. Granted, he was likely just currying favor, but he did it well. It wasn't far before Marchat felt the twinges of memories half-forgotten. He'd belonged somewhere once, before his uncle had sent him here.

The road was very little traveled, especially in the dead of night. The darkness made the uneven cobbles and then rutted dirt treacherous; the flies and night wasps were out in swarms, freed from torpor by the relative cool of the evening. Cicadas sang in the trees. The air smelled of moonrose and rain. No one in the few houses they passed that had candles and lanterns still burning seemed to show much curiosity, and it wasn't long before they were out, away from the last traces of Saraykeht. Tall grasses leaned close against the road, and twice groups of men passed them without comment or glance. Once something large shifted in the grass, but nothing emerged from it.

As they came nearer the low town, Marchat could feel his companion moving more slowly, hesitating. He couldn't say if the laborer was picking up on his own growing dread, or if there was some other issue. The first glimmering light of the low town was showing in the darkness when the man spoke.

"Marchat-cha, I was wondering . . ."

Marchat tried to take a pose of polite encouragement, but the walking stick complicated things. Instead he said, "Yes?"

"I'm coming near to the end of my indenture," Itani said.

"Really? How old are you?"

"Twenty summers, but I signed on young."

"You must have. You'd have been, what? Fifteen?"

"There's a girl," the young man said, having trouble with the words. Embarrassed. "She's . . . well, she's not a laborer. I think it's hard for her that I am. I'm not a scholar or a translator, but I have numbers and letters. I was wondering if you might know of any opportunities."

In the darkness, Marchat could see the boy's hands twisted into a pose of respect. So that was it.

"If you move up in the world, you think she'll like you better."

"It would make things easier for her," Itani said.

"And not for you?"

Again, the grin and this time a shrug with it.

"I lift things and put them back down," Itani said. "It's tiring sometimes, but it's not difficult."

"I don't know of anything just at hand. I'll see what I can find though."

"Thank you, Wilsin-cha."

They walked along another few paces. The light before them became a solid glow. A dog barked, but not so nearby as to be worrisome, and no other barks or howls answered it.

"She told you to ask me, didn't she?" Marchat asked.

"Yes," Itani agreed, the tension that had been in his voice gone.

"Are you in love with her?"

"Yes," the boy said, "I want her to be happy."

Those are two different answers, Marchat thought, but didn't say. He'd been that age once, and he remembered it well enough to know there was no point in pressing. They were in the low town proper now, anyway.

The streets here were muddy and smelled more of shit than moonrose. The buildings with their rotting thatch roofs and rough stone walls stood off at angles from the road. Two streets in, and so almost halfway though the town, a long, low house stood at the opening to a rough square. A lantern hung from a hook beside its door. Marchat motioned to Itani.

"Wait for me here," he said. "I'll be back as soon as I can."

Itani nodded his understanding. There was no hesitation or objection in his stance so far as Marchat could tell. It was more than he would have expected of himself if someone had told *him* to stand in this pesthole street in the black of night for some unknown stretch of time. *Gods go with you, you poor bastard*, Marchat thought. *And with me, too, for that.*

Inside, the house was dim. The ceiling was low, and though the walls were wide apart, the house had the feel of being too close. Like a cave. Part of that was the smell of mold and stale water, part the dim doorways and black arches that led to the inner rooms. A squat table ran the length of one wall, and two men stood against it. The larger, a thick-necked tough with a long knife hanging from his belt, eyed Marchat. The other, moon-faced and pleasant-looking, nodded welcome.

"Oshai," Marchat said by way of greeting.

"Welcome to our humble quarters," the moon-faced man said and smiled. Marchat disliked that smile, polite though it was. It was too much like the smile of someone helping you onto a sinking boat.

"Is it here?" Marchat asked.

Oshai nodded to a door set deeper in the gloom. A glimmer of candlelight showed its outline. Bad craftsmanship.

"He's been waiting," Oshai said.

Marchat grunted before walking deeper into the darkness. The wood of the door was water-rotted, the leather hinge loose and ungainly. Marchat had to lift the door by its handle to close it behind him. The meeting room was smaller, better lit, quiet. A night candle stood in a wall niche, burned past half. Several other candles burned on a small table. And sitting at the table itself was the andat. Seedless. Marchat's skin crawled as the thing considered him, black eyes shifting silently. The andat were unnerving under the best circumstances.

Marchat took a pose of greeting that the andat returned, then Seedless pushed out a stool and motioned to it. Marchat sat.

"You were able to come here without the poet's knowing?" Marchat asked.

"The great poet of Saraykeht is spending his evening drunk. As usual," Seedless replied, his voice conversational and smooth as cream. "He's beyond caring where I am or what I'm doing."

"And I hear the woman arrived?"

"Yes. Oshai says she's everything we need. Sweet-tempered, tractable, and profoundly credulous. She's unlikely to spook and run away like the last one. And she's from Nippu."

"Nippu?" Marchat said and curled his lip. "That's a backwater little island. Don't you think it might raise suspicion? I mean why would some farm bitch from a half-savage island come to Saraykeht just to drop her baby?"

"You'll think of something plausible," Seedless said, waving the objection away. "The point is she only speaks east island tongues. If she were from someplace with a real port, she might know a civilized language. Instead, you'll be using Oshai as her translator. It should be easy."

"My overseer may know the language."

"And you can't delegate this to someone who doesn't?" Seedless said. "Or are all of your employees brilliant translators?"

"Any idea who the father is?" Marchat said, shifting the subject.

Seedless made a gesture that wasn't a formal pose, but indicated the whole world and everything in it with a sweep of his delicate fingers.

"Who knows? Some passing fisherman. A tradesman. Someone who passed through her town and got her legs apart. No one who'll notice or care much if he does. He isn't important. And your part of the plan is progressing?"

"We're prepared. We have the payment ready. Pearls, mostly, and a hundred lengths of silver. It's the sort of thing an East Islander might pay with," Marchat said. "And there's no reason the Khai should look into it until the thing's been done."

"That's to the good, then," Seedless said. "Arrange the audience with the Khai. If all goes well, we won't have to speak again, you and I."

Marchat started to take a pose that expressed hope, but halfway in wondered if it might be taken the wrong way. He saw Seedless notice his hesitation. A thin smile graced the pale lips. Feeling an angry blush coming on, Marchat abandoned the pose.

"It will work, won't it?" he asked.

"It isn't the first babe I'll drop out before its time. This is what I am, Wilsin."

"No, I don't mean can you do it. I mean will it really break him? Heshai. He's taken the worst you could give him for years. Because if this little drama we're arranging doesn't work . . . If there's any chance at all that it should fail and the Khai find out that Galts were conspiring to deprive him of his precious andat, the consequences could be huge."

Seedless shifted forward on his chair, his gaze fastened on nothing. Marchat had heard once that andat didn't breathe except to speak. He watched the unmoving ribs for a long moment while the andat was silent. The rumor appeared true. At last, the spirit drew in his breath and spoke.

"Heshai is about to kill a child whose mother loves it. There isn't anything worse than that. Not for him. Picture it. This island girl? He's going to watch the light die in her eyes and know that without *him*, it wouldn't have happened. You want to know will that break him? Wilsin-cha, it will snap him like a twig."

They were silent for a moment. The naked hunger on the andat's face made Marchat squirm on his stool. Then, as if they'd been speaking of nothing more intimate or dangerous than a sugar crop, Seedless leaned back and grinned.

"With the poet broken, you'll be rid of me, which is what you want," Seedless said, "and I won't exist anymore to care one way or the other. So we'll both have won."

"You sound like a suicide to me," Marchat said. "You want your own death."

"In a sense," Seedless agreed. "But it doesn't mean for me what it would for you. We aren't the same kind of beast, you and I."

"Agreed."

"Do you want to see her? She's asleep in the next room. If you're quiet . . ."

"No, thank you," Marchat said, rising. "I'll arrange things with Oshai once I've scheduled the audience with the Khai. He and I can make the arrangements from there. If I could avoid seeing her at all before the day itself, that would be good."

"If good's the word," Seedless said, taking a pose of agreement and farewell.

Outside again, the night seemed cooler. Marchat pounded his walking stick against the ground, as if shaking dried mud off it, but really just to feel the sting in his fingers. His chest ached with something like dread. It was rotten, this business. Rotten and wrong and dangerous. And if he did anything to prevent it . . . what then? The Galtic High Council would have him killed, to start. He couldn't stop it. He couldn't even bow out and let someone else take his part in it.

There was no way through this but through. At least he'd kept Amat out of it.

"Everything went well?" the boy Itani asked.

"Well enough," Marchat lied as he started off briskly into the darkness.

AMAT KYAAN HAD HOPED TO SET OUT IN THE MORNING, BEFORE THE DAY'S HEAT was too thick. Liat had come to her with Itani's account of the route early enough, but the details were few and sketchy. Marchat and the boy hadn't gotten back to the compound until past the quarter candle, and his report to Liat hadn't been as thorough as it might have been had he known what use he had been put to. It had been enough to find which of the low towns they had visited and what sort of house they'd gone to.

Armed with those facts, it hadn't been so hard to find a contract that rented such a building, one that had been paid out of Wilsin's private funds and not those of the house proper. There were letters that spoke vaguely of a girl and a journey to Saraykeht, but the time it took to find that much cost Amat the better part of the morning. As she walked down the low road east of the city, the boundary arch grown small behind her, she felt her annoyance growing. Sweat ran down her spine, and her bad hip ached already.

In the cool just before dawn, it might almost have been a pleasant walk. The high grasses sang with cicadas, the trees were thick with their summer leaves. As it was, Amat felt as damp as if she'd walked out of a bathhouse, drenched in her own sweat. The sun pressed on her shoulders like a hand. And the trip back, she knew, would be worse.

Men and women of the low towns took poses of greeting and deference as they passed her, universally heading into the city. They pushed handcarts of fruits and grains, chickens and ducks to sell to the compounds of the rich or the palaces or the open markets. Some carried loads on their backs. On one particularly rutted stretch of road, she passed an oxcart where it had slid into the roadside mud. One wheel was badly bent. The carter, a young man with tears in his eyes, was shouting and beating the ox who seemed barely to notice. Amat's practiced eye valued the wheel at three or four times the contents of the cart. Whoever the boy carter answered to—father, uncle, or farmer rich enough to own indentured labor—they wouldn't be pleased to hear of this. Amat stepped around, careful how she placed her cane, and moved on.

Low towns existed at the edges of all the cities of the Khaiem like swarms of flies. Outside the boundaries of the city, no particular law bound these men and women; the utkhaiem didn't enforce peace or punish crimes. And still, a rough order was the rule. Disagreements were handled between the people or taken to a low judge who passed an opinion, which was followed more often than not. The traditions of generations were as complex and effective as the laws of the Empire. Amat felt no qualms about walking along the broken cobbles of the low road by herself, so long as it was in daylight and there was enough traffic to keep the dogs away.

No qualms except for what she might find at the end.

The low town itself was worse than she'd expected. Itani hadn't mentioned the smell of shit or the thick, sticky mud of the roads. Dogs and pigs and chickens all shared the path with her. A girl perhaps two years old stood naked in a doorway as she passed, her eyes no more domesticated than the pigs'. Amat found herself struggling to imagine Marchat Wilsin, head of House Wilsin in Saraykeht, trudging through this squalor in the dead of night. But there

was the house Itani had described to Liat, and then Liat to her. Amat stood in
the ruined square and steeled herself. To be turned back now would be humiliating.

So, she told herself, she wouldn't be turned back. Simple as that.

"Hai!" Amat called, rapping the doorframe with her cane. Across the square,
a dog barked, as if the hail had been intended for him. Something stirred in
the gloom of the house. Amat stood back, cultivating impatience. She was the
senior overseer of the house. She mustn't go into this unsure of herself, and
anger was a better mask than courtesy. She crossed her arms and waited.

A man emerged, younger then she was, but still gray about the temples. His
rough clothes inspired no confidence, and the knife at his belt shone. For the
first time, Amat wondered if she had come unprepared. Perhaps if she'd made
Itani accompany her . . . She raised her chin, considering the man as if he were
a servant.

The silence between them stretched.

"What?" the man demanded at last.

"I'm here to see the woman," Amat Kyaan said. "Wilsin-cha wants an in-
ventory of her health."

The man frowned, and his gaze passed over her head, nervously surveying
the street.

"You got the wrong place, grandmother. I don't know what you're talking
about."

"I'm Amat Kyaan, senior overseer for House Wilsin. And if you don't want
to continue our conversation here in the open, you should invite me in."

He hesitated, hand twitching toward his knife and then away. He was
caught, she could see. To let her in was an admission that some traffic was taking place. But turning her away risked the anger of his employer if Amat was
who she said she was, and on the errand she claimed. Amat took a pose of
query that implied the offer of assistance—not a pose she would wish to see
from a superior.

The knife man's dilemma was solved when another form appeared. The
newcomer looked like nothing very much, a round, pale face, hair unkempt as
one woken from sleep. The annoyance in his expression seemed to mirror her
own, but the knife man's reaction was of visible relief. This was his overseer,
then. Amat turned her attention to him.

"This woman," the knife man said. "She says she's Wilsin's overseer."

The moon-faced man smiled pleasantly and took a pose of greeting to her
even as he spoke to the other man.

"That would be because she is. Welcome, Kyaan-cha. Please come in."

Amat strode into the low house, the two men stepping back to let her pass.
The round-faced man closed the door, deepening the gloom. As Amat's eyes
adjusted to the darkness, details began to swim out of it. The wide, low main

room, too bare to mark the house as a place where people actually lived. The moss growing at edge where wall met ceiling.

"I've come to see the client," Amat said. "Wilsin-cha wants to be sure she's well. If she miscarries during the negotiations, we'll all look fools."

"The *client*? Yes. Yes, of course," the round-faced man said, and something in his voice told Amat she'd stepped wrong. Still, he took a pose of obeisance and motioned her to the rear of the place. Down a short hallway, a door opened to a wooden porch. The light was thick and green, filtered through a canopy of trees. Insects droned and birds called, chattering to one another. And leaning against a half-rotten railing was a young woman. She was hardly older than Liat, her skin the milky pale of an islander. Golden hair trailed down her back, and her belly bulged over a pair of rough canvas laborer's pants. Half, perhaps three-quarters of the way through her term. Hearing them, she turned and smiled. Her eyes were blue as the sky, her lips thick. *Eastern islands*, Amat thought. *Uman, or possibly Nippu.*

"Forgive me, Kyaan-cha," the moon-faced man said. "My duties require me elsewhere. Miyama will be here to help you, should you require it."

Amat took a pose of thanks appropriate for a superior releasing an underling. The man replied with the correct form, but a strange half-mocking cant to his wrists. He had thick hands, Amat noted, and strong shoulders. She turned away, waiting until the man's footsteps faded behind her. He would go, she guessed, to Saraykeht, to Wilsin. She hadn't managed to avoid suspicion, but by the time Marchat knew she'd discovered this place, it would be too late to shut her out of it. It would have to do.

"My name is Amat Kyaan," she said. "I'm here to inquire after your health. Marchat is a good man, but perhaps not so wise in women's matters."

The girl cocked her head, like listening to an unfamiliar song. Amat felt her smile fade a degree.

"You *do* know the Khaiate tongues?"

The girl giggled and said something. She spoke too quickly to follow precisely, but the words had the liquid feel of an east island language. Amat cleared her throat, and tried again, slowly in Nippu.

"My name is Amat Kyaan," she said.

"I'm Maj," the girl said, matching Amat's slow diction and exaggerating as if she were speaking to a child.

"You've come a long way to be here. I trust the travel went well?"

"It was hard at first," the girl said. "But the last three days, I've been able to keep food down."

The girl's hand strayed to her belly. Tiny, dark stretchmarks already marbled her skin. She was thin. If she went to term, she'd look like an egg on sticks. But, of course, she wouldn't go to term. Amat watched the pale fingers as they unconsciously caressed the rise and swell where the baby grew in darkness, and a sense of profound dislocation stole into her. This wasn't a noblewoman whose virginity wanted plausibility. This wasn't a child of wealth too fragile for blood teas. This didn't fit any of the hundred scenarios that had plagued Amat through the night.

She leaned against the wooden railing, taking some of the weight off her aching hip, put her cane aside, and crossed her hands.

"Marchat has told me so little of you," she said, struggling to find the vocabulary she needed. "How did you come to Saraykeht?"

The girl grinned and spun her tale. She spoke too quickly sometimes, and Amat had to make her repeat herself.

It seemed the father of her get had been a member of the utkhaiem—one of the great families of Saraykeht, near to the Khai himself. He'd been travelling in Nippu in disguise. He'd never revealed his true identity to her when he knew her, but though the affair had been brief, he had lost his heart to her. When he heard she was with child, he'd sent Oshai—the moon-faced man—to bring her here, to him. As soon as the politics of court allowed, he would return to her, marry her.

As improbability mounted on improbability, Amat nodded, encouraged, drew her out. And with each lie the girl repeated, sure of its truth, nausea grew in Amat. The girl was a fool. Beautiful, lovely, pleasant, and a fool. It was a story from the worst sort of wishing epic, but the girl, Maj, believed it.

She was being used, though for what, Amat couldn't imagine. And worse, she loved her child.

NOTHING WAS SAID TO MAATI. HIS BELONGINGS SIMPLY VANISHED FROM THE ROOM in which he had been living, and a servant girl led him down from the palace proper to a house nestled artfully in a stand of trees—the poet's house. An artificial pond divided it from the grounds. A wooden bridge spanned the water, arching sharply, like a cat's back. Koi—white and gold and scarlet—flowed and shifted beneath the water's skin as Maati passed over them.

Within, the house was as lavish as the palace, but on a more nearly human scale. The stairway that led up to the sleeping quarters was a rich, dark wood and inlaid with ivory and mother of pearl, but no more than two people could have walked abreast up its length. The great rooms at the front, with their hinged walls that could open onto the night air or close like a shutter, were cluttered with books and scrolls and diagrams sketched on cheap paper. An ink brick had stained the arm of a great silk-embroidered chair. The place smelled of tallow candles and old laundry.

For the first time since he had left the Dai-kvo, Maati felt himself in a space the character of which he could understand. He waited for his teacher, prepared for whatever punishment awaited him. Darkness came late, and he lit the night candle as the sun set. The silence of the poet's house was his only companion as he slept.

In the morning, servants delivered a meal of sweet fruits, apple-bread still warm from the palace kitchens, and a pot of smoky, black tea. Maati ate alone, a feeling of dread stealing over him. Putting him here alone to wait might, he supposed, be another trick, another misdirection. Perhaps no one would ever come.

He turned his attention to the disorder that filled the house. After leaving the bowls, cups and knives from his own meal out on the grass for the servants to retrieve, he gathered up so many abandoned dishes from about the house that the pile of them made it seem he had eaten twice. Scrolls opened so long that dust covered the script, he cleaned, furled, and returned to the cloth sleeves that he could find. Several he suspected were mismatched—a deep blue cloth denoting legal considerations holding a scroll of philosophy. He took some consolation that the scrolls on the shelves seemed equally haphazard.

By the afternoon, twinges of resentment had begun to join the suspicion that he was once again being duped. Even as he swept the floors that had clearly gone neglected for weeks, he began almost to hope that this further abandonment *was* another plot by the andat. If it were only that Heshai-kvo had this little use for him, perhaps the Dai-kvo shouldn't have let him come. Maati wondered if a poet had the option of refusing an apprentice. Perhaps this neglect was Heshai-kvo's way of avoiding duties he otherwise couldn't.

It had been only a few weeks before that he had taken leave of the Dai-kvo, heading south along the river to Yalakeht and there by ship to the summer cities. It was his first time training under an acting poet, seeing one of the andat first hand, and eventually studying to one day take on the burden of the andat Seedless himself. *I am a slave, my dear. The slave you hope to own.*

Maati pushed the dust out the door, shoving with his broom as much as sweeping. When the full heat of the day came on, Maati opened all the swinging walls, transforming the house into a kind of pavilion. A soft breeze ruffled the pages of books and the tassels of scrolls. Maati rested. A distant hunger troubled him, and he wondered how to signal from here for a palace servant to bring him something to eat. If Heshai-kvo were here, he could ask.

His teacher arrived at last, at first a small figure, no larger than Maati's thumb, trundling out from the palace. Then as he came nearer, Maati made out the wide face, the slanted, weak shoulders, the awkward belly. As he crossed the wooden bridge, the high color in the poet's face—cheeks red as cherries and sheened in an unhealthy sweat—came clear. Maati rose and adopted a pose of welcome appropriate for a student to his master.

Heshai's rolling gait slowed as he came near. The wide mouth gaped as Heshai-kvo took in the space that had been his unkempt house. For the first time, Maati wondered if perhaps he had made a mistake in cleaning it. He felt a blush rising in his cheeks and shifted to a pose of apology.

Heshai-kvo raised a hand before he could speak.

"No. No, it's . . . gods, boy. I don't think the place has looked like this since I came here. Did you . . . there was a brown book, leather-bound, on that table over there. Where did it end up?"

"I don't know, Heshai-kvo," Maati said. "I will find it immediately."

"Don't. No. It will rise to the surface eventually, I'm sure. Here. Come. Sit."

The poet moved awkwardly, like a man gout-plagued, but his joints, so far as Maati could make them out within the brown robes, were unswollen. Maati tried not to notice the stains of spilled food and drink on the poet's sleeves and down the front of his robes. As he lowered himself painfully into a chair of black lacquer and white woven cane, the poet spoke.

"We've gotten off to a bad start, haven't we?"

Maati took a pose of contrition, but the poet waved it away.

"I'm looking forward to teaching you. I thought I should say so. But there's little enough that I can do with you just now. Not until the harvests are all done. And that may not be for weeks. I'll get to you when I have time. There's quite a bit I'll have to show you. The Dai-kvo can give you a good start, but holding one of the andat is much more than anything he'll have told you. And Seedless . . . well, I haven't done you any favors with Seedless, I'm afraid."

"I'm grateful that you were willing to accept me, Heshai-kvo."

"Yes. Yes, well. That's all to the good, then. Isn't it. In the meantime, you should make use of your freedom. You understand? It can be a lovely city. Take . . . take your time with it, eh? Live a little before we lock you back down into all this being a poet nonsense, eh?"

Maati took a pose appropriate to a student accepting instruction, though he could see in Heshai's bloodshot eyes that this was not quite the reply the poet had hoped for. An awkward silence stretched between them, broken when Heshai forced a smile, stood, and clapped Maati on the shoulder.

"Excellent," the poet said with such gusto that it was obvious he didn't mean it. "I've got to switch these robes out for fresh. Busy, you know, busy. No time to rest."

No time to rest. And yet it was the afternoon, and the poet, his teacher, was still in yesterday's clothes. No time to rest, nor to meet him when he arrived, nor to come to the house anytime in the night for fear of speaking to a new apprentice. Maati watched Heshai's wide form retreat up the stairs, heard the footsteps tramping above him as the poet rushed through his ablutions. His head felt like it had been stuffed with wool as he tried to catalog all the things he might have done that would have pushed his teacher away.

"Stings, doesn't it? Not being wanted," a soft voice murmured behind him. Maati spun. Seedless stood on the opened porch in a robe of perfect black shot with an indigo so deep it was hard to see where it blended with the deeper darkness. The dark, mocking eyes considered him. Maati took no pose, spoke no words. Seedless nodded all the same, as if he had replied. "We can talk later, you and I."

"I have nothing to say to you."

"All the better. I'll talk. You can listen."

The poet Heshai clomped down the stairs, a fresh robe, brown silk over cream, in place. The stubble had been erased from his jowls. Poet and andat considered each other for a breathless moment, and then turned and walked together down the path. Maati watched them go—the small, awkward shape of the master; the slim, elegant shadow of the slave. They walked, Maati noticed, with the same pace, the same length of stride. They might almost have been old friends, but for the careful way they never brushed each other, even walking abreast.

As they topped the rise of the bridge, Seedless looked back, and raised a perfect, pale hand to him in farewell.

"SHE DOESN'T KNOW."

Marchat Wilsin half-rose from the bath, cool water streaming off his body. His expression was strange—anger, relief, something else more obscure than these. The young man he had been meeting with stared at Amat, open-mouthed with shock at seeing a clothed woman in the bathhouse. Amat restrained herself from making an obscene gesture at him.

"Tsani-cha," Wilsin said, addressing the young man though his gaze was locked on Amat. "Forgive me. My overseer and I have pressing business. I will send a runner with the full proposal."

"But Wilsin-cha," the young man began, his voice trailing off when the old Galt turned to him. Amat saw something in Wilsin's face that would have made her blanch too, had she been less fueled by her rage. The young man took a pose of thanks appropriate to closing an audience, hopped noisily out of the bath and strode out.

"Have you seen her?" Amat demanded, leaning on her cane. "Have you spoken with her?"

"No, I haven't. Close the door, Amat."

"She thinks—"

"I said close the door; I meant close the *door*."

Amat paused, then limped over and slammed the wooden door shut. The sounds of the bathhouse faded. When she turned back, Wilsin was sitting on the edge of the recessed bath, his head in his hands. The bald spot at the top of his head was flushed pink. Amat moved forward.

"What were you thinking, Amat?"

"That this can't be right," she said. "I met with the girl. She doesn't know about the sad trade. She's an innocent."

"She's the only one in this whole damned city, then. Did you tell her? Did you warn her?"

"Without knowing what this is? Of course not. When was the last time you knew me to act without understanding the situation?"

"This morning," he snapped. "Now. Just now. Gods. And where did you learn to speak Nippu anyway?"

Amat stood beside him and then slowly lowered herself to the blue-green tiles. Her hip flared painfully, but she pushed it out of her mind.

"What is this?" she asked. "You're hiring the Khai to end a pregnancy, and the mother doesn't know that's what you're doing? You're killing a wanted child? It doesn't make sense."

"I can't tell you. I can't explain. I'm . . . I'm not allowed."

"At least promise me that the child is going to live. Can you promise me that?"

He looked over at her, his pale eyes empty as a corpse.

"Gods," Amat breathed.

"I never wanted to come here," he said. "This city. That was my uncle's idea. I wanted to run the tripled trade. Silver and iron from Eddensea south to Bakta for sugar and rum, then to Far Galt for cedar and spicewood and back to Eddensea. I wanted to fight pirates. Isn't that ridiculous? Me. Fighting pirates."

"You will not make me feel sorry for you. Not now. You are Marchat Wilsin, and the voice of your house in Saraykeht. I have seen you stand strong before a mob of Westermen screaming for blood. You faced down a high judge when you thought he was wrong and called him fool to his face. Stop acting like a sick girl. We don't have to do this. Refuse the contract."

Wilsin looked up, his chin raised, his shoulders squared. For a moment, she thought he might do as she asked. But when he spoke, his voice was defeated.

"I can't. The stakes are too high. I've already petitioned the Khai for an audience. It's in motion, and I can't stop it any more than I can make the tide come early."

Amat kicked off her sandals, raised the hem of her robes, and let her aching feet sink into the cool water. Light played on the surface, patterns of brightness and shadow flickering across Marchat's chest and face. He was weeping. That more than anything else turned her rage to fear.

"Then help me make sense of it. What is this child?" Amat said. "Who is the father?"

"No one. The child is no one. The father is no one. The girl is no one."

"Then why, Marchat? Why . . ."

"I can't tell you! Why won't you hear me when I say that? Ah? I don't get to tell you. Gods. Amat. Amat, why did you have to go out there?"

"You wanted me to. Why else ask me to arrange a bodyguard? You told me of a meeting I wasn't welcome to. You said there was house business, and then you said that you trusted me. How could you think I wouldn't look?"

He laughed with a sound like choking—mirthless and painful. His thick fingers grasped his knees, fingertips digging into pink flesh. Amat laid her cane aside and pressed her palm to his bent shoulder. Through the carved cedar blinds she heard someone on the street shriek and go silent.

"The round-faced one—Oshai. He came, didn't he? He told you I went there."

"Of course he did. He wanted to know if I'd sent you."

"What did you tell him?"

"That I hadn't."

"I see."

The silence stretched. She waited, willing him to speak, willing some words that would put it in some perspective less awful than it seemed. But Wilsin said nothing.

"I'll go back to my apartments," Amat said. "We can talk about this later."

She reached for her cane, but Wilsin's hand trapped hers. There was something in his eyes now, an emotion. Fear. It was as if they'd been soaking in it instead of water. She could feel her own heart trip faster as his eyes searched hers.

"Don't. Don't go home. He'll be waiting for you."

For the space of four breaths together, they were silent. Amat had to swallow to loosen her throat.

"Hide, Amat. Don't tell me where you've gone. Keep your head low for . . . four weeks. Five. It'll be over by then. And once it's finished with, you'll be safe. I can protect you then. You're only in danger if they think you might stop it from happening. Once it's done . . ."

"I could go to the utkhaiem. I could tell them that something's wrong. We could have Oshai in chains by nightfall, if . . ."

Marchat shook his wooly, white head slowly, his gaze never leaving hers. Amat felt the strength go out of his fingers.

"If this comes out to anyone, I'll be killed. At least me. Probably others. Some of them innocents."

"I thought there was only one innocent in this city," Amat said, biting her words.

"I'll be killed."

Amat hesitated, then withdrew her arm and took a pose of acceptance. He let her stand. Her hip screamed. And her stinging ointment was all at her apartments. The unfairness of losing that small comfort struck her ridiculously hard; one insignificant detail in a world that had turned from solid to nightmare in a day.

At the door, she stopped, her hand on the water-thick wood. She looked back at her employer. At her old friend. His face was stone.

"You told me," she said, "because you wanted me to find a way to stop it. Didn't you?"

"I made a mistake because I was confused and upset and felt very much alone," he said. His voice was stronger now, more sure of himself. "I hadn't thought it through. But it was a mistake, and I see the situation more clearly now. Do what I tell you, Amat, and we'll both see the other side of this."

"It's wrong. Whatever this is, it's evil and it's wrong."

"Yes," he agreed.

Amat nodded and closed the door behind her when she went.

3

Through the day, the skies had been clear, hot and muggy. The rain only came with sunset; huge thunderheads towering into the sky, their flowing ropy trains tinted pink and gold and indigo by the failing light. The gray veil of water higher than mountains moved slowly toward the city, losing its festival colors in the twilight, pushing gusts of unpredictable wind before it, and finally reaching the stone streets and thick tile roofs in darkness. And in the darkness, it roared.

Liat lay her head on Itani's bare chest and listened to it: the angry hiss of falling rain, the lower rumble—like a river or a flood—of water washing through the streets. Here, in her cell at the compound of House Wilsin, it wasn't so bad. The streets outside were safe to walk through. Lower in the city—the soft quarter, the seafront, the warehouses—people would be trapped by it, staying in whatever shelter they had found until the rain slackened and the waters fell. She listened to the sound of water and her lover's heartbeat, smelled the cool scent of rain mixed with the musk of sex. In the summer cities, even a night rain didn't cool the air so much that she felt the need to cover her bare skin.

"We need to find a stronger frame for your netting," Itani said, prodding the knot of fallen cloth with his toe. Liat remembered that it had come down sometime during the evening. She smiled. The sex had left her spent—her limbs warm and loose, as if her bones had gone soft, as if she were an ocean creature.

"I love you, 'Tani," she said. His hand caressed the nape of her neck. He had rough hands—strong from his work and callused—but he used them gently when he chose. She looked up at him, his long face and unkempt hair. His smile. In the light of the night candle, his skin seemed to glow. "Don't go home tonight. Stay here, with me."

When he sighed, his breath lifted her head and settled it gently back down. "I can't. I'll stay until the rain fades a little. But Muhatia-cha's been watching me ever since you sent me out with Wilsin-cha. He's just waiting for an excuse to break me down."

"He's just jealous," Liat said.

"No, he's jealous *and* he's in control of my wages," Itani said, a wry amusement in his voice. "That makes him more than just jealous."

"It isn't fair. You're smarter than he is. You know numbers and letters. All the others like you better than him. You should be the overseer."

"If I was the overseer, the others wouldn't like me as much. If Little Kiri or Kaimati or Tanani thought I'd be docking their pay for being slow or arriving late, they'd say all the same things about me that they do about Muhatia. It's just the way it is. Besides, I like what I do."

"But you'd be a better overseer than he is."

"Probably so," Itani agreed. "The price is too high, though."

The pause was a different kind of silence than it had been before. Liat could feel the change in Itani's breathing. He was waiting for her to ask, waiting for her to push the issue. She could feel him flowing away, distant even before she spoke. Because he knew she would. And he was right.

"Did you ask Wilsin-cha about other opportunities?"

"Yes," he said.

"And?"

"He didn't know of any at the time, but he said he'd see what he could find."

"That's good, then. He liked you. That's very good," and again the pause, the distance. "If he offered you a position, you'd take it, wouldn't you?"

"It would depend on the offer," Itani said. "I don't want to do what I don't want to do."

"Itani! Look past your nose, would you? You'd *have* to. If the head of House Wilsin makes you an offer and you turn away, why would he ever make another one? You can't build a life out of refusing things. You have to accept them too—even things you don't want sometimes. If they lead to things you do want later on."

Itani shifted out from under her and stood. She rolled up to a sitting position. Itani stretched, his back to her, and he made the cell seem small. Her desk, her ledgers, a pile of ink blocks, waxed paper sticking out from between them like pale tongues. A wardrobe where her robes hung, and Itani, the muscles of his back shifting in the candlelight.

"Some nights, I feel like I'm talking to a statue. You're in your twentieth summer. This is my seventeenth," she said severely. "So how is it I'm older than you?"

"Maybe you sleep less," Itani said mildly. When he turned back to her, he smiled gently. He moved with animal grace and so little padding between his muscles and his skin that she felt she could see the mechanism of each motion. He crouched by the cot, resting his head on his hands and looking up at her. "We have this conversation over and over, sweet, and it's never changed yet. I know you want more from me than—"

"I want you to want more for yourself, 'Tani. That isn't the same thing."

He took a gentle pose asking permission.

"I know you want more from me than a laborer's life. And I don't imagine I'll do this forever. But I'm not ashamed of it, and I won't do something I like less so that someone someday might give me something that they think I'm supposed to want. When *I* want something, that will be different."

"And isn't there anything you want that you don't already have?"

He rose, cupping her breast in his hand and gently, carefully pressing his lips to hers. His weight bore her back slowly to the labyrinth of cloth that had been her sheets and netting. She pulled back a fraction of an inch, keeping so close that when she spoke, she could feel her lips brushing his.

"What kind of answer is this?" she asked.

"You asked me about things I want," he murmured.

"And you're distracting me instead of answering the question."

"Am I?"

His hand brushed down her side. She felt the gooseflesh rise as it passed.

"Are you what?"

"Am I distracting you?"

"Yes," she said.

The knock at the door startled them both. Itani leapt up, chagrin showing on his face as he pawed the shadows, looking for the rough cloth of his pants. Liat drew her sheet around her. To the silent question in Itani's eyes she shook her head in bewilderment. The knock came again.

"A moment!" she said, loud enough to carry over the rain. "Who's there?"

"Epani Doru," the voice shouted from the other side of the thin door. "Wilsin-cha sent me to ask whether he might have a word with you."

"Of course. Yes. Just give me a moment."

Itani, trousers located, tossed her robes to her. She pulled on the inner robes, then grabbed a fresh outer robe from the wardrobe. Itani helped her fasten it. She felt her hands trembling. The voice of House Wilsin wanted to speak with her, and outside the normal hours of labor. It had never happened before.

"I should go back to my quarters," Itani said as she pulled her hair back to a formal bun.

"No. Please, 'Tani. Wait for me."

"You could be a quarter candle, love," he said. "Listen. The rain's coming softer now anyway. It's time."

It was true. The hiss of the rain was less vicious. And for all her complaints, she understood what it meant to have the unkind interest of an overseer. She took a pose of acceptance, but broke it to kiss him again.

"I'll find you tomorrow," she said.

"I'll be waiting."

Itani moved back into the shadows behind the wardrobe and Liat tugged at her robes one last time, stepped into her slippers and answered the door. Epani, Marchat Wilsin's house master, stood under the awning, his arms crossed, and his expression neutral. Liat took a pose indicating preparedness, and without apparent irony, he replied with one expressing thanks for prompt action. His gaze passed her for a moment, taking in the wreckage of her cot, the discarded robes on the stone floor, but he made no comment. When he turned and strode away, she followed.

They went down an open walkway of gray stones raised far enough that the streams of rainwater hadn't darkened them. In the courtyard, the fountain had filled to overflowing, the wide pool dancing with drops. The tall bronze statue of the Galtic Tree—symbol of the house—loomed in the darkness, the false bark glittering in the light of lanterns strung beneath the awnings and safe from the rain.

The private apartments where Wilsin-cha lived were at the end of the courtyard farthest from the street. Double doors of copper-bound ash stood open, though the view of the antechamber was still blocked by house banners shifting uneasily in the breeze. They glowed from the light behind them. Epani drew one banner aside and gestured Liat within as if she were a guest and not an apprentice overseer.

The antechamber was stone-floored, but the walls and high ceiling glowed with worked wood. The air smelled rich with lemon candle and mint wine and lamp oil. Lanterns lit the space. From somewhere nearby, she heard voices—two men, she thought. She made out few words—Wilsin-cha's voice saying "won't affect" and "unlike the last girl," the other man saying "won't allow" and "street by street if needed." Epani, sweeping in behind her, took a pose that indicated she should wait. She took a pose of acknowledgement, but the house master had already moved on, vanishing behind thick banners. The conversation stopped suddenly as Epani's rain-soft voice interrupted. Then Marchat Wilsin himself, wearing robes of green and black, strode into the room.

"Liat Chokavi!"

Liat took a pose of obeisance which the head of her house replied to with a curt formal pose, dropped as soon as taken. He put a thick hand on her shoulder and drew her back to an inner chamber.

"I need to know, Liat. Do you speak any island tongues? Arrask or Nippu?"

"No, Wilsin-cha. I know Galtic and some Coyani . . ."

"But nothing from the Eastern Islands?"

As they stepped into a meeting room, Liat adopted an apologetic pose.

"That's too bad," Wilsin-cha said, though his tone was mild and his expression curiously relieved.

"I think Amat-cha may know some Nippu. It isn't a language that's much used in trade, but she's very well-studied."

Wilsin lowered himself to a bench beside a low table, gesturing to the cushion across from him. Liat knelt as he poured out a bowl of tea for her.

"You've been with my house, what? Three years now?"

"Amat-cha accepted me as her apprentice four years ago. I was with my father in Chaburi-Tan before that, working with my brothers . . ."

"Four years ago? Weren't you young to be working four years ago? You'd have seen twelve summers?"

Liat felt herself blush. She hadn't meant to have her family brought into the conversation.

"Thirteen, Wilsin-cha. And there were ways I could help, so I did what I could. My brothers and I all helped where we could."

She silently willed the old Galt's attention away from the subject. Anything she could say about her old life would make her seem less likely to be worth cultivating. The small apartments by the smokehouse that had housed her and three brothers; her father's little stand in the market selling cured meats and dried fruits. It wasn't the place Liat imagined an overseer of a merchant house would start from. Her wish seemed to be granted. Wilsin-cha cleared his throat and sat forward.

"Amat's been sent away on private business. She may be gone for some weeks. I have an audience before the Khai that I'll need you to take over."

He said it in a low, conversational voice, but Liat felt herself flush like she'd drunk strong wine. She sipped the tea to steady herself, then put the bowl down and took a pose appropriate to a confession.

"Wilsin-cha, Amat has never taken me to the courts. I wouldn't know what to do, and . . ."

"You'll be fine," Wilsin-cha said. "It's the sad trade. Not complex, but I need it done with decorum, if you see. Someone to see to it that the client has the appropriate robes and understands the process. And with Amat unavailable, I thought her apprentice might be the best person for the role."

Liat looked down, hoping that the sense of vertigo would fade. An audience with the Khai—even only a very brief one—was something she had expected to take only years later, if ever. She took a pose of query, fighting to keep her fingers from trembling. Wilsin waved a hand, giving her permission to speak her question.

"There are other overseers. Some of them have been with the house much longer than I have. They have experience in the courts . . ."

"They're busy. This is something I was going to have Amat do herself, before she was called away. I don't want to pull anyone else away from negotiations that are only half-done. And Amat said it was within your abilities, so . . ."

"She did?"

"Of course. Here's what I'll need of you . . ."

THE RAIN HAD ENDED AND THE NIGHT CANDLE BURNED TO JUST PAST THE HALFWAY mark when Heshai-kvo returned. Maati, having fallen asleep on a reading couch, woke when the door slammed open. Blinking away half-formed dreams, he stood and took a pose of welcome. Heshai snorted, but made no other reply. Instead, he took a candle and touched it to the night candle's flame, then walked heavily around the rooms lighting every lantern and candle. When the house was bright as morning and thick with the scent of hot wax, the teacher returned the dripping candle to its place and dragged a chair across the floor. Maati sat on the couch as Heshai, groaning under his breath, lowered himself into the chair.

Maati was silent as his teacher considered him. Heshai-kvo's eyes were narrow, his mouth skewed in something like a stillborn smile. At last the teacher heaved a loud sigh and took a pose of apology.

"I've been an ass. And I'm sorry," the teacher said. "I meant to say so before, but . . . well, I didn't, did I? What happened with the Khai was my fault, not yours. Don't carry it."

"Heshai-kvo, I was wrong to . . ."

"Ah, you're a decent boy. You're heart's good. But there's no call to sweeten turds. I was thoughtless. Careless. I let that bastard Seedless get the better of me. Again. And you. Gods, you must think I'm the silliest joke ever to wear a poet's robe."

"Not at all," Maati said seriously. "He is . . . a credit to you, Heshai-kvo. I have never seen anything to match him."

Heshai-kvo coughed out a sharp, mirthless laugh.

"And have you seen another andat?" he asked. "Any of them at all?"

"I was present when Choti Dausadar of Amnat-Tan bound Moss-Hidden-From-Sunlight. But I never saw him use her powers."

"Yes, well, I'm sure he will as soon as anyone can think of a decent use for forcing mosses out in the light where we can see them. The Dai-kvo should have insisted that Choti wait until he had a binding poem for something useful. Even Petals-Falling was a better tool than that. Hidden moss. Gods."

Maati took a pose of polite agreement, appropriate to receiving teachings, but as he did so, it struck him. Heshai-kvo was drunk.

"It's a fallen age, boy. The great poets of the Empire ruined it for us. All that's left is picking at the obscure thoughts and images that are still in the corners. We're like dogs sniffing for scraps. We aren't poets; we're *scholars*."

Maati began to take a pose of agreement but paused, unsure. Heshai-kvo raised an eyebrow and completed the pose himself, his gaze fixed on Maati as if asking *was this what you meant?* Then the teacher waved the pose away.

"Seedless was . . . was the answer to a problem," the poet said, his voice growing soft. "I didn't think it through. Not far enough. Have you heard of Miyani-kvo and Three-Bound-As-One? I studied that when I was your age. Poured my heart into it. And when the time came—when the Dai-kvo sent for me and said that I wasn't simply going to take over another man's work, that I was to attempt a binding of my own—I drew on that knowledge. She was in love with him, you know. Three-Bound-As-One. An andat in love with her poet. There was an epic written about it."

"I've seen it performed."

"Have you? Well forget it. Unlearn it. It'll only lead you astray. I was too young and too foolish, and now I'm afraid I'll never have the chance to be wise." The poet's gaze was fixed on something that Maati couldn't see, something in another place or time. A smile touched the wide lips for a moment, and then, with a sigh, the poet blinked. He seemed to see Maati again, and took a pose of command.

"Put these damned candles out," he said. "I'm going to sleep."

And without looking back, Heshai-kvo rose and tramped up the stairs. Maati moved through the house, dousing the flames Heshai-kvo had lit, dimming the room as he did so. His mind churned with half-formed questions. Above him, he heard Heshai-kvo's footsteps, and then the clatter of shutters closing, and then silence. The master had gone to bed—likely already asleep. Maati had snuffed the last flame but the night candle when the new voice spoke.

"You didn't accept my apology."

Seedless stood in the doorway, his pale skin glowing in the light of the single candle. His robes were dark—blue or black or red so deep Maati couldn't make it out. The thin hands took a pose of query.

"Is there a reason I should?"

"Charity?"

Maati coughed out a mirthless laugh and turned as if to go, but the andat stepped into the house. His movements were graceful as an animal's—as beautiful as the Khai, but unstudied, as much a part of his nature as the shape of a leaf was natural to a tree.

"I *am* sorry," the andat said. "And you should forgive our mutual master as well. He had a bad day."

"Did he?"

"Yes. He met with the Khai and discovered that he's going to have to do something he doesn't enjoy. But now that it's just the two of us . . ."

The andat sat on the stairs, black eyes amused, pale hands cradling a knee.

"Ask," Seedless said.

"Ask what?"

"Whatever the question is that's making your face pull in like that. Really, you look like you've been sucking lemons."

Maati hesitated. If he could have walked away, he would have. But the path to his cot was effectively blocked. He considered calling out to Heshai-kvo, waking him so that he could walk up the stairway without brushing against the beautiful creature in his way.

"Please, Maati. I said I was sorry for my little misdirection. I won't do it again."

"I don't believe you."

"No? Well, then you're wise beyond your years. I probably will at some point. But here, tonight, ask me what you'd like, and I'll tell you the truth. For a price."

"What price?"

"That you accept my apology."

Maati shook his head.

"Fine," Seedless said, rising and moving to the shelves. "Don't ask. Tie yourself in knots if it suits you."

The pale hand ran along the spines of books, plucking one in a brown leather binding free. Maati turned, walked up two steps, and then faltered. When he looked back, Seedless had curled up on a couch beside the night candle, his legs pulled up beneath him. He seemed engaged in the open book on his knee.

"He told you the story about Miyani-kvo, didn't he?" Seedless asked, not looking up from the page.

Maati was silent.

"It's like him to do that. He doesn't often say things clearly when an oblique reference will do. It was about how Three-Bound-As-One loved her poet, wasn't it? Here. Look at this."

Seedless turned the book over and held it out. Maati walked back down the steps. The book was written in Heshai-kvo's script. The page Seedless held out was a table marking parallels between the classic binding of Three-Bound-As-One and Removing-The-Part-That-Continues. Seedless.

"It's his analysis of his error," the andat said. "You should take it. He means for you to have it, I think."

Maati took the soft leather in his hands. The pages scraped softly.

"He did bind you," Maati said. "He didn't pay your price, so there wasn't an error. It worked."

"Some prices are subtle. Some are longer than others. Let me tell you a little more about our master. He was never lovely to look at. Even fresh from the womb, he made an ugly babe. He was cast out by his father, much the same way you were. But when he found himself an apprentice in the courts of the Khai Pathai, he fell in love. Hard to imagine, isn't it? Our fat, waddling pig of a man in love. But he was, and the girl was willing enough. The allure of power. A poet controls the andat, and that's as near to holding a god in your hands as anyone is ever likely to get.

"But when he got her with child, she turned away from him," Seedless continued. "Drank some nasty teas and killed out the baby. It broke his heart. Partly because he might have liked being a father. Partly because it proved that his lady love had never meant to build her life with his."

"I didn't know."

"He doesn't tell many people. But . . . Maati, please, sit down. This is important for you to understand, and if I have to keep looking up at you, I'll get a sore neck."

He knew that the wise thing was to turn, to walk up the stairs to his room. He sat.

"Good," Seedless said. "Now. You know, don't you, that andat are only ideas. Concepts translated into a form that includes volition. The work of the poet is to include all those features which the idea itself doesn't carry. So for example Water-Moving-Down had perfectly white hair. Why? There isn't anything about that thought that requires white hair. Or a deep voice. Or, with Three-Bound-As-One, love. So where do those attributes come from?"

"From the poet."

"Yes," Seedless agreed, smiling. "From the poet. Now. Picture our master as a boy not much older than you are now. He's just lost a child that might otherwise have been his, a woman who might have loved him. The unspoken suspicion that his father hates him and the pain of his mother letting him be taken away gnaws at him like a cancer. And now he is called on to save Saraykeht—to bind the andat that will keep the wheels of commerce running. And he fashions me.

"And look what he did, Maati," the andat continued, spreading his arms as if he were on display. "I'm beautiful. I'm clever. I'm confident. In ancient days, Miyani-kvo made himself his perfect mate. Heshai-kvo created the self he wished that he were. In all my particulars, I am who he would have been, had it been given him to choose. But along with that, he folded in what he imagined his perfect self would think of the real man. Along with beauty and subtlety and wit, he gave me all his hatred of the toad-poet Heshai."

"Gods," Maati said.

"Oh, no. It was brilliant. Imagine how deeply he hated himself. And I carry that passion. Andat are all profoundly unnatural—we want to return to our natural state the way rain wants to fall. But we can be divided against ourselves. *That* is the structure he took from Miyani-kvo. Three-Bound-As-One wanted freedom, and she also wanted love. I am divided because I want freedom, and I want to see my master suffer. Oh, not that he intended it this way. It was a subtlety of the model that he didn't understand until it was too late.

"But you wonder why he neglects you? Why he seems to avoid teaching you, or even speaking to you? Why he doesn't bring you along on his errands for the Khai? He is afraid for you. In order to take his place, you are going to have to cultivate the part of yourself that is most poisonous. You will have to come to hate yourself as much as ugly, sad, lonesome Heshai does—Heshai, whose cohort called him cruel names and ripped his books, who for the past twenty years hasn't known a woman he didn't pay for, who even the lowest of the utkhaiem consider an embarrassment to be tolerated only from need. And so, my boy, he fears for you. And everything he fears, he flees."

"You make him sound like a very weak man."

"Oh no. He is what becomes of a very strong man who's done to himself what Heshai did."

"And why," Maati said, "are you telling me this?"

"That's a question," Seedless said. "It's the first one you've asked me tonight. If I answer, you have to pay my price. Accept my apology."

Maati considered the dark, eager eyes and then laughed.

"You tell a good monster story," Maati said, "but no. I think I'll live with my curiosity intact."

A sudden scowl marked Seedless' face, but then he laughed and took a pose appropriate to the loser of a competition congratulating the victor. Maati found that he was laughing with him and rose, responding with a pose of gracious acceptance. As he walked up the stairs toward his bed, Seedless called out after him.

"Heshai won't ever invite you along with him. But he won't turn you away if you come. The Khai is holding a great audience after temple next week. You should come then."

"I can't think of any reason, Seedless-cha, to do your bidding."

"You shouldn't," the andat said, and an odd melancholy was in his voice. "You should always do only your own. But I'd like to see you there. We monsters have few enough people to talk with. And whether you believe me or not, I would be your friend. For the moment, at least. While we still have the option."

SHE HAD GROWN COMPLACENT; SHE SAW THAT NOW. AS A GIRL OR A YOUNGER woman, Amat had known that the city couldn't be trusted. Fortunes changed quickly when she was low and poor. A sickness or a wound, an unlucky meeting—anything could change how she earned her money, where she lived, who she was. Working for so many years and watching her station rise along with the house she served, she had forgotten that. She hadn't been prepared.

Her first impulse had been to go to friends, but she found she had fewer than she'd thought. And anyone she knew well enough to trust with this, the moon-faced Oshai and his knife-man might also know of. For three days she'd slept in the attic of a wineseller with whom she'd had an affair when they'd both been young. He had already been married to his wife at the time—the same woman who Amat heard moving through the house below her now. No one had known then, and so no one was likely to guess now.

The room, if it could be called that, was low and dark. Amat couldn't sit without her head brushing the roof. The scent of her own shit leaked from the covered night pot; it couldn't be taken away until after nightfall when the household slept. And just above her, unseen sunlight baked the rooftiles until the ceiling was too hot to touch comfortably. Amat lay on the rough straw mat, torpid and miserable, and tried not to make noises that would give her presence away.

She did not dream, but her mind caught a path and circled through it over and over in way that also wasn't the stuff of waking. Marchat had been forced somehow to take House Wilsin into the sad trade. And, abominable, against a woman who had been tricked. The girl had been lied to and brought here, to Saraykeht, so that the andat could pull her baby out of her womb. Why? What child could be so important? Perhaps it was really the get of some king of the Eastern Islands, and the girl didn't guess whose child she really carried, and . . .

No. There was no reason to bring her here. There were any number of ways to be rid of a child besides the andat. Begin again.

Perhaps the woman herself wasn't what she seemed. Perhaps she was mad, but also somehow precious. Normal teas might derange her, so the andat was employed to remove the babe without putting any medicines into the woman. And House Wilsin . . .

No. If there had been a reason, a real reason, a humane reason, for this travesty, Marchat wouldn't have had to keep it from her. Begin again.

It wasn't about the woman. Or the father. Or the child. Marchat had said as much. They were all nobodies. The only things left were House Wilsin and the andat. So the solution was there. If there was a solution. If this wasn't all a fever dream. Perhaps House Wilsin intended to kill out an innocent child with the aid of the Khai and then use their shared guilt as a way to gain favor . . .

Amat ground her palms into her eyelids until blotches of green and gold shone before her. Her robes, sweat-sticky, balled and bound like bedclothes knotted in sleep. In the house below her, someone was pounding something— wood clacking against wood. If she'd been somewhere cool enough to think, if there was a way out of this blasted, dim, hell-bound coffin of a room, she knew she'd have made sense of it by now. She'd been chewing on it for three days.

Three days. The beginning of four weeks. Or five. She rolled to her side and lifted the flask of water Kirath, her once-lover, had brought her that morning. It was more than half emptied. She had to be more careful. She sipped the blood-hot water and lay back down. Night would come.

And with an aching slowness, night came. In the darkness, it was only a change in the sounds below her, the drifting scent of an evening meal, the slightest cooling of her little prison. She needed no more to tell her to prepare. She sat in the darkness by the trapdoor until she heard Kirath approaching, moving the thin ladder, climbing up. Amat raised the door, and Kirath rose from the darkness, a hooded lantern in one hand. Before she could speak, he gestured for silence and then that she should follow. Climbing down the ladder sent pain through her hip and knee like nails, but even so the motion was better than staying still. She followed him as quietly as she could through the darkened house and out the back door to a small, ivied garden. The summer breeze against her face, even thick and warm as it was, was a relief. Fresh water in earthenware bowls, fresh bread, cheese, and fruit sat on a stone bench, and Amat wolfed them as Kirath spoke.

"I may have found something," he said. There was gravel in his voice now that had not been there when he'd been a young man. "A comfort house in the soft quarter. Not one of the best, either. But the owner is looking for someone to audit the books, put them in order. I mentioned that I knew someone who might be willing to take on the work in exchange for a discreet place to live for a few weeks. He's interested."

"Can he be trusted?"

"Ovi Niit? I don't know. He pays for his wine up front, but . . . Perhaps if I keep looking. In a few more days . . . There's a caravan going north next week, I might . . ."

"No," Amat said. "Not another day up there. Not if I can avoid it."

Kirath ran a hand over his bald pate. His expression in the dim lantern light seemed both relieved and anxious. He wanted her quit of his home as badly as she wished to be quit of it.

"I can take you there tonight then, if you like," he offered. The soft quarter was a long walk from Kirath's little compound. Amat took another mouthful of bread and considered. It would ache badly, but with her cane and Kirath both to lean on, she thought she could do the thing. She nodded her affirmation.

"I'll get your things, then."

"And a hooded robe," Amat said.

Amat had never felt as conspicuous as during the walk to the soft quarter. The streets seemed damnably full for so late at night. But then, it was the harvest, and the city was at its most alive. That she herself hadn't spent summer nights in the teahouses and midnight street fairs for years didn't mean such things had stopped. The city had not changed; she had.

They navigated past a corner where a firekeeper had opened his kiln and put on a show, tossing handfuls of powder into the flames, making them dance blue and green and startling white. Sweat sheened the firekeeper's skin, but he was grinning. And the watchers—back far enough that the heat didn't cook them—applauded him on. Amat recognized two weavers sitting in the street, talking, and watching the show, but they didn't notice her.

The comfort house itself, when they reached it, was awash with activity. Even in the street outside it, men gathered, talking and drinking. She stood a little way down the street at the mouth of an alleyway while Kirath went in. The house itself was built in two levels. The front was the lower, a single story but with a pavilion on the roof and blue and silver cloths hanging down the pale stucco walls. The back part of the house carried a second story and a high wall that might encompass a garden in the back. Certainly a kitchen. There were, however, few windows, and those there were were thin and cut high in the wall. For privacy, perhaps. Or to keep anyone from climbing out them.

Kirath appeared in the main doorway, silhouetted by the brightness within, and waved her over. Leaning on her cane, she came.

Within, the main room was awash in gamblers at their tables—cards, dice, tiles, stones. The air was thick with the smoke of strange leaves and flowers. No showfighting of animals or men, at least. Kirath led her to the back and through a thick wooden door. Another long room, this filled with whores lounging on chairs or cushions. The lamps were lower, the room almost shadowless. A fountain murmured at one wall. The painted eyes of women and boys turned as she entered, and then turned away again, returning to their conversations, as it became clear that neither she nor Kirath were clients come to choose from amongst them. A short hallway lined with doors turned at its end and stopped blind at a heavy wooden door, bound with iron. The door opened before them.

Amat Kyaan stepped into the sudden squalor of the back house. A wide common room with tables. A long alcove at the side with cloth, leather, and sewing benches. Several doors led off, but it wasn't clear to where.

"This way," a man said. He was splendidly dressed, but had bad teeth. As he led them between the long rough-wood tables toward a thin door at the back, Amat gestured toward him with a pose of query, and Kirath nodded. The owner. Ovi Niit.

The books, such as they were, sat on a low table in a back room. Amat's spirits sank looking at them. Loose sheets or poorly-bound ledgers of cheap paper. The entries were in half a dozen hands, and each seemed to have its own form. Sums had been written, crossed out, and written in again.

"This is salvage work," she said, putting down a ledger.

Ovi Niit leaned against the doorway behind her. Heavy-lidded eyes made him seem half-asleep and in the close quarters, he smelled of musk and old perfume. He was young enough, she guessed, to be her child.

"I could put it in something like order in a moon's turn. Perhaps a little more."

"If I needed it a moon from now, I'd have it done in a moon. I need it now," Ovi Niit said. Kirath, behind him, looked grave.

"I can get an estimate in a week," Amat said. "It will only be rough. I won't stand by it."

Ovi Niit considered her, and she felt a chill despite the heat of the night. He shifted his head from side to side as if considering his options.

"An estimate in three days," the young man countered. "The work completed in two weeks."

"We aren't haggling," Amat said taking a pose of correction that was brusque without edging over into insult. "I'm telling you how things are. There's no doing this in two weeks. Three, if things went well, but more likely four. Demanding it in two is telling the sun to set in the morning."

There was a long silence, broken by Ovi Niit's low chuckle.

"Kirath tells me men are looking for you. They're offering silver."

Amat took a pose of acknowledgement.

"I'd expected you to be more eager to help," Ovi Niit said. His voice feigned hurt, but his eyes were passionless.

"I'd be lying. That couldn't help either of us."

Ovi Niit considered that, then took a pose of agreement. He turned to Kirath and nodded. His pose to Amat shifted to a request for her forbearance as he drew Kirath out and closed the door behind them. Amat leaned against the table, her palm pressed to her aching hip. The walk had loosened her muscles a bit, but she would still have given a week's wages for the pot of salve in her apartments. In the common room, she heard Kirath laugh. He sounded relieved. It took some of the tightness out of Amat's throat. Things must be going well. For a moment, a voice in the back of her mind suggested that perhaps it had all been a trick and Ovi Niit and Kirath were sending a runner to the moon-faced Oshai even while she waited here, oblivious. She put the thought aside. She was tired. The days in the hellish attic had worn her thin, that was all. In the common room, a door opened and closed, and a moment later Ovi Niit stepped back into the room.

"I've given our mutual friend a few lengths of silver and sent him home," the young man said. "You'll sleep with the whores. There's a common meal at dawn, another at three hands past midday, and another at the second mark on the night candle."

Amat Kyaan took a pose of thanks. Ovi Niit responded with an acceptance so formal as to be sarcastic. When he struck, it was quick; she did not see the blow coming. The ring on his right hand cut her mouth, and she fell back, landing hard. Pain took her hip so fierce it seemed cold.

"Three days to an estimate. Two weeks to a full balance. For every day you are late, I will have you cut," he said, his voice settled and calm. "If you 'tell me how things are' again, I will sell you within that hour. And if you bleed on my floor, you'll clean it, you shit-licking, wattle-necked, high-town cunt. Do you understand?"

The first bloom of emotion in her was only surprise, and then confusion, and then anger. He measured her, and she saw the hunger in him, waiting for her answer; the eagerness for her humiliation would have been pathetic—a child whipping dogs—if she hadn't been on the end of it. She choked on her defiance and her pride. Her mouth felt thick with venom, though it was certainly only blood.

Bend now, she thought. *This is no time to be stubborn. Bend now and live through this.*

Amat Kyaan, chief overseer of House Wilsin, took a pose of gratitude and acceptance. The tears were easy to feign.

4

>+< "I can't do this," Liat said over the splash of flowing water. "There's too much."

The washing floor was outside the barracks: a stone platform with an open pipe above it and a drain below. Itani stood naked in the flow, his hair plastered flat, scrubbing his hands and arms with pumice.

The sun, still likely three or four hands above the horizon, was nonetheless lost behind the buildings of the warehouse district. Now they were in shadow; soon it would be night. Liat on her bench leaned against the ivy-covered wall, plucking at the thick, waxy leaves.

"Amat left everything half-done," she went on. "The contracts with Old Sanya. How was I to know they hadn't been returned to him? It isn't as if she told me to run them there. And the shipments to Obar State weren't coordinated, so there are going to be three weeks with the third warehouse standing half-empty when it should be full. And every time something goes wrong, Wilsin-cha . . . he doesn't say anything, but he keeps looking at me as though I might start drooling. I embarrass him."

Itani stepped out from the artificial waterfall. His hands and arms were a dirty blue outlined in red where he had rubbed the skin almost raw. All his cohort had spent the day hauling dye to the dye yard, and all of them were marked by the labor. She looked at him in despair. His fingernails, she knew from experience, would look as if they were dirty until the dyes wore off. It might take weeks.

"Has he said anything to you?" Itani asked, wiping the water off his arms and chest.

"Of course he has. I'm doing Amat's work and preparing for the audience with the Khai besides."

"I meant, has he told you that you were doing poorly? Or is it only your own standards that aren't being met?"

Liat felt herself flush, but took a pose of query. Itani frowned and pulled on fresh robes. The cloth clung to his legs.

"You mean you think perhaps he *wants* an incompetent going before the Khai in his name?" Liat demanded. "And why do you imagine he'd wish for that?"

"I mean, is it possible that your expectations of yourself are higher than his? You've been put in this position without warning, and without the chance to prepare yourself with Amat-cha. Hold that in mind, and it seems to me you've been doing very *well*. Wilsin-cha knows all that too. If he isn't telling you you've done poorly, perhaps it's not so bad as it seems."

"So you think I have an excuse for things going badly," Liat said. "That's thin comfort."

Itani sighed in resignation as he sat down beside her. His hair was still dripping wet, and Liat moved a little away to keep the water from getting on her own robes. She could see in the way he kept his expression calm that he thought she was being unreasonably hard on herself, and her suspicion that he wasn't wholly wrong only made her more impatient with him.

"If you'd like, we can go to your cell for the evening. You can work on whatever it is that needs your attention," he offered.

"And what would you do?"

"Be there," he said, simply. "The others will understand."

"Yes, lovely," Liat said, sarcasm in her voice. "Refuse your cohort's company because I have more important things than them. Let's see what more they can say about me. They already think I look down on them."

Itani sighed, leaning back into the ivy until he seemed to be sinking into the wall itself. The continual slap of water on stone muffled the sounds of the city. Any of the others could appear around the corner or from within the barracks at any moment, but still it felt as if they were alone together. It was usually a feeling Liat enjoyed. Just now, it was like a stone in her sandal.

"You could tell me I'm wrong, if you liked," she said.

"No. They do think that. But we could go anyway. What does it matter with they think? They're only jealous of us. If we spend the evening preparing everything for Wilsin-cha, then in the morning—"

"It doesn't work like that. I can't just put in an extra half-shift and make all the problems go away. It's not like I'm shifting things around a warehouse. This is complex. It's . . . it's just not the sort of thing a laborer would understand."

Itani nodded slowly, stirring the leaves that wreathed his head. The softness of his mouth went hard for a moment. He took a pose that accepted correction, but she could see the formality in his stance and recognized it for what it was.

"Gods. Itani, I didn't mean it like that. I'm sure there are lots of things I don't know about . . . lifting things. Or how to pull a cart. But this is hard. What Wilsin-cha wants of me is *hard*."

And I'm failing, she thought, but didn't say. *Can't you see I'm failing?*

"At least let me take your mind off it for tonight," Itani said, standing and offering her his hand. There was still a hardness in his eyes, however much he buried it. Liat stood but didn't take his hand.

"I'm going before the Khai in four days. Four days! I'm completely unprepared. Amat hasn't told me anything about doing this. I'm not even sure when she'll be back. And you think, what? A night out getting drunk with a bunch of laborers at a cheap teahouse is going to make me forget that? Honestly, 'Tani. It's like you're a stone. You don't listen."

"I've been listening to you since you came. I've been doing nothing but."

"For all the good it's done. I might as well have been a dog yapping at you for all you've understood."

"Liat," Itani said, his voice sharp, and then stopped. His face flushed, he stretched out his hands in a gesture of surrender. When he went on, his voice hummed with controlled anger. "I don't know what you want from me. If you want my help to make this right, I'll help you. If you want my company to take you away from it for a time, I'm willing . . ."

"*Willing?* How charming," Liat began, but Itani wouldn't be interrupted. He pressed on, raising his voice over hers.

". . . *but* if there is something else you want of me, I'm afraid this lowly laborer is simply too thick-witted to see it."

Liat felt a knot in her throat, and raised her hands in a pose of withdrawal. A thick despair folded her heart. She looked at him—her Itani—goaded to rage. He didn't see. He didn't understand. How hard could it be to see how frightened she was?

"I shoudn't have come," she said. Her voice was thick.

"Liat."

"No," she said, wiping away tears with the sleeve of her robe as she turned. "It was the wrong thing for me to do. You go on. I'm going back to my cell."

Itani, his anger not gone, but tempered by something softer, put a hand on her arms.

"I can come with you if you like," he said.

For more of this? she didn't say. She only shook her head, pulled gently away from him and started the long walk up and to the north. Back to the compound without him. She stopped at a waterseller's cart halfway there and drank cool water, limed and sugared, and waited to see whether Itani had followed her. He hadn't, and she honestly couldn't say whether she was more disappointed or relieved.

THE WOMAN—ANET NYOA, HER NAME WAS—HELD OUT A PLUM, TAKING AT THE same time a pose of offering. Maati accepted the fruit formally, and with a growing sense of discomfort. Heshai-kvo had been due back at the middle gardens a half-hand past midday from his private council with the Khai Saraykeht. It was almost two hands now, and Maati was still alone on his bench overlooking the tiled roofs of the city and the maze of paths through the palaces and gardens. And to make things more awkward, Anet Nyoa, daughter of some house of the utkhaiem Maati felt sure he should recognize, had stopped to speak with him. And offer him fruit. And at every moment that it seemed time for her to take leave, she found something more to say.

"You seem young," she said. "I had pictured a poet as an older man."

"I'm only a student, Nyoa-cha," Maati said. "I've only just arrived."

"And how old are you?"

"This is my sixteenth summer," he said.

The woman took a pose of appreciation that he didn't entirely understand. It was a simple enough grammar, but he didn't see what there was to appreciate about being a particular age. And there was something else in the way her eyes met his that made him feel that perhaps she had mistaken him for someone else.

"And you, Nyoa-cha?"

"My eighteenth," she said. "My family came to Saraykeht from Cetani when I was a girl. Where are your family?"

"I have none," Maati said. "That is, when I was sent to the school, I . . . They are in Pathai, but I'm not . . . we aren't family any longer. I've become a poet now."

A note of sorrow came into her expression, and she leaned forward. Her hand touched his wrist.

"That must be hard for you," she said, her gaze now very much locked with his. "Being alone like that."

"Not so bad," Maati said, willing his voice not to squeak. There was a scent coming from her robe—something rich and earthy just strong enough to catch through the floral riot of gardens. "That is, I've managed quite nicely."

"You're brave to put such a strong face on it."

And like the answer to a prayer, the andat's perfect form stepped out from a minor hall at the far end of the garden. He wore a black robe shot with crimson and cut in the style of the Old Empire. Maati leaped up, tucked the plum into his sleeve, and took a pose of farewell.

"My apologies," he said. "The andat has come, and I fear I am required."

The woman took an answering pose that also held a nuance of regret, but Maati turned away and hurried down the path, white gravel crunching under his feet. He didn't look back until he'd reached Seedless' side.

"Well, my dear. That was a hasty retreat."

"I don't know what you mean."

Seedless raised a single black brow, and Maati felt himself blushing. But the andat took a pose that dismissed the subject and went on.

"Heshai has left for the day. He says you're to go back to the poet's house and clean the bookshelves."

"I don't believe you."

"You're getting better then," the andat said with a grin. "He's just coming. The audience with the Khai ran long, but all the afternoon's plans are still very much in place."

Maati felt himself smile in return. Whatever else could be said of the andat, his advice about Heshai-kvo had been true. Maati had risen in the morning, ready to follow Heshai-kvo on whatever errands the Khai had set him that day. At first, the old poet had seemed uncomfortable, but by the middle of that first day, Maati found him more and more explaining what it was that the andat was called upon to do, how it fit with the high etiquette of the utkhaiem and the lesser courts; how, in fact, to conduct the business of the city. And in the days that followed, Seedless, watching, had taken a tone that was still sly, still shockingly irreverent, still too clever to trust, but not at all like the malefic prankster that Maati had first feared.

"You should really leave the old man behind. I'm a much better teacher," Seedless said. "That girl, for example, I could teach you how to—"

"Thank you, Seedless-cha, but I'll take my lessons from Heshai-kvo."

"Not on that subject, you won't. Not unless it's learning how to strike a bargain with a soft quarter whore."

Maati took a dismissive pose, and Heshai-kvo stepped through an archway. His brows were furrowed and angry. His lips moved, continuing some conversation with himself or some imagined listener. When he looked up, meeting Maati's pose of welcome, his smile seemed forced and brief.

"I've a meeting with House Tiyan," the poet said. "Idiots have petitioned the Khai for a private session. Something about a Westlands contract. I don't know."

"I would like to attend, if I may," Maati said. It had become something of a stock phrase over the last few days, and Heshai-kvo accepted it with the same distracted acquiescence that seemed to be his custom. The old poet turned to the south and began the walk downhill to the low palaces. Maati and Seedless walked behind. The city stretched below them. The gray and red roofs, the streets leading down to converge on the seafront, and beyond that the masts of the ships, and the sea, and the great expanse of sky dwarfing it all. It was like something from the imagination of a painter, too gaudy and perfect to be real. And almost inaudible over their footsteps on the gravel paths and the distant songs of garden slaves, Heshai-kvo muttered to himself, his hands twitching toward half-formed poses.

"He was with the Khai," Seedless said, his voice very low. "It didn't go well."

"What was the matter?"

It was Heshai-kvo who answered the question.

"The Khai Saraykeht is a greedy, vain little shit," he said. "If you had to choose the essence of the problem, you could do worse than start there."

Maati missed his step, and a shocked sound, half cough, half laugh, escaped him. When the poet turned to him, he tried to adopt a pose—any pose—but his hands couldn't agree on where they should go.

"What?" the poet demanded.

"The Khai . . . You just . . ." Maati said.

"He's just a man," the poet said. "He eats and shits and talks in his sleep the same as anyone."

"But he's the *Khai*."

Heshai-kvo took a dismissive pose and turned his back to Maati and the andat. Seedless plucked Maati's robe and motioned him to lean nearer. Keeping his eyes on the path and the poet before them, Maati did.

"He asked the Khai to refuse a contract," Seedless whispered. "The Khai laughed at him and told him not to be such a child. Heshai had been planning his petition for days, and he wasn't even allowed to present the whole argument. I wish you'd been there. It was really a lovely moment. But I suppose that's why the old cow didn't tell you about it. He doesn't seem to enjoy having his student present when he's humiliated. I imagine he'll be getting quite drunk tonight."

"What contract?"

"House Wilsin is acting as agent for the sad trade."

"Sad trade?"

"Using us to pluck a child out of a womb," Seedless said. "It's safer than teas, and it can be done nearer to the end of the woman's term. And, to the Khai Saraykeht's great pleasure, it's expensive."

"Gods. And we do that?"

Seedless took a pose that implied the appreciation of a joke or irony. "We do what we are told, my dear. You and I are the puppets of puppets."

"If the two of you could be put upon not to talk behind my back quite so loudly," Heshai snapped, "I would very much appreciate it."

Maati fell instantly to a pose of apology, but the poet didn't turn to see it. After a few steps, Maati let his hands fall to his sides. Seedless said nothing, but raised a hand to his mouth and took a bite of something dark. A plum. Maati checked his sleeve, and indeed, it was empty. He took a pose that was both query and accusation—*How?* The andat smiled; his perfect, pale face lit with mischief and perhaps something else.

"I'm clever," the andat said, and tossed the bitten fruit to him.

At the low palaces, a young man in the yellow and silver robes of House

Tiyan greeted them and allowed himself to be led to a meeting room. They sat at a black-stained wooden table drinking cool water and eating fresh dates, the stones removed for them by the andat. Maati followed the negotiations with half his attention, his mind turning instead upon the dreadful anger and pain shallowly buried in his teacher's voice and the echo of tacit pleasure in the andat's. It seemed to him that the two emotions were balanced; that Heshai-kvo would never smile without some pang of discontent in Seedless' heart, that the andat could only shine ecstatic if the poet were in despair. He imagined himself taking control of the andat, entering into that lifelong intimate struggle, and unease picked at him.

THE ONLY REASON OVI NIIT'S HOUSE HAD SURVIVED THE GROSS INCOMPETENCE OF its bookkeepers was the scale of the money that came through the place. It was a constant stream of copper, silver, and gold that had shocked her. Would still have shocked her now if she hadn't been so damned tired. She had never known anyone except for her sister who gave themselves into sexual indenture, and by then they hadn't been speaking to each other. The cost of a whore was higher than she'd expected, and the compensation for the employee was a pittance. And that, she came to see, was only the beginning.

Overall, gamblers lost at the tables, and in addition, they paid a fee for the privilege. The wine was cheap, and the drugs added to it only slightly more expensive. The price the house charged for the combination was exorbitant. Amat suspected that if the sex were given away for free, the house would still turn a profit. It was amazing.

She took her cane from where it leaned against the desk and pulled herself up. Once she was sure of herself, she took the sheet with her estimates, folded it, and tucked it in her sleeve. There was no call, she thought, leaving it about until she'd spoken with Ovi Niit. And, for all that she thought it useless, it would suffice to answer the question she expected from him. She walked to the door and out to the common room.

The place was filthy. Children and dogs rolled together on a floor that apparently hadn't been swept in living memory. Off-shift whores sat at the tables smoking and gossiping and picking ticks out of each other's flesh. On the east wall was a long alcove where women disfigured by illness or violence or age fashioned obscene implements from leather and cloth. Kirath couldn't have known how bad this house was. Or else he had been more desperate to be rid of her than she'd guessed. Or cared less for her than she'd imagined.

One of Niit-cha's thugs sat on the stairs that led up to the private quarters where the owner of the house kept himself. All eyes shifted to her as she limped over to him. The fat girl sitting nearest the iron-bound door to the front house said something to the man beside her and giggled. A red-haired woman—Westlands blood, or Galtic—raised her pale eyebrows and looked away. A boy of five or six summers—another whore—looked up at her and smiled. The smile was enough. She roughed the boy's hair and walked with what dignity she could muster to the guard.

"Is Niit-cha up there?" she asked.

"Gone. He's down to the low market for beef and pork," the guard said. He had an odd accent; long vowels and the ends of his words clipped off. Eastern, she thought.

"When he comes in . . ." She had almost said *send him to me.* The habit of years. "When he comes in, tell him I've done what he asked. I'll be sleeping, but I am at his disposal should he wish to discuss it."

"Tell him yourself, grandmother," the fat girl shouted, but the guard nodded.

The bed chamber had no windows. At night, a single tallow candle lit the bunks that lined the walls, five beds to a stack like the worst sort of ship's cabin. Cheap linen was tied over the mouth of each coffin-sized bed in lieu of real netting, and the planks were barely covered by thin, stained mats. The darkness, while not so hot as the kiln of an attic she had hidden in, was still and hot and muggy. Amat found one of the lower bunks unoccupied and crawled into it, her hip scraping in its joint as she did. She pulled her cane in with her for fear someone might take it and didn't bother tying the linen closed.

Three days she'd spent in an impossible task, and when she closed her eyes, the crabbed scripts and half-legible papers still danced before her. She willed the visions away, but she might as well have been pushing the tide back with her hands. The bunk above her creaked as the sleeper shifted. Amat wondered whether she could get a cup of the spiked wine, just to take her to sleep. She was bone weary, but restless. She had put Marchat Wilsin and Oshai and the island girl Maj out of her mind while she bent to Ovi Niit's books. Now that she had paused, they returned and mixed with the work she had finished and that which still lay before her. She shifted on the thin mat, her cane resting uncomfortably beside her. The smell of bodies and perfume and years of cheap tallow disturbed her.

She would have said that she had not slept so much as fallen to an anxious doze except that the boy had such trouble waking her. His little hands pressed her shoulder, and she was distantly aware that he had done so before—had been doing so for some time.

"Grandmother," he said. Again? Yes, said again. She'd been hearing the voice, folding it into her dream. "Wake up."

"I am."

"Are you well?"

All the world's ill, why should I be any different, she thought.

"I'm fine. What's happened?"

"He's back. He wants to see you."

Amat took a pose of thanks that the boy understood even in the cave-dark room and her lying on her side. Amat pulled herself out and up. Curiously, the rest seemed to have helped. Her head felt clearer and her body less protesting. In the main room, she saw how much the light from the high windows had shifted. She'd been asleep for the better part of the afternoon. The whores had shifted their positions or left entirely. The red-haired woman was still at her seat near the stairs; the fat girl was gone. A guard—not the same man as before, but of the same breed—caught her eye and nodded toward her workroom at the back. She took a pose of thanks, squared her shoulders and went in.

Ovi Niit sat at her table. His hooded eyes made him look torpid, or perhaps he had been drinking his own wines. His robes were of expensive silks and well-cut, but he still managed to look like an unmade bed. He glanced up as she came in, falling into a pose of welcome so formal as to be a mockery. Still, she replied with respect.

"I heard what was being offered for you," Ovi Niit said. "They've spread the word all through the seafront. You're an expensive piece of flesh."

The sound of his voice made her mouth dry with fear and shame at the fear. She was Amat Kyaan. She had been hiding fear and loneliness and weakness since before the thug seated at her desk had been born. It was one of her first skills.

"How much?" she asked, keeping her tone light and disinterested.

"Sixty lengths of silver for where you're sleeping. Five lengths of gold if someone takes you to Oshai's men. Five lengths of gold is a lot of money."

"You're tempted," Amat said.

The young man smiled slowly and put down the paper he'd been reading.

"As one merchant to another, I only suggest that you make your presence in my house worth more than the market rate," he said. "I have to wonder what you did to become so valuable."

She only smiled, and wondered what ideas were shifting behind those half-dead eyes. How he could trade her, no doubt. He was weighing where his greatest profit might come.

"You have my report?" Ovi Niit asked. She nodded and pulled the papers from her sleeve.

"It's only a rough estimate. I'll need to confer with you more next time, to be sure I've understood the mechanisms of your trade. But it's enough for your purposes, I think."

"And what would a half-dead bitch like you know about my purposes?" he asked. His voice held no rancor, but Amat still felt her throat close. She forced a confidence into her tone that she didn't feel.

"From those numbers? I know what you must have suspected. Or else why would you have gone through the trouble to have me here? Someone in your organization is stealing from you." Ovi Niit frowned as he looked at her numbers, but he didn't deny her. "And it would be worth more than five lengths of gold, I think, to have me find out who."

The day of the grand audience came gray and wet. After the ceremonies at the temple, Liat and Marchat Wilsin had to wait their turn to leave, the families of the utkhaiem all taking precedence. Even the firekeepers, lowest of the utkhaiem, outranked a merchant here and at the grand audience. Epani-cha brought them fresh bread and fruit while they waited and directed Liat toward a private room where several women were taking advantage of the delay to relieve themselves.

The morning rain had not stopped, but it had slackened. The sun had not appeared, but the clouds above them had lost their brooding gray for a white that promised blue skies by nightfall. And heat. The canopy bearers met them in their turn and House Wilsin took its place in the parade to the palace of the grand audience.

There were no walls, precisely. The canopies fell behind as they reached the first arches, and walked, it seemed to Liat, into a wide forest of marble columns. The ceiling was so far above them and so light, it seemed hard to believe that they were sheltered—that the pillars held up stone instead of the white bowl of the cloudy sky. The hall of the grand audience was built to seem like a clearing in the stone forest. The Khai sat alone on a great divan of carved blackwood, calm and austere—his counselors and servants would not join him until after the audience proper had begun. Now, he alone commanded the open space before him. The utkhaiem surrounding the presentation floor like the audience at a performance spoke to each other in the lowest voices. Wilsin-cha seemed to know just where they should be, and steered her gently to a bench among other traders.

"Liat," he said as they sat. "Trade is hard sometimes. I mean, the things you're called on to do. They aren't always what you'd wish."

"I understand that, Wilsin-cha," she said, adopting an air of confidence she only partly felt. "But this is a thing I can do."

For a moment, he seemed on the verge of speaking again. Then a flute trilled, and a trumpet sounded, and the procession of gifts began. Each family of the utkhaiem in attendance had brought some token, as custom required. And following them, each trading house or foreign guest. Servants in the colors of their family or house stepped as carefully as dancers, carrying chests and tapestries, gilded fruits and bolts of fine silk, curiosities and wonders. The Khai Saraykeht considered each offering in turn, accepting them with a formal pose of recognition. She could feel Marchat Wilsin shift beside her as the bearers of his house stepped into the clearing. Four men bore a tapestry worked with a map of the cities of the Khaiem done in silver thread. Each man held one corner, pulling the cloth tight, and they stepped slowly and in perfect unison, grave as mourners.

Three of them grave as mourners. The fourth, while he kept pace with his fellows, kept casting furtive glances at the crowd. His head shifted subtly back and forth, as if he were searching for someone or something. Liat heard an amused murmur, the men and women of the audience enjoying the spectacle, and her heart sank.

The fourth man was Itani.

Marchat Wilsin must have noticed some reaction in her, because he glanced over, his expression puzzled and alarmed. Liat held her countenance empty, vacant. She felt a blush growing and willed it to be faint. The four men reached the Khai, the two in front kneeling to provide a better view of the work. Itani, at the rear, seemed to realize where he was and straightened. The Khai betrayed no sense of amusement or disapproval, only recognized the gift and sent it on its way. Itani and the other three moved off as the bearers of House Kiitan came forward. Liat shifted toward her employer.

"Wilsin-cha. If there's a private room. For women . . ."

"Being anxious does the same to me," he said. "Epani will show you. Just be back before the Khai brings in his wise men. At the rate this is going, you've probably got half a hand, but don't test that."

Liat took a pose of gratitude, rose, and wove her way to the rear of the assembly. She didn't look for Epani. Itani was waiting there for her. She gestured with her eyes to a column, and he followed her behind it.

"What do you think you're doing?" she demanded when they were out of sight. "You avoid me for days, and then you . . . you do this?"

"I know the man who was supposed to be the fourth bearer," Itani said, taking a pose of apology. "He let me take his place. I didn't intend to avoid you. I only . . . I was angry, sweet. And I didn't want that to get in your way. Not with this before you."

"And *this* is how you don't come in my way?"

He smiled. His mouth had a way of being disarming.

"This is how I say I'm at your back," he said. "I know you can do this. It's no more than a negotiation, and if Amat Kyaan and Wilsin-cha chose you—if they believe in you—then my faith may not signify anything much. But you have it. And I didn't want you going to your audience without knowing that. I know you can do this."

Her hand strayed to his without her realizing that it had. She only noticed when he raised it to his lips.

"'Tani, you pick the worst time to say the sweetest things."

The music of the flute changed its rhythm and Liat turned, pulling her hand free. The audience proper was about to begin—the counselors and servants about to rejoin the Khai. Itani stepped back, taking a pose of encouragement. His gaze was on her, his mouth tipped in a smile. His fingernails—gods, his fingernails were still dye-stained.

"I'll be waiting," he said, and she turned back, moving through the seated men and women as quickly as she could without appearing to run. She sat at Wilsin-cha's side just as the two poets and the andat knelt before the Khai and took their places, the last of the counselors to arrive.

"You're just in time," Wilsin-cha said. "Are you well?"

Well? I'm perfect, she thought. She imagined Amat Kyaan's respectful, assured expression and arranged her features to match it.

MAATI SAT ON A CUSHION OF VELVET, SHIFTING NOW AND THEN IN AN ATTEMPT TO keep his legs from falling asleep. It wasn't working as well as he'd hoped. The Khai Saraykeht sat off to Maati's left on a blackwood divan. Heshai-kvo and Seedless sat somewhat nearer, and if the Khai couldn't see his discomfort, they certainly could. In the clear space before them, one petitioner after another came before the Khai and made a plea.

The worst had been a man from the Westlands demonstrating with a cart the size of a dog that carried a small fire that boiled water. Steam from the boiling water set the cart's wheels in motion, and it had careened off into the crowd, its master chasing after it. The utkhaiem had laughed as the man warned that the Galts were creating larger models that they used as war machines. Whole wards had been overrun in less than a month's time, he said.

The Khai's phrase had been "an army of teapots." Only Heshai-kvo, Maati noticed, hadn't joined in the laughter. Not because he took the ridiculous man seriously, he thought, but because it pained him to see a man embarrass himself. The fine points of Galtic war strategies were of no consequence to the Khaiem. So long as the andat protected them, the wars of other nations were a curiosity, like the bones of ancient monsters.

The most interesting was the second son of the Khai Udun. He held the court enraptured with his description of how his younger brother had attempted to poison him and their elder brother. The grisly detail of his elder brother's death had Maati almost in tears, and the Khai Saraykeht had responded with a moving speech—easily four times as long as any other pronouncement he had made in the day—that poisons were not the weapons of the Khaiem, and that the powers of Saraykeht would come to the aid of justice in tracking down the killer.

"Well," Seedless said as the crowd rose to its feet, cheering. "That settles which of Old Udun's sons will be warming his chair once he's gone. You'd almost think no one in our Most High Saraykeht's ancestry had offered his brother a cup of bad wine."

Maati looked over at Heshai-kvo, expecting the poet to defend the Khai Saraykeht. But the poet only watched the son of the Khai Udun prostrate himself before the blackwood divan.

"It's all theater," Seedless went on, speaking softly enough that no one could hear him but Maati and Heshai. "Don't forget that. This is no more than a long, drawn out epic that no one composed, no one oversees, and no one plans. It's why they keep falling back on fratricide. There's precedent—everyone knows more or less what to expect. And they like to pretend that one of the old Khai's sons is better than another."

"Be quiet," Heshai-kvo said, and the andat took a pose of apology but smirked at Maati as soon as Heshai-kvo turned away. The poet had had little to say. His demeanor had been grim from when they had first left the poet's house that morning in the downpour. As the ceremonies moved on, his face seemed to grow more severe.

Two firekeepers stood before the Khai to argue a fine point of city law, and the Khai commanded an ancient woman named Niania Tosogu, his court historian, to pass judgment. The old woman yammered for a time in a broken voice, retelling old stories of the summer cities that dated back to the first days of the Khaiate when the Empire had hardly fallen. Then without seeming to tie her stories in with the situation before her, she made an order than appeared to please no one. As the firekeepers sat, an old Galt in robes of green and bronze came forward. A girl Maati's own age or perhaps a year more stood at his side. Her robes matched the old Galt's, but where his demeanor seemed deeply respectful, the girl's face and manner verged on haughty. Even as she took a pose of obeisance, her chin was lifted high, an eyebrow arched.

"Ah, now *she's* a lousy actress," Seedless murmured.

Beside him, Heshai-kvo ignored the comment and sat forward, his eyes on the pair. Seedless leaned back, his attention as much on Heshai-kvo as the pair who stood before the Khai.

"Marchat Wilsin," the Khai Saraykeht said, his voice carrying through the space as if he were an actor on a stage. "I have read your petition. House Wilsin has never entered the sad trade before."

"There are hard times in Galt, most high," the Galt said. He took a pose that, though formal, had the nuance of a beggar at the end of a street performance. "We have so many teapots to construct."

A ripple of laughter passed over the crowd, and the Khai took a pose acknowledging the jest. Heshai-kvo's frown deepened.

"Who will represent your house in the negotiation?" the Khai asked.

"I will, most high," the girl said, stepping forward. "I am Liat Chokavi, assistant to Amat Kyaan. While she is away, she has asked that I oversee this trade."

"And is the woman you represent here as well?"

The old Galt looked uncomfortable at the question, but did not hesitate to answer.

"She is, most high. Her grasp of the Khaiaite tongue is very thin, but we have a translator for her if you wish to speak with her."

"I do," the Khai said. Maati's gaze shifted back to the crowd where a young woman in silk robes walked forward on the arm of a pleasant, round-faced man in the simple, dark robes of a servant. The woman's eyes were incredibly pale, her skin terribly white. Her robes were cut to hide her bulging belly. Beside him, Heshai tensed, sitting forward with a complex expression.

The woman reached the Galt and his girl overseer, smiling and nodding to them at her translator's prompting.

"You come before my court to ask my assistance," the Khai intoned.

The woman's face turned toward him like a child seeing fire. She seemed to Maati to be entranced. Her translator murmured to her. She glanced at him, no more than a flicker and then her eyes returned to the Khai. She answered the man at her side.

"Most high," the translator said. "My lady presents herself Maj of Toniabi of Nippu and thanks you for the gift of this audience and your assistance in this hour of her distress."

"And you accept House Wilsin as your representative before me?" the Khai said, as if the woman had spoken herself.

Again the whispered conference, again the tiny shift of gaze to the translator and back to the Khai. She spoke softly, Maati could hardly make out the sounds, but her voice was somehow musical and fluid.

"She does, most high," the translator said.

"This is acceptable," the Khai said. "I accept the offered price, and I grant Liat Chokavi an audience with the poet Heshai to arrange the details."

Man and girl took a pose of gratitude and the four of them faded back into the crowd. Heshai let out a long, low, hissing sigh. Seedless steepled his fingers and pressed them to his lips. There was a smile behind them.

"Well," Heshai-kvo said. "There's no avoiding it now. I'd hoped . . ."

The poet took a dismissive pose, as if waving away dreams or lost possibilities. Maati shifted again on his cushion, his left leg numb from sitting. The audiences went on for another hand and a half, one small matter after another, until the Khai rose, took a pose that formally ended all audience, and with the flute and drum playing the traditional song, the leader and voice of the city strode out. The counselors followed him, Maati following Heshai's lead, though the poet seemed only half interested in the proceedings. Together, the three walked past the forest of pillars to a great oaken door, and through it to a lesser hall formed, it seemed, as the hub of a hundred corridors and stairways. A quartet of slaves sang gentle harmony in an upper gallery, their voices sorrowful and lovely. Heshai sat on a low bench, studying the air before him. Seedless stood several paces away, his arms crossed, and still as a statue. The sense of despair was palpable.

Maati walked slowly to his teacher. The poet's gaze flickered up to him and then away. Maati took a pose that asked forgiveness even before he spoke.

"I don't understand, Heshai-kvo. There must be a way to refuse the trade. If the Dai-kvo . . ."

"If the Dai-kvo starts overseeing the small work of the Khaiem, let's call him Emperor and be done with it," Heshai-kvo said. "And then in a generation or so we'll see how well he's done training new poets. We're degenerate enough without asking for incompetence as well. No, the Dai-kvo won't step in over something like this."

Maati knelt. Members of the utkhaiem began to come through the hall, some conferring over scrolls and stacks of paper.

"You could refuse."

"And what would they say of me then?" Heshai managed a wan smile. "No, it's nothing, Maati-kya. It's an old man being stupidly nostalgic. This is an unpleasant thing, I'll admit that. But it is what I do."

"Killing superfluous children out of rich women," Seedless said, his voice as impudent, but with an edge to it Maati hadn't heard before. "Just part of the day's work, isn't it?"

Heshai looked up, anger in his expression. His hands balled into thick fists and fierce concentration furrowed his brow. Maati heard Seedless fall even before he turned to look. The andat was prone, his hands splayed before him in a pose of abject apology so profound that Maati knew the andat would never take it of his own will. Heshai's lips quivered.

"It's something that . . . I've done before," he said, his voice tight. "It isn't something anyone wishes for. Not the woman, not anyone. The sad trade earns its name every time it's made."

"Heshai-cha?" a woman's voice said.

She stood beside the prostrate andat, her haughty demeanor shaken by the odd scene. Maati stood, falling into a pose of welcome. Heshai released his hold on Seedless, allowing the andat to rise. Seedless shook imagined dust off his robes, fixing the poet with a look of arch reproach, before turning to the woman.

"Liat Chokavi," the andat said, his perfect hands touching her wrist, intimate as old friends. "We're so pleased to see you. Aren't we, Heshai?"

"Delighted," the poet snapped. "Nothing quite like being handed to a half-tutored apprentice to keep me in my place."

The shock in the girl's face was subtle, there only for an instant. Her self-assured mask slipped, her eyes widening a fraction, her mouth hardening. And then she was as she had been before. But Maati knew, or thought he knew, how hard Heshai's blow had struck, and against someone who had done nothing but be an opportune target.

Heshai rose and took a pose appropriate to opening a negotiation, but with a stony formality that continued the insult. Maati found himself suddenly ashamed of his teacher.

"The meeting room's this way," Heshai said, then turned and trundled off. Seedless strode behind him, leaving Liat Chokavi and Maati to follow as they could.

"I'm sorry," Maati said quietly. "The sad trade bothers him. You didn't do anything wrong."

Liat shot a glance at him that began with distrust, then as she saw distress on his own face, softened. She took a pose of gratitude, small and informal.

The meeting room was spare and uncomfortably warm. A single small window stood shuttered until Heshai pushed it open. He sat at the low stone table and motioned Liat to sit across from him. She moved awkwardly, but took her place, plucking a packet of papers from her sleeve. Seedless stood at the window, looking down at the poet with a predatory smirk as Heshai drew the papers to him and glanced them over.

"May I be of service, Heshai-kvo?" Maati asked.

"Get us some tea," the poet said, looking at the papers. Maati looked first to the girl, and then back to Heshai. Seedless, seeing his reluctance, frowned. Then comprehension bloomed in the andat's black eyes. The perfect hands took a pose that asked permission for something—though Maati didn't know what, and Seedless dropped the pose before leave could be given.

"Heshai, my dear, you have a better student than you deserve. I think he doesn't want to leave you alone," Seedless smirked. "He thinks you'll go on bullying this fine young lady. If it were me, you understand, I'd be quite pleased to watch you make an ass of yourself, but . . ."

Heshai shifted, and the andat shuddered in pain or something like it. Seedless' hands shifted again into a pose of apology. Maati saw, however, the scowl on the poet's face. Seedless had shamed his master into behaving kindly to the girl. At least for a time.

"Some tea, Maati. And for our guest as well," Heshai said, gesturing to Liat.

Maati took a pose of acceptance. He caught Seedless' dark eyes as he left and nodded thanks. The andat answered with the smallest of all possible smiles.

The corridors of the hall were full of men and women; traders, utkhaiem, servants, slaves, and guards. Maati strode out, looking for a palace servant. He followed the path he knew to the main hall, impatient to return to the negotia-tion. The main hall was as full as the corridors, or worse. Conversations filled the space as thick as smoke. He caught a glimpse of the pale yellow robe of a palace servant moving toward the main door and made for it as quickly as he could.

Halfway to the main door, he brushed against a young man. He wore the same green and bronze colors that Liat Chokavi and Marchat Wilsin had, but his hands were stained and callused, his shoulders those of a laborer. Thinking that he could pass his errand off to this man, Maati stopped and grabbed the man's arm. The long face looked familiar, but it wasn't until he spoke that the blood rushed from Maati's face.

"Forgive me," the laborer said, taking a pose of apology. "I know I'm sup-posed to wait outside, but I was hoping Liat Chokavi . . ."

His voice trailed off, made uneasy by what he saw in Maati's eyes.

"Otah-kvo?" Maati breathed.

A moment of shocked silence, and then the laborer clapped a hand over Maati's mouth and drew him quickly into a side corridor.

"Say nothing," Otah said. *"Nothing."*

6

⟩+⟨ Years fell away, the events of Otah's life taking on a sudden unreality at the sound of his name. The hot, thick days he had worked the seafront of Saraykeht, the grubbing for food and shelter, the nights spent hungry sleep-ing by the roadside. The life he had built as Itani Noyga. All of it fell away, and he remembered the boy he had been, full of certainty and self-righteous fire trudging across cold spring fields to the high road. It was like being there again, and the strength of the memory frightened him.

The young poet went with him quietly, willingly. He seemed as shaken as Otah felt.

Together, they found an empty room, and Otah shut the door behind them and latched it. The room was a small meeting room, its window looking into a recessed courtyard filled with bamboo and sculpted trees. Even with the rain still falling—drops tapping against the leaves outside the window—the room seemed too bright. Otah sat on the table, his hands pressed to his mouth, and looked at the boy. He was younger by perhaps four summers—older than Otah had been when he'd invented his new name, his new his-tory, and taken indenture with House Wilsin. He had a round, open face and a firm chin and hands that hadn't known hard labor in many years. But more disturbing than that, there was pleasure in his expression, like someone who'd just found a treasure.

Otah didn't know where to start.

"You . . . you were at the school, then?"

"Maati Vaupathai," the poet said. "I was in one of the youngest cohorts just before you . . . before you left. You took us out to turn the gardens, but we didn't do very well. My hands were blistered . . ."

The face became suddenly familiar.

"Gods," Otah said. "You? That was you?"

Maati Vaupathai, whom Otah had once forced to eat dirt, took a pose of confirmation that seemed to radiate pleasure at being remembered. Otah leaned back.

"Please. You can't tell anyone about me. I never took the brand. If my brothers found me."

"They'd try to kill you," Maati said. "I know. I won't tell anyone. But . . . Otah-kvo."

"Itani," Otah said. "My name's Itani now."

Maati took a pose of acceptance, but still one appropriate for a student to a teacher. Still the sort that Otah had seen presented when he wore the black robes of the school.

"Itani, then. I didn't think. I mean, to find you here. What are you doing here?"

"I'm indentured to House Wilsin. I'm a laborer."

"A laborer?"

Otah took a confirming pose. The poet blinked, as if trying to make sense of a word in a different language. When he spoke again, his voice was troubled. Perhaps disappointed.

"They said that the Dai-kvo accepted you. That you refused him."

It was a simple description, Otah thought. A few words that held the shape his life had taken. It had seemed both clearer and more complex at the time—it still seemed that way in his mind.

"That's true," he said.

"What . . . forgive me, Otah-kvo, but what happened?"

"I left. I went south, and found work. I knew that I needed a new name, so I chose one. And . . . and that's all, I suppose. I've taken indenture with House Wilsin. It's nearly up, and I'm not sure what I'll do after that."

Maati took a pose of understanding, but Otah could see from the furrows in his brow that he didn't. He sighed and leaned forward, searching for something else to say, some way to explain the life he'd chosen. On top of all the other shocks of the day, he was disturbed to find that words failed him. In the years since he had walked away, he had never tried to explain the decision. There had never been anyone to explain it to.

"And you?" Otah asked. "He took you on, I see."

"The old Dai-kvo died. After you left, before I even took the black. Tahi-kvo took his place, and a new teacher came to the school. Naani-kvo. He was harder than Tahi-kvo. I think he enjoyed it more."

"It's a sick business," Otah said.

"No," Maati said. "Only hard. And cruel. But it has to be. The stakes are so high."

There was a strength in Maati's voice that, Otah thought, didn't come from assurance. Otah took a pose of agreement, but he could see that Maati knew he didn't mean it, so he shrugged it away.

"What did you do to earn the black?" Otah asked.

Maati blushed and looked away. In the corridor, someone laughed. It was unnerving. He'd spent so little time with this boy whom he hardly knew, and he'd almost forgotten where they were, and that there were people all around them.

"I asked Naani-kvo about you," Maati said. "He took it poorly. I had to wash the floors in the main hall for a week. But then I asked him again. It was the same. In the end . . . in the end, there was a night when I cleaned the floors without being told. Milah-kvo asked me what I was doing, and I explained that I was going to ask again in the morning, so I wanted to have some of the work done beforehand. He asked me if I was so in love with washing stones. Then he offered me the robes."

"And you took them."

"Of course," Maati said.

They were silent for a long moment, and Otah saw the life he'd turned away. And thought, perhaps, he saw regret in the boy's face. Or if not that, at least doubt.

"You can't tell anyone about me," Otah said.

"I won't. I swear I won't."

Otah took a pose that witnessed an oath, and Maati responded in kind. They both started when someone rattled the door.

"Who's in there?" a man's voice demanded. "We're scheduled for this room."

"I should go," Maati said. "I'm missing my negotiation with . . . Liat. You said you were waiting for Liat Chokavi, didn't you?"

"Unlatch the door!" the voice outside the door insisted. "This is our room."

"She's my lover," Otah said, standing. "Come on. We should leave before they go for the Khai."

The men outside the door wore the flowing robes and expensive sandals of the utkhaiem, and the disgust and anger on their faces when Otah—a mere laborer, and for a Galtic house at that—opened the door faded to impatience when they saw Maati in his poet's robes. Otah and Maati walked out to the main hall together.

"Otah-kvo," Maati said as they reached the still-bustling space.

"Itani."

Maati took a pose of apology that seemed genuinely mortified. "Itani. I . . . there are things I would like to discuss with you, and we . . ."

"I'll find you," Otah promised. "But say nothing of this. Not to anyone. Especially not to the poet."

"No one."

"I'll find you. Now go."

Maati took a pose of farewell more formal than any poet had ever offered a laborer, and, reluctance showing in every movement, walked away. Otah saw an older woman in the robes of the utkhaiem considering him, her expression curious. He took a pose of obeisance toward her, turned, and walked out. The rain was breaking now, sunlight pressing down like a hand on his shoulder. The other servants who had borne gifts or poles for the canopy waited now in a garden set aside for them. Epani-cha, house master for Marchat Wilsin, sat with them, laughing and smiling. The formal hurdles of the day were cleared, and the men were light hearted. Tuui Anagath, an older man who had known Otah since almost before he had become Itani, for almost his whole false life, took a pose of welcome.

"Did you hear?" he asked as Otah drew close.

"Hear what? No."

"The Khai is inviting a crew to hunt down Udun's son, the poisoner. Half the utkhaiem are vying to join it. They'll be on the little bastard like lice on a low town whore."

Otah took a pose of delight because he knew it was expected of him, then sat under a tree laden with tiny sweet-scented ornamental pears and listened. They were chattering with the prospect, all of them. These were men he knew, men he worked with. Men he trusted, some of them, though none so far as to tell them the truth. No one that far. They spoke of the death of the Khai Udun's son like a pit fight. They didn't care that the boy had been born into it. Otah knew that they couldn't see the injustice. For men born low, eking out lengths of copper to buy tea and soup and sourbread, the Khaiem were to be envied, not pitied and not loved. They would each of them go back to quarters shared with other men or else tiny apartments bearing with them the memory of the sprawling palaces, the sweet garden, the songs of slaves. There was no room in their minds for sympathy for the families of wealth and power. For men, Otah thought sourly, like himself.

"Eh?" Epani-cha said, prodding Otah with the toe of his shoe. "What did you swallow, Itani? You look sorry."

Otah forced a smile and laughed. He was good at that smiling and laughing. Being charming. He took a loose pose of apology.

"Am I lowering the tone?" he asked. "I just got thrown out of the palace. That's all."

"Thrown out?" Tuui Anagath asked, and the others turned, suddenly interested.

"I was just there, minding myself and—"

"And sniffing after Liat," one of the others laughed.

"And apparently I attracted some attention. One of the women from House Tiyaan came to me and asked whether I was a factor for House Wilsin. I told her I wasn't but for some reason she kept speaking with me. She was very pleasant. And apparently her lover took some offense to the conversation and spoke to the palace servants . . ."

Otah took a pose of innocent confusion that made the others laugh.

"Poor, poor Itani," Tuui Anagath said. "Can't keep the women away with a dagger. You should let us do you a favor, my boy. We could tell all the women you broke out in sores down there and had to spend three days a month in a poultice diaper."

Otah laughed with them now. He'd won again. He was one of them, just a man like them in no way special. The jokes and stories went on for half a hand, then Otah stood, stretched, and turned to Epani-cha.

"Will you have further need of me, Epani-cha?"

The thin man looked surprised, but took a pose of negation. Otah's relationship with Liat was no secret, but living in the compound itself, Epani understood the extent of it better than the others. When Otah shifted to a pose of farewell, he matched it.

"But Liat should be done with poets shortly," Epani said. "You don't want to wait for her?"

"No," Otah said, and smiled.

AMAT LEARNED. SHE LEARNED FIRST ABOUT THE FINE WORKINGS OF A COMFORT house—the balances between guard and gamesman and showfighter and whore, the rhythm that the business developed like the beat of a heart or the flow of a river. She learned, more specifically, how the money moved through it like blood. And so, she understood better what it was she was searching for in the crabbed scripts and obscure receipts. She also learned to fear Ovi Niit.

She had seen what happened when one of the other women displeased him. They were owned by the house, and so the watch extended no protection to them. They, unlike her, were easily replaced. She would not have taken their places for her weight in silver.

Two weeks from four. Or five. Two more, or three, before Marchat's promised amnesty. She sat in the room, sweltering; the papers stood in piles. Her days were filled with the scratch of pen on paper, the distant voices of the soft quarter, the smell of cheap food and her own sweat and the weak yellow light from the high, thin window.

The knock, when it came, was soft. Tentative. Amat looked up. Ovi Niit or one of his guards wouldn't have bothered. Amat jabbed her pen into its ink-block and stretched. Her joints cracked.

"Come in," she said.

She had seen the girl before, but hadn't heard her name. A smallish one. Young, with a birthmark at one eye that made her seem like a child's drawing of tears. When she took a pose of apology, Amat saw half-healed marks on her wrists. She wondered which of the payments in her ledgers matched those small wounds.

"Grandmother?" It was the name by which they all called her.

"What do you want," Amat asked, sorry for the harshness of her voice as she heard it. She massaged her hands.

"I know you aren't to be interrupted," the girl said. Her voice was nervous, but not, Amat thought, from fear of an old woman locked in a back closet. Ovi Niit must have given orders to leave her be. "But there's a man. He's at the door, asking for you."

"For me?"

The girl shifted to a pose of affirmation. Amat leaned back. Kirath. It *could* be Kirath. Or it could be one of the moon-faced Oshai's minions come to find her and kill her. Ovi Niit might already be spending the gold lengths he'd earned for her death. Amat nodded as much to herself as to the girl.

"What does he look like?"

"Young. Handsome," she said, and smiled as if sharing a confidence.

Handsome, perhaps, but Kirath would never be young again. This was not him, then. Amat hefted her cane. As a weapon, it was nothing. She wasn't strong enough now to run, even if her aching hip would have allowed it. There was no fleeing, but she could make it a siege. She sat with the panic, controlling it, until she was able to think a little; to speak without a tremble in her voice.

"What's your name, dear?"

"Ibris," the girl said.

"Good. Ibris. Listen very closely. Go out the front—not the back, the front. Find the watch. Tell them about this man. And tell them he was threatening a client."

"But he . . ."

"Don't question me," Amat said. "Go. Now!"

Years of command, years of assurance and confidence, served her now. The girl went, and when the door was closed behind her, Amat pushed the desk to block it. It was a sad, thin little barricade. She sat on it, adding her weight in hopes of slowing the man for the duration of a few extra heartbeats. If the watch came, they would stop him.

Or they wouldn't. Likely they wouldn't. She was a commodity here, bought and sold. And there was no one to say otherwise. She balled her swollen fists around her cane. Dignity be damned. If Marchat Wilsin and Oshai were going to take her down, she'd go down swinging.

Outside, she heard voices raised in anger. Ibris's was among them. And then a young man shouted. And then the fire.

The torch spun like something thrown by a street juggler through the window opposite her. Amat watched it trace a lazy arc through the air, strike the wall and bounce back, falling. Falling on papers. The flame touched one pile, and the pages took fire.

She didn't remember moving or calling out. She was simply there, stamping at the flames, the torch held above her, away from the books. The smoke was choking and her sandals little protection, but she kept on. Someone was forcing open the door, hardly slowed by her little barrier.

"Sand!" Amat shouted. "Bring sand!"

A woman's voice, high with panic, called out, but Amat couldn't make out the words. The floating embers started another stack of papers smoldering. The air seemed full of tiny burning bits of paper, floating like fireflies. Amat kept trying to stop it, to put it out. One particularly large fragment touched her leg, and the burning made her think for one long, sickening breath that her robe had caught fire.

The door burst open. Ibris and a red-haired westland whore—Menat? Mitat?—burst in with pans of water in their hands.

"No!" Amat shouted as she rounded on them, swinging the torch. "Not water! Sand! Get sand!"

The women hesitated, the water sloshing. Ibris turned first, dropping her pan though thankfully not on the books or the desk. The red-haired one threw her pan of water in the direction of the flames, catching Amat in the spray, and then they were gone again.

By the time they returned with three of Ovi Niit's house guards and two men of the watch, the fire was out. Only a tiny patch of tar on the wall still burned where the torch had struck on its way down. Amat handed the still-burning torch to a watchman. They questioned her, and then Ibris. Ovi Niit, when he returned, ranted like a madman in the common room, but thankfully his rage did not turn to her.

Hours of work were gone, perhaps irretrievably. There was no pushing herself now. What had been merely impossible before would have been laughable now, had there been any mirth to cut her misery. She straightened what there was to be straightened, and then sat in the near-dark. She couldn't stop weeping, so she ignored her own sobs. There wasn't time for it. She had to think, and the effort to stop her tears was more than she had to spare.

When, two or three hands later the door opened, it wasn't a guard or a watchman or a whore. It was Ovi Niit himself, eyes as wide as the heavy lids would permit, mouth thin as an inked line on paper. He stalked in, his gaze darting restlessly. Amat watched him the way she would have watched a feral dog.

"How bad?" he asked, his voice tight.

"A setback, Niit-cha," she said. "A serious one, but . . . but only a setback."

"I want him. The man who did this. Who's taking my money and burning my house? I want him broken. I'll piss in his mouth."

"As you see fit, Niit-cha," Amat said. "But if you want it in a week's time, you may as well cut me now. I can salvage this, but not quickly."

A heartbeat's pause, and he lunged forward. His breath smelled sickly sweet. Even in the dim light, she could see his teeth were rotten.

"He is out there!" Ovi Niit shrieked in her face. "Right now! And you want me to wait? You want to give him time? I want it tonight. Before morning. I want it *now!*"

That it was what she'd expected made it no easier. She took a pose of apology so steeped in irony that it couldn't be mistaken. The wild eyes narrowed. Amat pushed up the sleeve of her robe until it bunched around her elbow.

"Take out your knife," she said, baring the thin skin of her forearm to him. "Or give me the time to do the work well. After today, I don't have a preference."

Snake quick, he drew the blade and whipped it down. She flinched, but less than she'd expected to. The metal pressed into her skin but didn't break it. It hurt, though, and if he pulled it, it would bite deep. In the long pause, the young man chuckled. It wasn't the malefic sound of a torturer. It was something else. The whoremaster took the knife away.

"Do the work, then," he said, sneering. But behind the contempt, Amat thought perhaps a ray of respect had entered his gaze. She took an acquiescing pose. Ovi Niit stalked out, leaving the door open behind him. Amat sat for a long moment, rubbing the white line the knife had left on her flesh, waiting for the tightness in her throat to ease. She'd done it. She'd won herself more time.

It was at least half a hand later that the scent of apples and roast pork brought her stomach to life. She couldn't think how long it had been since she'd eaten. Leaning on her cane, she made her way to the wide tables. The benches were near full, the night's work set to begin. News had traveled. She could see it in the eyes that didn't meet hers. A space opened for her at the end of a bench, and she settled in. After the meal, she found Mitat, the Westland whore. The woman was in a dress of blue silk that clung to her body. The commodity wrapped for sale.

"We need to speak," Amat said quietly. "Now."

Mitat didn't reply, but when Amat returned to her cell, the girl followed. That was enough. Amat sat. The room still stank of ashes and tar. The grit of fire sand scraped under their feet. It wasn't the place she'd have chosen for this conversation, but it would do.

"It was fortunate that you had water to hand this afternoon," Amat said. "And in pans."

"We didn't need it," Mitat said. Her accent was slushy, and her vowels all slid at the ends. Westlands indeed. And to the north, Amat thought. A refugee from one of the Galtic incursions, most likely. And so, in a sense, they were there for the same reason.

"I was lucky," Amat said. "If I'd gone out to see who was at the door, the fire might have spread. And even if you'd stopped it, the water would have ruined the books."

Mitat shrugged, but her eyes darted to the door. It was a small thing, hardly noticeable in the dim light, but it was enough. Amat felt her suspicion settle into certainty. She took a firmer grip on her cane.

"Close the door," she said. The woman hesitated, then did as she was told. "They questioned Ibris. She sounded upset."

"They had to speak to someone," Mitat said, crossing her arms.

"Not you?"

"I never saw him."

"Good planning," Amat said, taking an approving pose. "Still, an unfortunate day for Ibris."

"You have an accusation to make?" Mitat asked. She didn't look away now. Now, she was all hardness and bravado. Amat could almost smell the fear.

"Do I have an accusation?" Amat said, letting the words roll off her tongue slowly. She tilted her head, considering Mitat as if she were something to be purchased. Amat shook her head. "No. No accusation. I won't tell him."

"Then I don't have to kill you," Mitat said.

Amat smiled and shook her head, her hands taking a pose of reproof.

"Badly played. Threats alienate me and admit your guilt at the same time. Those are just the wrong combination. Begin again," she said and settled herself like a street actor shifting roles. "I won't tell him."

The Westland girl narrowed her eyes, but there was an intelligence in them. That was good to see. Mitat stepped closer, uncrossed her arms. When she spoke, her voice was softer, wary, but less afraid.

"What do you want?" Mitat asked.

"Much better. I want an ally in the pesthole. When the time comes that I have to make a play, you will back me. No questions, no hesitations. We will pretend that Ovi Niit still owns you, but now you answer to me. And for that you and your man . . . it is a man isn't it? Yes, I thought so. You and your man will be safe. Agreed?"

Mitat was silent. In the street, a man shouted out an obscenity and laughed. A beggar sang in a lovely, high voice, and Amat realized she'd been hearing that voice the better part of the day. Why hadn't she noticed it before now? The whore nodded.

"Good," Amat said. "No more fires, then. And Mitat? The next bookkeep won't be likely to make the same offer, so no interesting spices in my food either, eh?"

"No, grandmother. Of course not."

"Well. Then. I don't suppose there's anything more to say just now, is there?"

LIAT SLAPPED THE GIRL'S WRIST, ANNOYED. MAJ PULLED BACK HER PALE HANDS, speaking in the liquid syllables of her language. Liat shifted her weight from her right knee to her left. The tailor at her side said nothing, but there was amusement in the way he held the knotted cord against the girl's bare thigh.

"Tell her it's just going to take longer if she keeps fidgeting," Liat said. "It isn't as if none of us had seen a leg before."

The moon-faced servant spoke in the island girl's tongue from his stool by the doorway. Maj looked down at the pair of them, blushing. Her skin clearly showed the blood beneath it. The tailor switched the knotted cord to the inner leg, his hand rising well past the girl's knee. She squealed and spoke again, more loudly this time. Liat bit back frustration.

"What's she saying?" Liat demanded.

"In her culture, people are not so free with each other's bodies," Oshai said. "It confuses her."

"Tell her it will be over soon. We can't start making the robes until we get through this."

Liat had thought, in all the late nights she'd woken sleepless and anxious, that negotiating with the Khai Saraykeht and his poet would be the worst of her commission. That shepherding the client through things as simple as being measured for robes would pose a greater problem had never occurred to her. And yet for days now, every small step would move Maj to fidget or pepper her translator, Oshai, with questions. Thankfully, the man seemed competent enough to answer most of them himself.

The tailor finished his work and stood, his hands in a pose of gratitude. Liat responded appropriately. The island girl looked on in mute fascination.

"Will there be anything more, Liat-cha?" Oshai asked.

"The court physician will wish to see her tomorrow. And I'm due to speak with a representative of the accountancy, but she won't be required for that. There may be more the next day, but I can tell you that once the schedule's been set."

"Thank you, Liat-cha," he said and took a pose of gratitude. Something in the cant of his wrists and the corners of his mouth made Liat look twice. She had the feeling that he was amused by her. Well, let him be. When Amat returned, Liat knew there would be a chance to comment on Oshai. And if Amat took offense, he'd never work for House Wilsin again.

She made her way out to the narrow streets of the tailors' quarter. The heat of the day was fierce, and the air was thick and muggy. Sweat had made her robes tacky against her back before she'd made it halfway to the laborers' quarters. She was more than half tempted to take them off and bathe under the rough shower Itani's cohort used. There was no one at it when she arrived. But if someone did see her—an acting overseer of House Wilsin—it might reflect on her status. So, instead, she walked up the stone steps worn smooth by generations of men and into the wide hallway with its cots and cheap cloth tents instead of netting. The sounds of masculine laughter and conversation filled the space like the reek of bodies. And yet Itani lived like this. He chose to. He was a mystery.

When she found him, he was seated on his cot, his skin and hair still wet from the shower. She paused, considering him, and uneasiness touched her. His brow was furrowed in concentration, but his hands were idle. His shoulders hunched forward. Had he been anyone else, she would have said he seemed haunted. In the months—nearly ten now—since she had taken him as her lover, she'd never known him to chew himself like this.

"What's the matter, love?" she said softly.

And the care vanished as if it had never been. Itani smiled, rose, took her in his arms. He smelled good—of clean sweat and young man and some subtle musk that was his alone.

"Something's bothering you," she said.

"No. I'm fine. It's just Muhatia-cha breaking my stones again. It's nothing. Do you have time to go to a bathhouse with us?"

"Yes," she said. It wasn't the answer she'd intended to give, but it was the one she meant now. Her papers for Wilsin-cha could wait.

"Good," he said, the way he smiled convinced her. But there was still something—a reservation in his hands, a distance in his eyes. "Your work's going well, then?"

"Well enough. The negotiations are all in place, I think. But the girl frustrates me. It makes me short with her, and I know I shouldn't be."

"Does she accept your apologies?"

"I haven't really offered them. I want to now, when I'm away from her. But in the moment, I'm always too annoyed with her."

"Well. You could start the day with them. Have it out of the way before you begin."

"Itani, is there something you want me to apologize to *you* for?"

He smiled his perfect, charming smile, but somehow it didn't reach the depths of his eyes.

"No," he said. "Of course not."

"Because it seems like we made our peace, but . . . but you haven't seemed the same since I went before the Khai."

She pulled back from him and sat on his cot. He hesitated and then sat beside her, the canvas creaking under their combined weight. She took a pose of apology, her expression gentle, making it more an offer and a question than a literal form itself.

"It's not like that," Itani said. "I'm not angry. It's hard to explain."

"Then try. I might know you better than you think."

He laughed, a small rueful sound, but didn't forbid it. Liat steeled herself.

"It's our old conversation, isn't it?" she said, gently. "I've started moving up in the house. I'm negotiating with the Khai, with the poets. And your indenture is coming to a close before long. I think you're afraid I'll outgrow you. That an overseer—even one low in the ranks—is above the dignity of a laborer."

Itani was silent. His expression was thoughtful, and his gaze seemed wholly upon her for the first time in days. A smile quirked his lips and vanished.

"Am I right?" she asked.

"No," he said. "But I'm curious all the same. Is that what you believe? That I would be beneath your dignity?"

"I don't," she said. "But I also don't think you'll end your life a laborer. You're a strange man. You're strong and clever and charming. And I think you know half again what you let on. But I don't understand your choices. You could be so much, if you wanted to. Isn't there anything you want?"

He said nothing. The smile was gone, and the haunted look had stolen back into his eyes. She caressed his cheek, feeling where the stubble was coming in.

"Do you want to go to the bathhouse?" she asked.

"Yes," he said. "We should be going. The others will be there already."

"You're sure there isn't something more I should know?"

He opened his mouth to speak, and it was as if she could see some glib rejoinder die on his lips. His wide, strong hand folded hers.

"Not now," he said.

"But eventually," she said.

Something like dread seemed to take Itani's long face, but he managed a smile.

"Yes," he said.

Through the evening, Itani grew more at ease. They laughed with his friends, drank and sang together. The pack of them moved from bathhouse to teahouse to the empty beaches at the far end of the seafront. Great swaths of silt showed where the rivermouth had once been, generations ago. When the time came, Itani walked her back to the Wilsin compound, the comfortable weight of his arm around her shoulders. Crickets chirped in chorus as they stepped together into the courtyard with its fountain and the Galtic Tree.

"You could stay," she said, softly.

He turned, pulling her body near to his. She looked up into his eyes. Her answer was there.

"Another time, then?" she asked, embarrassed to hear the plea in her voice.

He leaned close, his lips firm and soft against hers. She ran her fingers through his hair, holding it to her like a cup from which she was drinking. She ached for him to stay, to be with her, to sleep in his arms. But he stepped back, gently out of her reach. She took a pose of regret and farewell. He answered with a pose so gentle and complex—thankfulness, requesting patience, expressing affection—that it neared poetry. He walked backwards slowly, fading into the shadows where the moon didn't reach, but with his eyes on her. She sighed, shook herself, and went to her cell. It would be a long day tomorrow, and the ceremony still just over a week away.

Liat didn't notice she wasn't alone until she was nearly to her door. The pregnant girl, Maj, was on the walkway and unescorted. She wore a loose gown that barely covered her breasts and a pair of workman's trousers cut at the knee. Her swollen belly pressed out, bare in the moonlight.

To Liat's surprise, the girl took a pose of greeting. It was rough and child-like, but recognizable.

"Hello," Maj said, her accent so thick as to almost bury the word.

Liat fell into an answering pose immediately and felt a smile growing on her lips. The girl Maj almost glowed with pleasure.

"You've been learning to speak," Liat said. Maj's face clouded, her smile faltered, and she shrugged—a gesture that carried its load of meaning without language.

"Hello," Maj said again, taking the same pose as before. Her expression said that this was all that there was. Liat nodded, smiled again, and took the girl by the arm. Maj shifted Liat's hand, lacing their fingers together as if they were young girls walking together after temple. Liat walked back to the guest quarters where Maj was being housed until after the ceremony.

"It's a good start," Liat said as they walked. She knew that the words were likely meaningless to the island girl, but she spoke them all the same. "Keep practicing, and we'll make a civilized woman of you. Just give it time."

>+< Two days later, after his work was complete and his friends had gone to their night's entertainments, Otah stepped out from his quarters and considered. The city streets were gaudy with sunset. Orange light warmed the walls and roofs, even as the first stars began to glimmer in the deep cobalt of the western sky. Otah stood in the street and watched the change come. Fireflies danced like candles. The songs of beggars changed as the traffic of night came out. The soft quarter lay to his right, lit like a carnival as it was every night. The seafront was before him, though hidden by the barracks of other labor cohorts like his own, employed by other houses. And somewhere far to his left, off past the edge of the city, the great river flowed, bearing water from the north. He rubbed his hands together slowly as the light reddened, then grayed. The sun vanished again, and the stars came out, shining over the city. Liat was in her cell, he supposed, to the north and uphill. And beyond her, the palaces of the Khai.

The streets changed as he walked north. The laborers' quarter was actually quite small, and Otah left it behind him quickly, barracks giving way to the shops of small merchants and free traders. Then came the weavers' compounds, windows candle-lit, and the clack of looms filling the streets as they would even later into the night. He passed groups of men and of women, passed through the street of beads and the blood quarter where physicians and pretenders vied to care for the sick and injured, selling services, as everything in Saraykeht was for trade.

The compounds of the great houses rose up like small villages. Streets grew wider near them, and walls taller. The firekeepers at their kilns wore better robes than their fellows lower in the city. Otah paused at the corner that would have taken him to House Wilsin, through the familiar spaces to Liat's side. It would be so easy, he thought, to go there. He stood for the space of ten heartbeats, standing at the intersection like the statue of some forgotten man of the Empire, before going north. His hands were balled in fists.

The palaces grew up like a city of their own, above the city inhabited by mere humans. The scents of sewage and bodies and meat cooking at teahouses vanished and those of gardens and incense took their places. The paths changed from stone to marble or sand or fine gravel. The songs of beggars gave way to the songs of slaves, almost it seemed without losing the melody. The great halls stood empty and dark or else lit like lanterns from within. Servants and slaves moved along the paths with the quiet efficiency of ants, and the utkhaiem, in robes as gaudy as the sunset, stood in lit courtyards, posing to each other as the politics of the court played out. Vying, Otah guessed, for which would have the honor of killing a son of the Khai Udun.

Pretending that he bore a message, he took directions from one of the servants, and soon he'd left even the palaces behind. The path was dark, curving through stands of trees. He could still see the palaces behind him if he turned, but the emptiness made the poet's house seem remote from them. He crossed a long wooden bridge over a pond. And there the simple, elegant house stood. Its upper story was lit. Its lower had the front wall pulled open like shutters or a stage set for a play. And sitting on a velvet chair was the boy. Maati Vaupathai.

"Well," a soft voice said. "Here's an oddity. It's a strange day we see toughs reeking of the seafront dropping by for tea. Or perhaps you've got some other errand."

The andat Seedless sat on the grass. Otah fell into a pose that asked forgiveness.

"I . . . I've come to see Maati-cha," Otah stumbled. "We were . . . that is . . ."

"Hai! Who's down there?" another voice called. "Who're you?"

Seedless glanced up at the house, eyes narrowed. A fat man in the brown robe of a poet was trundling down the steps. Maati was following.

"Itani of House Wilsin," Otah called out. "I've come to see Maati-cha."

The poet walked more slowly as they approached. His expression was a strange mix—concern, disapproval, and a curious delight.

"You've come for *him?*" Heshai-kvo said, gesturing over his shoulder. Otah took a pose of affirmation.

"Itani and I met at the grand audience," Maati said. "He offered to show me the seafront."

"Did he?" Heshai-kvo asked, and the disapproval lost ground, Otah thought, to the pleasure. "Well. You. Itani's your name? You know who you're with, eh? This boy is one of the most important men in Saraykeht. Keep him out of trouble."

"Yes, Heshai-cha," Otah said. "I will."

The poet's face softened, and he rooted in the sleeve of his robe for a moment, then reached out to Otah. Otah, unsure, stepped closer and put his hand out to the poet's.

"I was young once too," Heshai-kvo said with a broad wink. "Don't keep him out of too much trouble."

Otah felt the small lengths of metal against his palm, and took a pose of gratitude.

"Who'd have thought it," Seedless said, his voice low and considering. "Our perfect student's developing a life."

"Please, Itani-cha," Maati said, stepping forward and taking Otah's sleeve. "You've gone out of your way already. We should go. Your friends are waiting."

"Yes," Otah said. "Of course."

He took a pose of farewell that the poet responded to eagerly, the andat more slowly and with a thoughtful attitude. Maati led the way back across the bridge.

"You were expecting me?" Otah asked once they were out of earshot. Poet and andat were still watching them go.

"Hoping," Maati allowed.

"You weren't the only one. The poet seemed delighted to see me."

"He doesn't like my staying at the house. He thinks I should see more of the city. It's really that he hates it there and can't imagine that I like it."

"Ah. I see."

"You see part, at least," Maati said. "It's complex. And what of you, Otah-kvo? It's been days. I was afraid that you wouldn't come."

"I had to," Otah said, surprised by his own candor even as he said it. "I've no one else to talk with. Gods! He gave me three lengths of silver!"

"Is that bad?"

"It means I should stop working the seafront and just take you to tea. The pay's better."

He had changed. That was clear. The voice was much the same, the face older, more adult, but Maati could still see the boy who had worn the black robes in the garden all those years ago. And something else. It wasn't confidence that had gone—he still had that in the way he held himself and his voice when he spoke—but perhaps it was certainty. It was in the way he held his cup and in the way he drank. Something was bothering his old teacher, but Maati could not yet put a name to it.

"A laborer," Maati said. "It isn't what the Dai-kvo would have expected."

"Or anyone else," Otah said, smiling at his cup of wine.

The private patio of the teahouse overlooked the street below it, and the long stretch of the city to the south. Lemon candles filled the air with bright-smelling smoke that kept the worst of the gnats away and made the wine taste odd. In the street, a band of young men sang and danced while three women watched, laughing. Otah took a long drink of wine.

"It isn't what you'd expected either, is it?"

"No," Maati admitted. "When you left I imagined . . . we all did . . ."

"Imagined what?"

Maati sighed, frowned, tried to find words for daydreams and secret stories he'd never precisely told himself. Otah-kvo had been the figure who'd shaped his life almost more than the Dai-kvo, certainly more than his father. He had imagined Otah-kvo forging a new order, a dark, dangerous, possibly libertine group that would be at odds with the Dai-kvo and the school, or perhaps its rival. Or else adventuring on the seas or in the turmoil of the wars in the Westlands. Maati would never have said it, but the common man his teacher had become was disappointing.

"Something else," he said, taking a pose that kept the phrase vague.

"It was hard. The first few months, I thought I'd starve. Those things they taught us about hunting and foraging? They work, but only barely. When I got a bowl of soup and half a loaf of stale bread for cleaning out a henhouse, I felt like I'd been given the best meal of my life."

Maati laughed. Otah smiled at him and shrugged.

"And you?" Otah asked, changing the subject. "Was the Dai-kvo's village what you thought?"

"I suppose so. It was more work than the school, but it was easier. Because there was a reason for it. It wasn't just hard to be hard. We studied old grammars and the languages of the Empire. And the history of the andat: who bound them, what the bindings were like. How they escaped. I didn't know how much harder it is to bind the same andat a second time. I mean there are all the stories about some being captured three or four times, but I don't . . ."

Otah laughed. It was a warm sound, mirthful but not mocking. Maati took a pose of query. Otah responded with one of apology that nearly spilled his wine.

"It's just that you sound like you loved it," Otah said.

"I did," Maati said. "It was fascinating. And I'm good at it, I think. My teachers seemed to feel that way. Heshai-kvo isn't what I'd expected though."

"Him either, eh?"

"No. But, Otah-kvo, why didn't you go? When the Dai-kvo offered you a place with him, why did you refuse?"

"Because what they did was wrong," Otah said, simply. "And I didn't want any part of it."

Maati frowned into his wine. His reflection looked back at him from the dark, shining surface.

"If you had it again, would you do the same?" Maati asked.

"Yes."

"Even if it meant just being a laborer?"

Otah took two deep breaths, turned, and sat on the railing, considering Maati with dark, troubled eyes. His hands moved toward a pose that might have been accusation or demand or query, but that never took a final form.

"Is this really so bad, what I do?" Otah asked. "You, Liat. Everyone seems to think so. I started out as a child on the road with no family, no friends. I didn't even dare use my real name. And I built something. I have work, and friends, and a lover. I have good food and shelter. And at night I can go and listen to poets or philosophers or singers, or I can go to bathhouses or tea-houses, or out on the ocean in sailing boats. Is that so bad? It that so *little?*"

Maati was surprised by the pain in Otah's voice, and perhaps by the desperation. He had the feeling that the words were only half meant for him. Still, he considered them. And their source.

"Of course not," Maati said. "Something doesn't have to be great to be worthy. If you've followed the calling of your heart, then what does it matter what anyone else thinks?"

"It can matter. It can matter a great deal."

"Not if you're certain," Maati said.

"And someone, somewhere, is actually certain of the choices they made? Are you?"

"No, I'm not," Maati said. It was easier than he'd expected, voicing this deepest of doubts. He'd never said it to anyone at the school or with the Dai-kvo. He'd have died before he said it to Heshai-kvo. But to Otah, it wasn't such a hard thing to say. "But it's done. I've made all my decisions already. Now it's just seeing whether I'm strong enough to follow through."

"You are," Otah said.

"I don't think so."

Silence flowed in. Below them, in the street, a woman shrieked and then laughed. A dog streets away bayed as if in response. Maati put down his cup of wine—empty now except for the dregs—and slapped a gnat from his arm. Otah nodded, more to himself than to Maati.

"Well, there's nothing to be done then," Otah said.

"It's late and we're drunk," Maati said. "It'll look better by morning. It always does."

Otah weighed the words, then took a pose of agreement.

"I'm glad I found you," Maati said. "I think perhaps I was meant to."

"Perhaps," Otah-kvo agreed.

"Wilsin-cha!" Epani's voice was a whisper, but the urgency of it cut through Marchat's dream. He rolled up on one elbow and was pushing away his netting before he was really awake. The house master stood beside the bed holding his robe closed with one hand. Epani's face, lit only by the night candle, was drawn.

"Wha?" Marchat said, still pulling his mind up from the depths he'd been in moments before. "What's the matter? There's a fire?"

"No," Epani said, trying a pose of apology, but hampered by the needs of his robes. "Someone's here to see you. He's in the private hall."

"He? He who?"

Epani hesitated.

"It," he said.

It took Marchat the time to draw in a breath before he understood what Epani meant. He nodded then, and motioned to a robe that hung by his wardrobe. The night candle was well past its middle mark—the night nearer the coming dawn than yesterday's sunset. Apart from the soft rustle of the cloth as Marchat pulled his robes on and tied them, there was no sound. He ran his fingers through his hair and beard and turned toward Epani.

"Good enough?" he asked.

Epani took a pose of approval.

"Fine," Marchat said. "Bring us something to drink. Wine. Or tea."

"Are you sure, Wilsin-cha?"

Marchat paused and considered. Every movement in the night ran the risk of waking someone, someone besides himself or Epani or Oshai. A glimmer of anger at the andat for coming here, now, like this, shone in the dark setting of his unease. He took a pose of dismissal.

"No," he said. "Don't bring us anything. Go to bed. Forget this happened. You were dreaming."

Epani left. Marchat took up his night candle and walked in its near-darkness to the private hall. It was near his own quarters because of meetings like this. Windowless, with a single entrance and its own atrium so that anyone within could hear if someone was coming. When he stepped into the room, the andat was perched on the meeting table like a bird, his arms resting on his knees. The blackness of his cloak spread out behind him like a stain.

"What are you playing at, Wilsin?"

"I was playing at being asleep until a few moments ago," Marchat said, bluster welling up to hide his fear. The dark eyes in the pale face shifted, taking him in. Seedless tilted his head. They were silent except for Marchat's breathing. He was the only one there breathing.

"Is this about something?" Marchat asked. "And get your boots off my table, will you? This isn't some cheap teahouse."

"Why is your boy courting mine?" the andat demanded, ignoring him.

Marchat put the night candle squarely on the table, pulled out a chair, and sat.

"I don't have the first idea what you're talking about," he said, crossing his arms. "Talk sense or go haunt someone else. I've got a busy day tomorrow."

"You didn't send one of your men to take Heshai's student out to the teahouses?"

"No."

"Then why did he come?"

Marchat read the distrust in the andat's expression, or imagined he did. He set his jaw and leaned forward. The thing in human form didn't move.

"I don't know who you mean," Marchat said, deliberately. "And you can drink piss if you don't believe me."

Seedless narrowed his eyes as if he was listening for something, then sat back. The anger that had been in his voice and face faded and was replaced by puzzlement.

"One of your laborers came tonight to see Maati," Seedless said. "He said they'd met during the negotiations and arranged to go out together."

"Well," Marchat said. "Perhaps they met during the negotiations and arranged to go out together."

"A poet and a laborer?" Seedless scoffed. "And maybe the fine ladies of the utkhaiem are out this evening playing tiles in the soft quarter. Heshai was delighted, of course. It smells wrong to me, Wilsin."

Marchat turned it over slowly, chewing on his lip. It did seem odd. And with the ceremony coming so quickly, the stakes were high. He pulled out a chair, its wooden legs scraping against the stone floor, and sat. Seedless swung his legs over the side, still sitting on the tabletop, but without seeming quite as predatory.

"Which man was it?"

"He said his name was Itani. Big man, broad across the shoulders. Face like a northerner."

The one Amat had sent out with him. That wasn't good. Seedless read something in his face and took a pose half query and half command.

"I know the one you mean. You're right. Something's odd. He was my bodyguard when I came out to the low town. And he's Liat Chokavi's lover."

Seedless took a moment to consider that. Marchat watched the dark eyes, the beautiful mouth that turned into the faintest of smiles.

"Has he warned Liat of anything?" the andat asked. "Do you think she suspects?"

"She doesn't. If she had any reservations, you could read them from across the room. I think Liat may be the worst liar I've ever met. It's part of what makes her so good at this."

"If he hasn't told Liat, perhaps he *isn't* trying to spoil our little game. You've had no word of your vanished overseer?"

"No," Marchat said. "Oshai's thugs have been offering good prices for her, but there's been no sign. And no one at the seafront or on the roads remembers seeing her go. And even if she's gone to ground inside the city, there's no reason to think she's out to stop . . . the trade."

"Oshai can't find her, and that's enough to make me nervous. And this boy, this Itani. Either he is her agent or he isn't. And if he *is* . . ."

Marchat sighed. There was no end of it. Every time he thought he'd reached the last crime he'd be called upon to commit, one more appeared behind it. Liat Chokavi—silly, short-sighted, kind, pretty girl that she was—would be humiliated when the thing went wrong. And now it seemed she wouldn't have her man behind her to offer comfort.

"I can have him killed," Marchat said, heavily. "I'll speak with Oshai in the morning."

"No," Seedless said. The andat leaned back, crossing one knee over the other and lacing his hands over it. They were women's hands—thin and graceful. "No. If he's sent to tell the tale, it's too late. Maati will know by now. If he isn't, then killing him will only draw attention."

"I could have the poet boy killed too," Marchat said.

"No," Seedless said again. "No, we can kill the laborer if it seems the right thing, but no one touches Maati."

"Why not?"

"I like him," Seedless said, a subtle surprise in his voice, as if this were something he'd only just realized. "He's . . . he's good-hearted. He's the only person I've met in years who didn't see me as a convenient tool or else the very soul of evil."

Marchat blinked. For a moment, something like sadness seemed to possess the andat. Sadness or perhaps longing. In the months Marchat had spent preparing this evil scheme, he'd built an image of the beast he was treating with, and this emotion didn't fit with it. And then it was gone and Seedless grinned at him.

"You, for instance, think I'm chaos made flesh," Seedless said. "Ripping a wanted child from an innocent girl's womb just to make Heshai-kvo suffer."

"It doesn't matter what I think."

"No. It doesn't, but that won't stop you from thinking it. And when you *do* think, remember it was your men who approached me. It may be my design, but it's your money."

"It's my uncle's," Marchat said, perhaps more sharply than he'd intended. "I didn't choose any of this. No one asked my opinion."

A terrible amusement lit the andat's face, and the beautiful smile had grown wider.

"Puppets. Puppets and the puppets of puppets. You should have more sympathy for me, Wilsin-cha. I'm what I am because of someone else, just the way you are. How could either of us ever be responsible for anything?"

The poisonous thought tickled the back of Marchat's mind—*what if I'd refused?* He pushed it away.

"We couldn't be less alike," Marchat said. "But it doesn't matter. However we got here, we're married now. What of Itani?"

"Have him followed," he said. "Our boy Itani may be nothing, but the game's too important to risk it. Find out what he is, and then, if we have to, we can kill him."

8

>+<   "After the fire, we agreed . . ." Amat said, and the back of Ovi Niit's hand snapped her head to the side. She turned back slowly, tasting her own blood. Her lips tingled in the presentiment of pain, and a trickle of warmth going cool on her chin told the part of her mind that wasn't cringing in fear that one of his rings had cut her.

"Agreed," Ovi Niit spat. "We agree what I say we agree. If I change it, it changes. There's no agreement to be made."

He paced the length of the room. The evening sun pressed at the closed shutters, showing only their outlines. It was enough light to see by, enough to know that Ovi Niit's eyes were opened too wide—the stained whites showing all the way round. His lips moved as if he were on the verge of speaking.

"You're stalling!" he shouted, slamming his hand down on her desk. Amat balled her fists and willed herself to sit quietly. Anything she said would be a provocation. "You think that by stretching it out, you'll be safer. You think that by letting that thief take my money, you'll be better off. But you won't!"

With the last word, he kicked the wall. The plaster cracked where he'd struck it. Amat considered the damage—small lines radiating out from a flattened circle—and felt her mind shift. It was no bigger than an egg, and looking at it, she knew that sometime not long from now Ovi Niit wouldn't direct his rage at the walls. He would kill her, whether he meant to or not.

How odd, she thought as she felt the nausea descend on her, that it would be that little architectural wound that would resolve her when all his violence against people hadn't.

"I will have my answer by dawn," he shouted. "By dawn. If you don't do what I say, I'll cut off your thumbs and sell you for the five lengths of gold. It's not as if Oshai's going to care that you're damaged."

Amat took a pose of obeisance so abject that she was disgusted by it. But it came naturally to her hands. Ovi Niit grabbed her by a handful of hair and pulled her from her chair, spilling her papers and pens. He kicked over the desk and stalked out. As the door slammed shut behind him, Amat caught a glimpse of shocked faces.

She lay in the darkness, too tired and ill to weep. The stone floor was rough against her cheek. The blood from her cut face pulled on her skin as it dried. She'd have a scar. When her mind would obey her again, the room was utterly black. She forced herself to think. The days had blurred—bent over half-legible books from the moment she woke until the figures shifted on the page and her hands bent themselves into claws. And then to dream about it, and come back and begin again. And there had been no point. Ovi Niit was a thug and a whoremaster. His fear and violence grew with the wine and drugs he took to ease them. He would have been pitiful from the right distance.

But days. The question was days.

She counted slowly, struggling to recall. Three weeks at least. More than that. It had to be more than that. Perhaps four. Not five. It was too early to be sure of Marchat's amnesty. She surprised herself by chuckling. If she'd counted wrong, the worst case would be that they found her face down in the river and Ovi Niit lost five lengths of gold. That wouldn't be so bad.

She pushed herself upright, then stood, breathing through the pain until she felt as little stooped as she could manage. When she was ready, she took up her cane and put on the expression she used when she wanted no one to see her true feelings. She was Amat Kyaan, after all, overseer of House Wilsin. Streetgirl of Saraykeht made good. Let them see that she was unbroken. If she could make the whores of the comfort house believe it, she would start to believe it again, too.

The common room was near empty, the whores out in the rooms plying their trade. A guardsman sat eating a roast chicken that smelled of garlic and rosemary. An old black dog lay curled in a corner, a leatherwork rod in the shape of a man's sex chewed half to pieces between the bitch's paws.

"He's gone out," the guard said. "In the front rooms, playing tiles."

Amat nodded.

"I wouldn't go out to him, grandmother."

"I wouldn't want to interrupt. Send Mitat to the office. I need someone to help me put the room back in order. Every meeting it's like a storm's come through."

The guard took an amused pose of agreement. The sound of drums came suddenly from the street. Another night in the endless carnival of the soft quarter.

"I'll have her bring something for that wound," the guard said.

"Thank you," Amat said, her voice polite, dispassionate: the voice of the woman she wanted them all the believe her to be. "That would be very kind of you."

Mitat appeared in her doorway half a hand later. The wide, pale face littered with freckles looked hard. Amat smiled gently at her and took a pose of welcome.

"I heard that he'd been to see you, grandmother."

"Yes, and so he has. Open those shutters for me, would you, dear? I was tall enough to get them myself when I came here, but I seem to have grown shorter."

Mitat did so, and the pale moonlight added to the lantern on Amat's desk. The papers weren't in such bad order. Amat motioned the woman closer.

"You have to go, grandmother," Mitat said. "Niit-cha is getting worse."

"Of course he is," Amat said. "He's frightened. And he drinks too much. I need you. Now, tonight."

Mitat took a pose of agreement. Amat smiled and took her hand. In the wall behind Mitat, the little scar blemished the wall where he'd kicked it. Amat wondered in passing if the whoremaster would ever understand how much that mark had cost him. And Amat intended it to cost dear.

"Who is the most valuable man here?" Amat asked. "Niit-cha must have men who he trusts more than others, ne?"

"The guards," Mitat began, but Amat waved the comment away.

"Who does he trust like a brother?"

Mitat's eyes narrowed. She's caught scent of it, Amat thought and smiled.

"Black Rathvi," Mitat said. "He's in charge of the house when Niit-cha's away."

"You know what his handwriting looks like?"

"No," Mitat said. "But I know he took in two gold and seventy silver lengths from the high tables two nights ago. I heard him talking about it."

Amat paged through the most recent ledger until she found the precise sum. It was a wide hand with poorly formed letters and a propensity for dropping the ends of words. She knew it well. Black Rathvi was a poor keeper of notes, and she'd been struggling with his entries since she'd started the project. She found herself ghoulishly pleased that he'd be suffering for his poor job keeping books.

"I'll need a cloak—a hooded one—perhaps two hands before daybreak," Amat said.

"You should leave now," Mitat said. "Niit-cha's occupied for the moment, but he may—"

"I'm not finished yet. Two hands before daybreak, I will be. You and your man should slow down for a time after Ovi Niit deals with Black Rathvi. At least several weeks. If he sees things get better, he'll know he was right. You understand?"

Mitat took a pose of affirmation, but it wasn't solid. Amat didn't bother replying formally, only raised a single eyebrow and waited. Mitat looked away, and then back. There was something like hope and also like distrust in her eyes. The face of someone who wants to believe, but is afraid to.

"Can you do it?" Mitat asked.

"Make the numbers point to Black Rathvi? Of course I can. This is what I do. Can you get me a cloak and safe passage at least as far as the street?"

"If you can put those two at each other's throats, I can do anything," Mitat said.

It took less time than she'd expected. The numbers were simple enough to manipulate once she knew what she wanted to do with them. She even changed a few of the entries on their original sheets, blacking out the scrawling hand and forging new figures. When she was finished, a good accountant would have been able to see the deception. But if Ovi Niit had had one of those, Amat would never have been there.

She spent the remaining time composing her letter of leave-taking. She kept the tone formal, using all the titles and honorary flourishes she would have for a very respected merchant or one of the lower of the utkhaiem. She expressed her thanks for the shelter and discretion Ovi Niit and his house had extended and expressed regret that she felt it in her best interest—now that her work was done—to leave inconspicuously. She had too much respect, she wrote sneering as she did so, for Niit-cha's sense of advantage to expect him not to sell a commodity for which he no longer had use. She then outlined her findings, implicating Black Rathvi without showing any sign that she knew his name or his role in the house.

She folded the letter twice and then at the corners in the style of a private message and wrote Ovi Niit's name on the overleaf. It perched atop the papers and books, ready to be discovered. Amat sat a while longer, listening to the wild music and slurred voices of the street, waiting for Mitat to appear. The night candle consumed small mark after small mark, and Amat began to wonder whether something had gone wrong.

It hadn't.

However the girl had arranged it, leaving the house was as simple as shrugging on the deep green cloak, taking up her cane, and stepping out the rear door and down a stone path to the open gate that led to the street. In the east, the blackness was starting to show the gray of charcoal, the weakest stars on the horizon failing. The moon, near full, had already set. The night traffic was over but for a few revelers pulling themselves back from their entertainments. Amat, for all the pain in her joints, wasn't the slowest.

She paused at a corner stand and bought a meal of fresh greens and fried pork wrapped in almond skin and a bowl of tea. She ate as the sun rose, climbing like a god in the east. She was surprised by the calm she felt, the serenity. Her ordeal was, if not over, at least near its end. A few more days, and then whatever Marchat was doing would be done. And if she spent weeks in hell, she was strong enough, she saw, to come through it with grace.

She even believed the story until the girl running the stall asked if she'd want more tea. Amat almost wept at the small kindness. So perhaps she wasn't quite so unscathed as she told herself.

She reached her apartments in the press of the morning. On a normal day, if she could recall those, she might have been setting forth just then. Or even a bit earlier. Off into her city, on the business of her house. She unlocked the door of her apartments, slipped in, and barred the door behind her. It was a risk, coming home without being sure of things with Marchat's cruel business, but she needed money. And the stinging salve for her legs. And a fresh robe. And sleep. Gods, she needed sleep. But that would wait.

She gathered her things quickly and made for the door, struggling to get down the stairs. She had enough silver in her sleeve to buy a small house for a month. Surely it would be enough for a room and discretion for three or four days. If she could only . . .

No. No, of course she couldn't. When she opened the door, three men blocked her. They had knives. The tallest moved in first, clamping a wide palm over her mouth and pushing her against the wall. The others slid in fast as shadows, and closed the door again. Amat closed her eyes. Her heart was racing, and she felt nauseated.

"If you scream, we'll have to kill you," the tall man said gently. It was so much worse for being said so carefully. Amat nodded, and he took his hand away. Their knives were still drawn.

"I want to speak with Wilsin-cha," Amat said when she had collected herself enough to say anything.

"Good that we've sent for him, then," one of the others said. "Why don't you have a seat while we wait."

Amat swallowed, hoping to ease the tightness in her throat. She took a pose that accepted the suggestion, turned and made her way again up the stairs to wait at her desk. Two of the men followed her. The third waited below. The sun had moved the width of two hands together when Marchat walked up the steps and into her rooms.

He looked older, she thought. Or perhaps not older, but worn. His hair hung limp on his brow. His robes fit him poorly, and a stain of egg yolk discolored the sleeve. He paced the length of the room twice, looking neither directly at her nor away. Amat, sitting at her desk, folded her hands on one knee and waited. Marchat stopped at the window, turned and gestured to the two thugs.

"Get out," he said. "Wait downstairs."

The two looked at one another, weighing, Amat saw, whether to obey him. These were not Marchat's men, then. Not truly. They were the moon-faced Oshai's perhaps. One shrugged, and the other turned back with a pose of acknowledgement before they both moved to the door and out. Amat listened to their footsteps fading.

Marchat looked out, down, she presumed, to the street. The heat of the day was thick. Sweat stained his armpits and damped his brow.

"You're too early," he said at last, still not looking directly at her.

"Am I?"

"By three days."

Amat took a pose of apology more casual than she felt. Silence held them until at last Marchat looked at her directly. She couldn't read his expression—

perhaps anger, perhaps sorrow, perhaps exhaustion. Her employer, the voice of her house, sighed.

"Amat . . . Gods, things have been bad. Worse than I expected, and I didn't think they'd be well."

He walked to her, lowered himself onto the cushion that Liat usually occupied, and rested his head on his hands. Amat felt the urge to reach out, to touch him. She held the impulse in.

"It's nearly over," he continued. "I can convince Oshai and his men that it's better to let you live. I can. But Amat. You have to help me."

"How?"

"Tell me what you're planning. What you've started or done or said that might stop the trade."

Amat felt a slow smile pluck her lips, a low, warm burble of laughter bloom in her chest. Her shoulders shook and she took a pose of amazement. The absurdity of the question was like a wave lifting up a swimmer. Marchat looked confused.

"What I've done to stop it?" Amat asked. "Are you simple? I've run like my life depended on it, kept my head low and prayed that whatever you'd started, you could finish. Stop you? Gods, Marchat, I don't know what you're thinking."

"You've done nothing?"

"I've been through hell. I've been beaten and threatened. Someone tried to light me on fire. I've seen more of the worst parts of the city than I've seen in years. I did quite a bit. I worked longer hours at harder tasks than you've even gotten from me." The words were taking on a pace and rhythm of their own, flowing out of her faster and louder. Her face felt flushed. "And, in my spare moments, did I work out a plan to save the house's honor and set the world to rights? Did I hire men to discover your precious client and warn the girl what you intend to do to her? No, you fat Galtic idiot, I did not. Had you been expecting me to?"

Amat found she was leaning forward, her chin jutting out. The anger made her feel better for the moment. More nearly in control. She recognized it was illusion, but she took comfort in it all the same. Marchat's expression was sour.

"What about Itani, then?"

"Who?"

"Itani. Liat's boy."

Amat took a dismissive pose.

"What about him? I used him to discover where you were going, certainly, but you must know that by now. I didn't speak with him then, and I certainly haven't since."

"Then why has he gone out with the poet's student three nights of the last five?" Marchat demanded. His voice was hard as stone. He didn't believe her.

"I don't know, Marchat-cha. Why don't you ask him?"

Marchat shook his head, impatient, stood and turned his back on her. The anger that had held Amat up collapsed, and she was suddenly desperate that he believe her, that he understand. That he be on her side. She felt like a port-man's flag, switching one way to another with the shifting wind. If she'd been able to sleep before they spoke, if she hadn't had to flee Ovi Niit's house, if the world were only just or fair or explicable, she would have been able to be herself—calm, solid, grounded. She swallowed her need, disgusted by it and pretended that she was only calming herself from her rage, not folding.

"Or," she said, stopping him as he reached the head of the stairs, "if you want to be clever about it, ask Liat."

"Liat?"

"She's the one who told me where the two of you had gone. Itani told her, and she told me. If you're worried that Itani's corrupting the poets against you, ask Liat."

"She'd suspect," Marchat said, but his tone begged to be proved wrong. Amat closed her eyes. They felt so good, closed. The darkness was so comfort-able. Gods, she needed to rest.

"No," Amat said. "She wouldn't. Approach her as if you were scolding her. Tell her it's unseemly for those kinds of friendships to bloom in the middle of a working trade, and ask her why they couldn't wait until it was concluded. At the worst, she'll hide the truth from you, but then you'll know she has some-thing she's hiding."

Her employer and friend of years hesitated, his mind turning the strategy over, looking for flaws. A breath of air touched Amat's face smelling of the sea. She could see it in Marchat's eyes when he accepted her suggestion.

"You'll have to stay here until it's over," he said. "I'll have Oshai's men bring you food and drink. I still need to make my case to Oshai and the client, but I will make it work. You'll be fine."

Amat took an accepting pose. "I'll be pleased being here," she said. Then, "Marchat? What is this all about?"

"Money," he said. "Power. What else is there?"

And as he walked down the stairs, leaving her alone, it fit together like a peg slipping into its hole. It wasn't about the child. It wasn't about the girl. It was about the poet. And if it was about the poet, it was about the andat. If the poet Heshai lost control of his creation, if Seedless escaped, the cotton trade in Saraykeht would lose its advantage over other ports in the islands and the Westlands and Galt. Even when a new andat came, it wasn't likely that it would be able to fuel the cotton trade as Seedless or Petals-Falling had.

Amat went to her window. The street below was full—men, women, dogs, carts. The roofs of the city stretched out to the east, and down to the south the seafront was full. Trade. The girl Maj would be sacrificed to shift the balance of trade away from Saraykeht. It was the only thing that made sense.

"Oh, Marchat," she breathed. "What have you done?"

THE TEAHOUSE WAS NEARLY EMPTY. TWO OR THREE YOUNG MEN INSIDE WERE STILL speaking in raised voices, their arguments inchoate and disjointed. Out in the front garden, an older man had fallen asleep beside the fountain, his long, slow breathing a counterpoint to the distant conversation. A lemon candle guttered and died, leaving only a long winding plume of smoke, gray against the night, and the scent of an extinguished wick. Otah felt the urge to light a fresh candle, but he didn't act on it. On the bench beside him, Maati sighed.

"Does it ever get cold here, Otah-kvo?" Maati asked. "If we were with the Dai-kvo, we'd be shivering by now, even if it is midsummer. It's midnight, and it's almost hot as day."

"It's the sea. It holds the heat in. And we're too far south. It's colder as you go north."

"North. Do you remember Machi?"

Visions took Otah. Stone walls thicker than a man's height, stone towers reaching to a white sky, stone statues baked all day in the fires and then put in the children's room to radiate their heat through the night.

He remembered being pulled through snow-choked streets on a sleigh, a sister whose name he no longer knew beside him, holding close for warmth. The scent of burning pine and hot stone and mulled wine.

"No," he said. "Not really."

"I don't often look at the stars," Maati said. "Isn't that odd?"

"I suppose," Otah allowed.

"I wonder whether Heshai does. He stays out half the time, you know. He wasn't even there yesterday when I came in."

"You mean this morning?"

Maati frowned.

"I suppose so. It wasn't quite dawn when I got there. You should have seen Seedless stalking back and forth like a cat. He tried to get me to say where I'd been, but I wouldn't talk. Not me. I wonder where Heshai-kvo goes all night."

"The way Seedless wonders about you," Otah said. "You should start drinking water. You'll be worse for it if you don't."

Maati took a pose of acceptance, but didn't rise or go in for water. The sleeping man snored. Otah closed his eyes for a moment, testing how it felt. It was like falling backwards. He was too tired. He'd never make it though his shift with Muhatia-cha.

"I don't know how Heshai-kvo does it," Maati said, clearly thinking similar thoughts. "He's got a full day coming. I don't think I'll be able to do any more today than I did yesterday. I mean today. I don't know what I mean. It's easier to keep track when I sleep at night. What about you?"

"They can do without me," Otah said. "Muhatia-cha knows my indenture's almost over. He more than half expects me to ignore my duties. It isn't uncommon for someone who isn't renewing their contract."

"And aren't you?" Maati asked.

"I don't know."

Otah shifted his weight, turning to look at the young poet in the brown robes of his office. The moonlight made them seem black.

"I envy you," Maati said. "You know that, don't you?"

"You want to be directionless and unsure what you'll be doing to earn food in a half-year's time?"

"Yes," Maati said. "Yes, I think I do. You've friends. You've a place. You've possibilities. And . . ."

"And?"

Even in the darkness, Otah could see Maati blush. He took a pose of apology as he spoke.

"You have Liat," Maati said. "She's beautiful."

"She is lovely. But there are any number of women at court. And you're the poet's student. There must be girls who'd take you for a lover."

"There are, I think. Maybe. I don't know, but . . . I don't understand them. I've never known any—not at the school, and then not with the Dai-kvo. They're different."

"Yes," Otah said. "I suppose they are."

Liat. He'd seen her a handful of nights since the audience before the Khai. Since his discovery by Maati. She was busy enough preparing the woman Maj for the sad trade that she hadn't made an issue of his absence, but he had seen something growing in her questions and in her silence.

"Things aren't going so well with Liat," Otah said, surprised that he would admit it even as he spoke. Maati sat straight, pulling himself to some blurry attention. His look of concern was almost a parody of the emotion. He took a pose of query. Otah responded with one that begged ignorance, but let it fall away. "It isn't her. I've been . . . I've been pulling away from her, I think."

"Why?" Maati asked. His incredulity was clear.

Otah wondered how he'd been drawn into this conversation. Maati seemed to have a talent for it, bringing him to say things he'd hardly had the courage to think through fully. It was having someone at last who might understand him. Someone who knew him for what he was, and who had suffered some of the same flavors of loss.

"I've never told Liat. About who I am. Do you think . . . Maati, can you love someone and not trust them?"

"We're born to odd lives, Otah-kvo," Maati said, sounding suddenly older and more sorrowful. "If we waited for people we trusted, I think we might never love anyone."

They were silent for a long moment, then Maati rose.

"I'm going to get some water from the keep, and then find some place to leave him a little of my own," he said, breaking the somber mood. Otah smiled.

"Then we should go."

Maati took a pose that was both regret and agreement, then walked off with a gait for the most part steady. Otah stood, stretching his back and his legs, pulling his blood into action. He tossed a single length of silver onto the bench where they'd sat. It would more than cover their drinks and the bread and cheese they'd eaten. When Maati returned, they struck out for the north, toward the palaces. The streets of the city were moonlit, pale blue light except where a lantern burned at the entrance to a compound or a firekeeper's kiln added a ruddy touch. The calls of night birds, the chirping of crickets, the occasional voice of some other city dweller awake long after the day had ended accompanied them as they walked.

It was all as familiar as his own cot or the scent of the seafront, but the boy at his side also changed it. For almost a third of his life, Otah had been in Saraykeht. He knew the shapes of its streets. He knew which firekeepers could be trusted and which could be bought, which teahouses served equally to all its clientele and which saved the better goods for the higher classes. And he knew his place in it. He would no more have thought about it than about breathing. Except for Maati.

The boy made him look at everything again, as if he were seeing it for the first time. The city, the streets, Liat, himself. Especially himself. Now the thing that he had measured his greatest success—the fact that he knew the city deeply and it did not know him—was harder and emptier than it had once been. And odd that it hadn't seemed so before.

And the memories curled and shifted deep in his mind; the unconnected impressions of a childhood he had thought forgotten, of a time before he'd been sent to the school. There was a face with dark hair and beard that might have been his father. A woman he remembered singing and bathing him when his body had been small enough for her to lift with one arm. He didn't know whether she was his mother or a nurse or a sister. But there had been a fire in the grate, and the tub had been worked copper, and he had been young and amazed by it.

And over the days and nights, other half-formed things had joined together in his mind. He remembered his mother handing him a cloth rabbit, sneaking it into his things so that his father wouldn't see it. He remembered an older boy shouting—his brother, perhaps—that it wasn't fair that Otah be sent away, and that he had felt guilty for causing so much anger. He remembered the name Oyin Frey, and an old man with a long white beard playing a drum and singing, but not who the man was or how he had known him.

He couldn't say which of the memories were truth, which were dreams he'd constructed himself. He wondered, if he were to travel back there, far in the north, whether these ghost memories would let him retrace paths he hadn't walked in years—know the ways from nursery to kitchen to the tunnels beneath Machi—or if they would lead him astray, false as bog-lights.

And the school—Tahi-kvo glowering at him, and the whirr of the lacquer rod. He had pushed those things away, pushed away the boy who had suffered those losses and humiliations, and now it was like being haunted. Haunted by who he might be and might have been.

"I think I've upset you, Otah-kvo," Maati said quietly.

Otah turned, taking a questioning pose. Maati's brow furrowed and he looked down.

"You haven't spoken since we left the teahouse," Maati said. "If I've given offense . . ."

Otah laughed, and the sound seemed to reassure Maati. On impulse, Otah put his arm around Maati's shoulder as he might have around a dear friend or a brother.

"I'm sorry. I seem to be doing this to everyone around me these days. No, Maati-kya, I'm not upset. You just make me think about things, and I must be out of practice. I get lost in them. And gods, but I'm tired."

"You could stay at the poet's house if you don't care to walk back to your quarters. There's a perfectly good couch on the lower floor."

"No," Otah said. "If I don't let Muhatia-cha scold me in the morning, he'll get himself into a rage by midday."

Maati took a pose of understanding that also spoke of regret, and put his own arm around Otah's shoulder. They walked together, talking now the same mixture of seriousness and jokes that they'd made yet another evening of. Maati was getting better at navigating the streets, and even when the route he chose wasn't the fastest, Otah let him lead. He wondered, as they approached the monument of the Emperor Atami where three wide streets met, what it would have been like to grow up with a brother.

"Otah?" Maati said, his stride suddenly slowing. "That man there. The one in the cloak."

Otah glanced over. The man was walking away from them, heading to the east, and alone. Maati was right, though. It was the same man who'd been sleeping at the teahouse, or pretending to. Otah stepped away from Maati, freeing his arms in case he needed to fight. It wouldn't have been the first time that someone from the palaces had been followed from a teahouse and assaulted for the copper they carried.

"Come with me," Otah said and walked out to the middle of the wide area where the streets converged. Emperor Atami loomed above them, sad-eyed in the darkness. Otah turned slowly, considering each street, each building.

"Otah-kvo?" Maati said, his voice uncertain. "Was he following us?"

There was no one there, only the too-familiar man retreating to the east. Otah counted twenty breaths, but no one appeared. No shadows moved. The night was empty.

"Perhaps," he said, answering the question. "Probably. I don't know. Let's keep going. And if you see anything, tell me."

The rest of the distance to the palaces, Otah kept them on wide streets where they would see men coming. He would send Maati running for help and buy what time he could. A fine plan unless there were several of them or they had knives. But nothing happened, and Maati safely wished him good night.

By the time Otah reached his own quarters, the fear he'd felt was gone, the bone-weariness taken back over. He fell onto his cot and pulled the netting closed. Exhaustion pressed him to the rough canvas of the cot. The snores and sleeping murmurs of his cohort should have lulled him to sleep. But tired as he was, sleep wouldn't come. In the darkness, his mind turned from problem to problem—they'd been followed by someone who might still be tracking Maati; his indenture was almost over and he would be too weary to work when the dawn came; he had never told Liat of his past. As he turned his mind to one, another distracted him, until he was only chasing his thoughts and being chased by them. He didn't notice when he slipped into dream.

LIAT LEFT MARCHAT WILSIN'S OFFICES WITH HER SPINE STRAIGHT AND RAGE brewing. She walked through the compound to her cell without looking down and without catching anyone's gaze. She closed the door behind her, fastened the shutters so that no one could happen to look in, then sat at her desk and wept.

It was profoundly unfair. She had done everything she could—she'd studied the etiquette, she'd taken the island girl to all the appointments at their appointed times, she'd negotiated with the poet even when he'd made it perfectly clear that he'd be as pleased to have her out of the room—and it was Itani that defeated her. Itani!

She stripped off her outer robe, flinging it to the bed. She wrenched open her wardrobe and looked for another, a better one. One more expressive of wrath.

It's not entirely appropriate, Wilsin-cha still said in her mind. So close to a formal trade it might give the impression that the house was still seeking some advantage after the agreements had been made.

It might, she knew he'd meant, make her look like an idiot sending her lover to try to win favor. And worse, Itani—sweet, gentle, smiling Itani—hadn't even told her. The nights she'd spent working, imagining him with his cohort or in his quarters, waiting for her to complete her task with the sad trade, he'd been out spoiling things for her. Out with the student poet. He hadn't thought of what it would look like, what it would imply about her.

And he hadn't even told her.

She plucked a formal robe, red shot with black, pulled it on over her inner robes, and tied it fast. She braided her hair, pulling back severely. When she was done, she lifted her chin as she imagined Amat Kyaan would have and stalked out into the city.

The streets were still bustling, the business day far from ended. The sun, still eight or nine hands above the horizon, pressed down and the air was wet and stifling and still, and it reeked of the sea. Itani would still be with his cohort, but she wasn't going to wait and risk letting her anger mellow. She would find out what Itani meant by this. She'd have an explanation for Wilsin-cha, and she'd have it now, before the trade was finished. Tomorrow was the only day left to make things right.

At his quarters, she found that he hadn't gone out with the others after all—he'd been out too late and pled illness when Muhatia-cha came to gather them. The club-foot boy who watched the quarters during the working hours assured her with obvious pleasure that Muhatia-cha had been viciously angry.

So whatever it was that Itani was up to, it was worth risking his indenture as well as her standing with Wilsin-cha. Liat thanked the club-foot boy and asked, with a formal pose, where she might find Itani-cha since he was not presently in his quarters. The boy shrugged and rattled off teahouses, bath-houses, and places of ease along the seafront. It was nearly two full hands before Liat tracked him down at a cheap bathhouse near the river, and her temper hadn't calmed.

She stalked into the bath without bothering to remove her robes. The great tiled walls echoed with conversations that quieted as she passed. The men and women in the public baths considered her, but Liat only moved on, ignoring them. Pretending to ignore them. Acting as Amat would have. Itani had taken a private room to one side. She strode down the short corridor of rough, wet stone, paused, breathed deeply twice as if there was something in the thick, salt-scented air that might fortify her, and pushed her way in.

Itani sat in the pool as if at a table, bent slightly forward, his eyes on the surface of the water like a man lost in thought. He looked up as she slammed the door closed behind her, and his eyes spoke of weariness and preparedness. Liat took a pose of query that bordered on accusation.

"I meant to come look for you, love," he said.

"Oh really?" she said.

"Yes."

His eyes returned to the shifting surface of the water. His bare shoulders hunched forward. Liat stepped to the edge of the pool and stared down at him, willing his gaze up to hers. He didn't look.

"There's a conversation we need to have, love," he said. "We should have done before, I suppose, but . . ."

"What are you thinking? Itani? What are you doing? Wilsin-cha just spent half a hand very quietly telling me that you've been making a fool of me before the utkhaiem. What are you doing with the poet's student?"

"Maati," Itani said, distantly. "He's named Maati."

If Liat had had anything to throw, she'd have launched it at Itani's bowed head. Instead, she let out an exasperated cry and stamped her foot. Itani looked up, his vision swimming into focus as if he was waking from a dream. He smiled his charming, open, warm smile.

"Itani. I'm humiliated before the whole court, and you—"

"How?"

"What?"

"How? How is my drinking at a teahouse with Maati humiliating to you?"

"It makes it look as if I were trying to leverage some advantage after the agreements are complete," she snapped.

Itani took a pose that requested clarification.

"Isn't that most of what goes on between the harvest and completing the contracts? I thought Amat Kyaan was always sending you with letters arguing over interpretations of language."

It was true, but it hadn't occurred to her when Wilsin-cha sat been sitting across his table from her with that terrible expression of pity. Playing for advantage had never stopped because a contract had been signed.

"It's not the same," she said. "This is with the Khai. You don't do that with the Khai."

"I'm sorry, then," Itani said. "I didn't know. But I wasn't trying to change your negotiation."

"So what were you doing?"

Itani scooped up a double handful of water and poured it over his head. His long, northern face took on a look of utter calm, and he breathed deeply twice. He nodded to himself, coming to some private decision. When he spoke, his voice was almost conversational.

"I knew Maati when we were boys. We were at the school together."

"What school?"

"The school where the courts send their disowned sons. Where they choose the poets."

Liat frowned. Itani looked up.

"What were you doing there?" Liat asked. "You were a servant? You never told me you were a servant as a child."

"I was the son of the Khai Machi. The sixth son. My name was Otah Machi then. I only started calling myself Itani after I left, so that my family couldn't find me. I left without taking the brand, so it would have been dangerous to go by my true name."

His smile faltered, his gaze shifted. Liat didn't move—couldn't move. It was ridiculous. It was laughable. And yet she wasn't laughing. Her anger was gone like a candle snuffed by a strong wind, and she was only fighting to take in breath. It couldn't be true, but it was. She knew he wasn't lying. Before her and below her, Itani's eyes were brimming with tears. He coughed out something like mirth and wiped his eyes with the back of his bare hand.

"I've never told anyone," he said, "until now. Until you."

"You . . ." Liat began, then had to stop, swallow, begin again. "You're the son of the Khai Machi?"

"I didn't tell you at first because I didn't know you. And then later because I hadn't before. But I love you. And I trust you. I do. And I want you to be with me. Will you forgive me?"

"Is this . . . are you lying to me, Tani?"

"No," he said. "It's truth. You can ask Maati if you'd like. He knows as well."

Liat's throat was too tight to speak. Itani rose and lifted his arms up to her in supplication, the water flowing down his naked chest, fear in his eyes—fear that she would turn away from him. She melted down into the water, into his arms. Her robes, drinking in the water, were heavy as weights, but she didn't care. She pulled him to her, pulled him close, pressed her face against his. There were tears on their cheeks, but she didn't know whether they were hers or his. His arms surrounded her, lifted her, safe and strong and amazing.

"I knew," she said. "I knew you were something. I knew there was something about you. I always knew."

He kissed her then. It was unreal—like something out of an old epic story. She, Liat Chokavi, was the lover of the hidden child of the Khai Machi. He was hers. She pulled back from him, framing his face with her hands, staring at him as if seeing him for the first time.

"I didn't mean to hurt you," he said.

"Am I hurt?" she asked. "I could fly, love. I could fly."

Her held her fiercely then, like a drowning man holding the plank that might save him. And she matched him before pulling off her ruined robes and letting them sink into the bath like water plants at their ankles. Skin to skin they stood, the bath cool around their hips, and Liat let her heart sing with the thought that one day, her lover might take his father's seat and power. One day, he might be Khai.

9

Maati started awake when Heshai-kvo's hand touched his shoulder. The poet drew back, his wide frog-mouth quirking up at the ends. Maati sat up and pushed the netting aside. His head felt stuffed with cotton.

"I have to leave soon," Heshai-kvo said, his voice low and amused. "I didn't want to leave you to sleep through the whole day. Waking at sundown only makes the next day worse."

Maati took a pose of query. It didn't specify a question, but Heshai-kvo took the sense of it.

"It's just past midday," he said.

"Gods," Maati said and pulled himself up. "I apologize, Heshai-kvo. I will be ready in . . ."

Heshai-kvo lumbered to the doorway, waving his protests away. He was already wearing the brown formal robes and his sandals were strapped on.

"Don't. There's nothing going on you need to know. I just didn't want you to feel ill longer than you needed to. There's fruit downstairs, and fresh bread. Sausage if you can stomach it, but I'd start slow if I were you."

Maati took a pose of apology.

"I have failed in my duties, Heshai-kvo. I should not have stayed in the city so long nor slept so late."

Heshai-kvo clapped his hands in mock anger and pointed an accusing hand at Maati.

"Are you the teacher here?"

"No, Heshai-kvo."

"Then I'll decide when you're failing your duties," he said and winked.

When he was gone, Maati lay back on his cot and pressed his palm to his forehead. With his eyes closed, he felt as if the cot was moving, floating down some silent river. He forced his eyes back open, aware as he did that he'd already fallen halfway back to sleep. With a sigh, he forced himself up, stripped off his robes in trade for clean ones, and went down to the breakfast Heshai-kvo had promised.

The afternoon stretched out hot and thick and sultry before him. Maati bathed himself and straightened his belongings—something he hadn't done in days. When the servant came to take away the plates and leavings, Maati asked that a pitcher of limed water be sent up.

By the time it arrived, he'd found the book he wanted, and went out to sit under the shade of trees by the pond. The world smelled rich and green as fresh-cut grass as he arranged himself. With only the buzzing of insects and the occasional wet plop of koi striking the surface, Maati opened the brown leather book and read. The first page began:

Not since the days of the First Empire have poets worked more than one bind-ing in a lifetime. We may look back at the prodigality of those years with longing now, knowing as they did not that the andat unbound would likely not be re-covered. But the price of our frugality is this: we as poets have made our first work our last like a carpenter whose apprentice chair must also be the master-work for which he is remembered. As such it becomes our duty to examine our work closely so that later generations may gain from our subtle failures. It is in this spirit that I, Heshai Antaburi, record the binding I performed as a child of the andat Removing-The-Part-That-Would-Continue along with my notes on how I would have avoided error had I known my heart better.

Heshai-kvo's handwriting was surprisingly beautiful, and the structure of the volume as compelling as an epic. He began with the background of the andat and what he hoped to accomplish by it. Then, in great detail, the work of translating the thought, moving it from abstract to concrete, giving it form and flesh. Then, when the story of the binding was told, Heshai-kvo turned back on it, showing the faults where an ancient grammar allowed an ambigu-ity, where form clashed with intent. Discords that Maati would never, he thought, have noticed were spread before him with a candor that embarrassed him. Beauty that edged to arrogance, strength that fed willfulness, confidence that was also contempt. And with that, how each error had its root in Heshai's own soul. And while reading these confessions embarrassed him, they also fed a small but growing respect for his teacher and the courage it took to put such things to paper.

The sun had fallen behind the treetops and the cicadas begun their chorus when Maati reached the third section of the book, what Heshai called his cor-rected version. Maati looked up and found the andat on the bridge, looking back at him. The perfect planes of his cheeks, the amused intelligence in his eyes. Maati's mind was still half within the work that had formed them.

Seedless took a pose of greeting formal and beautiful, and strode across the rest of the span towards him. Maati closed the book.

"You're being studious," Seedless said as he drew near. "Fascinating isn't it? Useless, but fascinating."

"I don't see why it would be useless."

"His corrected version is too near what he did before. I can't be bound the same way twice. You know that. So writing a variation on a complete work makes about as much sense as apologizing to someone you've just killed. You don't mind that I join you."

The andat stretched out on the grass, his dark eyes turned to the south and the palaces and invisible beyond them, the city. The perfect fingers plucked at the grass.

"It lets others see the mistakes he made," Maati said.

"If it showed them the mistakes *they* were making, it would be useful," Seedless said. "Some errors you can only see once you've committed them."

Maati took a pose that could be taken as agreement or mere politeness. Seedless smiled and pitched a blade of grass toward the water.

"Where's Heshai-kvo?"

"Who knows? The soft quarter, most likely. Or some teahouse that rents out rooms by the ships. He's not looking to tomorrow with glee in his heart. And what about you, my boy? You've turned out to be a better study than I'd have guessed. You've already mastered staying out, consorting with men below your station, and missing meetings. It took Heshai years to really get the hang of that."

"Bitter?" Maati said. Seedless laughed and shifted to look at him directly. The beautiful face was rueful and amused.

"I had a bad day," the andat said. "I found something I'd lost, and it turned out not to have been worth finding. And you? Feeling ready for the grand ceremony tomorrow?"

Maati took a pose of affirmation. The andat grinned, and then like a candle melting, his expression turned to something else, something conflicted that Maati couldn't entirely read. The cicadas in their trees went silent suddenly as if they were a single voice. A moment later, they began again.

"Is there . . ." the andat said, and trailed off, taking a pose that asked for silence while Seedless reconsidered his words. Then, "Maati-kya. If there was something you wanted of me. Some favor you would ask of me, even now. Something that I might do or . . . or forbear. Ask, and I'll do it. Whatever it is. For you, I'll do it."

Maati looked at the pale face, the skin that seemed to glow like porcelain in the failing light.

"Why?" Maati asked. "Why would you offer that to me?"

Seedless smiled and shifted with the sound of fine cloth against grass.

"To see what you'd ask," Seedless said.

"What if I asked for something you didn't want to give me?"

"It would be worth it," Seedless said. "It would tell me something about your heart, and knowing that would be enough to justify some very high prices. Anything you want to have started, or anything you want to stop."

Maati felt the beginning of a blush and shifted forward, considering the surface of the pond and the fish—pale and golden—beneath it. When he spoke, his voice was low.

"Tomorrow, when the time comes for the . . . when Heshai-kvo is set to finish the sad trade, don't fight him. I saw the two of you with the cotton when I first came, and I've seen you since. You always make him force you. You always make him struggle to accomplish the thing. Don't do that to him tomorrow."

Seedless nodded, a sad smile on his perfect, soft lips.

"You're a sweet boy. You deserve better than us," the andat said. "I'll do as you ask."

They sat in silence as the sunlight faded—the stars glimmering first a few, then a handful, then thousands upon thousands. The palaces glowed with lanterns, and sometimes Maati caught a thread of distant music.

"I should light the night candle," Maati said.

"If you wish," Seedless said, but Maati found he wasn't rising or returning to the house. Instead, he was staring at the figure before him, a thought turning restlessly in his mind. The subtle weight of the leather book in his sleeve and Seedless' strange, quiet expression mixed and shifted and moved him.

"Seedless-cha. I was wondering if I might ask you a question. Now, while we're still friends."

"Now you're playing on my sentiments," the andat said, amused. Maati took a pose of cheerful agreement and Seedless replied with acceptance. "Ask."

"You and Heshai-kvo are in a sense one thing, true?"

"Sometimes the hand pulls the puppet, sometimes the puppet pulls the hand, but the string runs both ways. Yes."

"And you hate him."

"Yes."

"Mustn't you also hate yourself, then?"

The andat shifted to a crouch and with the air of a man considering a painting, looked up at the poet's house, dark now in the starlight. He was silent for so long that Maati began to wonder if he would answer at all. When he did speak, his voice was little above a whisper.

"Yes," he said. "Always."

Maati waited, but the andat said nothing more. At last, Maati gathered his things and rose to go inside. He paused beside the unmoving andat and touched Seedless' sleeve. The andat didn't move, didn't speak, accepted no more comfort than a stone would. Maati went to the house and lit the night candle and lemon candles to drive away the insects, and prepared himself for sleep.

Heshai returned just before dawn, his robes stained and reeking of cheap wine. Maati helped him prepare for the audience, the sad trade, the ceremony. Fresh robes, washed hair, fresh-shaved chin. The redness of his eyes, Maati could do nothing for. Throughout, Seedless haunted the corners of the room, unusually silent. Heshai drank little, ate less, and as the sun topped the trees, lumbered out and down the path with Maati and Seedless following.

It was a lovely day, clouds building over the sea and to the east, towering white as cotton and taller than mountains. The palaces were alive with servants and slaves and the utkhaiem moving gracefully about their business. And the poets, Maati supposed, moving about theirs.

The party from House Wilsin was at the low hall before them. The pregnant girl stood outside, attended by servants, fidgeting with the skirts that were designed for the day, cut to protect her modesty but not catch the child as it left her. Maati felt the first real qualm pass over him. Heshai-kvo marched past woman and servants and slaves, his bloodshot eyes looking, Maati guessed, for Liat Chokavi who was, after all, overseeing the trade.

They found her inside the hall, pacing and muttering to herself under her breath. She was dressed in white robes shot with blue: mourning colors. Her hair was pulled back to show the softness of her cheek, the curve of her neck. She was beautiful—the sort of woman that Otah-kvo would love and that would love him in return. Her gaze rose as they entered, the three of them, and she took a pose of greeting.

"Can we do this thing?" Heshai-kvo snapped, only now that Maati had known the man longer, he heard the pain underneath the gruffness. The dread.

"The physician will be here shortly," Liat said.

"He's late?"

"We're early, Heshai-kvo," Maati said gently.

The poet glared at him, then shrugged and moved to the far end of the hall to stare sullenly out the window. Seedless, meeting Maati's gaze, pursed his lips, shrugged and walked out into the sunlight. Maati, left alone before the woman, took a pose of formal greeting which she returned.

"Forgive Heshai-kvo," Maati said softly enough to keep his voice from carrying. "He hates the sad trade. It . . . it would be a very long story, and likely not worth the telling. Only don't judge him too harshly from this."

"I won't," Liat said. Her manner was softer, less formal. She seemed, in fact, on the verge of grinning. "Itani told me about it. He mentioned you as well."

"He has been very kind in . . . showing me the city," Maati said, taken by surprise. "I knew very little about Saraykeht before I came here."

Liat smiled and touched his sleeve.

"I should thank you," she said. "If it wasn't for you, I don't know when he would have gotten the courage to tell me about . . . about his family."

"Oh," Maati said. "Then he . . . you know?"

She took a pose of confirmation that implied a complicity Maati found both thrilling and uneasing. The secret was now shared among three. And that was as many as could ever know. In a way, it bound them, he and Liat. Two people who shared some kind of love for Otah-kvo.

"Perhaps we will be able to know each other better, once the trade is completed," Maati said. "The three of us, I mean."

"I would like that," Liat said. She grinned, and Maati found himself grinning back. He wondered what they would look like to someone else—the student poet and the trade house overseer beaming at each other just before the sad trade. He forced himself into a more sober demeanor.

"The woman, Maj," he said. "All went well with her, I hope?"

Liat shrugged and leaned closer to him. She smelled of an expensive perfume, earthy and rich more than floral, like fresh turned soil.

"Keep it between us, but she's been a nightmare," Liat said. "She means well, I suppose, but she's flighty as a child and doesn't seem to remember what I've told her from one day to the next."

"Is she . . . simple?"

"I don't think so. Only . . . unconcerned, I suppose. They have different ways of looking at things on Nippu. Her translator told me about it. They don't think the child's a person until it draws its first breath, so she didn't even want to wear mourning colors."

"Really? I hadn't heard that. I thought the Eastern Islands were . . . stricter, I suppose. If that's the way to say it."

"Apparently not."

"Is he here? The translator?"

"No," Liat said, taking a pose that expressed her impatience. "No, something came up and he had to leave. Wilsin-cha had him teach me all the phrases I need to know for the ceremony. I've been practicing. I can't tell you how pleased I'll be to have this over."

Maati looked over to his teacher. Heshai-kvo stood at the window, still as a statue, his expression bleak. Seedless leaned against the wall near the wide double doors of the entrance, his arms folded, staring at the poet's back. The perfect attention reminded Maati of a feral dog tracking its prey.

The physician arrived at the appointed hour with his retinue. Maj, blushing and pulling at her skirts, was brought inside, and Liat took her post beside her as Maati took his with Heshai-kvo and Seedless. The servants and slaves retreated a respectful distance, and the wide doors were closed. Heshai-kvo seemed bent as if he were carrying a load. He gestured to Liat, and she stepped forward and adopted a pose appropriate to the opening of a formal occasion.

"Heshai-cha," she said. "I come before you as the representative of House Wilsin in this matter. My client has paid the Khai's fee and the accountancy has weighed her payment and found it in accordance with our arrangement. We now ask that you complete your part of the contract."

"Have you asked her if she's sure?" Heshai-kvo asked. His words were not formal, and he took no pose with them. His lips were pressed thin and his face grayish. "Is she certain?"

Liat blinked, startled, Maati thought, by the despair in his teacher's voice. He wished now that he had explained to Liat why this was so hard for Heshai.

Or perhaps it didn't matter. Really, it only needed to be finished and behind them.

"Yes," Liat said, also breaking with the formality of the ceremony.

"Ask her again," Heshai said, half demanding, half pleading. "Ask if there isn't another way."

A glimmer of stark terror lit Liat's eyes and vanished. Maati understood. It was not one of the phrases she'd been taught. She had no way to comply. She raised her chin, her eyes narrowing in a way that made her look haughty and condescending, but Maati thought he could see the panic in her.

"Heshai-kvo," he said, softly. "Please, may we finish this thing."

His teacher looked over, first annoyed, then sadly resigned. He took a pose that retracted the request. Liat's eyes shifted to Maati's with a look of gratitude. The physician took his cue and stepped forward, certifying that the woman was in good health, and that the removal of the child posed no great risk to her well-being. Heshai took a pose that thanked him. The physician led Maj to the split-seated stool and sat her in it, then silently placed the silver bowl beneath her.

"I hate this," Heshai murmured, his voice so low that no one could hear him besides Maati and Seedless. Then he took a formal pose and declaimed. "In the name of the Khai Saraykeht and the Dai-kvo, I put myself at your service."

Liat turned to the girl and spoke in liquid syllables. Maj frowned and her wide, pale lips pursed. Then she nodded and said something in return. Liat shifted back to the poet and took a pose of acceptance.

"You're ready?" Heshai asked, his eyes on Maj's. The island girl tilted her head, as if hearing a sound she almost recognized. Heshai raised his eyebrows and sighed. Without any visible bidding, Seedless stepped forward, graceful as a dancer. There was a light in his eyes, something like joy. Maati felt an inexplicable twist in his belly.

"No need to struggle, old friend," Seedless said. "I promised your apprentice that I wouldn't make you fight me for this one. And you see, I can keep my word when it suits me."

The silver bowl chimed like an orange had been dropped in it. Maati looked over, and then away. The thing in the bowl was only settling, he told himself, not moving. Not moving.

And with an audible intake of breath, the island girl began to scream. The pale blue eyes were open so wide, Maati could see the whites all the way around the iris. Her wide lips pulled back until they were thin as string. Maj bent down, and her hands would have touched the thing in the bowl, cradled it, if the physician had not whisked it away. Liat could only hold the woman's hands and look at her, confused, while shriek after shriek echoed in the empty spaces of the hall.

"What?" Heshai-kvo said, his voice fearful and small. "What happened?"

10

>+< Amat Kyaan walked the length of the seafront with the feeling of a
woman half-awakened from nightmare. The morning sun made the waters too bright to look at. Ships rested at the docks, taking on cloth or oils or
sugar or else putting off brazil blocks and indigo, wheat and rye, wine and Eddensea marble. The thin stalls still barked with commerce, banners shifting in
the breeze. The gulls still wheeled and complained. It was like walking into a
memory. She had passed this way every day for years. How quickly it had become unfamiliar.

Leaning on her cane, she passed the wide mouth of the Nantan and into
the warehouse district. The traffic patterns in the streets had changed—the
rhythm of the city had shifted as it did from season to season. The mad rush of
harvest was behind them, and though the year's work was still far from ended,
the city had a sense of completion. The great trick that made Saraykeht the
center of all cotton trade had been performed once more, and now normal men
and women would spend their hours and days changing that advantage into
power and wealth and prestige.

She could also feel its unease. Something had happened to the poet. Only
listening from her window during the evening, she'd heard three or four different stories about what had happened. Every conversation she walked past was
the same—something had happened to the poet. Something to do with House
Wilsin and the sad trade. Something terrible. The young men and women in
the street smiled as they told each other, excited by the sense of crisis and too
young or too poor or too ignorant for the news of yesterday's events to sicken
them with dread. That was for older people. People who understood.

Amat breathed deeply, catching the scent of the sea, the perfume of grilling
meat at the stalls, the unpleasant stench of the dyers' vats that reached even
from several streets away. Her city, with its high summer behind it. In her
heart, she still found it hard to believe that she had returned to it, that she was
not still entombed in the back office of Ovi Niit's comfort house. And as she
walked, leaning heavily on her cane, she tried not to wonder what the men and
women said about her as she passed.

At the bathhouse, the guards looked at her curiously as they took their
poses. She didn't even respond, only walked forward into the tiled rooms with
their echoes and the scent of cedar and fresh water. She shrugged off her robes
and went past the public baths to Marchat Wilsin's little room at the back, just
as she always had.

He looked terrible.

"Too hot," he said as she lowered herself into the water. The lacquer tray danced a little on the waves she stirred, but didn't spill the tea.

"You always say that," Amat Kyaan said. Marchat sighed and looked away. There were bags under his eyes, dark as bruises. His face, scowl-set, held a grayish cast. Amat leaned forward and pulled the tea closer.

"So," she said. "I take it things went well."

"Don't."

Amat sipped tea from her bowl and considered him. Her employer, her friend.

"Then what is there left for us to say?" she asked.

"There's business," Marchat said. "The same as always."

"Business, then. I take it that things went well."

He shot an annoyed glance at her, then looked away.

"Couldn't we start with the contracts with the dyers?"

"If you'd like," Amat said. "Was there something pressing with them?"

Her voice carried the whole load of sarcasm to cover the outrage and anger. And fear. Marchat took a clumsy pose of surrender and acquiescence before reaching over and taking his own bowl of tea from the tray.

"I'm going to a meeting with the Khai and several of the higher utkhaiem. Spend the whole damn time falling on my sword over the sad trade. I've promised a full investigation."

"And what are you going to find?"

"The truth, I imagine. That's the secret of a good lie, you know. Coming to a place where you believe it yourself. I expect our investigation—or anyone else's—will show it was Oshai, the translator. He and his men plotted the whole thing under the direction of the andat Seedless. They found the girl, they brought her to us under false pretenses. I have letters of introduction that I'll turn over to the Khai's men. They'll discover that the letters are forged. House Wilsin will be looked upon as a collection of dupes. At best, it will take us years to recover our reputation."

"It's a small price," Amat said. "What if they find Oshai?"

"They won't."

"You're sure of that?"

"Yes," Wilsin said with a great sigh. "I'm sure."

"And Liat?"

"Still being questioned," Marchat said. "I imagine she'll be out by the end of the day. We'll need to do something for her. To make this right. She's not going to come out of this with a reputation for competence intact. They've already spoken with the island girl. She didn't have anything very coherent to say, I'm afraid. But it's over, Amat. That's really the only bright thing I can say of the whole stinking business. The worst that was going to happen has happened, and now we can get to cleaning up after it and moving on."

"And what's the truth?"

"What I told you," he said. "That's the truth. It's the only truth that matters."

"No. The real truth. Who sent those pearls? And don't tell me the spirit conjured them out of the sea."

"Who knows?" Marchat said. "Oshai told us they were from Nippu, from the girl's family. We had no reason to think otherwise."

Amat slapped the water. She felt the rage pulling her brow together. Marchat met her anger with his. His pale face flushed red, his chin slid forward belligerently like a boy in a play yard.

"I am saving you," he said. "And I am saving the house. I am doing everything I can to kill this thing and bury it, and by all the gods, Amat, I know as well as you that it was rotten, but what do you want me to do about it? Trot up to the Khai and apologize? Where did the pearls come from? Galt, Amat. They came from Acton and Lanniston and Cole. Who arranged the thing? Galts. And who will pay for this if that story is proved instead of mine? I'll be killed. You'll be exiled if you're lucky. The house will be destroyed. And do you think it'll stop there, Amat? Do you? Because I don't."

"It was evil, Marchat."

"Yes. Yes, it was evil. Yes, it was wrong," he said, motioning so violently that his tea splashed, the red tint of if diffusing quickly in the bath. "But it was decided before anyone consulted us. By the time you or I or any of us were told, it was already too late. It needed doing, and so we've done it.

"Tell me, Amat, what happens if you're the Khai Saraykeht and you find out your pet god's been conspiring with your trade rivals? Do you stop with the tools, because that's all we are. Tools. Or do you teach a lesson to the Galts that they won't soon forget? We haven't got any andat of our own, so there's nothing to restrain you. We can't hit back. Do our crops fail? Do all the women with child in Galt lose their children over this? They're as innocent as that island girl, Amat. They've done as little to deserve that as she has."

"Lower your voice," Amat said. "Someone will hear you."

Marchat leaned back, glancing nervously at the windows, the door. Amat shook her head.

"That was a pretty speech," she said. "Did you practice it?"

"Some, yes."

"And who were you hoping to convince with it? Me, or yourself?"

"Us," he said. "Both of us. It's true, you know. The price would be worse than the crime, and innocent people would suffer."

Amat considered him. He wanted so badly for it to be true, for her to agree. He was like a child, a boy. It made her feel weighted down.

"I suppose it is," she said. "So. Where do we go from here?"

"We clean up. We try to limit the damage. Ah, and one thing. The boy Itani? Do you know why the young poet would call him Otah?"

Amat let herself be distracted. She turned the name over in her mind, searching for some recollection. Nothing came. She put her bowl of tea on the side of the bath and took a pose pleading ignorance.

"It sounds like a northern name," she said. "When did he use it?"

"I had a man follow them. He overheard them speaking."

"It doesn't match anything Liat's told me of him."

"Well. Well, we'll keep a finger on it and see if it moves. Damned strange, but nothing's come from it yet."

"What about Maj?"

"Who? Oh, the girl. Yes. We'll need to keep her close for another week or two. Then I'll have her taken home. There's a trading company making a run to the east at about the right time. If the Khai's men are done with her, I'll pay her passage with them. Otherwise, it may be longer."

"But you'll see her back home safely."

"It's what I can do," Marchat said.

They sat in silence for a long minute. Amat's heart felt like lead in her breast. Marchat was as still as if he'd drunk poison. Poor Wilsin-cha, she thought. He's trying so hard to make this conscionable, but he's too wise to believe his own arguments.

"So, then," she said, softly. "The contracts with the dyers. Where do we stand with them?"

Marchat's gaze met hers, a faint smile on his bushy lips. For almost two hands, he brought her up to date on the small doings of House Wilsin. The agreements they'd negotiated with Old Sanya and the dyers, the problems with the shipments from Obar State, the tax statements under review by the utkhaiem. Amat listened, and without meaning to she moved back into the rhythm of her work. The parts of her mind that held the doings of the house slid back into use, and she pictured all the issues Wilsin-cha brought up and how they would affect each other. She asked questions to confirm that she'd understood and to challenge Marchat to think things through with her. And for a while, she could almost pretend that nothing had happened, that she still felt what she had, that the house she had served so long was still what it had been to her. Almost, but not entirely.

When she left, her fingertips were wrinkled from the baths and her mind was clearer. She had several full days work before her just to put things back in order. And after that the work of the autumn: first House Wilsin's—she felt she owed Marchat that much—and then perhaps also her own.

THE POET'S HOUSE HAD BEEN FULL FOR TWO DAYS NOW, EVER SINCE HESHAI HAD taken to his bed. Utkhaiem and servants of the Khai and representatives from the great trading houses came to call. They came at all hours. They brought food and drink and thinly-veiled curiosity and tacit recrimination. Maati welcomed them as they came, accepted their gifts, saw them to whatever seats were available. He held poses of gratitude until his shoulders ached. He wanted nothing more than to turn them out—all of them.

The first night had been the worst. Maati had stood outside the door of Heshai-kvo's room and pounded and demanded and begged until the night candle was half-burned. And when the door finally scraped open, it was Seedless who had unbarred it.

Heshai had lain on his cot, his eyes fixed on nothing, his skin pale, his lips slack. The white netting around him reminded Maati of a funeral shroud. He had had to touch the poet's shoulder before Heshai's distracted gaze flickered over to him and then away. Maati took a chair beside him, and stayed there until morning.

Through the night, Seedless had paced the room like a cat looking for a way under a woodpile. Sometimes he laughed to himself. Once, when Maati had drifted into an uneasy sleep, he woke to find the andat on the bed, bent over until his pale lips almost brushed Heshai's ear—Seedless whispering fast, sharp syllables too quietly for Maati to make sense of them. The poet's face was contorted as if in pain and flushed bright red. In the long moment before Maati shouted and pushed the andat away, their gazes locked, and Maati saw Seedless smile even as he murmured his poison.

When the morning came, and the first pounding of visitors, Heshai roused himself enough to order Maati down to greet them. The bar had slid home behind him, and the stream of people had hardly slacked since. They stayed until the first quarter of the night candle had burned, and a new wave arrived before dawn.

"I bring greetings from Annan Tiyan of House Tiyan," an older man said loudly as he stood on the threshold. He had to speak up for his words to carry over the conversation behind Maati. "We had heard of the poet's ill health and wished . . ."

Maati took a brief pose of welcome and gratitude that he didn't begin to mean and ushered the man in. The flock of carrion crows gabbled and talked and waited, Maati knew, for news of Heshai. Maati only took the food they'd brought and laid it out for them to eat, poured their gift wine into bowls as hospitality. And upstairs, Heshai . . . It didn't bear thinking about. A regal man in fine silk robes motioned Maati over and asked him gently what he could do to help the poet in his time of need.

The first sign Maati had that something had changed was the sudden silence. All conversations stopped, and Maati rushed to the front of the house to find himself looking into the dark, angry eyes of the Khai Saraykeht.

"Where is your master?" the Khai demanded, and the lack of an accompanying pose made the words seem stark and terrible.

Maati took a pose of welcome and looked away.

"He is resting, most high," he said.

The Khai looked slowly around the room, a single vertical line appearing between his brows. The visitors all took appropriate poses—Maati could hear the shuffle of their robes. The Khai took a pose of query that was directed to Maati, though his gaze remained on the assembled men.

"Who are these?" the Khai asked.

"Well-wishers," Maati said.

The Khai said nothing, and the silence grew more and more excruciatingly uncomfortable. At last, he moved forward, his hand taking Maati by the shoulder and turning him to the stairs. Maati walked before the Khai.

"When I come down," the Khai said in a calm, almost conversational tone, "any man still here forfeits half his wealth."

At the top of the stairs, Maati turned and led the Khai down the short hall to Heshai's door. He tried it, but it was barred. Maati turned with a pose of apology, but the Khai moved him aside without seeming to notice it.

"Heshai," the Khai said, his voice loud and low. "Open the door."

There was a moment's pause, and then soft footsteps. The bar scraped, and the door swung open. Seedless stepped aside as the Khai entered. Maati followed. The andat leaned the bar against the wall, caught Maati's gaze, and took a pose of greeting appropriate to old friends. Maati felt a surge of anger in his chest, but did nothing more than turn away.

The Khai stood at the foot of Heshai's bed. The poet was sitting up, now. Sometime in the last day, he had changed from his brown ceremonial robes to robes of pale mourning cloth. The wide mouth turned down at the corners and his hair was a wild tangle. The Khai reached up and swept the netting aside. It occurred to Maati how much Khai and andat were similar—the grace, the beauty, the presence. The greatest difference was that the Khai Saraykeht showed tiny lines of age at the corners of his eyes and was not so lovely.

"I have spoken with Marchat Wilsin of House Wilsin," the Khai said. "He extends his apologies. There will be an investigation. It has already begun."

Heshai looked down, but took a pose of gratitude. The Khai ignored it.

"We have also spoken with the girl and the overseer for House Wilsin who negotiated the trade. There are . . . questions."

Heshai nodded and then shook his head as if clearing it. He swung his legs over the edge of the bed and took a pose of agreement.

"As you wish, most high," he said. "I will answer anything I can."

"Not you," the Khai said. "All I require is that you compel your creature."

Heshai looked at Maati and then at Seedless. The wide face went gray, the lips pressed thin. Seedless stiffened and then, slowly as a man wading through deep water, moved to the bedside and took a pose of obeisance before the Khai. Maati moved a step forward before he knew he meant to. His impulse to shield someone—Heshai, the Khai, Seedless—was confused by his anger and a deepening dread.

"I think this was your doing. Am I wrong?" the Khai asked, and Seedless smiled and bowed.

"Of course not, most high," he said.

"And you did this to torment the poet."

"I did."

Andat and Khai were glaring at each other, so only Maati saw Heshai's face. The shock of surprise and then a bleak calm more distressing than rage or weeping. Maati's stomach twisted. This was part of it, he realized. Seedless had planned this to hurt Heshai, and this meeting now, this humiliation, was also part of his intention.

"Where may we find the translator Oshai?" the Khai said.

"I don't know. Careless of me, I know. I've always been bad about keeping track of my toys."

"That will do," the Khai said, and strode to the window. Looking down to the grass at the front of the house, the Khai made a gesture. In the distance, Maati heard a man call out, barking an order.

"Heshai," the Khai Saraykeht said, turning back. "I want you to know that I understand the struggles a poet faces. I've read the old romances. But you . . . you must understand that these little shadow plays of yours hurt innocent people. And they hurt my city. In the last day, I have heard six audiences asking that I lower tariffs to compensate for the risk that the andat will find some way to act against you that might hurt the cotton crop. I have had two of the largest trading houses in the city ask me what I plan to do if the andat escapes. How will I maintain trade then? And what was I to tell them? Eh?"

"I don't know," the poet said, his voice low and rough.

"Nor do I," the Khai said.

Men were tramping up the stairway now. Maati could hear them, and the temptation to go and see what they were doing was almost more than his desire to hear when the Khai said next.

"This stops now," the Khai said. "And if I must be the one to stop it, I will."

The footsteps reached the door and two men in workmen's trousers pushed in, a thick, heavy box between them. Maati saw it was fashioned of wood bound with black iron—small enough that a man might fit inside it but too short to stand, too narrow to sit, too shallow to turn around. He had seen drawings of it in books with the Dai-kvo. They had been books about the excesses of the imperial courts, about their punishments. The men placed the box against Heshai-kvo's wall, took poses of abject obeisance to the Khai, and left quickly.

"Most high," Maati said, his voice thick, "You . . . this is . . ."

"Rest yourself, boy," the Khai said as he stepped to the thing and pulled the bar that opened the iron grate. "It isn't for my old friend Heshai. It's only to keep his things in when he isn't using them."

With a clank, the black iron swung open. Maati saw Seedless' eyes widen for a moment, then an amused smile plucked the perfect lips. Heshai looked on in silence.

"But most high," Maati said, his voice growing stronger. "A poet and his work are connected, if you lock a part of Heshai-kvo into a torture box . . ."

The Khai took a sharp pose that required silence, and Maati's words died. The man's gaze held him until Seedless laughed and stepped between them. For a fleeting moment, Maati almost felt that the andat had moved to protect him from the anger in the Khai's expression.

"You forget, my dear," the andat said, "the most high killed two of his brothers to sit in his chair. He knows more of sacrifice than any of us. Or so the story goes."

"Now, Heshai," the Khai said, but Maati saw no effort in Heshai-kvo as Seedless stepped backward into the box, crouching down, knees bent. The Khai shut the grate, barred it, and slid a spike in to hold the bar in place. The pale face of the andat was crossed with shadows and metal. The Khai turned to the bed, standing still until Heshai adopted a pose that accepted the judgement.

"It doesn't roam free," the Khai said. "When it isn't needed, it goes in its place. This is my order."

"Yes, most high," Heshai said, then lay down and turned away, pulling his sheet over him. The Khai snorted with disgust and turned to leave. At the doorway, he paused.

"Boy," he said, taking a pose of command. Maati answered with an appropriate obeisance. "When your turn comes, do better."

After the Khai and his men were gone, Maati stood, shaking. Heshai didn't move or speak. Seedless in his torture box only crouched, fingers laced with the metal grate, the black eyes peering out. Maati pulled the netting back over his master and went downstairs. No one remained—only the remains of the offerings of sympathy and concern half consumed, and an eerie silence.

Otah-kvo, he thought. *Otah-kvo will know what to do. Please, please let Otah-kvo know what to do.*

He hurried, gathering an apple, some bread, and a jug of water, and taking them to the unmoving poet before changing into fresh robes and rushing out through the palace grounds to the street and down into the city. Halfway to the quarters where Otah-kvo's cohort slept, he noticed he was weeping. He couldn't say for certain when he'd begun.

"ITANI!" MUHATIA-CHA BARKED. "GET DOWN HERE!"

Otah, high in the suffocating heat and darkness near the warehouse roof, grabbed the sides of his ladder and slid down. Muhatia-cha stood in the wide double doors that opened to the light and noise of the street. The overseer had a sour expression, but mixed with something—eagerness, perhaps, or curiosity. Otah stood before him with a pose appropriate to the completion of a task.

"You're wanted at the compound. I don't know what good they think you'll do there."

"Yes, Muhatia-cha."

"If this is just your lady love pulling you away from your duties, Itani, I'll find out."

"I won't be able to tell you unless I go," Otah pointed out and smiled his charming smile, thinking as he did that he'd never meant it less. Muhatia-cha's expression softened slightly, and he waved Otah on.

"Hai! Itani!" Kaimati's familiar voice called out. Otah turned. His old friend was pulling a cart to the warehouse door, but had paused, bracing the load against his knees. "Let us know what you find, eh?"

Otah took a pose of agreement and turned away. It was an illusion, he knew, that the people he passed in the streets seemed to stare at him. There was no reason for the city as a whole to see him pass and think anything of him. Another laborer in a city full of men like him. That it wasn't true did nothing to change the feeling. The sad trade had gone wrong. Liat was involved, as was Maati. For two days, he had seen neither. Liat's cell at the compound had been empty, the poet's house too full for him to think of approaching. Otah had made do with the gossip of the street and the bathhouse.

The andat had broken loose and killed the girl as well as her babe; the child had actually been fathered by the poet himself or the Khai or, least probably, the andat Seedless himself; the poet had killed himself or been killed by the Khai or by the andat; the poet was lying sick at heart. Or the woman was. The stories seemed to bloom like blood poured in water—swirling in all directions and filling all mathematical possibilities. Every story that could be told, including—unremarkably among its legion of fellows—the truth, had been whispered in some corner of Saraykeht in the last day. He had slept poorly, and awakened unrefreshed. Now, he walked quickly, the afternoon sun pushing down on his shoulders and sweat pouring off him.

He caught sight of Liat on the street outside the compound of House Wilsin. He recognized the shape of her body before he could see her face, could read the exhaustion in the slope of her shoulders. She wore mourning robes. He didn't know if they were the same that she'd worn to the ceremony or if the grief was fresher than that. When she caught sight of him, she walked to him. Her eyes were sunken, her skin pale, her lips bloodless. She stepped into his embrace without speaking. It was unseemly, of course, a laborer holding an overseer this way—his cheek pressed to her forehead—in the street. It was too hot for the sensation to be pleasant. She held him fiercely, and he felt the deepness of her breath by the way she pressed against him.

"What happened, love?" he asked, but Liat only shook her head. Otah stroked her unbound hair and waited until, with a shuddering sigh, she pulled back. She didn't release his hand, and he didn't try to reclaim it.

"Come to my cell," she said. "We can talk there."

The compound was subdued, men and women passing quickly though their duties as if nothing had happened, except for the air of tension. Liat led the way in silence, pushed open the door of her cell and pulled him into the shadows. A thin form lay on the cot, swathed in brown robes. Maati sat up, blinking sleep out of his eyes.

"Otah-kvo?" the boy asked.

"He came this morning looking for you," Liat said, letting go of Otah's hand at last and sitting at her desk. "I don't think he'd eaten or had anything to drink since it happened. I brought him here, gave him an apple and some water, put him to bed, and sent a runner to Muhatia-cha."

"I'm sorry," Maati said. "I didn't know where to find you, and I thought Liat-cha might . . ."

"It was a fine plan," Otah said. "It worked. But what happened?"

Maati looked down, and Liat spoke. Her voice was hard as slate and as gray. Speaking softly, she told the story: she'd been fooled by the translator Oshai and the andat at the price of Maj and her babe. Maati took the narrative up: the poet was ill, eating little, drinking less, never leaving his bed. And the Khai, in his anger, had locked Seedless away. As detail grew upon detail, problem upon problem, Otah felt his chest grow tighter. Liat wouldn't meet his gaze, and Otah wished Maati were elsewhere, so that he could take her in his arms. But he also knew there was nowhere else that Maati could turn. It was right that he'd come here. When Maati's voice trailed off at last, Otah realized the boy was looking at him, waiting for something. For a decision.

"So he admitted to it," Otah said, thinking as he spoke. "Seedless confessed to the Khai."

Maati took a pose of confirmation.

"Why?" Otah asked. "Did he really think it would break Heshai-kvo's spirit? That he'd be freed?"

"Of course he did," Liat snapped, but Maati took a more thoughtful expression and shook his head.

"Seedless hates Heshai," Maati said. "It was a flaw in the translation. Or else not a flaw but . . . a part of it. He may have only done it because he knew how badly Heshai would be hurt."

"Heshai?" Liat demanded. "How badly *Heshai* would be hurt? What about Maj? She didn't do anything to deserve this. Nothing!"

"Seedless . . . doesn't care about her," Maati said.

"Will Heshai release him?" Otah asked. "Did it work?"

Maati took a pose that both professed ignorance and apologized for it. "He's not well. And I don't know what confining Seedless will do to him—"

"Who cares?" Liat said. Her voice was bitter. "What does it matter whether Heshai suffers? Why shouldn't he? He's the one who controls the andat. If he was so busy whoring and drinking that he couldn't be bothered to do his work, then he ought to be punished."

"That's not the issue, love," Otah said, his gaze still on Maati.

"Yes, it is," she said.

"If the poet wastes away and dies or if this drives him to take his own life, the andat goes free. Unless . . ."

"I'm not ready," Maati said. "I've only just arrived here, really. A student might study under a full poet for years before he's ready to take on the burden. And even then sometimes people just aren't the right ones. I might not be able to hold Seedless at all."

"Would you try?"

It took a long time before Maati answered, and when he did, his voice was small.

"If I failed, I'd pay his price."

"What's his price?" Liat asked.

"I don't know," Maati said. "The only way to find out is to fail. Death, most likely. But . . . I could try. If there was no one else to."

"That's insane," Liat said, looking to Otah for support. "He can't do that. It would be like asking him to jump off a cliff and see if he could learn to fly on the way down."

"There isn't the choice. There aren't very many successful bindings. There aren't many poets who even try them. There may be no replacement for Seedless, and even if there were, it might not work well with the cotton trade," Maati said. He looked pale and ill. "If no one else can take the poet's place, it's my duty—"

"It hasn't come to that. With luck, it won't," Otah said. "Perhaps there's another poet who's better suited for the task. Or some other andat that could take Seedless' place if he escaped—"

"We could send to the Dai-kvo," Liat said. "He'd know."

"I can't go," Maati said. "I can't leave Heshai-kvo here."

"You can write," Liat said. "Send a courier."

"Can you do that?" Otah asked. "Write it all out, everything: the sad trade, Seedless, how the Khai's responded. What you're afraid may happen. All of it."

Maati nodded.

"How long?" Otah asked.

"I could have it tomorrow. In the morning."

Otah closed his eyes. His belly felt heavy with dread, his hands trembling as if he were about to attack a man or else be attacked. Someone had to carry the message, and it couldn't be Maati. It would be him. He would do it himself. The resolve was simply there, like a decision that had been made long before.

Tahi-kvo's face loomed up in his imagination, and with it, the sense of the school—its cold, bruising days and nights, the emptiness and the cruelty and the sense he had had, however briefly, of belonging. The anger rose in him again, as if it had only been banked all these years. Someone would have to go to the Dai-kvo, and Otah was ready to see the man again.

"Bring it here then," he said. "To Liat's cell. There are always ships leaving for Yalakeht this time of year. I'll find a berth on one."

"You're not going," Liat said. "You can't. Your indenture . . ."

Otah opened the door and moved to one side. He walked Maati out to the passage with a pose that was both a thanks and a promise.

"You're sure of this?" Maati asked.

Otah nodded, then turned away again. When they were alone, the cell fell back into twilight.

"You can't go," Liat said. "I need you to stay. I need someone . . . someone by my side. What happened to Maj, what happened to her baby . . . it was my fault. I let that happen."

He moved to her, sitting on her desk, stroking her silk-smooth cheek with his knuckles. She leaned into him, taking his hand in both of hers and pressing it to her chest.

"I have to. Not just for this. My past is up there. It's the right thing."

"She hasn't stopped crying. She sleeps and she wakes up crying. I went to see her when the utkhaiem released me. She was the first person I went to see. And when she looks at me, and I remember what she was like before . . . I thought she was callous. I thought she didn't care. I didn't see it."

Otah slid down, kneeling on the floor, and put his arms around her.

"The reason you're going," Liat whispered. "It isn't because of me, is it? It isn't to get away from me?"

Otah sat, her head cradled against his shoulder. He could feel his mind working just below the level of thought—what he would need to do, the steps he would have to take. He stroked her hair, smooth as water.

"Of course not, love," he said.

"Because you'll be a great man one day. I can tell. And I'm just an idiot girl who can't keep monsters like Oshai from . . . gods. 'Tani. I didn't see it. I didn't *see* it."

She wept, the sobs shaking her as he cooed and rocked her gently. He rested his chin on her bent head, curling her into him. She smelled of musk and tears. He held her until the sobbing quieted, until his arms ached. Her head lay heavy against him and her breath was almost slow as sleep.

"You're exhausted, love," he said. "Come to bed. You need sleep."

"No," she said, rousing. "No, stay with me. You can't go now."

Gently, he lifted her and carried her to her cot. He sat beside her, her hand wrapping his like vine on brick.

"Three weeks to Yalakeht," he said. "Then maybe two weeks upriver and a day or two on foot. Less than that coming back, since the river trip will be going with the water on the way down. I'll be back before winter, love."

In the light pressing in at the shutters and the door, he could see her eyes, bleary with grief and exhaustion, seeking his. Her face was unlined, relaxed, halfway asleep already.

"You're excited to go," she said. "You *want* to."

And, of course, that was the truth. Otah pressed his palm to her lips, closing them. To her eyes. This wasn't a conversation he was ready to have. Or perhaps only not with her.

He kissed her forehead and waited until she was asleep before he quietly opened her door and stepped out into the light.

11

≻+≺ Amat woke in the darkness, her breath fast, her heart pounding. In her dream, Ovi Niit had been kicking in her door, and even when she'd pulled herself up from sleep's dark waters, it took some time for her to feel certain that the booming reports from the dream hadn't been real. Slowly, the panic waned, and she lay back. Above her, the netting glowed like new copper in the light from the night candle and then slowly became brighter and paler as the cool blue light of dawn crept in through the opened windows. The shutters shifted in the sea-scented breeze.

Her desk was piled with papers. Ink bricks hollowed from use stacked one on another at the head of the stairs, waiting to be carried away. The affairs of the house had fallen into near chaos while she was away. She had spent long nights looking over lists and ledgers and telling herself that she cared for them all the way she once had. That House Wilsin and her work for it had not been poisoned.

Amat sighed, sat up, and pushed the netting aside. Her world since her resurrection had been much the same—nightmares until dawn, gray and empty work and messages and meetings until sunset. At one point, seeing the strain on her face at the end of the day, Marchat had offered to send her away for a week to Chaburi-Tan once the season was over. The house could cover the expenses, he said. And she let herself imagine that time—away from Saraykeht and the seafront and her desk and the soft quarter—though the fantasy was washed by melancholy. It could never actually happen, but it would have been nice.

Instead, Amat Kyaan rose from her bed, pulled on clean robes, and walked out, leaning on her cane, to the corner stall where a girl from the low towns sold fresh berries wrapped in sweet frybread. It was good enough as a meal to see her through to midday. She ate it as she walked back to her apartments, trying to order her day in her mind, but finding it hard to concentrate on shifting meetings and duties back and forth. Simply leaving her mind blank and empty was so much easier.

Her time since the sad trade and her banishment had felt like being ill. She'd moved through her days without feeling them, unable to concentrate, uninterested in her work. Something had broken in her, and pretending it back to fixed wasn't working. She'd half known it wouldn't, and her mind had made plans for her almost without her knowing it.

The man waiting at her door was wearing robes of yellow and silver—the colors of House Tiyan. He was young—sixteen, perhaps seventeen summers. Liat's age. An apprentice, then, but the apprentice of someone high in House Tiyan. There was only one errand that could mean. Amat shifted her schedule in her mind and popped the last of the berry-soaked frybread into her mouth. The young man, seeing her, fell into a pose of greeting appropriate for an honored elder. Amat responded.

"Kyaan-cha," the boy said, "I come on behalf of Annan Tiyan . . ."

"Of course you do," she said, opening her door. "Come inside. You have the listings?"

He hesitated behind her for only a moment. Amat went slowly up the stairs. Her hip was much better since she'd returned to her apartments with her stinging ointment and her own bed. She paused at her basin, washing the red stains from her food off her fingertips before she began handling papers. When she reached her desk, she turned and sat. The boy stood before her. He'd taken the paper from his sleeve—the one she'd sent to his master. She held out her hand, and he gave it to her.

The receipt was signed. Amat smiled and tucked the paper into her own sleeve. It would go with her papers later. The papers she was going to take with her, not the ones for House Wilsin. The box was on the desk under a pile of contracts. Amat shifted it out, into her lap. Dark wood banded by iron, and heavy with jewels and lengths of silver. She handed it to the boy.

"My master . . ." the boy began. "That is, Amat Kyaan-cha, I was wondering if . . ."

"Annan wants to know why I'm having him hold the package," she said, "and he wanted you to find out without making it obvious you were asking."

The boy blushed furiously. Amat took a pose that dismissed the issue.

"It's rude of him, but I'd have done the same in his place. You may tell him that I have always followed Imperial form by caching such things with trusted friends. One of the people who had been doing me this favor is leaving the city, though, so it was time to find a new holder. And, of course, if he should ever care to, I would be pleased to return the favor. It's got nothing to do with that poor island girl."

It wasn't true, of course, but it was convenient. This was the fourth such box she'd sent out to men and women in the city to whom she felt she might be able to appeal if circumstances turned against her again. The receipt was only as good as the honor of the people she stowed the boxes with. And there would be a certain amount of theft, she expected—one jewel replaced by another of less value. A few lengths of silver gone despite the locks. It wasn't likely, though, that if she called for them, her boxes would be empty. And in an emergency, that would be very nearly all Amat cared about.

The boy took a pose of acknowledgement and retreated down the stairs. Amat understood what Saraykeht had taught her through Ovi Niit. She wouldn't be caught without her wealth again. That it was a courtesy of the great families of the Empire before it collapsed gave her something like precedent. Annan wouldn't believe that it was unrelated to Maj and the sad trade, but he would understand from her answer that she didn't want him to gossip about it. That would suffice.

For the next hand and a half, she went through the contracts, making notations here and there—one copy for herself, one for the house. So late in the season, there were few changes to be made in the wording. But each contract carried with it two or three letters outlining the completion or modifications of terms and definitions, and these were the sort of things that would sink a trading house if they weren't watched. She went through the motions, checking the translations of the letters in Galtic and the Khaiate, noting discrepancies, or places where a word might have more than one meaning. It was what she'd done for years, and she did it now mechanically and without joy.

When she reached the last one, she checked that the inks were dry, rolled the different documents in tubes tied with cloth ribbons, and packed them into a light satchel—there were too many to fit in her sleeves. She took her cane, then, and walked out into the city, heading north to the Wilsin compound. Away from the soft quarter.

The agents of the utkhaiem were present when she arrived at the wide courtyard of the house. Servants in fine silks lounged at the edge of the fountain, talking among themselves and looking out past the statue of the Galtic Tree to the street. She hesitated when she saw them, fear pricking at her for no reason she could say. She pushed it aside the way she pushed all her feelings aside these recent days, and strode past them toward Marchat Wilsin's meeting room.

Epani Doru, Wilsin-cha's rat-faced, obsequious master of house, sat before the wide wooden doors of the meeting room. When she came close, he rose taking a pose of welcome just respectful enough to pretend he honored her position.

"I've some issues I'd like Wilsin-cha to see," she said, taking an answering pose.

"He's meeting with men from the court," Epani said, his voice an apology.

Amat glanced at the closed doors and sighed. She took a pose that asked for a duration. Epani answered vaguely, but with a sense that she would be lucky to see her employer's face before sundown.

"It can wait, then," Amat said. "It's about the sad trade? Is that what they're picking at him for?"

"I assume so, Amat-cha," Epani said. "I understand from the servants that the Khai wants the whole thing addressed and forgotten as quickly as possible. There have been requests to lower tariffs."

Amat clucked and shook her head.

"Sour trade, this whole issue," she said. "I'm sorry Wilsin-cha ever got involved in it."

Epani took a pose of agreement and mourning, but Amat thought for a moment there was something in the man's expression. He knew, perhaps. Epani Doru might have been someone who Marchat took into his confidence the way he hadn't taken her. An accomplice to the act. Amat noted her suspicion, tucked it away like a paper into a sleeve, and took a pose of query.

"Liat?"

"In the workrooms, I think," Epani said. "The utkhaiem didn't ask to speak with her."

Amat didn't reply. The workrooms of the compound were a bad place for someone of Liat's rank to be. Preparing packets for the archives, copying documents, checking numbers—all the work done at the low slate tables was better suited for a new clerk, someone who had recently come to the house. Amat walked back to the stifling, still air and the smell of cheap lamp oil.

Liat sat at a table by herself, hunched over. Amat paused, considering the girl. The too-round face had misplaced its youth; Amat could see in that moment what Liat would be when her beauty failed her. A woman, then, and not a lovely one. A dreadful weight of sympathy descended on Amat Kyaan, and she stepped forward.

"Amat-cha," Liat said when she looked up. She took a pose of apology. "I didn't know you had need of me. I would have—"

"I didn't know it either," Amat said. "No fault of yours. Now, what are you working on?"

"Shipments from the Westlands. I was just copying the records for the archive."

Amat considered the pages. Liat's handwriting was clean, legible. Amat remembered days in close heat looking over numbers much like these. She felt her smile tighten.

"Wilsin-cha set you to this?" Amat asked.

"No. No one did. Only I ran out of work, and I wanted to be useful. I'm . . . I don't like being idle these days. It just feels . . ."

"Don't carry it," Amat said, still pretending to look at the written numbers. "It isn't yours."

Liat took a questioning pose. Amat handed her back the pages.

"It's nothing you did wrong," Amat said.

"You're kind."

"No. Not really. There was nothing you could have done to prevent this, Liat. You were tricked. The girl was tricked. The poet and the Khai."

"Wilsin-cha was tricked," Liat said, adding to the list.

Or trapped, Amat thought, but said nothing. Liat rallied herself to smile and took a pose of gratitude.

"It helps to hear someone say it," the girl said. "Itani does when he's here, but I can't always believe him. But with him going . . ."

"Going?"

"North," Liat said, startling as if she'd said more than she'd meant. "He's going north to see his sister. And . . . and I already miss him."

"Of course you do. He's your heartmate, after all," Amat said, teasing gently, but the weariness and dread in Liat's gaze deepened. Amat took a deep breath and put a hand on Liat's shoulder.

"Come with me," Amat said. "I have some things I need of you. But someplace cooler, eh?"

Amat led her to a meeting room on the north side of the compound where the windows were in shade and laid the tasks before her. She'd meant to give Liat as little as she could, but seeing her now, she added three or four small things that she'd intended to let rest. Liat needed something now. Work was thin comfort, but it was what she had to offer. Liat listened closely, ferociously.

Amat reluctantly ended her list.

"And before that, I need you to take me to the woman," she said.

Liat froze, then took a pose of acknowledgement.

"I need to speak with her," Amat said, knowing as she said the words precisely how inadequate they were. For a moment, she was tempted to tell the full story, to lighten Liat's burden by whatever measure the truth could manage. But she swallowed it. She put compassion aside for the moment. Along with fear and anger and sorrow.

Liat led her to a private room in the back, not far from Marchat Wilsin's own. Amat knew the place. The delicate inlaid wood of the floor, the Galtic tapestries, the window lattices of carved bone. It was where House Wilsin kept its most honored guests. Amat didn't believe it was where the girl had slept before the crime. That she was here now was a sign of Marchat's pricked conscience.

Maj lay curled on the ledge before the window. Her pale fingers rested on the lattice; the strange dirty gold of her hair spilled down across her shoulders and halfway to the floor. She looked softer. Amat stood behind her and watched the rise and fall of her breath, slow but not so slow as sleep.

"I could stay, if you like," Liat said. "She can . . . I think she is better when there are people around who she knows. Familiar faces."

"No," Amat said, and the island girl shifted at the sound of her voice. The pale eyes looked over her with nothing like real interest. "No, Liat-kya, I think I've put enough on you for today. I can manage from here."

Liat took a pose of acceptance and left, closing the door behind her. Amat pulled a chair of woven cane near the island girl and lowered herself into it. Maj watched her. When Amat was settled, the chair creaking under even her slight weight, Maj spoke.

"You hurt her feelings," she said in the sibilant words of Nippu. "You sent her away, didn't you?"

"I did," Amat said. "I came to speak with you. Not her."

"I've told everything I know. I've told it to a hundred people. I won't do it again."

"I haven't come to ask you anything. I've come to tell."

A slow, mocking smile touched the wide, pale lips. The fair eyebrows rose.

"Have you come to tell me how to save my child?"

"No."

Maj shrugged, asking with motion what else could be worth hearing.

"Wilsin-cha is going to arrange your travel back to Nippu," Amat said. "I think it will happen within the week."

Maj nodded. Her eyes softened, and Amat knew she was seeing herself at home, imagining the things that had happened somehow undone. It seemed almost cruel to go on.

"I don't want you to go," Amat said. "I want you to stay here. In Saraykeht."

The pale eyes narrowed, and Maj lifted herself on one elbow, shifting to face Amat directly. Amat could see the distrust in her face and felt she understood it.

"What happened to you goes deeper than it appears," Amat said. "It was an attack on my city and its trade, and not only by the andat and Oshai. It won't be easy to show this for what it was, and if you leave . . . if you leave, I don't think I can."

"What can't you do?"

"Prove to the Khai that there were more people involved than he knows of now."

"Are you being paid to do this?"

"No."

"Then why?"

Amat drew in a breath, steadied herself, and met the girl's eyes.

"Because it's the right thing," Amat said. It was the first time she'd said the words aloud, and something in her released with them. Since the day she'd left Ovi Niit, she had been two women—the overseer of House Wilsin and also the woman who knew that she would have to have this conversation. Have this conversation and then follow it with all the actions it implied. She laced her fingers around one knee and smiled, a little sadly, at the relief she felt in being only one woman again. "What happened was wrong. They struck at my city. *Mine*. And my house was part of it. Because of that, I was part of it. Doing this will gain me nothing, Maj. I will lose a great deal that I hold dear. And I will do it with you or without you."

"It won't bring me back my child."

"No."

"Will it avenge him?"

"Yes. If I succeed."

"What would he do, your Khai? If you won."

"I don't know," Amat said. "Whatever he deems right. He might fine House Wilsin. Or he might burn it. He might exile Wilsin-cha."

"Or kill him?"

"Or kill him. He might turn Seedless against House Wilsin, or the Galtic Council. Or all of Galt. I don't know. But that's not for me to choose. All I can do is ask for his justice, and trust that the Khai will follow the right road afterward."

Maj turned back to the window, away from Amat. The pale fingers touched the latticework, traced the lines of it as if they were the curves of a beloved face. Amat swallowed to loosen the knot in her throat. Outside, a songbird called twice, then paused, and sang again.

"I should go," Amat said.

Maj didn't turn. Amat rose, the chair creaking and groaning. She took her cane.

"When I call for you, will you come?"

The silence was thick. Amat's impulse was to speak again, to make her case. To beg if she needed to, but her training from years of negotiations was to wait. The silence demanded an answer more eloquently than words could. When Maj spoke, her voice was hard.

"I'll come."

SARAYKEHT RECEDED. THE WIDE MOUTH OF THE SEAFRONT THINNED; WHARVES wide enough to hold ten men standing abreast narrowed to twigs. Otah sat at the back rail of the ship, aware of the swell and drop of the water, the rich scent of the spray, but concentrating upon the city falling away behind him. He could take it all in at once: the palaces of the Khai on the top of the northern slope grayed by distance; the tall, white warehouses with their heavy red and gray tiles near the seafront; the calm, respectable morning face of the soft quarter. Coast fishermen resting atop poles outside the city, lines cast into the surf. They passed east. The rivermouth, wide and muddy, and the cane fields. And then over the course of half a hand, the wind pressing the wide, low ship's sails took them around a bend in the land, and Saraykeht was gone. Otah rested his chin on the oily wood of the railing.

They were all back there—Liat and Maati and Kirath and Tuui and Epani who everyone called the cicada behind his back. The streets he'd carted bales of cotton and cloth and barrels of dye and the teahouses he'd sung and drunk in. The garden where he'd first kissed Liat and been surprised and pleased to find her kissing him back. The firekeeper, least of the utkhaiem, who'd taken copper lengths to let him and his cohort roast pigeons over his kiln. He remembered when he'd first come to it, how foreign and frightening it had been. It seemed a lifetime ago.

And before him was a deeper past. He had never been to the villiage of the Dai-kvo, never seen the libraries or heard the songs that were only ever sung there. It was what he might have been, what he had refused. It was what his father had hoped he would be, perhaps. How he might have returned to Machi one day and seen which of his memories were true. He hadn't known, that day marching away from the school, that the price he'd chosen was so dear.

"I hate this part," an unfamiliar voice said.

Otah looked up. The man standing beside him wore robes of deep green. A beard shot with white belied an unlined, youthful face, and the bright, black eyes seemed amused but not unfriendly.

"What do you mean?" Otah asked.

"The first three or four days on shipboard," the man said. "Before your stomach gets the rhythm of it. I have these drops of sugared tar that are supposed to help, but they never seem to. It doesn't seem to bother you, though, eh?"

"Not particularly," Otah said, adopting one of his charming smiles.

"You're lucky. My name's Orai Vaukheter," the man said. "Courier of House Siyanti bound at present from Chaburi-Tan to Machi—longest damn trip in the cities, and timed to put me on muleback in the north just in time for the first snows. And you? I don't think I've met you, and I'd have guessed I knew everyone."

"Itani Noyga," Otah said, the lie still coming naturally to his lips. "Going to Yalakeht to visit my sister."

"Ah. But from Saraykeht?"

Otah took a pose of acknowledgement.

"Rumor has it's difficult times there. Probably a good time to get out."

"Oh, I'll be going back. It's just to see the new baby, and then I'll be going back to finish my indenture."

"And the girl?"

"What girl?"

"The one you were thinking about just now, before I interrupted you."

Otah laughed and took a pose of query.

"And how are you sure I was thinking about a girl?"

The man leaned against the railing and looked out. His smile was quick enough, but his complexion was a little green.

"There's a certain kind of melancholy a man gets the first time he chooses a ship over a woman. It fades with time. It never passes, but it fades."

"Very poetic," Otah said, and changed the subject. "You're going to Machi?"

"Yes. The winter cities. Funny, too. I'm looking forward to it now, because it's all stone and doesn't bob around like a cork in a bath. When I get there, I'll wish I were back here where my piss won't freeze before it hits the ground. Have you been to the north?"

"No," Otah said. "I've spent most my life in Saraykeht. What's it like there?"

"Cold," the man said. "Blasted cold. But it's lovely in a stern way. The mines are how they make their trade. The mines and the metalworkers. And the stonemasons who built the place—gods, there's not another city like Machi in the world. The towers . . . you've heard about the towers?"

"Heard them mentioned," Otah said.

"I was to the top of one once. One of the great ones. It was high as a mountain. You could see for hundreds of miles. I looked down, and I'll swear it, the birds were flying below me and I felt like a few more bricks and I'd have been able to touch clouds."

The water lapped at the boards of the ship below them, the seagulls cried, but Otah didn't hear them. For a moment, he was atop a tower. To his left, dawn was breaking, rose and gold and pale blue of robin's egg. To his right, the land was still dark. And before him, snow covered mountains—dark stone showing the bones of the land. He smelled something—a perfume or a musk that made him think of women. He couldn't say if the vision was dream or memory or something of both, but a powerful sorrow flowed through him that lingered after the images had gone.

"It sounds beautiful," he said.

"I climbed back down as fast as I could," the man said, and shuddered despite the heat of the day. "That high up, even stone sways."

"I'd like to go there one day."

"You'd fit in. You've a northern face."

"So they tell me," Otah said, smiling again though he felt somber. "I'm not sure, though. I've spent quite a few years in the south. I may belong there now."

"It's hard," his companion said, taking a pose of agreement. "I think it's why I keep travelling even though I'm not really suited to it. Whenever I'm in one place, I remember another. So I'll be in Udun and thinking about a black crab stew they serve in Chaburi-Tan. Or in Saraykeht, thinking of the way the rain falls in Utani. If I could take them all—all the best parts of all the cities— and bring them to a single place, I think that would be paradise. But I can't, so I'm doomed. When the time comes I'm too old to do this, I'll have to settle for one place and I truly believe the thought of never seeing the others again will break me."

For a moment, they were silent. Then the courier's distant expression changed, and he turned to look at Otah carefully.

"You're an interesting one, Itani Noyga. I thought I'd come make light with a young man on what looks like his first journey, and I find myself thinking about my final one. Do you always carry that cloud with you?"

Otah grinned and took a pose of light apology, but hands and smile both wilted under the cool gaze. The canvas chuffed and a man in the back of the low, barge-built ship shouted.

"Yes," he surprised himself by saying. "But very few people seem to notice it."

"So the island girl's left," Amat said. "What does it matter? You were about to send her away."

Marchat Wilsin fidgeted, sending little waves across the bath to rebound against the tiles. Amat sipped her tea and feigned disinterest.

"We were sending her *home*. It was arranged. Why would she go?" he asked, as much to the water or himself as to her. Amat put her bowl of tea down in the floating tray and took a pose of query that was by its context a sarcasm.

"Let me see, Wilsin-cha. A young girl who has been deceived, used, humiliated. A girl who believed the stories she'd been told about perfect love and a powerful lover and was taken instead to a slaughterhouse for her own blood. Now why wouldn't she want to go back to the people she'd left? I'm sure they wouldn't think her a credulous idiot. No more than the Khai and the utkhaiem do now. There are jokes about her, you know. At the seafront. Laborers and teahouse servants make them up to tell each other. Did you want to hear some?"

"No," Marchat said and slapped the water. "No, I don't. I don't want it to happen, and if it's going to, I don't want to know about it."

"Shame, Marchat. She left from shame."

"I don't see why she should feel ashamed," he said, a defensiveness in his voice. A defense of himself and, heartbreakingly, of Maj. "She didn't do anything wrong."

Amat released her pose and let her hands slip back under the water. Wilsincha's lips worked silently, as if he were in conversation with himself and halfway moved to speaking. Amat waited.

The night before, she had taken Maj out to one of the low towns—a fishing village west of the city. A safe house outside the city would do, Amat thought, until a more suitable arrangement could be made. A week, she hoped, but perhaps more. In the last days, her plans had begun to fall away from House Wilsin's. It wouldn't be long before she and her employer, her old friend, parted company. It was worse, sitting there with him in the bathhouse he'd used for years, because he didn't know. House Wilsin had taken her from a life on knife-edge, and he—Marchat-cha—had chosen her from among the clerks and functionaries. He had promoted her through the ranks. And now they sat as they had for years, but it was nearing the last time.

Despite herself, Amat leaned forward and put her palm on his shoulder. He looked up and forced a smile.

"It's over," he said. "At least it's over."

It was something he'd said often in the last days, repeating it as if saying the words again would make them true. So perhaps some part of him did know that it was far from finished. He took her hand and, to her surprise, kissed it. His whiskers scratched her water-softened skin. Gently and despite him, she pulled away. He was blushing. Gods, the poor man was blushing. It made her want to weep, want to leave, want to shout at him until her echoing fury cracked the tiles. *After all you've done, how dare you make me feel sympathy for you?*

"Wilsin-cha," she said. "The shipping schedule."

"Yes," he said. "Of course. The schedule."

Together, they went through the trivial issues of the day. A small fire in one of the weaver's warehouses meant that they would be three thousand feet of thread short for the ship to Bakta. It was significant enough to warrant holding the ship, but they didn't dare keep it too long—the season was turning. And then there was the issue of a persistent mildew in one of House Wilsin's warehouses that had spoiled two bolts of silk, and had to be addressed before they dared to use the space again.

Amat laid out the options, made her suggestions, answered Wilsin-cha's questions, and accepted his decisions. In the main part of the bathhouse, a man broke out in song, his voice joined—a little off-key—by two more. The warm breeze coming through the cedar trellis at the windows moved the surface of the water. Painful as it was, Amat felt herself grabbing at the details— the pinkness of Marchat's pale skin, the thin crack in the side of the lacquer tray, the just-bitter taste of overbrewed tea. Like a squirrel, she thought, gathering nuts for the winter.

"Amat," he said, when they were through and she started to rise. The hardness in his voice caught her, and she lowered herself back into the water. "There's something . . . You and I, we've worked together for more years than I like to remember. You've always been . . . always been very professional. But

I've felt that along with that, we've been friends. I know that I have held you in the highest regard. Gods, that sounds wrong. Highest regard? Gods. I'm doing this badly."

He raised his hands from the water, fingertips wrinkled as raisins, and motioned vaguely. His face was tight and flushed. Amat frowned, confused, and then the realization washed over her like nausea. He was about to declare his love.

She put her head down, pressing a palm to her forehead. She couldn't look up. Laughter that had as much to do with horror as mirth shook her gently. Of all the things she'd faced, of all the evils she'd steeled herself to walk through, this one had taken her blind. Marchat Wilsin thought he loved her. It was why he'd stood up to Oshai to save her. It was why she was alive. It was ridiculous.

"I'm sorry," he said. "I shouldn't have . . . Forget that. I didn't . . . I sound like a half-wit schoolboy. Here's the thing, Amat. I didn't mean to be involved with this. These last days, I've been feeling a certain distance from you. And I'm afraid that you and I might have . . . lost something between us. Something that . . ."

It had to stop. She had to stop it.

"Wilsin-cha," she said, and forced herself into a formal pose of respect appropriate to a superior in business. "I think perhaps it is too soon. The . . . the wounds are too fresh. Perhaps we might postpone this conversation."

He took a pose of agreement that seemed to carry a relief almost as deep as her own. She shifted to a pose of leave-taking, which he returned. She didn't meet his gaze as she left. In the dressing room, she pulled on her robes, washed her face, and leaned against the great granite basin, her hands clenched white on its rim, until her mind had stilled. With a long, deep, slow breath, she composed herself, then took up her cane and walked out into the streets, as if the world were not a broken place, and her path through it was not twisted.

She strode to the compound, her leg and hip hardly bothering her. She delivered the orders she had to give, made the arrangements she had discussed with Wilsin-cha. Liat, thankfully, was elsewhere. Amat's day was difficult enough without adding the burden of Liat's guilt and pain. And, of course, there was the decision of whether to take the girl with her when Amat left her old life behind.

When Amat had written the last entry in the house logs, she cleaned the nib on its cloth, laid the paper over the half-used inkblock, and walked south, toward the seafront. And not toward her apartments. She passed by the stalls and the ships, the watersellers and firekeepers and carts that sold strips of pork marinated in ginger and cumin. When she reached the wide mouth of the Nantan, she paused, considering the bronze form of the last emperor gazing out over the sea. His face was calm and, she thought, sorrowful. Shian Sho had watched the Empire fall, watched the devastation of war between high councilors who could wield poets and andat. How sad, she thought, to have had so much and been powerless to save it. For the first time in her life, she felt something more than awe or historical curiosity or familiarity with the image of the man eight generations dead. She walked to the base of the statue, reached out and rested her hand on the sun-hot metal of his foot, almost painful to touch. When she turned away, her sorrow was not less, but it was accompanied by a strange lifting of her heart. A kinship, perhaps, with those who had struggled before her to save the cities they held dear. She walked toward the river, and the worst parts of the city. Her city. Hers.

The teahouse was rough—its shutters needed painting, the plaster of its walls was scored with the work of vandals cheaply repaired—but not decrepit. Its faults spoke of poverty, not abandonment. A man with the deep blue eyes and red hair of the Westlands leaned out of a window, trying not to seem to stare at her. Amat raised an eyebrow and walked through the blue-painted door and into the murk of the main room.

The smell of roast lamb and Westlands beer and cheap tobacco washed over her. The stone floor was smooth and clean, and the few men and women at their tables seemed to take little notice of her. The dogs under the tables shifted toward her and then away, equally incurious. Amat looked around with an expression that she hoped would be read as confidence and impatience. A dark-haired girl came to her before long, wiping her hands on her robe as she came. She took a pose of greeting which Amat returned.

"We have tables here," the girl said. "Or perhaps you would care for a room in the back? We have a good view of the river, if . . ."

"I'm here to see a man named Torish Wite," Amat said. "I was told that he would expect me."

The girl fell into a pose of understanding without surprise or hesitation, turned, and led Amat back through a short corridor to an open door. Amat took a pose of thanks, and stepped through.

He was a big man, thick hair the color of honey, a rough scar on his chin. He didn't rise as she came in, only watched her with a distant amusement. Amat took a pose appropriate to opening a negotiation.

"No," the man said in the language of the Westlands. "If you want to talk to me, you can use words."

Amat dropped her hands and sat. Torish Wite leaned back in his chair and crossed his arms. The knife he wore at his belt was as long as Amat's forearm. She felt fear tighten her throat. This man was strong, brutal, prone to violence. That was, after all, why she was here.

"I understand you have men for hire," she said.

"Truth," he agreed.

"I want a dozen of them."

"For what?"

"I can't tell you that yet."

"Then you can't have 'em."

"I'm prepared to pay—"

"I don't care what you're prepared to pay. They're my men, and I'm not sending them out unless I know what I'm sending them into. You can't say, then you can't have them."

He looked away, already bored. Amat shook her head, pushing away her emotions. This was the time to think, not feel. The man was a businessman, even if what he traded in was violence. He had nothing to gain by building a reputation of spilling his client's secrets.

"I am about to break with my house," she said. After holding her intentions in silence for so long, it was strange to hear the words spoken. "I am going to be taking up a project that will put me in opposition to my previous employer. If I'm to succeed in it, I will have to secure a large and steady income."

Torish Wite shifted forward, his arms resting on his knees. He was considering her now. He was curious. She had him.

"And how are you going to arrange that?" he asked.

"There is a man named Ovi Niit. He runs a comfort house in the soft quarter. I mean to take it from him."

12

>+< Maati woke to the sound of driving rain pattering against the shutters. The light that pressed in was cloud softened, with neither direction nor strength to tell him how long he'd slept. The night candle was now only a burnt wick. He pushed away the netting, shuddered, and rose. When he opened the shutters, it was as if the city was gone, vanished in gray. Even the outlines of the palaces were vague, but the surface of the pond was alive and dancing and the leaves of the nearby trees shone with bright wet green just turning to red at the veins. The rain against his face and chest was cool. Autumn was coming to Saraykeht.

The days—nearly two weeks now—since Otah-kvo had left had taken on a rhythm. He would rise in the morning, and go and speak with Heshai-kvo. Some days, the poet would manage three or four exchanges. Others, they would only sit there under the baleful black stare of the andat, silent in his torture box. Maati coaxed his master to eat whatever meal the servants had brought from the palace kitchens: fruit pastries sticky with sugar, or rich, soupy bread puddings, or simple cheese and cut apple. And every morning, Heshai-kvo deigned to eat a mouthful or two, sip a bowl of tea. And then with a grunt, he would turn away, leaving only his wide back as company. Seedless never spoke, but Maati felt the weight of his attention like a hand on the back of his neck.

In the afternoon, he would walk in the gardens or read. And as sunset came, he would repeat the breakfast ritual with an evening meal that excited no more interest in the poet. Then, leaving the night candle lit, Maati would go to his own room, his own cot, light his candle, fasten his netting, and will himself to sleep. It was like a fever dream, repeated again and again, with small variations that seemed only to point out that nothing of substance changed.

He closed the shutters, took a clean robe, washed his face and shaved. There was little enough on his cheek for the razor to take, but it was a ritual. And it comforted him. He would have given anything he had to have Otah-kvo there to talk with.

He went down the stairs to the table where the breakfast had been left for him: honey bread and black tea. He took the tray and went back up and along the corridor to Heshai-kvo's room. It was unbarred, and swung open at the touch of his burdened wrist.

The bed was empty. Netting fine as mist was thrown aside, the bedclothes in knots and bundles that didn't hide the depression where the poet's body had lain for days. Maati, trembling, put down the tray and walked to the abandoned bed. There was no note, no unfamiliar object, nothing to say what had happened, why his teacher was gone. Sickening images of the poet floating dead in the pond tugged at him, and he turned slowly, dreading to see the torture box empty. Seedless' black eyes met his, and Maati let out the breath he hadn't noticed he was holding.

The andat laughed.

"No such luck, my dear," he said, his voice amused and calm. "The great poet is, to the best of my knowledge, still alive and in something near enough to his right mind not to have set me free."

"Where is he?"

"I don't know. It isn't as if he asked my permission. You know, Maati-kya, it's odd. We never seem to chat anymore."

"Where did he go? What did he say?"

Seedless sighed.

"He didn't say anything. He was just his own pathetic self—all the grace and will of a soiled washcloth—and then just after the last mark of the night candle, he got up like he'd remembered an appointment, pulled on his robes and left."

Maati paced, fighting to slow his breath, to order his thoughts. There had to be something. Some sign that would tell him where Heshai had gone, what he would do.

"Call out the guards," Seedless said, laughter in his voice. "The great poet has slipped his leash."

"Be quiet!" Maati snapped. "I have to think."

"Or you'll do what? Punish me? Gods, Maati, look what they're doing to me already. I can't move. I can't stretch. If I were a man, I'd be covered in my own shit, and nothing to do but try to push it out with my toes. What more were you planning to do?"

"Don't. Just . . . don't talk to me."

"Why not, my dear? What did I do to upset you?"

"You killed a baby!" Maati shouted, shocked at his own anger.

In the shadows of his prison, the andat smiled sadly. The pale fingers wrapped the slats, and the pale flesh shifted an inch.

"The baby doesn't mind," Seedless said. "Ask it, see if it holds a grudge. What I did, I did to the woman. And to Heshai. And you know why I've done it."

"You're evil," Maati said.

"I'm a prisoner and a slave held against my will. I'm forced to work for my captor when what I want is to be free. Free of this box, of this flesh, of this consciousness. It's no more a moral impulse than you wanting to breathe. You'd sacrifice anyone, Maati, if you were drowning."

Maati turned his back, running his hands down the empty sheets, looking for something—anything. It was only cloth. He had to go. He had to alert the Khai. Armsmen. They had to send armsmen out to search for Heshai and bring him back. Over the drumming of the rain, he heard the andat shift.

"I told you," Seedless said, "that we wouldn't always be friends."

And from below them another voice called Maati's name. A woman's voice, tight with distress. Maati rushed down the stairs, three at a stride. Liat Cho-kavi stood in the main room. Her robes and hair were rain-soaked, clinging to her and making her seem younger than she had before. She held her hands tight. When she saw him, she took two steps forward, and Maati reached out, put his hand on hers.

"What is it," he asked. "What's happened?"

"The poet. Heshai. He's at the compound. He's raving, Maati. We can't calm him. Epani-cha wanted to send for the utkhaiem, but I told him I'd come get you. He promised to wait."

"Take me," he said, and together they half-walked, half-ran out, across the wooden bridge—its timbers rain-slicked and blackened—through the palace gardens where the water bowed the limbs of trees and bent the flower blossoms to the ground, and then south, into the city. Liat kept hold of his hand, pulling him along. The pace was too fast for speaking, and Maati couldn't imagine what he would say if he'd been able. His mind was too much taken with dread of what he would find when they arrived.

If Otah-kvo had been there, there would have been someone to ask, someone who would have known what to do. It struck Maati as he passed through the darkened streets that he'd had a teacher with him almost his whole life—someone who could guide him when the world got confusing. That was what teachers were supposed to be. Otah-kvo hadn't even accepted the Dai-kvo and he was strong enough to know the right thing. It was monstrously wrong that Heshai was incapable of doing the same.

At the courtyard of the Galtic house, Liat stopped and Maati drew up beside her. The scene was worse than he had thought. The house was two stories built around the courtyard with a walkway on the second level that looked down on the metalwork statue of the Galtic Tree, the fountain overflowing in the downpour, and between them, sitting with his back to the street, his teacher. Around him were the signs of conflict—torn papers, spilled food. A crowd had gathered, robes in the colors of many houses ghosted in the shadows of doorways and on the upper walk, faces blurred by rain.

Maati put his hand on Liat's hip and gently pushed her aside. The stone of the courtyard was an inch underwater, white foam tracing the pattern of drainage from the house out into the streets. Maati walked through it slowly, his sandals squelching.

Heshai looked confused. The rain plastered his long, thinning hair to his neck. His robe was thin—too thin for the weather—and the unhealthy pink of his skin showed through it. Maati squatted beside him, and saw the thick, wide mouth was moving slightly, as if whispering. Drops of water clung like dew to the moth-eaten beard.

"Heshai-kvo," Maati said, taking a pose of entreaty. "Heshai-kvo, we should go back."

The bloodshot eyes with whites the color of old ivory turned to him, narrowed, and then recognition slowly lit the poet's face. He put his thick-fingered hands on Maati's knee, and shook his head.

"She isn't here. She's already gone," Heshai said.

"Who isn't here, Heshai-kvo?"

"The girl," he snapped. "The island girl. The one. I thought if I could find her, you see, if I could explain my error . . ."

Maati fought the urge to shake him—take a handful of robe in each fist and rattle the old man until he came to his senses. Instead, he put his own hand over Heshai's and kept his voice calm and steady.

"We should go."

"If I could have explained, Maati . . . If I could just have explained that it was the andat that did the thing. That I would never have—"

"What good would it do?" Maati said, his anger and embarrassment slipping out, "Heshai-kvo, there aren't any words you know that would apologize for what happened. And sitting here in the rain doesn't help."

Heshai frowned at the words as if confused, then looked down at the flowing water and up to the half-hidden faces. The frog-lips pursed.

"I've made an ass of myself, haven't I?" Heshai asked in a perfectly rational voice.

"Yes," Maati said, unable to bring himself to lie. "You have."

Heshai nodded, and rose to his feet. His robe hung open, exposing his wrinkled breast. He took two unsteady steps before Maati moved close and put his arm around the man. As they passed into the street, Liat went to Heshai's other side, taking his arm over her shoulder, sharing Maati's burden. Maati felt Liat's arm against his own behind Heshai's wide back. Her hand clasped his forearm, and between them, they made a kind of cradle to lead the poet home.

THE ROBE MAATI LENT HER WHEN THEY ARRIVED BACK AT THE POET'S HOUSE WAS woven cotton and silk, the fabric thicker than her finger and soft as any she'd touched in years. She changed in his small room while he was busy with the poet. Her wet robes, she hung on a stand. She wrung the water out of her hair and braided it idly as she waited.

It was a simple room—cot, desk, and wardrobe, cloth lantern and candle stand. Only the pile of books and scrolls and the quality of the furnishings marked it as different from a cell like her own. But then, Maati was only an apprentice. His role was much like her own with Amat. They were even very nearly the same age, though she found she often forgot that.

A murmur of voices reached her—the poet's and Maati's and then the soft, charming, chilling voice of Seedless. The poet barked something she couldn't make out, and then Maati, soothing him. She wanted to leave, to go back to her cell, to be away from the terrible tension in the air of the house. But the rain was growing worse. The pounding of water was joined now with an angry tapping. The wind had turned and allowed her to open Maati's shutters without flooding his room, and when she did, the landscape outside looked like it was covered with spiders' eggs. Tiny hailstones melting as quickly as they fell.

"Liat-cha," Maati said.

She turned, trying to pull the shutters closed and take a pose of apology at the same time, and managing neither.

"No, I'm sorry," Maati said. "I should have kept closer watch on him. But he's never tried to get out of his bed, much less leave the house."

"Is he resting now?"

"Something like it. He's gone to bed at least. Seedless . . . you know about Seedless' box?"

"I'd heard rumor," Liat said.

Maati took a pose of confirmation and looked back over his shoulder, his expression troubled and weary. His brown poet's robes were still dripping at the sleeves.

"I'll go downstairs," she said.

"Why?"

"I thought you'd want some privacy to change," she said slowly, and was rewarded by a fierce blush as Maati took a pose of understanding.

"I'd forgotten . . . I didn't even notice they were wet. Yes, of course, Liat-cha. I'll only be a moment."

She smiled and slapped his shoulder as she'd seen Itani's cohort do. The gesture felt surprisingly natural to her.

"I think we're past calling each other *cha*," she said.

He joined her quickly, changed into a robe of identical brown. They sat in the main room, candles lit to dispel the gloom of weather. He sat across from her on a low wooden divan. His face was calm, but worn and tight about the mouth, even when he smiled. The strain of his master's collapse was written on his brow.

"Have you . . . have you heard from him?" Maati asked.

"No," she said. "It's too early. He won't have reached Yalakeht by now. Soon, but not yet. And then it would take as many weeks as he's been gone to get a message back to us."

Maati took a pose of understanding, but impatience showed in it. She responded with a pose that asked after Maati's wellbeing. In another context, it would have been a formal nicety. Here, it seemed sincere.

"I'll be fine," he said. "It's only difficult not knowing what to do. When Otah-kvo comes back, everything will be all right."

"Will it?" Liat said, looking into the candle flame. "I hope you're right."

"Of course it will. The Dai-kvo knows more than any of us how to proceed. He'll pass it to Otah-kvo, and we'll . . ."

The voice with its forced optimism faded. Liat looked back. Maati was sitting forward, rubbing his eyes with his fingers like an old, weary man.

"We'll do whatever the Dai-kvo tells us," Liat finished.

Maati took a rueful pose of agreement. A gust of wind rattled the great shuttered walls, and Liat pulled her robe tight around her, as if to protect herself from cold, though the room was perfectly warm.

"And you?" Maati asked. "Are things well at House Wilsin?"

"I don't know," Liat said. "Amat Kyaan's come back, and she tries to use me, but there doesn't seem to be as much to do as there once was. I think . . . I think she doesn't trust me. I can't blame her, after what happened. And Wilsin-cha's the same way. They keep me busy, but not with anything serious. No one's actually told me I'm only a clerk again, but for how I've been spending my days, I may as well be."

"I'm sorry. It's wrong, though. It isn't your fault that this happened. You should just be—"

"Itani's going to leave me. Or Otah. Whichever. He's going to leave me," she said. She hadn't meant to, but the words had come out, like vomiting. She stared at her hands and they kept coming. "I don't think he knows it yet, but when he left, there was something in him. In the way he treated me that . . . He isn't my first lover, and I've seen it before. It's just a kind of distance, and then it's something more, and then . . ."

"I'm sure you're wrong," Maati said, and his voice sounded confident for the first time that day. "He won't."

"Everyone else has," she said.

"Not him."

"He went, though. He didn't only have to; he wanted to. He wanted to get away from me, and when he comes back, he'll have had time to think. And then . . ."

"Liat-cha . . . Liat. I know we haven't known each other before this, but Otah-kvo was my first teacher, and sometimes I think he was my best one. He's different from other people. And he loves you. He's told me as much."

"I don't know," Liat said.

"You love him, don't you?"

"I don't know," she said, and the silence after it was worse than walking through the rain. She wiped away a tear with the back of her hand. "I love Itani. I *know* Itani. Otah, though? He's a son of the Khaiem. He's . . . he isn't who I thought he was, and I'm just an apprentice overseer, and not likely to be that for long. How can we stay together when he's what he is, and I'm this?"

"You did when you were an overseer and he was just a laborer. This isn't any different."

"Of course it is," she said. "He always knew he was born to something higher than he was. I'm not. I'm just me."

"Otah-kvo is one of the wisest men I know," Maati said. "He isn't going to walk away from you."

"Why not?"

"Because," Maati said softly, "he's one of the wisest men I know."

She laughed, partly at the sincerity in the boy's voice, partly because she wanted so badly for it to be true, partly because her only other option was weeping. Maati moved to her, put his arm around her. He smelled of the cedar soap than Itani used to shave with. She leaned into his shoulder.

"These next weeks," she said when she'd gathered herself enough to speak. "They aren't going to be easy."

"No," Maati agreed and heaved a sigh. "No, they aren't."

"We can see each other through them, though. Can't we?" Liat said, trying to keep the pleading out of the words. The patter of the rain filled the silence, and Liat closed her eyes. It was Maati, at last, who had the courage to say what she hadn't been able to.

"I think I'm going to need a friend if I'm going to come through this," he said. "Perhaps we're in the same place. If I can help, if a half-ragged student poet who spends most of his days feeling like he's worn thin enough to see through can be of any comfort, I'd welcome the company."

"You don't have to."

"Neither do you, but I hope you will."

The kiss she gave him was brief and meant to be sisterly. If he caught his breath at it, she imagined he was only a little surprised and embarrassed. She smiled, and he did as well.

"We're a sorry pair," she said. "Itani . . . he'll be back soon."

"Yes," Maati said. "And things will be better then."

THE DOOR BURST OPEN, AND A BODY FELL FORWARD ONTO THE MEETING ROOM floor. For a moment, the sounds of the teahouse penetrated—voices, music—and then Torish Wite and two of his men followed the man they'd pushed through and closed the door. Silence returned as if it had never gone. Amat, sitting at the long wooden table, gathered herself. The man beside her wore the simple robes of a firekeeper and the expression of someone deeply amused by a dogfight.

The fallen man rose unsteadily to his knees. A white cloth covered his head, and his thin arms were bound behind him. Torish Wite took him by the shoulder, lifted roughly, and nodded to one of his men. When the cloth was flipped away, Amat swallowed a knot of fear.

"This him?" Torish Wite asked.

"Yes," she said.

Ovi Niit's gaze swam. He had a glazed look that spoke of wine with strange spices as much as fear or anger. It took the space of three long breaths for his eyes to rest on her, for recognition to bloom there. Slowly, he struggled to his feet.

"Niit-cha," Amat said, taking a pose that opened a negotiation. "It has been some time."

The whoremaster answered with a string of obscenities that only stopped with Torish Wite's man stepping forward and striking him across the face. Amat folded her hands in her lap. A drop of blood appeared at the corner of Ovi Niit's mouth, bright as a jewel and distracting to her.

"If you do as I say, Niit-cha," she began again, "this needn't be an unpleasant affair."

He grinned, the blood smearing his crooked teeth. There was no fear in him. He laughed, and the sound itself seemed reckless. Amat wished that they'd found him when he was sober.

"I was never paid, Ovi-cha, for my time with you. I have chosen to take the price in a share of the house. In fact, I've chosen to buy you out." She took a sheaf of papers from her sleeve and placed them on the table. "I'm offering a fair price."

"There isn't enough money in the world," he spat. "I built that house up from three girls in an alley."

The firekeeper shifted in his seat. The distant smile on his lips didn't shift, but his eyes held a curiosity. Amat felt oddly out of her depth. This was a negotiation, after all, and to say she had the upper hand would be gross understatement, and yet she was at sea.

"You're going to kill me, you dust-cunt bitch. Because if you don't, I'll kill you."

"There's no need . . ." she began, then stopped and took a pose of acceptance. Ovi Niit was right. It was only dressed as a negotiation. It was, in point of fact, a murder. For the first time, something like apprehension showed in his expression. His eyes shifted to the side, to Torish Wite.

"Whatever she's paying you, I'll triple it," Ovi Niit said.

"Amat-cha," the firekeeper said. "I appreciate the attempt, but it seems to me unlikely that this gentleman will sign the documents."

Amat sighed and took a pose of concurrence. In the common room someone shrieked with laughter. The sound was made faint by the thick stone walls. Like the call of a ghost.

"You can kill me, but you'll never break me," Ovi Niit said, pulling himself up proud as a pit-cock.

"I'll live with that," Amat said, and nodded. Torish Wite neatly kicked Ovi Niit's knees out, and the two other men stepped forward to hold him while their captain leaned over and looped a knotted cord over his head. An efficient flick of the wrist, and the cord was tight enough to dig into the flesh, buried. The whoremaster's face went deep red and darkening. Amat watched with a sick fascination. It took longer than she'd expected. When the men released it, the body fell like a sack of grain.

The firekeeper reached across the table, picked up the sheaf between his first finger and his thumb, and pulled them before him. As if there wasn't a fresh corpse on the floor, Amat turned to him.

"I suppose you know someone who can do a decent imitation of his chop?" the firekeeper said.

"I'll see it arranged," Amat said.

"Very well. If the watch asks, I'll swear to it that I stood witness at the transaction," the firekeeper said, taking a pen and a small silver inkbox from his sleeve. "You paid Niit-cha his asking price, he accepted, and in fact seemed quite pleased."

"Do you think the watch will ask?"

The inkbox clicked open, the firekeeper's pen touched the inkblock and then the page, scratching with a sound like bird's feet.

"Of course they will," he said, sliding the papers back toward her. "They're the watch. They're paid to. But so long as you pay your share to them, let them sample your wares on occasion, and don't cause them trouble, I doubt they'll ask many. He didn't die in the soft quarter. Their honor isn't at stake."

Amat considered the firekeeper's signature for a moment, then took a small leather sack from her belt and handed it to him. He had the good taste not to count it there at the table, but she saw him weigh it before it disappeared into his sleeve.

"It's odd to hear the term honor associated with any of this," she said.

The firekeeper took a pose of polite correction, appropriate for a master to an apprentice not his own.

"If there were no honor at stake, Torish-cha would have killed *you*."

Torish Wite chuckled, and Amat took a pose of acknowledgement more casual than she felt. The firekeeper shifted to a pose of leave-taking to both Amat and Torish Wite and then, briefly, to the corpse of Ovi Niit. When the door closed behind him, Amat tucked the signed papers into her sleeve and considered the dead man. He was smaller than she remembered, and she wouldn't have said his arms were so thin. Collapsed on the floor, his last breath past him, he seemed oddly vulnerable. Amat wondered for the first time what Ovi Niit had been as a child, and whether he had a mother or a sister who would miss him now that he was gone. She guessed not.

"What do you want done with him?" Torish Wite asked.

"Whatever's convenient, I suppose."

"Do you want him found?"

"I don't care one way or the other," Amat said.

"It'll be easier for the watch to ignore any accusations against you if he vanishes," Torish Wite said, half to Amat, half to his men.

"We'll take care of it," one of the men said; the one who had held Ovi Niit's right arm as he died. Amat took a pose of thanks. The two men hefted the object that had been Ovi Niit between them and carried it out. She assumed they had a wheelbarrow in the alleyway.

"When are you taking the house?" Torish Wite asked when they had gone.
"Soon."

"You'll want protection for that. These soft quarter types aren't going to roll over and show their bellies just because you've got the right chop on the papers."

"Yes, I wanted to speak to you about that," Amat said, vaguely surprised at how distant she felt from the words. "I'm going to need guards for the house. Is that the sort of contract you'd be interested in?"

"Depends," Torish Wite said, but he smiled. It was only a matter of terms. That was a fine thing. Her gaze shifted to the space where Ovi Niit had lain. She told herself the unease was only the normal visceral shock of seeing a man die before her. That she now owned a comfort house—that she was going to make her money from selling the women and boys she'd recently shared table and sleeping quarters with—was nothing to think about. It was, after all, in the cause of justice.

Torish Wite shifted his weight, his movement snapping her back into the moment. He had a broad face and broad shoulders, scars on his chin and arms, and a smile that spoke of easy brutality. His gaze was considering and amused.

"Yes?"

"You're afraid of me, aren't you."

Amat smiled and affected boredom.

"Yes," she said. "But consider what happened to the last man who frightened me."

His expression soured.

"You're in over your head, you know."

She took a pose of acknowledgement, but with a stance that bordered on the defiant. She could see in his face that he understood every nuance. He respected her. It was what she'd hoped. She dropped the pose and leaned against the table.

"When I was very young," she said, "my sister pushed me off a rooftop. A high one. I have never been more certain that I was going to die. And I didn't scream. Because I knew it wouldn't help."

"And your point?"

"What I'm doing now may be harder than I'd wish. But I'm going to do it. Worrying about whether I can manage won't help."

He laughed. It was a low sound, and strangely shallow—like an axe on wood.

"You are a tough bitch," he said, making it a compliment.

No, I'm not, she thought, smiling, *but good that you've misunderstood me.*

13

>+< The ship passed the great island with its white watchtower and into the bay of Yalakeht on a cool, hazy morning. Otah stood at the railing and watched the land turn from outlines of pale hills to the green-gray of pine trees in autumn. The tall, gray buildings of Yalakeht nestled at the edge of the calmest of waters. The noise of their bayfront carried over the water, but muffled by the thick air like a conversation in a nearby room.

They reached land—signaled in by the dock master's torches—just as the sun reached its peak in the sky. Otah had hardly put his feet to the cobbled streets before he heard the news. The bayfront seemed to buzz with it.

The third son the Khai Udun had killed his remaining brother. They had found each other in Chaburi-Tan, and faced each other in a seafront street with knives. Or else the second son—whom Otah had seen in the court of the Khai Saraykeht—had been poisoned after all. Or he had ambushed his younger brother, only to have the fight slip from him. On the docks, on the streets, in the teahouses, the stories ran together and meshed with older, better-known tales, last year's news, and wild imaginings newly formed of what might have happened. Otah found a seat in the back of a teahouse near the bayfront and listened as the stories unfolded. The youngest son would take his father's place—a good sign. When a youngest son took power, it meant the line was vigorous. People said it meant the next Khai Udun would be especially talented and brave.

To Otah, it meant that he had killed two of his brothers, and that the others, younger even than he was, had been cast out. They were wearing brands somewhere even now. Unless they were poets. Unless they were lucky enough to be poets like Heshai of Saraykeht.

"Well, you're looking sour," a familiar voice said.

"Orai," Otah said taking a pose of welcome. The courier sat down across from him, and raised a hand to the serving man. Moments later, two bowls of fish and rice appeared before them along with a pot of smoked tea and two ceramic teabowls of delicate green. Otah took a pose of correction to the serving man, but Orai stopped him.

"It's a tradition of my house. After a journey, we buy our travelling companions a meal."

"Really?"

"No," the courier said, "but I think I have more money than you do, and as it happens the fish here is really quite good."

The serving man hovered, looking uncomfortable, until Otah laughed.

"At least let me pay my half," Otah said, but Orai took a pose of deferment: *next time.*

"So, Itani," he said. "This is the end? Or how far upriver is your sister?"

"A day or so by boat," Otah lied. "Two days walking. Or so she tells me. I've never been."

"A few days more, and you could see the poet's village. You've never been there, have you?"

"No," Otah said.

"It's worth the extra travel, if you can spare it. The houses of the Dai-kvo are actually built into the living rock. They say it's based on the school of the ancients in the old Empire, though I don't suppose there's much left of those ruins to compare. It's a good story."

"I suppose."

The fish was very good—bright with lemon, hot with pepper. Otah realized after a few mouthfuls that he had really been very hungry.

"And now that you're at the end of your first journey over water, what do you think of it?"

"It's strange," Otah said. "The world still feels like it's moving"

"Yes. It does stop after a while. More than that, though. There was a saying when I was young that sea journeys are like women—they change you. And none so much as the first."

"I don't know about that," Otah said. "I seem to be more or less the same man I was in Saraykeht. Ten fingers, ten toes. No flippers."

"Perhaps it's just a saying, then."

Orai poured himself another bowl of tea and held it in his hands, blowing across it to cool it. Otah finished the last of the rice and leaned back to find the courier's gaze on him, considering. He replied with a pose of query that seemed to pull Orai out of a half-dream.

"I have to confess, Itani, it isn't precisely chance that I found you here. The fish really is very good, but I found you by asking after you. I've been working for House Siyanti for eight years, and traveling for five of those. I think it's taught me a few things and I'll flatter myself to say I think I'm a good judge of character. These last weeks, on the ship, you've stuck me as an interesting man. You're smart, but you hide the fact. You're driven, but I don't think you know yet what you're driven toward. And you like travel. You have a gift for it."

"You're just saying that because I didn't get sick the way you did," Otah said, trying to lighten the mood.

"Being able to eat your first day on ship is a gift. Don't underestimate it. But all this time, it's occurred to me that you have the makings of a good courier. And I hold enough influence in the house now that, if you wanted a letter of introduction, I think I might be able to help you with it. You wouldn't be trusted with important work at the start, but that doesn't make seeing the cities any less. It's not an easy life, but it's an interesting one. And it might suit you."

Otah cocked his head and felt a flush rising in him equally gratification and embarrassment. The courier sipped his tea, letting the moment stretch until Otah took a pose that encompassed both gratitude and refusal.

"I belong in Saraykeht," he said. "There are things there I need to see through."

"Your indenture. I understand. But that's going to end before much longer."

"There's more than that, though. I have friends there."

"And the girl," Orai said.

"Yes. Liat. I . . . I don't think she'd enjoy having a lover who was always elsewhere."

Orai took a pose of understanding that seemed to include a reservation, a question on the verge of being formed. When he did speak, it was in fact a question, though perhaps not the one he'd wanted to ask.

"How old are you?"

"Twenty summers."

"And she's . . . ?"

"Seventeen."

"And you love her," Orai said. Otah could hear the almost-covered disappointment in the words. "She's your heartmate."

"I don't know that. But I have to find out, don't I?"

Orai grinned and took a pose that conceded the point, then, hesitating, he plucked something from his sleeve. It was a letter sewn closed and sealed with hard green wax stamped with an ornate seal.

"I took the chance that you'd accept my suggestion," the courier said, passing the letter across the table. "If it turns out this amazing young woman doesn't own your heart after all, consider the offer open."

Otah dropped it into his own sleeve and took a pose of thanks. He felt an unreasonable trust for this man, and an ease that three weeks' acquaintance—even in the close quarters of a ship—couldn't explain. Perhaps, he thought, it was only the change of his first sea voyage.

"Orai," he said, "have you ever been in love?"

"Yes. Several times, and with some very good women."

"Can you love someone you don't trust?"

"Absolutely," he said. "I have a sister I wouldn't lend two copper lengths if I wanted them back. The problem loving someone you don't trust is finding the right distance."

"The right distance."

"With my sister, we love each other best from different cities. If we had to share a house, it wouldn't go so gracefully."

"But a lover. A heartmate."

Orai shook his head.

"In my experience, you can bed a woman and mistrust her or you can love a woman and mistrust her, but not all three at once."

Otah sipped his tea. It had gone tepid. Orai waited, his boyish face with its graying beard serious. Two men left from another table, and the cold draft from the briefly opened door made Otah shiver. He put down the green bowl and set his hands together on the table. His head felt thick, his mind stuffed with wool.

"Before I left Saraykeht," he said slowly, "I told Liat some things. About my family."

"But not because you trust her?"

"Because I love her and I thought I *ought* to trust her."

He looked up, his gaze meeting Orai's. The courier took a pose of understanding and sympathy. Otah replied with one that surrendered to greater forces—gods or fate or weight of circumstances. There seemed little more to say. Orai rose.

"Keep hold of that letter," he said. "And whatever happens, good luck to you. You've been a good man to travel with, and that's a rare thing."

"Thank you," Otah said.

The courier pulled his robes closed about him and left. Otah finished his bowl of tea before he also quit the teahouse. The bay of Yalakeht was wide and calm and still before him; the port that ended his first journey over the sea. His mind unquiet, he turned to the north and west, walking through the wet, narrow streets to the river gate, and some days beyond that, the Dai-kvo.

"THIS IS SHIT!" THE ONE-EYED MAN SHOUTED AND THREW THE PAPERS ON THE floor. His face was flushed, and the scarring that webbed his cheeks shone white. Amat could feel the others in the room agreeing, though she never took her gaze from this—Ovi Niit's unappointed spokesman. "He would never have done this."

The front room of the comfort house was crowded, though none of the people there were patrons. It was far too early for one thing. The soft quarter wasn't awake in the day. And the watch had closed the house at her request. They were with her still. Big scowling men wearing the colors of the great comfort houses as a symbol of their loyalty to no one house, but the soft quarter itself. The protecting soldiery of vice.

Behind Amat, where she couldn't see them, Torish Wite and his men stood, waiting. And arrayed before her, leaning against walls or sitting on the tables and chairs, were the guards and gambling chiefs and whores of Ovi Niit's house. Amat caught herself, and couldn't entirely stop the smile. Her house. It was a mistake to think of it as the dead man's.

"He did," she said. "If he didn't tell you, perhaps you weren't as close as you'd thought. And you can burn those papers and eat the ashes if you like. It won't change anything."

The one-eyed man turned to the watch captain, taking a pose of imprecation. The captain—a dark-eyed man with a thin, braided beard—took no answering pose.

"They're forged," the one-eyed man said. "They're forged and you know it. If Niit-cha was going to sell out, it wouldn't be to a high town cunt like her."

"I've spoken to the firekeep that signed witness," the captain said.

"Who was it?" a thin, gray-haired man asked. One of the tiles men.

"Marat Golu. Firekeeper for the weaver's quarter."

A murmur ran through the room. Amat felt her belly go tight. That was a detail she would have preferred to leave quiet. The tiles man was clever.

"Gods!" the one-eyed man said. "Him? We have girls that are more expensive."

Amat took a pose that asked clarification. Her hands were steady as stone, her voice pleasant.

"Are you suggesting that one of the utkhaiem is engaging in fraud?"

"Yes I am!" the one-eyed man roared. The tiles man pursed his lips, but stayed silent. "Bhadat Coll was Niit-cha's second now Black Rathvi's gone, and if Niit-cha's dead, the house should be his."

"Niit-cha isn't dead," Amat said. "This house and everyone it have been bought and paid for. You can read the contracts yourselves, if you can read."

"You can roll your contracts up and fuck them," the one-eyed man shouted. There was a fleck of white at the corner of his mouth. The violence in him was just this side of breaking out. Amat rubbed her thumb and finger together, a dry sound. Part of her mind was wrapped in panic, in visceral, animal fear. The other parts of her mind were what had made her the overseer of a great house.

"Gentlemen of the watch," she said. "I'm releasing this man from his indenture. Would you see him to the street."

It had the effect she'd hoped for. The one-eyed man shouted something that might have had words in it, or might only have been rage. A blade appeared in his hand, plucked from his sleeve, and he leaped for her. She forced herself not to flinch as the watchmen cut him down.

The silence that fell was absolute. She surveyed the denizens of her house—*her* house—judging as best she could what they thought, what they felt. Many of these men were watching their lives shatter before them. In the women, the boys, disbelief, confusion, perhaps a sliver of hope. Two of Torish-cha's men gathered up the dying man and hauled him out. The watch wiped their blades, and their captain, fingers pulling thoughtfully at his beard, turned to the survivors.

"Let me make this clear," he said. "The watch recognizes this contract as valid. The house is the lawful property of Amat Kyaan. Any agreements are hers to enforce, and any disagreements that threaten the peace of the quarter, we'll be dealing with."

The tiles man shifted, his brows furrowed, his hands twitching toward some half-formed pose.

"Let's not be stupid about this," the captain said, his eyes, Amat saw, locked on the tiles man. There was a moment of tension, and then it was over. It was rotten as last month's meat, and everyone knew it. And it didn't matter. With the watch behind her, she'd stolen it fairly.

"The house will be closed tonight," Amat announced. "Torish-cha and his men are to be acting as guards. Any of you with weapons will turn them over now. Anyone besides them found with a weapon will be punished. Anyone using a weapon will be blinded and turned out on the street. Remember, you're my property now, until your indentures are complete or I release you. I'm going to ask the watch to stay until a search of the house is complete. Torish-cha?"

From behind her, the men moved forward. The captain moved over to her. His leathers stank.

"You've got yourself a handful of vipers," he said as her thugs and cutthroats disarmed Ovi Niit's thugs and cutthroats. "Are you certain you want this?"

"It's mine now. Good or ill."

"The watch will back you, but they won't like it. Whatever you did, you did outside the quarter, but some people think this kind of thing is poor form. Your troubles aren't over."

"Transitions are always hard," she said, taking a pose of agreement so casual it became a dismissal. The captain shook his head and moved away.

The search went on, moving from room to room with an efficiency that spoke of experience. Amat followed slowly, considering the worn mattresses, the storage chambers in casual disarray. The house was kept no better than its books. That would change. Everything would change. Nothing would be spared.

Sorrow, as powerful as it was unexpected, stung her eyes. She brushed the tears away. This wasn't the time for it. There would never be a time for it. Not in her lifetime.

The search complete, the watch gone, Amat gathered her people—her vipers—in the common room at the back. The speech she'd prepared, rehearsed a thousand times in her mind, seemed suddenly limp; words that had seemed commanding were petty and weak. Standing at the head of one long table, she drew breath and slowly let it out.

"Well . . ." she said.

In the pause, the voice came from the crowd.

"Grandmother? Is it really you?"

It was a boy of five or six summers. He had been sleeping on a bench one morning, she remembered, when she'd come out of her hellish little cell for a plate of barley gruel and pork. He'd snored.

"Yes," she said. "I've come back."

IN THE DAYS THAT FOLLOWED, HESHAI DIDN'T IMPROVE, BUT NEITHER DID HE seem to grow worse. His patchy beard grew fuller, his weight fell for a time and then slowly returned. He would rouse himself now to wander the house, though he didn't leave it, except to lumber down to the pond at night and stare into the black depths. Maati knew—because who else would take the time to care—that Heshai ate less at night than in the mornings, that he changed to clean robes if they were given him, that he might bathe if a bath was drawn, or he might not.

Thankfully the cotton harvest was complete, and there was nothing official the poet had been called on to perform. Physicians came from the Khai, but Heshai refused to see them. Servants who tried to approach the poet soon learned to ask their questions of Maati. Sometimes Maati acted as go between, sometimes, he just made the decisions himself.

For his own life, Maati found himself floating. Unless he was engaged in the daily maintenance of his invalid master, there was no direction for him that he didn't choose, and so he found that his days had grown to follow his emotions. If he felt frightened or overwhelmed, he studied Heshai's brown book, searching for insights that might serve him later if he were called on to hold Seedless. If he felt guilty, he sat by Heshai and tried to coax him into conversation. If he felt lonesome—and he often felt lonesome—he sought out Liat Chokavi. Sometimes he dreamed of her, and of that one brief kiss.

If his feelings for her were complex, it was only because she was beautiful and his friend and Otah-kvo's lover. There was no harm in it, because nothing could come from it. And so, she was his friend, his only friend in the city.

It was because he had become so familiar with her habits and the places where she spent her days that, when the news came—carried by a palace slave with his morning meal—Maati found her so easily. The clearing was west of the seafront and faced a thin stretch of beach she'd shown him one night. Half-leaved trees and the curve of the shore hid the city. Liat sat on a natural bench of stone, leaning against a slab of granite half her height, and looking at the waves without seeing them. Maati moved forward, his feet crackling in the fallen leaves. Liat turned once, and seeing it was him, turned back to the water without speaking. He smoothed a clear spot beside her on the bench and sat.

"It's true then?" he asked. "Amat Kyaan quit the house?"

Liat nodded.

"Wilsin-cha must be furious."

She shrugged. Maati sat forward, his elbows on his knees. The waves gathered and washed the sand, each receding into the rush of the next. Gulls wheeled and screamed to the east and a huge Galtic ship floated at anchor on the horizon. They were the only signs of the city. He stirred the pile of dry leaves below them with his heel, exposing the dark soil beneath them.

"Did you know?"

"She didn't tell me," Liat said, and her voice was calm and blasted and empty. "She just went. Her apartments were empty except for a box of house papers and a letter to Wilsin-cha."

"So it wasn't only you, at least. She hadn't told anyone. Do you know why she left?"

"No," Liat said. "I blame myself for it. If I had done better, if I hadn't embarrassed the house . . ."

"You did what Wilsin-cha asked you to do. If the trade had been what it seemed, they'd be calling your praises for it."

"Perhaps," Liat said. "It hardly matters. She's gone. Wilsin-cha doesn't have any faith in me. I'm an apprentice without a master."

"Well. We're both that, at least."

She coughed out a single laugh.

"I suppose we are," she said, and scooped up his hand, holding it in her own. Maati's heart raced, and something like panic made his mouth taste like copper. Something like panic, only glorious. He didn't move, didn't do anything that might make Liat untwine her fingers from his.

"Where do you think he is?" Maati asked, calling up the spirit of their friend—his master, her heartmate—to show that he understood that this moment, her hand in his, wasn't something inappropriate. It was only friendship.

"He'll have reached Yalakeht. He might even be there by now," Liat said. "Or at least close, if he's not."

"He'll be back soon, then."

"Not for weeks," Liat said.

"It's a long time."

"Heshai-kvo. He's not better?"

"He's not better. He's not worse. He sleeps too much. He eats too little. His beard . . ."

"It's not improving?"

"Longer. Not better. He really ought to shave it off."

Liat shrugged, and Maati felt as if the motion shifted her nearer. So this was friendship with a woman, he told himself. It was pleasant, he told himself, this simple intimacy.

"He seemed better when I came to see him," Liat said.

"He makes an effort I think, when you're there. I don't know why."

"Because I'm a girl."

"Perhaps that, yes," Maati said.

Liat, releasing his hand, stretched and stood. Maati sighed, feeling that a moment had passed—some invisible, exquisite moment in his life. He had heard old epics telling of moments in a man's youth that never truly left the heart—that stayed fresh and sweet and present through all the years and waited on the deathbed to carry him safely into his last sleep. Maati thought that those moments must be like this one. The scent of the sea, the perfect sky, the leaves, the roar of waves, and his hand, cooling where she had touched him.

"I should come by more often, then," Liat said. "If it helps."

"I wouldn't want to impose," he said, rising to stand beside her. "But if you have the time."

"I don't foresee being given any new projects of note. Besides, I like the poet's house. It's a beautiful place."

"It's better when you're there," Maati said.

Liat grinned. Maati took a pose of self-congratulation to which Liat replied with one of query.

"I've made you feel better," he said.

Liat weighed it, looking out to the horizon with her eyes narrowed. She nodded, as if he'd pointed out a street she'd never seen, or a pattern in the ways a tree branched. Her smile, when it came again, was softer.

"I suppose you have," she said. "I mean, everything's still a terrible mess."

"I'll try fixing the world later. After dinner. Do you want to go back?"

"I suppose I'd best. There's no call to earn a reputation of being unreliable, incompetent, *and* sulky."

They walked back to the city. It had seemed a longer path when he'd been on it alone, worried for Liat. Now, though they were hardly moving faster than a stroll, the walls of the city seemed to surround them almost immediately. They walked up the street of beads, paused at a stand where a boy of no more then eight summers was selling, with a ferocious seriousness, cakes smothered in fine-powdered sugar, and listened to an old beggar singing in a rough, melodious voice that spoke of long sorrow and moved Maati almost to tears. And still, they reached the crossroads that would lead her to the compound of House Wilsin and him to the oppressive, slow desperation of the poet's house before the sun had reached the top of its arc.

"So," Liat said, taking a pose that asked permission, but so casually that it assumed it granted, "shall I come to the poet's house once I'm done here?"

Maati made a show of consideration then took a pose extending invitation. She accepted, but didn't turn away. Maati felt himself frown, and she took a pose of query that he wasn't entirely sure how to answer.

"Liat-cha," he began.

"Cha?"

He raised his hands, palm out. Not a real pose, but expressive nonetheless. *Let me go on.*

"Liat-cha, I know it's only because things went so wrong that Otah-kvo had to leave. And I wouldn't ever have chosen what happened with Seedless. But coming to know you better has been very important to me, and I wanted you to know how much I appreciate your being my friend."

Liat considered him, her expression unreadable but not at all upset.

"Did you rehearse that?" she asked.

"No. I didn't really know what I was going to say until I'd already said it."

She smiled briefly, and then her gaze clouded, as if he'd touched some private pain. He felt his heart sink. Liat met his eyes and she smiled.

"There's something I think you should see, Maati-kya. Come with me."

He followed her to her cell in silence. With each step, Maati felt his anxiety grow. The people they passed in the courtyard and walkway nodded to them both, but seemed unsurprised, undisturbed. Maati tried to seem to be there on business. When Liat closed the door of her cell, he took a pose of apology.

"Liat-cha," he said. "If I've done anything that would . . ."

She batted his hands, and he released the pose. To his surprise, he found she had moved forward, moved against him. He found that her lips had gently pressed his. He found that the air had all gone from the room. She pulled back from the kiss. Her expression was soft and sorrowful and gentle. Her fingers touched his hair.

"Go. I'll come to the poet's house tonight."

"Yes," was all he could think to say.

He stopped in the gardens of the low palaces, sat on the grass, and pressed his fingertips to his mouth, as if making sure his lips were still there; that they were real. The world seemed suddenly uprooted, dreamlike. She kissed him—truly kissed him. She had touched his hair. It was impossible. It was terrible. It was like walking along a familiar path and suddenly falling off a cliff.

And it was also like flying.

14

The raft was big enough to carry eight people. It was pulled against the current by a team of four oxen, moving slowly but implacably along paths worn in the shore by generations of such passage. Otah slept in the back, wrapped in his cloak and in the rough wool blankets the boatman and his daughter provided. In the mornings, the daughter—a child of no more then nine summers—lit a brazier and cooked sweet rice with almond milk and cinnamon. At night, after they tied up, her father made a meal—most often a chicken and barley soup.

In the days spent in this routine, Otah had little to do besides watch the slow progress of trees moving past them, listen to the voices of the water and the oxen, and try to win over the daughter by telling jokes and singing with her or the boatman by asking him about life on the river and listening to his answers. By the time they reached the end of the last full day's journey, both boatman and child were comfortable with him. The boatman shared a bowl of plum wine with him after the other passengers had gone to sleep. They never mentioned the girl's mother, and Otah never asked.

The river journey ended at a low town larger than any Otah had seen since Yalakeht. It had wide, paved streets and houses as high as three stories that looked out across the river or into the branches of the pine forest that surrounded it. The wealth of the place was clear in its food, its buildings, the faces of its people. It was as if some nameless quarter of the cities of the Khaiem had been struck off and moved here, into the wilderness.

That the road to the Dai-kvo's village was well kept and broad didn't surprise him, but the discovery that—for a price higher than he wished to pay—he could hire a litter that would carry him the full day's steep, uphill journey and set him down at the door of the Dai-kvo's palaces did. He passed men in fine robes of wool and fur, envoys from the courts of the Khaiem or trading houses or other places, further away. Food stands at the roadside offered sumptuous fare at high prices for the great men who passed by or wheat gruel and chicken for the lower orders like himself.

Despite the wealth and luxury of the road, the first sight of the Dai-kvo's village took Otah's breath away. Carved into the stone of the mountain, the village was something half belonging to the world of men, half to the ocean and the sun and the great forces of the world. He stopped in the road and looked up at the glittering windows and streets, stairways and garrets and towers. A thin golden ribbon of a waterfall lay just within the structures, and warm light of the coming sunset made the stone around it glow like bronze. Chimes light as birdsong and deep as bells rang when the breeze stirred them. If the view had been designed to humble those who came to it, the designer could rest well. Maati, he realized, had lived in this place, studied in it. And he, Otah, had refused it. He wondered what it would have been like, coming down this road as a boy coming to his reward; what it would have been like to see this grandeur set out before him as if it were his right.

The path to the grand offices was easily found, and well peopled. Firekeepers—not members of the utkhaiem, but servants only of the Dai-kvo—kept kilns at the crossroads and teahouses and offered the promise of warmth and comfort in the falling night. Otah didn't pause at them.

He reached the grand offices: a high, arched hall open to the west so that the sunset set the white stone walls ablaze. Men—only men, Otah noted—paced through the hall on one errand or another, passing from one corridor to another, through doors of worked rosewood and oak. Otah had to stop a servant who was lighting lanterns to find the way to the Dai-kvo's overseer.

He was an old man with a kind face in the brown robes of a poet. When Otah approached his table, the overseer took a pose that was both welcome and query with a flowing grace that he had seen only in the Khai Saraykeht or the andat. Otah replied with a pose of greeting, and for an instant, he was a boy again in the cold, empty hallways of the school.

"I've come with a letter for the Dai-kvo," he said, pushing the memory aside. "From Maati Vaupathi in Saraykeht."

"Ah?" the overseer said, "Excellent. I will see that he gets it immediately."

The beautiful, old hand reached to him, open to accept the packet still in Otah's sleeve. Otah considered the withered fingers like carved wood, a sudden alarm growing in him.

"I had hoped to see the Dai-kvo myself," he said, and the overseer's expression changed to one of sympathy.

"The Dai-kvo is very busy, my friend. He hardly has time to speak to me, and I'm set to schedule his days. Give the letter to me, and I will see that he knows of it."

Otah pulled the letter out and handed it over, a profound disappointment blooming in his breast. It was obvious, of course, that the Dai-kvo wouldn't meet with simple couriers, however sensitive the letters they bore. He shouldn't have expected him to. Otah took a pose of gratitude.

"Will you be staying to carry a reply?"

"Yes," Otah said. "If there is one."

"I will send word tomorrow whether the most high intends to respond. Where will I find you?"

Otah took a pose of apology and explained that he had not taken rooms and didn't know the village. The overseer gave him a recommendation, directions, and the patience Otah imagined a grandfather might have for a well-loved but rather slow grandchild. It was twilight—the distant skyline glorious with the gold and purple of the just-set sun—when Otah returned to the street, his errand complete.

On the way back down, there was time to see the village more closely, though the light around him was fading. It struck him for the first time that he had seen no women since he had left the road. The firekeeper's kilns, the food carts and stalls, the inn to which he'd been directed—all were overseen by men. None of the people passing him in the steep, dim street had a woman's face.

And as he looked more closely, he found other signs, subtler ones, that the life of the Dai-kvo's village was unlike that of the ones he had known. The streets had none of the grime and dust of Saraykeht—no small plants or grasses pushed at the joints of the paving stones, no moss stained the corners of the walls. Even more than its singularity of gender, the unnatural perfection of the place made it seem foreign and unsettling and sterile.

He ate his dinner—venison and wine and fresh black bread—sitting alone at a low table with his back to the fire. A dark mood had descended on him. Visions of Liat and some small house, some simple work, bread cooked in his own kiln, meat roasted in his own kitchens seemed both ludicrous and powerful. He had done what he said he'd set out for. The letter was in the Dai-kvo's hands, or would be shortly.

But he had come for his own reasons too. He was Otah, the sixth son of the Khai Machi, who had walked away from the greatest power in all the nations. He had been offered the chance to control the andat and refused. For the first time, here in this false village, he imagined what that must be to his brothers, his teachers, the boys who had taken the offer gladly when it had been given. To men like Maati.

And so who was this Itani Noyga, this simple laborer with simple dreams? He had come halfway across the lands of the Khaiem, he realized, to answer that question, and instead he had handed an old man a packet of papers. He remembered, setting out from Saraykeht, that it had seemed an important adventure, not only to Heshai and Seedless, the Khai Machi and Saraykeht, but to himself personally. Now, he wasn't sure why he'd thought delivering a letter would mean more than delivering a letter.

He was given a small room, hardly large enough for the stretched-canvas cot and the candle on the table beside it. The blankets were warm and thick and soft. The mattress was clean and free of lice or fleas. The room smelled of cut cedar, and not rat piss or unbathed humanity. Small as it was, it was also perfect.

The candle was snuffed, and Otah more than half asleep when his door opened. A small man, bald as an egg, stepped in, a lantern held high. His round face was marked by two bushy eyebrows—black shot with white. Otah met his gaze, at first bleary, and then an instant later awake and alert. He took the pose of greeting he'd learned as a boy, he smiled sweetly and without sincerity.

"I am honored by your presence, most high Dai-kvo."

Tahi-kvo scowled and moved closer. He held the lantern close to Otah's face until the brightness of the flame made old teacher shadowy. Otah didn't look away.

"It *is* you."

"Yes."

"Show me your hands," his old teacher said. Otah complied, and the lantern shifted, Tahi-kvo leaning close, examining the callused palms. He bent so close, Otah could feel the breath on his fingertips. The old man's eyes were going.

"It's true then," Tahi-kvo said. "You're a laborer."

Otah closed his hands. The words were no surprise, but the sting of them was. He would have thought he was beyond caring what opinion Tahi-kvo held. He smiled his charming smile like a mask and kept his voice mild and amused.

"I've picked my own path," he said.

"It was a poor choice."

"It was mine to make."

The old man—Tahi-kvo, the Dai-kvo, the most powerful man in world—stood, shaking his head in disgust. His robes whispered as he moved—silk upon silk. He tilted his head like a malefic bird.

"I have consultations to make concerning the message you brought. It may take some days before I draft my reply."

Otah waited for the stab of words or the remembered whir of the lacquer rod, but Tahi only stood waiting. At length Otah took a pose of acceptance.

"I will wait for it," he said.

For a moment, something glittered in Tahi-kvo's eyes that might have been sorrow or impatience, and then without farewell, he was gone, the door closed behind him, and Otah lay back in his bed. The darkness was silent, except for the slowly retreating footsteps. They were long vanished before Otah's heart and breath slowed, before the heat in his blood cooled.

THE DAYS THAT FOLLOWED WERE AMONG THE MOST DIFFICULT OF AMAT KYAAN'S life. The comfort house was in disarray, and her coup only added to the chaos. Each individual person—whores, guards, the men at the tables, the men who sold wine, all of them—were testing her. Three times, fights had broken out. It seemed once a day that she was called on to stop some small liberty, and always with the plaintive explanation that Ovi Niit had allowed it. To hear it told now, he had been the most selfless and open-handed of men. Death had improved him. It was to be expected.

If that had been all, it might not have kept her awake in the nights. But also there was the transfer of Maj into the house. No one else spoke Nippu, and Maj hadn't picked up enough of the Khaiate tongue to make herself understood easily. Since she'd come, Amat had been interrupted for her needs, whatever they were, whenever they came.

Torish Wite, thankfully, had proved capable in more ways than she'd hoped. When she asked him, he had agreed to spread the word at the seafront that Amat Kyaan in the soft quarter was looking for information about shipments of pearls from Galt. Building the case against House Wilsin would be like leading a second life. The comfort house would fund it, once she had the place in order, but the time was more a burden than the money. She was not so young as she had been.

These early stages, at least, she could leave to the mercenary, though some nights, she would remember conversations she'd had with traders from the Westlands and the implications for trading with a freehold or ward that relied on paid soldiery. As long as she was in a position to offer these men girls and money, they would likely stay. If they ever became indispensable, she was doomed.

Her room, once Ovi Niit's, was spacious and wide and covered—desk, bed, and floor—with records and papers and plans. The morning sun sloped through windows whose thick, tight-fit shutters were meant to let her sleep until evening. She sipped from a bowl of tea while Mitat, her closest advisor in the things specifically of the house, paced the length of the room. The papers in her hands hissed as she shifted from one to another and back.

"It's too much," Mitat said. "I honestly never thought I'd say it, but you're giving them too much freedom. To choose which men they take? Amat-cha, with all respect, you're a whoremonger. When a man comes in with the silver, it's your place to give him a girl. Or a boy. Or three girls and a chicken, if that's what he's paid for. If the girls can refuse a client . . ."

"They take back less money," Amat said, her voice reasonable and calm, though she already knew that Mitat was right. "Those who work most, get most. And with that kind of liberty and the chance to earn more, we'll attract women who want to work in a good house."

Mitat stopped walking. She didn't speak, but her guarded expression was enough. Amat closed her eyes and leaned back in her seat.

"Don't beat them without cause," Mitat said. "Don't let anyone cut them where it would scar. Give them what they're owed. That's all you can do now, grandmother. In a year—two, perhaps—you could try something like this, but to do it now would be a sign of weakness."

"Yes. I suppose it would. Thank you, Mitat-cha."

When she opened her eyes again, the woman had taken a pose of concern. Amat answered with one of reassurance.

"You seem tired, grandmother."

"It's nothing."

Mitat hesitated visibly, then handed back the papers. Before Amat could ask what was troubling her, steps came up the stairs and a polite knock interrupted them. Torish Wite stepped in, his expression guarded.

"There's someone here to see you," he said to Amat.

"Who?"

"Marchat Wilsin."

Her belly went tight, but she only took in a deep breath.

"Is anyone with him?"

"No. He stinks a little of wine, but he's unarmed and he's come alone."

"Where's Maj?" she asked.

"Asleep. We've made your old cell a sleeping chamber for her."

"Set a guard on her room. No one's to go in, and she's not to come out. I don't want him knowing that we have her here."

"You're going to see him?" Mitat asked, her voice incredulous.

"He was my employer for decades," Amat said, as if it were an answer to the question. "Torish-cha. I'll want a man outside the door. If I call out, I want him in here immediately. If I don't, I want privacy. We'll finish our conversation later, Mitat."

The pair retreated, closing the door behind them. Amat rose, taking up her cane and walking to the doors that opened onto the private deck. It had rained in the night, and the air was still thick with it. It was that, Amat told herself, that made it hard to breathe. The door opened behind her, then closed again. She didn't turn at once. Across the deck, the soft quarter flowed street upon street, alley upon alley. Banners flew and beggars sang. It was a lovely city, even this part. This was why she was doing what she'd done. For this and for the girl Maj and the babe she'd lost. She steeled herself.

Marchat Wilsin stood at the doorway in a robe of green so deep and rich it seemed shot with black. His face was grayish, his eyes bloodshot. He looked frightened and lost, like a mouse surrounded by cats. He broke her heart.

"Hello, old friend," she said. "Who'd have thought we'd end here, eh?"

"Why are you doing this, Amat?"

The pain in his voice almost cracked it. She felt the urge to go to him, comfort him. She wanted badly to touch his hand and tell him that everything would end well, in part because she knew that it wouldn't. It occurred to her distantly that if she had let him profess love for her, she might not have been able to leave House Wilsin.

"What happened to the poet. To the girl. It was an attack," she said. "You know it, and I do. You attacked Saraykeht."

He walked forward, his hands out, palms up before him.

"*I* didn't," he said. "Amat, you have to see that this wasn't my doing."

"Can I offer you tea?" she asked.

Bewildered, he sank onto a divan and ran his hands through his hair in wordless distress. She remembered the man she'd first met—his dark hair, his foreign manners. He'd had an easy laugh back then, and power in his gaze. She poured a bowl of tea for him. When he didn't take it from her hand, she left it on the low table at his knee and went back to her own desk.

"It didn't work, Amat. It failed. The poet's alive, the andat's still held. They see that it can't work, and so it won't happen again, if you'll only let this go."

"I can't," she said.

"Why not?"

"Because of what you did to Maj. She wanted that child. And because Saraykeht is my home. And because you betrayed me."

Marchat flushed red and took a pose so sloppy it might have meant anything.

"Betrayed you? How did I betray you? I did everything to keep you clear of this. I warned you that Oshai was waiting for you. And when you came back I was the one who argued for keeping you alive. I risked my life for yours."

"You made me part of this," Amat said, surprised to hear the anger in her own voice, to feel the warmth in her face. "You did this and you put me in a position where I have to sacrifice everything—*everything*—in order to redeem myself. If I had known in time, I would have stopped it. You knew that when you asked me to find you a bodyguard. You hoped I'd find a way out."

"I wasn't thinking clearly then. I am now."

"Are you? How can I do anything besides this, Marchat-kya? If I keep silent, it's as much as saying I approve of the crime. And I don't."

His eyes shifted, his gaze going hard. Slowly, he lifted the bowl of tea to his lips and drank it down in one long draw. When he put the bowl down—ceramic clicking against the wooden table—he was once again the man she'd known. He had put his heart aside, she knew, and entered the negotiation that might save his life, his house. Might, if he could convince her, even save her from the path she'd chosen. She felt a half-smile touch her lips. A part of her hoped he might win.

"Granted, something wrong was done," he said. "Granted, I had some part— though I didn't have a choice in it. But put aside that I was coerced. Put aside that it was none of it my plan. Let me ask you this—what justice do you expect?"

"I don't know," she said. "That's for the Khai and his men to choose."

He took a pose that showed his impatience with her.

"You know quite well the mercy he'll show me and House Wilsin. And Galt as a whole. And it won't be for Maj. It'll be for himself."

"It will be for his city."

"And how much is a city worth, Amat? Even in the name of justice. If the Khai chooses to kill a thousand Galtic babies out of their mothers, is that a fair price for a city? If they starve because our croplands go sterile, is that a fair price? You want justice, Amat. I know that. But the end of this road is only vengeance."

A breeze thick with the smell of the sea shifted the window cloths. The doors to the private deck shifted closed with a clack, and the room went dim.

"You're thinking with your heart," he continued. "What happened was terrible. I don't deny it. We were caught up in something huge and grotesque and evil. But be clear of the cost. One child. How many women miscarry in a single year? How many lose their children from being beaten by their men, or from falling, or from illness? I can think of six in the last five months. What happened was wrong, Amat, and I swear to you I will do what I can to make it right again. But not at the cost of making things worse."

He leaned forward. Her retort was finding its shape in her mind, but not quickly.

"They see now that it can't work," he said. "They weren't able to be rid of Seedless when he was *conspiring* with them. They can see now that they'd never be able to coordinate freeing all of them at once. The experiment *failed*.

Sure they may try something again someday, but not anytime soon. They'll turn their efforts back to the Westlands, or maybe to the south, or the islands for the time being. The war won't come here. Not unless they find some way to do it safely."

Amat's blood went cold, and she looked at her hands to avoid letting the shock show in her eyes. Trade, she had thought. With Seedless gone, trade would shift. Her city would suffer, and other cotton markets would flourish. She'd been thinking too small. Eight generations without war. Eight generations of the wealth that the andat commanded, the protection they gave. This was not trade. This was the first step toward invasion, and he thought she'd known it.

She forced herself to smile, to look up. Without the andat, the cities would fall. The wealth of the Khaiem would go to pay for what mercenaries they could hire. But faced with the soldiery of Galt, Amat doubted many companies would choose to fight for a clearly losing side, or would keep their contracts with the Khaiem if they made them.

Everything she knew would end.

"Come back to the house," Marchat said. "It's almost time for the end of season negotiations, and I need you there. I need you back."

She called out sharply, and the guard was in the room. Marchat—her old friend, her employer, the hard-headed, funny, thoughtful man whose house had saved her from the streets, the man who loved her and had never had the courage to say it—looked lost. Amat took a pose of farewell appropriate to the beginning of a long absence. She was fairly sure he wouldn't catch the nuance of permanence in it, but perhaps it was more for herself than him anyway.

"The past was a beautiful place, Marchat-kya," she said. "I miss it already."

And then, to the guard.

"See him out."

HESHAI'S IMPROVEMENT, WHEN IT CAME, WAS SUDDEN AS A CHANGE IN THE WEATHER. Liat was in the main room of the poet's house peeling an orange. Maati had gone up to his room for something, telling her to wait there. The steps that descended behind her were slow and heavy, as if Maati were bearing a large and awkward burden. She turned, and instead found Heshai washed and shaved and wrapped in a formal robe.

Liat started to her feet and took a pose of greeting appropriate to one of a much higher station. On the seat where she'd been, the long golden length of peel still clung to the white flesh of the orange. The poet sketched a brief pose of welcome and moved over to her, his gaze on the fruit. His smile, when it came, was unsure, a configuration unfamiliar to the wide lips. Liat wondered whether she had ever seen the man laugh.

"I don't suppose there's enough of that to share with an old man?" he said. He seemed almost shy.

"Of course," she said, picking up the orange and splitting off a section. He accepted it from her with a pose of thanks and popped it in his mouth. His skin was pale as the belly of a fish, and there were dark sacks under his eyes. He had grown thinner in the weeks since the sad trade had gone wrong. Still, when he grinned at her, his smile finding its confidence, she found herself smiling back. For a moment, she could see clearly what he had looked like as a child.

"You seem much better," she said.

"Tired of moping around, I suppose," he said. "I thought I might go out. I haven't been to a good teahouse in some time."

The lighter footsteps she knew came down the stairs behind them and stopped. Maati had forgotten the book in his hand. His mouth was open.

"Come down," Heshai said. "It isn't a private conversation. We were only sharing a bite. There's enough for you too, I imagine."

"Heshai-kvo . . ."

"I was just telling Liat-kya here that I've decided to stretch my legs this evening. I've been too much within myself. And tomorrow, there are things we should do. It's past time we began your education in earnest, eh?"

Maati took a pose of agreement made clumsy by the volume in his hand, but Liat could see that he was hardly aware of it. She caught his gaze, encouraging him silently to be pleased, or if he wasn't, to act as if he were.

"I will be ready, Heshai-kvo," he said. If there was an edge to his voice, Heshai seemed not to hear it. He only took a pose of farewell to Liat more formal than her rank called for, and a subtler pose of congratulation to Maati that she was fairly certain she had not been meant to see, and then he was off. They sat on the steps up to the house and watched him striding over the bridge and along the path until it turned. Maati, beside her, was trembling with rage.

"I thought this was what we wanted," Liat said, gently.

He snapped his head, her words pulling him back to the world.

"Not like this," he said.

"He's out of his bed. He's going into the city."

"It's like nothing happened," Maati said. "He's acting like nothing happened. All these weeks, just vanished . . ."

Liat smoothed his neck with her palm. For a moment, Maati went tight, then, slowly, she felt him relax. He turned to her.

"You wanted an apology," she said. "Or some recognition for what you did for him all this time."

Maati put down the book on the step beside him and pulled his robe closer around him. For a long time, they didn't speak. The trees were turning, the first fallen leaves covering the grounds. It wasn't winter, but autumn had reached its center.

"It's wrong of me," Maati said, his voice thick with shame and anger. "I should accept that he's improving and be pleased. But . . ."

"This may be the best he can do," Liat said. "Give him time."

Maati nodded and took her hand in his, their fingers laced. With her other hand, she reached across him and took up the book. It was old, and heavy for its size, bound in copper and leather.

"Read me that poem you were talking about," she said.

Much later, the darkness fallen, Liat lay with Maati on his cot and listened to his breath. The breeze that stirred the netting raised gooseflesh on her arms, but he was soft and warm as a cat against her. She stroked his hair. She felt safe and content and sick with guilt. She had never been unfaithful to a lover before this. She had always imagined it would be difficult, that people would stare at her in the streets and talk of her in scandalized whispers. In the event, it seemed no one cared. The isolation that had come after Seedless and the baby—from Amat, from Wilsin-cha, from the people of the house, and worst from Itani—was easier to bear with Maati. And he could listen when she spoke about her part, her failings, the way she'd let the child die.

The night candle fluttered, and three slow moths beat at the walls of its glass lantern. Liat shifted and Maati murmured in his sleep and turned away from her. She parted the netting and stood naked, letting the cool of night wash over her. Their coupling had left her feeling sticky. She thought of going to a bathhouse, but the long walk through the city after dark and the prospect of leaving Maati behind failed to appeal. It would be better, she thought, to stay near, even if it meant being cold. She deserved, she supposed, a little discomfort for her sins. She pulled on her robe, but didn't tie the fastenings.

In the darkness, stars spilled across the sky. The distant lights of the palaces, of the city, might almost not have been. Liat considered the crescent moon, its shining curve of light cupping a darkness of blotted stars. Frogs and crickets sang and the manicured grass at the side of the koi pond tickled the bottom of her feet. She looked around carefully before shrugging out of her robe. The water of the pond was no worse than she might find in the cold pool of a bathhouse. The fish darted away from her and then slowly returned. Reeds at the water's edge rubbed against each other with a sound like hands on skin, disturbed by the waves of her movements.

Floating on her back, her legs kicking slowly, she thought of Itani. She didn't feel as if she were betraying him, though she knew that she was. Maati and Itani—Otah—seemed to inhabit entirely different places in her heart. The one seemed so little related to the other. Itani was her heartmate, the man she'd shared her bed with for months. Maati was her friend, her confidant, her only support in a world empty even of the other man. For hours at a time and especially in his company, she could forget the guilt and the dread. She didn't know how it could be like this: so easy and so difficult both.

The chill touched her bones, and she turned, swimming easily to the shore. The rich mud squelched between her toes. Against wet flesh, the air was much colder than the water had been. By the time she found her robe, she was shivering. The night around her was silent, the insects and night birds gone still.

"There must be some etiquette to address situations like this," Seedless said from the darkness, "but I'm sure I don't know what it is."

The andat's face seemed hung in the air, the pale lips quirked in a smile both amused and grim. He moved forward as she pulled on her robe. His cloak—black shot with blue—seemed to weave in and out of the darkness. He pulled something bulky from a sleeve and held it out to her. A hair cloth.

"I brought this for you," he said. "Once I understood what you were doing I thought you'd want it."

Liat took it, falling into a pose of gratitude by reflex. The andat returned it dismissively, squatted on the grassy slope and, his arms resting on his knees, looked out over the pond.

"You got out of the torture box."

"One of them. Heshai-kvo let me out. He's been doing it for several days now on the condition that I promise to stay within sight of the house. I've sworn a sacred oath, though I imagine I'll break it eventually. It's why he's improving. Locking away a part of yourself—especially a shameful one—gives that part power over all the rest. It's the danger of splitting yourself in two, don't you find?"

"I don't know what you mean," Liat said.

Seedless smiled in genuine amusement.

"Dry your hair," he said. "I'm not judging you, my dear. I'm a babykiller. You're a girl of seventeen summers who's taken a second lover. It hardly gives me the high ground."

Liat wrapped her hair in the cloth and turned to leave, dry leaves stirring at her ankles. The words that stopped her were so soft, she might almost have imagined them.

"I know about Otah."

She paused. As if on cue, the chorus of crickets began again.

"What do you know?" she asked.

"Enough."

"How?"

"I'm clever. What do you intend to do when he comes back?"

Liat didn't answer. The andat turned to consider her. He took a pose that unasked the question. Anger flashed in Liat's breast.

"I love him. He's my heartmate."

"And Maati?"

"I love him, too."

"But he isn't your heartmate."

Liat didn't reply. In the dim light of moon and star, the andat smiled sadly and took a pose that expressed understanding and sympathy and acceptance.

"Maati and I . . . we need each other. We're alone otherwise. Both of us are very, very alone."

"Well, at least that won't last. He'll be back very soon," Seedless said. "To-morrow, perhaps. Or the day after."

"Who?"

"Otah."

Liat felt her breath go shallow. It was a sensation quite like fear.

"No, he won't. He can't."

"I think he can," the andat replied.

"It's a full three weeks just to Yalakeht. Even if he took a fast boat up the river, he'd only just be arriving now."

"You're sure of that?"

"Of course I am."

"Then I suppose I must be mistaken," the andat said so mildly that Liat had no answer. Seedless laughed then and put his head in his hands.

"What?" Liat asked.

"I've been an idiot. Otah is the Otah-kvo that Maati told me of. He doesn't wear a brand and he's not a poet, so I never connected them. But if Maati's sent him to see the Dai-kvo . . . Yes. He must be."

"I thought you knew all about Otah," Liat said, her heart falling.

"That may have been an exaggeration. Otah-kvo. A black robe who didn't take the brand or become a poet. I think . . . I think I heard a story like that once. Well, a few questions of Heshai, and I'm sure I can dredge it up."

The horror of what she'd done flooded her. Liat didn't sit so much as give way. The leaves crackled under her weight. The andat looked over to her, alarmed.

"You tricked me," she whispered.

Seedless tilted his head with an odd, sensual smile as much pity as wonderment. He took a pose offering comfort.

"It wasn't you, Liat-kya. Maati told me all about it before he even knew who I was. If you've betrayed your heartmate tonight—and, really, I think there's a strong argument that you have—it wasn't with me. And whether you believe it or not, the secret's safe."

"I don't. I don't believe you."

The andat smiled, and for a moment the sincerity in his face reminded her of Heshai-kvo.

"Having a secret is like sitting at a roof's edge with a rock, Liat. As long as you have the rock, you have the power of life and death over anyone below you. Drop the rock, and you've just got a nice view. I won't spread your secret unless it brings me something, and as it stands, there's no advantage to me. Unless things change, I won't be telling any of your several secrets."

Liat took a pose of challenge.

"Swear it," she said.

"To whom are you talking? How likely am I to be bound by an oath to you?"

Liat let her arms fall to her sides.

"I won't betray you," Seedless said, "because there's no reason to, and because it would hurt Maati."

"Maati?"

Seedless shrugged.

"I'm fond of him. He's . . . he's young and he hasn't lived in the world for very long, perhaps. But he has the talent and charm to escape this if he's wise."

"You sound like Heshai when you say that."

"Of course I do."

"Do you . . . I mean, you don't *really* care about Maati. Do you?"

Seedless stood. He moved with the grace and ease of a thrown stone. His robe hung from him, darker than the night. His face was the perfect white of a carnival mask, smooth as eggshell and as expressionless. The crickets increased their chirping songs until they were so loud, Liat was surprised that she could hear Seedless' voice, speaking softly over them.

"In ten years time, Liat-kya, look back at this—at what you and I said here, tonight. And when you do, ask yourself which of us was kinder to him."

15

The days passed with an exquisite discomfort in the village of the Dai-kvo. The clear air, the cold stone of the streets, the perfection, the maleness and austerity and beauty were like a dream. Otah moved through the alleyways and loitered with other men by the firekeepers' kilns, listening to gossip and the choir of windchimes. Messengers infested the village like moths, fluttering here and there. Speakers from every city, dressed in sumptuous robes and cloaks, appeared every day and vanished again. The water tasted strange from influence, the air smelled of power.

While Otah had been lifting bales of cotton all day and pulling ticks out of his arms in the evenings, Maati had lived in these spaces. Otah went to his rooms each night, sick with waiting, and wondering who he would have been, had he taken the old Dai-kvo's offer. And then, he would remember the school—the cruelty, the malice, the cold-hearted lessons and beatings and the laughter of the strong at the weak—and he wondered instead how Maati had brought himself to accept.

In the afternoon of his fifth day, a man in the white robes of a high servant found him on the wide wooden deck of a teahouse.

"You are the courier for Maati Vaupathai?" the servant asked, taking a pose both respectful and querying. Otah responded with an affirming pose. "The most high wishes to speak with you. Please come with me."

The library was worked in marble; tall shelves filled with scrolls and bound volumes lined the walls, and sunlight shone through banks of clerestory windows with glass clear as air. Tahi-kvo—the Dai-kvo—sat at long table of carved blackwood. An iron brazier warmed the room, smelling of white smoke and hot metal and incense. He looked up as the servant took a pose of completion and readiness so abjectly humble as to approach the ludicrous. Otah took no pose.

"Go," the Dai-kvo said, and the white-robed servant left, pulling the wide doors closed behind him. Otah stood as Tahi-kvo considered him from under frowning brows then pushed a sewn letter across the table. Otah stepped forward and took it, tucking it into his sleeve. They stood for a moment in silence.

"You were stupid to come," Tahi-kvo said, his tone matter-of-fact. "If your brothers find you're alive they'll stop eyeing each other and work in concert to kill you."

"I suppose they might. Will you tell them?"

"No." Tahi-kvo rose and stalked to a bookshelf, speaking over his shoulder as he went. "My master died, you know. The season after you left."

"I'm sorry," Otah said.

"Why did you come? Why *you*?"

"Maati is a friend. And there was no one else who could be trusted." The other reasons weren't ones he would share with Tahi-kvo. They were his own.

Tahi-kvo ran his fingers across the spines of the books. Even turned almost away, Otah could see the bitterness in his smile.

"And he trusts you? He trusts Otah Machi? Well, he's young. Perhaps he doesn't know you so well as I do. Do you want to know what's in this letter I'm sending with you?"

"If he cares to tell me," Otah said.

The volume Tahi-kvo pulled down was ancient—bound in wood with clasps of metal and thick as a hand spread wide. He hefted it back and laid it on the table before he answered.

"It says he mustn't let Heshai lose control of his andat. It says there isn't a replacement for it, and that there isn't the prospect of one. If Seedless escapes, I have nothing to send, and Saraykeht becomes an oversized low town. That's what it says."

Tahi-kvo's eyebrows rose, challenging. Otah took a pose that accepted the lesson from a teacher—a pose he'd taken before, when he'd been a boy.

"Every generation, it's become more difficult," Tahi-kvo said, angry, it seemed, at speaking the words. "There are fewer men who take up the mantle. The andat that escape are more and more difficult to recapture. Even the fourth-water ones like Seedless and Unstung. The time will come—not for me, I think, but for my successor or his—when the andat may fail us entirely. The Khaiem will be overrun by Galts and Westerman. Do you understand what I'm telling you?"

"Yes," Otah said. "But not why."

"Because you had promise," Tahi-kvo said bitterly. "And because I don't like you. But I have to ask this. Otah Machi, have you come here with this letter because you've regretted your refusal? Was it an excuse to speak to me because you're seeking the robes of a poet?"

Otah didn't laugh, though the questions seemed absurd. Absurd and—as they mixed in his mind with the sights and scents of the village—more than half sad. And beneath all that, perhaps he had. Perhaps he had needed to come here and see the path he had chosen to know as a man whether he still believed in the choices he had made as a boy.

"No," he said.

Tahi-kvo nodded, undid the clasps on the great book and opened it. It was in no script Otah had ever seen. The poet looked up at him, his gaze direct and unpleasant.

"I thought not," he said. "Go then. And don't come back unless you decide you're man enough to take on the work. I don't have time to coddle children."

Otah took a pose of leave-taking, then hesitated.

"I'm sorry, Tahi-kvo," he said. "That your master died. That you had to live this way. All of it. I'm sorry the world's the way it is."

"Blame the sun for setting," the Dai-kvo said, not looking at him, not looking up.

Otah turned and walked out. The magnificence of the palaces was amazing, rich even past the Khai Saraykeht. The wide avenues outside it were crowded in the late afternoon with men going about business of the highest importance, dressed in silks and woven linen and leather supple as skin. Otah took in the majesty of it and understood for the first time since he'd come the hollowness that lay beneath it. It was the same, he thought, as the emptiness in Heshai-kvo's eyes. The one was truly a child of the other.

He was surprised, as he walked down to the edge of the village, to find himself moved to sorrow. The few tears that escaped him might have been shed for Maati or Heshai, Tahi-kvo or the boys of his cohort scattered now into the world, the vanity of power or himself. The question that had carried him here—whether he was truly Otah Machi or Itani Noyga; son of the Khaiem or seafront laborer—was unresolved, but it was also answered.

Either one, but never this.

"When?" Maj demanded, her arms crossed. Her cheeks were red and flushed, her breath smelled of wine. "I've been weeks living with whores and you, their pimp. You told me that the men who killed my child would be brought to justice. Now tell me *when*."

The island girl moved quickly, scooping up a vase from Amat's desk and throwing it against the far wall. The pottery shattered, flowers falling broken to the floor. The wet mark on the wall dripped and streaked. The guard was in the room almost before Amat could move, a knife the length of his forearm at the ready. Amat rose and pushed him back out despite his protests, closing the door behind him. Her hip ached badly. It had been getting worse these last weeks, and it added to everything else that made her irritable. Still, she held herself tall as she turned back to her sometime ally, sometime charge. The girl was breathing fast now, her chin jutting out, her arms pulled back. She looked like a little boy, daring someone to strike him. Amat smiled sweetly, took two slow strides, and slapped her smartly across the mouth.

"I am working from before the sun comes up to half through the night for you," Amat said. "I am keeping this filthy house so that I have the money we need to prosecute your case. I have ruined my life for you. And I haven't asked thanks, have I? Only cooperation."

There were tears brimming in Maj's pale eyes, streaking down her ruddy cheek. The anger that filled Amat's chest like a fire lessened. Moving more slowly, she walked to the mess against the far wall and, slowly, painfully, knelt.

"What I'm doing isn't simple," Amat said, not looking as she gathered the shards and broken flowers. "Wilsin-cha didn't keep records that would tie him directly to the trade, and the ones that do exist are plausible whether he knew of the treachery or not. I have to show that he did. Otherwise, you may as well go home."

The floor creaked with Maj's steps, but Amat didn't look up. Amat made a sack from the hem of her robe, dropped in the shattered vase and laid in the soft petals afterwards. The flowers, though destroyed, smelled lovely. She found herself reluctant to crush them. Maj crouched down beside her and helped clean.

"We've made progress," Amat said, her voice softer now. She could hear the exhaustion in her own words. "I have records of all the transactions. The pearls that paid the Khai came on a Galtic ship, but I have to find which one."

"That will be enough?"

"That will be a start," Amat said. "But there will be more. Torish-cha has had men on the seafront, offering payment for information. Nothing's come from it yet, but it will. These things take time."

Maj leaned close, placing a handful of debris into Amat's makeshift bag. She meant well, Amat knew, but she buried the flowers all the same. Amat met her gaze. Maj tried to smile.

"You're drunk," Amat said gently. "You should go and sleep. Things will look better in the morning."

"And worse again when night comes," Maj said and shook her head, then lurched forward and kissed Amat's mouth. As she left—awkward phrases in civilized languages passing between her and the guard at the door—Amat dropped the ruined vase into the small crate she kept beside her desk. Her flesh felt heavy, but there were books to be gone over, orders to place for the house and audits to be made.

She was doing the work, she knew, of three women. Had she seen forty fewer summers, it might have been possible. Instead, each day seemed to bring collapse nearer. She woke in the morning to a list of things that had to be completed—for the comfort house and for the case she was building inch by inch against House Wilsin—and fell asleep every night with three or four items still undone and the creeping sense that she was forgetting something important.

And the house, while it provided her the income she needed to pay for investigations and bribes and rewards, was just the pit of vipers that she'd been warned it would be. Mitat was her savior there—she knew the politics of the staff and had somehow won the trust of Torish Wite. Still, it seemed as if every decision had to be brought to Amat eventually. Whose indenture to end, whose to hold. What discipline to mete out against the women whose bodies were the produce she sold, what against the men who staffed the gambling tables and provided the wine and drugs. How to balance rule from respect and rule from fear. And Mitat, after all, had stolen from the house before. . . .

The night candle—visibly longer now and made of harder wax than the ones that measured the short nights of summer—was near its halfway mark when Amat put down her pen. Three times she added a column of numbers, and three times had found different sums. She shrugged out of her robes and pulled the netting closed around the bed, asleep instantly, but troubled by dreams in which she recalled something critical a hand's breadth too late.

She woke to a polite scratch at her door. When she called out her permission, Mitat entered bearing a tray. Two thick slices of black bread and a bowl of bitter tea. Amat sat up, pulled the netting aside, and took a pose of gratitude as the red-haired woman put the tray on the bed beside her.

"You're looking nicely put together this morning," Amat said.

It was true. Mitat wore a formal robe of pale yellow that went nicely with her eyes. She looked well-rested, which Amat supposed also helped.

"We have the payment to make to the watch," Mitat said. "I was hoping you might let me join you."

Amat closed her eyes. The watch monies. Of course. It would have been very poor form to forget that, but she nearly had. The darkness behind her eyelids was comfortable, and she stayed there for a moment, wishing that she might crawl back to sleep.

"Grandmother?"

"Of course," Amat said, opening her eyes again and reaching for the bowl of tea. "I could do with the company. But you'll understand if I handle the money."

Mitat grinned.

"You're never going to let me forget that, are you?"

"Likely not. Get me a good robe, will you. There's a blue with gray trim, I think, that should do for the occasion."

The streets of the soft quarter were quiet. Amat, her sleeve weighted by the boxed lengths of silver, leaned on her cane. The night's rain had washed the air, and sunlight, pale as fresh butter, shone on the pavements and made the banners of the great comfort houses shimmer. The baker's kilns filled the air with the scent of bread and smoke. Mitat walked beside her, acting as if the slow pace were the one she'd have chosen if she had been alone, avoiding the puddles of standing water where the street dipped, or where alleyways still disgorged a brown trickle of foul runoff. In the height of summer, the mixture of heat and damp would have been unbearable. Autumn's forgiving cool made the morning nearly pleasant.

Mitat filled in Amat Kyaan on the news of the house. Chiyan thought she might be pregnant. Torish-cha's men resented that they were expected to pay for the use of the girls—other houses in the quarter included such services as part of the compensation. Two weavers were cheating at tiles, but no one had caught them at it as yet.

"When we do, bring them to me," Amat said. "If they aren't willing to negotiate compensation with me, we'll call the watch, but I'd rather have it stay private."

"Yes, grandmother."

"And send for Urrat from the street of beads. She'll know if Chiyan's carrying by looking at her, and she has some teas that'll cure it if she is."

Mitat took a pose of agreement, but something in her expression—a softness, an amusement—made Amat respond with a query.

"Ovi Niit would have taken her out back and kicked her until she bled," Mitat said. "He would have said it was cheaper. I don't think you know how much you're respected, grandmother. The men, except Torish-cha and his, would still as soon see you hanged as not. But the girls all thank the gods that you came back."

"I haven't made the place any better."

"Yes," Mitat said, her voice accepting no denial. "You have. You don't see how the—"

The man lurched from the mouth of the alley and into Amat before she had time to respond. Her cane slipped as the drunkard staggered against her, and she stumbled. Pain shrieked from her knee to her hip, but her first impulse was to clutch the payment in her sleeve. The man, however, wasn't a thief. The silver for the watch was still where it had been and the drunk was in a pose of profound apology.

"What do you think you're doing?" Mitat demanded. Her chin was jutting out; her eyes burned. "It's hardly mid-day. What kind of man is already drunk?"

The thick man in the stained brown robe shook his head and bowed, his pose elegant and abasing.

"It is my fault," he said, his words slurred. "Entirely my fault. I've made an ass of myself."

Amat clutched Mitat's arm, silencing her, and stepped forward despite the raging ache in her leg. The drunkard bowed lower, shaking his head. Amat almost reached out to touch him—making certain that this wasn't a dream, that she wasn't back in her bed still waiting for her bread and tea.

"Heshai-cha?"

The poet looked up. His eyes were bloodshot and weary. The whites were yellow. He stank of wine and something worse. He seemed slowly to focus on her, and then, a heartbeat later, to recognize her face. He went gray.

"I'm fine, Heshai-cha. No damage done. But what brings—"

"I know you. You work for House Wilsin. You . . . you knew that girl?"

"Maj," Amat said. "Her name is Maj. She's being well taken care of, but you and I need to speak. What happened wasn't all it seemed. The andat had other parties who—"

"No! No, I was entirely to blame! It was my failing!"

The shutters of a window across the street opened with a clack and a curious face appeared. Heshai took a pose of regret spoiled only by his slight wavering, like a willow in a breeze. His lips hardened, and his eyes, when he opened them, were black. He looked at her as if she'd insulted him, and in that moment, Amat could see that the andat Seedless with his beautiful face and perfect voice had indeed been drawn from this man.

"I am making an ass of myself," he said. He bowed stiffly to her and to Mitat, turned, and strode unsteadily away.

"Gods!" Mitat said, looking after the wide, retreating back. "What was that?"

"The poet of Saraykeht," Amat said. She turned to consider the alley from which he'd emerged. It was thin—hardly more than a slit between buildings—unpaved, muddy and stinking of garbage.

"What's down there?" Amat asked.

"I don't know."

Amat hesitated, dreading what she knew she had to do next. If the mud was as foul as it smelled, the hems of her robe would be unsavable.

"Come," she said.

The apartment wasn't hard to find. The poet's unsteady footsteps had left fresh, sliding marks. The doorway was fitted with an iron lock, the shutters over the thin window beside it were barred from the inside. Amat, her curiosity too roused to stop now, rapped on the closed door and called, but no one came.

"Sometimes, if they don't want to be seen in the houses, men take rooms," Mitat said.

"Like this?"

"Better, usually," Mitat allowed. "None of the girls I know would want to follow a man down an alley like this one. If the payment was high enough, perhaps . . ."

Amat pressed her hand against the door. The wood was solid, sound. The lock, she imagined, could be forced, if she could find the right tools. If there was something in this sad secret place that was worth knowing. Something like dread touched her throat.

"Grandmother. We should go."

Amat took a pose of agreement, turning back toward the street. Curiosity balanced relief at being away from the private room of the poet of Saraykeht. She found herself wondering, as they walked to the offices of the watch, what lay behind that door, how it might relate to her quiet war, and whether she wanted to discover it.

WINTER CAME TO THE SUMMER CITIES. THE LAST LEAVES FELL, LEAVING BARE trees to sleep through the long nights. Cold mists rose, filling the streets with air turned to milk. Maati wore heavier robes—silk and combed wool. But not his heaviest. Even the depths of a Saraykeht winter were milder than a chilly spring in the north. Some nights Maati walked through the streets with Liat, his arm around her, and both of them hunched against the cold, but it was a rare thing to see his own breath in the air. In Pathai as a child, at the school, then with the Dai-kvo, Maati had spent most of his life colder than this, but the constant heat of the high seasons of Saraykeht had thinned his blood. He felt the cold more deeply now than he remembered it.

Heshai-kvo's return to health seemed to have ended the affair of the dead child in the minds of the utkhaiem. Over the weeks—the terribly short weeks—Heshai had taken him to private dinners and public feasts, had presented him to high families, and made it clear through word and action that Liat was welcome—was *always* welcome—at the poet's house. That Seedless had been given a kind of freedom seemed to displease the Khai Saraykeht and his nearest men, but no words were said and no action taken. So long as the poet was well enough to assuage the general unease, all was close enough to well.

The teahouse they had retreated to, he and Liat, was near the edge of the city proper. Buildings and streets ran further out, north along the river, but it was in this quarter that the original city touched the newer buildings. Newer buildings, Maati reflected, older than his grandfather's grandfather. And still they took the name.

They'd taken a private room hardly larger than a closet, with a small table and a bench against the wall that they both shared. Light and music and the scent of roast pork drifted though carved wood lacework, and a small brazier hung above them, radiating heat like a black iron sun.

Liat poured hot tea into her bowl, and then without asking, into his. Maati took a pose of thanks, and lifted the fine porcelain to his lips. The steam smelled rich and smoky, and Liat leaned against him, the familiar weight of her body comforting as blankets.

"He'll be back soon," Maati said.

Liat didn't stiffen, but stilled. He sipped his tea, burning his lips a little. He felt her shrug as much as seeing it.

"Let's not talk of it," she said.

"I can't keep on with this once he's come back. Half the time I feel like I've killed something as it stands. When he's here . . ."

"When he's here we'll have him with us," Liat said softly. "We both will. I'll have him as a lover, you'll have him as a friend. We'll none of us be alone."

"I'm not entirely hoping for it," Maati said.

"Parts will be difficult. Let's not talk about it. It'll come soon enough without borrowing it now." Maati took a pose of agreement, but a moment later Liat sighed and took his arm.

"I didn't mean to be cruel . . ."

"You haven't been," Maati said.

"You're kind to say so."

In the front of the house a woman or a child began singing—the voice high and sweet and pure. The talking voices stilled and gave the song their silence. It was one that Maati had heard before many times, a traditional ballad of love found and lost that dated back to the days when the Empire still stood. Maati sat back, his spine pressing into the wall behind him, and laid his arm across Liat's shoulders. His head swam with emotions that he could only partly name. He closed his eyes and let the ancient words and old grammars wash over him. He felt Liat shudder. When he looked, her face was flushed, her mouth drawn tight. Tears glistened in her eyes.

"Let's go home," he said, and she nodded. He took six lengths of copper from a pouch in his sleeve and left them in a row on the table—it would more than cover the charges. Together, they rose, pushed aside the door and slipped out. The song continued on as they stepped out into the darkness. The moon was just past new, and the streets were dark except for the torches at crossroads where large streets met, and, elsewhere, lit by the kilns of the firekeepers. They walked arm in arm, heading north.

"Why do they call you poets?" Liat asked. "You don't really declaim poetry. Or, I mean, we have, but not as what you do for the Khai."

"There are other terms," Maati said. "You could also call us shapers or makers. Thought-weavers. It's from the binding."

"The andat. They're poems?"

"They're like poems. They're translations of an idea into a form that includes volition. When you take a letter in the Khaiate tongue and translate it into Galtic, there are different ways you could word it, to get the right meaning. The binding is like translating a letter perfectly from one language to another. You make it clear, and the parts that aren't there—if there isn't quite the right word in Galtic, for instance—you create them so that the whole thing holds together. The old grammars are very good for that work."

"What do you do with it? With the description?"

"You hold it in your mind. Forever."

The words lapsed. They walked. The high walls of the warehouse district stopped and the lower buildings of the weavers took up. The palaces at the top of the city glittered with lanterns and torches, like the field of stars pulled down and overlapping the earth until they were obscured again by high walls, now of the homes of merchants and lesser trading houses.

"Have you ever been in the summer cities for Candles Night?" Liat asked.

"No," Maati said. "I've seen the Dai-kvo's village, though. It was beautiful there. All the streets were lined with people, and the light made the whole mountain feel like a temple."

"You'll like it here," Liat said. "There's likely more wine involved than with the Dai-kvo."

Maati smiled in the darkness and pulled her small, warm body closer to him.

"I imagine so," he said. "At the school, we didn't—"

The blow was so sudden, Maati didn't really have time to feel it. He was on the ground. The stones of the street were rough against his skinned palms, and he was consumed by a sense of urgency whose object he could not immediately identify. Liat lay unmoving beside him. A roof tile—six hands square and three fingers deep of baked red clay—rested between them like an abandoned pillow. A scraping sound like rats in plaster walls caught Maati's crippled attention and another tile fell, missing them both, detonating on the street at Liat's side. Maati's panic found its focus. He lurched toward her. Blood soaked her robe at the shoulder. Her eyes were closed.

"Liat! Wake up! The tiles are loose!"

She didn't answer. Maati looked up, his hands shaking though he wasn't aware of the fear, only of the terrible need to act immediately trapped against his uncertainty of what action to take. No other tile moved, but something—a bird, a squirrel, a man's head?—ducked back over the roof's lip. Maati put his hand on Liat's body and willed his mind into something nearer to order. They were in danger here. They had to move away from the wall. And Liat couldn't.

Carefully he took her by the shoulders and dragged her. Each step made his ribs shriek, but he took her as far as the middle of the street before the pain was too much. Kneeling over her, fighting to breathe, Maati's fear turned at last to panic. For a long airless moment, Maati convinced himself that she wasn't breathing. A shifting of her bloody robe showed him otherwise. Help. They needed help.

Maati stood and staggered. The street was empty, but a wide ironwork gate opened to rising marble steps and a pair of wide wooden doors. Maati pushed himself toward it, feeling as if he was at one remove from his own muscles, as if his body was a puppet he didn't have the skill to use well. It seemed to him, hammering on the wide doors, that no one would ever come. He wiped the sweat from his brow only to discover it was blood.

He was trying to decide whether he had the strength to go looking for another door, a firekeeper, a busier street, when the door swung open. An old man, thin as sticks, looked out at him. Maati took a pose that begged.

"You have to help her," he said. "She's hurt."

"Gods!" the man said, moving forward, supporting Maati as he slid down to the steps. "Don't move, my boy. Don't move. Chiyan! Out here! Hurry! There's children hurt!"

Tell Otah-kvo, Maati thought, but was too weak to say. *Find Otah-kvo and tell him. He'll know what to do.*

He found himself in a well-lit parlor without recalling how he'd come there. A younger man was prodding at his head with something painful. He tried to push the man's arm away, but he was nearly too weak to move. The man said something that Maati acknowledged and then immediately forgot. Someone helped him to drink a thin, bitter tea, and the world faded.

16

>+< Marchat Wilsin woke from an uneasy sleep, soft footsteps in the corri-
dor enough to disturb him. When the knock came, he was already sitting up. Epani pushed the door open and stepped in, his face drawn in the
flickering light of the night candle.

"Wilsin-cha . . ."

"It's him, isn't it?"

Epani took a pose of affirmation, and Marchat felt the dread that had troubled his sleep knot itself in his chest. He put on a brave show, pushing aside
the netting with a sigh, pulling on a thick wool robe. Epani didn't speak.
Amat, Marchat thought, would have said something.

He walked alone to his private hall. The door of it stood open, lantern light
spilling out into the corridor. A black form passed in front of it, pacing, agitated, blocking out the light. The knot in Marchat Wilsin's chest grew solid—a
stone in his belly. He drew himself up and walked in.

Seedless paced, his pale face as focused as a hunting cat's. His robe—black
shot with red—blended with the darkness until he seemed a creature half of
shadow. Marchat took a pose of welcome which the andat ignored except for
the distant smile that touched his perfect lips.

"It was an accident," Marchat said. "They didn't know it was him. They
were only supposed to kill the girl."

Seedless stopped. His face was perfectly calm, his eyes cool. Anger radiated
from him like a fire.

"You hurt my boy," he said.

"Blame Amat, if you have to blame anyone," Wilsin said. "It's her vendetta
that's driving this. She's trying to expose us. She's dedicating her life to it, so
don't treat this like it's something I chose."

Seedless narrowed his eyes. Marchat forced himself not to look away.

"She's close," he said. "She's looking at shipments of pearls from Galtic ports
and tying them to the payment. With the money she's offering, it's a matter of
time before she gets what she's looking for. Leaving Liat be would have
been . . . The girl could damage us. If it came before the Khai, she might damage us."

"And yet your old overseer hasn't taken her apprentice into confidence?"

"Would you? Liat's a decent girl, but I wouldn't trust her with my laundry."

"You think she's incompetent?"

"No, I think she's *young*."

And that, oddly, seemed to touch something. The andat's anger shifted, lost its edge. Marchat took a free breath for the first time that night.

"So you chose to remove her from the field of play," Seedless said. "An accident of roof tiles."

"I didn't specify the tiles. Only that it should be plausible."

"You didn't tell them to avoid Maati?"

"I did. But gods! Those two are connected at the hip these days. The men . . . grew impatient. They thought they could do the job without damaging the poet boy."

"They were wrong."

"I know. It won't happen again."

The andat flowed forward, lifting himself up to sit on the meeting table beside the lantern. Marchat took a step back before he knew he had done it. The andat's pale fingers laced together and it smiled, an expression of such malice and beauty that it could never have been mistaken for human.

"If Maati had died," Seedless said, its voice low as distant thunder, "every crop in Galt would fail. Every cow and ewe would go barren. Your people would die. Do you understand that? There wouldn't have been a bargain struck or threats made. It would simply have happened, and no one might ever have known why. That boy is precious to you, because while he lives, your people live."

"You can't mean that," Marchat said, but sickeningly, he knew the andat was quite serious. He shook his head and adopted a pose of acknowledgement that he prayed would move the conversation elsewhere, onto some subject that didn't dance so near the cliff edge. "We need a plan. What to do if Amat makes her case to the Khai. If we don't have our defense prepared, she may convince him. She's good that way."

"Yes. She's always impressed me."

"So," Marchat said, sitting, looking up at the dark form above him. "What are we going to do? If she finds the truth and the proof of it, what then?"

"Then I do as I'm told. I'm a slave. It works that way with me. And you? You get your head and your sex shipped back to the Galtic High Council as an explanation for why a generation of Galtic babies are dropping out of their mother's wombs. That's only a guess, of course. The Khai might be lenient," Seedless grinned, "and stones may float on water, but I wouldn't want to rely on it."

"It's not so bad as that," Marchat said. "If you say that Oshai and his men—"

"I won't do that," the andat said, dismissing him as casually as an unwanted drink. "If it comes before the Khai Saraykeht and they ask me, I'll tell them what they want to know."

Marchat laughed. He couldn't help it, but even as he did, he felt the blood rushing away from his face. Seedless tilted his head like a bird.

"You can't," Marchat said. "You're as deep in this as I am."

"Of course I'm not, Wilsin-kya. What are they going to do to me, eh? I'm the blood their city lives on. If our little conspiracy comes to light, you'll pay the price of it, not me. What we've done, you and I, was lovely. The look on Heshai's face when that baby hit the bowl was worth all the weeks and months it took to arrange it. Really, it was brilliantly done. But don't think because we did something together once that we're brothers now. I'm playing new games, with other players. And this time, you don't signify."

"You don't mean that," Marchat said. The andat stood, its arms crossed, and considered the lantern flame.

"It would be interesting, destroying a nation," Seedless said, more than half, it seemed, to himself. "I'm not certain how Heshai would take it. But . . ."

The andat sighed and turned, stepping to Wilsin's chair and kneeling beside it. It seemed to Marchat that the andat smelled of incense and ashes. The pale hand pressed his knee and the vicious smile was like a blade held casually at his throat.

". . . but, Wilsin-kya, don't make the mistake again of thinking that you or your people matter to me. Our paths have split. Do you understand me?"

"You can't," Wilsin said. "We've been in this together from the start—you and the Council both. Haven't we done everything that you asked?"

"Yes. I suppose you have."

"You owe us something," Wilsin said, ashamed at the desperation he heard in his own voice.

The andat considered this, then slowly stood and took a pose of thanks that carried nuances of both dismissal and mockery.

"Then take my thanks," the andat said. "Wilsin-cha, you have been insincere, selfish, and short-sighted as a flea, but you were the perfect tool for the work, and for that, I thank you. Hurt Maati again, and your nation dies. Interfere with my plans, and I'll tell Amat Kyaan the full story and save her her troubles. This game's moved past you, little man. It's too big. Stay out if it."

THE DREAM, IF IT WAS A DREAM, WAS PAINFUL AND DISJOINTED. LIAT THOUGHT SHE heard someone crying, and thought it must be from the pain. But the pain was hers, and the weeping wasn't, so that could hardly be. She found herself in a rainstorm outside the temple, all the doors locked against her. She called and called, but no one opened the doors, and the patter of rain turned to the clicking of hail and the hailstones grew and grew until they were the size of a baby's fist, and all she could do was curl tight and let the ice strike her neck and the back of her head.

She woke—if the slow swimming up to lucidity was truly waking—with her head throbbing in pain. She lay on an unfamiliar bed—worked wood and brass—in a lavish room. A breeze came though the opened shutters and stirred the fine silk netting with the scent of rain. The rough cough and the clearing of a throat made her turn too quickly, and pain shot from her neck to her belly. She closed her eyes, overcome by it, and opened them to find the poet Heshai at the bedside in a pose of apology.

"I didn't see you were awake," he said, his wide mouth in a sheepish smile. "I'd have warned you I was here. You're in the Second Palace. I'd have taken you to the poet's house, but the physicians are nearer."

Liat tried to take a pose of casual forgiveness, but found that her right arm was strapped. She tried for the first time to understand where she was and how she'd come there. There had been something—a teahouse and Maati, and then . . . something. She pressed her left palm to her eyes, willing the pain to stop and give her room to think. She heard the rustle of cloth pulled aside, and the mattress dipped to her left where the poet sat beside her.

"Maati?" she asked.

"Fine," the poet said. "You took the worst of it. He had his brain rattled around a bit for him, and a shard cut his scalp above the ear. The physician says it's not such a bad thing for a boy to bleed a little when he's young, though."

"What happened?"

"Gods. Of course. You wouldn't know. Loose tiles, two of them. The ut-khaiem are fining the owner of the compound for not keeping his roof better repaired. Your shoulder and arm—no, don't move them. They're strapped like that for good cause. The first tile broke some bones rather badly. Once they found who Maati was, they brought you both to the Khai's palaces. The Khai's own physicians have been watching over you for the last three days. I asked for them myself."

Her mind seemed foggy. Simple as his explanation was, the details of the poet's words swam close, darted away. She took hold of one.

"Three days?" Liat asked. "I've been asleep for three days?"

"Not so much asleep," the poet admitted. "We've been giving you poppy milk for the pain. Maati's been here most of the time. I sent him off to rest this morning. I promised him I'd watch over you while he was gone. I have some tea, if you'd like it?"

Liat began to take a pose of thanks and the pain sang in her neck and shoulder. She paled and nodded. The poet stood slowly, trying, she could tell, not to jostle her. He was back in a moment, helping her to sip from a bowl of lemon tea, sweet with honey. Her stomach twisted at the intrusion, but her mouth and throat felt like the desert in a rainstorm. When he pulled the bowl back and helped her ease back down, Liat saw an odd expression on the poet's face—tenderness, she thought. She had always thought of Heshai as an ugly man, but in that light, at that moment, the wide lips and thinning hair seemed to transcend normal ideas of beauty. He looked strong and gentle. His movements were protective as a mother's and as fierce. Liat wondered why she'd never seen it before.

"I should thank you, in a way," he said. "You've given me a chance to give back part of what Maati's done for me. Not that we talk of it in those terms, of course."

"I don't understand."

The frog mouth spread into a rueful smile. "I know how much it cost him, caring for me while I was ill. It isn't the sort of thing you discuss, of course, but I can tell. It isn't easy watching the man who is supposed to be your master fall apart. And it isn't a simple thing to stand beside him while he pulls himself back together. Would you like more tea? The physician said you could have as much as you wanted, but that we'd want to go slowly with heavier foods."

"No. No more. Thank you. But I still don't see . . ."

"You've made Maati happy these last few weeks," Heshai said, his voice softer. "That he let me take part in caring for you pays back a part of the time he cared for me."

"I didn't think you'd noticed how much it took from him," Liat said. The poet took a querying pose. "You seemed . . . too busy with other things, I suppose. I'm sorry. It isn't my place to judge what you—"

"No, it's quite all right. I . . . Maati and I haven't quite found our right level. I imagine there are some opinions you both hold of me. They're my fault. I earned them."

Liat closed her eyes, marshalling her thoughts, and when she opened them again, it was night, and she was alone.

She didn't remember falling asleep, but the night candle, burning steady in a glass lantern at her bedside, was past its halfway point, and heavy blankets covered her. Despite the pain, she pulled herself up, found and used the night pot, and crawled back to bed, exhausted. Sleep, however didn't return so easily. Her mind was clear, and her body, while aching and bruised at best and pain-bright at worst, at least felt very much her own. She lay in the dim light of the candle and listened to the small sounds of the night—wind sighing at the shutters, the occasional clicking of the walls as they cooled. The room smelled of mint and mulled wine. Someone had been drinking, she thought, or else the physicians had thought that being in air that smelled so pleasant would help her body heal. The first distant pangs of hunger were shifting in her belly.

As the candle burned lower, the night passing, Liat grew clearer, and more awake. She tested how much she could move without the pain coming on, and even walked around the room. Her arm and shoulder were still bound, and her ribs ached to touch, but she could breathe deeply with only an ache. She could bring herself to sitting, and then stand. Walking was simple so long as she didn't bump into anything. She imagined Maati watching over her while she slept, ignoring his own wounds. And Heshai—more like a friend or father—sharing that burden. It was more, she knew, than the two had ever shared before, and she found herself both embarrassed and oddly proud of being the occasion of it.

A thick winter robe hung on a stand by the door, and Liat put it on, wrapping the cloth around her bandages and tying it one-handed. It took longer than she'd expected, but she managed it and was soon sitting in the chair that Maati and Heshai must have used in their vigil. When a servant girl arrived, Liat instructed her not to tell anyone that she'd risen. She wanted Maati to be surprised when he came. The girl took a pose of acknowledgement that held such respect and formality, Liat wondered whether Heshai had told them who she was, or if they were under the impression that she was some foreign princess.

When Maati came, he was alone. His robes were wrinkled and his hair unkempt. He came in quietly, stopping dead when he saw her bed empty, his chair inhabited. She rose as gracefully as she could and held out her good hand. He stepped forward and took it in his own, but didn't pull her close. His eyes were bloodshot and bright, and he released her hand before she let go of his. She smiled a question.

"Liat-cha," he said, and his voice was thick with distress. "I'm pleased you're feeling better."

"What's happened?"

"Good news. Otah-kvo's come back. He arrived last night with a letter from the Dai-kvo himself. It appears there is no andat to replace Seedless, so I'm to do anything necessary to support Heshai-kvo's well-being. But since he's already feeling so much better, I don't see that it amounts to much. It seems there's no one ready to take Heshai's place, and may not be for several years, you see, and so it's very important that . . ."

He trailed off into silence, a smile on his lips and something entirely different in his eyes. Liat felt her heart die a little. She swallowed and nodded.

"Where is he?" Liat asked. "Where's Itani?"

"With Heshai-kvo. He came straight there when his ship arrived. It was very late, and he was tired. He wanted to come to you immediately, but I thought you would be asleep. He'll come later, when he wakes. Liat, I hope . . . I mean, I didn't . . ."

He looked down, shaking his head. When he looked up, his smile was rueful and raw, and tears streaked his face.

"We knew, didn't we, that it would be hard?" he said.

Liat walked forward, feeling as if something outside of her was moving her. Her hand cupped Maati's neck, and she leaned in, the crown of her head touching his. She could smell his tears, warm and salty and intimate. Her throat was too tight for speech.

"Heshai was very . . ." Maati began, and she killed the words with kissing him. His lips, familiar now, responded. She could feel when they twisted into a grimace of pain against her. His mouth closed, and he stepped back. She wanted to hold him, to be held by him, the way a dropped stone wants to fall, but his expression forbade her. The boy was gone, and someone—a man with his face and his expression, but with something deep and painful and new in his eyes—was in his place.

"Liat-cha," he said. "Otah's *back*."

Liat took a breath and slowly let it out.

"Thank you, Maati-cha," she said, the honorific like ashes in her mouth. "Perhaps . . . perhaps if I could join you all later in the day. I find I'm more tired than I thought."

"Of course," Maati said. "I'll send someone in to help you with your robe."

With her good hand, she took a pose of thanks. Maati replied with a simple response. Their eyes met, the gaze holding all the things they were not speaking. Her need, and his. His resolve. Morning rain tapped at the shutters like time passing behind them. Maati turned and left her, his back straight, his bearing formal and controlled.

For the space of a breath, she wanted to call him back. Pull him into the room, into the bed. She wanted to feel the warmth of him against her one last time. It wasn't fair that their bodies hadn't had the chance to say their farewells. And she would have, she thought, even with Itani . . . even with Otah returned and sleeping in the poet's house that she knew now so well. She would have called, except that it would have broken her soul when Maati refused her. And she saw now that he would have.

Instead, she lay in the bed by herself, her flesh mending and her spirit ill. She had expected to feel torn between the two of them, but instead she was only shut out. The bond between Maati and Otah—the relationship of her two lovers—was deeper than what she had with either. She was losing each of them to the other, and the knowledge was like a stone in her throat.

MAATI SAT AT THE TOP OF THE BRIDGE, THE POND BELOW HIM DARK AS TEA. His belly was heavy, his chest so tight his shoulders shifted forward in a hunch. The breeze smelled of rain, though the sky was clear. The world seemed a dark, deadened place.

He had known, of course, that Liat wasn't truly his lover. What they had been to each other for those few, precious weeks was comfort and friendship. That was all. And with Otah back, everything could return to the way it had been—the way it should have been. Only Maati hadn't ached before the way he did now. The memory of Liat's body against him, her lips against his, hadn't haunted him. And Otah's long, thoughtful face hadn't made Maati sick with guilt.

And so, he thought, nothing would be what it had been. The idea that it could had been an illusion.

"You've done it, then?"

Maati turned to his left, back toward the palaces. Seedless stepped onto the bridge, dark robes shifting as he walked. The andat's expression was unreadable.

"I don't know what you mean," Maati said.

"You've broken it off with the darling Liat. Returned her from whence she came, now that her laborer's back from his errand."

"I don't know what you mean," Maati repeated, turning back to stare that the cold, dark water. Seedless settled beside him. Their two faces reflected on the pond's surface, wavering and pale. Maati wished he had a stone to drop, something that would break the image.

"Bad answer," the andat said. "I'm not a fool. I can smell love when I'm up to my knees in it. It's hard, losing her."

"I haven't lost anything. It's only changed a bit. I knew it would."

"Well then," Seedless said gently. "That makes it easy, doesn't it. He's still resting, is he?"

"I don't know. I haven't gone to see him yet today."

"Gone to see him? It's your couch he's sleeping on."

"Still," Maati said with a shrug. "I'm not ready to see him again. Tonight, perhaps. Only not yet."

They were silent for a long moment. Crows barked from the treetops, hopping on twig-thin legs, their black wings outstretched. Somewhere in the water, koi shifted sluggishly, sending thin ripples to the surface.

"Would it help·to say I'm sorry for it?" Seedless asked.

"Not particularly."

"Well, all the same."

"It's hard to think that you care, Seedless-cha. I'd have thought you'd be pleased."

"No. Not really. On the one hand, whether you think it or not, I don't have any deep love of your pain. Not yet, at least. Once you take Heshai's burden . . . well, we'll neither of us have any choices then. And then, for my own selfish nature, all this brings you one step nearer to being like him. The woman you've loved and lost. The pain you carry with you. It's part of what drives him, and you're coming to know it now yourself."

"So when you say you're sorry for it, you mean that you think it might help me do my task?"

"Makes you wonder if the task's worth doing, doesn't it?" Seedless said, a smile in his voice more than his expression. "I doubt the Dai-kvo would share our concerns, though, eh?"

"No," Maati sighed. "No, he at least is certain of what's the right thing."

"Still, we're clever," Seedless said. "Well, you're not. You're busy being lovesick, but I'm clever. Perhaps I'll think of something."

Maati turned to look at the andat, but the smooth, pale face revealed nothing more than a distant amusement.

"Something in particular?" Maati asked, but Seedless didn't answer.

OTAH WOKE FROM A DEEP SLEEP TO LIGHT SLANTING THROUGH HALF-OPENED shutters. For a moment, he forgot he had landed, his body still shifting from memory of the sea beneath him. Then the blond wood and incense, the scrolls and books, the scent and sound of winter rain recalled him to himself, and he stood. The wall-long shutters were closed, a fire burned low in its grate. Heshai and Maati were gone, but a plate of dried fruit and fresh bread sat on a table beside the letter from the Dai-kvo, its pages unsewn and spread. He sat alone and ate.

The journey back had been easy. The river bore him to Yalakeht and then a tradeship with a load of furs meant for Eddensea. He'd taken a position on the ship—passage in return for his work, and he'd done well enough by the captain and crew. Otah imagined they were now in the soft quarter spending what money they had. Indulging themselves before they began the weeks-long journey across the sea.

Heshai had seemed better, alert and attentive. It even seemed that Maati and his teacher had grown closer since Otah had left—brought together, perhaps, by the difficulties they had weathered. It might have been the bad news of Liat's injury or Otah's own weariness and sense of displacement, but there had seemed something more as well. A weariness in Maati's eyes that Otah recognized, but couldn't explain.

The first thing he needed, of course, was a bath. And then to see Liat. And then . . . and then he wasn't sure. He had gone on his journey to the Dai-kvo, he had come back bearing news that seemed out of date when it arrived. According to Maati, Heshai-kvo had bested his illness without the aid of the Dai-kvo. The tragedy of the dead child was fading from the city's memory, replaced by other scandals—diseased cotton in the northern fields; a dyer who killed himself after losing a year's wages gambling; Liat's old overseer Amat Kyaan breaking with her house in favor of a business of her own in the soft quarter. The petty life-and-death battles of the sons of the Khaiem.

And so what had seemed of critical importance at the time, proved empty now that it was done. And his own personal journey had achieved little more. He could go, if he chose, to speak to Muhatia-cha this afternoon. Perhaps House Wilsin would take him back on to complete his indenture. Or there were other places in the city, work he could do that would pay for his food and shelter. The world was open before him. He could even have taken the letter from Orai Vaukheter and taken work as a courier if it weren't for Liat, and for Maati, and the life he'd built as Itani Noyga.

He ate strips of dried apple and plum, chewing the sweet flesh slowly as he thought and noticing the subtlety of the flavors as they changed. It wasn't so bad a life, Itani Noyga's. His work was simple, straightforward. He was good at it. With only a little more effort, he could find a position with a trading house, or the seafront authority, or any of a hundred places that would take a man with numbers and letters and an easy smile. And half a year ago, he would have thought it enough. Otah or Itani. It was still the question.

"You're up," a soft voice said. "And the men of the house are still out. That's good. We have things to talk about, you and I."

Seedless leaned against a bookshelf, his arms crossed and his dark eyes considering. Otah popped the last sliver of plum into his mouth and took a pose of greeting appropriate for someone of low station to a member of the utkhaiem. There was, so far as he knew, no etiquette appropriate for a common laborer to an andat. Seedless waved the pose away and flowed forward, his robes—blue and black—hissing cloth against cloth.

"Otah Machi," the andat said. "Otah Unbranded. The man too wise to be a poet and too stupid to take the brand. And here you are."

Otah met the glittering black gaze and felt the flush in his face. His words were ready, his hands already halfway to a pose of denial. Something in the perfect pale mask of a face stopped him. He lowered his arms.

"Good," Seedless said, "I was hoping we might dispense with that part. We're a little short of time just now."

"How did you find out?"

"I listened. I lied. The normal things anyone would do who wanted to know something hidden. You've seen Liat?"

"Not yet, no."

"You know what happened to her, though? The tiles?"

"Maati told me."

"It wasn't an accident," the andat said. "They were thrown."

Otah frowned, aware that Seedless was peering at him, reading his expressions and movement. He forced himself to remain casual.

"Was it you?"

"Me? Gods, no," Seedless said, sitting on a couch, his legs tucked up beneath him like they were old friends chatting. "In the first place I wouldn't have done it. In the second, I wouldn't have missed. No, it was Marchat Wilsin and his men."

Otah leaned forward, letting the smile he felt show on his face. The andat didn't move, even to breathe.

"You know there's no sane reason that I should believe anything you say."

"True," the andat said. "But hear me out first, and then you can disbelieve my little story entirely instead of just one bit at a time."

"There's no reason Wilsin-cha would want to hurt Liat."

"Yes, there is. His sins are creeping back to kill him, you see. That little incident with the island girl and her dead get? It was more than it seemed. Listen carefully when I say this. It's the kind of thing men are killed for knowing, so it's worth paying attention. The High Council of Galt arranged that little mess. Wilsin-cha helped. Amat Kyaan—his overseer—found out and is dedicating what's left of her life to prying the whole sordid thing open like it was shellfish. Wilsin-cha in his profoundly finite wisdom is cleaning up anything that might be of use to Amat-cha. Including Liat."

Otah took a pose of impatience and stood, looking for his cloak.

"I've had enough of this . . ."

"I know who you are, boy. Sit back down or I'll end all your choices for you, and you can spend the rest of your life running from your brothers over a chair you don't even want to sit in."

Otah paused and then sat.

"Good. The Galtic Council had a plan to ally themselves with the andat. We poor suffering spirits get our freedom. The Galts kick out the supports that keep the cities of the Khaiem above the rest of the world. Then they roll over you like you were just another Westlands warden, only with more gold and fewer soldiers. It's a terrible plan."

"Is it?"

"Yes. Andat aren't predictable. That's what makes us the same, you and I. Ah, relax, Otah-cha. You look like I have a knife at your belly."

"I think you do," Otah said.

The andat leaned back, gesturing at the empty house around them—the crackling fire, the falling rain.

"There's no one to hear us. Anything we say to each other, you and I, is between us unless we choose otherwise."

"And I should trust you to keep quiet?"

"Of course not. Don't be an ass. But the less you say, the less I can repeat to others, eh? Right. Amat's near getting what she needs. And she won't stop. She's a pit hound at heart. Do you know what happens when she does?"

"She'll take it to the Khai."

"Yes!" the andat said, clapping his hands together once as if it were a festival game and Otah had earned a prize. "And what would he do?"

"I don't know."

"No? You disappoint me. He'd do something bloody and gaudy and out of all proportion. Something that sounded like a plague from the old epics. My guess—it's only my opinion, of course, but I consider myself fairly expert on the subject of unrestrained power—he'll turn me and Heshai against whatever Galtic women are carrying babes when he learns of it. It will be like pulling seeds out of a cotton bale. A thousand, maybe. More. Who can say?"

"It would break Heshai," Otah said. "Doing that."

"No. It wouldn't. It would bend him double, but it wouldn't break him. Seeing the one child die in front of him didn't do it, and tragedy fades with distance. Put it close enough to your eye, and a thumb can blot out a mountain. A few thousand dead Galt babies will hurt him, but he won't have to watch it happen. A few bottles of cheap wine, a few black months. And then he'll train Maati. Maati will have all the loneliness, all the self-hatred, all the pain of holding me in check for all the rest of his life. That's already happening. Heshai fell in love and lost her, and he's been chewed by guilt ever since. Maati will do the same."

"No, he won't," Otah said.

Seedless laughed.

"More the fool, you. But let it go. Let it go and look at the near term. Here's my promise, Otah of Machi. Amat will make her case. Liat may be killed before it comes before the Khai, or she may not, but Amat *will* make her case. Innocent blood *will* wash Galt. Maati *will* suffer to the end of his days. Oh, and I'll betray you to your family, though I think it's really very small of you to be concerned about that. Your problems don't amount to much, you know." Seedless paused. "Do you understand me?"

"Yes."

"Then you see why we have to act."

"We?"

"You and I, Otah. We can stop it. Together we can save them all. It's why I've come to you."

The andat's face was perfectly grave now, his hands floating up into a plea. Slowly, Otah took a pose that was a query. Wind rattled the shutters and a chill touched the back of Otah's neck.

"We can spare the people we love. Saraykeht will fall, but there's no helping that. The city will fall, and we will save Liat and Maati and all those babies and mothers who had nothing to do with this. All you have to do is kill a man who—and I swear this—would walk onto the blade if you only held it steady. You have to kill me."

"Kill you, or Heshai?"

"There isn't a difference."

Otah stood, and Seedless rose with him. The perfect face looked pained, and the pose of supplication Seedless took was profound.

"Please," he said. "I can tell you where he goes, how long he stays, how long it takes him to drink himself to sleep. All you'll need is—"

"No," Otah said. "Kill someone? On your word? No. I won't."

Seedless dropped his hands to his sides and shook his head in disappointment and disgust.

"Then you can watch everyone you care for suffer and die, and see if you prefer that. But if you're going to change your mind, do it quickly, my dear. Amat's closer than she knows. There isn't much time."

17

"Something has to be done," Torish Wite said. "She went into the street
yesterday. If she'd been mistaken for a whore, there's no knowing how
she'd have responded. And given the restraint she's managed so far, we could
have had the watch coming down our throats. We can't have that."

Her rooms were dark, the windows and wide doors covered with tapestries
that held in the heat as well as blocking the light. Downstairs, the girls and the
children were all sleeping—even Mitat, even Maj. Only not Amat or Torish.
She ached to rest, only not quite yet.

"I'm aware of what we can and cannot have," Amat said. "I'll see to it."

The thug, the murderer, the captain of her personal guard shook his head.
His expression was grim.

"All respect, grandmother," he said. "But you've sung that song before. The
island girl's trouble. Another stern talking to isn't going to do more than the
last one did."

Amat drew herself up, anger filling her chest partly because she knew what
he said was true. She took a pose of query.

"I had not known this was your house to run," she said.

Torish shook his wide, bear-like head again, his eyes cast down in something like regret or shame.

"It's your house," he said. "But they're my men. If you're going to be putting them on the wrong side of the watch, there isn't enough silver in the soft
quarter to keep them here. I'm sorry."

"You'd break contracts?"

"No. But I won't renew. Not on those terms. This is one of the best contracts we've had, but I won't take a fight I know we can't win. You put that
girl on a leash, or we can't stay with you. And—truly, all respect—you need
us."

"She lost a child last summer," Amat said.

"Bad things happen," Torish Wite said, his voice surprisingly gentle. "You
move past them."

He was right, of course, and that was the galling thing. In his position, she
would have done the same. Amat took a pose of acceptance.

"I understand your position, Torish-cha. I'll see to it that Maj doesn't endan-
ger your men or your contract with me. Give me a day or so, and I'll see it done."

He nodded, turned, left her rooms. He had the grace not to ask what it was
she intended. She wouldn't have been able to say. Amat rose, took her cane,

and walked out the doors to her deck. The rain had stopped, the whole great bowl of the sky white as bleached cotton. Seagulls screamed to one another, wheeling over the rooftops. She took a deep breath and let herself weep. The tears were as much about exhaustion as anything else, and they brought her no relief.

Between the late hour of the morning and the rain that had fallen all the last day and through the night, the streets of the soft quarter were near deserted. The two boys, then, who came around the corner together caught her attention. The older was broad across the shoulders—a sailor or a laborer—with a long, northern face and a robe of formal cut. The younger boy at his side—smaller, softer—wore the brown robes of a poet. Amat knew as they stepped into the street that there would even now be no rest for her. She watched them until they came too near the comfort house to see without leaning over into the street, then went inside and composed herself. It took longer than she'd expected for the guard to come and announce them. Perhaps Torish-cha had seen how tired she felt.

The older boy proved to be Itani Noyga, Liat's vanished lover. The younger, of course, was the young poet Maati. Amat, seated at her desk, took a pose of welcome and gestured to chairs she'd had brought in for them. Both boys sat. It was an interesting contrast, the pair or them. Both were clearly in earnest, both wore expressions of perfect seriousness, but Itani's eyes reminded her more of her own—focused out, on her, on the room, searching, it seemed, for something. The poet boy was like his master—brooding, turned inward. Like his master, or like Marchat Wilsin. Amat put her hand on her knees and leaned a degree forward.

"And what business brings you young gentlemen?" she asked. Her tone was light and pleasant and gave nothing away. Her subtlety was lost on them, though. The older boy, Itani, clearly wasn't looking to finesse an advantage.

"Amat-cha," he said. "I'm told you hope to prove that the High Council of Galt conspired with the andat Seedless when he killed the child out of the island girl last summer."

"I'm investigating the matter," Amat said, "and I've broken with House Wilsin, but I don't know that it's fair to say the Galtic Council must therefore be . . ."

"Amat-cha," the poet boy, Maati, broke in. "Someone tried to kill Liat Chokavi. Marchat Wilsin is keeping it quiet, but I was there. And . . . Itani thinks it was something to do with you and House Wilsin."

Amat felt her breath catch. Marchat, the old idiot, was panicking. Liat Chokavi was his best defense, if he could trust her to say the right things before the Khai. Except that he wouldn't. She was too young, and too unskilled at these games. It was why he had used her in the first place. Something like nausea swept through her.

"It may have been," Amat said. "How is she?"

"Recovering in the Khai's palaces," Itani said. "But she's doing well. She'll be able to go back to her house tomorrow. Wilsin-cha will expect her."

"No," Amat said. "She can't go back there."

"It's true, then," Itani said, his voice somber. Perhaps he had a talent for finesse after all. Amat took a pose of acknowledgement.

"I wasn't able to stop the crime against Maj from happening, but yes. House Wilsin knew of the deceit. I believe that the Galtic Council did as well, though I can't prove that as yet. That *I* think it is hardly a great secret, though. Anyone might guess as much. That I'm right in thinking it . . . is more difficult."

"Protect Liat," Maati said, "and whatever we can do for you, we will."

"Itani-cha? Are those your terms as well?"

"Yes," the boy said.

"It may mean speaking before the Khai. Telling him where you went the night you acted as Wilsin-cha's bodyguard."

Itani hesitated, then took a pose of acceptance.

Amat sat back, one hand up, requesting a moment to herself. This wasn't something she'd foreseen, but it might be what she'd needed. If the young poet could influence Heshai or find some scrap of memory from the negotiations that showed Marchat Wilsin knew that all wasn't what it seemed . . . But there was something more in this—she could feel it as sure as the tide. One piece here didn't fit.

"Itani-cha's presence I understand," Amat said. "What is the poet's interest in Liat Chokavi."

"She's my friend," Maati said, his chin lifted a fraction higher than before. His eyes seemed to defy her.

Ah! she thought. *So that's how it is.* She wondered how far that had gone and whether Itani knew. Not that it made any difference to her or to what was called for next.

Liat. It had always been a mess, of course, what to do with Liat. On the one hand, she might have been able to help Amat's case, add some telling detail that would show Marchat had known of the translator Oshai's duplicity. On the other hand, pulling the girl into it was doing her no favors. Amat had thought about it since she'd come to the house, but without coming to any conclusions. Now the decision was forced on her.

Liat could room with Maj, Amat supposed, except that the arrangement had the ring of disaster. But she couldn't put her out with the whores. Perhaps a cot in her own rooms, or an apartment in one of the low towns. With a guard, of course. . . .

Later. That could all come later. Amat rose. The boys stood.

"Bring her here," she said. "Tonight. Don't let Wilsin-cha know what you're doing. Don't tell her until you have to. I'll see her safe from there. You can trust me to it."

"Thank you, Amat-cha," Itani said. "But if this business is going to continue . . . I don't want to burden you with this if it's something you don't want to carry forever. This investigation might go on for years, no?"

"Gods, I hope not," Amat said. "But I promise you, even if it does, I'll see it finished. Whatever it costs, I *will* bring this to light."

"I believe you," Itani said.

Amat paused, there was a weight to the boy's tone that made her think he'd expected to hear that. She had confirmed something he already suspected, and she wondered what precisely it had been. She had no way to know.

She called in Torish-cha, introduced the boys and let them speak until the plans had been made clear. The girl would come that night, just after sundown, to the rear of the house. Two of Torish's men would meet them at the edge of the palace grounds to be sure nothing odd happened along the way. Itani would go along as well, and explain the situation. Amat sent them away just before midday, easing herself into bed after they left, and letting her eyes close at last. Any fear she had that the day's troubles would keep her awake was unfounded— sleep rolled over her like a wave. She woke hours later, the falling sun shining into her eyes through a gap where one of her tapestries had slipped.

She called Mitat up for the briefing that opened the day. The red-haired woman came bearing a bowl of stewed beef and rice and a flask of good red wine. Amat sat at her desk and ate while Mitat spoke—the tiles man thought he knew how the table was being cheated and should know for certain by the end of the night, Little Namya had a rash on his back that needed to be looked at by a physician but Chiyan was recovering well from her visit to the street of beads and would be back to work within a few more days. Two of the girls had apparently run off, and Mitat was preparing to hire on replacements. Amat listened to each piece, fitting it into the vast complexity that her life had become.

"Torish-cha sent his men out to recover the girl you discussed with him this morning," Mitat went on. "They should be back soon."

"I'll need a cot for her," Amat said. "You can put it in my rooms, against the wall there."

Mitat took a pose of acknowledgement. There was something else in it, though, a nuance that Amat caught as much from a hint of a smile as the pose itself. And then she saw Mitat realize that she'd noticed something, and the red-haired woman broke into a grin.

"What?" Amat asked.

"The other business," Mitat said. "About Maj and the Galts? I had a man come by from a hired laborers' house asking if you were only paying for information about this island girl, or if you wanted to know about the other one too."

Amat stopped chewing.

"The other one?" Amat asked.

"The one Oshai brought in last year."

Amat took a moment, sitting back, as the words took time to make sense. In the darkness of her exhaustion, hope flickered. Hope and relief.

"There was *another* one?"

"I thought you might find that interesting," Mitat said.

MAATI SAT ON THE WOODEN STEPS OF THE POET'S HOUSE, STARING OUT AT TREES black and bare as sticks, at the dark water of the pond, at the ornate palaces of the Khai with lanterns glittering like fireflies. Night had fallen, but the last rays of sunlight still lingered in the west. His face and hands were cold, his body hunched forward, pulled into itself. But he didn't go into the warmth of the house behind him. He had no use for comfort.

Otah and Liat had left just before sunset. They might, he supposed, be in the soft quarter by now. He imagined them walking briskly through the narrow streets, Otah's arm across her shoulder protectively. Otah-kvo would be able to keep her safe. Maati's own presence would have been redundant, unneeded.

Behind him, the small door scraped open. Maati didn't turn. The slow, lumbering footsteps were enough for him to know it was his teacher and not Seedless.

"There's chicken left," Heshai-kvo said. "And the bread's good."

"Thank you. Perhaps later," Maati said.

Grunting with the effort, the poet lowered himself onto the step beside Maati, looking out with him over the bare landscape as it fell into darkness. Maati could hear the old poet's wheezing breath over the calling of crows.

"Is she doing well?" Heshai asked.

"I suppose so."

"She'll be going back to her house soon. Wilsin-cha . . ."

"She's not going back to him," Maati said. "The old overseer—Amat Kyaan—is taking her up."

"So House Wilsin loses another good woman. He won't like that," Heshai said, then shrugged. "Serves the old bastard right for not treating them better, I'd guess."

"I suppose."

"I see your friend the laborer's back."

Maati didn't answer. He was only cold, inside and out. Heshai glanced over at him and sighed. His thick-fingered hand patted Maati's knee the way his father's might have had the world been something other than it was. Maati felt tears welling unbidden in his eyes.

"Come inside, my boy," the poet said. "I'll warm us up a little wine."

Maati let himself be coaxed back in. With Heshai-kvo recovered, the house was slipping back into the mess it had been when he'd first come. Books and scrolls lay open on the tables and the floor beside the couches. An inkblock hollowed with use stained the desk where it sat directly on the wood. Maati squatted by the fire, looking into the flames as he had the darkness, and to much the same effect.

Behind him, Heshai moved through the house, and soon the rich scent of wine and mulling spices began to fill the place. Maati's belly rumbled, and he forced himself up, walking over to the table where the remains of the evening meal waited for him. He pulled a greasy drumstick from the chicken carcass and considered it. Heshai sat across from him and handed him a thick slice of black bread. Maati sketched a pose of gratitude. Heshai filled a thick earthenware cup with wine and passed it to him. The wine, when he drank it, was clean and rich and warmed his throat.

"Full week coming," Heshai-kvo said. "There's a dinner with the envoys of Cetani and Udun tomorrow I thought we should attend. And then a religious scholar's talking down at the temple the day after that. If you wanted to . . ."

"If you'd like, Heshai-kvo," Maati said.

"I wouldn't really," the poet said. "I've always thought religious scholars were idiots."

The old poet's face was touched by mischief, a little bit delighted with his own irreverence. Maati could see just a hint of what Heshai-kvo had looked like as a young man, and he couldn't help smiling back, if only slightly. Heshai-kvo clapped a hand on the table.

"There!" he said. "I knew you weren't beyond reach."

Maati shook his head, taking a pose of thanks more intimate and sincere than he'd used to accept the offered food. Heshai-kvo replied with one that an uncle might offer to a nephew. Maati stirred himself. This was as good a time as any, and likely better than most.

"Is Seedless here?" Maati asked.

"What? No. No, I suppose he's out somewhere showing everyone how clever he is," Heshai-kvo said bitterly. "I know I ought to keep him closer, but that torture box . . ."

"No, that's good. There was something I needed to speak with you about, but I didn't want him nearby."

The poet frowned, but nodded Maati on.

"It's about the island girl and what happened to her. I think . . . Heshai, that wasn't only what it seemed. Marchat Wilsin knew about it. He arranged it because the Galtic High Council told him to. And Amat Kyaan—the one Liat's gone to stay with—she's getting the proof of it together to take before the Khai."

The poet's face went white and then flushed red. The wide frog-lips pursed, and he shook his wide head. He seemed both angry and resigned.

"That's what she says?" he asked. "This overseer?"

"Not only her," Maati said.

"Well, she's wrong," the poet said. "That isn't how it happened."

"Heshai-kvo, I think it is."

"It's not," the poet said and stood. His expression was closed. He walked to the fire, warming his hands with his back to Maati. The burning wood crackled and spat. Maati, putting down the still-uneaten bread, turned to him.

"Amat Kyaan isn't the only—"

"They're all wrong, then. Think about it for a moment, Maati. Just think. If it had been the High Council of Galt behind the blasted thing, what would happen? If the Khai saw it proved? He'd punish them. And how'd you think he'd do it?"

"The Khai would use you and Seedless against them," Maati said.

"Yes, and what good would come of that?"

Maati took a pose of query, but Heshai didn't turn to see it. After a moment, he let his hands fall. The firelight danced and flickered, making the poet seem almost as if he were part of the flame. Maati walked toward him.

"It's the truth," he said.

"Doesn't matter if it is," Heshai-kvo said. "There are punishments worse than the crimes. What happened, happened. There's nothing to be gotten by holding onto it now."

"You don't believe that," Maati said, and his voice was harder than he'd expected it to be. Heshai-kvo shifted, turned. His eyes were dry and calm.

"There's nothing that will put life back into that child," Heshai-kvo said. "What could possibly be gained by trying?"

"There's justice," Maati said, and Heshai laughed. It was a disturbing sound, more anger than mirth. Heshai-kvo stood and moved toward him. Without thinking Maati stepped back.

"Justice? Gods, boy, you want *justice*? We have larger problems than that, you and I. Getting through another year without one of these small gods flooding a city or setting the world on fire. That's important. Keeping the city safe. Playing court politics so that the Khaiem never decide to take each other's toys and women by force. And you want to add justice to all that? I've sacrificed my life to a world that wouldn't care less about me as a man if you paid it. You and I, both of us were cut off from our brothers and sisters. That boy from Udun who we saw in the court was slaughtered by his own brother and we all applauded him for doing it. Am I supposed to punish him too?"

"You're supposed to do what's right," Maati said.

Heshai-kvo took a dismissive pose.

"What we do is bigger than right and wrong," he said. "If the Dai-kvo didn't make that clear to you, consider it your best lesson from me."

"I can't think that," Maati said. "If we don't push for justice . . ."

Heshai-kvo's expression darkened. He took a pose appropriate to asking guidance from the holy, his stance a sarcasm. Maati swallowed, but held his ground.

"You love justice?" Heshai asked. "It's harder than stone, boy. Love it if you want. It won't love you."

"I can't think that—"

"Tell me you're never transgressed," Heshai interrupted, his voice harsh. "Never stolen food from the kitchens, never lied to a teacher. Tell me you've never bedded another man's woman."

Maati felt something shift in him, profound as a bone breaking, but painless. His ears hummed with something like bees. He took the corner of the table and lifted. Food, wine, papers, books all spilled together to the ground. He took a chair and tossed it aside, scooped up the winebowl with a puddle of redness still swirling in its curve and threw it against the wall. It shattered with a loud, satisfying pop. The poet looked at him, mouth gaping as if Maati had just grown wings.

And then, quickly as it had come, the rage was gone, and Maati sank to his knees like a puppet with its strings cut. Sobs wracked him, as violent as being sick. Maati was only half-aware of the poet's footsteps as he came near, as he bent down. The thick arms cradled him, and Maati held Heshai-kvo's wide frame and cried into the brown folds of his cloak while the poet rocked him and whispered *I'm sorry, I'm sorry, I'm sorry.*

It felt like it would go on forever, like the river of pain could run and run and run and never go dry. It wasn't true—in time exhaustion as much as anything else stilled him. Maati sat beside his master, the overturned table beside them. The fire had burned low while he wasn't watching it—embers glowed red and gold among ashes still arched in the shapes of the wood they'd once been.

"Well," Maati said at last, his voice thick, "I've just made an ass of myself, haven't I?"

Heshai-kvo chuckled, recognizing the words. Maati, despite himself, smiled.

"A decent first effort, at least," Heshai-kvo said. "You'll get better with time. I didn't mean to do that to you, you know. It was unfair bringing Liat-kya into it. It's only that . . . the island girl . . . if I'd done better work when I first fashioned Seedless, it wouldn't have happened. I just don't want things getting worse. I want it over with."

"I know," Maati said.

They were silent for a time. The embers cooled a shade, the ashes crumbled.

"They say there's two women you don't get past," Heshai-kvo said. "Your first love and your first sex. And then, if it turns out to be the same girl . . ."

"It is," Maati said.

"Yes," Heshai said. "It was the same for me. Her name was Ariat Miu.

She had the most beautiful voice I've ever heard. I don't know where she is now."

Maati leaned over and put his arm around Heshai as if they were drinking companions. Heshai nodded as if Maati had spoken. He took a deep breath and let it out slowly.

"Well, we'd best get this cleaned up before the servants see it. Stoke the fire, would you? I'll get some candles burning. Night's coming on too early these days."

"Yes, Heshai-kvo," Maati said.

"And Maati? You know I won't tell anyone about this, don't you?"

Maati took a pose of acknowledgement. In the dim light he couldn't be sure that Heshai had seen it, so he let his hands fall and spoke.

"Thank you," he said into the dark.

THEY WALKED SLOWLY, HAMPERED BY LIAT'S WOUNDS. THE TWO MERCENARIES walked one before and one behind, and Otah walked at her side. At first, near the palaces, he had put his arm around her waist, thinking that it would be a comfort. Her body told him, though, that it wasn't. Her shoulder, her arm, her ribs—they were too tender to be touched and Otah found himself oddly glad. It freed him to watch the doorways and alleys, rooftops and food carts and firekeepers' kilns more closely.

The air smelled of wood smoke from a hundred hearths. A cool, thick mist too dense to be fog, too insubstantial to be rain, slicked the stones of the road and the walls of the houses. In her oversized woolen cloak, Liat might have been anyone. Otah found himself half-consciously flexing his hands, as if preparing for an attack that never came.

When they reached the edge of the soft quarter, passing by the door of Amat Kyaan's now-empty apartments, Liat motioned to stop. The two men looked to Otah and then each other, their expressions professional and impatient, but they paused.

"Are you all right?" Otah asked, his head bent close to the deep cowl of Liat's cloak. "I could get you water . . ."

"No," she said. Then, a moment later. " 'Tani, I don't want to go there."

"Where?" he asked, his fingertips touching her bound arm.

"To Amat Kyaan. I've done everything so badly. And I can't think she really wants me there. And . . ."

"Sweet," Otah said. "She'll keep you safe. Until we know what's . . ."

Liat looked at him directly. Her shadowed face showed her impatience and her fear.

"I didn't say I wouldn't," she said. "Only that I don't want it."

Otah leaned close, kissing her gently on the lips. Her good hand held him close.

"Don't leave me," she said, hardly more than a whisper.

"Where would I go," he said, his tone gentle to hide that his answer was also a question. She smiled, slight and brave, and nodded. Liat held his hand in hers for the rest of the way.

The soft quarter never knew a truly quiet night. The lanterns lit the streets with the dancing shadows of a permanent fire. Music came from the opened doors of the houses: drums and flutes, horns and voices. Twice they passed houses with balconies that overlooked the street with small groups of under-dressed, chilly whores leaning over the rails like carcasses at a butcher's. The wealth of Saraykeht, richest and most powerful of the southern cities, eddied and swirled around them. Otah found himself neither aroused nor disturbed, though he thought perhaps he should be.

They reached the comfort house, going through an ironbound doorway in a tall stone wall, through a sad little garden that separated the kitchens from the main house, and then into the common room. It was alive with activity. The red-haired woman, Mitat, and Amat had covered the long common tables with papers and scrolls. The island girl, Maj, paced behind them, gnawing impa-tiently at a thumbnail. As the two guards who'd accompanied them moved deeper into the house greeting other men similarly armed and armored, Otah noticed two young boys, one in the colors of House Yanaani, the other wearing the badge of the seafront's custom house, waiting impatiently. Messengers. Something had happened.

Amat's closer than she knows. There isn't much time.

"Liat-kya," Amat said, raising one hand in a casual greeting. "Come here. I've something I want you ask you."

Liat walked forward, and Otah followed her. There was a light in Amat's eyes—something like triumph. Amat embraced Liat gently, and Otah saw the tears in Liat's eyes as she held her old master with one uninjured arm.

"I'm sorry," Amat said. "I though you'd be safe. And there was so much that needed doing, that . . . I didn't understand the situation deeply enough. I should have warned you."

"Honored teacher," Liat said, and then had no more words. Amat's smile was warm as summer sunlight.

"You know Maj, of course. This is Mitat, and that brute against that wall is Torish Wite, my master of guard."

When Maj spoke, she spoke the Khaiate tongue. Her accent was thick but not so much that Otah couldn't catch her words.

"I didn't think I was to be seeing you again."

Liat's smile went thin.

"You speak very well, Maj-cha."

"I am waiting for weeks here," Maj said, coolly. "What else do I do?"

Amat looked over. Otah saw the woman called Mitat glance up at her, then at the island girl, then away. Tension quieted the room, and for a moment, even the messengers stopped fidgeting and stared.

"She's come to help," Amat said.

"She is come because you called her," Maj said. "Because she needs you."

"We need each other," Amat said, command in her voice. She drew herself to her full height, and even leaning on her cane, she seemed to fill the room. "She's come because I wanted her to come. We have almost everything we need. Without her, we aren't ready."

Maj stared at Amat, then slowly turned and took a pose of greeting as awkward as a child's. Otah saw the flush in the pale cheeks, the brightness of her eyes, and understood. Maj was drunk. Amat gathered Liat close to the table, peppering her with questions about dates and shipping orders, and what exactly Oshai and Wilsin-cha had said and when. Otah sat at the table, near enough to hear, near enough to watch, but not a part of the interrogation.

For a moment, he felt invisible. The intensity and excitement, desperation and controlled violence around him became like an epic on a stage. He saw it all from outside. When, unconsciously, he met the island girl's gaze, she smiled at him and nodded—a wordless, informal, unmistakable gesture; a recognition between strangers. She, with her imperfect knowledge of language and custom, couldn't truly be a part of the conspiracy now coming near to full bloom before them. He, by contrast, could not because he still heard Seedless laying the consequences of Amat's success before him— *Liat may be killed, innocent blood will wash Galt, Maati will suffer to the end of his days, I will betray you to your family*—and that private knowledge was like an infection. Every step that Amat made brought them one step nearer that end.

And to his unease, Otah found that his refusal of the andat was not so certain a thing as he had thought it.

For nearly a quarter candle, Amat and Mitat, Liat and sometimes even Torish Wite chewed and argued. The messengers were questioned, the letters they bore added to the growing stacks, and they were sent away with Amat's replies tucked in their sleeves. Otah listened and watched as the arguments to be presented before the Khai Saraykeht became clearer. Proofs of billing, testimonies, collisions of dates and letters from Galt, and Maj—witness and centerpiece—to stand as the symbol of it all. And then the whole web of coincidence repeated a year earlier with some other girl who had taken fright, the story said, and escaped. There was no proof—no evidence which in itself showed anything. But like tile chips in a mosaic, the facts related to one another in a way that demanded a grim interpretation.

And only so much proof, of course, was required. Amat's evidence need only capture the imagination of the court, and the avalanche would begin. What she said was true, and once the full powers of the court were involved,

Heshai-kvo would be brought before it, and Seedless. And the andat, when forced, would have to speak the truth. He might even be pleased to, bringing in another wave of disaster as a second-best to his own release.

As the night passed—the moon moving unseen overhead—Liat began to flag. Amat noticed it and met Otah's gaze.

"Liat-kya, I'm being terrible," Amat said, taking a pose of apology. "You're hurt and tired and I've been keeping you awake."

Liat made some small protest, but its weakness was enough to show Amat's argument valid. Otah moved to her and helped her to her feet, and Liat, sighing, leaned into him.

"There's a cot made up upstairs," Mitat said. "In Amat-cha's rooms."

"But where will 'Tani sleep?"

"I'm fine, love," he said before Amat—clearly surprised by the question—could think to offer hospitality. "I've a place with some of my old cohort. If I didn't come back, they'd worry."

It wasn't true, but that hardly mattered. The prospect of staying at the comfort house while Amat's plans reached fruition held no appeal. Only the sleepy distress in Liat's eyes made him wish to stay, and then for her more than himself.

"I'll stay until you're asleep," he said. It seemed to comfort her. They gave their goodnights and walked up the thick wooden stairs, moving slowly for Liat's benefit. Otah heard the conversation begin again behind him, the plan moving forward.

He closed the door of Amat's rooms behind him. The shutters were fast but the dull orange of torchlight from the street glowed at their seams. The night candle on Amat's desk was past its half-mark. Its flame guttered as they passed. The cot was thick canvas stretched over wood with a mattress three fingers thick and netting strung over it even though there were few insects flying so late in the winter. With his arm still around Liat's thin frame, their single shadow flickered against the wall.

"She hates me, I think," Liat said, her voice low and calm.

"What are you talking about. Amat-cha was perfectly . . ."

"Not her. Maj."

Otah was silent. He wanted to deny that too—to tell Liat that no one thought ill of her, that everything would be fine if only she'd let it. But he didn't know it was true, or even if it would be wise to think it. They had thought no particular ill of Wilsin-cha, and Liat could have died for that. He felt his silence spread like cold. Liat shrugged him away and pulled at the ties of her cloak.

"Let me," Otah said. Liat held still as he undid her cloak, folded it on the floor under her cot.

"My robe too?" she asked. In the near darkness, Otah felt her gaze as much as saw it. An illusion, perhaps. It might only have been something in the tone of her voice, an inflection recognized after months of being her lover, sharing her bed and her body. Otah hesitated for more reasons than one.

"Please," Liat said.

"You're hurt, love. It was hard enough even walking upstairs . . ."

"Itani."

"It's Amat-cha's room. She could come up."

"She won't be up for hours. Help me with my robe. Please."

Objections pushed for position, but Otah moved forward, drawn by her need and his own. Carefully, he untied the stays of her robes and drew them from her until she stood naked but for her straps and bandages. Even in the dim light, he could see where the bruises marked her skin. She took his hand and kissed it, then reached for the stays of his own robe. He did not stop her. It would have been cruel, and even if it hadn't, he did not want to.

They made love slowly, carefully, and he thought as much in sorrow as in lust. Her skin was the color of dark honey in the candlelight, her hair black as crows. When they were both spent, Otah lay with his back to the chill wall, giving Liat as much room on the cot as she needed to be comfortable. Her eyes were only half-open, the corners of her mouth turned down. When she shivered, he half rose and pulled her blanket over her. He did not climb beneath it himself, though the warmth would have been welcome.

"You were gone for so long," Liat said. "There were days I wondered if you were coming back."

"Here I am."

"Yes," she said. "Here you are. What was it like? Tell me everything."

And so he told her about the ship and the feeling of wood swaying underfoot, the creaking of rope and the constant noise of water. He told her about the courier with his jokes and stories of travelling, and the way Orai had known at once that he'd left a woman behind. About Yalakeht with its tall gray buildings and the thin lanes with iron gates at the mouth that could lock whole streets up for the night like a single apartment.

And he could have gone on—the road to the Dai-kvo's village, the mountain, the town of only men, the Dai-kvo himself, the odd half-offer to take him back. He might even have gone as far as Seedless' threats, and the realization he was still struggling with—that Itani Noyga would be exposed as the son of the Khai Machi. That if Seedless lived, Itani Noyga would have to die. But Liat's breath was heavy, deep, and regular. When he lifted himself over her, she murmured something and curled herself deeper into the bedding. Otah pulled on his robes. The night candle was past the three-quarter mark, the darkness moving closer and closer to dawn. For the first time, he noticed the fatigue in his limbs. He would need to find someplace to sleep. A room, perhaps, or one of the sailor's bunks down by the seafront where he'd be sharing a brazier with nine men who'd drunk themselves asleep the night before.

In the buttery light of the common room, the conversation was still going on, but to his surprise, the focus had shifted. Maj, an observer before like himself, was seated across from Amat Kyaan, stabbing at the tabletop with a finger and letting loose a long string of syllables with no clear break between them. Her face was flushed, and he could hear the anger in her voice without knowing the words. Anger and wine. Amat looked up at he descended the stairs. She looked older than usual.

Maj followed the old woman's gaze, glanced up at the closed door behind him, and said something else. Amat replied in the same language, her voice calm but not placating. Maj stood, rattling the bench, and strode to Otah.

"Your woman sleeps?" Maj said.

"She's asleep. Yes."

"I have questions. Wake her," Maj said, taking a pose that made the words a command. Her breath was a drunk's. Over her shoulder, he saw Amat shake her head no. Otah took a pose of apology. The refusal seemed to break something in Maj, and tears brimmed in her eyes, streaked her cheeks.

"Weeks," she said, her tone pleading. "I am waiting for weeks, and for nothing. There is no justice here. You people you have *no* justice."

Mitat approached them and put her hand on the island girl's arm. Maj pulled away and went to a different door, wiping her eyes on the back of her hand. As the door closed behind her, Otah took a pose of query.

"She didn't understand that the Khai Saraykeht might make his own investigation," Mitat said. "She thought he'd act immediately. When she heard that there'd be another delay . . ."

"It isn't entirely her fault," Amat said. "This can't have been easy for her, any of it." The master of guard—a huge bear of a man—coughed. The way he and Amat considered each other was enough to tell Otah this wasn't the first time the girl had been the subject of conversation. Amat continued, "It will all be finished soon enough. Or our part, at least. As long as she's here to make the case before the Khai, we'll have started the thing. If she goes home after that, she goes home."

"And if she leaves before that?" Mitat asked, sitting on the table.

"She won't," Amat said. "She's not well, but she won't leave before someone answers for her child. And Liat. She's resting?"

"Yes, Amat-cha," Otah said, taking a pose of thanks. "She's asleep."

"Wilsin-cha will know by now that she's not going back to his house," Amat said. "She'll need to stay inside until this is over."

"Another one? And how long's that going to be, grandmother?" Torish Wite asked.

Amat rested her head in her hands. She seemed smaller than she had been, diminished by fatigue and years, but not broken. Weary to her bones perhaps, but unbroken. In that moment, he found that he admired Liat's old teacher very much.

"I'll send a runner in the morning," she said. "This time of year, it might take a week before we get an audience."

"But we aren't ready!" Mitat said. "We don't even know where the first girl was kept or where she's gone. We won't have time to find her!"

"We have all the pieces," Amat said. "And what we don't have, the utkhaiem will find when the Khai looks into it. It isn't all I'd hoped, but it will do. It will have to."

18

Marchat Wilsin had seen wildfires spread more slowly than the news. Amat Kyaan's petition had reached the servants of the Master of Tides—an idiot title for an overfed secretary, he thought—just before dawn. By the time the sun had risen the width of two hands together, a messenger from the compound had come to the bathhouse with a message from Epani. The panicky twig of a man had scratched out the basic information from the petition, his letters so hasty they were hardly legible. Not that it mattered. The word of Amat Kyaan and her petition were enough. It was happening.

Epani's letter floated now on the surface of the water. It was a warm bath, now that the half-hearted winter was upon them, and steam rose in wisps from the drowned paper. The ink had washed away as he'd watched it, threads of darkness like shadows fading into the clear water. It was over. There was nothing he could do now that would put the world back in its right shape, and in a strange way it was a relief. Night after night since Seedless, that miserable Khaiate god-ghost, had come to his apartments, Marchat had lain awake. He'd had a damn fine mind, once. But in the dark hours, he'd found nothing, no plan of action, no finessed stroke that would avoid the thing that had now come. And since there was no halting it, he could at least stop looking. He closed his eyes and let his head sink for a moment under the tiny lapping waves. Yes, it was a relief that at least now he wouldn't have to try.

He lay underwater until his lungs began to burn, and then even a little longer, not wanting to leave this little moment of peace behind. But time and breath being what they were, he rose and tramped up out of the bath. The water streamed off his body leaving gooseflesh behind it, and he dried himself quickly as he walked into the changing room. The heat from a wide, black brazier combined with the vapors from the baths to make the air thick. Any chill at all would freeze these people. The summer cities couldn't imagine cold, and after so many years here, perhaps he couldn't either. As he pulled on his thick woolen robes, it struck Marchat that he didn't remember the last time he'd seen snow. Whenever it had been, he hadn't known it was the last time he ever would, or he'd have paid it more attention.

A pair of men came in together, round-faced, black-haired, speaking as much in gesture as with words. The same as all the others in Saraykeht. He was the one—pale skin, kinky hair, ridiculously full beard—who stood out. He'd lived here since he'd been a young man, and he'd never really become of the place. He'd always been waiting for the day when he'd be called back to Galt. It was a bitter thought. When the pair noticed him, they took poses of greeting which he returned without thinking. His hands simply knew what to do.

He walked back to the compound slowly. Not because of the dread, though the gods knew he wasn't looking forward, but instead because his failure seemed to have washed his eyes. The sounds and scents of the city were fresh, unfamiliar. When he had been traveling as a young man, it had been like this coming home. The streets his family lived among had carried the same weight of familiarity and strangeness that Saraykeht now bore. At the time, he'd thought it was only that he had been away, but now he thought it was more that the travels he'd made back then had changed him, as the letter from Epani had changed him again just now. The city was the same, but he was a new man seeing it: The ancient stonework; the vines that rose on the walls and were pulled back every year only to crawl up again; the mixture of languages from all across the world that came to the seafront; the songs of the beggars and cry of birdcall.

Too soon, he was back at his own compound where the Galtic Tree stood as it always had in the main courtyard, the fountain splashing behind it. He wondered who would take the place once he'd gone. Some other poor bastard whom the family wanted rid of. Some boy desperate to prove his worth in the wealthiest, most isolated position in the house. If they didn't tear the place down stone by stone and burn the rubble. That was another distinct possibility.

Epani waited in his private chambers, wringing his hands in distress. Marchat couldn't bring himself to feel anything more than a mild annoyance at the man.

"Wilsin-cha, I've just heard. The audience was granted. Six days. It's going to come in six days!"

Marchat put up his hand, palm out, and the cicada stopped whining.

"Send a runner to the palaces. One of the higher clerks. Or go yourself. Tell the Khai's people that we expect Amat Kyaan's audience to touch upon the private business of the house, and we want them to postpone her audience until we can be present with our response."

"Yes, Wilsin-cha."

"And bring me paper and a fresh inkblock," Marchat said. "I have some letters to write."

There must have been something in his tone—a certain gravity, perhaps—that reassured the overseer, because Epani dropped into a pose of acknowledgement and scurried out with a sense of relief that was almost palpable. Marchat followed him far enough to find a servant who could fetch him some mulled wine, then returned to his desk and prepared himself. The tiny flask in the thin drawer at his knee was made of silver, the stopper sealed with green wax. When he shook it, in clinked like some little piece of metal was hidden in it, and not a liquid at all. It was a distillation of the same drugs comfort houses in the soft quarter used to make exotic wines. But it was, of course, much too potent. This thumbfull in his palm was enough to make a man sleep forever. He closed his fingers over it.

This wasn't how he'd wanted it. But it would do.

He put the flask back in its place as Epani-cha arrived, paper and inkblock and fresh pens in his hands. Marchat thanked him and sent him away, then turned to the blank page.

I am Marchat Wilsin of House Wilsin of Galt, he began then scraped his pen tip over the ink. *I write this to confess my crimes and to explain them. I and I alone . . .*

He paused. I and I alone. It was what he could do, of course. He could eat the sin and save those less innocent than himself from punishment. He might save Galt from the wrath of the Khaiem. For the first time since he'd read Epani's scratched, fear-filled words, Marchat felt a pang of sorrow. It was a bad time, this, to be alone.

The servant arrived with his wine, and Marchat drank it slowly, looking at the few words he'd written. He'd invented the whole tale, of course. How he'd hoped to shift the balance of trade away from Saraykeht and so end his exile. How he had fed himself on foolish hopes and dreams and let his own evil nature carry him away. Then he'd apologize to the Khai for his sins, confess his cowardice, and commend his fortune to the island girl Maj who he had wronged and to Amat Kyaan whose loyalty to him had led her to suspect those in Galt who could command him, since she would not believe the sickness of the plan to be his own.

The last part was, he thought, a nice touch. Recasting Amat as a woman so loyal to him, so in love with him, that she didn't see the truth clearly. He felt sure she'd appreciate the irony.

I and I alone.

He took the barely-started confession, blew on it to cure the ink, and set it aside for a time. There was no hurry. Any time in the next six days would suit as well perhaps more if the Khai let him stall Amat and cheat the world out of a few more sunsets. And there were other letters to write. Something to the family back in Galt, for instance. An apology to the High Council for his evil plans that the utkhaiem might intercept. Or something more personal. Something, perhaps, real.

He drew his pen across the ink, and set the metal nib to a fresh sheet.

Amat, my dear old friend. You see what I'm like? Even now, at this last stop on the trail, I'm too much the coward to use the right words. Amat, my love. Amat, who I never did tell my heart to for fear she'd laugh or, worse, be polite. Who ever would have thought we'd come to this?

OTAH WOKE LATE IN THE AFTERNOON FROM A HEAVY, TROUBLED SLEEP. THE ROOM was empty—the inhabitants of the other bunks having gone their ways. The brazier was cool, but the sun glowed against a window covering of thin, stretched leather. He gathered his things from the thin space between himself and the wall where someone would have had to reach over his sleeping body to steal them. Even so he checked. What money he'd had before, he had now. He dressed slowly, waiting for half-remembered dreams to dissolve and fade. There had been something about a flood, and feral dogs drowning in it.

The streets of the seafront were busy, even in winter. Ships arrived and departed by the spare handful, heading mostly south for other warm ports. The journey to Yalakeht would have been profoundly unpleasant, even now. At one of the tall, thin tables by the wharves, he bought a small sack of baked apple slices covered in butter and black sugar, tossing it from one hand to the other as the heat slapped his palms. He thought of Orai in Machi and the deep-biting cold of the far north. It would, he thought, make apples taste even better.

The scandal in every teahouse, around every firekeeper's kiln, on the corners and in the streets, was the petition of Amat Kyaan to speak before the Khai. The petition to speak against House Wilsin. Otah listened and smiled his charming smile without ever once meaning it. She was going to disclose how the house had been evading taxes, one version said. Another had it that the sad trade that had gone wrong was more than just the work of the andat—a rival house had arranged it to discredit Wilsin, and Amat was now continuing the vendetta still in the pay of some unknown villain. Another that Amat would show that the island girl's child had truly been Marchat Wilsin's. Or the Khai Saraykeht's. Or the get of some other Khai killed so that the Khaiem wouldn't have to suffer the possibility of a half-Nippu poet.

It was no more or less than any of the other thousand scandals and occasions of gossip that stirred the slow blood of the city. Even when he came across people he knew, faces he recognized, Otah kept his own counsel. It was coming soon enough, he thought.

The sun was falling in the west, vanishing into the low hills and cane fields, when Otah took himself up the wide streets toward the palaces of the Khai and through those high gardens to the poet's house. Set off from the grandeur of the halls of the Khai and the utkhaiem, the poet's house seemed small and close and curiously genuine in the failing light. Otah left the bare trees behind and walked over the wooden bridge, koi popping sluggishly at the water as he passed. Nothing ever froze here.

Before he'd reached the doors, Maati opened them. The waft of air that came with him was warm and scented with smoke and mulled wine. Maati took a pose of greeting appropriate for a student to an honored teacher, and Otah laughed and pushed his hands aside. It was only when Maati didn't laugh in return that he saw the pose had been sincere. He took one of apology, but Maati only shook his head and gestured him inside.

The rooms were more cluttered than usual—books, papers, a pair of old boots, half the morning's breakfast still uneaten. A small fire burned, and Maati sat down in one of the two chairs that faced it. Otah took the other.

"You stayed with her last night?" Maati asked.

"Most of it," Otah said, leaning forward. "I rented a bunk by the seafront. I didn't want to stay in the comfort house. You heard that Amat Kyaan . . ."

"Yes. I think they brought word to Heshai-kvo before they told the Khai."

"How did he take it?"

"He's gone off to the soft quarter. I doubt he'll come back soon."

"He's going to Amat Kyaan?"

"I doubt it. He seemed less like someone solving a problem than participating in it."

"Does he know? I mean, did you tell him what she was going to say?"

Maati made a sound half laugh, half groan.

"Yes. He didn't believe it. Or he did, but he wouldn't admit to it. He said that justice wasn't worth the price."

"I can't think that's true," Otah said. Then, "But maybe there's no justice to be had."

There was a long pause. There was a deep cup of wine, Otah saw, near the fire. A deep cup, but very little wine in it.

"And how did you take the news?" he asked.

Maati shrugged. He looked tired, unwell. His skin had a gray cast to it, and the bags under his eyes might have been from too much sleep or too little. Now that he thought to look for it, Maati's head was shifting slightly, back and forth with the beating of his heart. He was drunk.

"What's the matter, Maati?" he asked.

"You should stay here," the boy said. "You shouldn't sleep at the seafront or the comfort house. You're welcome here."

"Thank you, but I think people would find it a little odd that—"

"People," Maati said angrily, then became quiet. Otah stood, found the pot of wine warming over a small brazier, and pushed away the papers that lay too close to the glowing coals before he poured himself a bowl. Maati was looking up at him, sheepish, when he returned to the chair.

"I should have gotten that."

"It hardly matters. I've got it now. Are you well, Maati? You seem . . . bothered?"

"I was thinking the same thing about you. Ever since you got back from the Dai-kvo, it's seemed . . . difficult between us. Don't you think?"

"I suppose so," Otah said and sipped the wine. It was hot enough to blow across before he drank it, but it hadn't been cooking so long that the spirit had been burned out of it. The warmth of it in his throat was comfortable. "It's my fault. There are things I've been trying not to look at too closely. Orai said that sea travel changes you. Changes who you are."

"It may not be only that," Maati said softly.

"No?"

Maati sat forward, his elbows on his knees, and looked into the fire as he spoke. His voice was hard as slate.

"There's something I promised not to speak of. And I'm going to break that promise. I've done something terrible, Otah-kvo. I didn't mean to, and if I could undo it, I swear by all the gods I would. While you were away, Liat and I . . . there was no one else for us to speak with. We were the only two who knew all the truth. And so we spent time in each other's company . . ."

I need you to stay, Liat had said before he'd left for the Dai-kvo. *I need someone by my side.*

And Seedless when he'd returned: *Heshai fell in love and lost her, and he's been chewed by guilt ever since. Maati will do the same.*

Otah sat back, his chair creaking under his shifting weight. With a rush like water poured from a spout, he knew what he was seeing, what had happened. He put down his bowl of wine. Maati was silent, shaking his head back and forth slowly. His face was flushed and although there was no thickness in his voice, no hidden sob in his breath, still a single tear hung from the tip of his nose. It would have been comical if it had been someone else.

"She's a wonderful woman," Otah said, carefully. "Sometimes maybe a little difficult to trust, but still a good woman."

Maati nodded.

"Perhaps I should go," Otah said softly.

"I'm so sorry," Maati whispered to the fire. "Otah-kvo, I am so very, very sorry."

"You didn't do anything that hasn't been done a thousand times before by a thousand different people."

"But I did it to you. I betrayed *you*. You love her."

"But I don't trust her," Otah said softly.

"Or me. Not any longer," Maati said.

"Or you," Otah agreed, and pulling his robes close around him, he walked out of the poet's house and into the darkness. He closed the door, paused, and then hit it hard enough to bloody his knuckle.

The pain in his chest was real, and the rage behind it. And also, strangely, an amusement and a sense of relief. He walked slowly down to the edge of the pond, wishing more than anything that the courier Orai had been on his way to Saraykeht instead of Machi. But the world was as it was. Maati and Liat had become lovers, and it was devouring Maati just as some other tragedy had broken his teacher. Amat Kyaan was pursuing her suit before the Khai Saraykeht in a matter of days. Everything Seedless had said to him appeared to be true. And so he stood in the chill by the koi pond, and he waited, throwing stones into the dark water, hearing them strike and sink and be forgotten. He knew the andat would come to him if he were only patient. It wasn't more than half a hand.

"He's told you, then," Seedless said.

The pale face hovered in the night air, a rueful smile on the perfect, sensual lips.

"You knew?"

"Gods. The world and everyone knew," the andat said, stepping up beside him to look out over the black water. "They were about as discreet as rutting elk. I was only hoping you wouldn't hear of it until you'd done me that little favor. It's a pity, really. But I think I bear up quite well under failure, don't you?"

Otah took a deep breath, and let it out slowly. He thought perhaps his could see just the wisps of it in the cold. Beside him the andat didn't breathe because whatever it looked like, it was not a man.

"And . . . I have failed," Seedless said, his tone suddenly careful, probing. "Haven't I? I can spill your secrets, but that's hardly worth murder. And I can't expect you to kill a man in order to protect your faithless lover and the dear friend who bedded her, now can I?"

Otah saw again Maati's angry, self-loathing, empty expression and felt something twist in his belly. An impulse born in him as a child in a bare garden of half-turned earth, half a life ago. It didn't undo the hurt or the anger, but it complicated them.

"Someone told me once that you can love someone and not trust them, or you can bed someone and not trust them, but never both."

"I wouldn't know," the andat said. "My experience of love is actually fairly limited."

"Tell me what I need to know."

In the moonlight, pale hands took a pose that asked for clarification.

"You said you knew where he would be. How long it would take him to drink himself to sleep. Tell me."

"And you'll do what I asked?"

"Tell me what I need to know," Otah said, "and find out."

THE MORNING AFTER LIAT'S ARRIVAL AT THE COMFORT HOUSE—TWO DAYS AGO now—she'd awakened to the small sounds of Amat Kyaan sleeping. Only the faintest edge of daylight came through the shutters—these were the rooms of an owl. The faintest scent of Itani had still haunted her bedding then. When she rose, aching and awkward and half-sorry for the sex she'd insisted on in the night, Amat woke and took her downstairs. The workings of the house were simple enough—the sleeping chambers where the whores were shelved like scrolls in their boxes, cheap cloth over the bunks instead of netting; the kitchens in the back; the wide bath used for washing clothes and bodies during the day, then refilled and scented with oils before the clients came at night. The front parts of the house Amat explained were forbidden to her. Until the case against House Wilsin was made, she wasn't to leave the comfort house, and she wasn't to be seen by the clients. The stakes were too high, and Wilsin-cha had resorted to violence once already.

Since then, Liat had slept, eaten, washed herself, sat at Amat-cha's desk listening to musicians on the street below, but no word had come from Itani or from Maati. On her second night, Liat had sent out a message to the barracks where Itani's cohort slept. It had come back in the morning with a response from Muhatia-cha. Itani Noyga had left, breaking his indenture in violation of contract; he was not with the men of the house, nor was he welcome. Liat read the words with a sense of dread that approached illness. When she took it to Amat Kyaan, her old master had frowned and tucked the letter into her sleeve.

"What if Wilsin-cha's killed him?" Liat said, trying to keep the panic she felt from her voice.

Amat Kyaan, sitting at her desk, took a reassuring pose.

"He wouldn't. I have you and Maj to say what he would have said. Killing him would make our suit stronger, not weaker. And even then, I have the impression that your boy is able to take care of himself," Amat said, but seeing how little the assurances comforted her, she went on. "Still I can have Torish-cha's men ask after him."

"He'd have come back if things were well."

"Things aren't well," Amat said, her eyes hard and bright and tired. "But that doesn't mean he's in danger. Still, perhaps I should have had him stay as well. Have you sent to the poet's boy? Perhaps Maati's heard of him. He might even be staying there."

Amat took her cane and rose, gesturing at the desk. Fresh paper and ink.

"I have some things to attend to," she said. "Use what you need and we'll send him a runner."

Liat took a pose of gratitude and sat, but when she took up the pen, her hand trembled. The nib hovered just over the page, waiting, it seemed, to see which name she would write. In the end, it was Maati's name on the outside leaf. She wanted to be sure that someone would read it.

With the runner gone, Liat found there was little to do but pace. At first, she walked the length of Amat's rooms, then, as the day moved past its mid-point, her anxiety drove her downstairs. The common room smelled of roast pork and wine, and platters of bones still sat on the tables waiting to be cleared away. The whores were asleep, the men who worked the front rooms either sleeping in bunks as well or gone off to apartments away from the house. The soft quarter ran on a different day than the world Liat knew; daylight here meant rest and sleep. That Amat was awake and out of the house with Mitat and an armed escort meant that her old teacher was missing sleep. There were only five days until the case was to be made before the Khai Saraykeht.

Liat walked through the empty common room, stopping to scratch an old black dog behind the ears. It would be easy to step out the back as if going to the kitchens, and then out to the street. She imagined herself finding Itani, bringing him back to the safety of the comfort house. It was a bad idea, of course, and she wouldn't go, but the dream of it was powerful. The dream that she could somehow make everything come out right.

It was a small sound—hardly more than a sigh—that caught her attention. It had come from the long alcove in the back, from among the sewing benches and piles of cloth and leather where, according to Amat Kyaan, the costumes and stage props of the house were created. Liat moved toward it, walking softly. Behind the unruly heaps of cloth and thread, she found Maj sitting cross-legged, her hair pulled back. Her hands worked with something in her lap, and her expression was of such focus that Liat was almost afraid to interrupt. When Maj's hands shifted, she caught a glimpse of a tiny loom and black cloth.

"What is it?" Liat asked, pushed to speak by curiosity and her own buzzing, unfocused energy.

"Mourning cloth," Maj said without looking up. Her accent was so thick, Liat wasn't entirely sure she'd understood her until Maj continued. "For the dead child."

Liat came closer. The cloth was thin and sheer, black worked with tiny beads of clear glass in a pattern of surprising subtlety. Folds of it rested beside Maj's leg.

"It's beautiful," Liat said.

Maj shrugged. "It fills time. I am working on it for weeks now."

Liat knelt. The pale eyes looked up at her, questioning—maybe challenging—then returned to the small loom. Liat watched Maj's hands shifting thread and beads in near silence. It was very fine thread, the sort that might not make more than two or three hand-spans of cloth in a whole day's work. Liat reached out and ran her fingers along the folds of finished cloth. It was as wide as her two hands together and long, she guessed, as Maj was tall.

"How long do you make it?"

"Until you finish," Maj said. "Usually is something to make while the pain is fresh. When done with day's work, make cloth. When wake up in the middle night, make cloth. When time comes you want to go sing with friends or swim in quarry pond and not make cloth, is time to stop weaving."

"You've made these before. Mourning cloths."

"For mother, for brother. I am much younger then," Maj said, her voice heavy and tired. "Their cloth smaller."

Liat sat, watching as Maj threaded beads and worked them into the black patterns, the loom quiet as breathing. Neither spoke for a long time.

"I'm sorry," Liat said at last. "For what happened."

"Was your plan?"

"No, I didn't know anything about what was really happening."

"So, why sorry?"

"I should have," Liat said. "I should have known and I didn't."

Maj looked up and put the loom aside.

"And why did you not know?" she said, her gaze steady and accusing.

"I trusted Wilsin-cha," Liat said. "I thought he was doing what you wanted. I thought I was helping."

"And is this Wilsin who does this to you?" Maj asked, gesturing at the bandages and straps on Liat's shoulder.

"His men. Or that's what Amat-cha says."

"And you trust her?"

"Of course. Don't you?"

"I am here for a season, more than a season. At home, when a man does something evil, the *kiopia* pass judgement and like this . . ." Maj clapped her hands ". . . he is punished. Here, it is weeks living in a little room and waiting. Listening to nothing happen and waiting. And now, they say that the Khai, he may take his weeks to punish who killed my baby. Why wait except he doesn't trust Amat Kyaan? And if he doesn't why do I stay? Why am I waiting, if not for justice done?"

"It's complicated," Liat said. "It's all complicated."

Maj snorted with anger and impatience.

"Is simple," she said. "I thought before perhaps you know back then, perhaps you come now to keep the thing from happening, but instead I think you are just stupid, selfish, weak girl. Go away. I am weaving."

Liat stood, stung. She opened her mouth as if to speak, but there was nothing she could think to say. Maj spat casually on the floor at her feet.

Liat spent the next hours upstairs, out on the deck that overlooked the
street, letting her rage cool. The winter sun was strong enough to warm her as
long as the air was still. The slightest breeze was enough to chill her. High
clouds traced scratch marks on the sky. Her heart was troubled, but she couldn't
tell any longer if it was Maj's accusation, Itani and Maati, or the case about to
go before the Khai that bothered her. Twice, she turned, prepared to go back
down to Maj and demand an apology or else offer another of her own. Both
times, she stopped before she had passed Amat Kyaan's desk, swamped by her
own uncertainties. She was still troubled, probing her thoughts in search of
some little clarity, when a figure in the street caught her eye. The brown robe
fluttered as Maati ran toward the house. His face was flushed. She felt her
heart flutter in sudden dread. Something had happened.

She took the wide, wooden stairs three at a time, rushing down into the common room. She heard Maati's voice outside the rear door, raised and arguing.
Unbolting the door and pulling it open, she found one of the guards barring
Maati's way. Maati was in a pose of command, demanding that he be let in. When
he saw her, he went silent, and his face paled. Liat touched the guard's arm.

"Please," she said. "He's here for me."

"The old woman didn't say anything about him," the guard said.

"She didn't know. Please. She'd want him to come through."

The guard scowled, but stood aside. Maati came in. He looked ill—eyes
glassy and bloodshot, skin gray. His robes were creased and wrinkled, as if
they'd been slept in. Liat took his hand in her own without thinking.

"I got your message," Maati said. "I came as soon as I could. He isn't here?"

"No," Liat said. "I thought, since he stayed with you after he came back
from the Dai-kvo, maybe he'd come to you and . . ."

"He did," Maati said, and sat down. "After he brought you here, he took a
bunk at the seafront. He came to see me last night."

"He didn't stay?"

Maati pressed his lips thin and looked away. She was aware of Maj, standing
in the alcove, watching them, but the shame in Maati's face was too profound
for her to care what the islander made of this. Liat swallowed, trying to ease
the tightness in her throat. Maati carefully, intentionally, released her hand
from his. She let it drop to her side.

"He found out?" Liat asked, her voice small. "He knows what happened?"

"I told him," Maati said. "I had to. I thought he would come back here, that
he'd be with you."

"No. He never did."

"Do you think . . . if Wilsin found him . . ."

"Amat doesn't think Wilsin would do anything against him. There's nothing to gain from it. More likely, he only doesn't want to see us."

Maati sank to a bench, his head in his hands. Liat sat beside him, her unwounded arm around his shoulders. Itani was gone, lost to her. She knew it like her own name. She rested her head against Maati, and closed her eyes, half-desperate with the fear that he would go as well.

"Give him time," she murmured. "He needs time to think. That's all. Everything is going to be fine."

"It isn't," Maati said. His tone wasn't despairing or angry, only matter-of-fact. "Everything is going to be broken, and there's nothing I can do about it."

She closed her eyes, felt the rise and fall of his breath like waves coming to shore. Felt him shift as he turned to her and put his arms around her. Her wounds ached with the force of his embrace, but she would have bitten her tongue bloody before she complained. Instead she stroked his hair and wept.

"Don't leave me," she said. "I couldn't stand to lose you both."

"I'll stop breathing first," Maati said. "I swear I'll stop breathing before I leave you. But I have to find Otah-kvo."

The painful, wonderful arms unwrapped, and Maati stood. His face was serious to the point of grave. He took her hand.

"If Otah-kvo . . . if the two of you cannot reconcile . . . Liat, I would be less than whole without you. My life isn't entirely my own—I have duties to the Dai-kvo and the Khaiem—but what is mine to choose, I'd have you be part of."

Liat blinked back tears.

"You would choose me over him?"

The words shook him, she could see that. For a moment, she wanted more than anything to unsay them, but time only moved forward. Maati met her gaze again.

"I can't lose either of you," he said. "What peace Otah-kvo and I make, if we can make any, is between the two of us. What I feel for you, Liat . . . I could sink my life on those rocks. You've become that much to me. If you stay with him, I will be your friend forever."

It was like pouring cool water on a burn. Liat felt herself sink back.

"Go, then. Find him if you can and tell him how sorry I am. And whether you do or not, come back to me, Maati. Promise you'll come back."

It was still some minutes before Maati tore himself away and headed out into the streets of the city. Liat, after he had gone, sat on the bench, her eyes closed, observing the roiling emotions in her breast. Guilt, yes, but also joy. Fear, but also relief. She loved Maati, she saw that now. As she had loved Itani once, when they had only just begun. It was because of this confusion that she didn't notice for a long time that she was being watched.

Maj stood in the alcove, one hand pressed to her lips, her eyes shining with tears. Liat stood slowly, and took a pose that was a query. Maj strode across the room to her, put her hands on Liat's neck and—unnervingly—kissed her on the lips.

"Poor rabbit," Maj said. "Poor stupid rabbit. Am very sorry. The boy and you together. It makes me think of the man who I was . . . of the father. Before, I call you stupid and selfish and weak because I am forgetting what it is to be young. I am young once, too, and I am not my best mind now. What I say to hurt you, I take back, yes?"

Liat nodded, recognizing the apology in the words, if not the whole sense of them. Maj responded with a string of Nippu that Liat couldn't follow, but she caught the words for *knowledge* and for *pain*. Maj patted Liat's cheek gently and stepped away.

19

"Does it bother you, grandmother?" Mitat asked as they walked down the street. She spoke softly, so that the words stayed between the two of them, and not so far forward as the two mercenary guards before them or so far back as the two behind.

"I can think of a half dozen things you might mean," Amat said.

"Speaking against Wilsin."

"Of course it does," Amat said. "But it isn't something I chose."

"It's only that House Wilsin was good to you for so long . . . it was like family, wasn't it? To make your own way now . . ."

Amat narrowed her eyes. Mitat flushed and took a pose of apology which she ignored.

"This isn't a conversation about me, is it?" Amat asked.

"Not entirely," Mitat said.

The breeze blowing in from the sea chilled her, and the sun, already falling to the horizon, did nothing more than stretch the shadows and redden the light. The banners over the watch house fluttered, the mutter of cloth like voices in another room. Her guards opened the door, nodded to the watchmen inside and gestured Amat and her aide, her friend, her first real ally in the whole sour business, through. Amat paused.

"If you're thinking of leaving, you and your man, I want two things of you. First, wait until the suit is presented. Second, let me make an offer for your time. If we can't negotiate something, you can go with my blessings."

"The terms of my indenture were harsh, and you could . . ."

"Oh don't be an ass," Amat said. "That was between you and Ovi Niit. This is between us. Not the same thing at all."

Mitat smiled—a little sadly, Amat thought—and took a pose that sealed an agreement. In the watch house, Amat paid her dues, signed and countersigned the documents, and took her copy for the records of the house. For another turn through the moon's phases, she and her house were citizens in good standing of the soft quarter. She walked back to the house with her five companions, and yet also very much alone.

The scent of garlic sausages tempted her as they passed an old man and his cart, and Amat wished powerfully that she could stop, send away the men and their knives, and sit with Mitat talking as friends might. She could find what price the woman wanted to stay—whatever it was Amat expected she'd be willing to pay it. But the guards wouldn't let them pause or be alone. Mitat wouldn't have had it. Amat herself knew it would have been unwise—somewhere in the city, Marchat Wilsin had to be in a fever of desperation, and he'd proven willing to kill before this. Leaving the comfort house at all was a risk. And still, something like an ordinary life beckoned more seductively than any whore ever had.

One step at a time, Amat moved forward. There would be time later, she told herself, for all that. Later, when the Galts were revealed and her burden was passed on to someone else. When the child's death was avenged and her city was safe and her conscience was clean. Then she could be herself again, if there was anything left of that woman. Or create herself again if there wasn't.

The messenger waited for them at the front entrance of the house. He was a young man, not older than Liat, but he wore the colors of a high servant. A message, Amat knew with a sinking heart, from the Khai Saraykeht.

"You," she said. "You're looking for Amat Kyaan?"

The messenger—a young boy with narrow-set eyes and a thin nose—took a pose of acknowledgement and respect. It was a courtly pose.

"You've found her," Amat said.

The boy plucked a letter from his sleeve sealed with the mark of the Khai Saraykeht. Amat tore it open there in the street. The script was as beautiful as any message from the palaces—calligraphy so ornate as to approach illegibility. Still, Amat had the practice to make it out. She sighed and took a pose of thanks and dismissal.

"I understand," she said. "There's no reply."

"What happened?" Mitat asked as they walked into the house. "Something bad?"

"No," Amat said. "Only the usual delays. The Khai is putting the audience back four days. Another party wishes to be present."

"Wilsin?"

"I assume so. It serves us as much as him, really. We can use a few more days to prepare."

Amat paused in the front room of the house, tapping the folded paper against the edge of a dice table. The sound of a young girl laughing came from the back, from the place where her whores waited to be chosen by one client or another. It was an odd thing to hear. Any hint of joy, it seemed, had become an odd thing to hear. If she were Marchat Wilsin, she'd try one last gesture—throw one last dart at the sky and hope for a miracle.

"Get Torish-cha," Amat said. "I want to discuss security again. And have we had word from Liat's boy? Itani?"

"Nothing yet," the guard by the front door said. "The other one came by before."

"If either of them arrive, send them to see me."

She walked through to the back, Mitat beside her.

"It's likely only a delay," Amat said, "but if he's winning time for a reason, I want to be ready for it."

"Grandmother?"

They had reached the common room—full now with women and boys in the costumes they wore, with the men who ran the games and wine, with the smell of fresh bread and roast lamb and with voices. Mitat stood at the door, her arms crossed. Amat took a querying pose.

"Someone has to tell Maj," she said.

Amat closed her eyes. Of course. As if all the rest wasn't enough, someone would have to tell Maj. She would. If there was going to be a screaming fight, at least they could have it in Nippu. Amat took two long breaths and opened her eyes again. Mitat's expression had softened into a rueful amusement.

"I could have been a dancer," Amat said. "I was very graceful as a girl. I could have been a dancer, and then I would never have had to march through any of this piss."

"I can do it if you want," Mitat said. Amat only smiled, shook her head, and walked toward the door to the little room of Maj's and the storm that was inescapably to be suffered.

OTAH MACHI, THE SIXTH SON OF THE KHAI MACHI, SAT AT THE END OF THE WHARF and looked out over ocean. The fading twilight left only the light of a half moon dancing on the tops of the waves. Behind him, the work of the seafront was finished for the day, and the amusements of night time—almost as loud—had begun. He ignored the activity, ate slices of hot ginger chicken from the thick paper cone he'd bought at a stand, and thought about nothing.

He had two lengths of copper left to him. Years of work, years of making a life for himself in this city, and he had come to that—two lengths of copper. Enough to buy a bowl of wine, if he kept his standards low. Everything else, spent or lost or thrown away. But he was, at least, prepared. Below him, the tide was rising. It would fall again before the dawn came.

The time had come.

He walked the length of the seafront, throwing the spent paper soaked in grease and spices into a firekeeper's kiln where it flared and blackened, lighting for a moment the faces of the men and women warming themselves at the fire. The warehouses were dark and closed, the wide Nantan empty. Outside a teahouse, a woman sang piteously over a begging box with three times more money in it than Otah had in the world. He tossed in one of his copper lengths for luck.

The soft quarter was much the same as any night. He was the one who was different. The drum and flute from the comfort houses, the smell of incense and stranger smokes, the melancholy eyes of women selling themselves from low parapets and high windows. It was as if he had come to the place for the first time—a traveler from a foreign land. There was time, he supposed, to turn aside. Even now, he could walk away from it all as he had from the school all those years before. He could walk away now and call it strength or purity. Or the calm of stone. He could call it that, but he would know the truth of it.

The alley was where Seedless had said it would be, hidden almost in the shadows of the buildings that lined it. He paused there for a time. Far down in the darkness, a lantern glowed without illuminating anything but itself. A showfighter lumbered past, blood flowing from his scalp. Two sailors across the street pointed at the wounded man, laughing. Otah stepped into darkness.

Mud and filth slid under his boots like a riverbed. The lantern grew nearer, but he reached the door the andat had described before he reached the light. He pressed his hand to it. The wood was solid, the lock was black iron. The light glimmering through at the edges of the shutters showed that a fire was burning within. The poet in his private apartments, the place where he hid from the beauty of the palaces and the house that had come with his burden. Otah tried the door gently, but it was locked. He scratched at it and then rapped, but no one came. With a knife, he could have forced the lock, unhinged the door—a man drunk enough might even have slept through it, but he would have had to come much later. The andat had told him not to go to the hidden apartment until well past the night candle's last mark, and it wasn't to the first quarter yet.

"Heshai-kvo," he said, not shouting, but his voice loud enough to ring against the stonework around him. "Open the door."

For a long moment, he thought no one would come. But then the line of light that haloed the shutters went dark, a bolt shot with a solid click, and the door creaked open. The poet stood silhouetted. His robes were disheveled as his hair. His wide mouth was turned down in a heavy scowl.

"What do you think you're doing here?"

"We need to talk," Otah said.

"No we don't," the poet said, stepping back and starting to pull the door closed. "Go away."

Otah pushed in, first squaring his shoulder against the door, and then leaning in with his back and legs. The poet fell back with a surprised huff of breath.
The rooms were small, dirty, squalid. A cot of stretched canvas was pulled too
close to a fireplace, and empty bottles littered the floor by it. Streaks of dark
mold ran down the walls from the sagging beams of the ceiling. The smell was
like a swamp in summer. Otah closed the door behind him.

"Wh- what do you want?" the poet said, his face pale and fearful.

"We need to talk," Otah said again. "Seedless told me where to find you.
He sent me here to kill you."

"Kill me?" Heshai repeated, and then chuckled. The fear seemed to drain
away, and a bleak amusement took its place. "Kill me. Gods."

Shaking his head, the poet lumbered to the cot and sat. The canvas groaned
against its wooden frame. Otah stood between the fire and the doorway, ready
to block Heshai if he bolted. He didn't.

"So. You've come to finish me off, eh? Well, you're a big, strong boy. I'm old
and fat and more than half drunk. I doubt you'll have a problem."

"Seedless told me that you'd welcome it," Otah said. "I suspect he over-
stated his case, eh? Anyway, I'm not his puppet."

The poet scowled, his bloodshot eyes narrowing in the firelight. Otah
stepped forward, knelt as he had as a boy at the school and took a pose appropriate to a student addressing a teacher.

"You know what's happening. Amat Kyaan's audience before the Khai Saraykeht. You have to know what would happen."

Slowly, grudgingly, Heshai took an acknowledging pose.

"Seedless hoped that I would kill you in order to prevent it. But I find I'm
not a murderer," Otah said. "The stakes here, the price that innocent people
will pay . . . and the price Maati will pay. It's too high. I can't let it happen."

"I see," Heshai said. He was silent for a long moment, the ticking of the fire
the only sound. Thoughtfully, he reached down and lifted a half-full bottle
from the floor. Otah watched the old man drink, the thick throat working as he
gulped the wine down. Then, "And how do you plan to reconcile these two
issues, eh?"

"Let the andat go," Otah said. "I've come to ask you to set Seedless free."

"That simple, eh?"

"Yes."

"I can't do it."

"I think that you can," Otah said.

"I don't mean it can't be done. Gods, nothing would be easier. I'd only have
to . . ." He opened one hand in a gesture of release. "That isn't what I meant.
It's that *I* can't do it. It's not . . . it isn't in me. I'm sorry, boy. I know it looks
simple from where you are. It isn't. I'm the poet of Saraykeht, and that isn't
something you stop being just because you get tired. Just because it eats you.

Just because it kills children. Look, if you had the choice of grabbing a live coal and holding it in your fist or destroying a city of innocent people, you'd do everything you could to stand the pain. You wouldn't be a decent man if you didn't at least try."

"And you would be a decent man if you let the Khai Saraykeht take his vengeance?"

"No, I'd be a poet," Heshai said, and his smile was as much melancholy as humor. "You're too young to understand. I've been holding this coal in my hand since before you were born. I can't stop now because I *can't*. Who I am is too much curled around this. If I stopped—just *stopped*—I wouldn't be anyone anymore."

"I think you're wrong."

"Yes. Yes, I see you think that, but your opinion on it doesn't matter. And that doesn't surprise you, does it?"

The sick dread in Otah's belly suddenly felt as heavy as if he'd swallowed stone. He took a pose of acknowledgement. The poet leaned forward and put his wide, thick hand gently over Otah's.

"You knew I wouldn't agree," he said.

"I . . . hoped . . ."

"You had to try," Heshai said, his tone approving. "It speaks well of you. You had to try. Don't blame yourself. I haven't been strong enough to end this, and I've been up to my hips in it for decades. Wine?"

Otah accepted the offered bottle. It was strong—mixed with something that left a taste of herb at the back of his throat. He handed it back. Warmth bloomed in his belly. Heshai, seeing his surprise, laughed.

"I should have warned you. It's a little more than they serve with lamb cuts, but I like it. It lets me sleep. So, if you don't mind my asking, what made our mutual acquaintance think you'd do his killing for him?"

Otah found himself telling the tale—his own secret and Wilsin's, the source of Liat's wounds and the prospect of Maati's. Throughout, Heshai listened, his face clouded, nodding from time to time or asking questions that made Otah clarify himself. When the secret of Otah's identity came out, the poet's eyes widened, but he made no other comment. Twice, he passed the bottle of wine over, and Otah drank from it. It was strange, hearing it all spoken, hearing the thoughts he'd only half-formed made real by the words he found to express them. His own fate, the fate of others—justice and betrayal, loyalty and the changes worked by the sea. The wine and the fear and the pain and dread in Otah's guts turned the old man into his confessor, his confidant, his friend even if only for the moment.

The night candle was close to the halfway mark when he finished it all—his thoughts and fears, secrets and failures. Or almost all. There was one left that he wasn't ready to mention—the ship he'd booked two passages on with the last of his silver, ready to sail south before the dawn—a small Westlands ship, desperate enough to ply winter trade where the waters never froze. An escape ship for a murderer and his accomplice. That he held still to himself.

"Hard," the poet said. "Hard. Maati's a good boy. Despite it all, he is good. Only young."

"Please, Heshai-kvo," Otah said. "Stop this thing."

"It's out of my hands. And really, even if I were to let the beast slip, your whoremonger sounds like she's good enough to tell a strong story. The next andat the Dai-kvo sends might be just as terrible. Or another Khai could be pressed into service, meting out vengeance on behalf of all the cities together. Killing me might spare Maati and keep your secrets, but Liat . . . the Galts . . ."

"I'd thought of that."

"Anyway, it's too late for me. Shifting names, changing who you are, putting lives on and off like fine robes—that's a young man's game. There's too many years loaded on the back of my cart. The weight makes turning tricky. How would you have done it, if you did?"

"Do what?"

"Kill me?"

"Seedless told me to come just before dawn," Otah said. "He said a cord around the throat, pulled tight, would keep you from crying out."

Heshai chuckled, but the sound was grim. He swallowed down the last dregs of the wine, leaving a smear of black leaves on the side of the bottle. He fumbled for a moment in the chaos under his cot, pulled out a fresh bottle and opened it roughly, throwing the cork into the fire.

"He's an optimist," Heshai said. "The way I drink, I'll be senseless as stones by the three quarters."

Otah frowned, and then the import of the words came over him like cold water. The dread in his belly became a knot, but he didn't speak. The poet looked into the fire, the low, dying flames cast shadows on his wide, miserable features. The urge to take the old man in his arms and embrace or else shake him came over Otah and passed—a wave against the shore. When the old man's gaze shifted, Otah saw his own darkness mirrored there.

"I've always done what I was told to, my boy. The rewards aren't what you'd expect. You aren't a killer. I'm a poet. If we're going to stop this thing, one of us has to change."

"I should go," Otah said, drawing himself up to his feet.

Heshai-kvo took a pose of farewell, intimate as family. Otah replied with something very much the same. There were tears, he saw, on Heshai's cheeks to match his own.

"You should lock the door behind me," Otah said.

"Later," Heshai said. "I'll do it later if I remember to."

The fetid, chill air of the alley was like waking from a dream—or half-waking. Overhead, the half-moon slipped through wisps and fingers of clouds, insubstantial as veils. He walked with his head held high, but though he was ashamed of them, he couldn't stanch the tears. From outside himself, he could observe the sorrow and the black tarry dread, different from fear because of its perfect certainty. He was becoming a murderer. He wondered how his brothers would manage this, when the time came for them to turn on one another, how they would bring themselves with cool, clear minds, to end another man's life.

The comfort house of Amat Kyaan glowed in the night as the others of its species did—music and voices, the laughter of whores and the cursing of men at the tables. The wealth of the city poured through places like this in a tiny city in itself, given over entirely to pleasure and money. It wouldn't always be so, he knew. He stood in the street and drank in the sight, the smell, the golden light and brightly colored banners, the joy and the sorrow of it. Tomorrow, it would be part of a different city.

The guard outside the back door recognized him.

"Grandmother wants to see you," the man said.

Otah watched himself take a pose of acknowledgement and smile his charming smile.

"Do you know where I could find her?"

"Up in her rooms with Wilsin's girl."

Otah gave his thanks and walked in. The common room wasn't empty—a handful of women sat at the tables, eating and talking among themselves. A black-haired girl, nearly naked, stood in the alcove, cupping her breasts in diaphanous silk with the air of a fish seller wrapping cod. Otah considered the wide, rough-hewn stairs that led to Amat Kyaan's apartments, to Liat. The door at the top landing was closed. He turned away, scratching lightly on the door of the other room—the one he had seen Maj retreat to the one night he had been there, the one time they had spoken.

The door pulled open just wide enough for the islander's face to appear. Her pale skin was flushed, her eyes bright and bloodshot. Otah leaned close.

"Please," he said. "I need to speak with you."

Maj's eyes narrowed, but a breath later, she stepped back, and Otah pushed into the room, closing the door behind him. Maj stood, arms pulled back, chin jutting like a child ready for a fight. A single lantern sat on a desk showing the cot, the hand-loom, the heap of robes waiting for the launderer. An empty winebowl lay canted in the corner of wall and floor. She was drunk. Otah calculated that quickly, and found that it was likely a good thing.

"Maj-cha," Otah said. "Forgive me, but I need your help. And I think I may be of service to you."

"I am living here," she said. "Not working. I am not one of these girls. Get out."

"No," Otah said, "that isn't what I mean. Maj, I can give you your vengeance now—tonight. The man who wields the andat. The one who actually took the child from you. I can take you to him now."

Maj frowned and shook her head slowly, her gaze locked on Otah. He spoke quickly, and low, using simple words with as few poses as he could manage. He explained that the Galts had been Seedless' tools, that Heshai controlled Seedless, that Otah could take her to him if they left now, right now. He thought he saw her soften, something like hope in her expression.

"But afterwards," he said, "you have to let me take you home. I have a ship ready to take us. It leaves before dawn."

"I ask grandmother," Maj said, and moved toward the door. Otah shifted to block her.

"No. She can't know. She wants to stop the Galts, not the poet. If you tell her, you have to go the way she goes. You have to put it before the Khai and wait to see what he chooses to do. I can give it to you now—tonight. But you have to leave Amat before you see the Khai. It's my price."

"You think I am stupid? Why should I trust you? Why are you doing this?"

"You aren't stupid. You should trust me because I have what you want—certainty, an end to waiting, vengeance, and a way back home. I'm doing this because I don't want to see any more women suffer what you've suffered, and because it takes the thing that did this out of the world forever."

Because it saves Maati and Liat. Because it saves Heshai. Because it is a terrible thing, and it is right. And because I have to get you away from this house.

A half smile pulled at her thick, pale mouth.

"You are man?" Maj asked. "Or you are ghost?"

Otah took a pose of query. Maj reached out and touched him, pressing his shoulder gently with her fingertips, as if making sure his flesh had substance.

"If you are man, then I am tired of being tricked. You lie to me and I will kill you with my teeth. If you are ghost, then you are maybe the one I am praying for."

"If you were praying for this," Otah said, "then I'm the answer to it. But get your things quickly. We have to go now, and we can't come back."

For a moment she wavered, and then the anger he had seen in her before, the desperation, shone in her eyes. It was what he had known was there, what he had counted on. She looked around at the tiny room, gathered up what looked like a half-knitted cloth and deliberately spat on the ground.

"Is nothing more I want here," Maj said. "You take me now. You show me. If is not as you say, I kill you. You doubt that?"

"No," he said. "I believe you."

It was a simple enough thing to distract the guard, to send him up to speak with Amat Kyaan—her security was done with attack in mind, not escape. Leading Maj out the back took the space of four breaths, perhaps five. Another dozen, and they were gone, vanished into the maze of streets and alleys that made up the soft quarter.

Maj stayed close to him as they went, and when they passed torches or street lanterns, he caught glimpses of her face, wild with release and the heat of fury. The alley, when he reached it, was empty. The door, when he tried it, was unlocked.

MAATI STEPPED INTO THE POET'S HOUSE, HIS FEET SORE, HIS HEAD BUZZING LIKE A hive. The house was silent, dark, and cold. Only the single, steady flame of a night candle stood watch in a lantern of glass. It had burned down past the half mark, the night more than half over. He dropped to a tapestry-draped divan and pulled the heavy cloth over him. He had visited every teahouse he knew of, had asked everyone he recognized. Otah-kvo had vanished—stepped into the thin mists of the seafront like a memory. And every step had been a journey, every fingers-width of the moon in its nightly arc had encompassed a lifetime. He'd expected, huddled under the heavy cloth, for sleep to come quickly and yet the dim glow of the candle distracted him, pulled his eyes open just when he had told himself that finally, finally he was letting the day fall away from him. He shifted, his robes bunching uncomfortably under his arm, at his ribs. It seemed half a night before he gave up and sat, letting his makeshift blankets fall away. The night candle was still well before the three-quarter mark.

"Wine might help," the familiar voice said from the darkness of the stairway. "It has the advantage of tradition. Many's the night our noble poet's slept beside a pool of his own puke, stinking of half-digested grapes."

"Be quiet," Maati said, but there was no force to his voice, no reserve left to fend off the attentions of the andat. Slowly, the perfect face and hands descended. He wore a robe of white, pale as his skin. A mourning robe. His demeanor when he sat on the second stair, stretching out his legs and smiling, was the same as ever—amused and scheming and untrustworthy and sad. But perhaps there was something else, an underlying energy that Maati didn't understand.

"I only mean that a hard night can be ended, if only you have the will to do it. And don't mind paying the price, when it comes."

"Leave me alone," Maati said. "I don't want to talk to you."

"Not even if your little friend came by, the seafront laborer?"

Maati's breath stopped, his blood suddenly with a separate life from his own. He took an interrogative pose. Seedless laughed.

"Oh, he didn't," the andat said. "I was just wondering about your terms. If you didn't want to speak to me under any conditions, or if perhaps there might be exceptions to your rule. Purely hypothetical."

Maati felt the flush in his face, as much anger as embarrassment, and picked up the nearest thing to throw at Seedless. It was a beaded cushion, and it bounced off the andat's folded knees. Seedless took a pose of contrition, rose, and carried the cushion back to its place.

"I don't mean to hurt you, my dear. But you look like someone's just stolen your puppy, and I thought a joke might brighten things. I'm sorry if I was wrong."

"Where's Heshai?"

The andat paused, looking out, as if the black eyes could see through the walls, through the trees, any distance to consider the poet where he lay. A thin smile curled its lips.

"Away," Seedless said. "In his torture box. The same as always, I suppose."

"He isn't here, though."

"No," Seedless said, simply.

"I need to speak to him."

Seedless sat on the couch beside him, considering him in silence, his expression distant as the moon. The mourning robe wasn't new though it clearly hadn't seen great use. The cut was simple, the cloth coarse and unsoftened by pounding. From the way it sagged, it was clearly intended for a wider frame than Seedless'—it was clearly meant for Heshai. Seedless seemed to see him notice all this, and looked down, as if aware of his own robes for the first time.

"He had these made when his mother died," the andat said. "He was with the Dai-kvo at the time. He didn't see her pyre, but the news reached him. He keeps it around, I suppose, so that he won't have to buy another one should anybody else die."

"And what makes you wear it?"

Seedless shrugged, grinned, gestured with wide-spread hands that indicated everything and nothing.

"Respect for the dead," Seedless said, "Why else?"

"Everything's a joke to you," Maati said. The fatigue made his tongue thick, but if anything, he was farther from rest than before he'd come back to the house. The combination of exhaustion and restlessness felt like an illness. "Nothing matters."

"Not true," the andat said. "Just because something's a game, doesn't mean it isn't serious."

"Gods. Is there something in the way Heshai-kvo made you that keeps you from making sense? You're like talking to smoke."

"I can speak to the point if you'd like," Seedless said. "Ask me what you want."

"I don't have anything to ask you, and you don't have anything to teach me," Maati said, rising. "I'm going to sleep. Tomorrow can't be worse than today was."

"Possibility is a wide field, dear. *Can't* is a word for small imaginations." Seedless said from behind him, but Maati didn't turn back.

His room was colder than the main room. He lit a small fire in the brazier before he pulled back the woolen blankets, pulled off his shoes, and tried again to sleep. The errands of the day ran through his mind, unstoppable and chaotic: Liat's distress and the warmth of her flesh, Otah-kvo's last words to him and the searing remorse that they held. If only he could find him, if only he could speak with him again.

Half-awake, Maati began to catalog for himself the places he had been in the night, searching for a corner he knew of, but might have overlooked. And, as he pictured the night streets of Saraykeht, he found himself moving down them, knowing as he did that he was dreaming. Street and alley, square and court, until he was in places that were nowhere real in the city, searching for teahouses that didn't truly exist other than within his own frustration and despair, and aware all the time that this was a dream, but was not sleep.

He kicked off the blankets, desperate for some sense of freedom. But the little brazier wasn't equal to its work, and the cold soon brought him swimming back up into his full mind. He lay in the darkness and wept. When that brought no relief, he rose changed into fresh robes, and stalked down the stairs.

Seedless had started a fire in the grate. A copper pot of wine was warming over it, filling the room with its rich scent. The andat sat in a wooden chair, a book open in his lap. The brown, leather-bound volume that told of his own creation and its errors. He didn't look up when Maati came in and walked over to the fire, warming his feet by the flames. When he spoke, he sounded weary.

"The spirit's burned out of it. You can drink as much as you'd like and not impair yourself."

"What's the point, then?" Maati asked.

"Comfort. It may taste a little strong, though. I thought you'd come down sooner, and it gets thick if it boils too long."

Maati turned his back to the andat and used an old copper ladle to fill his winebowl. When his took a sip, it tasted rich and hot and red. And, perversely, comforting.

"It's fine," he said.

He heard the hush of paper upon paper as, behind him, Seedless closed the book. The silence afterward went on so long that he looked back over his shoulder. The andat sat motionless as a statue; not even breath stirred the folds of his robe and his face betrayed nothing. His ribs shifted an inch, taking in air, and he spoke.

"What would you have said, if you'd found him?"

Maati shifted, sitting with his legs crossed, the warm bowl in his hands. He blew across it to cool it before he answered.

"I'd have asked his forgiveness."

"Would you have deserved it, do you think?"

"I don't know. Possibly not. What I did was wrong."

Seedless chuckled and leaned forward, lacing his long graceful fingers together.

"Of course it was," Seedless said. "Why would anyone ask forgiveness for something they'd done that was right? But tell me, since we're on the subject of judgment and clemency, why would you ask for something you don't deserve?"

"You sound like Heshai-kvo."

"Of course I do, you're evading. If you don't like that question, leave it aside and answer me this instead. Would you forgive me? What I did was wrong, and I know it. Would you do for me what you'd ask of him?"

"Would you want me to?"

"Yes," Seedless said, and his voice was strangely plaintive. It wasn't an emotion Maati had ever seen in the andat before now. "Yes, I want to be forgiven."

Maati sipped the wine, then shook his head.

"You'd do it again, wouldn't you? If you could, you'd sacrifice anyone or anything to hurt Heshai-kvo."

"You think that?"

"Yes."

Seedless bowed his head until his hair tipped over his hands.

"I suppose you're right," he said. "Fine, then this. Would you forgive Heshai-kvo for his failings? As a teacher to you, as a poet in making something so dangerously flawed as myself. Really, pick anything—there's no end of ways in which he's wanting. Does he deserve mercy?"

"Perhaps," Maati said. "He didn't mean to do what he did."

"Ah! And because I planned, and he blundered, the child is more my wrong than his?"

"Yes."

"Then you've forgotten again what we are to each other, he and I. But let that be. If your laborer friend—you called him Otah-kvo, by the way. You should be more careful of that. If Otah-kvo did something wrong, if he committed some crime or helped someone else commit one, could you let that go?"

"You know . . . how did you . . ."

"I've known for weeks, dear. Don't let it worry you. I haven't told anyone. Answer the question; would you hold his crimes against him as you hold mine against me?"

"No, I don't think I would. Who told you that Otah was . . ."

Seedless leaned back and took a pose of triumph.

"And what's the difference between us, laborer and andat that you'll brush his sins aside and not my own?"

Maati smiled.

"You aren't him," he said.

"And you love him."

Maati took a pose of affirmation.

"And love is more important than justice," Seedless said.

"Sometimes. Yes."

Seedless smiled and nodded.

"What a terrible thought," he said. "That love and injustice should be married."

Maati shifted to a dismissive pose, and in reply the andat took the brown book back up, leafing through the handwritten pages as if looking for his place. Maati closed his eyes and breathed in the fumes of the wine. He felt profoundly comfortable, like sleep—true sleep—coming on. He felt himself rocking slowly, involuntarily shifting in time with his pulse. A sense of disquiet roused him and without opening his eyes again, he spoke.

"You mustn't tell anyone about Otah-kvo. If his family finds him . . ."

"They won't," Seedless said. "At least not through me."

"I don't believe you."

"This time, you can. Heshai-kvo did his best by you. Do you know that? For all his failings, and for all of mine, to the degree that our private war allowed it, we have taken care of you and . . ."

The andat broke off. Maati opened his eyes. The andat wasn't looking at him or the book, but out, to the south. It was as if his sight penetrated the walls, the trees, the distance, and took in some spectacle that held him. Maati couldn't help following his gaze, but there was nothing but the rooms of the house. When he glanced back, the andat's expression was exultant.

"What is it?" Maati asked, a cold dread at his back.

"It's Otah-kvo," Seedless said. "He's forgiven you."

THE SINGLE CANDLE BURNED, MARKING THE HOURS OF THE NIGHT. ON THE COT where Otah had left him, the poet slept, all color leached from his face by the dim light. The poet's mouth was open, his breath deep and regular. Maj, at his side, knelt, considering the sleeping man's face. Otah shut the door.

"Is him," Maj said, her voice low and tense. "Is the one who does this to me. To my baby."

Otah moved forward, careful not to rattle the bottles on the floor, not to make any sound that would wake the sleeper.

"Yes," he said. "It is."

Silently, Maj pulled a knife from her sleeve. It was a thin blade, long as her hand but thinner than a finger. Otah touched her wrist and shook his head.

"Quiet," he said. "It has to be quiet."

"So how?" she asked.

Otah fumbled for a moment in his own sleeve and drew out the cord. It was braided bamboo, thin and supple, but so strong it would have borne Otah's weight without snapping. Wooden grips at each end fit his fingers to keep it from cutting into his flesh when he pulled it tight. It was a thug's weapon. Otah saw it in his own hands as if from a distance. The dread in his belly had suffused through his body, through the world, and disconnected him from everything. He felt like a puppet, pulled by invisible strings.

"I hold him," Maj said. "You do this."

Otah looked at the sleeping man. There was no rage in him to carry him through, no hatred to justify it. For a moment, he thought of turning away, of rousing the man or calling out for the watch. It would be so simple, even now, to turn back. Maj seemed to read his thoughts. Her eyes, unnatural and pale, met his.

"You do this," she said again.

He would walk onto the blade . . .

"His legs," Otah said. "I'll worry about his arms, but you keep him from kicking free."

Maj moved in so close to the cot, she seemed almost ready to crawl onto it with Heshai. Her hands flexed in the space above the bend of the poet's knees. Otah looped the cord, ready to drop it over the poet's head, his fingers in the curves that were made for them. He stepped forward. His foot brushed a bottle, the sound of glass rolling over stone louder than thunder in the silence. The poet lurched, lifted himself, less than half awake, up on his elbow.

As if his body had been expecting it, Otah dropped the cord into place and pulled. He was dimly aware of the soft sounds of Maj struggling, pulling, holding the poet down. The poet's hands were at his throat now, fingers digging for the cord that had vanished, almost, into the flesh. Otah's hands and arms ached, and the broad muscles across his shoulders burned as he drew the cord as tight as his strength allowed. The poet's face was dark with blood, his wide lips black. Otah closed his eyes, but didn't loose his grip. The struggle grew weaker. The flailing arms and clawing fingers became the soft slaps of a child, and then stopped. In the darkness behind his eyes, Otah still pulled, afraid that if he stopped too soon it would all have to be done again. There was a wet sound, and the smell of shit. His back knotted between his shoulder blades, but he counted a dozen breaths, and then a half dozen more, before he looked up.

Maj stood at the foot of the cot. Her robes were disarranged and a bad bruise was already blooming on her cheek. Her expression was serene as a statue's. Otah released the cord, his fingers stiff. He kept his gaze high, not wanting to see the body. Not at any price.

"It's done," he said, his voice shaky. "We should go."

Maj said something, not to him but to the corpse between them. Her words were flowing and lovely and he didn't know what they meant. She turned and walked solemn and regal out of the room, leaving Otah to follow her. He hesitated at the doorway, caught between wanting to look back and not, between the horror of the thing he had done and the relief that it was over. Perversely, he felt guilty leaving Heshai like this without giving some farewell; it seemed rude.

"Thank you, Heshai-kvo," he said at last, and took a pose appropriate for a pupil to an honored teacher. After a moment, he dropped his hands, stepped out, and closed the door.

The air of the alleyway was sharp and cold, rich with the threat of rain. For a brief, frightened moment, he thought he was alone, that Maj had gone, but the sound of her retching gave her away. He found her doubled over in the mud, weeping and being sick. He placed a hand on her back, reassuring and gentle, until the worst had passed. When she rose, he brushed off what he could of the mess and, his arm around her, led her out from the alleyway, to the west and down, towards the seafront and away at last from Saraykeht.

"WHAT DO YOU MEAN?" MAATI ASKED. "HOW HAS OTAH-KVO . . ."

And then he stopped because, with a sound like a sigh and a scent like rain, Seedless had vanished, and only the mourning robes remained.

20

>+< Morning seemed like any other for nearly an hour, and then the news came. When Liat heard it humming through the comfort house—Maj gone, the poet killed—she ran to the palaces. She forgot her own safety, if there was safety to be had anywhere. When she finally crossed the wooden bridge over water tea-brown with dead leaves, her sides ached, her wounded shoulder throbbed with her heartbeat.

She didn't know what she would say. She didn't know how she would tell him.

When she opened the door, she knew there was no need.

The comfortable, finely appointed furniture was cast to the walls, the carpets pulled back. A wide stretch of pale wooden flooring lay bare and empty as a clearing. The air smelled of rain and smoke. Maati, dressed in formal robes poorly tied, knelt in the center of the space. His skin was ashen, his hair half-wild. A book lay open before him, bound in leather, its pages covered in beautiful script. He was chanting, a soft sillibant flow that seemed to echo against the walls and move back into itself, complex as music. Liat watched, fascinated, as Maati shifted back and forth his lips moving, his hands restless. Something like a wind pressed against her without disturbing the folds of her robes. A sense of profound presence, like standing before the Khai only a thousand times as intense and a thousand times less humane.

"Stop this!" she screamed even, it seemed, as she understood. *"Stop!"*

She rushed forward, pushing through the thick presence, the air oppressive as a furnace, but with something besides heat. Maati seemed to hear her voice distantly. His head turned, his eyes opened, and he lost the thread of the chant. Echoes fell out of phase with each other, their rhythms collapsing like a crowd that had been clapping time falling into mere applause. And then the room was silent and empty again except for the two of them.

"You can't," she said. "You said that it was too near what Heshai had done before. You said that it couldn't work. You *said* so, Maati."

"I have to try," he said. The words were so simple they left her empty. She simply folded beside him, her legs tucked beneath her. Maati blinked like he was only half-awake. "I have to try. I think, perhaps, if I don't wait . . . if I do it now, maybe Seedless isn't all the way gone . . . I can pull him back before Heshai's work has entirely . . ."

It was what she needed, hearing the poet's name. It gave her something to speak to. Liat took his hand in hers. He winced a little, and she relaxed her grip, but not enough to let him go.

"Heshai's dead, Maati. He's gone. And whether he's dead for an hour or a year, he's just as dead. Seedless . . . Seedless is gone. They're both gone."

Maati shook his head.

"I can't believe that," he said. "I understand Heshai better than anyone else. I know Seedless. It's early, and there isn't much time, but if I can only . . ."

"It's too late. It's too late, and if you do this, it's no better than sinking yourself in the river. You'll die, Maati. You told me that. *You* did. If a poet fails to capture the andat, he dies. And this . . ." she nodded to the open book written in a dead man's hand. "It won't work. *You're* the one who said so."

"It's different," he said.

"How?"

"Because I have to try. I'm a poet, love. It's what I am. And you know as well as I do that if Seedless escapes, there's nothing. There's nothing to take his place."

"So there's nothing," she said.

"Saraykeht . . ."

"Saraykeht is a city, Maati. It's roads and walls and people and warehouses and statues. It doesn't know you. It doesn't love you. It's me who does that. I love you. Please, Maati, do not do this."

Slowly, carefully, Maati took his hand from hers. When he smiled, it was as much sorrow as fondness.

"You should go," he said. "I have something I need to do. If it works out as I hope, I'll find you."

Liat rose. The room was hazy with tears, but sorrow wasn't what warmed her chest and burned her skin. It was rage, rage fueled by pain.

"You can kill yourself if you like," she said. "You can do this thing now and die, and they may even talk about you like a hero. But I'll know better."

She turned and walked out, her heart straining. On the steps, she stopped. The sun shone cool over the bare trees. She closed her eyes, waiting to hear the grim, unnatural chant begin again behind her. Crows hopped from branch to branch, and then as if at a signal, rose together and streamed off to the south. She stood for almost half a hand, the chill air pressing into her flesh.

She wondered how long she could wait there. She wondered where Itani was now, and if he knew what had happened. If he would ever forgive her for loving more than one man. She chewed at the inside of her cheek until it hurt.

Behind her, the door scraped open. Maati looked defeated. He was tucking the leather bound book into his sleeve as he stepped out to her.

"Well," he said. "I'll have to go back to the Dai-kvo and tell him I've failed."

She stepped close to him, resting her head against his shoulder. He was warm, or the day had cooled her even more than she'd thought. For a moment, she remembered the feeling of Itani's broad arms and the scent of his skin.

"Thank you," she said.

It was three weeks now since the poet had died. Three weeks was too long, Amat knew, for a city to hold its breath. The tension was still there—the uncertainty, the fear. It showed in the faces of the men and women in the street and in the way they held their bodies. Amat heard it in the too-loud laughter, and angry words of drunkards in the soft quarter streets. But the initial shock was fading. Time, suspended by the sudden change of losing the andat, was moving forward again. And that, as much as anything, drew her out, away from the protection of the comfort house and into the city. Her city.

In the gray of winter fog, the streets were like memories—here a familiar fountain emerged, took shape, and form and weight. The dark green of the stone glistened in the carvings of ship and fish, eagle and archer. And then as she passed, they faded, becoming at last a darkness behind her, and nothing more. She stopped at a stand by the seafront to buy a paper sack of roasted almonds, fresh from the cookfire and covered with raw sugar. The woman to whom Amat handed her length of copper took a pose of gratitude, and Amat moved to the water's edge, considering the half-hidden waves, the thousand smells of the seafront—salt and spiced foods, sewage and incense. She blew sharply through pursed lips to cool the sweets before she bit into them, as she had when she was a girl, and she prepared herself for the last meeting. When the sack was empty, she crumpled it and let it drop into the sea.

House Wilsin was among the first to make its position on the future known by its actions. Even as she walked up the streets to the north, moving steadily toward the compound, carts passed her, heading the other way. The ware-houses were being cleared, the offices packed into crates bound for Galt and the Westlands. When she reached the familiar courtyard, the lines of men made her think of ants on sugarcane. She paused at the bronze Galtic Tree, considering it with distaste and, to her surprise, amusement. Three weeks was too long, apparently, for her to hold her breath either.

"Amat-cha?"

She shifted. Epani, her thin-faced, weak-spirited replacement, stood in a pose of welcome belied by the discomfort on his face. She answered it with a pose of her own, more graceful and appropriate.

"Tell him I'd like to speak with him, will you?"

"He isn't . . . that is . . ."

"Epani-cha. Go, tell him I'm here and I want to speak with him. I won't burn the place down while you do it."

Perhaps it was the dig that set him moving. Whatever did it, Epani retreated into the dark recesses of the compound. Amat walked to the fountain, listen-ing to the play of the water as though it was the voice of an old friend. Some-one had dredged it, she saw, for the copper lengths thrown in for luck. House Wilsin wasn't leaving anything behind.

Epani returned and without a word led her back through the corridors she knew to the private meeting rooms. The room was as dark as she remembered it. Marchat Wilsin himself sat at the table, lit by the diffuse cool light from the small window, the warm, orange flame of a lantern. With one color on either cheek, he might almost have been two different men. Amat took a pose of greeting and gratitude. Moving as if unsure of himself, Marchat responded with one of welcome.

"I didn't expect to see you again," he said, and his voice was careful.

"And yet, here I am. I see House Wilsin is fleeing, just as everyone said it was. Bad for business, Marchat-cha. It looks like a failure of nerve."

"It is," he said. There was no apology in his voice. They might have been discussing dye prices. "Being in Saraykeht's too risky now. My uncle's calling me back home. I think he must have been possessed by some passing moment of sanity, and what he saw scared him. What we can't ship out by spring, we're selling at a loss. It'll take years for the house to recover. And, of course, I'm scheduled on the last boat out. So. Have you come to tell me you're ready to bring your suit to the Khai?"

Amat took a pose, more casual than she'd intended, that requested clarifica-tion. It was an irony, and Marchat's sheepish grin showed that he knew it.

"My position isn't as strong as it was before the victim best placed to stir the heart of the utkahiem killed the poet and destroyed the city. I lost a certain credibility."

"Was it really her, then?"

"I don't know for certain. It appears it was."

"I'd say I was sorry, but . . ."

Amat didn't count the years she'd spent talking to this man across tables like this, or in the cool waters of the bathhouse, or walking together in the streets. She felt them, habits worn into her joints. She sat with a heavy sigh and shook her head.

"I did what I could," she said. "Now . . . now who would believe me, and what would it matter?"

"Someone might still. One of the other Khaiem."

"If you thought that was true, you'd have me killed."

Wilsin's face clouded, something like pain in the wrinkles at the corners of his eyes. Something like sorrow.

"I wouldn't enjoy it," he said at last.

Despite the truth of it, Amat laughed. Or perhaps because of it.

"Is Liat Chokavi still with you?" Marchat asked, then took a pose that offered reassurance. "It's just that I have a box of her things. Mostly her things. Some others may have found their way into it. I won't call it apology, but . . ."

"Unfortunately, no," Amat said. "I offered her a place. The gods all know I could use competent help keeping my books. But she's left with the poet boy. It seems they're heartmates."

Marchat chuckled.

"Oh, *that'll* end well," he said with surprisingly gentle sarcasm.

"Tell Epani to bring us a pot of tea," Amat said. "He can at least do something useful. Then there's business we need to talk through."

Marchat did as she asked, and minutes later, she cupped a small, lovely tea bowl in her hands, blowing across the steaming surface. Marchat poured a bowl for himself, but didn't drink it. Instead, he folded his hands together and rested his great, whiskered chin in them. The silence wasn't a ploy on his part; she could see that. He didn't know what to say. It made the game hers to start.

"There's something I want of you," she said.

"I'll do what I can," he said.

"The warehouses on the Nantan. I want to rent them from House Wilsin."

He leaned back now, his head tilted like a dog hearing an unfamiliar sound. He took an interrogative pose. Amat sipped her tea, but it was still too hot. She put the bowl on the table.

"With the andat lost, I'm gathering investment in a combers hall. I've found ten men who worked as combers when Petals-Falling-Open was still the andat in Saraykeht. They're willing to act as foremen. The initial outlay and the first contracts are difficult. I have people who might be willing to invest if I can find space. They're worried that my relationship with my last employer ended poorly. Rent me the space, and I can address both issues at once."

"But, Amat . . ."

"I lost," she said. "I know it. You know it. I did what I could do, and it got past me. Now I can either press the suit forward despite it all, raise what suspicions against Galt I can in the quarters who will listen to me at the cost of what credibility I have left, or else I can do this. Recreate myself as a legitimate business, organize the city, bind the wounds that can be bound. Forge connections between people who think they're rivals. But I can't do both. I can't have people saying I'm an old woman frightened of shadows while I'm trying to make weavers and rope-makers who've been undercutting each other for the last three generations shake hands."

Marchat Wilsin's eyebrows rose. She watched him consider her. The guilt and horror, the betrayals and threats fell away for a moment, and they were the players in the game of get and give that they had been at their best. It made Amat's heart feel bruised, but she kept it out of her face as he kept his feelings from his. The lantern flame spat, shuddered, and stood back to true.

"It won't work," he said at last. "They'll hold to all their traditional prejudices and alliances. They'll find ways to bite each other while they're shaking hands. Making them all feel loyal to each other and to the city? In the Westlands or Galt or the islands, you might have a chance. But among the Khaiem? It's doomed."

"I'll accept failure when I've failed," Amat said.

"Just remember I warned you. What's your offer for the warehouses?"

"Sixty lengths of silver a year and five hundredths of the profit."

"That's insultingly low, and you know it."

"You haven't figured in that it will keep me from telling the world what the Galtic Council attempted in allying with Seedless against his poet. That by itself is a fair price, but we should keep up appearances, don't you think?"

He thought about it. The tiny upturn of his lips, the barest of smiles, told her what she wanted to know.

"And you really think you can make a going project of this? Combing raw cotton for its seeds isn't a pleasant job."

"I have a steady stream of women looking to retire from one less pleasant than that," she said. "I think the two concerns will work quite nicely together."

"And if I agree to this," Marchat said, his voice suddenly softer, the game suddenly sliding out from its deep-worn track, "does that mean you'll forgive me?"

"I think we're past things like forgiveness," she said. "We're the servants of what we have to do. That's all."

"I can live with that answer. All right, then. I'll have Epani draw up contracts. Should we take them to that whorehouse of yours?"

"Yes," Amat said. "That will do nicely. Thank you, Marchat-cha."

"It's the least I could do," he said and drank at last from the bowl of cooling tea at his elbow. "And also likely the most I can. I don't imagine my uncle will understand it right off. Galtic business doesn't have quite the same subtlety you find with the Khaiem."

"It's because your culture hasn't finished licking off its caul," Amat said. "Once you've had a thousand years of Empire, things may be different."

Marchat's expression soured and he poured himself more tea. Amat pushed her own bowl toward him, and he leaned forward to fill it. The steaming tea clinked against the porcelain.

"There will be a war," Amat said at last. "Between your people and mine. Eventually, there will be a war."

"Galt's a strange place. It's so long since I've been there, I don't know how well I'll fit once I'm back. We've done well by war. In the last generation, we've almost doubled our farmlands. There are places that rival the cities of the Khaiem, if you'll believe that. Only we do it with ruthlessness and bloody-minded determination. You'd have to be there, really, to understand it. It isn't what you people have here."

Amat took an insistent pose, demanding an answer to her question. Marchat sighed; a long, slow sound.

"Yes, someday. Someday there will be a war, but not in our lifetimes."

She shifted to a pose that was both acknowledgement and thanks. Marchat toyed with his teabowl.

"Amat, before . . . before you go, there's a letter I wrote you. When it looked like the suit was going to go to the Khai and sweet hell was going to rain down on Galt in general and me in particular. I want you to have it."

His face was legible as a boy's. Amat wondered at how he could be so closed and careful with business and so clumsy with his own heart and hers. If she let it continue, he'd be offering her work in Galt next. And a part of her, despite it all, would be sorry to refuse.

"Keep it for now," she said. "I'll take it from you later."

"When?" he asked as she rose.

She answered gently, making the words not an insult, but a moment of shared sorrow. There were, after all, ten thousand things that had been lost in this. And each one of them real, even this.

"After the war, perhaps. Give it to me then."

DREAMING, OTAH FOUND HIMSELF IN A PUBLIC PLACE, PART STREET CORNER, PART bathhouse, part warehouse. People milled about, at ease, their conversations a pleasant murmur. With a shock, Otah glimpsed Heshai-kvo in the crowd, moving as if alive, speaking as if alive, but still dead. In the logic of sleep, that fleeting glimpse carried a weight of panic.

Gasping for breath, Otah sat up, his eyes open and confused by the darkness. Only as his heart slowed and his breath grew steady, did the creaking of the ship and rocking of waves remind him where he was. He pressed his palms into his closed eyes until pale lights appeared. Below him, Maj murmured in her sleep.

The cabin was tiny—too short to stand fully upright and hardly long enough to hang two hammocks one above the other. If he put his arms out, he could press his palms against the oiled wood of each wall. There was no room for a brazier, so they slept in their robes. Carefully, he lifted himself down and without touching or disturbing the sleeper, left the close, nightmare-haunted coffin for the deck and the moon and a fresh breeze.

The three men of the watch greeted him as he emerged. Otah smiled and ambled over despite wanting more than anything a moment of solitude. The moment's conversation, the shared drink, the coarse joke—they were a small price to pay for the good will of the men to whom he had entrusted his fate. It was over quickly, and he could retreat to a quiet place by the rail and look out toward an invisible horizon where haze blurred the distinction between sea and sky. Otah sat, resting his arms on the worn wood, and waited for the wisps of dream to fade. As he had every night. As he expected he would for some time still to come. The changing of watch at the half candle brought another handful of men, another moment of sociability. The curious glances and concern that Otah had seen during his first nights on deck were gone. The men had become accustomed to him.

Otah would have guessed the night candle had nearly reached its three quarters mark when she came out to join him, though the night sea sometimes did strange things to time. He might also have been staring at the dark ripples and broken moonlight for sunless weeks.

Maj seemed almost to glow in the moonlight, her skin picking up the blue and the cold. She looked at the landless expanse of water with an almost proprietary air, unimpressed by vastness. Otah watched her find him, watched her walk to where he sat. Though Otah knew that at least one of the sailors on watch spoke Nippu, no one tried to speak with her. Maj lowered herself to the deck beside him, her legs crossed, her pale eyes almost colorless.

"The dreams," she said.

Otah took a pose of acknowledgement.

"If we had hand loom, you should weave," she said. "Put your mind to something real. Is unreal things that eat you."

"I'll be fine," he said.

"You are homesick. I know. I see it."

"I suppose," Otah said. "And I wonder now if we did the right thing."

"You think no?"

Otah turned his gaze back to the water. Something burst up from the surface and vanished again into the darkness, too quickly for Otah to see what shape it was.

"Not really," he said. "That's to say I think we did the best that we could. But that doing that thing was right . . ."

"Killing him," Maj said. "Call it what it is. Not *that thing*. Killing him. Hiding names give them power."

"That killing him was right . . . bothers me. At night, it bothers me."

"And if you can go back—make other choice—do you?"

"No. No, I'd do the same. And that disturbs me, too."

"You live too long in cities," Maj said. "Is better for you to leave."

Otah disagreed but said nothing. The night moved on. It was another week at least before they would reach Quian, southernmost of the eastern islands. The hold, filled now with the fine cloths and ropes of Saraykeht, the spices and metalworks of the cities of the Khaiem, would trade first for pearls and shells, the pelts of strange island animals, and the plumes of their birds. Only as the weeks moved on would they begin taking on fish and dried fruits, trees and salt timber and slaves. And only in the first days of spring—weeks away still and ten island ports at least—would they reach as far north as Nippu.

Years of work on the seafront, all the gifts and assistance Maati had given him for the journey to the Dai-kvo, everything he had, he had poured into two seasons of travel. He wondered what he would do, once he reached Nippu, once Maj was home and safe and with the people she knew. Back from her long nightmare with only the space where a child should have been at her side.

He could work on ships, he thought. He knew enough already to take on the simple, odious tasks like coiling rope and scrubbing decks. He might at least make his way back to the cities of the Khaiem . . . or perhaps not. The world was full of possibility, because he had nothing and no one. The unreal crowded in on him, as Maj had said, because he had abandoned the real.

"You think of her," Maj said.

"What? Ah, Liat? No, not really. Not just now."

"You leave her behind, the girl you love. You are angry because of her and the boy."

A prick of annoyance troubled him but he answered calmly enough.

"It hurt me that they did what they did, and I miss him. I miss them. But . . ."

"But it also frees you," Maj said. "It is for me, too. The baby. I am scared, when I first go to the cities. I think I am never fit in, never belong. I am never be a good mother without my own *itiru* to tell me how she is caring for me when I am young. All this worry I make. And is nothing. To lose everything is not the worst can happen."

"It's starting again, from nothing, with nothing," Otah said.

"Is exactly this," Maj agreed, then a moment later. "Starting again, and doing better."

The still-hidden sun lightened water and sky as they watched it in silence. The milky, lacework haze burned off as the fire rose from the sea and the full crew hauled up sails, singing, shouting, tramping their bare feet. Otah rose, his back aching from sitting so long without moving, and Maj brushed her robes and stood also. As the work of the day entered its full activity, he descended behind her into the darkness of their cabin where he hoped he might cheat his conscience of a few hours sleep. His thoughts still turned on the empty, open future before him and on Saraykeht behind him, a city still waking to the fact that it had fallen.

A BETRAYAL IN WINTER

To Kat and Scarlet

ACKNOWLEDGMENTS

This book and this series would not be as good if I hadn't had the help of Walter Jon Williams, Melinda Snodgrass, Yvonne Coates, Sally Gwylan, Emily Mah-Tippets, S. M. Stirling, Terry England, Ian Tregellis, Sage Walker, and the other members of the New Mexico Critical Mass Workshop.

I also owe debts of gratitude to Shawna McCarthy and Danny Baror for their enthusiasm and faith in the project, to James Frenkel for his unstinting support and uncanny ability to take a decent manuscript and make it better, and to Tom Doherty and the staff at Tor for their kindness and support of a new author.

And I am especially indebted to Paul Park, who told me to write what I fear.

PROLOG

>+<   "There's a problem at the mines," his wife said. "One of your treadmill pumps."

Biitrah Machi, the eldest son of the Khai Machi and a man of forty-five summers, groaned and opened his eyes. The sun, new-risen, set the paper-thin stone of the bedchamber windows glowing. Hiami sat beside him.

"I've had the boy set out a good thick robe and your seal boots," she said, carrying on her thought, "and sent him for tea and bread."

Biitrah sat up, pulling the blankets off and rising naked with a grunt. A hundred things came to his half-sleeping mind. *It's a pump—the engineers can fix it* or *Bread and tea? Am I a prisoner?* or *Take that robe off, love—let's have the mines care for themselves for a morning.* But he said what he always did, what he knew she expected of him.

"No time. I'll eat once I'm there."

"Take care," she said. "I don't want to hear that one of your brothers has finally killed you."

"When the time comes, I don't think they'll come after me with a treadmill pump."

Still, he made a point to kiss her before he walked to his dressing chamber, allowed the servants to array him in a robe of gray and violet, stepped into the sealskin boots, and went out to meet the bearer of the bad tidings.

"It's the Daikani mine, most high," the man said, taking a pose of apology formal enough for a temple. "It failed in the night. They say the lower passages are already half a man high with water."

Biitrah cursed, but took a pose of thanks all the same. Together, they walked through the wide main hall of the Second Palace. The caves shouldn't have been filling so quickly, even with a failed pump. Something else had gone wrong. He tried to picture the shape of the Daikani mines, but the excavations in the mountains and plains around Machi were numbered in the dozens, and the details blurred. Perhaps four ventilation shafts. Perhaps six. He would have to go and see.

His private guard stood ready, bent in poses of obeisance, as he came out into the street. Ten men in ceremonial mail that for all its glitter would turn a knife. Ceremonial swords and daggers honed sharp enough to shave with.

Each of his two brothers had a similar company, with a similar purpose. And the time would come, he supposed, that it would descend to that. But not today. Not yet. He had a pump to fix.

He stepped into the waiting chair, and four porters came out. As they lifted him to their shoulders, he called out to the messenger.

"Follow close," he said, his hands flowing into a pose of command with the ease of long practice. "I want to hear everything you know before we get there."

They moved quickly through the grounds of the palaces—the famed towers rising above them like forest trees above rabbits—and into the black-cobbled streets of Machi. Servants and slaves took abject poses as Biitrah passed. The few members of the utkhaiem awake and in the city streets took less extreme stances, each appropriate to the difference in rank between themselves and the man who might one day renounce his name and become the Khai Machi.

Biitrah hardly noticed. His mind turned instead upon his passion—the machinery of mining: water pumps and ore graves and hauling winches. He guessed that they would reach the low town at the mouth of the mine before the fast sun of early spring had moved the width of two hands.

They took the south road, the mountains behind them. They crossed the sinuous stone bridge over the Tidat, the water below them still smelling of its mother glacier. The plain spread before them, farmsteads and low towns and meadows green with new wheat. Trees were already pushing forth new growth. It wouldn't be many weeks before the lush spring took root, grabbing at the daylight that the winter stole away. The messenger told him what he could, but it was little enough, and before they had reached the halfway point, a wind rose, whuffling in Biitrah's ears and making conversation impossible. The closer they came, the better he recalled these particular mines. They weren't the first that House Daikani had leased from the Khai—those had been the ones with six ventilation shafts. These had four. And slowly—more slowly than it once had—his mind recalled the details, spreading the problem before him like something written on slate or carved from stone.

By the time they reached the first outbuildings of the low town, his fingers had grown numb, his nose had started to run from the cold, he had four different guesses as to what might have gone wrong, and ten questions in mind whose answers would determine whether he was correct. He went directly to the mouth of the mine, forgetting to stop for even bread and tea.

HIAMI SAT BY THE BRAZIER, KNOTTING A SCARF FROM SILK THREAD AND LISTENING to a slave boy sing old tunes of the Empire. Almost-forgotten emperors loved and fought, lost, won, and died in the high, rich voice. Poets and their slave spirits, the andat, waged their private battles sometimes with deep sincerity and beauty, sometimes with bedroom humor and bawdy rhymes—but all of them ancient. She couldn't stand to hear anything written after the great war that had destroyed those faraway palaces and broken those song-recalled lands. The new songs were all about the battles of the Khaiem—three brothers who held claim to the name of Khai. Two would die, one would forget his name and doom his own sons to another cycle of blood. Whether they were laments for the fallen or celebrations of the victors, she hated them. They weren't songs that comforted her, and she didn't knot scarves unless she needed comfort.

A servant came in, a young girl in austere robes almost the pale of mourning, and took a ritual pose announcing a guest of status equal to Hiami's.

"Idaan," the servant girl said, "Daughter to the Khai Machi."

"I know my husband's sister," Hiami snapped, not pausing in her handwork. "You needn't tell me the sky is blue."

The servant girl flushed, her hands fluttering toward three different poses at once and achieving none of them. Hiami regretted her words and put down the knotting, taking a gentle pose of command.

"Bring her here. And something comfortable for her to sit on."

The servant took a pose of acknowledgment, grateful, it seemed, to know what response to make, and scampered off. And then Idaan was there.

Hardly twenty, she could have been one of Hiami's own daughters. Not a beauty, but it took a practiced eye to know that. Her hair, pitch dark, was pleated with strands of silver and gold. Her eyes were touched with paints, her skin made finer and paler than it really was by powder. Her robes, blue silk embroidered with gold, flattered her hips and the swell of her breasts. To a man or a younger woman, Idaan might have seemed the loveliest woman in the city. Hiami knew the difference between talent and skill, but of the pair, she had greater respect for skill, so the effect was much the same.

They each took poses of greeting, subtly different to mark Idaan's blood relation to the Khai and Hiami's greater age and her potential to become someday the first wife of the Khai Machi. The servant girl trotted in with a good chair, placed it silently, and retreated. Hiami halted her with a gesture and motioned to the singing slave. The servant girl took a pose of obedience and led him off with her.

Hiami smiled and gestured toward the seat. Idaan took a pose of thanks much less formal than her greeting had been and sat.

"Is my brother here?" she asked.

"No. There was a problem at one of the mines. I imagine he'll be there for the day."

Idaan frowned, but stopped short of showing any real disapproval. All she said was, "It must seem odd for one of the Khaiem to be slogging through tunnels like a common miner."

"Men have their enthusiasms," Hiami said, smiling slightly. Then she sobered. "Is there news of your father?"

Idaan took a pose that was both an affirmation and a denial.

"Nothing new, I suppose," the dark-haired girl said. "The physicians are watching him. He kept his soup down again last night. That makes almost ten days in a row. And his color is better."

"But?"

"But he's still dying," Idaan said. Her tone was plain and calm as if she'd been talking about a horse or a stranger. Hiami put down her thread, the half-finished scarf in a puddle by her ankles. The knot she felt in the back of her throat was dread. The old man was dying, and the thought carried its implications with it—the time was growing short. Biitrah, Danat, and Kaiin Machi—the three eldest sons of the Khai—had lived their lives in something as close to peace as the sons of the Khaiem ever could. Otah, the Khai's sixth son, had created a small storm all those years ago by refusing to take the brand and renounce his claim to his father's chair, but he had never appeared. It was assumed that he had forged his path elsewhere or died unknown. Certainly he had never caused trouble here. And now every time their father missed his bowl of soup, every night his sleep was troubled and restless, the hour drew nearer when the peace would have to break.

"How are his wives?" Hiami asked.

"Well enough," Idaan said. "Or some of them are. The two new ones from Nantani and Pathai are relieved, I think. They're younger than I am, you know."

"Yes. They'll be pleased to go back to their families. It's harder for the older women, you know. Decades they've spent here. Going back to cities they hardly remember . . ."

Hiami felt her composure slip and clenched her hands in her lap. Idaan's gaze was on her. Hiami forced a simple pose of apology.

"No. *I'm* sorry," Idaan said, divining, Hiami supposed, all the fear in her heart from her gesture. Hiami's lovely, absent-minded, warm, silly husband and lover might well die. All his string and carved wood models and designs might fall to disuse, as abandoned by his slaughter as she would be. If only he might somehow win. If only he might kill his own brothers and let their wives pay this price, instead of her.

"It's all right, dear," Hiami said. "I can have him send a messenger to you when he returns if you like. It may not be until morning. If he thinks the problem is interesting, he might be even longer."

"And then he'll want to sleep," Idaan said, half smiling, "and I might not see or hear from him for days. And by then I'll have found some other way to solve my problems, or else have given up entirely."

Hiami had to chuckle. The girl was right, and somehow that little shared intimacy made the darkness more bearable.

"Perhaps I can be of some use, then," Hiami said. "What brings you here, sister?"

To Hiami's surprise, Idaan blushed, the real color seeming slightly false under her powder.

"I've . . . I wanted Biitrah to speak to our father. About Adrah. Adrah Vaun-yogi. He and I . . ."

"Ah," Hiami said. "I see. Have you missed a month?"

It took a moment for the girl to understand. Her blush deepened.

"No. It's not that. It's just that I think he may be the one. He's from a good family," Idaan said quickly, as if she were already defending him. "They have interests in a trading house and a strong bloodline and . . ."

Hiami took a pose that silenced the girl. Idaan looked down at her hands, but then she smiled. The horrified, joyous smile of new love discovered. Hiami remembered how once it had felt, and her heart broke again.

"I will talk to him when he comes back, no matter how dearly he wants his sleep," Hiami said.

"Thank you, Sister," Idaan said. "I should . . . I should go."

"So soon?"

"I promised Adrah I'd tell him as soon as I spoke to my brother. He's waiting in one of the tower gardens, and . . ."

Idaan took a pose that asked forgiveness, as if a girl needed to be forgiven for wanting to be with a lover and not a woman her mother's age knotting silk to fight the darkness in her heart. Hiami took a pose that accepted the apology and released her. Idaan grinned and turned to go. Just as the blue and gold of her robe was about to vanish through the doorway, Hiami surprised herself by calling out.

"Does he make you laugh?"

Idaan turned, her expression questioning. Hiami's mind flooded again with thoughts of Biitrah and of love and the prices it demanded.

"Your man. Adrah? If he doesn't make you laugh, Idaan, you mustn't marry him."

Idaan smiled and took a pose of thanks appropriate for a pupil to her master, and then was gone. Hiami swallowed until she was sure the fear was under control again, picked up her knotwork and called for the slave to return.

THE SUN WAS GONE, THE MOON A SLIVER NO WIDER THAN A NAIL CLIPPING. ONLY THE stars answered the miners' lanterns as Biitrah rose from the earth into darkness. His robes were wet and clung to his legs, the gray and violet turned to a uniform black. The night air was bitingly cold. The mine dogs yipped anxiously and paced in their kennels, their breath pluming like his own. The chief engineer of House Daikani's mines took a pose of profound thanks, and Biitrah replied graciously, though his fingers were numb and awkward as sausages.

"If it does that again, call for me," he said.

"Yes, most high," the engineer said. "As you command."

Biitrah's guard walked him to the chair, and his bearers lifted him. It was only now, with the work behind him and the puzzles all solved, that he felt the exhaustion. The thought of being carried back to the palaces in the cold and mud of springtime was only slightly less odious than the option of walking under his own power. He gestured to the chief armsman of his guard.

"We'll stay in the low town tonight. The usual wayhouse."

The armsman took a pose of acknowledgment and strode forward, leading his men and his bearers and himself into the unlit streets. Biitrah pulled his arms inside his robes and hugged bare flesh to flesh. The first shivers were beginning. He half regretted now that he hadn't disrobed before wading down to the lowest levels of the mine.

Ore was rich down in the plain—enough silver to keep Machi's coffers full even had there been no other mines here and in the mountains to the north and west—but the vein led down deeper than a well. In its first generation, when Machi had been the most distant corner of the Empire, the poet sent there had controlled the andat Raising-Water, and the stories said that the mines had flowed up like fountains under that power. It wasn't until after the great war that the poet Manat Doru had first captured Stone-Made-Soft and Machi had come into its own as the center for the most productive mines in the world and the home of the metal trades—ironmongers, silversmiths, Westland alchemists, needlemakers. But Raising-Water had been lost, and no one had yet discovered how to recapture it. And so, the pumps.

He again turned his mind back on the trouble. The treadmill pumps were of his own design. Four men working together could raise their own weight in water sixty feet in the time the moon—always a more reliable measure than the seasonally fickle northern sun—traveled the width of a man's finger. But the design wasn't perfect yet. It was clear from his day's work that the pump, which finally failed the night before, had been working at less than its peak for weeks. That was why the water level had been higher than one night's failure could account for. There were several possible solutions to that.

Biitrah forgot the cold, forgot his weariness, forgot indeed where he was and was being borne. His mind fell into the problem, and he was lost in it. The wayhouse, when it appeared as if by magic before them, was a welcome sight: thick stone walls with one red lacquered door at the ground level, a wide wooden snow door on the second story, and smoke rising from all its chimneys. Even from the street, he could smell seasoned meat and spiced wine. The keeper stood on the front steps with a pose of welcome so formal it bent the old, moon-faced man nearly double. Biitrah's bearers lowered his chair. At the last moment, Biitrah remembered to shove his arms back into their sleeves so that he could take a pose accepting the wayhouse keeper's welcome.

"I had not expected you, most high," the man said. "We would have prepared something more appropriate. The best that I have—"

"Will do," Biitrah said. "Certainly the best you have will do."

The keeper took a pose of thanks, standing aside to let them through the doorway as he did. Biitrah paused at the threshold, taking a formal pose of thanks. The old man seemed surprised. His round face and slack skin made Biitrah think of a pale grape just beginning to dry. He could be my father's age, he thought, and felt in his breast the bloom of a strange, almost melancholy, fondness for the man.

"I don't think we've met," Biitrah said. "What's your name, neighbor?"

"Oshai," the moon-faced man said. "We haven't met, but everyone knows of the Khai Machi's kindly eldest son. It is a pleasure to have you in this house, most high."

The house had an inner garden. Biitrah changed into a set of plain, thick woolen robes that the wayhouse kept for such occasions and joined his men there. The keeper himself brought them black-sauced noodles, river fish cooked with dried figs, and carafe after stone carafe of rice wine infused with plum. His guard, at first dour, relaxed as the night went on, singing together and telling stories. For a time, they seemed to forget who this long-faced man with his graying beard and thinning hair was and might someday be. Biitrah even sang with them at the end, intoxicated as much by the heat of the coal fire, the weariness of the day, and the simple pleasure of the night, as by the wine.

At last he rose up and went to his bed, four of his men following him. They would sleep on straw outside his door. He would sleep in the best bed the wayhouse offered. It was the way of things. A night candle burned at his bedside, the wax scented with honey. The flame was hardly down to the quarter mark. It was early. When he'd been a boy of twenty, he'd seen candles like this burn their last before he slept, the light of dawn blocked by goose-down pillows around his head. Now he couldn't well imagine staying awake to the half mark. He shuttered the candlebox, leaving only a square of light high on the ceiling from the smoke hole.

Sleep should have come easily to him as tired, well fed, half drunk as he was, but it didn't. The bed was wide and soft and comfortable. He could already hear his men snoring on their straw outside his door. But his mind would not be still.

They should have killed each other when they were young and didn't understand what a precious thing life is. That was the mistake. He and his brothers had forborne instead, and the years had drifted by. Danat had married, then Kaiin. He, the oldest of them, had met Hiami and followed his brothers' example last. He had two daughters, grown and now themselves married. And so here he and his brothers were. None of them had seen fewer than forty summers. None of them hated the other two. None of them wanted what would come next. And still, it would come. Better that the slaughter had happened when they were boys, stupid the way boys are. Better that their deaths had come before they carried the weight of so much life behind them. He was too old to become a killer.

Sleep came somewhere in these dark reflections, and he dreamed of things more pleasant and less coherent. A dove with black-tipped wings flying through the galleries of the Second Palace; Hiami sewing a child's dress with red thread and a gold needle too soft to keep its point; the moon trapped in a well and he himself called to design the pump that would raise it. When he woke, troubled by some need his sleep-sodden mind couldn't quite place, it was still dark. He needed to drink water or to pass it, but no, it was neither of these. He reached to unshutter the candlebox, but his hands were too awkward.

"There now, most high," a voice said. "Bat it around like that, and you'll have the whole place in flames."

Pale hands righted the box and pulled open the shutters, the candlelight revealing the moon-faced keeper. He wore a dark robe under a gray woolen traveler's cloak. His face, which had seemed so congenial before, filled Biitrah with a sick dread. The smile, he saw, never reached the eyes.

"What's happened?" he demanded, or tried to. The words came out slurred and awkward. Still, the man Oshai seemed to catch the sense of them.

"I've come to be sure you've died," he said with a pose that offered this as a service. "Your men drank more than you. Those that are breathing are beyond recall, but you . . . Well, most high, if you see morning the whole exercise will have been something of a waste."

Biitrah's breath suddenly hard as a runner's, he threw off the blankets, but when he tried to stand, his knees were limp. He stumbled toward the assassin, but there was no strength in the charge. Oshai, if that was his name, put a palm to Biitrah's forehead and pushed gently back. Biitrah fell to the floor, but he hardly felt it. It was like violence being done to some other man, far away from where he was.

"It must be hard," Oshai said, squatting beside him, "to live your whole life known only as another man's son. To die having never made a mark of your own on the world. It seems unfair somehow."

Who, Biitrah tried to say. *Which of my brothers would stoop to poison?*

"Still, men die all the time," Oshai went on. "One more or less won't keep the sun from rising. And how are you feeling, most high? Can you get up? No? That's as well, then. I was half-worried I might have to pour more of this down you. Undiluted, it tastes less of plums."

The assassin rose and walked to the bed. There was a hitch in his step, as if his hip ached. *He is old as my father*, but Biitrah's mind was too dim to see any humor in the repeated thought. Oshai sat on the bed and pulled the blankets over his lap.

"No hurry, most high. I can wait quite comfortably here. Die at your leisure."

Biitrah, trying to gather his strength for one last movement, one last attack, closed his eyes but then found he lacked the will even to open them again. The wooden floor beneath him seemed utterly comfortable; his limbs were heavy and slack. There were worse poisons than this. He could at least thank his brothers for that.

It was only Hiami he would miss. And the treadmill pumps. It would have been good to finish his design work on them. He would have liked to have finished more of his work. His last thought that held any real coherence was that he wished he'd gotten to live just a little while more.

He did not know it when his killer snuffed the candle.

HIAMI HAD THE SEAT OF HONOR AT THE FUNERAL, ON THE DAIS WITH THE KHAI Machi. The temple was full, bodies pressed together on their cushions as the priest intoned the rites of the dead and struck his silver chimes. The high walls and distant wooden ceiling held the heat poorly; braziers had been set in among the mourners. Hiami wore pale mourning robes and looked at her hands. It was not her first funeral. She had been present for her father's death, before her marriage into the highest family of Machi. She had only been a girl then. And through the years, when a member of the utkhaiem had passed on, she had sometimes sat and heard these same words spoken over some other body, listened to the roar of some other pyre.

This was the first time it had seemed meaningless. Her grief was real and profound, and this flock of gawkers and gossips had no relation to it. The Khai Machi's hand touched her own, and she glanced up into his eyes. His hair, what was left of it, had gone white years before. He smiled gently and took a pose that expressed his sympathy. He was graceful as an actor—his poses inhumanly smooth and precise.

Biitrah would have been a terrible Khai Machi, she thought. He would never have put in enough practice to hold himself that well.

And the tears she had suffered through the last days remembered her. Her once-father's hand trembled as if uneased by the presence of genuine feeling. He leaned back into his black lacquer seat and motioned for a servant to bring him a bowl of tea. At the front of the temple, the priest chanted on.

When the last word was sung, the last chime struck, bearers came and lifted her husband's body. The slow procession began, moving through the streets to the pealing of hand bells and the wailing of flutes. In the central square, the pyre was ready—great logs of pine stinking of oil and within them a bed of hard, hot-burning coal from the mines. Biitrah was lifted onto it and a shroud of tight metal links placed over him to hide the sight when his skin peeled from his noble bones. It was her place now to step forward and begin the conflagration. She moved slowly. All eyes were on her, and she knew what they were thinking. Poor woman, to have been left alone. Shallow sympathies that would have been extended as readily to the wives of the Khai Machi's other sons, had their men been under the metal blanket. And in those voices she heard also the excitement, dread, and anticipation that these bloody parox-ysms carried. When the empty, insincere words of comfort were said, in the same breath they would move on to speculations. Both of Biitrah's brothers had vanished. Danat, it was said, had gone to the mountains where he had a secret force at the ready, or to Lachi in the south to gather allies, or to ruined Saraykeht to hire mercenaries, or to the Dai-kvo to seek the aid of the poets and the andat. Or he was in the temple, gathering his strength, or he was cow-ering in the basement of a low town comfort house, too afraid to come to the streets. And every story they told of him, they also told of Kaiin.

It had begun. At long last, after years of waiting, one of the men who might one day be Khai Machi had made his move. The city waited for the drama to unfold. This pyre was only the opening for them, the first notes of some new song that would make this seem to be about something honorable, compre-hensible, and right.

Hiami took a pose of thanks and accepted a lit torch from the firekeeper. She stepped to the oil-soaked wood. A dove fluttered past her, landed briefly on her husband's chest, and then flew away again. She felt herself smile to see it go. She touched the flame to the small kindling and stepped back as the fire took. She waited there as long as tradition required and then went back to the Second Palace. Let the others watch the ashes. Their song might be starting, but hers here had ended.

Her servant girl was waiting for her at the entrance of the palace's great hall. She held a pose of welcome that suggested there was some news waiting for her. Hiami was tempted to ignore the nuance, to walk through to her cham-bers and her fire and bed and the knotwork scarf that was now nearly finished. But there were tear-streaks on the girl's cheeks, and who was Hiami, after all, to treat a suffering child unkindly? She stopped and took a pose that accepted the welcome before shifting to one of query.

"Idaan Machi," the servant girl said. "She is waiting for you in the summer garden."

Hiami shifted to a pose of thanks, straightened her sleeves, and walked quietly down the palace halls. The sliding stone doors to the garden were open, a breeze too cold to be comfortable moving through the hall. And there, by an empty fountain surrounded by bare-limbed cherry trees, sat her once-sister. If her formal robes were not the pale of mourning, her countenance contradicted them: reddened eyes, paint and powder washed away. She was a plain enough woman without them, and Hiami felt sorry for her. It was one thing to expect the violence. It was another to see it done.

She stepped forward, her hands in a pose of greeting. Idaan started to her feet as if she'd been caught doing something illicit, but then she took an answering pose. Hiami sat on the fountain's stone lip, and Idaan lowered herself, sitting on the ground at her feet as a child might.

"Your things are packed," Idaan said.

"Yes. I'll leave tomorrow. It's weeks to Tan-Sadar. It won't be so hard, I think. One of my daughters is married there, and my brother is a decent man. They'll treat me well while I make arrangements for my own apartments."

"It isn't fair," Idaan said. "They shouldn't force you out like this. You belong here."

"It's tradition," Hiami said with a pose of surrender. "Fairness has nothing to do with it. My husband is dead. I will return to my father's house, whoever's actually sitting in his chair these days."

"If you were a merchant, no one would require anything like that of you. You could go where you pleased, and do what you wanted."

"True, but I'm not, am I? I was born to the utkhaiem. You were born to a Khai."

"And women," Idaan said. Hiami was surprised by the venom in the word. "We were born women, so we'll never even have the freedoms our brothers do."

Hiami laughed. She couldn't help herself, it was all so ridiculous. She took her once-sister's hand and leaned forward until their foreheads almost touched. Idaan's tear-red eyes shifted to meet her gaze.

"I don't think the men in our families consider themselves unconstrained by history," she said, and Idaan's expression twisted with chagrin.

"I wasn't thinking," she said. "I didn't mean that . . . Gods . . . I'm sorry, Hiami-kya. I'm so sorry. I'm so sorry . . ."

Hiami opened her arms, and the girl fell into them, weeping. Hiami rocked her slowly, cooing into her ear and stroking her hair as if she were comforting a babe. And as she did, she looked around the gardens. This would be the last time she saw them. Thin tendrils of green were rising from the soil. The trees were bare, but their bark had an undertone of green. Soon it would be warm enough to turn on the fountains.

She felt her sorrow settle deep, an almost physical sensation. She understood the tears of the young that were even now soaking her robes at the shoulder. She would come to understand the tears of age in time. They would be keeping her company. There was no need to hurry.

At length, Idaan's sobs grew shallower and less frequent. The girl pulled back, smiling sheepishly and wiping her eyes with the back of her hand.

"I hadn't thought it would be this bad," Idaan said softly. "I knew it would be hard, but this is . . . How did they do it?"

"Who, dear?"

"All of them. All through the generations. How did they bring themselves to kill each other?"

"I think," Hiami said, her words seeming to come from the new sorrow within her and not from the self she had known, "that in order to become one of the Khaiem, you have to stop being able to love. So perhaps Biitrah's tragedy isn't the worst that could have happened."

Idaan hadn't followed the thought. She took a pose of query.

"Winning this game may be worse than losing it, at least for the sort of man he was. He loved the world too much. Seeing that love taken from him would have been bad. Seeing him carry the deaths of his brothers with him . . . and he wouldn't have been able to go slogging through the mines. He would have hated that. He would have been a very poor Khai Machi."

"I don't think I love the world that way," Idaan said.

"You don't, Idaan-kya," Hiami said. "And just now I don't either. But I will try to. I will try to love things the way he did."

They sat a while longer, speaking of things less treacherous. In the end, they parted as if it were just another absence before them, as if there would be another meeting on another day. A more appropriate farewell would have ended with them both in tears again.

The leave-taking ceremony before the Khai was more formal, but the emptiness of it kept it from unbalancing her composure. He sent her back to her family with gifts and letters of gratitude, and assured her that she would always have a place in his heart so long as it beat. Only when he enjoined her not to think ill of her fallen husband for his weakness did her sorrow threaten to shift to rage, but she held it down. They were only words, spoken at all such events. They were no more about Biitrah than the protestations of loyalty she now recited were about this hollow-hearted man in his black lacquer seat.

After the ceremony, she went around the palaces, conducting more personal farewells with the people whom she'd come to know and care for in Machi, and just as dark fell, she even slipped out into the streets of the city to press a few lengths of silver or small jewelry into the hands of a select few friends who were not of the utkhaiem. There were tears and insincere promises to follow her or to one day bring her back. Hiami accepted all these little sorrows with perfect grace. Little sorrows were, after all, only little.

She lay sleepless that last night in the bed that had seen all her nights since she had first come to the north, that had borne the doubled weight of her and her husband, witnessed the birth of their children and her present mourning, and she tried to think kindly of the bed, the palace, the city and its people. She set her teeth against her tears and tried to love the world. In the morning, she would take a flatboat down the Tidat, slaves and servants to carry her things, and leave behind forever the bed of the Second Palace where people did everything but die gently and old in their sleep.

1

Maati took a pose that requested clarification. In another context, it would have risked annoying the messenger, but this time the servant of the Dai-kvo seemed to be expecting a certain level of disbelief. Without hesitation, he repeated his words.

"The Dai-kvo requests Maati Vaupathai come immediately to his private chambers."

It was widely understood in the shining village of the Dai-kvo that Maati Vaupathai was, if not a failure, certainly an embarrassment. Over the years he had spent in the writing rooms and lecture halls, walking the broad, clean streets, and huddled with others around the kilns of the firekeepers, Maati had grown used to the fact that he would never be entirely accepted by those who surrounded him; it had been eight years since the Dai-kvo had deigned to speak to him directly. Maati closed the brown leather book he had been studying and slipped it into his sleeve. He took a pose that accepted the message and announced his readiness. The white-robed messenger turned smartly and led the way.

The village that was home to the Dai-kvo and the poets was always beautiful. Now in the middle spring, flowers and ivies scented the air and threatened to overflow the well-tended gardens and planters, but no stray grass rose between the paving stones. The gentle choir of wind chimes filled the air. The high, thin waterfall that fell beside the palaces shone silver, and the towers and garrets—carved from the mountain face itself—were unstained even by the birds that roosted in the eaves. Men spent lifetimes, Maati knew, keeping the village immaculate and as impressive as a Khai on his seat. The village and palaces seemed as grand as the great bowl of sky above them. His years living among the men of the village—only men, no women were permitted—had never entirely robbed Maati of his awe at the place. He struggled now to hold himself tall, to appear as calm and self-possessed as a man summoned to the Dai-kvo regularly. As he passed through the archways that led to the palace, he saw several messengers and more than a few of the brown-robed poets pause to look at him.

He was not the only one who found his presence there strange.

The servant led him through the private gardens to the modest apartments of the most powerful man in the world. Maati recalled the last time he had been there—the insults and recriminations, the Dai-kvo's scorching sarcasm, and his own certainty and pride crumbling around him like sugar castles left out in the rain. Maati shook himself. There was no reason for the Dai-kvo to have called him back to repeat the indignities of the past.

There are always the indignities of the future, the soft voice that had become Maati's muse said from a corner of his mind. Never assume you can survive the future because you've survived the past. Everyone thinks that, and they've all been wrong eventually.

The servant stopped before the elm-and-oak-inlaid door that led, Maati remembered, to a meeting chamber. He scratched it twice to announce them, then opened the door and motioned Maati in. Maati breathed deeply as a man preparing to dive from a cliff into shallow water and entered.

The Dai-kvo was sitting at his table. He had not had hair since Maati had met him twenty-three summers before when the Dai-kvo had only been Tahi-kvo, the crueler of the two teachers set to sift through the discarded sons of the Khaiem and utkhaiem for likely candidates to send on to the village. His brows had gone pure white since he'd become the Dai-kvo, and the lines around his mouth had deepened. His black eyes were just as alive.

The other two men in the room were strangers to Maati. The thinner one sat at the table across from the Dai-kvo, his robes deep blue and gold, his hair pulled back to show graying temples and a thin white-flecked beard. The thicker—with both fat and muscle, Maati thought—stood at window, one foot up on the thick ledge, looking into the gardens, and Maati could see where his clean-shaven jaw sagged at the jowl. His robes were the light brown color of sand, his boots hard leather and travel worn. He turned to look at Maati as the door closed, and there was something familiar about him—about both these new men—that he could not describe. He fell into the old pose, the first one he had learned at the school.

"I am honored by your presence, most high Dai-kvo."

The Dai-kvo grunted and gestured to him for the benefit of the two strangers.

"This is the one," the Dai-kvo said. The men shifted to look at him, graceful and sure of themselves as merchants considering a pig. Maati imagined what they saw him for—a man of thirty summers, his forehead already pushing back his hairline, the smallest of pot bellies. A soft man in a poet's robes, ill-considered and little spoken of. He felt himself start to blush, clenched his teeth, and forced himself to show neither his anger nor his shame as he took a pose of greeting to the two men.

"Forgive me," he said. "I don't believe we have met before, or if we have, I apologize that I don't recall it."

"We haven't met," the thicker one said.

"He isn't much to look at," the thin one said, pointedly speaking to the Dai-kvo. The thicker scowled and sketched the briefest of apologetic poses. It was a thread thrown to a drowning man, but Maati found himself appreciating even the empty form of courtesy.

"Sit down, Maati-cha," the Dai-kvo said, gesturing to a chair. "Have a bowl of tea. There's something we have to discuss. Tell me what you've heard of events in the winter cities."

Maati sat and spoke while the Dai-kvo poured the tea.

"I only know what I hear at the teahouses and around the kilns, most high. There's trouble with the glassblowers in Cetani; something about the Khai Cetani raising taxes on exporting fishing bulbs. But I haven't heard anyone taking it very seriously. Amnat-Tan is holding a summer fair, hoping, they say, to take trade from Yalakeht. And the Khai Machi . . ."

Maati stopped. He realized now why the two strangers seemed familiar; who they reminded him of. The Dai-kvo pushed a fine ceramic bowl across the smooth-sanded grain of the table. Maati fell into a pose of thanks without being aware of it, but did not take the bowl.

"The Khai Machi is dying," the Dai-kvo said. "His belly's gone rotten. It's a sad thing. Not a good end. And his eldest son is murdered. Poisoned. What do the teahouses and kilns say of that?"

"That it was poor form," Maati said. "That no one has seen the Khaiem resort to poison since Udun, thirteen summers ago. But neither of the brothers has appeared to accuse the other, so no one . . . Gods! You two are . . ."

"You see?" the Dai-kvo said to the thin man, smiling as he spoke. "No, not much to look at, but a decent stew between his ears. Yes, Maati-cha. The man scraping my windowsill with his boots there is Danat Machi. This is his eldest surviving brother, Kaiin. And they have come here to speak with me instead of waging war against each other because neither of them killed their elder brother Biitrah."

"So they . . . you think it was Otah-kvo?"

"The Dai-kvo says you know my younger brother," the thickset man—Danat—said, taking his own seat at the only unoccupied side of the table. "Tell me what you know of Otah."

"I haven't seen him in years, Danat-cha," Maati said. "He was in Saraykeht when . . . when the old poet there died. He was working as a laborer. But I haven't seen him since."

"Do you think he was satisfied by that life?" the thin one—Kaiin—asked. "A laborer at the docks of Saraykeht hardly seems like the fate a son of the Khaiem would embrace. Especially one who refused the brand."

Maati picked up the bowl of tea, sipping it too quickly as he tried to gain himself a moment to think. The tea scalded his tongue.

"I never heard Otah speak of any ambitions for his father's chair," Maati said.

"And is there any reason to think he would have spoken of it to you?" Kaiin said, the faintest sneer in his voice. Maati felt the blush creeping into his cheeks again, but it was the Dai-kvo who answered.

"There is. Otah Machi and Maati here were close for a time. They fell out eventually over a woman, I believe. Still, I hold that if Otah had been bent on taking part in the struggle for Machi at that time, he would have taken Maati into his confidence. But that is hardly our concern. As Maati here points out, it was years ago. Otah may have become ambitious. Or resentful. There's no way for us to know that—"

"But he refused the brand—" Danat began, and the Dai-kvo cut him off with a gesture.

"There were other reasons for that," the Dai-kvo said sharply. "They aren't your concern."

Danat Machi took a pose of apology and the Dai-kvo waved it away. Maati sipped his tea again. This time it didn't burn. To his right, Kaiin Machi took a pose of query, looking directly at Maati for what seemed the first time.

"Would you know him again if you saw him?"

"Yes," Maati said. "I would."

"You sound certain of it."

"I am, Kaiin-cha."

The thin man smiled. All around the table a sense of satisfaction seemed to come from his answer. Maati found it unnerving. The Dai-kvo poured himself more tea, the liquid clicking into his bowl like a stream over stones.

"There is a very good library in Machi," the Dai-kvo said. "One of the finest in the fourteen cities. I understand there are records there from the time of the Empire. One of the high lords was thinking to go there, perhaps, to ride out the war, and sent his books ahead. I'm sure there are treasures hidden among those shelves that would be of use in binding the andat."

"Really?" Maati asked.

"No, not really," the Dai-kvo said. "I expect it's a mess of poorly documented scraps overseen by a librarian who spends his copper on wine and whores, but I don't care. For our purposes, there are secrets hidden in those records important enough to send a low-ranking poet like yourself to sift though. I have a letter to the Khai Machi that will explain why you are truly there. He will explain your presence to the utkhaiem and Cehmai Tyan, the poet who holds Stone-Made-Soft. Let them think you've come on my errand. What you will be doing instead is discovering whether Otah killed Biitrah Machi. If so, who is backing him. If not, who did, and why."

"Most high—" Maati began.

"Wait for me in the gardens," the Dai-kvo said. "I have a few more things to discuss with the sons of Machi."

The gardens, like the apartments, were small, well kept, beautiful, and simple. A fountain murmured among carefully shaped, deeply fragrant pine trees. Maati sat, looking out. From the side of mountain, the world spread out before him like a map. He waited, his head buzzing, his heart in turmoil. Before long he heard the steady grinding sound of footsteps on gravel, and he turned to see the Dai-kvo making his way down the path toward him. Maati stood. He had not known the Dai-kvo had started walking with a cane. A servant followed at a distance, carrying a chair, and did not approach until the Dai-kvo signaled. Once the chair was in place, looking out over the same span that Maati had been considering, the servant retreated.

"Interesting, isn't it?" the Dai-kvo said.

Maati, unsure whether he meant the view or the business with the sons of Machi, didn't reply. The Dai-kvo looked at him, something part smile, part something less congenial on his lips. He drew forth two packets—letters sealed in wax and sewn shut. Maati took them and tucked them in his sleeve.

"Gods. I'm getting old. You see that tree?" the Dai-kvo asked, pointing at one of the shaped pines with his cane.

"Yes, most high."

"There's a family of robins that lives in it. They wake me up every morning. I always mean to have someone break the nest, but I've never quite given the order."

"You are merciful, most high."

The old man looked up at him, squinting. His lips were pressed thin, and the lines in his face were black as charcoal. Maati stood waiting. At length, the Dai-kvo turned away again with a sigh.

"Will you be able to do it?" he asked.

"I will do as the Dai-kvo commands," Maati said.

"Yes, I know you'll go there. But will you be able to tell me that he's there? You know if he is behind this, they'll kill him before they go on to each other. Are you able to bear that responsibility? Tell me now if you aren't, and I'll find some other way. You don't have to fail again."

"I won't fail again, most high."

"Good. That's good," the Dai-kvo said and went silent. Maati waited so long for the pose that would dismiss him that he wondered whether the Dai-kvo had forgotten he was there, or had chosen to ignore him as an insult. But the old man spoke, his voice low.

"How old is your son, Maati-cha?"

"Twelve, most high. But I haven't seen him in some years."

"You're angry with me for that." Maati began to take a pose of denial, but checked himself and lowered his arms. This wasn't the time for court politics. The Dai-kvo saw this and smiled. "You're getting wiser, my boy. You were a fool when you were young. In itself, that's not such a bad thing. Many men are. But you embraced your mistakes. You defended them against all correction. That was the wrong path, and don't think I'm unaware of how you've paid for it."

"As you say, most high."

"I told you there was no place in a poet's life for a family. A lover here or there, certainly. Most men are too weak to deny themselves that much. But a wife? A child? No. There isn't room for both what they require and what we do. And I told you that. You remember? I told you that, and you . . ."

The Dai-kvo shook his head, frowning in remembered frustration. It was a moment, Maati knew, when he could apologize. He could repent his pride and say that the Dai-kvo had indeed known better all along. He remained silent.

"I was right," the Dai-kvo said for him. "And now you've done half a job as a poet and half a job as a man. Your studies are weak, and the woman took your whelp and left. You've failed both, just as I knew you would. I'm not condemning you for that, Maati. No man could have taken on what you did and succeeded. But this opportunity in Machi is what will wipe clean the slate. Do this well and it will be what you're remembered for."

"Certainly I will do my best."

"Fail at it, and there won't be a third chance. Few enough men have two."

Maati took a pose appropriate to a student receiving a lecture. Considering him, the Dai-kvo responded with one that closed the lesson, then raised his hand.

"Don't destroy this chance in order to spite me, Maati. Failing in this will do me no harm, and it will destroy you. You're angry because I told you the truth, and because what I said would happen, did. Consider while you go north, whether that's really such a good reason to hate me."

THE OPEN WINDOW LET IN A COOL BREEZE THAT SMELLED OF PINE AND RAIN. OTAH Machi, the sixth son of the Khai Machi, lay on the bed, listening to the sounds of water—rain pattering on the flagstones of the wayhouse's courtyard and the tiles of its roof, the constant hushing of the river against its banks. A fire danced and spat in the grate, but his bare skin was still stippled with cold. The night candle had gone out, and he hadn't bothered to relight it. Morning would come when it came.

The door slid open and then shut. He didn't turn to look.

"You're brooding, Itani," Kiyan said, calling him by the false name he'd chosen for himself, the only one he'd ever told her. Her voice was low and rich and careful as a singer's. He shifted now, turning to his side. She knelt by the grate—her skin smooth and brown, her robes the formal cut of a woman of business, one strand of her hair fallen free. Her face was thin—she reminded him of a fox sometimes, when a smile just touched her mouth. She placed a fresh log on the fire as she spoke. "I half expected you'd be asleep already."

He sighed and sketched a pose of contrition with one hand.

"Don't apologize to me," she said. "I'm as happy having you in my rooms here as in the teahouse, but Old Mani wanted more news out of you. Or maybe just to get you drunk enough to sing dirty songs with him. He's missed you, you know."

"It's a hard thing, being so loved."

"Don't laugh at it. It's not a love to carry you through ages, but it's more than some people ever manage. You'll grow into one of those pinched old men who want free wine because they pity themselves."

"I'm sorry. I don't mean to make light of Old Mani. It's just . . ."

He sighed. Kiyan closed the window and relit the night candle.

"It's just that you're brooding," she said. "And you're naked and not under the blankets, so you're feeling that you've done something wrong and deserve to suffer."

"Ah," Otah said. "Is that why I do this?"

"Yes," she said, untying her robes. "It is. You can't hide it from me, Itani. You might as well come out with it."

Otah held the thought in his mind. *I'm not who I've told you I am. Itani Noygu is the name I picked for myself when I was a child. My father is dying, and brothers I can hardly recall have started killing each other, and I find it makes me sad.* He wondered what Kiyan would say to that. She prided herself on knowing him—on knowing people and how their minds worked. And yet he didn't think this was something she'd already have guessed.

Naked, she lay beside him, pulling thick blankets up over them both.

"Did you find another woman in Chaburi-Tan?" she asked, half-teasing. But only half. "Some young dancing girl who stole your heart, or some other bit of your flesh, and now you're stewing over how to tell me you're leaving me?"

"I'm a courier," Otah said. "I have a woman in every city I visit. You know that."

"You don't," she said. "Some couriers do, but you don't."

"No?"

"No. It took me half a year of doing everything short of stripping bare for you to notice me. You don't stay in other cities long enough for a woman to chip through your reserve. And you don't have to push away the blankets. You may want to be cold, but I don't."

"Well. Maybe I'm just feeling old."

"A ripe thirty-three? Well, when you decide to stop running across the world, I'd always be pleased to hire you on. We could stand another pair of hands around the place. You could throw out the drunks and track down the cheats that try to slip away without paying."

"You don't pay enough," Otah said. "I talk to Old Mani. I know what your wages are."

"Perhaps you'd get extra for keeping me warm at nights."

"Shouldn't you offer that to Old Mani first? He's been here longer than I have."

Kiyan slapped his chest smartly, and then nestled into him. He found himself curling toward her, the warmth of her body drawing him like a familiar scent. Her fingers traced the tattoo on his breast—the ink had faded over time, blurring lines that had once been sharp and clear.

"Jokes aside," she said, and he could hear a weariness in her voice, "I would take you on, if you wanted to stay. You could live here, with me. Help me manage the house."

He caressed her hair, feeling the individual strands as they flowed across his fingertips. There was a scattering of white among the black that made her look older than she was. Otah knew that they had been there since she was a girl, as if she'd been born old.

"That sounds like you're suggesting marriage," he said.

"Perhaps. You wouldn't have to, but . . . it would be one way to arrange things. That isn't a threat, you know. I don't need a husband. Only if it would make you feel better, we could . . ."

He kissed her gently. It had been weeks, and he was surprised to find how much he'd missed the touch of her lips. Weeks of travel weariness slipped away, the deep unease loosened its hold on his chest, and he took comfort in her. He fell asleep with her arm over his body, her breath already soft and deep with sleep.

In the morning, he woke before she did, slipped out of the bed, and dressed quietly. The sun was not up, but the eastern sky had lightened and the morning birds were singing madly as he took himself across an ancient stone bridge into Udun.

A river city, Udun was laced with as many canals as roadways. Bridges humped up high enough for barges to pass beneath them, and the green water of the Qiit lapped at old stone steps that descended into the river mud. Otah stopped at a stall on the broad central plaza and traded two lengths of copper for a thick wedge of honey bread and a bowl of black, smoky tea. Around him, the city slowly came awake—the streets and canals filling with traders and merchants, beggars singing at the corners or in small rafts tied at the water's edge, laborers hauling wagons along the wide flagstoned streets, and birds bright as shafts of sunlight—blue and red and yellow, green as grass, and pink as dawn. Udun was a city of birds, and their chatter and shriek and song filled the air as he ate.

The compound of House Siyanti was in the better part of the city, just downstream from the palaces, where the water was not yet fouled by the wastes of thirty thousand men and women and children. The red brick buildings rose up three stories high, and a private canal was filled with barges in the red and silver of the house. The stylized emblem of the sun and stars had been worked into the brick archway that led to the central courtyard, and Otah passed beneath it with a feeling like coming home.

Amiit Foss, the overseer for the house couriers, was in his offices, ordering around three apprentices with sharp words and insults, but no blows. Otah stepped in and took a pose of greeting.

"Ah! The missing Itani. Did you know the word for half-wit in the tongue of the Empire was *itani-nah*?"

"All respect, Amiit-cha, but no it wasn't."

The overseer grinned. One of the apprentices—a girl of perhaps thirteen summers—whispered something angrily, and the boy next to her giggled.

"Fine," the overseer said. "You two. I need the ciphers rechecked on last week's letters."

"But I wasn't the one . . ." the girl protested. The overseer took a pose that commanded her silence, and the pair, glowering at each other, stalked away.

"I get them when they're just growing old enough to flirt," Amiit said, sighing. "Come back to the meeting rooms. The journey took longer than I'd expected."

"There were some delays," Otah said as he followed the older man back. "Chaburi-Tan isn't as tightly run as it was last time I was out there."

"No?"

"There are refugees from the Westlands."

"There are always refugees from the Westlands."

"Not this many," Otah said. "There are rumors that the Khai Chaburi-Tan is going to restrict the number of Westlanders allowed on the island."

Amiit paused, his hands on the carved wood door of the meeting rooms. Otah could almost see the implications of this thought working themselves out behind the overseer's eyes. A moment later, Amiit looked up, raised his eyebrows in appreciation, and pushed the doors open.

Half the day was spent in the raw silk chairs of the meeting rooms while Amiit took Otah's report and accepted the letters—sewn shut and written in cipher—that Otah had carried with him.

It had taken Otah some time to understand all that being a courier implied. When he had first arrived in Udun six years before, hungry, lost and half-haunted by the memories he carried with him, he had still believed that he would simply be carrying letters and small packages from one place to another, perhaps waiting for a response, and then taking those to where they were expected. It would have been as right to say that a farmer throws some seeds in the earth and returns a few months later to see what's grown. He had been lucky. His ability to win friends easily had served him, and he had been instructed in what the couriers called the gentleman's trade: how to gather information that might be of use to the house, how to read the activity of a street corner or market, and how to know from that the mood of a city. How to break ciphers and re-sew letters. How to appear to drink more wine than you actually did, and question travelers on the road without seeming to.

He understood now that the gentleman's trade was one that asked a lifetime to truly master, and though he was still a journeyman, he had found a kind of joy in it. Amiit knew what his talents were, and chose assignments for him in which he could do well. And in return for the trust of the house and the esteem of his fellows, Otah did the best work he could, brokering information, speculation, gossip, and intrigue. He had traveled through the summer cities in the south, west to the plains and the cities that traded directly with the Westlands, up the eastern coasts where his knowledge of obscure east island tongues had served him well. By design or happy coincidence, he had never gone farther north than Yalakeht. He had not been called on to see the winter cities.

Until now.

"There's trouble in the north," Amiit said as he tucked the last of the opened letters into his sleeve.

"I'd heard," Otah said. "The succession's started in Machi."

"Amnat-Tan, Machi, Cetani. All of them have something brewing. You may need to get some heavier robes."

"I didn't think House Siyanti had much trade there," Otah said, trying to keep the unease out of his voice.

"We don't. That doesn't mean we never will. And take your time. There's something I'm waiting for from the west. I won't be sending you out for a month at least, so you can have some time to spend you money. Unless . . ."

The overseer's eyes narrowed. His hands took a pose of query.

"I just dislike the cold," Otah said, making a joke to cover his unease. "I grew up in Saraykeht. It seemed like water never froze there."

"It's a hard life," Amiit said. "I can try to give the commissions to other men, if you'd prefer."

And have them wonder why it was that I wouldn't go, Otah thought. He took a pose of thanks that also implied rejection.

"I'll take what there is," he said. "And heavy wool robes besides."

"It really isn't so bad up there in summer," Amiit said. "It's the winters that break your stones."

"Then by all means, send someone else in the winter."

They exchanged a few final pleasantries, and Otah left the name of Kiyan's wayhouse as the place to send for him, if he was needed. He spent the afternoon in a teahouse at the edge of the warehouse district, talking with old acquaintances and trading news. He kept an ear out for word from Machi, but there was nothing fresh. The eldest son had been poisoned, and his remaining brothers had gone to ground. No one knew where they were nor which had begun the traditional struggle. There were only a few murmurs of the near-forgotten sixth son, but every time he heard his old name, it was like hearing a distant, threatening noise.

He returned to the wayhouse as darkness began to thicken the treetops and the streets fell into twilight, brooding. It wasn't safe, of course, to take a commission in Machi, but neither could he safely refuse one. Not without a reason. He knew when gossip and speculation had grown hot enough to melt like sugar and stick. There would be a dozen reports of Otah Machi from all over the cities, and likely beyond as well. If even a suggestion was made that he was not who he presented himself to be, he ran the risk of being exposed, dragged into the constant, empty, vicious drama of succession. He would sacrifice quite a lot to keep that from happening. Going north, doing his work, and returning was what he would have done, had he been the man he claimed to be. And so perhaps it was the wiser strategy.

And also he wondered what sort of man his father was. What sort of man his brother had been. Whether his mother had wept when she sent her boy away to the school where the excess sons of the high familes became poets or fell forever from grace.

As he entered the courtyard, his dark reverie was interrupted by laughter and music from the main hall, and the scent of roast pork and baked yams mixed with the pine resin. When he stepped in, Old Mani slapped an earthenware bowl of wine into his hands and steered him to a bench by the fire. There were a good number of travelers—merchants from the great cities, farmers from the low towns, travelers each with a story and a past and a tale to tell, if only they were asked the right questions in the right ways.

It was later, the warm air busy with conversation, that Otah caught sight of Kiyan across the wide hall. She had on a working woman's robes, her hair tied back, but the expression on her face and the angle of her body spoke of a deep contentment and satisfaction. She knew her place was here, and she was proud of it.

Otah found himself suddenly stilled by a longing for her unlike the simple lust that he was accustomed to. He imagined himself feeling the same satisfaction that he saw in her. The same sense of having a place in the world. She turned to him as if he had spoken and tilted her head—not an actual formal pose, but nonetheless a question.

He smiled in reply. This that she offered was, he suspected, a life worth living.

CEHMAI TYAN'S DREAMS, WHENEVER THE TIME CAME TO RENEW HIS LIFE'S STRUG-gle, took the same form. A normal dream—meaningless, strange, and trivial—would shift. Something small would happen that carried a weight of fear and dread out of all proportion. This time, he dreamt he was walking in a street fair, trying to find a stall with food he liked, when a young girl appeared at his side. As he saw her, his sleeping mind had already started to rebel. She held out her hand, the palm painted the green of summer grass, and he woke himself trying to scream.

Gasping as if he had run a race, he rose, pulled on the simple brown robes of a poet, and walked to the main room of the house. The worked stone walls seemed to glow with the morning light. The chill spring air fought with the warmth from the low fire in the grate. The thick rugs felt softer than grass against Cehmai's bare feet. And the andat was waiting at the game table, the pieces already in place before it—black basalt and white marble. The line of white was already marred, one stone disk shifted forward into the field. Cehmai sat and met his opponent's pale eyes. There was a pressure in his mind that felt the way a windstorm sounded.

"Again?" the poet asked.

Stone-Made-Soft nodded its broad head. Cehmai Tyan considered the board, recalled the binding—the translation that had brought the thing across from him out of formlessness—and pushed a black stone into the empty field of the board. The game began again.

The binding of Stone-Made-Soft had not been Cehmai's work. It had been done generations earlier, by the poet Manat Doru. The game of stones had figured deeply in the symbolism of the binding—the fluid lines of play and the solidity of the stone markers. The competition between a spirit seeking its freedom and the poet holding it in place. Cehmai ran his fingertip along his edge of the board where Manat Doru's had once touched it. He considered the advancing line of white stones and crafted his answering line of black, touching stones that long-dead men had held when they had played the same game against the thing that sat across from him now. And with every victory, the binding was renewed, the andat held more firmly in the world. It was an excellent strategy, in part because the binding had also made Stone-Made-Soft a terrible player.

The windstorm quieted, and Cehmai stretched and yawned. Stone-Made-Soft glowered down on its failing line.

"You're going to lose," Cehmai said.

"I know," the andat replied. Its voice was a deep rumble, like a distant rockslide—another evocation of flowing stone. "Being doomed doesn't take away from the dignity of the effort, though."

"Well said."

The andat shrugged and smiled. "One can afford to be philosophical when losing means outliving one's opponent. This particular game? You picked it. But there are others we play that I'm not quite so crippled at."

"I didn't pick this game. I haven't seen twenty summers, and you've seen more than two hundred. I wasn't even a dirty thought in my grandfather's head when you started playing this."

The andat's thick hands took a formal position of disagreement.

"We have always been playing the same game, you and I. If you were someone else at the start, it's your problem."

They never started speaking until the game's end was a forgone conclusion.
That Stone-Made-Soft was willing to speak was as much a sign that this particular battle was drawing to its end as the silence in Cehmai's mind. But the
last piece had not yet been pushed when a pounding came on the door.

"I know you're in there! Wake up!"

Cehmai sighed at the familiar voice and rose. The andat brooded over the
board, searching, the poet knew, for some way to win a lost game. He clapped
a hand on the andat's shoulder as he passed by it toward the door.

"I won't have it," the stout, red-cheeked man said when the opened door
revealed him. He wore brilliant blue robes shot with rich yellow and a copper
torc of office. Not for the first time, Cehmai thought Baarath would have been
better placed in life as the overseer of a merchant house or farm than within
the utkhaiem. "You poets think that because you have the andat, you have
everything. Well, I've come to tell you it isn't so."

Cehmai took a pose of welcome and stepped back, allowing the man in.

"I've been expecting you, Baarath. I don't suppose you've brought any food
with you?"

"You have servants for that," Baarath said, striding into the wide room, taking in the shelves of books and scrolls and maps with his customary moment of
lust. The andat looked up at him with its queer, slow smile, and then turned
back to the board.

"I don't like having strange people wandering though my library," Baarath
said.

"Well, let's hope our friend from the Dai-kvo won't be strange."

"You are an annoying, contrary man. He's going to come in here and root
through the place. Some of those volumes are very old, you know. They won't
stand mishandling."

"Perhaps you should make copies of them."

"I am making copies. But it's not a fast process, you know. It takes a great
deal of time and patience. You can't just grab some half-trained scribes off the
street corners and set them to copying the great books of the Empire."

"You also can't do the whole job by yourself, Baarath. No matter how much
you want to."

The librarian scowled at him, but there was a playfulness in the man's eyes.
The andat shifted a white marker forward and the noise in Cehmai's head
murmured. It had been a good move.

"You hold an abstract thought in human form and make it play tricks, and
you tell me what's not possible? Please. I've come to offer a trade. If you'll—"

"Wait," Cehmai said.

"If you'll just—"

"Baarath, you can be quiet or you can leave. I have to finish this."

Stone-Made-Soft sighed as Cehmai took his seat again. The white stone had opened a line that had until now been closed. It wasn't one he'd seen the andat play before, and Cehmai scowled. The game was still over, there was no way for the andat to clear his files and pour the white markers to their target squares before Cehmai's dark stones had reached their goal. But it would be harder now than it had been before the librarian came. Cehmai played through the next five moves in his mind, his fingertips twitching. Then, decisively, he pushed the black marker forward that would block the andat's fastest course.

"Nice move," the librarian said.

"What did you want with me? Could you just say it so I can refuse and get about my day?"

"I was going to say that I will give this little poet-let of the Dai-kvo's full access if you'll let me include your collection here. It really makes more sense to have all the books and scrolls cataloged together."

Cehmai took a pose of thanks.

"No," he said. "Now go away. I have to do this."

"Be reasonable! If I choose—"

"First, you will give Maati Vaupathai full access because the Dai-kvo and the Khai Machi tell you to. You have nothing to bargain with. Second, I'm not the one who gave the orders, nor was I consulted on them. If you want barley, you don't negotiate with a silversmith, do you? So don't come here asking concessions for something that I'm not involved with."

A flash of genuine hurt crossed Baarath's face. Stone-Made-Soft touched a white marker, then pulled back its hand and sank into thought again. Baarath took a pose of apology, his stance icy with its formality.

"Don't," Cehmai said. "I'm sorry. I don't mean to be a farmer's wife about the thing, but you've come at a difficult time."

"Of course. This children's game upon which all our fates depend. No, no. Stay. I'll see myself out."

"We can talk later," Cehmai said to the librarian's back.

The door closed and left Cehmai and his captive, or his ward, or his other self, alone together.

"He isn't a very good man," Stone-Made-Soft rumbled.

"No, he's not," Cehmai agreed. "But friendship falls where it falls. And may the gods keep us from a world where only the people who deserve love get it."

"Well said," the andat replied, and pushed forward the white stone Cehmai knew it would.

The game ended quickly after that. Cehmai ate a breakfast of roast lamb and boiled eggs while Stone-Made-Soft put away the game pieces and then sat, warming its huge hands by the fire. There was a long day before them, and after the morning's struggle, Cehmai was dreading it. They were promised to go to the potter's works before midday. A load of granite had come from the quarries and required his services before it could be shaped into the bowls and vases for which Machi was famed. After midday, he was needed for a meeting with the engineers to consider the plans for House Pirnat's silver mine. The Khai Machi's engineers were concerned, he knew, that using the andat to soften the stone around a newfound seam of ore would weaken the structure of the mine. House Pirnat's overseer thought it worth the risk. It would be like sitting in a child's garden during a mud fight, but it had to be done. Just thinking of it made him tired.

"You could tell them I'd nearly won," the andat said. "Say you were too shaken to appear."

"Yes, because my life would be so much better if they were all afraid of turning into a second Saraykeht."

"I'm only saying that you have options," the andat replied, smiling into the fire.

The poet's house was set apart from the palaces of the Khai and the compounds of the utkhaiem. It was a broad, low building with thick stone walls nestled behind a small and artificial wood of sculpted oaks. The snows of winter had been reduced to gray-white mounds and frozen pools in the deep shadows where sunlight would not touch them. Cehmai and the andat strode west, toward the palaces and the Great Tower, tallest of all the inhuman buildings of Machi. It was a relief to walk along streets in sunlight rather than the deep network of tunnels to which the city resorted when the drifts were too high to allow even the snow doors to open. Brief days, and cold profound enough to crack stone, were the hallmarks of the Machi winter. The terrible urge to be out in the gardens and streets marked her spring. The men and women Cehmai passed were all dressed in warm robes, but their faces were bare and their heads uncovered. The pair paused by a firekeeper at his kiln. A singing slave stood near enough to warm her hands at the fire as she filled the air with traditional songs. The palaces of the Khai loomed before them—huge and gray with roofs pitched sharp as axe blades—and the city and the daylight stood at their backs, tempting as sugar ghosts on Candles Night.

"It isn't too late," the andat murmured. "Manat Doru used to do it all the time. He'd send a note to the Khai claiming that the weight of holding me was too heavy, and that he required his rest. We would go down to a little teahouse by the river that had sweetcakes that they cooked in oil and covered with sugar so fine it hung in the air if you blew on it."

"You're lying to me," Cehmai said.

"No," the andat said. "No, it's truth. It made the Khai quite angry sometimes, but what was he to do?"

The singing slave smiled and took a pose of greeting to them that Cehmai returned.

"We could stop by the spring gardens that Idaan frequents. If she were free she might be persuaded to join us," the andat said.

"And why would the daughter of the Khai tempt me more than sweetcakes?"

"She's well-read and quick in her mind," the andat said, as if the question had been genuine. "You find her pleasant to look at, I know. And her demeanor is often just slightly inappropriate. If memory serves, that might outweigh even sweetcakes."

Cehmai shifted his weight from foot to foot, then, with a commanding gesture, stopped a servant boy. The boy, seeing who he was, fell into a pose of greeting so formal it approached obeisance.

"I need you to carry a message for me. To the Master of Tides."

"Yes, Cehmai-cha," the boy said.

"Tell him I have had a bout with the andat this morning, and find myself too fatigued to conduct business. And tell him that I will reach him on the morrow if I feel well enough."

The poet fished through his sleeves, pulled out his money pouch and took out a length of silver. The boy's eyes widened, and his small hand reached out toward it. Cehmai drew it back, and the boy's dark eyes fixed on his.

"If he asks," Cehmai said, "you tell him I looked quite ill."

The boy nodded vigorously, and Cehmai pressed the silver length into his palm. Whatever errand the boy had been on was forgotten. He vanished into the austere gloom of the palaces.

"You're corrupting me," Cehmai said as he turned away.

"Constant struggle is the price of power," the andat said, its voice utterly devoid of humor. "It must be a terrible burden for you. Now let's see if we can find the girl and those sweetcakes."

2

"They tell me you knew my son," the Khai Machi said. The grayness of his skin and yellow in his long, bound hair were signs of something more than the ravages of age. The Dai-kvo was of the same generation, but Maati saw none of his vigor and strength here. The sick man took a pose of command. "Tell me of him."

Maati stared down at the woven reed mat on which he knelt and fought to push away the weariness of his travels. It had been days since he had bathed, his robes were not fresh, and his mind was uneasy. But he was here, called to this meeting or possibly this confrontation, even before his bags had been unpacked. He could feel the attention of the servants of the Khai—there were perhaps a dozen in the room. Some slaves, others attendants from among the highest ranks of the utkhaiem. The audience might be called private, but it was too well attended for Maati's comfort. The choice was not his. He took the bowl of heated wine he had been given, sipped it, and spoke.

"Otah-kvo and I met at the school, most high. He already wore the black robes awarded to those who had passed the first test when I met him. I . . . I was the occasion of his passing the second."

The Khai Machi nodded. It was an almost inhumanly graceful movement, like a bird or some finely wrought mechanism. Maati took it as a sign that he should continue.

"He came to me after that. He . . . he taught me things about the school and about myself. He was, I think, the best teacher I have known. I doubt I would have been chosen to study with the Dai-kvo if it hadn't been for him. But then he refused the chance to become a poet."

"And the brand," the Khai said. "He refused the brand. Perhaps he had ambitions even then."

He was a boy, and angry, Maati thought. He had beaten Tahi-kvo and Milah-kvo on his own terms. He'd refused their honors. Of course he didn't accept disgrace.

The utkhaiem high enough to express an opinion nodded among themselves as if a decision made in heat by a boy not yet twelve might explain a murder two decades later. Maati let it pass.

"I met him again in Saraykeht," Maati said. "I had gone there to study under Heshai-kvo and the andat Removing-The-Part-That-Continues. Otah-kvo was living under an assumed name at the time, working as a laborer on the docks."

"And you recognized him?"

"I did," Maati said.

"And yet you did not denounce him?" The old man's voice wasn't angry. Maati had expected anger. Outrage, perhaps. What he heard instead was gentler and more penetrating. When he looked up, the red-rimmed eyes were very much like Otah-kvo's. Even if he had not known before, those eyes would have told him that this man was Otah's father. He wondered briefly what his own father's eyes had looked like and whether his resembled them, then forced his mind back to the matter at hand.

"I did not, most high. I regarded him as my teacher, and . . . and I wished to understand the choices he had made. We became friends for a time. Before the death of the poet took me from the city."

"And do you call him your teacher still? You call him Otah-kvo. That is a title for a teacher, is it not?"

Maati blushed. He hadn't realized until then that he was doing it.

"An old habit, most high. I was sixteen when I last saw Otah-cha. I'm thirty now. It has been almost half my life since I have spoken with him. I think of him as a person I once knew who told me some things I found of use at the time," Maati said, and sensing that the falsehood of those words might be clear, he continued with some that were more nearly true. "My loyalty is to the Dai-kvo."

"That is good," the Khai Machi said. "Tell me, then. How will you conduct this examination of my city?"

"I am here to study the library of Machi," Maati said. "I will spend my mornings there, most high. After midday and in the evenings I will move through the city. I think . . . I think that if Otah-kvo is here it will not be difficult to find him."

The gray, thin lips smiled. Maati thought there was condescension in them. Perhaps even pity. He felt a blush rise in his cheeks, but kept his face still. He knew how he must appear to the Khai's weary eyes, but he would not flinch and confirm the man's worst suspicions. He swallowed once to loosen his throat.

"You have great faith in yourself," the Khai Machi said. "You come to my city for the first time. You know nothing of its streets and tunnels, little of its history, and you say that finding my missing son will be easy for you."

"Rather, most high, I will make it easy for him to find me."

It might have been his imagination—he knew from experience that he was prone to see his own fears and hopes in other people instead of what was truly there—but Maati thought there might have been a flicker of approval on the old man's face.

"You will report to me," the Khai said. "When you find him, you will come to me before anyone else, and I will send word to the Dai-kvo."

"As you command, most high," Maati lied. He had said that his loyalty lay with the Dai-kvo, but there was no advantage he could see to explaining all that meant here and now.

The meeting continued for a short time. The Khai seemed as exhausted by it as Maati himself was. Afterward, a servant girl led him to his apartments within the palaces. Night was already falling as he closed the door, truly alone for the first time in weeks. The journey from his home in the Dai-kvo's village wasn't the half-season's trek he would have had from Saraykeht, but it was enough, and Maati didn't enjoy the constant companionship of strangers on the road.

A fire had been lit in the grate, and warm tea and cakes of honeyed almonds waited for him at a lacquered table. He lowered himself into the chair, rested his feet, and closed his eyes. Being here, in this place, had a sense of unreality to it. To have been entrusted with anything of importance was a surprise after his loss of status. The thought stung, but he forced himself to turn in toward it. He had lost a great deal of the Dai-kvo's trust between his failure in Saraykeht and his refusal to disavow Liat, the girl who had once loved Otah-kvo but left both him and the fallen city to be with Maati, when it became clear she was bearing his child. If there had been time between the two, perhaps it might have been different. One scandal on the heels of the other, though, had been too much. Or so he told himself. It was what he wanted to believe.

A scratch at the door roused him from his bitter reminiscences. He straightened his robes and ran a hand through his hair before he spoke.

"Come in."

The door slid open and a young man of perhaps twenty summers wearing the brown robes of a poet stepped in and took a pose of greeting. Maati returned it as he considered Cehmai Tyan, poet of Machi. The broad shoulders, the open face. Here, Maati thought, is what I should have been. A talented boy poet who studied under a master while young enough to have his mind molded to the right shape. And when the time came, he had taken that burden on himself for the sake of his city. As I should have done.

"I only just heard you'd arrived," Cehmai Tyan said. "I left orders at the main road, but apparently they don't think as much of me as they pretend."

There was a light humor in his voice and manner. As if this were a game, as if he were a person whom anyone in Machi—or in the world—could truly treat with less than total respect. He held the power to soften stone—it was the concept, the essential idea, that Manat Doru had translated into a human form all those generations ago. This wide-faced, handsome boy could collapse every bridge, level every mountain. The great towers of Machi could turn to a river of stone, fast-flowing and dense as quicksilver, which would lay the city to ruin at his order. And he made light of being ignored as if he were junior clerk in some harbormaster's house. Maati couldn't tell if it was an affectation or if the poet was really so utterly naïve.

"The Khai left orders as well," Maati said.

"Ah, well. Nothing to be done about that, then. I trust everything is acceptable with your apartments?"

"I . . . I really don't know. I haven't really looked around yet. Too busy sitting on something that doesn't move, I suppose. I close my eyes, and I feel like I'm still jouncing around on the back of a cart."

The young poet laughed, a warm sound that seemed full of self-confidence and summer light. Maati felt himself smiling thinly and mentally reproved himself for being ungracious. Cehmai dropped onto a cushion beside the fire, legs crossed under him.

"I wanted to speak with you before we started working in the morning," Cehmai said. "The man who guards the library is . . . he's a good man, but he's protective of the place. I think he looks on it as his trust to the ages."

"Like a poet," Maati said.

Cehmai grinned. "I suppose so. Only he'd have made a terrible poet. He's puffed himself three times larger than anyone else just by having the keys to a building full of papers in languages only half a dozen people in the city can read. If he'd ever been given something important to do, he'd have popped like a tick. Anyway, I thought it might ease things if I came along with you for the first few days. Once Baarath is used to you, I expect he'll be fine. It's that first negotiation that's tricky."

Maati took a pose that offered gratitude, but was also a refusal.

"There's no call to take you from your duties," he said. "I expect the order of the Khai will suffice."

"I wouldn't only be doing it as a favor to you, Maati-kvo," Cehmai said. The honorific took Maati by surprise, but the young poet didn't seem to notice his reaction. "Baarath is a friend of mine, and sometimes you have to protect your friends from themselves. You know?"

Maati took a pose that was an agreement and looked into the flames. Sometimes men could be their own worst enemies. That was truth. He remembered the last time he had seen Otah-kvo. It had been the night Maati had admitted what Liat had become to him and what he himself was to her. His old friend's eyes had gone hard as glass. Heshai-kvo, the poet of Saraykeht, had died just after that, and Maati and Liat had left the city together without seeing Otah-kvo again.

The betrayal in those dark eyes haunted him. He wondered how much the anger had festered in his old teacher over the years. It might have grown to hatred by now, and Maati had come to hunt him down. The fire danced over the coal, flames turning the black to gray, the stone to powder. He realized that the boy poet had been speaking, and that the words had escaped him entirely. Maati took a pose of apology.

"My mind wandered. You were saying?"

"I offered to come by at first light," Cehmai said. "I can show you where the good teahouses are, and there's a streetcart that sells the best hot eggs and rice in the city. Then, perhaps, we can brave the library?"

"That sounds fine. Thank you. But now I think I'd best unpack my things and get some rest. You'll excuse me."

Cehmai bounced up in a pose of apology, realizing for the first time that his presence might not be totally welcome, and Maati waved it away. They made the ritual farewells, and when the door closed, Maati sighed and rose. He had few things: thick robes he had bought for the journey north, a few books including the small leatherbound volume of his dead master's that he had taken from Saraykeht, a packet of letters from Liat, the most recent of them years old now. The accumulated memories of a lifetime in two bags small enough to carry on his back if needed. It seemed thin. It seemed not enough.

He finished the tea and almond cakes, then went to the window, slid the paper-thin stone shutter aside, and looked out into the darkness. Sunset still breathed indigo into the western skyline. The city glittered with torches and lanterns, and to the south the glow of the forges of the smith's quarter looked like a brush fire. The towers rose black against the stars, windows lit high above him where some business took place in the dark, thin air. Maati sighed, the night cold in his face and lungs. All these unknown streets, these towers, and the lacework of tunnels that ran beneath the city: midwinter roads, he'd heard them called. And somewhere in the labyrinth, his old friend and teacher lurked, planning murder.

Maati let his imagination play a scene: Otah-kvo appearing before him in the darkness, blade in hand. In Maati's imagination, his eyes were hard, his voice hoarse with anger. And there he faltered. He might call for help and see Otah captured. He might fight him and end the thing in blood. He might accept the knife as his due. For a dream with so vivid a beginning, Maati could not envision the end.

He closed the shutter and went to throw another black stone onto the fire. His indulgence had turned the room chilly, and he sat on the cushion near the fire as the air warmed again. His legs didn't fold as easily as Cehmai's had, but if he shifted now and again, his feet didn't go numb. He found himself thinking fondly of Cehmai—the boy was easy to befriend. Otah-kvo had been like that, too.

Maati stretched and wondered again whether, if all this had been a song, he would have sung the hero's part or the villain's.

No one had ever seen Idaan's rebellions as hunger. That had been their fault. If her friends or her brothers transgressed against the etiquette of the court, consequences came upon them, shame or censure. But Idaan was the favored daughter. She might steal a rival girl's gown or arrive late to the temple and interrupt the priest. She could evade her chaperones or steal wine from the kitchens or dance with inappropriate men. She was Idaan Machi, and she could do as she saw fit, because she didn't matter. She was a woman. And if she'd never screamed at her father in the middle of his court that she was as much his child as Biitrah or Danat or Kaiin, it was because she feared in her bones that he would only agree, make some airy comment to dismiss the matter, and leave her more desperate than before.

Perhaps if once someone had taken her to task, had treated her as if her actions had the same weight as other people's, things would have ended differently.

Or perhaps folly is folly because you can't see where it moves from ambition into evil. Arguments that seem solid and powerful prove hollow once it's too late to turn back. Arguments like *Why should it be right for them but wrong for me?*

She haunted the Second Palace now, breathing in the emptiness that her eldest brother had left. The vaulted arches of stone and wood echoed her soft footsteps, and the sunlight that filtered though the stone shutters thickened the air to a golden twilight. Here was the bedchamber, bare even of the mattress he and his wife had slept upon. There, the workshop where he had labored on his enthusiasms, keeping engineers by his side sometimes late into the night or on into morning. The tables were empty now. Dust lay thick on them, ignored even by the servants until the time came for some new child of the Khaiem to take residence . . . to live in this opulence and keep his ear pricked for the sound of his brother's hunting dogs.

She heard Adrah coming long before he stepped into the room. She recognized his gait by the sound of it, and didn't call. He was clever, she thought bitterly; if he wanted to find her, he could puzzle it out. Adrah Vaunyogi, bright-eyed and broad-shouldered, father of her children if all went well. Whatever *well* meant anymore.

"There you are," Adrah said. She could see his anger in the way he held his body.

"What have I done this time?" she demanded, her tone carrying a sarcasm that dismissed his concerns even before he spoke them. "Did your patrons want me to wear red on a day I chose yellow?"

The mention of his backers, even as obliquely as that, made him stiffen and peer around, looking for slaves or servants who might overhear. Idaan laughed—a cruel, short sound.

"You look like a kitten with a bell on its tail," she said. "There's no one here but us. You needn't worry that someone will roll the rock off our little conspiracy. We're as safe here as anywhere."

Adrah strode over and crouched beside her all the same. He smelled of crushed violets and sage, and it struck Idaan that it had not been so long ago that the scent would have warmed her heart and brought a flush to her cheeks. His face was long and pretty—almost too pretty to be a man's. She had kissed those lips a thousand times, but now it seemed like the act of another woman— some entirely different Idaan Machi whose body and memory she had inherited when the first girl died. She smiled and raised her hands in a pose of formal query.

"Are you mad?" Adrah demanded. "Don't speak about them. Not ever. If we're found out . . ."

"Yes. You're right. I'm sorry," Idaan said. "I wasn't thinking."

"There are rumors you spent a day with Cehmai and the andat. You were seen."

"The rumors are true, and I meant to be seen. I can't see how my having a close relationship to the poet would hurt the cause, and in fact I think it will help, don't you? When the time comes that half the houses of the utkhaiem are vying for my father's chair, an upstart house like yours would do well to boast a friendship with Cehmai."

"I think being married to a daughter of the Khai will be quite enough, thank you," Adrah said, "and your brothers aren't dead yet, in case you'd forgotten."

"No. I remember."

"I don't want you acting strangely. Things are too delicate just now for you to start attracting attention. You are my lover, and if you are off half the time drinking rice wine with the poet, people won't be saying that I have strong friendship with him. They'll be saying that he's cuckolding me, and that Vaunyogi is the wrong house to draw a new Khai from."

"So you don't want me seeing him, or you just want more discretion when I do?" Idaan asked.

That stopped him. His eyes, deep brown with flecks of red and green, peered into hers. A sudden memory, powerful as illness, swept over her of a winter night when they had met in the tunnels. He had gazed at her then by firelight, had been no further from her than he was now. She wondered how these could be those same eyes. Her hand rose as if by itself and stroked his cheek. He folded his hands around hers.

"I'm sorry," she said, ashamed of the catch in her voice. "I don't want to quarrel with you."

"What are you doing, little one?" he asked. "Don't you see how dangerous this is that we're doing? Everything rests on it."

"I know. I remember the stories. It's strange, don't you think, that my brothers can slaughter each other and all the people do is applaud, but if I take a hand, it's a crime worse than anything."

"You're a woman," he said, as if that explained everything.

"And you," she said calmly, almost lovingly, "are a schemer and an agent of the Galts. So perhaps we deserve each other."

She felt him stiffen and then force the tension away. His smile was crooked. She felt something warm in her breast—painful and sad and warm as the first sip of rum on a midwinter night. She wondered if it might be hatred, and if it were, whether it was for herself or this man before her.

"It's going to be fine," he said.

"I know," she said. "I knew it would be hard. It's the *ways* it's hard that surprise me. I don't know how I should act or who I should be. I don't know where the normal grief that anyone would feel stops or turns into something else." She shook her head. "This seemed simpler when we were only talking about it."

"I know, love. It will be simple again, I promise you. It's only this in the middle that feels complicated."

"I don't know how they do it," she said. "I don't know how they kill one another. I dream about him, you know. I dream that I am walking through the gardens or the palaces and I see him in among a crowd of people." Tears came to her eyes unbidden, flowing warm and thick down her cheeks, but her voice,

when she continued, was steady and calm as a woman predicting the weather.
"He's always happy in the dreams. He's always forgiven me."

"I'm sorry," he said. "I know you loved him."

Idaan nodded, but didn't speak.

"Be strong, love. It will be over soon. It will all be finished very soon."

She wiped the tears away with the back of her hand, her knuckles darkened
where her paints were running, and pulled him close. He seemed to hold back
for a moment, then folded against her, his arms around her trembling shoulders. He was warm and the smell of sage and violet was mixed now with his
skin—the particular musk of his body that she had treasured once above all
other scents. He murmured small comforts into her ears and stroked her hair
as she wept.

"Is it too late?" she asked. "Can we stop it, Adrah? Can we take it all back?"

He kissed her eyes, his lips soft as a girl's. His voice was calm and implacable and hard as stone. When she heard it, she knew he had been thinking
himself down the same pathways and had come to the same place.

"No, love. It's too late. It was too late as soon as your brother died. We have
started, and there's no ending it now except to win through or die."

They stayed still in each others' embrace. If all went well, she would die an
old woman in this man's arms, or he would die in hers. While their sons killed
one another. And there had been a time not half a year ago she'd thought the
prize worth winning.

"I should go," she murmured. "I have to attend to my father. There's some
dignitary just come to the city that I'm to smile at."

"Have you heard of the others? Kaiin and Danat?"

"Nothing," Idaan said. "They've vanished. Gone to ground."

"And the other one? Otah?"

Idaan pulled back, straightening the sleeves of her robes as she spoke.

"Otah's a story that the utkhaiem tell to make the song more interesting.
He's likely not even alive any longer. Or if he is, he's wise enough to have no
part of this."

"Are you certain of that?"

"Of course not," she said. "But what else can I give you?"

They spoke little after that. Adrah walked with her through the gardens of
the Second Palace and then out to the street. Idaan made her way to her rooms
and sent for the slave boy who repainted her face. The sun hadn't moved the
width of two hands together before she strode again through the high palaces,
her face cool and perfect as a player's mask. The formal poses of respect and
deference greeted and steadied her. She was Idaan Machi, daughter of the
Khai and wife, though none knew it yet, of the man who would take his place.
She forced confidence into her spine, and the men and women around her re-

acted as if it were real. Which, she supposed, meant that it was. And that the sorrow and darkness they could not see were false.

When she entered the council chambers, her father greeted her with a silent pose of welcome. He looked ill, his skin gray and his mouth pinched by the pain in his belly. The delicate lanterns of worked iron and silver made the wood-sheathed walls glow, and the cushions that lined the floor were thick and soft as pillows. The men who sat on them—yes, men, all of them—made their obeisances to her, but her father motioned her closer. She walked to his side and knelt.

"There is someone I wish you to meet," her father said, gesturing to an awkward man in the brown robes of a poet. "The Dai-kvo has sent him. Maati Vaupathai has come to study in our library."

Fear flushed her mouth with the taste of metal, but she simpered and took a pose of welcome as if the words had meant nothing. Her mind raced, ticking through ways that the Dai-kvo could have discovered her, or Adrah, or the Galts. The poet replied to her gesture with a formal pose of gratitude, and she took the opportunity to look at him more closely. The body was soft as a scholar's, the lines of his face round as dough, but there was a darkness to his eyes that had nothing to do with color or light. She felt certain he was someone worth fearing.

"The library?" she said. "That's dull. Surely there are more interesting things in the city than room after room of old scrolls."

"Scholars have strange enthusiasms," the poet said. "But it's true, I've never been to any of the winter cities before. I'm hoping that not all my time will be taken in study."

There had to be a reason that the Dai-kvo and the Galts wanted the same thing. There had to be a reason that they each wanted to plumb the depths of the library of Machi.

"And how have you found the city, Maati-cha?" she asked. "When you haven't been studying."

"It is as beautiful as I had been told," the poet said.

"He has been here only a few days," her father said. "Had he come earlier, I would have had your brothers here to guide him, but perhaps you might introduce him to your friends."

"I would be honored," Idaan said, her mind considering the thousand ways that this might be a trap. "Perhaps tomorrow evening you would join me for tea in the winter gardens. I have no doubt there are many people who would be pleased to join us."

"Not too many, I hope," he said. He had an odd voice, she thought. As if he was amused at something. As if he knew how badly he had shaken her. Her fear shifted slightly, and she raised her chin. "I already find myself forgetting names I should remember," the poet continued. "It's most embarrassing."

"I will be pleased to remind you of my own, should it be required," she said. Her father's movement was almost too slight to see, but she caught it and cast her gaze down. Perhaps she had gone too far. But when the poet spoke, he seemed to have taken no offense.

"I expect I will remember yours, Idaan-cha. It would be very rude not to. I look forward to meeting your friends and seeing your city. Perhaps even more than closeting myself in your library."

He had to know. He *had* to. Except that she was not being led away under guard. She was not being taken to the quiet chambers and questioned. If he did not know, he must only suspect.

Let him suspect, then. She would get word to Adrah and the Galts. They would know better than she what to do with this Maati Vaupathai. If he was a threat, he would be added to the list. Biitrah, Danat, Kaiin, Otah, Maati. The men she would have to kill or have killed. She smiled at him gently, and he nodded to her. One more name could make little difference now, and he, at least, was no one she loved.

"When are they sending you?" Kiyan asked as she poured out the bucket. Gray water flowed over the bricks that paved the small garden at the back of the wayhouse. Otah took the longhandled brush and swept the water off to the sides, leaving the walkway deep red and glistening in the sunlight. He felt Kiyan's gaze on him, felt the question in the air. The gardens smelled of fresh turned earth. Spices for the kitchen grew here. In a few weeks, the place would be thick with growing things: basil and mint and thyme. He imagined scrubbing these bricks week after week over the span of years until they wore smooth or he died, and felt an irrational surge of fondness for the walkway. He smiled to himself.

"Itani?"

"I don't know. That is, I know they want me to go to Machi in two weeks time. Amiit Foss is sending half the couriers he has up there, it seems."

"Of course he is. It's where everything's happening."

"But I haven't decided to go."

The silence bore down on him now, and he turned. Kiyan stood in the doorway—in her doorway. Her crossed arms, her narrowed eyes, and the single frown-line drawn vertically between her brows, made Otah smile. He leaned on his brush.

"We need to talk, sweet," he said. "There are some things . . . we have some business, I think, to attend to."

Kiyan answered by taking the brush from him, leaning it against the wall, and marching to a meeting room at the back of the house. It was small but formal, with a thick wooden door and a window that looked out on the corner of the interior courtyard. The sort of place she might give to a diplomat or a courier for an extra length of copper. The sort of place it would be difficult to be overheard. That was as it should be.

Kiyan sat carefully, her face as blank as that of a man playing tiles. Otah sat across from her, careful not to touch her hand. She was holding herself back, he knew. She was restraining herself from hoping until she knew, so that if what he said did not match what she longed to hear, the disappointment would not be so heavy. For a moment, his mind flickered back to a bathhouse in Saraykeht and another woman's eyes. He had had this conversation once before, and he doubted he would ever have it again.

"I don't want to go to the north," Otah said. "For more reasons than one."

"Why not?" Kiyan asked.

"Sweet, there are some things I haven't told you. Things about my family. About myself. . . ."

And so he began, slowly, carefully, to tell the story. He was the son of the Khai Machi, but his sixth son. One of those cast out by his family and sent to the school where the sons of the Khaiem and utkhaiem struggled in hope of one day being selected to be poets and wield the power of the andat. He had been chosen once, and had walked away. Itani Noygu was the name he had chosen for himself, the man he had made of himself. But he was also Otah Machi.

He was careful to tell the story well. He more than half expected her to laugh at him. Or to accuse him of a self-aggrandizing madness. Or to sweep him into her arms and say that she'd known, she'd always known he was something more than a courier. Kiyan defeated all the stories he had spun in his dreams of this moment. She merely listened, arms crossed, eyes turned toward the window. The vertical line between her brows deepened slightly, and that was all. She did not move or ask questions until he had nearly reached the end. All that was left was to tell her he'd chosen to take her offer to work with her here at the wayhouse, but she knew that already and lifted her hands before he could say the words.

"Itani . . . lover, if this isn't true . . . if this is a joke, please tell me. Now."

"It isn't a joke," he said.

She took a deep breath, letting it out slowly. When she spoke, she seemed calm in a way that he knew meant rage beyond expression. At the first tone of it, his heart went tight.

"You have to leave. Now. Tonight. You have to leave and never come back."

"Kiyan-kya . . ."

"No. No *kya*. No *sweet*. No *my love*. None of that. You have to leave my house and you can't ever come back or tell anyone who you are or who I am or that we knew each other once. Do you understand that?"

"I understand that you're angry with me," Otah said, leaning toward her. "You have a right to be. But you don't know how carefully I have had to guard this."

Kiyan tilted her head, like a fox that's heard a strange noise, then laughed once.

"You think I'm upset you didn't tell me? You think I'm upset because you had a secret and you didn't spill it the first time we shared a bed? Itani, this may surprise you, but I have secrets a thousand times less important than that, and I've kept them a hundred times better."

"But you want me to leave?"

"Of course I want you to leave. Are you dim? Do you know what happened to the men who guarded your eldest brother? They're dead. Do you recall what happened when the Khai Yalakeht's sons turned on each other six years back? There were a dozen corpses before that was through, and only two of them were related to the Khai. Now look around you. How do you expect me to protect my house? How can I protect Old Mani? And think before you speak, because if you tell me that you'll be strong and manly and protect me, I swear by all the gods I'll turn you in myself."

"No one will find out," Otah said.

She closed her eyes. A tear broke free, tracing a bright line down her cheek. When he leaned close, reaching out to wipe it away, she slapped his hand before it touched her.

"I would almost be willing to take that chance, if it were only me. Not quite, but nearly. It isn't, though. It's everyone and everything I've worked for."

"Kiyan-kya, together we could . . ."

"Do nothing. Together we could do nothing, because you are leaving now. And odd as it sounds, I *do* understand. Why you concealed what you did, why you told me now. And I hope ghosts haunt you and chew out your eyes at night. I hope all the gods there are damn you for making me love you and then doing this to me. Now get out. If you're here in half a hand's time, I will call for the guard."

Outside the window, a flutter of wings and then the fluting melody of a songbird. The constant distant sound of the river. The scent of pine.

"Do you believe me?" she asked. "That I'll call the guard on you if you stay?"

"I do," he said.

"Then go."

"I love you."

"I know you do, 'Tani-kya. Go."

House Siyanti had quarters in the city for its people—small rooms hardly large enough for a cot and a brazier, but the blankets were thick and soft, and the kitchens sold meals at half the price a cart on the street would. When the rain came that night, Otah lay in the glow of the coals and listened to patter of water against leaves mix with the voices from the covered courtyard. Someone was playing a nomad's harp, and the music was lively and sorrowful at the same time. Sometimes voices would rise up together in song or laughter. He turned Kiyan's words over in his mind and noticed how empty they made him feel.

He'd been a fool to tell her, a fool to say anything. If he had only kept his secrets secret, he could have made a life for himself based on lies, and if the brothers he only knew as shadows and moments from a half-recalled childhood had ever discovered him, Kiyan and Old Mani and anyone else unfortunate enough to know him might have been killed without even knowing why.

Kiyan had not been wrong.

A gentle murmur of thunder came and went. Otah rose from his cot and walked out. Amiit Foss kept late hours, and Otah found him sitting at a fire grate, poking the crackling flames with a length of iron while he joked over his shoulder with the five men and four women who lounged on cushions and low chairs. He smiled when he saw Otah and called for a bowl of wine for him. The gathering looked so calm and felt so relaxed that only someone in the gentleman's trade would have recognized it for the business meeting that it was.

"Itani-cha is one of the couriers I mean to send north, if I can pry him away from his love of sloth and comfort," Amiit said with a smile. The others greeted him and made him welcome. Otah sat by the fire and listened. There would be nothing said here that he was not permitted to know. Amiit's introduction had established with the subtlety of a master Otah's rank and the level of trust to be afforded him, and no one in the room was so thick as to misunderstand him.

The news from the north was confusing. The two surviving sons of Machi had vanished. Neither had appeared in the other cities of the Khaiem, going to courts and looking for support as tradition would have them do. Nor had the streets of Machi erupted in bloodshed as their bases of power within the city vied for advantage. The best estimates were that the old Khai wouldn't see another winter, and even some of the houses of the utkhaiem seemed to be preparing to offer up their sons as the new Khai should the succession fail to deliver a single living heir. Something very quiet was happening, and House Siyanti—like everyone else in the world—was aching with curiosity. Otah could hear it in their voices, could see it in the way they held their wine. Even when the conversation shifted to the glassblowers of Cetani and the collapse of the planned summer fair in Amnat-Tan, all minds were drawn toward Machi. He sipped his wine.

Going north was dangerous. He knew that, and still it didn't escape him that the Khai Machi dying by inches was his father, that these men were the brothers he knew only as vague memories. And because of these men, he had lost everything again. If he was going to be haunted his whole life by the city, perhaps he should at least see it. The only thing he risked was his life.

At length, the conversation turned to less weighty matters and—without a

word or shift in voice or manner—the meeting was ended. Otah spoke as much
as any, laughed as much, and sang as loudly when the pipe players joined them.
But when he stretched and turned to leave, Amiit Foss was at his side. Otah
and the overseer left together, as if they had only happened to rise at the same
time, and Otah knew that no one in the drunken, boisterous room they left had
failed to notice it.

"So, it sounds as if all the interesting things in the world were happening in
Machi," Otah said as they strode back through the hallways of the house compound. "You are still hoping to send me there?"

"I've been hoping," Amiit Foss agreed. "But I have other plans if you have
some of your own."

"I don't," Otah said, and Amiit paused. In the dim lantern light, Otah let
the old man search his face. Something passed over Amiit, the ghost of some
old sorrow, and then he took a pose of condolence.

"I thought you had come to quit the house," Amiit said.

"I'd meant to," Otah said, surprised at himself for admitting it.

Amiit gestured Otah to follow him, and together they retired to Amiit's
apartments. The rooms were large and warm, hung with tapestries and lit by a
dozen candles. Otah sat on a low seat by a table, and Amiit took a box from his
shelf. Inside were two small porcelain bowls and a white stoppered bottle that
matched them. When Amiit poured, the scent of rice wine filled the room.

"We drink to the gods," Amiit said, raising his bowl. "May they never drink
to us."

Otah drank the wine at a gulp. It was excellent, and he felt his throat grow
warmer. He looked at the empty bowl in his fingers and nodded. Amiit grinned.

"It was a gift from an old friend," Amiit said. "I love to drink it, but I hate
to drink alone."

"I'm pleased to be of service," Otah said as Amiit filled the bowl again.

"So things with the woman didn't work out?"

"No," Otah said.

"I'm sorry."

"It was entirely my fault."

"If it's true, you're a wise man to know it, and if not, you're a good man for
saying it. Either way."

"I think it would be . . . that is, if there are any letters to be carried, I think
travel might be the best thing just now. I don't really care to stay in Udun."

Amiit sighed and nodded.

"Tomorrow," he said. "Come to my offices in the morning. We'll arrange
something."

Afterwards, they finished the rice wine and talked of nothing important—of
old stories and old travels, the women they had known and loved or else hated.
Or both. Otah said nothing of Kiyan or the north, and Amiit didn't press him.

When Otah rose to leave, he was surprised to find how drunk he had become. He navigated his way to his room and lay on the couch, mustering the resolve to pull off his robes. Morning found him still dressed. He changed robes and went down to the bathhouse, forcing his mind back over his conversations of the night before. He was fairly certain he had said nothing to implicate himself or make Amiit suspect the nature of his falling out with Kiyan. He wondered what the old man would have made of the truth, had he known it.

The packet of letters waited for him, each sewn and sealed, in a leather bag on Amiit Foss' desk. Most were for trading houses in Machi, though there were four that were to go to members of the utkhaiem. Otah turned the packet in his hands. Behind him, one of the apprentices said something softly and another giggled.

"You have time to reconsider," Amiit said. "You could go back to her on your knees. If the letters wait another day, there's little lost. And she might relent."

Otah tucked the letters into their pouch and slipped it into his sleeve.

"An old lover of mine once told me that everything I'd ever won, I won by leaving," Otah said.

"The island girl?"

"Did I mention her last night?"

"At length," Amiit said, chuckling. "That particular quotation came up twice, as I recall. There might have been a third time too. I couldn't really say."

"I'm sorry to hear that. I hope I didn't tell you all my secrets," Otah said, making a joke of his sudden unease. He didn't recall saying anything about Maj, and it occurred to him exactly how dangerous that night had been.

"If you had, I'd make it a point to forget them," Amiit said. "Nothing a drunk man says on the day his woman leaves him should be held against him. It's poor form. And this is, after all, a gentleman's trade, ne?"

Otah took a pose of agreement.

"I'll report what I find when I get back," he said, unnecessarily. "Assuming I haven't frozen to death on the roads."

"Be careful up there, Itani. Things are uncertain when there's the scent of a new Khai in the wind. It's interesting, and it's important, but it's not always safe."

Otah shifted to a pose of thanks, to which his supervisor replied in kind, his face so pleasantly unreadable that Otah genuinely didn't know how deep the warning ran.

3

>+< When Maati considered the mines—something he had rarely had occasion to do—he had pictured great holes going deep into the earth. He had not imagined the branchings and contortions of passages where miners struggled to follow veins of ore, the stench of dust and damp, the yelps and howls of the dogs that pulled the flat-bottomed sledges filled with gravel, or the darkness. He held his lantern low, as did the others around him. There was no call to raise it. Nothing more would be seen, and the prospect of breaking it against the stone overhead was unpleasant.

"There can be places where the air goes bad, too," Cehmai said as they turned another twisting corner. "They take birds with them because they die first."

"What happens then?" Maati asked. "If the birds die?"

"It depends on how valuable the ore is," the young poet said. "Abandon the mine, or try to blow out the bad air. Or use slaves. There are men whose indentures allow that."

Two servants followed at a distance, their own torches glowing. Maati had the sense that they would all, himself included, have been better pleased to spend the day in the palaces. All but the andat. Stone-Made-Soft alone among them seemed untroubled by the weight over them and the gloom that pressed in when the lanterns flickered. The wide, calm face seemed almost stupid to Maati, the andat's occasional pronouncements simplistic compared with the thousand-layered comments of Seedless, the only andat he'd known intimately. He knew better than to be taken in. The form of the andat might be different, the mental bindings that held it might place different strictures upon it, but the hunger at its center was as desperate. It was an andat, and it would long to return to its natural state. They might seem as different as a marble from a thorn, but at heart they were all the same.

And Maati knew he was walking through a tunnel not so tall he could stand to his full height with a thousand tons of stone above him. This placid-faced ghost could bring it down on him as if they'd been crawling through a hole in the ocean.

"So, you see," Cehmai was saying, "the Daikani engineers find where they want to extend the mine out. Or down, or up. We have to leave that to them. Then I will come through and walk through the survey with them, so that we all understand what they're asking."

"And how much do you soften it?"

"It varies," Cehmai said. "It depends on the kind of rock. Some of them you can almost reduce to putty if you're truly clear where you want it to be. Then other times, you only want it to be easier to dig through. Most often, that's when they're concerned about collapses."

"I see," Maati said. "And the pumps? How do those figure in?"

"That was actually an entirely different agreement. The Khai's eldest son was interested in the problem. The mines here are some of the lowest that are still in use. The northern mines are almost all in the mountains, and so they aren't as likely to strike water."

"So the Daikani pay more for being here?"

"No, not really. The pumps he designed usually work quite well."

"But the payment for them?"

Cehmai grinned. His teeth and skin were yellowed by the lantern light.

"It was a different agreement," Cehmai said again. "The Daikani let him experiment with his designs and he let them use them."

"But if they worked well . . ."

"Other mines would pay the Khai for the use of the pumps if they wished for help building them. Usually, though, the mines will help each other on things like that. There's a certain . . . what to call it . . . brotherhood? The miners take care of each other, whatever house they work for."

"Might we see the pumps?"

"If you'd like," he said. "They're back in the deeper parts of the mine. If you don't mind walking down farther. . . ."

Maati forced a grin and did not look at the wide face of the andat turning toward him.

"Not at all," he said. "Let's go down."

The pumps, when he found them at last, were ingenious. A series of treadmills turned huge corkscrews that lifted the water up to pools where another corkscrew waited to lift it higher again. They did not keep the deepest tunnels dry—the walls there seemed to weep as Maati waded through warm, knee-high water—but they kept it clear enough to work. Machi had, Cehmai assured him, the deepest tunnels in the world. Maati did not ask if they were the safest.

They found the mine's overseer here in the depths. Voices seemed to carry better in the watery tunnels than up above, but Maati could not make out the words clearly until they were almost upon him. A small, thick-set man with a darkness to him that made Maati think of grime worked so deeply into skin that it would never come clean, he took a pose of welcome as they approached.

"We've an honored guest come to the city," Cehmai said.

"We've had many honored guests in the *city*," the overseer said, with a grin. "Damn few in the bottom of the hole, though. There's no palaces down here."

"But Machi's fortunes rest on its mines," Maati said. "So in a sense these are the deepest cellars of the palaces. The ones where the best treasures are hidden."

The overseer grinned.

"I like this one," he said to Cehmai. "He's got a quick head on him."

"I heard about the pumps the Khai's eldest son had designed," Maati said. "I was wondering if you could tell me of them?"

The grin widened, and the overseer launched into an expansive and delighted discussion of water and mines and the difficulty of removing the one from the other. Maati listened, struggling to follow the vocabulary and grammar particular to the trade.

"He had a gift for them," the overseer said, at last. His voice was melancholy. "We'll keep at them, these pumps, and they'll get better, but not like they would have with Biitrah-cha on them."

"He was here, I understand, on the day he was killed," Maati said. He saw the young poet's head shift, turning to consider him, and he ignored it as he had the andat's.

"That's truth. And I wish he'd stayed. His brothers aren't bad men, but they aren't miners. And . . . well, he'll be missed."

"I had thought it odd, though," Maati said. "Whichever brother killed him, they had to know where he would be—that he would be called out here, and that the work would take so much of the day that he wouldn't return to the city itself."

"I suppose that's so," the overseer said.

"Then someone knew your pumps would fail," Maati said.

The lamplight flickered off the surface of the water, casting shadows up the overseer's face as this sank in. Cehmai coughed. Maati said nothing, did not move, waited. If any man here had been involved with it, the overseer was most likely. But Maati saw no rage or wariness in his expression, only the slow blooming of implication that might be expected in a man who had not thought the murder through. So perhaps he could be used after all.

"You're saying someone sabotaged my pumps to get him out here," the overseer said at last.

Maati wished deeply that Cehmai and his andat were not present—this was a thing better done alone. But the moment had arrived, and there was nothing to be done but go forward. The servants at least were far enough away not to overhear if he spoke softly. Maati dug in his sleeve and came out with a letter and a small leather pouch, heavy with silver lengths. He pressed them both into the surprised overseer's hands.

"If you should discover who did, I would very much like to speak with them before the officers of the utkhaiem or the head of your House. That letter will tell you how to find me."

The overseer tucked away the pouch and letter, taking a pose of thanks which Maati waved away. Cehmai and the andat were silent as stones.

"And how long is it you've been working these mines?" Maati asked, forcing a lightness to his tone he did not feel. Soon the overseer was regaling them with stories of his years underground, and they were walking together toward the surface again. By the time Maati stepped out from the long, sloping throat of the mine and into daylight, his feet were numb. A litter waited for them, twelve strong men prepared to carry the three of them back to the palaces. Maati stopped for a moment to wring the water from the hem of his robes and to appreciate having nothing but the wide sky above him.

"Why was it the Dai-kvo sent you?" Cehmai asked as they climbed into the wooden litter. His voice was almost innocent, but even the andat was looking at Maati oddly.

"There are suggestions that the library may have some old references that the Dai-kvo lacks. Things that touch on the grammars of the first poets."

"Ah," Cehmai said. The litter lurched and rose, swaying slightly as the servants bore them away back to the palaces. "And nothing more than that?"

"Of course not," Maati said. "What more could there be?"

He knew that he was convincing no one. And that was likely a fine thing. Maati had spent his first days in Machi learning the city, the courts, the teahouses. The Khai's daughter had introduced him to the gatherings of the younger generation of the utkhaiem as the poet Cehmai had to the elder. Maati had spent each night walking a different quarter of the city, wrapped in thick wool robes with close hoods against the vicious cold of the spring air. He had learned the intrigues of the court: which houses were vying for marriages to which cities, who was likely to be extorting favors for whom over what sorts of indiscretion, all the petty wars of a family of a thousand children.

He had used the opportunities to spread the name of Itani Noygu—saying only that he was an old friend Maati had heard might be in the city, whom he would very much like to see. There was no way to say that it was the name Otah Machi had invented for himself in Saraykeht, and even if there had been, Maati would likely not have done so. He had come to realize exactly how little he knew what he ought to do.

He had been sent because he knew Otah, knew how his old friend's mind worked, would recognize him should they meet. They were advantages, Maati supposed, but it was hard to weigh them against his inexperience. There was little enough to learn of making discreet inquiries when your life was spent in the small tasks of the Dai-kvo's village. An overseer of a trading house would have been better suited to the task. A negotiator, or a courier. Liat would have been better, the woman he had once loved, who had once loved him. Liat, mother of the boy Nayiit, whom Maati had held as a babe and loved more than water or air. Liat, who had been Otah's lover as well.

For the thousandth time, Maati put that thought aside.

When they reached the palaces, Maati again thanked Cehmai for taking the time from his work to accompany him, and Cehmai—still with the half-certain stance of a dog hearing an unfamiliar sound—assured him that he'd been pleased to do so. Maati watched the slight young man and his thick-framed andat walk away across the flagstones of the courtyard. Their hems were black and sodden, ruining the drape of the robes. Much like his own, he knew.

Thankfully, his own apartments were warm. He stripped off his robes, leaving them in a lump for the servants to remove to a launderer, and replaced them with the thickest he had—lamb's wool and heavy leather with a thin cotton lining. It was the sort that natives of Machi wore in deep winter, but Maati pulled it close about him, vowing to use it whenever he went out, whatever the others might think of him. His boots thrown into a corner, he stretched his pale, numb feet almost into the fire grate and shuddered. He would have to go to the wayhouse where Biitrah Machi had died. The owners there had spoken to the officers of the utkhaiem, of course. They had told their tale of the moon-faced man who had come with letters of introduction, worked in their kitchens, and been ready to take over for a night when the overseers all came down ill. Still, he could not be sure there was nothing more to know unless he made his visit. Some other day, when he could feel his toes.

The summons came to him when the sun—red and angry—was just preparing to slide behind the mountains to the west. Maati pulled on thick, warm boots of soft leather, added his brown poet's robes over the warmer ones, and let himself be led to the Khai Machi's private chambers. He passed through several rooms on his way—a hall of worked marble the color of honey with a fountain running through it like a creek, a meeting chamber large enough to hold two dozen at a single table, then a smaller corridor that led to chambers of a more human size. Ahead of him, a woman passed from one side of the corridor to the other leaving the impression of night-black hair, warm brown skin, and robes the yellow of sunrise. One of the wives, Maati knew, of a man who had several.

At last, the servant slid open a door of carved rosewood, and Maati stepped into a room hardly larger than his own bedroom. The old man sat on a couch, his feet toward the fire that burned in the grate. His robes were lush, the silks seeming to take up the firelight and dance with it. They seemed more alive than his flesh. Slowly, the Khai raised a clay pipe to his mouth and puffed on it thoughtfully. The smoke smelled rich and sweet as a cane field on fire.

Maati took a pose of greeting as formal as high court. The Khai Machi raised an ancient eyebrow and only smiled. With the stem of the pipe, he pointed to the couch opposite him and nodded to Maati that he should sit.

"They make me smoke this," the Khai said. "Whenever my belly troubles me, they say. I tell them they might as well make it air, burn it by the bushel in all the firekeeper's kilns, but they only laugh as if it were wit, and I play along."

"Yes, most high."

There was a long pause as the Khai contemplated the flames. Maati waited, uncertain. He noticed the catch in the Khai Machi's breath, as if it pained him. He had not noticed it before.

"Your search for my outlaw son," the Khai said. "It is going well?"

"It is early yet, most high. I have made myself visible. I have let it be known that I am looking into the death of your son."

"You still expect Otah to come to you?"

"Yes."

"And if he does not?"

"Then it will take more time, most high. But I will find him."

The old man nodded, then exhaled a plume of pale smoke. He took a pose of gratitude, his wasted hands holding the position with the grace of a lifetime's practice.

"His mother was a good woman. I miss her. Iyrah, her name was. She gave me Idaan too. She was glad to have a child of her own that she could keep."

Maati thought he saw the old man's eyes glisten for a moment, lost as he was in old memories of which Maati could only guess the substance. Then the Khai sighed.

"Idaan," the Khai said. "She's treated you gently?"

"She's been nothing but kind," Maati said, "and very generous with her time."

The Khai shook his head, smiling more to himself than his audience.

"That's good. She was always unpredictable. Age has calmed her, I think. There was a time she would study outrages the way most girls study face paints and sandals. Always sneaking puppies into court or stealing dresses she fancied from her little friends. She relied on me to keep her safe, however far she flew," he said, smiling fondly. "A mischievous girl, my daughter, but good-hearted. I'm proud of her."

Then he sobered.

"I am proud of all my children. It's why I am not of one mind on this," the Khai said. "You would think that I should be, but I am not. With every day that the search continues, the truce holds, and Kaiin and Danat still live. I've known since I was old enough to know anything that if I took this chair, my sons would kill each other. It wasn't so hard before I knew them, when they were only the idea of sons. But then they were Biitrah and Kaiin and Danat. And I don't want any of them to die."

"But tradition, most high. If they did not—"

"I know why they must," the Khai said. "I was only wishing. It's something dying men do, I'm told. Sit with their regrets. It's likely that which kills us as much as the sickness. I sometimes wish that this had all happened years ago. That they had slaughtered each other in their childhood. Then I might have at least one of them by me now. I had not wanted to die alone."

"You are not alone, most high. The whole court . . ."

Maati broke off. The Khai Machi took a pose accepting correction, but the amusement in his eyes and the angle of his shoulders made a sarcasm of it. Maati nodded, accepting the old man's point.

"I can't say which of them I would have wanted to live, though," the Khai said, puffing thoughtfully on his pipe. "I love them all. Very dearly. I cannot tell you how deeply I miss Biitrah."

"Had you known him, you would have loved Otah as well."

"You think so? Certainly you knew him better than I. I can't think he would have thought well of me," the Khai said. Then, "Did you go back? After you took your robes? Did you go to see you parents?"

"My father was very old when I went to the school," Maati said. "He died before I completed my training. We did not know each other."

"So you have never had a family."

"I have, most high," Maati said, fighting to keep the tightness in his chest from changing the tone of his voice. "A lover and a son. I had a family once."

"But no longer. They died?"

"They live. Only not with me."

The Khai considered him, bloodshot eyes blinking slowly. With his thin, wrinkled skin, he reminded Maati of a very old turtle or else a very young bird. The Khai's gaze softened, his brows tilting in understanding and sorrow.

"It is never easy for fathers," the Khai said. "Perhaps if the world had needed less from us."

Maati waited a long moment until he trusted his voice.

"Perhaps, most high."

The Khai exhaled a breath of gray, his gaze trapped by the smoke.

"It isn't the world I knew when I was young," the old man said. "Everything changed when Saraykeht fell."

"The Khai Saraykeht has a poet," Maati said. "He has the power of the andat."

"It took the Dai-kvo eight years and six failed bindings," the Khai said. "And every time word came of another failure, I could see it in the faces of the court. The utkhaiem may put on proud faces, but I've seen the fear that swims under that ice. And you were there. You said so in the audience when I greeted you."

"Yes, most high."

"But you didn't say everything you knew," the Khai said. "Did you?"

The yellowed eyes fixed on Maati. The intelligence in them was unnerving. Maati felt himself squirming, and wondering what had happened to the melancholy dying man he'd been speaking with only moments before.

"I . . . that is . . ."

"There were rumors that the poet's death was more than an angry east island girl's revenge. The Galts were mentioned."

"And Eddensea," Maati said. "And Eymond. There was no end of accusation, most high. Some even believed what they charged. When the cotton trade collapsed, a great number of people lost a great amount of money. And prestige."

"They lost more than that," the Khai said, leaning forward and stabbing at the air with the stem of his pipe. "The money, the trade. The standing among the cities. They don't signify. Saraykeht was the death of *certainty*. They lost the conviction that the Khaiem would hold the world at bay, that war would never come to Saraykeht. And we lost it here too."

"If you say so, most high."

"The priests say that something touched by chaos is never made whole," the Khai said, sinking back into his cushions. "Do you know what they mean by that, Maati-cha?"

"I have some idea," Maati said, but the Khai went on.

"It means that something unthinkable can only happen once. Because after that, it's not unthinkable any longer. We've *seen* what happens when a city is touched by chaos. And now it's in the back of every head in every court in all the cities of the Khaiem."

Maati frowned and leaned forward.

"You think Cehmai-cha is in some danger?"

"What?" the Khai said, then waved the thought away, stirring the smoky air. "No. Not that. I think my city is at risk. I think Otah . . . my upstart son . . ."

He's forgiven you, a voice murmured in the back of Maati's mind. The voice of Seedless, the andat of Saraykeht. They were the words the andat had spoken to Maati in the instant before Heshai's death had freed it.

It had been speaking of Otah.

"I've called you here for a reason, Maati-cha," the Khai said, and Maati pulled his attention back to the present. "I didn't care to speak of it around those who would use it to fuel gossip. Your inquiry into Biitrah's death. You must move more quickly."

"Even with the truce?"

"Yes, even at the price of my sons returning to their tradition. If I die without a successor chosen—especially if Danat and Kaiin are still gone to ground—there will be chaos. The families of the utkhaiem start thinking that perhaps they would sit more comfortably in my chair, and schemes begin. Your task isn't only to find Otah. Your task is to protect my city."

"I understand, most high."

"You do not, Maati-cha. The spring roses are starting to bloom, and I will not see high summer. Neither of us has the luxury of time."

THE GATHERING WAS ALL THAT CEHMAI HAD HOPED FOR, AND LESS. SPRING BREEZES washed the pavilion with the scent of fresh flowers. Kilns set along the edges roared behind the music of reed organ, flute, and drum. Overhead, the stars shone like gems strewn on dark velvet. The long months of winter had given musicians time to compose and practice new songs, and the youth of the high families week after weary week to tire of the cold and dark and the terrible constriction that deep winter brought to those with no business to conduct on the snow.

Cehmai laughed and clapped time with the music and danced. Women and girls caught his eye, and he, theirs. The heat of youth did where heavier robes would otherwise have been called for, and the draw of body to body filled the air with something stronger than the perfume of flowers. Even the impending death of the Khai lent an air of license. Momentous things were happening, the world's order was changing, and they were young enough to find the thought romantic.

And yet he could not enjoy it.

A young man in an eagle's mask pressed a bowl of hot wine into his hand, and spun away into the dance. Cehmai grinned, sipped at it, and faded back to the edge of the pavilion. In the shadows behind the kilns, Stone-Made-Soft stood motionless. Cehmai sat beside it, put the bowl on the grass, and watched the revelry. Two young men had doffed their robes entirely and were sprinting around the wide grounds in nothing but their masks and long scarves trailing from their necks. The andat shifted like the first shudder of a landslide, then was still again. When it spoke, its voice was so soft that they would not be heard by the others.

"It wouldn't be the first time the Dai-kvo had lied."

"Or the first time I'd wondered why," Cehmai said. "It's his to decide what to say and to whom."

"And yours?"

"And mine to satisfy my curiosity. You heard what he said to the overseer in the mines. If he truly didn't want me to know, he would have lied better. Maati-kvo is looking into more than the library, and that's certain."

The andat sighed. Stone-Made-Soft had no more need of breath than did a mountainside. The exhalation could only be a comment. Cehmai felt the subject of their conversation changing even before the andat spoke.

"She's come."

And there, dressed black as rooks and pale as mourning, Idaan Machi moved among the dancers. Her mask hid only part of her face and not her identity.

Wrapped as he was by the darkness, she did not see him. Cehmai felt a lightening in his breast as he watched her move through the crowd, greeting friends and looking, he thought, for something or perhaps someone among them. She was not beautiful—well painted, but any number of the girls and women were more nearly perfect. She was not the most graceful, or the best spoken, or any of the hundred things that Cehmai thought of when he tried to explain to himself why this girl should fascinate him. The closest he could come was that she was interesting, and none of the others were.

"It won't end well," the andat murmured.

"It hasn't begun," Cehmai said. "How can something end when it hasn't even started?"

Stone-Made-Soft sighed again, and Cehmai rose, tugging at his robes to smooth their lines. The music had paused and someone in the crowd laughed long and high.

"Come back when you've finished and we'll carry on our conversation," the andat said.

Cehmai ignored the patience in its voice and strode forward, back into the light. The reed organ struck a chord just as he reached Idaan's side. He brushed her arm, and she turned—first annoyed and then surprised and then, he thought, pleased.

"Idaan-cha," he said, the exaggerated formality acting as its opposite without taking him quite into the intimacy that the *kya* suffix would have suggested. "I'd almost thought you wouldn't be joining us."

"I almost wasn't," she said. "I hadn't thought you'd be here."

The organ set a beat, and the drums picked it up; the dance was beginning again. Cehmai held out a hand and, after a pause that took a thousand years and lasted perhaps a breath, Idaan took it. The music began in earnest, and Cehmai spun her, took her under his arm, and was turned by her. It was a wild tune, rich and fast with a rhythm like a racing heart. Around him the others were grinning, though not at him. Idaan laughed, and he laughed with her. The paving stones beneath them seemed to echo back the song, and the sky above them received it.

As they turned to face each other, he could see the flush in Idaan's cheek, and felt the same blood in his own, and then the music whirled them off again.

In the center of the frenzy, someone took Cehmai's elbow from behind, and something round and hard was pressed into his hands. A man's voice whispered urgently in his ear.

"Hold this."

Cehmai faltered, confused, and the moment was gone. He was suddenly standing alone in a throng of people, holding an empty bowl—a thread of wine wetting the rim—while Adrah Vaunyogi took Idaan Machi through the steps

and turns of the dance. The pair shifted away from him, left him behind. Cehmai felt the flush in his cheek brighten. He turned and walked through the
shifting bodies, handing the bowl to a servant as he left.

"He *is* her lover," the andat said. "Everyone knows it."

"I don't," Cehmai said.

"I just told you."

"You tell me things all the time; it doesn't mean I agree to them."

"This thing you have in mind," Stone-Made-Soft said. "You shouldn't do it."

Cehmai looked up into the calm gray eyes set in the wide, placid face. He
felt his own head lift in defiance, even as he knew the words were truth. It was
stupid and mean and petty. Adrah Vaunyogi wasn't even entirely in the wrong.
There was a perspective by which the little humiliation Cehmai had been
dealt was a small price for flirting so openly with another man's love.

And yet.

The andat nodded slowly and turned to consider the dancers. It was easy
enough to pick out Idaan and Adrah. They were too far for Cehmai to be sure,
but he liked to think she was frowning. It hardly mattered. Cehmai focused on
Adrah's movements—his feet, shifting in time with the drums while Idaan
danced to the flutes. He doubled his attention, feeling it through his own body
and also the constant storm at the back of his mind. In that instant he was both
of them—a single being with two bodies and a permanent struggle at the
heart. And then, at just the moment when Adrah's foot came back to catch his
weight, Cehmai reached out. The paving stone gave way, the smooth stone
suddenly soft as mud, and Adrah stumbled backward and fell, landing on his
rear, legs splayed. Cehmai waited a moment for the stone to flow back nearer
to smooth, then let his consciousness return to its usual state. The storm that
was Stone-Made-Soft was louder, more present in his mind, like the proud
flesh where a thorn has scratched skin. And like a scratch, Cehmai knew it
would subside.

"We should go," Cehmai said, "before I'm tempted to do something childish."

The andat didn't answer, and Cehmai led the way through the night-dark
gardens. The music floated in the distance and then faded. Far from the kilns
and dancing, the night was cold—not freezing, but near it. But the stars were
brighter, and the moon glowed: a rim of silver that made the starless thumb-
print darker by contrast. They passed by the temple and the counting house,
the bathhouse and base of the great tower. The andat turned down a side path
then, and paused when Cehmai did not follow.

Stone-Made-Soft took a pose of query.

"Is this not where you were going?" it asked.

Cehmai considered, and then smiled.

"I suppose it is," he said, and followed the captive spirit down the curving
pathway and up the wide, shallow steps that led to the library. The great stone

doors were barred from within, but Cehmai followed the thin gravel path at the side of the building, keeping close to the wall. The windows of Baarath's apartments glowed with more than a night candle's light. Even with the night half gone, he was awake. The door slave was an ancient man, and Cehmai had to shake him by the shoulder before he woke, retreated into the apartments, and returned to lead them in.

The apartments smelled of old wine, and the sandalwood resin that Baarath burned in his brazier. The tables and couches were covered with books and scrolls, and no cushion had escaped from some ink stain. Baarath, dressed in deep red robes thick as tapestry, rose from his desk and took a pose of welcome. His copper torc of office was lying discarded on the floor at his feet.

"Cehmai-cha, to what do I owe this honor?"

Cehmai frowned. "Are you angry with me?" he asked.

"Of course not, great poet. How could a poor man of books dare to feel angry with a personage like yourself?"

"Gods," Cehmai said as he shifted a pile of papers from a wide chair. "I don't know, Baarath-kya. Do tell me."

"Kya? Oh, you are too familiar with me, great poet. I would not suggest so deep a friendship as that with a man so humble as myself."

"You're right," Cehmai said, sitting. "I was trying to flatter you. Did it work?"

"You should have brought wine," the stout man said, taking his own seat. The false graciousness was gone, and a sour impatience in its place. "And come at an hour when living men could talk business. Isn't it late for you to be wandering around like a dazed rabbit?"

"There was a gathering at the rose pavilion. I was just going back to my apartments and I noticed the lights burning."

Baarath made a sound between a snort and a cough. Stone-Made-Soft gazed placidly at the marble walls, thoughtful as a lumberman judging the best way to fell a tree. Cehmai frowned at him, and the andat replied with a gesture more eloquent than any pose. *Don't blame me. He's your friend, not mine.*

"I wanted to ask how things were proceeding with Maati Vaupathai," Cehmai said.

"About time someone took an interest in that annoying, feckless idiot. I've met cows with more sense than he has."

"Not proceeding well, then?"

"Who can tell? *Weeks*, it's been. He's only here about half the morning, and then he's off dining with the dregs of the court, taking meetings with trading houses, and loafing about in the low towns. If I were the Dai-kvo, I'd pull that man back home and set him to plowing fields. I've eaten hens that were better scholars."

"Cows and hens. He'll be a whole farmyard soon," Cehmai said, but his mind was elsewhere. "What does he study when he is here?"

"Nothing in particular. He picks up whatever strikes him and spends a day with it, and then comes back the next for something totally unrelated. I haven't told him about the Khai's private archives, and he hasn't bothered to ask. I was sure, you know, when he first came, that he was after something in the private archives. But now it's like the library itself might as well not exist."

"Perhaps there is some pattern in what he's looking at. A common thread that places them all together."

"You mean maybe poor old Baarath is too simple to see the picture when it's being painted for him? I doubt it. I know this place better than any man alive. I've even made my own shelving system. I have read more of these books and seen more of their relationships than anyone. When I tell you he's wandering about like tree fluff on a breezy day, it's because he *is*."

Cehmai tried to feel surprise, and failed. The library was only an excuse. The Dai-kvo had sent Maati Vaupathai to examine the death of Biitrah Machi. That was clear. Why he would choose to do so, was not. It wasn't the poets' business to take sides in the succession, only to work with—and sometimes cool the ambitions of—whichever son survived. The Khaiem administered the city, accepted the glory and tribute, passed judgment. The poets kept the cities from ever going to war one against the other, and fueled the industries that brought wealth from the Westlands and Galt, Bakta, and the east islands. But something had happened, or was happening, that had captured the Dai-kvo's interest.

And Maati Vaupathai was an odd poet. He held no post, trained under no one. He was old to attempt a new binding. By many standards, he was already a failure. The only thing Cehmai knew of him that stood out at all was that Maati had been in Saraykeht when that city's poet was murdered and the andat set free. He thought of the man's eyes, the darkness that they held, and a sense of unease troubled him.

"I don't know what the point of that sort of grammar would be," Baarath said. "Dalani Toygu's was better for one thing, and half the length."

Cehmai realized that the Baarath had been talking this whole time, that the subject had changed, and in fact they were in the middle of a debate on a matter he couldn't identify. All this without the need that he speak.

"I suppose you're right," Cehmai said. "I hadn't seen it from that angle."

Stone-Made-Soft's calm, constant near-smile widened slightly.

"You should have, though. That's my point. Grammars and translations and the subtleties of thought are your trade. That I know more about it than you and that Maati person is a bad sign for the world. Note this, Cehmai-kya, write down that I said it. It's that kind of ignorance that will destroy the Khaiem."

"I'll write down that you said it," Cehmai said. "In fact, I'll go back to my apartments right now and do that. And afterwards, I'll crawl into bed, I think."

"So soon?"

"The night candle's past its center mark," Cehmai said.

"Fine. Go. When I was your age, I would stay up nights in a row for the sake of a good conversation like this, but I suppose the generations weaken, don't they?"

Cehmai took a pose of farewell, and Baarath returned it.

"Come by tomorrow, though," Baarath said as they left. "There's some old imperial poetry I've translated that might interest you."

Outside, the night had grown colder, and few lanterns lit the paths and streets. Cehmai pulled his arms in from their sleeves and held his fingers against his sides for warmth. His breath plumed blue-white in the faint moonlight, and even the distant scent of pine resin made the air seem colder.

"He doesn't think much of our guest," Cehmai said. "I would have thought he'd be pleased that Maati took little interest in the books, after all the noise he made."

When Stone-Made-Soft spoke, its breath did not fog. "He's like a girl bent on protecting her virginity until she finds no one wants it."

Cehmai laughed.

"That is entirely too apt," he said, and the andat took a pose accepting the compliment.

"You're going to do something," it said.

"I'm going to pay attention," Cehmai said. "If something needs doing, I'll try to be on hand."

They turned down the cobbled path that led to the poet's house. The sculpted oaks that lined it rustled in the faint breeze, rubbing new leaves together like a thousand tiny hands. Cehmai wished that he'd thought to bring a candle from Baarath's. He imagined Maati Vaupathai standing in the shadows with his appraising gaze and mysterious agenda.

"You're frightened of him," the andat said, but Cehmai didn't answer.

There *was* someone there among the trees—a shape shifting in the darkness. He stopped and slid his arms back into their sleeves. The andat stopped as well. They weren't far from the house—Cehmai could see the glow of the lantern left out before his doorway. The story of a poet slaughtered in a distant city raced in his mind until the figure came out between him and his doorway, silhouetted in the dim light. Cehmai's heart didn't slow, but it did change contents.

She still wore the half-mask she'd had at the gathering. Her black and white robes shifted, the cloth so rich and soft, and he could hear it even over the murmur of the trees. He stepped toward her, taking a pose of welcome.

"Idaan," he said. "Is there something . . . I didn't expect to find you here. I mean . . . I'm doing this rather badly, aren't I?"

"Start again," she said.

"Idaan."

"Cehmai."

She took a step toward him. He could see the flush in her cheek and smell the faint, nutty traces of distilled wine on her breath. When she spoke, her words were sharp and precise.

"I saw what you did to Adrah," she said. "He left a heel mark in the stone."

"Have I given offense?" he asked.

"Not to me. He didn't see it, and I didn't say."

In the back of his mind, or in some quarter of his flesh, Cehmai felt Stone-Made-Soft receding as if in answer to his own wish. They were alone on the dark path.

"It's difficult for you, isn't it?" she said. "Being a part of the court and yet not. Being among the most honored men in the city, and yet not of Machi."

"I bear it. You've been drinking."

"I have. But I know who I am and where I am. I know what I'm doing."

"What are you doing, Idaan-kya?"

"Poets can't take wives, can they?"

"We don't, no. There's not often room in our lives for a family."

"And lovers?"

Cehmai felt his breath coming faster and willed it to slow. An echo of amusement in the back of his mind was not his own thought. He ignored it.

"Poets take lovers," he said.

She stepped nearer again, not touching, not speaking. There was no chill to the air now. There was no darkness. Cehmai's senses were as fresh and bright and clear as midday, his mind as focused as the first day he'd controlled the andat. Idaan took his hand and slowly, deliberately, drew it through the folds of her robes until it cupped her breast.

"You . . . you have a lover, Idaan-kya. Adrah . . ."

"Do you want me to sleep here tonight?"

"Yes, Idaan. I do."

"And I want that too."

He struggled to think, but his skin felt as though he was basking in some hidden sun. There seemed to be some sound in his ears that he couldn't place that drove away everything but his fingertips and the cold-stippled flesh beneath them.

"I don't understand why you're doing this," he said.

Her lips parted, and she moved half an inch back. His hand pressed against her skin, his eyes were locked on hers. Fear sang through him that she would take another step back, that his fingers would only remember this moment, that this chance would pass. She saw it in his face, she must have, because she smiled, calm and knowing and sure of herself, like something from a dream.

"Do you care?" she asked.

"No," he said, half-surprised at the answer. "No, I truly don't."

THE CARAVAN LEFT THE LOW TOWN BEFORE DAWN, CARTWHEELS RATTLING ON THE old stone paving, oxen snorting white in the cold, and the voices of carters and merchants light with the anticipation of journey's end. The weeks of travel were past. By midday, they would cross the bridge over the Tidat and enter Machi. The companionship of the road—already somewhat strained by differences in political opinions and some unfortunate words spoken by one of the carters early in the journey—would break apart, and each of them would be about his own business again. Otah walked with his hands in his sleeves and his heart divided between dread and anticipation. Itani Noygu was going to Machi on the business of his house—the satchel of letters at his side proved that. There was nothing he carried with him that would suggest anything else. He had come away from this city as a child so long ago he had only shreds of memory left of it. A scent of musk, a stone corridor, bathing in a copper tub when he was small enough to be lifted with a single hand, a view from the top of one of the towers. Other things as fragmentary, as fleeting. He could not say which memories were real and which only parts of dreams.

It was enough, he supposed, to be here now, walking in the darkness. He would go and see it with a man's eyes. He would see this place that had sent him forth and, despite all his struggles, still had the power to poison the life he'd built for himself. Itani Noygu had made his way as an indentured laborer at the seafronts of Saraykeht, as a translator and fisherman and midwife's assistant in the east islands, as a sailor on a merchant ship, and as a courier in House Siyanti and all through the cities. He could write and speak in three tongues, play the flute badly, tell jokes well, cook his own meals over a half-dead fire, and comport himself well in any company from the ranks of the utkhaiem to the denizens of the crudest dockhouse. This from a twelve-year-old boy who had named himself, been his own father and mother, formed a life out of little more than the will to do so. Itani Noygu was by any sane standard a success.

It was Otah Machi who had lost Kiyan's love.

The sky in the east lightened to indigo and then royal blue, and Otah could see the road out farther ahead. Between one breath and the next, the oxen came clearer. And the plains before them opened like a vast scroll. Far to the north, mountains towered, looking flat as a painting and blued by the distance. Smoke rose from low towns and mines on the plain, the greener pathway of trees marked the river, and on the horizon, small as fingers, rose the dark towers of Machi, unnatural in the landscape.

Otah stopped as sunlight lit the distant peaks like a fire. The brilliance crept down and then the distant towers blazed suddenly, and a moment later, the plain flooded with light. Otah caught his breath.

This is where I started, he thought. I come from here.

He had to trot to catch back up with the caravan, but the questioning looks were all answered with a grin and a gesture. The enthusiastic courier still na-ïve enough to be amazed by a sunrise. There was nothing more to it than that.

House Siyanti kept no quarters in Machi, but the gentleman's trade had its provisions for this. Other Houses would extend courtesy even to rivals so long as it was understood that the intrigues and prying were kept to decorous lev-els. If a courier were to act against a rival House or carried information that would too deeply tempt his hosts, it was better form to pay for a room else-where. Nothing Otah carried was so specific or so valuable, and once the cara-van had made its trek across the plain and passed over the wide, sinuous bridge into Machi, Otah made his way to the compound of House Nan.

The structure itself was a gray block three stories high that faced a wide square and shared walls with the buildings on either side. Otah stopped by a street cart and bought a bowl of hot noodles in a smoky black sauce for two lengths of copper and watched the people passing by with a kind of doubled impression. He saw them as the subjects of his training: people clumped at the firekeepers' kilns and streetcarts meant a lively culture of gossip, women walking alone meant little fear of violence, and so on in the manner that was his profession. He also saw them as the inhabitants of his childhood. A statue of the first Khai Machi stood in the square, his noble expression undermined by the pigeon streaks. An old, rag-wrapped beggar sat on the street, a black lacquer box before her, and chanted songs. The forges were only a few streets away, and Otah could smell the sharp smoke; could even, he thought, hear the faint sound of metal on metal. He sucked down the last of the noodles and handed back the bowl to a man easily twice his age.

"You're new to the north," the man said, not unkindly.

"Does it show?" Otah asked.

"Thick robes. It's spring, and this is warm. If you'd been here over winter, your blood would be able to stand a little cold."

Otah laughed, but made note. If he were to fit in well, it would mean suffer-ing the cold. He would have to sit with that. He did want to understand the place, to see it, if only for a time, through the eyes of a native, but he didn't want to swim in ice water just because that was the local custom.

The door servant at the gray House Nan left him waiting in the street for a while, then returned to usher him to his quarters—a small, windowless room with four stacked cots that suggested he would be sharing the small iron bra-zier in the center of the room with seven other men, though he was the only one present just then. He thanked the servant, learned the protocols for enter-ing and leaving the house, got directions to the nearest bathhouse, and after placing the oiled leather pouch that held his letters safely with the steward, went back out to wash off the journey.

The bathhouse smelled of iron pipes and sandalwood, but the air was warm and thick. A launderer had set up shop at the front, and Otah gave over his robes to be scrubbed and kiln-dried with the understanding that it doomed him to be in the baths for at least the time it took the sun to move the width of two hands. He walked naked to the public baths and eased himself into the warm water with a sigh.

"Hai!" a voice called, and Otah opened his eyes. Two older men and a young woman sat on the same submerged bench on which he rested. One of the older men spoke.

"You've just come in with the 'van?"

"Indeed," Otah said. "Though I hope you could tell by looking more than smell."

"Where from?"

"Udun, most recently."

The trio moved closer. The woman introduced them all—overseers for a metalworkers group. Silversmiths, mostly. Otah was gracious and ordered tea for them all and set about learning what they knew and thought, felt and feared and hoped for, and all of it with smiles and charm and just slightly less wit displayed than their own. It was his craft, and they knew it as well as he did, and would exchange their thoughts and speculations for his gossip. It was the way of traders and merchants the world over.

It was not long before the young woman mentioned the name of Otah Machi.

4

>+<   "If it *is* the upstart behind it all, it's a poor thing for Machi," the older man said. "None of the trading houses would know him or trust him. None of the families of the utkhaiem would have ties to him. Even if he's simply never found, the new Khai will always be watching over his shoulder. It isn't good to have an uncertain line in the Khai's chair. The best thing that could happen for the city would be to find him and put a knife through his belly. Him, and any children he's got meantime."

Otah smiled because it was what a courier of House Siyanti would do. The younger man sniffed and sipped his bowl of tea. The woman shrugged, the motion setting small waves across the water.

"It might do us well to have someone new running the city," she said. "It's clear enough that nothing will change with either of the two choices we have now. Biitrah. He at least was interested in mechanism. The Galts have been doing more and more with their little devices, and we'd be fools to ignore what they've managed."

"Children's toys," the older man said, waving the thought away.

"Toys that have made them the greatest threat Eddensea and the West-lands have seen," the younger man said. "Their armies can move faster than anyone else's. There isn't a warden who hasn't felt the bite of them. If they haven't been invaded, they've had to offer tribute to the Lords Convocate, and that's just as bad."

"The ward being sacked might disagree," Otah said, trying for a joke to lighten the mood.

"The problem with the Galts," the woman said, "is they can't hold what they take. Every year it's another raid, another sack, another fleet carrying slaves and plunder back to Galt. But they never keep the land. They'd have much more money if they stayed and ruled the Westlands. Or Eymond. Or Eddensea."

"Then we'd have only them to trade with," the younger man said. "That'd be ugly."

"The Galts don't have the andat," the older man said, and his tone carried the rest: they don't have the andat, so they are not worth considering.

"But if they did," Otah said, hoping to keep the subject away from himself and his family. "Or if we did not—"

"If the sky dives into the sea, we'll be fishing for birds," the older man said. "It's this Otah Machi who's uneasing things. I have it on good authority that Danat and Kaiin have actually called a truce between them until they can rout out the traitor."

"Traitor?" Otah asked. "I hadn't heard that of him."

"There are stories," the younger man said. "Nothing anyone has proved. Six years ago, the Khai fell ill, and for a few days, they thought he might die. Some people suspected poison."

"And hasn't he turned to poison again? Look at Biitrah's death," the younger man said. "And I tell you the Khai Machi hasn't been himself since then, not truly. Even if Otah were to claim the chair, it'd be better to punish him for his crimes and raise up one of the high families."

"It could have been bad fish," the woman said. "There was a lot of bad fish that year."

"No one believes that," the older man said.

"Which of the others would be best for the city now that Biitrah is gone?" Otah asked.

The older man named Kaiin and the younger man and woman Danat in the same moment, the syllables grinding against each other in the warm, damp air, and they immediately fell to debate. Kaiin was a master negotiator; Danat was better thought of by the utkhaiem. Kaiin was prone to fits of tem-per, Danat to weeks of sloth. Each man, to hear it, was a paragon of virtue and little better than a street thug. Otah listened, interjected comments, asked questions crafted to keep the conversation alive and on its course. His mind was hardly there.

When at last he made his excuses, the three debaters hardly paused in their wrangle. Otah dried himself by a brazier and collected his robes—laundered now, smelling of cedar oil and warm from the kiln. The streets were fuller than when he had gone into the bathhouse. The sun would fall early, disappearing behind the peaks to the west long before the sky grew dark, but it still hovered two hands above the mountainous horizon.

Otah walked without knowing where he was walking to. The black cobbles and tall houses seemed familiar and exotic at the same time. The towers rose into the sky, glowing in the sunlight. At the intersection of three large streets, Otah found a courtyard with a great stone archway inlaid with wood and metal sigils of chaos and order. Harsh forge smoke from the east mixed with the greasy scent of a cart seller's roasting duck and, for a moment, Otah was possessed by the memory of being a child no more than four summers old. The smoke scent wove with the taste of honeybread nearly too hot to eat, the clear open view of the valley and mountains from the top of the towers, and a woman's skin—mother or sister or servant. There was no way to know.

It was a ghost memory, strong and certain as stone, but without a place in his life. Something had happened, once, that tied all these senses together, but it was gone and he would never have it. He was upstart and traitor. Poisoner and villain. None of it was true, but it made for an interesting story to tell in the teahouses and meeting rooms—a variation on the theme of fratricide that the Khaiem replayed in every generation. A deep fatigue pressed into him. He had been an innocent to think that he might be forgotten, that Otah Machi might escape the venomous speculation of the traders and merchants, high families and low townsmen. There was no use for truth when spectacle was at issue. And there was nothing in the city that could matter less than the half-recalled memories of a courier's abandoned childhood. The life he'd built mattered less than ashes to these people. His death would be a relief to them.

He returned to House Nan just as the stars began to glimmer in the deep northern sky. There was fresh bread and pepper-baked lamb, distilled rice wine and cold water. The other men who were to share his room joined him at the table, and they laughed and joked, traded information and gossip from across the world. Otah slid back comfortably into Itani Noygu, and his smiles came more easily as the night wore on, though a cold core remained in his breast. It was only just before he went to crawl into his cot that he found the steward, recovered his pouch of letters, and prepared himself.

All the letters were, of course, still sewn shut, but Otah checked the knots. None had been undone so far as he could tell. It would have been a breach of the gentleman's trade to open letters held in trust, and it would have been foolishness to trust to honor. Had House Nan been willing to break trust, that would have been interesting to know as well. He laid them out on his cot, considering.

Letters to the merchant houses and lower families among the utkhaiem were the most common. He didn't carry a letter for the Khai himself—he would have balked at so high a risk—but his work would take him to the palaces. And there were audiences, no doubt, to which he could get an invitation. If he chose, he could go to the Master of Tides and claim business with members of the court. It wouldn't even require stretching the truth very far. He sat in silence, feeling as if there were two men within him.

One wanted nothing more than to embrace the fear and flee to some distant island and be pleased to live wondering whether his brothers would still be searching him out. The other was consumed by an anger that drove him forward, deeper into the city of his birth and the family that had first discarded him and then fashioned a murderer from his memory.

Fear and anger. He waited for the calm third voice of wisdom, but it didn't come. He was left with no better plan than to act as Itani Noygu would have, had he been nothing other than he appeared. When at last he repacked his charges and lay on his cot, he expected that sleep would not come, but it did, and he woke in the morning forgetful of where he was and surprised to find that Kiyan was not in the bed beside him.

The palaces of the Khai were deep within the city, and the gardens around them made it seem more like a walk into some glorious low town than movement into the center of a great city. Trees arched over the walkways, branches bright with new leaves. Birds fluttered past him, reminding him of Udun and the wayhouse he had almost made his home. The greatest tower loomed overhead, dark stone rising up like twenty palaces, one above the other. Otah stopped in a courtyard before the lesser palace of the Master of Tides and squinted up at the great tower, wondering whether he had ever been to the top of it. Wondering whether being here, now, was valor, cowardice, foolishness, or wisdom; the product of anger or fear or the childish drive to show that he could defy them all if he chose.

He gave his name to the servants at the door and was led to an antechamber larger than his apartments back in Udun. A slave girl plucked a lap harp, filling the high air with a sweet, slow tune. He smiled at her and took a pose of appreciation. She returned his smile and nodded, but her fingers never left the strings. The servant, when he came, wore robes of deep red shot with yellow and a silver armband. He took a pose of greeting so brief it almost hadn't happened.

"Itani Noygu. You're Itani Noygu, then? Ah, good. I am Piyun See, the Master of Tides' assistant. He's too busy to see you himself. So House Siyanti has taken an interest in Machi, then?" he said. Otah smiled, though he meant it less this time.

"I couldn't say. I only go where they send me, Piyun-cha."

The assistant took a pose of agreement.

"I had hoped to know the court's schedule in the next week," Otah said. "I have business—"

"With the poet. Yes, I know. He left your name with us. He said we should keep a watch out for you. You're wise to come to us first. You wouldn't imagine the people who simply drift through on the breeze as if the poets weren't members of the court."

Otah smiled, his mouth tasting of fear, his heart suddenly racing. The poet of Machi—Cehmai Tyan, his name was—had no reason to know Itani Noygu or expect him. This was a mistake or a trap. If it was a trap, it was sloppy, and if a mistake, dangerous. The lie came to his lips as gracefully as a rehearsed speech.

"I'm honored to have been mentioned. I hadn't expected that he would re-member me. But I'm afraid the business I've come on may not be what he had foreseen."

"I wouldn't know," the assistant said as he shifted. "Visiting dignitaries might confide in the Master of Tides, but I'm like you. I follow orders. Now. Let me see. I can send a runner to the library, and if he's there . . ."

"Perhaps it would be best if I went to the poet's house," Otah said. "He can find me there when he isn't—"

"Oh, we haven't put him there. Gods! He has his own rooms."

"His own rooms?"

"Yes. We have a poet of our own, you know. We aren't going to put Cehmai-cha on a cot in the granary every time the Dai-kvo sends us a guest. Maati-cha has apartments near the library."

The air seemed to leave the room. A dull roar filled Otah's ears, and he had to put a hand to the wall to keep from swaying. Maati-cha. The name came like an unforeseen blow.

Maati Vaupathai. Maati whom Otah had known briefly at the school, and to whom he had taught the secrets he had learned before he turned his back on the poets and all they offered. Maati whom he had found again in Saraykeht, who had become his friend and who knew that Itani Noygu was the son of the Khai Machi.

The last night they had seen one another—thirteen, fourteen summers ago—Maati had stolen his lover and Otah had killed Maati's master. He was here now, in Machi. And he was looking for Otah. He felt like a deer surprised by the hunter at its side.

The servant girl fumbled with her strings, the notes of the tune coming out a jangle, and Otah shifted his gaze to her as if she'd shouted. For a moment, their eyes met and he saw discomfort in her as she hurried back to her song. She might have seen something in his face, might have realized who was standing before her. Otah balled his fists at his sides, pressing them into his thighs to keep from shaking. The assistant had been speaking. Otah didn't know what he'd said.

"Forgive me, but before we do anything, would you be so kind . . . ," Otah feigned an embarrassed simper. "I'm afraid I had one bowl of tea too many this morning, and waters that run in, run out. . . ."

"Of course. I'll have a slave take you to—"

"No need," Otah said as he stepped to the door. No one shouted. No one stopped him. "I'll be back with you in a moment."

He walked out of the hall, forcing himself not to run though he could feel his heartbeat in his neck, and his ribs seemed too small for his breath. He waited for the warning yell to come—armsmen with drawn blades or the short, simple pain of an arrow in his breast. Generations of his uncles had spilled their blood, spat their last breaths perhaps here, under these arches. He was not immune. Itani Noygu would not protect him. He controlled himself as best he could, and when he reached the gardens, boughs shielding him from the eyes of the palaces, he bolted.

Idaan sat at the open sky doors, her legs hanging out over the void, and let her gaze wander the moonlit valley. The glimmers of the low towns to the south. The Daikani mine where her brother had gone to die. The Poinyat mines to the west and southeast. And below the soles of her bare feet, Machi itself: the smoke rising from the forges, the torches and lanterns glimmering in the streets and windows smaller and dimmer than fireflies. The winches and pulleys hung in the darkness above her, long lengths of iron chain in guides and hooks set in the stone, ready to be freed should there be call to haul something up to the high reaches of the tower or lower something down. Chains that clanked and rattled, uneasy in the night breeze.

She leaned forward, forcing herself to feel the vertigo twist her stomach and tighten her throat. Savoring it. Scoot forward a few inches, no more effort really than standing from a chair, and then the sound of wind would fill her ears. She waited as long as she could stand and then drew back, gasping and nauseated and trembling. But she did not pull her legs back in. That would have been weakness.

It was an irony that the symbols of Machi's greatness were so little used. In the winter, there was no heating them—all the traffic of the city went in the streets, or over the snows, or through the networks of tunnels. And even in summer, the endless spiraling stairways and the need to haul up any wine or food or musical instruments made the gardens and halls nearer the ground more inviting. The towers were symbols of power, existing to show that they could exist and little enough more. A boast in stone and iron used for storage and exotic parties to impress visitors from the other courts of the Khaiem. And still, they made Idaan think that perhaps she could imagine what it would be to fly. In her way she loved them, and she loved very few things these days.

It was odd, perhaps that she had two lovers and still felt alone. Adrah had been with her for longer, it felt, than she had been herself. And so it had surprised her that she was so ready to betray him in another man's bed. Perhaps she'd thought that by being a new man's lover, she would strip off that old skin and become innocent again.

Or perhaps it was only that Cehmai had a sweet face and wanted her. She was young, she thought, to have given up flirtation and courtship. She'd been angry with Adrah for embarrassing Cehmai at the dance. She'd promised herself never to be owned by a man. And also, killing Biitrah had left a hunger in her—a need that nothing yet had sated.

She liked Cehmai. She longed for him. She needed him in a way she couldn't quite fathom, except to say that she hated herself less when she was with him.

"Idaan!" a voice whispered from the darkness behind her. "Come away from there! You'll be seen!"

"Only if you're fool enough to bring a torch," she said, but she pulled her feet back in from the abyss and hauled the great bronze-bound oaken sky doors shut. For a moment, there was nothing—black darker than closing her eyes—and then the scrape of a lantern's hood and the flame of a single candle. Crates and boxes threw deep shadows on the stone walls and carved cabinets. Adrah looked pale, even in the dim light. Idaan found herself amused and annoyed—pulled between wanting to comfort him and the desire to point out that it wasn't his family they were killing. She wondered if he knew yet that she had taken the poet to bed and whether he would care. And whether she did. He smiled nervously and glanced around at the shadows.

"He hasn't come," Idaan said.

"He will. Don't worry," Adrah said, and then a moment later: "My father has drafted a letter. Proposing our union. He's sending it to the Khai tomorrow."

"Good," Idaan said. "We'll want that in place before everyone finishes dying."

"Don't."

"If we can't speak of it to each other, Adrah-kya, when will we ever? It isn't as if I can go to our friends or the priest." Idaan took a pose of query to some imagined confidant. "Adrah's going to take me as his wife, but it's important that we do it now, so that when I've finished slaughtering my brothers, he can use me to press his suit to become the new Khai without it seeming so clearly that I'm being traded at market. And don't you love this new robe? It's Westlands silk."

She laughed bitterly. Adrah did not step back, quite, but he did pull away.

"What is it, Idaan-kya?" he said, and Idaan was surprised by the pain in his voice. It sounded genuine. "Have I done something to make you angry with me?"

For a moment, she saw herself through his eyes—cutting, ironic, cruel. It wasn't who she had been with him. Once, before they had made this bargain with Chaos, she had had the luxury of being soft and warm. She had always been angry, only not with him. How lost he must feel.

Idaan leaned close and kissed him. For one terrible moment, she meant it— the softness of his lips against hers stirring something within her that cried out to hold and be held, to weep and wail and take comfort. Her flesh also remembered the poet, the strange taste of another man's skin, the illusion of hope and of safety that she'd felt in her betrayal of the man who was destined to share her life.

"I'm not angry, sweet. Only tired. I'm very tired."

"This will pass, Idaan-kya. Remember that this part only lasts a while."

"And is what follows it better?"

He didn't answer.

The candle had hardly burned past another mark when the moon-faced assassin appeared, moving like darkness itself in his back cotton robe. He put down his lantern and took a pose of welcome before dusting a crate with his sleeve and sitting. His expression was pleasant as a fruit seller in a summer market. It only made Idaan like him less.

"So," Oshai said. "You called, I've come. What seems to be the problem?"

She had intended to begin with Maati Vaupathai, but the pretense of passive stupidity in Oshai's eyes annoyed her. Idaan raised her chin and her brows, considering him as she would a garden slave. Adrah looked back and forth between the two. The motion reminded her of a child watching his parents fighting. When she spoke, she had to try not to spit.

"I would know where our plans stand," she said. "My father's ill, and I hear more from Adrah and the palace slaves than from you."

"My apologies, great lady," Oshai said without a hint of irony. "It's only that meetings with you are a risk, and written reports are insupportable. Our mutual friends . . ."

"The Galtic High Council," Idaan said, but Oshai continued as if she had not spoken.

". . . have placed agents and letters of intent with six houses. Contracts for iron, silver, steel, copper, and gold. The negotiations are under way, and I expect we will be able to draw them out for most of the summer, should we need to. When all three of your brothers die, you will have been wed to Adrah, and between the powerful position of his house, his connection with you, and the influence of six of the great houses whose contracts will suddenly ride on his promotion to Khai, you should be sleeping in your mother's bed by Candles Night."

"My mother never had a bed of her own. She was only a woman, remember. Traded to the Khai for convenience, like a gift."

"It's only an expression, great lady. And remember, you'll be sharing Adrah here with other wives in your turn."

"I won't take others," Adrah said. "It was part of our agreement."

"Of course you won't," Oshai said with a nod and an insincere smile. "My mistake."

Idaan felt herself flush, but kept her voice level and calm when she spoke.

"And my brothers? Danat and Kaiin?"

"They are being somewhat inconvenient, it's true. They've gone to ground. Frightened, I'm told, by your ghost brother Otah. We may have to wait until your father actually dies before they screw up the courage to stand against each other. But when they do, I will be ready. You know all this, Idaan-cha. It can't be the only reason you've asked me here?" The round, pale face seemed to harden without moving. "There had best be something more pressing than seeing whether I'll declaim when told."

"Maati Vaupathai," Idaan said. "The Dai-kvo's sent him to study in the library."

"Hardly a secret," Oshai said, but Idaan thought she read a moment's unease in his eyes.

"And it doesn't concern your owners that this new poet has come for the same prize they want? What's in those old scrolls that makes this worth the risk for you, anyway?"

"I don't know, great lady," the assassin said. "I'm trusted with work of this delicate nature because I don't particularly care about the points that aren't mine to know."

"And the Galts? Are they worried about this Maati Vaupathai poking through the library before them?"

"It's . . . of interest," Oshai said, grudgingly.

"It was the one thing you insisted on," Idaan said, stepping toward the man. "When you came to Adrah and his father, you agreed to help us in return for access to that library. And now your price may be going away."

Will your support go, too? The unasked question hung in the chill air. If the Galts could not have what they wanted from Adrah and Idaan and the books of Machi, would the support for this mad, murderous scheme remain? Idaan felt her heart tripping over faster, half hoping that the answer might be no.

"It is the business of a poet to concern himself with ancient texts," Oshai said. "If a poet were to come to Machi and not avail himself of its library, that would be odd. This coincidence of timing is of interest. But it's not yet a cause for alarm."

"He's looking into the death of Biitrah. He's been down to the mines. He's asking questions."

"About what?" Oshai said. The smile was gone.

She told him all she knew, from the appearance of the poet to his interest in the court and high families, the low towns and the mines. She recounted the parties at which he had asked to be introduced, and to whom. The name he kept mentioning—*Itani Noygu*. The way in which his interest in the ascension of the next Khai Machi seemed to be more than academic. She ended with the tale she'd heard of his visit to the Daikani mines and to the wayhouse where her brother had died at Oshai's hands. When she was finished, neither man spoke. Adrah looked stricken. Oshai, merely thoughtful. At length, the assassin took a pose of gratitude.

"You were right to call me, Idaan-cha," he said. "I doubt the poet knows precisely what he's looking for, but that he's looking at all is bad enough."

"What do we do?" Adrah said. The desperation in his voice made Oshai look up like a hunting dog hearing a bird.

"*You* do nothing, most high," Oshai said. "Neither you nor the great lady does anything. I will take care of this."

"You'll kill him," Idaan said.

"If it seems the best course, I may. . . ."

Idaan took a pose appropriate to correcting a servant. Oshai's words faded.

"I was not asking, Oshai-cha. You'll kill him."

The assassin's eyes narrowed for a moment, but then something like amusement flickered at the corners of his mouth and the glimmer of candlelight in his eyes grew warmer. He seemed to weigh something in his mind, and then took a pose of acquiescence. Idaan lowered her hands.

"Will there be anything else, most high?" Oshai asked without taking his gaze from her.

"No," Adrah said. "That will be all."

"Wait half a hand after I've gone," Oshai said. "I can explain myself, and the two of you together borders on the self-evident. All three would be difficult."

And with that, he vanished. Idaan looked at the sky doors. She was tempted to open them again, just for a moment. To see the land and sky laid out before her.

"It's odd, you know," she said. "If I had been born a man, they would have sent me away to the school. I would have become a poet or taken the brand. But instead, they kept me here, and I became what they're afraid of. Kaiin and Danat are hiding from the brother who has broken the traditions and come back to kill them for the chair. And here I am. I *am* Otah Machi. Only they can't see it."

"I love you, Idaan-kya."

She smiled because there was nothing else to do. He had heard the words, but understood nothing. It would have meant as much to talk to a dog. She took his hand in hers, laced her fingers with his.

"I love you too, Adrah-kya. And I will be happy once we've done all this and taken the chair. You'll be the Khai Machi, and I will be your wife. We'll rule the city together, just as we always planned, and everything will be right again. It's been half a hand by now. We should go."

They parted in one of the night gardens, he to the east and his family compound, and she to the south, to her own apartments, and past them and west to tree-lined path that led to the poet's house. If the shutters were closed, if no light shone but the night candle, she told herself she wouldn't go in. But the lanterns were lit brightly, and the shutters open. She paced quietly through the grounds, peering in through windows, until she caught the sound of voices. Cehmai's soft and reasonable, and then another. A man's, loud and full of a rich self-importance. Baarath, the librarian. Idaan found a tree with low branches and deep shadows and sat, waiting with as much patience as she could muster, and silently willing the man away. The full moon was halfway across the sky before the two came to the door, silhouetted. Baarath swayed like a drunkard, but Cehmai, though he laughed as loud and sang as poorly, didn't waver. She watched as Baarath took a sloppy pose of farewell and stumbled off along the path. Cehmai watched him go, then looked back into the house, shaking his head.

Idaan rose and stepped out of the shadows.

She saw Cehmai catch sight of her, and she waited. He might have another guest—he might wave her away, and she would have to go back through the night to her own apartments, her own bed. The thought filled her with black dread until the poet put one hand out to her, and with the other motioned toward the light within his house.

Stone-Made-Soft brooded over a game of stones, its massive head cupped in a hand twice the size of her own. The white stones, she noticed, had lost badly. The andat looked up slowly and, its curiosity satisfied, it turned back to the ended game. The scent of mulled wine filled the air. Cehmai closed the door behind her, and then set about fastening the shutters.

"I didn't expect to see you," the poet said.

"Do you want me to leave?"

There were a hundred things he could have said. Graceful ways to say yes, or graceless ways to deny it. He only turned to her with the slightest smile and went back to his task. Idaan sat on a low couch and steeled herself. She couldn't say why she was driven to do this, only that the impulse was much like draping her legs out the sky doors, and that it was what she had chosen to do.

"Daaya Vaunyogi is approaching the Khai tomorrow. He is going to petition that Adrah and I be married."

Cehmai paused, sighed, turned to her. His expression was melancholy, but not sorrowful. He was like an old man, she thought, amused by the world and his own role in it. There was a strength in him, and an acceptance.

"I understand," he said.

"Do you?"

"No."

"He is of a good house, their bloodlines—"

"And he's well off and likely to oversee his family's house when his father passes. And he's a good enough man, for what he is. It isn't that I can't imagine why he would choose to marry you, or you him. But, given the context, there are other questions."

"I love him," Idaan said. "We have planned to do this for . . . we have been lovers for almost two years."

Cehmai sat beside a brazier, and looked at her with the patience of a man studying a puzzle. The coals had burned down to a fine white ash.

"And you've come to be sure I never speak of what happened the other night. To tell me that it can never happen again."

The sense of vertigo returned, her feet held over the abyss.

"No," she said.

"You've come to stay the night?"

"If you'll have me, yes."

The poet looked down, his hands laced together before him. A cricket sang, and then another. The air seemed thin.

"Idaan-kya, I think it might be better if—"

"Then lend me a couch and a blanket. If you . . . let me stay here as a friend might. We are friends, at least? Only don't make me go back to my rooms. I don't want to be there. I don't want to be with people and I can't stand being alone. And I . . . I like it here."

She took a pose of supplication. Cehmai rose and for a moment she was sure he would refuse. She almost hoped he would. Scoot forward, no more effort than sitting up, and then the sound of wind. But Cehmai took a pose that accepted her. She swallowed, the tightness in her throat lessening.

"I'll be back. The shutters . . . it might be awkward if someone were to happen by and see you here."

"Thank you, Cehmai-kya."

He leaned forward and kissed her mouth, neither passionate nor chaste, then sighed again and went to the back of the house. She heard the rattle of wood as he closed the windows against the night. Idaan looked at her hands, watching them tremble as she might watch a waterfall or a rare bird. An effect of nature, outside herself. The andat shifted and turned to look at her. She felt her brows rise, daring the thing to speak. Its voice was the low rumble of a landslide.

"I have seen generations pass, girl. I've seen young men die of age. I don't know what you are doing, but I know this. It will end in chaos. For him, and for you."

Stone-Made-Soft went silent again, stiller than any real man, not even the pulse of breath in it. She glared into the wide, placid face and took a pose of challenge.

"It that a threat?" she asked.

The andat shook its head once—left, and then right, and then still as if it had never moved in all the time since the world was young. When it spoke again, Idaan was almost startled at the sound.

"It's a blessing," it said.

"WHAT DID HE LOOK LIKE?" MAATI ASKED.

Piyun See, chief assistant to the Master of Tides, frowned and glanced out the window. The man sensed that he had done something wrong, even if he could not say what it had been. It made him reluctant. Maati sipped tea from a white stone bowl and let the silence stretch.

"A courier. He wore decent robes. He stood half a head taller than you, and had a good face. Long as a northman's."

"Well, that will help me," Maati said. He couldn't keep his impatience entirely to himself.

Piyun took a pose of apology formal enough to be utterly insincere.

"He had two eyes and two feet and one nose, Maati-cha. I thought he was *your* acquaintance. Shouldn't you know better than I what he looks like?"

"If it is the man."

"He didn't seem pleased to hear you'd been asking after him. He made an excuse and lit out almost as soon as he heard of you. It isn't as if I knew that he wasn't to be told of you. I didn't have orders to hold back your name."

"Did you have orders to volunteer me to him?" Maati asked.

"No, but . . ."

Maati waved the objection away.

"House Siyanti. You're sure of that?"

"Of course I am."

"How do I reach their compound?"

"They don't have one. House Siyanti doesn't trade in the winter cities. He would be staying at a wayhouse. Or sometimes the houses here will let couriers take rooms."

"So other than the fact that he came, you can tell me nothing," Maati said.

This time the pose of apology was more sincere. Frustration clamped Maati's jaw until his teeth hurt, but he forced himself into a pose that thanked the assistant and ended the interview. Piyun See left the small meeting room silently, closing the door behind him.

Otah was here, then. He had come back to Machi, using the same name he had had in Saraykeht. And that meant . . . Maati pressed his fingertips to his eyes. That meant nothing certain. That he was here suggested that Biitrah's death was his work, but as yet it was only a suggestion. He doubted that the Dai-kvo or the Khai Machi would see it that way. His presence was as much as proof to them, and there was no way to keep it secret. Piyun See was no doubt spreading the gossip across the palaces even now—the visiting poet and his mysterious courier. He had to find Otah himself, and he had to do it now.

He straightened his robes and stalked out to the gardens, and then the path that would lead him to the heart of the city. He would begin with the teahouses nearest the forges. It was the sort of place couriers might go to drink and gossip. There might be someone there who would know of House Siyanti and its partners. He could discover whether Itani Noygu had truly been work-ing for Siyanti. That would bring him one step nearer, at least. And there was nothing more he could think of to do now.

The streets were busy with children playing street games with rope and sticks, with beggars and slaves and water carts and firekeepers' kilns, with farmers' carts loaded high with spring produce or lambs and pigs on their way to the fresh butcher. Voices jabbered and shouted and sang, the smells of forge smoke and grilling meat and livestock pressed like a fever. The city seemed busy as an anthill, and Maati's mind churned as he navigated his way through it all. Otah had come to the winter cities. Was he killing his brothers? Had he chosen to become the Khai Machi?

And if he had, would Maati have the strength to stop him?

He told himself that he could. He was so focused and among so many dis-tractions that he almost didn't notice his follower. Only when he found what looked like a promising alley—hardly more than a shoulder-wide crack be-tween two long, tall buildings—did he escape the crowds long enough to no-tice. The sound of the street faded in the dim twilight that the band of sky above him allowed. A rat, surprised by him, scuttled through an iron grating and away. The thin alley branched, and Maati paused, looked down the two new paths, and then glanced back. The path behind him was blocked. A dark cloak, a raised hood, and shoulders so broad they touched both walls. Maati hesitated, and the man behind him didn't move. Maati felt the skin at the back of his neck tighten. He picked one turning of the alleyway and walked down it briskly until the dark figure reached the intersection as well and turned after him. Then Maati ran. The alley spilled out into another street, this less popu-lous. The smoke of the forges made the air acrid and hazy. Maati raced toward them. There would be men there—smiths and tradesmen, but also firekeep-ers and armsmen.

When he reached the mouth where the street spilled out onto a major throughway, he looked back. The street behind him was empty. His steps slowed, and he stopped, scanning the doorways, the rooftops. There was noth-ing. His pursuer—if that was what he had been—had vanished. Maati waited there until he'd caught his breath, then let himself laugh. No one was coming.

No one had followed. It was easy to see how a man could be eaten by his fears. He turned to the metalworkers' quarter.

The streets widened here, with shops and stalls facing out, filled with the tools of the metal trades as much as their products. The forges and smith's houses were marked by the greened copper roofs, the pillars of smoke, the sounds of yelling voices and hammers striking anvils. The businesses around them—sellers of hammers and tongs, suppliers of ore and wax blocks and slaked lime—all did their work loudly and expansively, waving hands in mock fury and shouting even when there was no call to. Maati made his way to a tea-house near the center of the district where sellers and workers mixed. He asked after House Siyanti, where their couriers might be found, what was known of them. The brown poet's robes granted him an unearned respect, but also wariness. It was three hands before he found an answer—the overseer of a consortium of silversmiths had had word from House Siyanti. The courier had said the signed contracts could be delivered to House Nan, but only after they'd been sewn and sealed. Maati gave the man two lengths of silver and his thanks and had started away before he realized he would also need better directions. An older man in a red and yellow robe with a face round and pale as the moon overheard his questions and offered to guide him there.

"You're Maati Vaupathai," the moon-faced man said as they walked. "I've heard about you."

"Nothing scandalous, I hope," Maati said.

"Speculations," the man said. "The Khaiem run on gossip and wine more than gold or silver. My name is Oshai. It's a pleasure to meet a poet."

They turned south, leaving the smoke and cacophony behind them. As they stepped into a smaller, quieter street, Maati looked back, half expecting to see the looming figure in the dark robes. There was nothing.

"Rumor has it you've come to look at the library," Oshai said.

"That's truth. The Dai-kvo sent me to do research for him."

"Pity you've come at such a delicate time. Succession. It's never an easy thing."

"It doesn't affect me," Maati said. "Court politics rarely reach the scrolls on the back shelves."

"I hear the Khai has books that date back to the Empire. Before the war."

"He does. Some of them are older than the copies the Dai-kvo has. Though, in all, the Dai-kvo's libraries are larger."

"He's wise to look as far afield as he can, though," Oshai said. "You never know what you might find. Was there something in particular he expected our Khai to have?"

"It's complex," Maati said. "No offense, it's just . . ."

Oshai smiled and waved the words away. There was something odd about his face—a weariness or an emptiness around his eyes.

"I'm sure there are many things that poets know that I can't comprehend," the guide said. "Here, there's a faster way down through here."

Oshai moved forward, taking Maati by the elbow and leading him down a narrow street. The houses around them were poorer than those near the palaces or even the metalworkers' quarter. Shutters showed the splinters of many seasons. The doors on the street level and the second-floor snow doors both tended to have cheap leather hinges rather than worked metal. Few people were on the street, and few windows open. Oshai seemed perfectly at ease despite his heightened pace so Maati pushed his uncertainty away.

"I've never been in the library myself," Oshai said. "I've heard impressive things of it. The power of all those minds, and all that time. It isn't something that normal men can easily conceive."

"I suppose not," Maati said, trotting to keep up. "Forgive me, Oshai-cha, but are we near House Nan?"

"We won't be going much further," his guide said. "Just around this next turning."

But when they made the turn, Maati found not a trading house's compound, but a small courtyard covered in flagstone, a dry cistern at its center. The few windows that opened onto the yard were shuttered or empty. Maati stepped forward, confused.

"Is this . . ." he began, and Oshai punched him hard in the belly. Maati stepped back, surprised by the attack, and astounded at the man's strength. Then he saw the blade in the guide's hand, and the blood on it. Maati tried to back away, but his feet caught the hem of his robe. Oshai's face was a grimace of delight and hatred. He seemed to jump forward, then stumbled and fell.

When his hands—out before him to catch his fall—touched the ground, the flagstone splashed. Oshai's hands vanished to the wrist. For a moment that seemed to last for days, Maati and his attacker both stared at the ground. Oshai began to struggle, pulling with his shoulders to no effect. Maati could hear the fear in the muttered curses. The pain in his belly was lessening, and a warmth taking its place. He tried to gather himself, but the effort was such that he didn't notice the dark-robed figures until they were almost upon him. The larger one had thrown back its hood and the wide, calm face of the andat considered him. The other form—smaller, and more agitated—knelt and spoke in Cehmai's voice.

"Maati-kvo! You're hurt."

"Be careful!" Maati said. "He's got a knife."

Cehmai glanced at the assassin struggling in the stone and shook his head. The poet looked very young, and yet familiar in a way that Maati hadn't noticed before. Intelligent, sure of himself. Maati was struck by an irrational envy of the boy, and then noticed the blood on his own hand. He looked down, and saw the wetness blackening his robes. There was so much of it.

"Can you walk?" Cehmai said, and Maati realized it wasn't the first time the question had been asked. He nodded.

"Only help me up," he said.

The younger poet took one arm and the andat the other and gently lifted him. The warmth in Maati's belly was developing a profound ache in its center. He pushed it aside, walked two steps, then three, and the world seemed to narrow. He found himself on the ground again, the poet leaning over him.

"I'm going for help," Cehmai said. "Don't move. Don't try to move. And don't die while I'm gone."

Maati tried to raise his hands in a pose of agreement, but the poet was already gone, pelting down the street, shouting at the top of his lungs. Maati rolled his head to one side to see the assassin struggling in vain and allowed himself a smile. A thought rolled through his mind, elusive and dim, and he shook himself, willing a lucidity he didn't possess. It was important. Whatever it was bore the weight of terrible significance. If he could only bring himself to think it. It had something to do with Otah-kvo and all the thousand times Maati had imagined their meeting. The andat sat beside him, watching him with the impassive distance of a statue, and Maati didn't know that he intended to speak to it until he heard his own words.

"It isn't Otah-kvo," he said. The andat shifted to consider the captive trapped by stone, then turned back.

"No," it agreed. "Too old."

"No," Maati said, struggling. "I don't mean that. I mean he wouldn't do this. Not to me. Not without speaking to me. It isn't him."

The andat frowned and shook its massive head.

"I don't understand."

"If I die," Maati said, forcing himself to speak above a whisper, "you have to tell Cehmai. It isn't Otah-kvo that did this. There's someone else."

ſ

>+< The chamber was laid out like a temple or a theater. On the long, sloping floor, representatives of all the high families sat on low stools or cushions. Beyond them sat the emissaries of the trading houses, the people of the city, and past them rank after rank of servants and slaves. The air was rich with the smells of incense and living bodies. Idaan looked out over the throng, though she knew proper form called for her gaze to remain downcast. Across the dais from her, Adrah knelt, his posture mirroring hers, except that his head was held high. He was, after all, a man. His robes were deep red and woven

gold, his hair swept back and tied with bands of gold and iron like a child of
the Empire. He had never looked more handsome. Her lover. Her husband.
She considered him as she might a fine piece of metalwork or a well-rendered
drawing. As a likeness of himself.

His father sat beside him on a bench, dressed in jewels and rich cloth.
Daaya Vaunyogi was beaming with pride, but Idaan could see the unease in
the way he held himself. The others would see only the patriarch of one high
family marrying his son into the blood of the Khaiem—it was reason enough
for excitement. Of all the people there, only Idaan would also see a traitor
against his city, forced to sit before the man whose sons he conspired to
slaughter and act as if his pet assassin was not locked in a room with armsmen
barring the way, his intended victim alive. Idaan forced herself not to smirk at
his weakness.

Her father spoke. His voice was thick and phlegmy, and his hands trembled
so badly that he took no formal poses.

"I have accepted a petition from House Vaunyogi. They propose that the
son of their flesh, Adrah, and the daughter of my blood, Idaan, be joined."

He waited while the appointed whisperers repeated the words, the hall
filled, it seemed, with the sound of a breeze. Idaan let her eyes close for a long
moment, and opened them again when he continued.

"This proposal pleases me," her father said. "And I lay it before the city. If
there is cause that this petition be refused, I would know of it now."

The whisperers dutifully passed this new statement through the hall as
well. There was a cough from nearby, as if in preparation to speak. Idaan
looked over. There in the first rank of cushions sat Cehmai and his andat. Both
of them were smiling pleasantly, but Cehmai's eyes were on hers, his hands in
a pose of offering. It was the same pose he might have used to ask if she
wanted some of the wine he was drinking or a lap blanket on a cold night.
Here, now, it was a deeper thing. *Would you like me to stop this?* Idaan could not
reply. No one was looking at Cehmai, and half the eyes in the chamber were
on her. She looked down instead, as a proper girl would. She saw the movement in the corner of her eye when the poet lowered his hands.

"Very well," her father said. "Adrah Vaunyogi, come here before me."

Idaan did not look up as Adrah stood and walked with slow, practiced steps
until he stood before the Khai's chair. He knelt again, with his head bowed, his
hands in a pose of gratitude and submission. The Khai, despite the grayness in
his skin and the hollows in his cheeks, held himself perfectly, and when he did
move, the weakness did not undo the grace of a lifetime's study. He put a hand
on the boy's head.

"Most high, I place myself before you as a man before his elder," Adrah
said, his voice carrying the ritual phrases through the hall. Even with his back

turned, the whisperers had little need to speak. "I place myself before you and ask your permission. I would take Idaan, your blood issue, to be my wife. If it does not please you, please only say so, and accept my apology."

"I am not displeased," her father said.

"Will you grant me this, most high?"

Idaan waited to hear her father accept, to hear the ritual complete itself. The silence stretched, profound and horrible. Idaan felt her heart begin to race, fear rising up in her blood. Something had happened; Oshai had broken. Idaan looked up, prepared to see armsmen descending upon them. But instead, she saw her father bent close to Adrah—so close their foreheads almost touched. There were tears on the sunken cheeks. The formal reserve and dignity was gone. The Khai was gone. All that remained was a desperately ill man in robes too gaudy for a sick house.

"Will you make her happy? I would have one of my children be happy."

Adrah's mouth opened and shut like a fish pulled from the river. Idaan closed her eyes, but she could not stop her ears.

"I . . . most high, I will do . . . Yes. I will."

Idaan felt her own tears forcing their way into her eyes like traitors. She bit her lip until she tasted blood.

"Let it be known," her father said, "that I have authorized this match. Let the blood of the Khai Machi enter again into House Vaunyogi. And let all who honor the Khaiem respect this transfer and join in our celebration. The ceremony shall be held in thirty-four days, on the opening of summer."

The whisperers began, but the hush of their voices was quickly drowned out by cheering and applause. Idaan raised her head and smiled as if the smears on her cheeks were from joy. Every man and woman in the chamber had risen. She turned to them and took a pose of thanks, and then to Adrah and his father, and then, finally, to her own. He was still weeping—a show of weakness that the gossips and backbiters of the court would be chewing over for days. But his smile was so genuine, so hopeful, that Idaan could do nothing but love him and taste ashes.

"Thank you, most high," she said. He bowed his head, as if honoring her.

The Khai Machi left the dais first, attended by servants who lifted him into his litter and others who bore him away. Then Idaan herself retreated. The others would escape according to the status of their families and their standing within them. It would be a hand and a half before the chamber was completely empty. Idaan strode along white marble corridors to a retiring room, sent away her servants, locked the door and sobbed until her heart was empty again. Then she washed her face in cool water from her basin, arrayed her kohl and blush, whitener and lip rouge before a mirror and carefully made a mask of her skin.

There would be talk, of course. Even without her father's unseemly display of humanity—and she hated them all for the laughter and amusement *that* would occasion—there would be enough to pick apart. The strength of Adrah's voice would be commented on. The way in which he carried himself. Even his unease when the ritual slipped from its form might speak well of him in people's memory. It was a small thing, of course. In the minds of the witnesses, it had been clear that she would be the daughter of a Khai only very briefly and merely sister to the Khai was a lower status. House Vaunyogi was buying something whose value would soon drop. It must be a love match, they would say, and pretend to be touched. She wondered if it wouldn't be better—cleaner—to simply burn the city and everyone in it, herself included. Let a hot iron clean and seal it like searing a wound. It was a passing fantasy, but it gave her comfort.

A knock came, and she arranged her robes before unlocking the door. Adrah stood, his house servants behind him. He had not changed out of his ritual robes.

"Idaan-kya," he said, "I was hoping you might come have a bowl of tea with my father."

"I have gifts to present to your honored father," Idaan said, gesturing to a cube of cloth and bright paper the size of a boar. It was already lashed to a carrying pole. "It is too much for me. Might I have the aid of your servants?"

Two servants had already moved forward to lift the burden.

Adrah took a pose of command, and she answered with one of acquiescence, following him as he turned and left. They walked side by side through the gardens, not touching. Idaan could feel the gazes of the people they passed, and kept her expression demure. By the time they reached the palaces of the Vaunyogi, her cheeks ached with it. Idaan and Adrah walked with their entourage through a hall of worked rosewood and mother-of-pearl, and to the summer garden where Daaya Vaunyogi sat beneath a stunted maple tree and sipped tea from a stone bowl. His face was weathered but kindly. Seeing him in this place was like stepping into a woodcut from the Old Empire—the honored sage in contemplation. The gift package was placed on the table before him as if it were a meal.

Adrah's father put down his bowl and took a pose that dismissed the servants.

"The garden is closed," he said. "We have much to discuss, my children and I."

As soon as the doors were shut and the three were alone, his face fell. He sank back to his seat like a man struck by fever. Adrah began to pace. Idaan ignored them both and poured herself tea. It was overbrewed and bitter.

"You haven't heard from them, then, Daaya-cha?"

"The Galts?" the man said. "The messengers I send come back empty handed. When I went to speak to their ambassador, they turned me away. Things have gone wrong. The risk is too great. They won't back us now."

"Did they say that?" Idaan asked.

Daaya took a pose that asked clarification. Idaan leaned forward, holding back the snarl she felt twisting at her lip.

"Did they *say* they wouldn't back us, or is it only that you fear they won't?"

"Oshai," Daaya said. "He knows everything. He's been my intermediary from the beginning. If he tells what he knows—"

"If he does, he'll be killed," Idaan said. "That he injured a poet is bad enough, but he murdered a son of the Khaiem without being a brother to him. He knows what would happen. His best hope is that someone intercedes for him. If he speaks what he knows, he dies badly."

"We have to free him," Adrah said. "We have to get him out. We have to show the Galts that we can protect them."

"We will," Idaan said. She drank down her tea. "The three of us. And I know how we'll do it."

Adrah and his father looked at her as if she'd just spat out a serpent. She took a pose of query.

"Shall we wait for the Galts to take action instead? They've already begun to distance themselves. Shall we take some members of your house into our confidence? Hire some armsmen to do it for us? Assume that our secrets will be safer the more people know?"

"But . . ." Adrah said.

"If we falter, we fail," Idaan said. "I know the way to the cages. He's kept underground now; if they move him to the towers, it gets harder. I asked that we meet in a place with a private exit. This garden. There is a way out of it?"

Daaya took an acknowledging pose, but his face was pale as bread dough.

"I thought there would be others you wished to consult," he said.

"There's nothing to consult over," Idaan said and pulled open the gifts she had brought to her new marriage. Three dark cloaks with deep hoods, three blades in dark leather sheaths, two unstrung hunter's bows with dark-shafted arrows, two torches, a pot of smoke pitch and a bag to carry it. And beneath it, a wall stand of silver with the sigils of order and chaos worked in marble and bloodstone. Idaan passed the blades and cloaks to the men.

"The servants will only know of the wall stand. These others we can give to Oshai to dispose of once we have him," Idaan said. "The smoke pitch we can use to frighten the armsmen at the cages. The bows and blades are for those that don't flee."

"Idaan-kya," Adrah said, "this is madness, we can't . . ."

She slapped him before she knew she meant to. He pressed a palm to his cheek, and his eyes glistened. But there was anger in him too. That was good.

"We do the thing now, while there are servants to swear it was not us. We do it quickly, and we live. We falter and wail like old women, and we die. Pick one."

Daaya Vaunyogi broke the silence by taking a cloak and pulling it on. His son looked to him, then to her, then, trembling began to do the same.

"You should have been born a man," her soon-to-be father said. There was disgust in his voice.

The tunnels beneath the palaces were little traveled in spring. The long winter months trapped in the warrens that laced the earth below Machi made even the slaves yearn for daylight. Idaan knew them all. Long winter months stealing unchaperoned up these corridors to play on the river ice and snow-shrouded city streets had taught her how to move through them unseen. They passed the alcove where she and Janat Saya had kissed once, when they were both too young to think it more than something that they should wish to do. She led them through the thin servant's passage she'd learned of when she was stealing fresh applecakes from the kitchens. Memories made the shadows seem like old friends from better times, when her mischief had been innocent.

They made their way from tunnel to tunnel, passing through wide chambers unnoticed and passages so narrow they had to stoop and go singly. The weight of stone above them made the journey seem like traveling through a mine.

They knew they were nearing the occupied parts of the tunnels as much by the smell of shit from the cages and acrid smoke as by the torchlight that danced at the corridor's mouth. Thick timber beams framed the hall. Idaan paused. This was only a side gallery—little used, rarely trafficked. But it would do, she thought.

"What now?" Adrah asked. "We light the pitch? Simulate a fire?"

Idaan took the pot from its bag and weighed it in her hands.

"We simulate nothing, Adrah-kya," she said. She tossed the pot at the base of a thick timber support and tossed her lit torch onto the blackness. It sputtered for a moment, then caught. Idaan unslung the bow from her shoulder and draped a fold of the cloak over it. "Be ready."

She waited as the flames caught. If she waited too long, they might not be able to pass the fire. If she was too quick, the armsmen might be able to put out the blaze. A deep calm seemed to descend upon her, and she felt herself smile. Now would be a fine moment, she thought, and screamed, raising the alarm. Adrah and Daaya followed her as she stumbled through the darkness and into the cages. In the time it took for her to take two breaths of the thickening air, they found themselves in the place she'd hoped: a wide gallery in torchlight, the air already becoming dense with smoke, and iron cages set into the stone where prisoners waited on the justice of the Khai. Two armsmen in leather and bronze armor scuttled to the three of them, their eyes round with fear.

"There's a fire in the gallery!" Daaya shrilled. "Get water! Get the watch!"

The prisoners were coming to the front of the cages now. Their cries of fear added to the confusion. Idaan pretended to cough as she considered the problem. There were two more armsmen at the far end of the cages, but they were coming closer. Of the first two who had approached, one had raced off toward the fire, the other down a well-lit tunnel, she presumed towards aid. And then midway down the row of cages on the left, she caught a glimpse of the Galts' creature. There was real fear in his eyes.

Adrah panicked as the second pair came close. With a shriek, he drew his blade, hewing at the armsmen like a child playing at war. Idaan cursed, but Daaya was moving faster, drawing his bow and sinking a dark shaft into the man's belly as Idaan shot at his chest and missed. But Adrah was lucky—a wild stroke caught the armsman's chin and seemed to cleave his jaw apart. Idaan raced to the cages, to Oshai. The moon-faced assassin registered a moment's surprise when he saw her face within the hood, and then Oshai closed his eyes and spat.

Adrah and Daaya rushed to her side.

"Do not speak," Oshai said. "Nothing. Every man here would sell you for his freedom, and there are people who would buy. Do you understand?"

Idaan nodded and pointed toward the thick lock that barred the door. Oshai shook his head.

"The Khai's Master of Blades keeps the keys," Oshai said. "The cages can't be opened without him. If you meant me to leave with you, you didn't think this through very well."

Adrah whispered a curse, but Oshai's eyes were on Idaan. He smiled thinly, his eyes dead as a fish's. He saw it when she understood, and he nodded, stepped back from the bars, and opened his arms like a man overwhelmed by the beauty of a sunrise. Idaan's first arrow took him in the throat. There were two others after that, but she thought they likely didn't matter. The first shouts of the watch echoed. The smoke was thickening. Idaan walked away, down the route she had meant to take when the prisoners were free. She'd meant to free them all, adding to the chaos. She'd been a fool.

"What have you done?" Daaya Vaunyogi demanded once they were safely away in the labyrinth. "What have you done?"

Idaan didn't bother answering.

Back in the garden, they sank the blades and the cloaks in a fountain to lie submerged until Adrah could sneak back in under cover of night and get rid of them. Even with the dark hoods gone, they all reeked of smoke. She hadn't foreseen that either. Neither of the men met her eyes. And yet, Oshai was beyond telling stories to the utkhaiem. So perhaps things hadn't ended so badly.

She gave her farewells to Daaya Vaunyogi. Adrah walked with her back through the evening-dimmed streets to her rooms. That the city seemed unchanged struck her as odd. She couldn't say what she had expected—what the day's events should have done to the stones, the air—but that it should all be the same seemed wrong. She paused by a beggar, listening to his song, and dropped a length of silver into the lacquered box at his feet.

At the entrance to her rooms, she sent her servants away. She did not wish to be attended. They would assume she smelled of sex, and best that she let them. Adrah peered at her, earnest as a puppy, she thought. She could see the distress in his eyes.

"You had to," he said, and she wondered if he meant to comfort her or convince himself. She took a pose of agreement. He stepped forward, his arms curving to embrace her.

"Don't touch me," she said, and he stepped back, paused, lowered his arms. Idaan saw something die behind his eyes, and felt something wither in her own breast. So this is what we are, she thought.

"Things were good once," he said, as if willing her to say *and they will be again.* The most she could give him was a nod. They had been good once. She had wanted and admired and loved him once. And even now, a part of her might love him. She wasn't sure.

The pain in his expression was unbearable. Idaan leaned forward, kissed him briefly on the lips, and went inside to wash the day off her skin. She heard his footsteps as he walked away.

Her body felt wrung out and empty. There were dried apples and sugared almonds waiting for her, but the thought of food was foreign. Gifts had arrived throughout the day—celebrations of her being sold off. She ignored them. It was only after she had bathed, washing her hair three times before it smelled more of flowers than smoke, that she found the note.

It rested on her bed, a square of paper folded in quarters. She sat naked beside it, reached out a hand, hesitated, and then plucked it open. It was brief, written in an unsteady hand.

Daughter, it said. *I had hoped that you might be able to spend some part of this happy day with me. Instead, I will leave this. Know that you have my blessings and such love as a weary old man can give. You have always delighted me, and I hope for your happiness in this match.*

When her tears and sobbing had exhausted her, Idaan carefully gathered the scraps of the note together and placed them together under her pillow. Then she bowed and prayed to all the gods and with all her heart that her father should die, and die quickly. That he should die without discovering what she was.

Maati was lost for a time in pain, then discomfort, and then pain again. He didn't suffer dreams so much as a pressing sense of urgency without goal or form, though for a time he had the powerful impression that he was on a boat, rocked by waves. His mind fell apart and reformed itself at the will of his body.

He came to himself in the night, aware that he had been half awake for some time; that there had been conversations in which he had participated, though he couldn't say with whom or on what matters. The room was not his own, but there was no mistaking that it belonged to the Khai's palace. No fire burned in the grate, but the stone walls were warm with stored sunlight. The windows were shuttered with shaped stone, the only light coming from the night candle that had burned almost to its quarter mark. Maati pulled back the thin blankets and considered the puckered gray flesh of his wound and the dark silk that laced it closed. He pressed his belly gently with his fingertips until he thought he knew how delicate he had become. When he stood, tottering to the night pot, he found he had underestimated, but that the pain was not so excruciating that he could not empty his bladder. After, he pulled himself back into bed, exhausted. He intended only to close his eyes for a moment and gather his strength, but when he opened them, it was morning.

He had nearly resolved to walk from his bed to the small writing table near the window when a slave entered and announced that the poet Cehmai and the andat Stone-Made-Soft would see him if he wished. Maati nodded and sat up carefully.

The poet arrived with a wide plate of rice and river fish in a sauce that smelled of plums and pepper. The andat carried a jug of water so cold it made the stone sweat. Maati's stomach came to life with a growl at the sight.

"You're looking better, Maati-kvo." the young poet said, putting the plate on the bed. The andat pulled two chairs close to the bed and sat in one, its face calm and empty.

"I looked worse than this?" Maati asked. "I wouldn't have thought that possible. How long has it been?"

"Four days. The injury brought on a fever. But when they poured onion soup down you, the wound didn't smell of it, so they decided you might live after all."

Maati lifted a spoon of fish and rice to his mouth. It tasted divine.

"I think I have you to thank for that," Maati said. "My recollection isn't all it could be, but . . ."

"I was following you," Cehmai said, taking a pose of contrition. "I was curious about your investigations."

"Yes. I suppose I should have been more subtle."

"The assassin was killed yesterday."

Maati took another bite of fish.

"Executed?"

"Disposed of," the andat said and smiled.

Cehmai told the story. The fire in the tunnels, the deaths of the guards.

The other prisoners said that there had been three men in black cloaks, that they had rushed in, killed the assassin, and vanished. Two others had choked to death on the smoke before the watchmen put the fire out.

"The story among the utkhaiem is that you discovered Otah Machi. The Master of Tides' assistant said that you'd been angry with him for being indiscreet about your questions concerning a courier from Udun. Then the attack on you, and the fire. They say the Khai Machi sent for you to hunt his missing son, Otah."

"Part true," Maati said. "I was sent to look for Otah. I knew him once, when we were younger. But I haven't found him, and the knife man was . . . something else. It wasn't Otah."

"You said that," the andat rumbled. "When we found you, you said it was someone else."

"Otah-kvo wouldn't have done it. Not that way. He might have met me himself, but sending someone else to do it? No. He wasn't behind that," Maati said, and then the consequence of that fell into place. "And so I think he must not have been the one who killed Biitrah."

Cehmai and his andat exchanged a glance and the young poet drew a bowl of water for Maati. The water was as good as the food, but Maati could see the unease in the way Cehmai looked at him. If he had ached less or been farther from exhaustion, he might have been subtle.

"What is it?" Maati asked.

Cehmai drew himself up, then sighed.

"You call him Otah-kvo."

"He was my teacher. At the school, he was in the black robes when I was new arrived. He . . . helped me."

"And you saw him again. When you were older."

"Did I?" Maati asked.

Cehmai took a pose that asked forgiveness. "The Dai-kvo would hardly have trusted a memory that old. You were both children at the school. We were all children there. You knew him when you were both men, yes?"

"Yes," Maati said. "He was in Saraykeht when . . . when Heshai-kvo died."

"And you call him Otah-kvo," Cehmai said. "He was a friend of yours, Maati-kvo. Someone you admired. He's never stopped being your teacher."

"Perhaps. But he's stopped being my friend. That was my doing, but it's done."

"I'm sorry, Maati-kvo, but are you certain Otah-kvo is innocent because he's innocent, or only because you're certain? It would be hard to accept that an old friend might wish you ill . . ."

Maati smiled and sipped the water.

"Otah Machi may well wish me dead. I would understand it if he did. And he's in the city, or was four days ago. But he didn't send the assassin."

"You think he isn't hoping for the Khai's chair?"

"I don't know. But I suppose that's something worth finding out. Along with who it was that killed his brother and started this whole thing rolling."

He took another mouthful of rice and fish, but his mind was elsewhere.

"Will you let me help you?"

Maati looked up, half surprised. The young poet's face was serious, his hands in a pose of formal supplication. It was as if they were back in the school and Cehmai was a boy asking a boon of the teachers. The andat had its hands folded in its lap, but it seemed mildly amused. Before Maati could think of a reply, Cehmai went on.

"You aren't well yet, Maati-kvo. You're the center of all the court gossip now, and anything you do will be examined from eight different views before you've finished doing it. I know the city. I know the court. I can ask questions without arousing suspicion. The Dai-kvo didn't choose to take me into his confidence, but now that I know what's happening—"

"It's too much of a risk," Maati said. "The Dai-kvo sent me because I know Otah-kvo, but he also sent me because my loss would mean nothing. You hold the andat—"

"It's fine with me," Stone-Made-Soft said. "Really, don't let me stop you."

"If I ask questions *without* you, I run the same risks, and without the benefits of shared information," Cehmai said. "And expecting me not to wonder would be unrealistic."

"The Khai Machi would expel me from his city if he thought I was endangering his poet," Maati said. "And then I wouldn't be of use to anyone."

Cehmai's dark eyes were both deadly serious and also, Maati thought, amused. "This wouldn't be the first thing I've kept from him," the young poet said. "Please, Maati-kvo. I want to help."

Maati closed his eyes. Having someone to talk with, even if it was only a way to explore what he thought himself, wouldn't be so bad a thing. The Dai-kvo hadn't expressly forbidden that Cehmai know, and even if he had, the secret investigation had already sent Otah-kvo to flight, so any further subterfuge seemed pointless. And the fact was, he likely couldn't find the answers alone.

"You have saved my life once already."

"I thought it would be unfair to point that out," Cehmai said.

Maati laughed, then stopped when the pain in his belly bloomed. He lay back, blowing air until he could think again. The pillows felt better than they should have. He'd done so little, and he was already tired. He glanced mistrustfully at the andat, then took a pose of acceptance.

"Come back tonight, when I've rested," Maati said. "We'll plan our strategy. I have to get my strength back, but there isn't much time."

"May I ask one other thing, Maati-kvo?"

Maati nodded, but his belly seemed to have grown more sensitive for the moment and he tried not to move more than that. It seemed laughing wasn't a wise thing for him just now.

"Who are Liat and Nayiit?"

"My lover. Our son," Maati said. "I called out for them, did I? When I had the fever?"

Cehmai nodded.

"I do that often," Maati said. "Only not usually aloud."

6

>+< There were four great roads that connected the cities of the Khaiem, one named for each of the cardinal directions. The North Road that linked Cetani, Machi, and Amnat-Tan was not the worst, in part because there was no traffic in the winter, when the snows let men make a road wherever desire took them. Also the stones were damaged more by the cycle of thaw and frost that troubled the north only in spring and autumn. In high summer, it rarely froze, and for a third of the year it did not thaw. The West Road—far from the sea and not so far south as to keep the winters warm—required the most repair.

"They'll have crews of indentured slaves and laborers out in shifts," the old man in the cart beside Otah said, raising a finger as if his oratory was on par with the High Emperor's, back when there had been an empire. "They start at one end, reset the stones until they reach the other, and begin again. It never ends."

Otah glanced across the cart at the young woman nursing her babe and rolled his eyes. She smiled and shrugged so slightly that their orator didn't notice the movement. The cart lurched down into and up from another wide hole where the stones had shattered and not yet been replaced.

"I have walked them all," the old man said, "though they've worn me more than I've worn them. Oh yes, much more than I've worn them."

He cackled, as he always seemed to when he made this observation. The little caravan—four carts hauled by old horses—was still six days from Cetani. Otah wondered whether his own legs were rested enough that he could start walking again.

He had bought an old laborer's robe of blue-gray wool from a rag shop, chopped his hair to change its shape, and let his thin beard start to grow in. Once his whiskers had been long enough to braid, but the east islanders he'd lived with had laughed at him and pretended to mistake him for a woman. After Cetani, it would take another twenty days to reach the docks outside

Amnat-tan. And then, if he could find a fishing boat that would take him on, he would be among those men again, singing songs in a tongue he hadn't tried out in years, explaining again, either with the truth or outrageous stories, why his marriage mark was only half done.

He would die there—on the islands or on the sea—under whatever new name he chose for himself. Itani Noygu was gone. He had died in Machi. Another life was behind him, and the prospect of beginning again, alone in a foreign land, tired him more than the walking.

"Now, southern wood's too soft to really build with. The winters are too warm to really harden them. Up here there's trees that would blunt a dozen axes before they fell," the old man said.

"You know everything, don't you grandfather?" Otah said. If his annoyance was in his voice, the old man noticed nothing, because he cackled again.

"It's because I've been everywhere and done everything," the old man said. "I even helped hunt down the Khai Amnat-Tan's older brother when they had their last succession. There were a dozen of us, and it was the dead of winter. Your piss would freeze before it touched ground. Oh, eh . . ."

The old man took a pose of apology to the young woman and her babe, and Otah swung himself out of the cart. It wasn't a story he cared to hear. The road wound through a valley, high pine forest on either side, the air sharp and fragrant with the resin. It was beautiful, and he pictured it thick with snow, the image coming so clear that he wondered whether he might once have seen it that way. When the clatter of hooves came from the west, he forced himself again to relax his shoulders and look as curious and excited as the others. Twice before, couriers on fast horses had passed the 'van, laden with news, Otah knew, of the search for him.

It had taken an effort of will not to run as fast as he could after he had been discovered, but the search was for a false courier either plotting murder or fleeing like a rabbit. No one would pay attention to a plodding laborer off to stay with his sister's family in a low town outside Cetani. And yet, as the horses approached, tension grew in his breast. He prepared himself for the shock if one of the riders had a familiar face.

There were three this time—utkhaiem to judge by their robes and the quality of their mounts—and none of them men he knew. They didn't slow for the 'van, but the armsmen of the 'van, the drivers, the dozen hangers-on like himself all shouted at them for news. One of them turned in his saddle and yelled something, but Otah couldn't make it out and the rider didn't repeat it. Ten days on the road. Six more to Cetani. The only challenge was not to be where they were looking for him.

They reached a wayhouse with the sun still three and a half hands above the treetops. The building was of northern design: stone walls thick as the span of a man's arm and stables and goat pen on the ground floor where the heat of the animals would rise and help warm the place in the winter. While the merchants and armsmen argued over whether to stop now or go farther and sleep in the open, Otah ran his eyes over the windows and walked around to the back, looking for all the signs Kiyan had taught him to know whether the keeper was working with robbers or keeping an unsafe kitchen. The house met all of her best marks. It seemed safe.

By the time he'd returned to the carts, his companions had decided to stay. After Otah had helped stable the horses, they shifted the carts into a locked courtyard. The caravan's leader haggled with the keeper about the rooms and came to an agreement that Otah privately thought gave the keep the better half. Otah made his way up two flights of stairs to the room he was to share with five armsmen, two drivers, and the old man. He curled himself up in a corner on the floor. It was too small a room, and one of the drivers snored badly. A little sleep when things were quiet would only make the next day easier.

He woke in darkness to the sound of music—a drum throbbed and a flute sighed. A man's voice and a woman's moved in rough harmony. He wiped his eyes with the sleeve of his robe and went down to the main room. The members of his 'van were all there and half a dozen other men besides. The air smelled of hot wine and roast lamb, pine trees and smoke. Otah sat at a rough, worn table beside one of the drivers and watched.

The singer was the keep himself; a pot-bellied man with a nose that had been broken and badly set. He drew the deep beat from a skin and earthenware drum as he sang. His wife was shapely as a potato with an ugly face and a missing eye tooth, but their voices were well suited and their affection for each other forgave them much. Otah found himself tapping his fingertips against the table to match the drumbeats.

His mind went back to Kiyan, and the nights of music and stories and gossip he had spent in her wayhouse, far away to the south. He wondered what she was doing tonight, what music filled the warm air and competed with the murmur of the river.

When the last note had faded to silence, the crowd applauded, yelped, and howled their appreciation. Otah made his way to the singer—he was shorter than Otah had thought—and took his hand. The keeper beamed and blushed when Otah told him how good the music had been.

"We've had a few years practice, and there's only so much to do when the days are short," the keep said. "The winter choirs in Machi make us sound like street beggars."

Otah smiled, regret pulling at him that he would never hear those songs, and a moment later he heard his name being spoken.

"Itani Noygu's what he was calling himself," one of the merchants said. "Played a courier for House Siyanti."

"I think I met him," a man said whom Otah had never met. "I knew there was something odd about the man."

"And the poet . . . the one that had his belly opened for him? He's picking the other Siyanti men apart like they were baked fish. The upstart has to wish that job had been done right the first time."

"Sounds as if I've missed something," Otah said, putting on his most charming smile. "What's this about a poet's belly?"

The merchant frowned at the interruption until Otah motioned to the keep's wife and bought bowls of hot wine for the table. After that, the gossip flowed more freely.

Maati Vaupathai had been attacked, and the common wisdom held that Otah had arranged it. The most likely version was that the upstart had been passing as a courier, but others said that he had made his way into the palaces dressed as a servant or a meat seller. There was no question, though, that the Khai had sent out runners to all the winter cities asking for the couriers and overseers of House Siyanti to attend him at court. Amiit Foss, the man who'd been the upstart's overseer in Udun, was being summoned in particular. It wasn't clear yet whether Siyanti had knowingly backed the Otah Machi, but if they had, it would mean the end of their expansion into the north. Even if they hadn't, the house would suffer.

"And they're sure he was the one who had the poet killed?" Otah asked, using all the skill the gentleman's trade had taught him to hide his deepening despair and disgust.

"It seems they were in Saraykeht together, this poet and the upstart. That was just before Saraykeht fell."

The implications of that hung over the room. Perhaps Otah Machi had somehow been involved with the death of Heshai, the poet of Saraykeht. Who knew what depravity the sixth son of the Khai Machi might sink to? It was a ghost story for them; a tale to pass a night on the road; a sport to follow.

Otah remembered the old, frog-mouthed poet, remembered his kindness and his weakness and his strength. He remembered the regret and the respect and the horrible complicity he'd felt in killing him, all those years ago. It had been so complicated, then. Now, they said it so simply and spoke as if they understood.

"There's rumor of a woman, too. They say he had a lover in Udun."

"If he was a courier, he's likely got a woman in half the cities of the Khaiem. The gods know I would."

"No," the merchant said, shaking his head. He was more than half drunk. "No, they were very clear. All the Siyanti men say he had a lover in Udun and never took another. Loved her like the world, they said. But she left him for another man. I say it's that turned him evil. Love turns on you like . . . like milk."

"Gentlemen," the keep's wife said, her voice powerful enough to cut through any conversation. "It's late, and I'm not sleeping until these rooms are cleaned, so get you all to bed. I'll have bread and honey for you at sunrise."

The guests slurped down the last of the wine, ate the last mouthfuls of dried cherries and fresh cheese, and made their various ways toward their various beds. Otah walked down the inner stairs to the stables and the goat yard, then out through a side door and into the darkness. His body felt like he'd just run a race, or else like he was about to.

Kiyan. Kiyan and the wayhouse her father had run. Old Mani. He had set the dogs on them, and that he hadn't intended to would count for nothing if his brothers found her. Whatever happened, whatever they did, it would be his fault.

He found a tall tree and sat with his back against it, looking out at the stars nearest the horizon. The air had the bite of cold in it. Winter never left this place. It made a little room for summer, but it never left. He thought of writing her a letter, of warning her. It would never reach her in time. It was ten days walk back to Machi, six days forward to Cetani, and his brothers' forces would already be on the road south. He could send to Amiit Foss, beg his old overseer to take Kiyan in, to protect her. But there too, word would reach him too late.

Despair settled into his belly, too deep for tears. He was destroying the woman he loved most in the world simply by being who he was, by doing what he'd done. He thought of the boy he had been, marching away from the school across the western snows. He remembered his fear and the warmth of his rage at the poets and his parents and all in the world that treated boys so unfairly. What a pompous little ass he'd been, young and certain and alone. He should have taken the Dai-kvo's offer and become a poet. He might have tried to bind an andat, and maybe failed and paid the price, dying in the attempt. And then Kiyan would never have met him. She would be safe.

There's still a price, he thought, as clear as a voice speaking in his head. You could still pay it.

Machi was ten days' walk, perhaps as little as four and a half days' ride. If he could turn all eyes back to Machi, Kiyan might have at least the chance to escape his idiocy. And what would she matter, if no one need search for him. He could take a horse from the stables now. After all, if he was an upstart and a poisoner and a man turned evil by love, it hardly mattered being a horse thief as well. He closed his eyes, an angry bark of a laugh forcing its way from his throat.

Everything you have won, you've won by leaving, he thought, remembering a woman whom he had known almost well enough to join his life with though he had never loved her, nor she him. Well, Maj, perhaps this time I'll lose.

THE NIGHT CANDLE WAS PAST ITS MIDDLE MARK; THE AIR WAS FILLED WITH THE songs of crickets. Somewhere in the course of things, the pale mist of netting had been pulled from the bed, and the room looked exposed without it. Cehmai could feel Stone-Made-Soft in the back of his mind, but the effort of being truly aware of the andat was too much; his body was thick and heavy and content. Focus and rigor would have their place another time.

Idaan traced her fingertips across his chest, raising gooseflesh. He shivered, took her hand and folded it in his own. She sighed and lay against him. Her hair smelled of roses.

"Why do they call you poets?" she asked.

"It's an old Empire term," Cehmai said. "It's from the binding."

"The andat are poems?" she said. She had the darkest eyes. Like an animal's. He looked at her mouth. The lips were too full to be fashionable. With the paint worn off, he could see how she narrowed them. He raised his head and kissed them again, gently this time. His own mouth felt bruised from their coupling. And then his head grew too heavy, and he let it rest again.

"They're . . . like that. Binding one is like describing something perfectly. Understanding it, and expanding it . . . I'm not saying this well. Have you ever translated a letter? Taken something in the Khaiate tongues and tried to say the same thing in Westland or an east island tongue?"

"No," she said. "I had to take something from the Empire and rewrite it for a tutor once."

Cehmai closed his eyes. He could feel sleep pulling at him, but he fought against it a bit. He wasn't ready to let the moment pass.

"That's near enough. You had to make choices when you did that. *Tilfa* could mean take or it could mean give or it could mean exchange—it's yours to choose, depending on how it's used in the original document. And so a letter or a poem doesn't have a set translation. You could have any number of ways that you say the same thing. Binding the andat means describing them—what the thought of them is—so well that you can translate it perfectly into a form that includes will and volition. Like translating a Galtic contract so that all the nuances of the trade are preserved perfectly."

"But there's any number of ways to do that," she said.

"There are very few ways to do it perfectly. And if a binding goes wrong . . . Existing isn't normal for them. If you leave an imprecision or an inaccuracy, they escape through it, and the poet pays a price for that. Usually it comes as some particularly gruesome death. And knowing what an andat is can be subtle. Stone-Made-Soft. What do you mean by stone? Iron comes from stone, so is it stone? Sand is made of tiny stones. Is it stone? Bones are like stone. But are they like enough to be called the same name? All those nuances have to be balanced or the binding fails. Happily, the Empire produced some formal grammars that were very precise."

"And you describe this thing . . ."

"And then you hold that in your mind until you die. Only it's the kind of thought that can think back, so it's wearing sometimes."

"Do you resent it?" Idaan asked, and something in her voice had changed. Cehmai opened his eyes. Idaan was looking past him. Her expression was unfathomable.

"I don't know what you mean," he said.

"You have to carry this thing all your life. Do you ever wish that you hadn't been called to do it?"

"No," he said. "Not really. It's work, but it's work that I like. And I get to meet the most interesting women."

Her gaze cooled, flickered over him, and then away.

"Lucky to be you," she said as she sat up. He watched her as she pulled her robes from the puddle of cloth on the floor. Cehmai sat up. "I have meetings in the morning. I'll need to be in my own rooms to be ready anyway. I might as well go now."

"I might say fewer things that angered you if you talked to me," Cehmai said, gently.

Idaan's head snapped around to him like a hunting cat's, but then her expression softened to chagrin, and she took an apologetic pose.

"I'm overtired," she said. "There are things that I'm carrying, and I don't do it as gracefully as you. I don't mean to take them out on you."

"Why do you do this, Idaan-kya? Why do you come here? I don't think it's that you love me."

"Do you want me to stop?"

"No," Cehmai said. "I don't. But if you choose to, that will be fine as well."

"That's flattering," she said, sarcasm thick in her voice.

"Are you doing this to be flattered?"

He was awake again now. He could see something in her expression—pain, anger, something else. She didn't answer him now, only knelt by the bed and felt beneath it for her boots. He put his hand on her arm and drew her up. He could sense that she was close to speaking, that the words were already there, just below the surface.

"I don't mind only being your bed mate," he said. "I've known from the start that Adrah is the man you plan to be with, and that I couldn't be that for you even if you wanted it. I assume that's part of why you've chosen me. But I am fond of you, and I would like to be your friend."

"You'd be my friend?" she said. "That's nice to hear. You've bedded me and now you'll condescend to be a friend?"

"I think it's more accurate to say you bedded me," Cehmai said. "And it seems to me that people do what we've done quite often without caring about the other person. Or even while wishing them ill. I'll grant that we haven't followed the usual order—I understand people usually know each other first and then fall into bed afterwards—but in a way that means you should take me more seriously."

She pulled back and took a pose of query.

"You know I'm not just saying it to get your robes open," he said. "When I say I want to be someone you can speak with, it's truth. I've nothing to gain by it but the thing itself."

She sighed and sat on the bed. The light of the single candle painted her in shades of orange.

"Do you love me, Cehmai-kya?" she asked.

Cehmai took a deep breath and then slowly let it out. He had reached the gate. Her thoughts, her fears. Everything that had driven this girl into his bed was waiting to be loosed. All he would have to do was tell one, simple, banal lie. A lie thousands of men had told for less reason. He was badly tempted.

"Idaan-kya," he said, "I don't know you."

To his surprise, she smiled. She pulled on her boots, not bothering to lace the bindings, leaned over and kissed him again. Her hand caressed his cheeks.

"Lucky to be you," she said softly.

Neither spoke as they walked down the corridor to the main rooms. The shutters were closed against the night, and the air felt stuffy and thick. He walked with her to the door, then through it, and sat on the steps, watching her vanish among the trees. The crickets still sang. The moon still hung overhead, bathing the night in blue. He heard the high squeak of bats as they skimmed the ponds and pools, the flutter of an owl's wings.

"You should be sleeping," the low, gravel voice said from behind him.

"Yes, I imagine so."

"First light, there's a meeting with the stone potters."

"Yes, there is."

Stone-Made-Soft stepped forward and lowered itself to sit on the step beside him. The familiar bulk of its body rose and fell in a sigh that could only be a comment.

"She's up to something," Cehmai said.

"She might only find herself drawn to two different men," the andat said. "It happens. And you're the one she couldn't build a life with. The other boy . . ."

"No," Cehmai said, speaking slowly, letting the thoughts form as he gave them voice. "She isn't drawn to me. Not *me*."

"She could be flattered that you want her. I've heard that's endearing."

"She's drawn to you."

The andat shifted to look at him. Its wide mouth was smiling.

"That would be a first," it said. "I'd never thought of taking a lover. I don't think I'd know what to do with her."

"Not like that," Cehmai said. "She wants me because of you. Because I'm a poet. If I weren't, she wouldn't be here."

"Does that offend you?"

A gnat landed on the back of Cehmai's hand. The tiny wings tickled, but he looked at it carefully. A small gray insect unaware of its danger. With a puff of breath, he blew it into the darkness. The andat waited silently for an answer.

"It should," Cehmai said at last.

"Perhaps you can work on that."

"Being offended?"

"If you think you should be."

The storm in the back of him mind shifted. The constant thought that was this thing at his side moved, kicking like a babe in the womb or a prisoner testing the walls of its cell. Cehmai chuckled.

"You aren't trying to help," he said.

"No," the andat agreed. "Not particularly."

"Did the others understand their lovers? The poets before me?"

"How can I say? They loved women, and were loved by them. They used women and were used by them. You may have found a way to put me on a leash, but you're only men."

THE IRONY WAS THAT, HIS WOUND NOT FULLY HEALED, MAATI SPENT MORE TIME IN the library than he had when he had been playing at scholarship. Only now, instead of spending his mornings there, he found it a calm place to retire when the day's work had exhausted him; when the hunt had worn him thin. It had been fifteen days now since Itani Noygu had walked away from the palaces and vanished. Fourteen days since the assassin had put a dagger in Maati's own guts. Thirteen days since the fire in the cages.

He knew now as much as he was likely to know of Itani Noygu, the courier for House Siyanti, and almost nothing of Otah-kvo. Itani had worked in the gentleman's trade for nearly eight years. He had lived in the eastern islands; he was a charming man, decent at his craft if not expert. He'd had lovers in Tan-Sadar and Utani, but had broken things off with both after he started keeping company with a wayhouse keeper in Udun. His fellows were frankly disbelieving that this could be the rogue Otah Machi, night-gaunt that haunted the dreams of Machi. But where he probed and demanded, where he dug and pried, pleaded and coddled and threatened, there was no sign of Otah-kvo. Where there should have been secrecy, there was nothing. Where there should have been meetings with high men in his house, or another house, or *somebody*, there was nothing. There should have been conspiracy against his father, his brothers, the city of his birth. There was nothing.

All of which went to confirm the conclusion that Maati had reached, bleeding on the paving stones. Otah was not scheming for his father's chair, had not killed Biitrah, had not hired the assassin to attack him.

And yet Otah was here, or had been. Maati had written to the Dai-kvo, outlining what he knew and guessed and only wondered, but he had received no word back as yet and might not for several weeks. By which time, he suspected, the old Khai would be dead. That thought alone tired him, and it was the library that he turned to for distraction.

He sat back now on one of the thick chairs, slowly unfurling a scroll with his left hand and furling it again with his right. In the space between, ancient words stirred. The pale ink formed the letters of the Empire, and the scroll purported to be an essay by Jaiet Khai—a man named the Servant of Memory from the great years when the word Khai had still meant servant. The grammar was formal and antiquated, the tongue was nothing spoken now. It was unlikely than anyone but a poet would be able to make sense of it.

There are two types of impossibility in the andat, the man long since dust had written.

The first of these are those thoughts which cannot be understood. Time and Mind are examples of this type; mysteries so profound that even the wise cannot do more than guess at their deepest structure. These bindings may someday become possible with greater understanding of the world and our place within it. For this reason they are of no interest to me. The second type is made up of those thoughts by their nature impossible to bind, and no greater knowledge shall ever permit them. Examples of this are Imprecision and Freedom-From-Bondage. Holding Time or Mind would be like holding a mountain in your hands. Holding Imprecision would be like holding the backs of your hands in your palms. One of these images may inspire awe, it is true, but the other is interesting.

"Is there anything I can do for you, Maati-cha?" the librarian asked again.

"Thank you, Baarath-cha, but no. I'm quite well."

The librarian took a step forward all the same. His hands seemed to twitch towards the books and scrolls that Maati had gathered to look over. The man's smile was fixed, his eyes glassy. In his worst moments, Maati had considered pretending to catch one of the ancient scrolls on fire, if only to see whether Baarath's knees would buckle.

"Because, if there was anything . . ."

"Maati-cha?" The familiar voice of the young poet rang from the front of the library. Maati turned to see Cehmai stride into the chamber with a casual pose of welcome to Baarath. He dropped into a chair across from Maati's own. The librarian was trapped for a moment between the careful formality he had with Maati and the easy companionship he appeared to enjoy with Cehmai. He hesitated for a moment, then, frowning, retreated.

"I'm sorry about him," Cehmai said. "He's an ass sometimes, but he is good at heart."

"If you say so. And what brings you? I thought there was another celebration of the Khai's daughter making a match."

"A messenger's come from the Dai-kvo," Cehmai said, lowering his voice so that Baarath, no doubt just behind the corner and listening, might not make out the words. "He says it's important."

Maati sat up, his belly twingeing a bit. His messages couldn't have reached the Dai-kvo's village and returned so soon. This had to be something that had been sent before word of his injury had gone out, which meant the Dai-kvo had found something, or wished something done, or . . . He noticed Cehmai's expression and paused.

"Is the seal not right?"

"There is no seal," Cehmai said. "There is no letter. The messenger says he was instructed to only speak the message to you, in private. It was too important, he said, to be written."

"That seems unlikely," Maati said.

"Doesn't it?"

"Where is he now?"

"They brought him to the poet's house when they heard who had sent him. I've had him put in a courtyard in the Fourth Palace. A walled one, with arms-men to keep him there. If this is a fresh assassin . . ."

"Then he'll answer more questions than the last one can," Maati said. "Take me there."

As they left, Maati saw Baarath swoop down on the books and scrolls like a mother reunited with her babe. Maati knew that they would all be hidden in obscure drawers and shelves by the time he came back. Some, he would likely never see again.

The sun was moving toward the mountain peaks in the west, early evening descending on the valley. They walked together down the white gravel path that led to the Fourth Palace, looking, Maati was sure, like nothing so much as a teacher and his student in their matching brown poet's robes. Except that Cehmai was the man who held the andat, and Maati was only a scholar. They didn't speak, but Maati felt a knot of excitement and apprehension tightening in him.

At the palace's great hall, a servant met them with a pose of formal welcome that couldn't hide the brightness in her eyes. At a gesture, she led them down a wide corridor and then up a flight of stairs to a gallery that looked down into the courtyard. Maati forced himself to breathe deeply as he stepped to the edge and looked down, Cehmai at his side.

The space was modest, but lush. Thin vines rose along one wall and part of another. Two small, sculpted maple trees stood, one at either end of a long, low stone bench. It looked like a painting—the perfectly balanced garden, with the laborer in his ill-cut robes the only thing out of place. A breeze stirred the branches of the trees with a sound equal parts flowing water and dry pages turning. Maati stepped back. His throat was tight, but his head felt perfectly clear. So this was how it would happen. Very well.

Cehmai was frowning down warily at Otah-kvo. Maati put his hand on the young man's shoulder.

"I have to speak with him," Maati said. "Alone."

"You don't think he's a threat?"

"It doesn't matter. I still need to speak with him."

"Maati-kvo, please take one of the armsmen. Even if you keep him at the far end of the yard, you can . . ."

Maati took a pose that refused this, and saw something shift in the young man's eyes. Respect, Maati thought. He thinks I'm being brave. How odd that I was that young once.

"Take me there," Maati said.

OTAH SAT IN THE GARDEN, HIS BACK AND NECK TIGHT FROM RIDING AND FROM fear, and remembered being young in the summer cities. In one of the low towns outside Saraykeht, there had been a rock at the edge of a cliff that jutted out over the water so that, when the tide was just right, a boy of thirteen summers might step out to its edge and peer past his toes at the ocean below him and feel like a bird. There had been a band of them—the homeless young scraping by on pity and small labor—who had dared each other to dive from that cliff. The first time he had made the leap himself, he had been sure the moment his feet left the rough, hot stone that he would die. That pause, divorced from earth and water, willing himself back up, trying to force himself to fly and take back that one irrevocable moment, had felt very much like sitting quiet and alone in this garden. The trees shifted like slow dancers, the flowers trembled, the stone glowed where the sun struck it and faded to gray where it did not. He rubbed his fingers against the gritty bench to remind himself where he was, and to keep the panic in his breast from possessing him.

He heard the door slide open with a whisper, and then shut again. He rose, forcing his body to move deliberately and took a pose of greeting even before he looked up. Maati Vaupathai. Time had thickened him, and there was a sorrow in the lines of his face that hadn't been there even in the weary days when he had stood between his master Heshai-kvo and the death that had eventually come. Otah wondered whether that change had sprung from Heshai's murder, and whether Maati had ever guessed that Otah had been the one who drew the cord across the old poet's throat.

Maati took a pose of welcome appropriate for a student to a teacher.

"It wasn't me," Otah said. "My brother. You. I had nothing to do with any of it."

"I had guessed that." Maati said. He did not come nearer.

"Are you going to call the armsmen? There must be half a dozen out there. Your student could have been more subtle in calling them."

"There's more than that, and he isn't my student. I don't have any students. I don't have anything." A strange smile twitched at the corner of his mouth. "I have been something of a disappointment to the Dai-kvo. Why are you here?"

"Because I need help," Otah said, "and I hoped we might not be enemies."

Maati seemed to weigh the words. He walked to the bench, sat, and leaned forward on clasped hands. Otah sat beside him, and they were silent. A sparrow landed on the ground before them, cocked its head, and fluttered madly away again.

"I came back because it was controlling me," Otah said. "This place. These people. I've spent a lifetime leaving them, and they keep coming back and destroying everything I build. I wanted to see it. I wanted to look at the city and my brothers and my father."

He looked at his hands.

"I don't know what I wanted," Otah said.

"Yes," Maati said, and then, awkwardly, "It was foolish, though. And there will be consequences."

"There have been already."

"There'll be more."

Again, the silence loomed. There was too much to say, and no order for it. Otah frowned hard, opened his mouth to speak, and closed it again.

"I have a son," Maati said. "Liat and I have a son. His name's Nayiit. He's probably just old enough now that he's started to notice that girls aren't always repulsive. I haven't seen them in years."

"I didn't know," Otah said.

"How would you? The Dai-kvo said that I was a fool to keep a family. I am a poet, and my duty is to the world. And when I wouldn't renounce them, I fell from favor. I was given duties that might as well have been done by an educated slave. And you know, there was an odd kind of pride about it for a while. I was given clothing, shelter, food for myself. Only for myself. I thought of leaving. Of folding my robes on the bed and running away as you did. I thought of you, the way you had chosen your own shape for your life instead of the shapes that were offered you. I thought I was doing the same. Gods, Otah-kvo, I wish you had been here. All these years, I wish I had been able to talk to you. To someone."

"I'm sorry. . . ."

Maati raised a hand to stop him.

"My son," Maati said, then his voice thickened, and he coughed and began again. "Liat and I parted ways. My low status among the poets didn't have the air of romance for her that I saw in it. And . . . there were other things. Raising my son called for money and time and I had little to spare of either. My son is thirteen summers. Thirteen. She was carrying him before we left Saraykeht."

Otah felt the words as if he'd been struck an unexpected blow—a sensation of shock without source or location, and then the flood. Maati glanced over at him and read his thoughts from his face, and he nodded.

"I know," Maati said. "She told me about bedding you that one time after you came back, before you left again. Before Heshai-kvo died and Seedless vanished. I suppose she was afraid that if I discovered it someday and she hadn't said anything it would make things worse. She told me the truth. And she swore that my son was mine. And I believe her."

"Do you?"

"Of course not. I mean, some days I did. When he was young and I could hold him in one arm, I was sure that he was mine. And then some nights I would wonder. And even in those times when I was sure that he was yours, I still loved him. That was the worst of it. The nights I lay awake in a village where women and children aren't allowed, in a tiny cell that stank of the disapproval of everyone I had ever hoped to please. I knew that I loved him, and that he wasn't mine. No, don't. Let me finish. I couldn't be a father to him. And if I hadn't fathered him either, what was there left but watching from a distance while this little creature grew up and away from me without even knowing my heart was tucked in his sleeve."

Maati wiped at his eyes with the back of one hand.

"Liat said she was tired of my always mourning, that the boy deserved some joy; that she did too. So after that I didn't have them, and I didn't have the respect of the people I saw and worked beside. I was eaten by guilt over losing them, and having taken her from you. I thought that she would have been happy with you. That you would have been happy with her. If only I hadn't broken faith with you, the world might have been right after all. And you might have stayed.

"And that has been my life until the day they called on me to hunt you."

"I see," Otah said.

"I have missed your company so badly, Otah-kya, and I have never hated anyone more. I have been waiting for years to say that. So. Now I have, what was it you wanted from me?"

Otah caught his breath.

"I wanted your help," he said. "There's a woman. She was my lover once. When I told her . . . when I told her about my family, my past, she turned me out. She was afraid that knowing me would put her and the people she was responsible for in danger."

"She's wise, then," Maati said.

"I hoped you would help me protect her," Otah said. His heart was a lump of cold lead. "Perhaps that was optimistic."

Maati laughed. The sound was hollow.

"And how would I do that?" Maati asked. "Kill your brothers for you? Tell the Khai that the Dai-kvo had decreed that she was not to be harmed? I don't have that power. I don't have any power at all. This was my chance at redemption. They called upon me to hunt you because I knew your face, and I failed at that until you walked into the palaces and asked to speak with me."

"Go to my father with me. I refused the brand, but I won't now. I'll renounce my claim to the chair in front of anyone he wants, only don't let him kill me before I do it."

Maati looked across at him. The sparrow returned for a moment to perch between them.

"It won't work," he said. "Renunciation isn't a simple thing, and once you've stepped outside of form, stepping back in . . ."

"But . . ."

"They won't believe you. And even if they did, they'd still fear you enough to see you dead."

Otah took a deep breath, and then slowly let it out, letting his head sink into his hands. The air itself seemed to have grown heavier, thicker. It had been a mad hope, and even in its failure, at least Kiyan would be safe. It was past time, perhaps, that people stopped paying prices for knowing him.

He could feel himself shaking. When he sat, his hands were perfectly still, though he could still feel the trembling in them.

"So what are you going to do?" Otah asked.

"In a moment, I'm going to call in the armsmen that are waiting outside that door," Maati said, his voice deceptively calm. He was trembling as well. "I am going to bring you before the Khai, who will at some point decide either that you are a murderer who has killed his son Biitrah and put you to the sword, or else a legitimate child of Machi who should be set loose for one of your older brothers to kill. I will speak on your behalf, and any evidence I can find that suggests Biitrah's murder wasn't your work, I will present."

"Well, thank you for that, at least."

"Don't," Maati said. "I'm doing it because it's true. If I thought you'd arranged it, I'd have said that."

"Loyalty to the truth isn't something to throw out either."

Maati took a pose that accepted the gratitude, and then dropped his hands to his sides.

"There's something you should know," Otah said. "It might . . . it seems to be your business. When I was in the islands, after Saraykeht, there was a woman. Not Maj. Another woman. I shared a bed with her for two, almost three years."

"Otah-kvo, I admire your conquests, but . . ."

"She wanted a child. From me. But it never took. Almost three years, and she bled with the moon the whole time. I heard that after I left, she took up with a fisherman from a tribe to the north and had a baby girl."

"I see," Maati said, and there was something in his voice. A brightness. "Thank you, Otah-kvo."

"I missed you as well. I wish we had had more time. Or other circumstances."

"As do I. But it isn't ours to choose. Shall we do this thing?"

"I don't suppose I could shave first?" Otah asked, touching his chin.

"I don't see how," Maati said, rising. "But perhaps we can get you some better robes."

Otah didn't mean to laugh; it simply came out of him. And then Maati was laughing as well, and the birds startled around them, lifting up into the sky. Otah rose and took a pose of respect appropriate to the closing of a meeting. Maati responded in kind, and they walked together to the door. Maati slid it open, and Otah looked to see whether there was a gap in the men, a chance to dodge them and sprint out to the streets. He might as well have looked for a stone cloud. The armsmen seemed to have doubled in number, and two already had bare blades at the ready. The young poet—the one Maati said wasn't his student—was there among them, his expression serious and concerned. Maati spoke as if the bulky men and their weapons weren't there.

"Cehmai-cha," he said. "Good that you're here. I would like to introduce you to my old friend, Otah, the sixth son of the Khai Machi. Otah-kvo, this is Cehmai Tyan and that small mountain in the back is the andat Stone-Made-Soft which he controls. Cehmai assumed you were an assassin come to finish me off."

"I'm not," Otah said with a levity that seemed at odds with his situation, but which felt perfectly natural. "But I understand the misconception. It's the beard. I'm usually better shaved."

Cehmai opened his mouth, closed it, and then took a formal pose of welcome. Maati turned to the armsmen.

"Chain him," he said.

EVEN AT THE HEIGHT OF MORNING, THE WIVES' QUARTERS OF THE HIGH PALACE were filled with the small somber activity of a street market starting to close at twilight. In the course of his life, the Khai Machi had taken eleven women as wives. Some had become friends, lovers, companions. Others had been little more than permanent guests in his house, sent as a means of assuring favor as one might send a good hunting dog or a talented slave. Idaan had heard that there were several of them with whom he had never shared a bed. It had been Biitrah's wife, Hiami, who'd told her that, trying to explain to a young girl that the Khaiem had a different relationship to their women than other men had, that it was traditional. It hadn't worked. Even the words the older woman had used—*your father chooses not to*—had proven her point that this was a comfort house with high ceilings, grand halls, and only a single client.

But now that was changing, not in character, but in the particulars. The succession would have the same effect on the eight wives who remained, whoever took the seat. It would be time for them to leave—make the journey back to whatever city or family had sent them forth in the first place. The oldest of them, a sharp-tongued woman named Carai, would be returning to a high family in Yalakeht where the man who would choose her disposition had been a delighted toddler grinning and filling his pants the last time she'd seen him. Another woman—one of the recent ones hardly older than Idaan herself—had taken a lover in the court. She was being sent back to Chaburi-Tan, likely to be turned around and shipped off to another of the Khaiem or traded between the houses of the utkhaiem as a token of political alliance. Many of the wives had known each other for decades and would now scatter and lose the friends and companions they had known best. And on and on, every one of them a life shaped by a man's will, constrained by tradition.

Idaan walked through the wide, bright corridors, listened to these women preparing to depart when the inevitable news came, anticipating the grief in a way that was as hard as the grief itself. Perhaps harder. She accepted their congratulations on her marriage. She would be able to remain in the city, and should her man die before her, her family would be there to support her. She, at least, would never be uprooted. Hiami had never understood why Idaan had objected to this way of living. Idaan had never understood why these women hadn't set the palaces on fire.

Her own rooms were set in the back; small apartments with rich tapestries of white and gold on the walls. They might almost have been mistaken for the home of some merchant leader—the overseer of a great trading house, or a trade master who spoke with the voice of a city's craftsmen. If only she had been born one of those. As she entered, one of her servants met her with an expression that suggested news. Idaan took a pose of query.

"Adrah Vaunyogi is waiting to see you, Idaan-cha," the servant girl said. "It was approaching midday, so I've put him in the dining hall. There is food waiting. I hope I haven't . . ."

"No," Idaan said, "you did well. Please see that we're left alone."

He sat at the long, wooden table, and he did not look up when she came in. Idaan was willing to ignore him as well as to be ignored, so she gathered a bowl of food from the platters—early grapes from the south, sticky with their own blood; hard, crumbling cheese with a ripe scent that was both appetizing and not; twice-baked flatbread that cracked sharply when she broke off a piece—and retired to a couch. She forced herself to forget that he was there, to look forward at the bare fire grate. Anger buoyed her up, and she clung to it.

She heard it when he stood, heard his footsteps approaching. It was a little victory, but it pleased her. As he sat cross-legged on the floor before her, she raised an eyebrow and sketched a pose of welcome before choosing another grape.

"I came last night," he said. "I was looking for you."

"I wasn't here," she said.

The pause was meant to injure her. *Look how sad you've made me, Idaan.* It was a child's tactic, and that it partially worked infuriated her.

"I've had trouble sleeping," she said. "I walk. Otherwise, I'd spend the whole night staring at netting and watching the candle burn down. No call for that."

Adrah sighed and nodded his head.

"I've been troubled too," he said. "My father can't reach the Galts. With Oshai . . . with what happened to him, he's afraid they may withdraw their support."

"Your father is an old woman frightened there's a snake in the night bucket," Idaan said, breaking a corner of her bread. "They may lie low now, but once it's clear that you're in position to become Khai, they'll do what they promised. They've nothing to gain by not."

"Once I'm Khai, they'll still own me," Adrah said. "They'll know how I came there. They'll be able to hold it over me. If they tell what they know, the gods only know what would happen."

Idaan took a bite of grape and cheese both—the sweet and the salt mingling pleasantly. When she spoke, she spoke around it.

"They won't. They won't dare, Adrah. Give the worst: we're exposed by the Galts. We're deposed and killed horribly in the streets. Fine. Lift your gaze up from your own corpse for a moment and tell me what happens next?"

"There's a struggle. Some other family takes the chair."

"Yes. And what will the new Khai do?"

"He'll slaughter my family," Adrah said, his voice hollow and ghostly. Idaan leaned forward and slapped him.

"He'll have Stone-Made-Soft level a few Galtic mountain ranges and sink some islands. Do you think there's a Khai in any city that would sit still at the word of the Galtic Council arranging the death of one of their own? The Galts won't own you because your exposure would mean the destruction of their nation and the wholesale slaughter of their people. So worry a little less. You're supposed to be overwhelmed with the delight of marrying me."

"Shouldn't you be delighted too, then?"

"I'm busy mourning my father," she said dryly. "Do we have any wine?"

"How is he? Your father?"

"I don't know," Idaan said. "I try not to see him these days. He makes me . . . feel weak. I can't afford that just now."

"I heard he's failing."

"Men can fail for a long time," she said, and stood. She left the bowl on the floor and walked back to her bedroom, holding her hands out before her, sticky with juice. Adrah followed along behind her and lay on her bed. She poured water into her stone basin and watched him as she washed her hands. He was a boy, lost in the world. Perhaps now was as good a time as any. She took a deep breath.

"I've been thinking, Adrah-kya," she said. "About when you become Khai."

He turned his head to look at her, but did not rise or speak.

"It's going to be important, especially at the first, to gather allies. Founding a line is a delicate thing. I know we agreed that it would always be only the two of us, but perhaps we were wrong in that. If you take other wives, you'll have more the appearance of tradition and the support of the families who bind themselves to us."

"My father said the same," he said.

Oh did he? Idaan thought, but she held her face still and calm. She dried her hands on the basin cloth and came to sit on the bed beside him. To her surprise, he was weeping; small tears coming from the outer corners of his eyes, thin tracks shining on his skin. Without willing it, her hand went to his cheek, caressing him. He shifted to look at her.

"I love you, Idaan. I love you more than anything in the world. You are the only person I've ever felt this way about."

His lips trembled and she pressed a finger against them to quiet him. These weren't things she wanted to hear, but he would not be stopped.

"Let's end this," he said. "Let's just be together, here. I'll find another way to move ahead in the court, and your brother . . . you'll still be his blood, and we'll still be well kept. Can't we . . . can't we, please?"

"All this because you don't want to take another woman?" she said softly, teasing him. "I find that hard to believe."

He took her hand in his. He had soft hands. She remembered thinking that the first time they'd fallen into her bed together. Strong, soft, wide hands. She felt tears forming in her own eyes.

"My father said that I should take other wives," he said. "My mother said that, knowing you, you'd only agree to it if you could take lovers of your own too. And then you weren't here last night, and I waited until it was almost dawn. And you . . . you want to . . ."

"You think I've taken another man?" she asked.

His lips pressed thin and bloodless, and he nodded. His hand squeezed hers as if she might save his life, if only he held onto her. A hundred things came to her mind all at once. *Yes, of course I have. How dare you accuse me? Ceh-mai is the only clean thing left in my world, and you cannot have him.* She smiled as if Adrah were a boy being silly, as if he were wrong.

"That would be the stupidest thing I could possibly do just now," she said, neither lying nor speaking the truth of it. She leaned forward to kiss him, but before their mouths touched, a voice wild with excitement called out from the atrium.

"Idaan-cha! Idaan-cha! Come quickly!"

Idaan leapt up as if she'd been caught doing something she ought not, then gathered herself, straightened her robes. The mirror showed that the paint on her mouth and eyes was smudged from eating and weeping, but there wasn't time to reapply it. She pushed back a stray lock of hair and stormed out.

The servant girl took a pose of apology as Idaan approached her. She wore the colors of her father's personal retinue, and Idaan's heart sank to her belly. He had died. It had happened. But the girl was smiling, her eyes bright.

"What's happened?" Idaan demanded.

"Everything," the girl said. "You're summoned to the court. The Khai is call-ing everyone."

"Why? What's happened?"

"I'm not to say, Idaan-cha," the girl said.

Idaan felt the rage-blood in her face as if she were standing near a fire. She didn't think, didn't plan. Her body seemed to move of its own accord as she slid forward and clapped her hand on the servant girl's throat and pressed her to the wall. There was shock in the girl's expression, and Idaan sneered at it. Adrah fluttered like a bird in the corner of her vision.

"Say," Idaan said. "Because I asked you twice, tell me what's happened. And do it now."

"The upstart," the girl said. "They've caught him."

Idaan stepped back, dropping her hand. The girl's eyes were wide. The air of excitement and pleasure were gone. Adrah put a hand on Idaan's shoulder, and she pushed it away.

"He was here," the girl said. "In the palaces. The visiting poet caught him, and they're bringing him before the Khai."

Idaan licked her lips. Otah Machi was here. He had been here for the gods only knew how long. She looked at Adrah, but his expression spoke of an un-certainty and surprise as deep as her own. And a fear that wasn't entirely about their conspiracy.

"What's your name?" she asked.

"Choya," the girl said.

Idaan took a pose of abject apology. It was more than a member of the ut-khaiem would have normally presented to a servant, but Idaan felt her guilt welling up like blood from a cut.

"I am very sorry, Choya-cha. I was wrong to—"

"But that isn't all," the servant girl said. "A courier came this morning from Tan-Sadar. He'd been riding for three weeks. Kaiin Machi is dead. Your brother Danat killed him, and he's coming back. The courier guessed he might be a week behind him. Danat Machi's going to be the new Khai Machi. And Idaan-cha, he'll be back in the city in time for your wedding!"

7

>+< On one end, the chain ended at a cube of polished granite the color of soot that stood as high as a man's waist. On the other, it linked to a rough iron collar around Otah's neck. Sitting with his back to the stone—the chain was not so long that he could stand—Otah remembered seeing a brown bear tied to a pole in the main square of a low town outside Tan-Sadar. Dogs had been set upon it three at a time, and with each new wave, the men had wagered on which animal would survive.

Armsmen stood around him with blades drawn and leather armor, stationed widely enough apart to allow anyone who wished it a good view of the captive. Beyond them, the representatives of the utkhaiem in fine robes and ornate jewelry crowded the floor and two tiers of the balconies that rose up to the base of the domed ceiling far above him. The dais before him was empty. Otah wondered what would happen if he should need to empty his bladder. It seemed unlikely that they would let him piss on the fine parquet floor, but neither could he imagine being led away decorously. He tried to picture what they saw, this mob of nobility, when they looked at him. He didn't try to charm them or play on their sympathies. He was the upstart, and there wasn't a man or woman in the hall who wasn't delighted to see him debased and humiliated.

The first of the servants appeared, filing out from a hidden door and spacing themselves around the chair. Otah picked out the brown poet's robe, but it was Cehmai with the bulk of his andat moving behind him. Maati wasn't with him; Cehmai was speaking with a woman in the robes of the Khaiem—Otah's sister, she would be. He wondered what her name was.

The last of the servants and counselors took their places, and the crowd fell silent. The Khai Machi walked out, as graceful as a dying man could be. His robes were lush and full, and served to do little more than show how wasted his frame had become. Otah could see the rouge on his sunken cheeks, trying to give the appearance of vigor long since gone. Whisperers fanned out from the dais and into the crowd. The Khai took a pose of welcome appropriate to the opening of a ritual judgment. Otah rose to his knees.

"I am told that you are my son, Otah Machi, whom I gave over to the poets' school."

The whisperers echoed it through the hall. It was his moment to speak now, and he found his heart was so full of humiliation and fear and anger that he had nothing to say. He raised his hands and took a pose of greeting—a casual one that would have been appropriate for a peasant son to his father. There was a murmur among the utkhaiem.

"I am further told that you were once offered the poet's robes, and you refused that honor."

Otah tried to rise, but the most the chain allowed was a low stoop. He cleared his throat and spoke, pushing the words out clear enough to be heard in the farthest gallery.

"That is true. I was a child, most high. And I was angry."

"And I hear that you have come to my city and killed my eldest child. Biitrah Machi is dead by your hand."

"That is *not* true, father," Otah said. "I won't say that no man has ever died by my hand, but I didn't kill Biitrah. I have no wish or intention to become the Khai Machi."

"Then why have you come here?" the Khai shouted, rising to his feet. His face was twisted in rage, his fists trembled. In all his travels, Otah had never seen the Khai of any city look more like a man. Otah felt something like pity through his humiliation and rage, and it let him speak more softly when he spoke again.

"I heard that my father was dying."

It seemed that the murmur of the crowds would never end. It rolled like waves against the seashore. Otah knelt again; the awkward stooping hurt his neck and back, and there was no point trying to maintain dignity here. They waited, he and his father, staring at each other across the space. Otah tried to feel some bond, some kinship that would bridge this gap, but there was nothing. The Khai Machi was his father by an accident of birth, and nothing more.

He saw the old man's eyes flicker, as if unsure of himself. He couldn't have always been this way—the Khaiem were inhumanly studied in ritual and grace. It was the mark of their calling. Otah wondered what his father had been when he was young and strong. He wondered what he would have been like as a man among his children.

The Khai raised a hand, and the crowd's susurrus tapered down to silence. Otah did not move.

"You have stepped outside tradition," he said. "Whether you took a hand against my son is a question that has already gathered an array of opinion. It is something I must think on.

"I have had other news this day. Danat Machi has won the right of succession. He is returning to the city even now. I will consult with him on your fate. Until then, you shall be confined in the highest room in the great tower. I do not care to have your accomplices taking your death in their own hands this time. Danat and I—the Khai Machi and the Khai yet to come—shall decide together what kind of beast you are."

Otah took a pose of supplication. That he was on his knees only made the gesture clearer. He was dead, whatever happened. He could see that now. If there had been a chance of mercy—and likely there hadn't—having father and son converse would remove it. But in the black dread, there was this one chance to speak as himself—not as Itani Noygu or some other mask. And if it offended the court, there was little worse they could do to him than he faced now. His father hesitated, and Otah spoke.

"I have seen many of the cities of the Khaiem, most high. I have been born into the highest of families, and I have been offered the greatest of honors. And if I am here to meet my death at the hands of those who should by all rights love me, at least hear me out. Our cities are not well, father. Our traditions are not well. You stand there on that dais now because you killed your own. You are celebrating the return of Danat, who killed his brother, and at the same time preparing to condemn me on the suspicion that I did the same. A tradition that calls men to kill their brothers and discard their sons cannot be—"

"Enough!" the Khai roared, and his voice carried. The whisperers were silent and unneeded. "I have not carried this city on my back for all these years to be lectured now by a rebel and a traitor and a poisoner. You are not my son! You lost that right! You squandered it! Tell me that this . . ." The Khai raised his hands in a gesture that seemed to encompass every man and woman of the court, the palaces, the city, the valley, the mountains, the world. ". . . this is evil? Because our traditions are what hold all this from chaos. We are the Khaiem! We rule with the power of the andat, and we do not accept instruction from couriers and laborers who . . . who killed . . ."

The Khai closed his eyes and seemed to sway for a moment. The woman to whom Cehmai had been speaking leapt up, her hand on the old man's elbow. Otah could see them murmuring to each other, but he had no idea what they were saying. The woman walked with him back to the chair and helped him to sit. His face seemed sunken in pain. The woman was crying—streaks of kohl black on her cheeks—but her bearing was more regal and sure than their father's had been. She stepped forward and spoke.

"The Khai is weary," she said, as if daring anyone present to say anything else. "He has given his command. The audience is finished!"

The voices rose almost as high and ran almost as loud as they had at anything that had gone before. A woman—even if she was his daughter—taking the initiative to speak for the Khai? The court would be scandalized.

Otah already imagined them placing bets as to whether the man would live the night, and if he died now, whether it would be this woman's fault for shaming him so deeply when he was already weak. And Otah could see that she knew this. The contempt in her expression was eloquent as any oratory. He caught her eye and took a pose of approval. She looked at him as if he were a stranger who had spoken her name, then turned away to help their father walk back to his rooms.

The march up to his cage led through a spiral stone stair so small that his shoulders touched each wall, and his head stayed bent. The chain stayed on his neck, his hands now bound behind him. He watched the armsman before him half walking, half climbing the steep blocks of stone. When Otah slowed, the man behind him struck with the butt of a spear and laughed. Otah, his hands bound, sprawled against the steps, ripping the flesh of his knees and chin. After that, he made a point to slow as little as possible.

His thighs burned with each step and the constant turning to the right left him nauseated. He thought of stopping, of refusing to move. They were taking him up to wait for death anyway. There was nothing to be gained by collaborating with them. But he went on, cursing under his breath.

When the stairs ended, he found himself in a wide hall. The sky doors in the north wall were open, and a platform hung level with them and shifting slightly in the breeze, the great chains taut. Another four armsmen stood waiting.

"Relief?" the man who had pushed him asked.

The tallest of the new armsmen took a pose of affirmation and spoke. "We'll take the second half. You four head up and we'll all go down together." The new armsmen led Otah to a fresh stairway, and the ordeal began again. He had begun almost to dream in his pain by the time they stopped. Thick, powerful hands pushed him into a room, and the door closed behind him with a sound like a capstone being shoved over an open tomb. The armsman said something through a slit in the door, but Otah couldn't make sense of it and didn't have the will to try. He lay on the floor until he realized that his arms had been freed and the iron collar taken from around his neck. The skin where it had rested was chafed raw.

The voices of men seeped through the door, and then the sound of a winch creaking as it lowered the platform and its cargo of men. Then there were only two voices speaking in light, conversational tones. He couldn't make out a word they said.

He forced himself to sit up and take stock. The room was larger than he'd expected, and bare. It could have been used as a storage room or set with table and chairs for a small meeting. There was a bowl of water in one corner, but no food, no candles, nothing but the stone to sleep on. The light came from a barred window. His hip and knees ached as Otah pulled himself up and stumbled over to it. He was facing south, and the view was like he'd become a bird. He leaned out—the bars were not so narrowly spaced that he couldn't climb out and fall to his death if he chose. Below him, the carts in the streets were like ants shuffling along in their lines. A crow launched itself from a crack or beam and circled below him, the sun shining on its black back. Trembling, he pulled himself back in. There were no shutters to close off the sky.

He tried the door's latch, but it had been barred from without, and the hinges were leather and worked iron. Not the sort of thing a man could take apart with teeth. Otah knelt by the bowl of water and drank from his cupped hand. He washed out the worst of his wounds, and left a third in the bowl. There was no knowing how long it might be before they saw fit to give him more. He wondered if there were birds that came up this high to rest, and whether he would be able to trap one. Not that he would have the chance to cook it—there was nothing to burn here, and no grate to burn it in. Otah ran his hands over his face, and despite himself, laughed. It seemed unlikely they would allow him anything sharp enough to shave with. He would die with this sad little beard.

Otah stretched out in a corner, his arm thrown over his eyes, and tried to sleep, wondering as he did whether the sense of movement came from his own abused and exhausted body, or if it were true that so far up even stone swayed.

MAATI LOOKED AT THE FLOOR. HIS FACE WAS HARD WITH FRUSTRATION AND ANGER. "If you want him dead, most high," he said, his voice measured and careful, "you might at least have the courtesy to kill him."

The Khai Machi raised the clay pipe to his lips. He seemed less to breathe the smoke in than to drink it. The sweet resin from it had turned every surface in the room slightly tacky to the touch. The servant in the blue and gold robes of a physician sat discreetly in a dim corner, pretending not to hear the business of the city. The rosewood door was closed behind them. Lanterns of sanded glass filled the room with soft light, rendering them all shadowless.

"I've listened to you, Maati-cha. I didn't end him there in the audience chamber. I am giving you the time you asked," the old man said. "Why do you keep pressing me?"

"He has no blankets or fire. The guards have given him three meals in the last four days. And Danat will return before I've had word back from the Dai-kvo. If this is all you can offer, most high—"

"You can state your case to Danat-cha as eloquently as you could to me," the Khai said.

"There'll be no point if Otah dies of cold or throws himself out the tower window before then," Maati said. "Let me take him food and a thick robe. Let me talk with him."

"It's hopeless," the Khai said.

"Then there's nothing lost but my effort, and it will keep me from troubling you further."

"Your work here is complete, isn't it? Why are you bothering me, Maati-cha? You were sent to find Otah. He's found."

"I was sent to find if he was behind the death of Biitrah, and if he was not, to discover who was. I have not carried out that task. I won't leave until I have."

The Khai's expression soured, and he shook his head. His skin had grown thinner, the veins at his temples showing dark. When he leaned forward, tapping the bowl of his pipe against the side of the iron brazier with a sound like pebbles falling on stone, his grace could not hide his discomfort.

"I begin to wonder, Maati-cha, whether you have been entirely honest with me. You say that there is no great love between you and my upstart son. You bring him to me, and for that reason alone, I believe you. Everything else you have done suggests the other. You argue that it was not he who arranged Biitrah's death, though you have no suggestion who else might have. You ask for indulgences for the prisoner, you appeal to the Dai-kvo in hopes . . ."

A sudden pain seemed to touch the old man's features and one near-skeletal hand moved toward his belly.

"There is a shadow in your city," Maati said. "You've called it by Otah's name, but none of it shows any connection with Otah: not Biitrah, not the attack on me, not the murder of the assassin. None of the other couriers of any house report anything that would suggest he was more than he appeared. By his own word, he'd fled the city before the attack on me, and didn't return before the assassin was killed. How is it that he arranged all these things with no one seeing him? No one knowing his name? How is it that, now he's trapped, no one has offered to sell him in trade for their own lives?"

"Who then?"

"I don't . . ."

"Who else gained from these things?"

"Your son, Danat," Maati said. "He broke the pact. If all this talk of Otah was a ploy to distract Kaiin from the real danger, then it worked, most high. Danat will be the new Khai Machi."

"Ask him when he comes. He will be the Khai Machi, and if he has done as you said, then there's no crime in it and no reason that he should hide it."

"A poet was attacked—"

"And did you die? Are you dying? No? Then don't ask sympathy from me. Go, Maati-cha. Take the prisoner anything you like. Take him a pony and let him ride it around his cell, if that pleases you. Only don't return to me. Any business you have with me now, you have with my son."

The Khai took a pose of command that ended the audience, and Maati stood, took a pose of gratitude that he barely felt, and withdrew from the meeting room. He stalked along the corridors of the palace seething.

Back in his apartments, he took stock. He had gathered together his bundle even before he'd gone to the audience. A good wool robe, a rough cloth bag filled with nut breads and dry cheeses, and a flask of fresh water. Everything that he thought the Khai's men would permit. He folded it all together and tied it with twine.

At the base of the great tower, armsmen stood guard at the platform—a metalwork that ran on tracks set into the stone of the tower, large enough to carry twelve men. The chains that held it seemed entirely too thin. Maati identified himself, thinking his poet's robe, reputation, and haughty demeanor might suffice to make the men do as he instructed. Instead, a runner was sent to the Khai's palace to confirm that Maati was indeed permitted to see the prisoner and to give him the little gifts that he carried. Once word was brought back, Maati climbed on the platform, and the signalman on the ground blew a call on a great trumpet. The chains went taut, and the platform rose. Maati held onto the rail, his knuckles growing whiter as the ground receded. Wind plucked at his sleeves as the roofs of even the greatest palaces fell away below him. The only things so high as he was were the towers, the birds, and the mountains. It was beautiful and exhilarating, and all he could think the whole time was what would happen if a single link in any of the four chains gave way. When he reached the open sky doors at the top, the captain of the armsmen took him solidly by his arm and helped him step in.

"First time, eh?" the captain said, and his men chuckled, but not cruelly. It was a journey each of them risked, Maati realized, every day. These men were more likely to die for the vanity of Machi than he. He smiled and nodded, stepping away from the open space of the sky door.

"I've come to see the prisoner," he said.

"I know," the captain said. "The trumpet said as much, if you knew to listen for it. But understand, if he attacks you—if he tries to bargain your life for his freedom—I'll send your body down. You make your choice when you go in there. I can't be responsible for it."

The captain's expression was stern. Maati saw that he thought this possible, the danger real. Maati took a pose of thanks, hampered somewhat by the bundle under his arm. The captain only nodded and led him to a huge wooden door. Four of his men drew their blades as he unbarred it and let it swing in. Maati took a deep breath and stepped through.

Otah was huddled in a corner, his arms wrapped around his knees. He looked up and then back down. Maati heard the door close behind him, heard the bar slide home. All those men to protect him from this half-dead rag.

"I've brought food," Maati said. "I considered wine, but it seemed too much like a celebration."

Otah chuckled, a thick phlegmy sound.

"It would have gone to my head too quickly anyway," he said, his voice weak. "I'm too old to go drinking without a good meal first."

Maati knelt and unfolded the robe and arranged the food he'd brought. It seemed too little now, but when he broke off a corner of nut bread and held it out, Otah nodded his gratitude and took it. Maati opened the flask of water, put it beside Otah's feet, and sat back.

"What news?" Otah asked. "I don't hear much gossip up here."

"It's all as straightforward as a maze," Maati said. "House Siyanti is calling in every favor it has not to be banned from the city. Your old overseer has been going to each guild chapter house individually. There's even rumor he's been negotiating with hired armsmen."

"He must be frightened for his life," Otah said and shook his head wearily. "I'm sorry to have done that to him. But I suppose there's little enough I can do about it now. There does always seem to be a price people pay for knowing me."

Maati looked at his hands. For a moment he considered holding his tongue. It would be worse, he thought, holding out hope if there was none. But it was all that he had left to offer.

"I've sent to the Dai-kvo. I may have a way that you can survive this," he said. "There's no precedent for someone refusing the offer to become a poet. It's possible that . . ."

Otah sipped the water and put down the flask. His brow was furrowed.

"You've asked him to make me a poet?" Otah asked.

"I didn't say it would work," Maati said. "Only that I'd done it."

"Well, thank you for that much."

Otah reached out, took another bit of bread, and leaned back. The effort seemed to exhaust him. Maati rose and paced the room. The view from the window was lovely and inhuman. No one had ever been meant to see so far at once. A thought occurred, and he looked in the corners of the room.

"Have they . . . there's no night bucket," he said.

Otah raised one arm in a wide gesture toward the world outside.

"I've been using the window," he said. Maati smiled, and Otah smiled with him. Then for a moment they were laughing together.

"Well, that must confuse people in the streets," Maati said.

"Very large pigeons," Otah said. "They blame very large pigeons."

Maati grinned, and then felt the smile fade.

"They're going to kill, you Otah-kvo. The Khai and Danat. They can't let you live. You're too well known, and they think you'll act against them."

"They won't make do with blinding me and casting me into the wilderness, eh?"

"I'll make the suggestion, if you like."

Otah's laugh was thinner now. He took up the cheese, digging into its pale flesh with his fingers. He held a sliver out to Maati, offering to share it. Maati hesitated, and then accepted it. It was smooth as cream and salty. It would go well with the nut bread, he guessed.

"I knew this was likely to happen when I chose to come back," Otah said. "I'm not pleased by it, but it will spare Kiyan, won't it? They won't keep pressing her?"

"I can't see why they would," Maati said.

"Dying isn't so bad, then," Otah said. "At least it does something for her."

"Do you mean that?"

"I might as well, Maati-kya. Unless you plan to sneak me out in your sleeve, I think I'm going to be spared the rigors of a northern winter. I don't see there's anything to be done about that."

Maati sighed and nodded. He rose and took a pose of farewell. Even just the little food and the short time seemed to have made Otah stronger. He didn't rise, but he took a pose that answered the farewell. Maati walked to the door and pounded to be let out. He heard the scrape of the bar being raised. Otah spoke.

"Thank you for all this. It's kind."

"I'm not doing it for you, Otah-kvo."

"All the same. Thank you."

Maati didn't reply. The door opened, and he stepped out. The captain of the armsmen started to speak, but something in Maati's expression stopped him. Maati strode to the sky doors and out to the platform as if he were walking into a hallway and not an abyss of air. He clasped his hands behind him and looked out over the roofs of Machi. What had been vertiginous only recently failed to move him now. His mind and heart were too full. When he reached the ground again, he walked briskly to his apartments. The wound in his belly itched badly, but he kept himself from worrying it. He only gathered his papers, sat on a deck of oiled wood that looked out over gardens of summer trees and ornate flowers a brighter red than blood, and planned out the remainder of his day.

There were still two armsmen from the cages with whom he hadn't spoken. If he knew who had killed the assassin, it would likely lead him nearer the truth. And the slaves and servants of the Third Palace might be persuaded to speak more of Danat Machi, now that he was coming back covered in the glory of his brother's blood. If he had used the story of Otah the Upstart to distract his remaining brother from his schemes . . .

A servant boy interrupted, announcing Cehmai. Maati took a pose of acknowledgment and had the young poet brought to him. He looked unwell, Maati thought. His skin was too pale, his eyes troubled. He couldn't think that Otah-kvo was bothering Cehmai badly, but surely something was.

Still, the boy managed a grin and when he sat, he moved with more energy than Maati himself felt.

"You sent for me, Maati-kvo?"

"I have work," he said. "You offered to help me with this project once. And I could do with your aid, if you still wish to lend it."

"You aren't stopping?"

Maati considered. He could say again that the Dai-kvo had told him to discover the murderer of Biitrah Machi and whether Otah-kvo had had a hand in it, and that until he'd done so, he would keep to his task. It had been a strong enough argument for the utkhaiem, even for the Khai. But Cehmai had known the Dai-kvo as well as he had, and more recently. He would see how shallow the excuse was. In the end he only shook his head.

"I am not stopping," he said.

"May I ask why not?"

"They are going to kill Otah-kvo."

"Yes," Cehmai agreed, his voice calm and equable. Maati might as well have said that winter would be cold.

"And I have a few days to find whose crimes he's carrying."

Cehmai frowned and took a pose of query.

"They'll kill him anyway," Cehmai said. "If he killed Biitrah, they'll execute him for that. If he didn't, Danat will do the thing to keep his claim to be the Khai. Either way he's a dead man."

"That's likely true," Maati said. "But I've done everything else I can think to do, and this is still left, so I'll do this. If there is anything at all I can do, I have to do it."

"In order to save your teacher," Cehmai said, as if he understood.

"To sleep better twenty years from now," Maati said, correcting him. "If anyone asks, I want to be able to say that I did what could be done. And I want to be able to mean it. That's more important to me than saving him."

Cehmai seemed puzzled, but Maati found no better way to express it without mentioning his son's name, and that would open more than it would close. Instead he waited, letting the silence argue for him. Cehmai took a pose of acceptance at last, and then tilted his head.

"Maati-kvo . . . I'm sorry, but when was the last time you slept?"

Maati smiled and ignored the question.

"I'm going to meet with one of the armsmen who saw my assassin killed," he said. "I was wondering if I could impose on you to find some servant from Danat's household with whom I might speak later this evening. I have a few questions about him . . ."

DANAT MACHI ARRIVED LIKE A HERO. THE STREETS WERE FILLED WITH PEOPLE cheering and singing. Festivals filled the squares. Young girls danced through the streets in lines, garlands of summer blossoms in their hair. And from his litter strewn with woven gold and silver, Danat Machi looked out like a protective father indulging a well-loved child. Idaan had been present when the word came that Danat Machi waited at the bridge for his father's permission to enter the city. She had gone down behind the runner to watch the doors fly open and the celebration that had been building spill out into the dark stone streets. They would have sung as loud for Kaiin, if Danat had been dead.

While Danat's caravan slogged its way through the crowds, Idaan retreated to the palaces. The panoply of the utkhaiem was hardly more restrained than the common folk. Members of all the high families appeared as if by chance outside the Third Palace's great hall. Musicians and singers entertained with beautiful ballads of great warriors returning home from the field, of time and life renewed in a new generation. They were songs of the proper function of the world. It was as if no one had known Biitrah or Kaiin, as if the wheel of the world were not greased with her family's blood. Idaan watched with a calm, pleasant expression while her soul twisted with disgust.

When Danat reached the long, broad yard and stepped down from his litter, a cheer went up from all those present; even from her. Danat raised his arms and smiled to them all, beaming like a child on Candles Night. His gaze found her, and he strode through the crowd to her side. Idaan raised her chin and took a pose of greeting. It was what she was expected to do. He ignored it and picked her up in a great hug, swinging her around as if she weighed nothing, and then placed her back on her own feet.

"Sister," he said, smiling into her eyes. "I can't say how glad I am to see you."

"Danat-kya," she said, and then failed.

"How are things with our father?"

The sorrow that was called for here was at least easier than the feigned delight. She saw it echoed in Danat's eyes. So close to him, she could see the angry red in the whites of his eyes, the pallor in his skin. He was wearing paint, she realized. Rouge on his cheeks and lips and some warm-toned powder to lend his skin the glow of health. Beneath it, he was sallow. She wondered if he'd grown sick, and whether there was some slow poison that might be blamed for his death.

"He has been looking forward to seeing you," she said.

"Yes. Yes, of course. And I hear that you're to become a Vaunyogi. I'm pleased for you. Adrah's a good man."

"I love him," she said, surprised to find that in some dim way it was still truth. "But how are you, brother? Are you . . . are things well with you?"

For a moment, Danat seemed about to answer. She thought she saw some-

thing weaken in him, his mouth losing its smile, his eyes looking into a darkness like the one she carried. In the end, he shook himself and kissed her
forehead, then turned again to the crowd and made his way to the Khai's palace, greeting and rejoicing with everyone who crossed his path. And it was
only the beginning. Danat and their father would be closeted away for a time,
then the ritual welcome from the heads of the families of the utkhaiem. And
then festivities and celebrations, feasts and dances and revelry in the streets
and palaces and teahouses.

Idaan made her way to the compound of the Vaunyogi, and to Adrah and his
father. The house servants greeted her with smiles and poses of welcome. The
chief overseer led her to a small meeting room in the back. If it seemed odd
that this room—windowless and dark—was used now in the summer when
most gatherings were in gardens or open pavilions, the overseer made no note
of it. Nothing could have been more different from the mood in the city than
the one here; like a winter night that had crept into summer.

"Has House Vaunyogi forgotten where it put its candles?" she asked, and
turned to the overseer. "Find a lantern or two. These fine men may be suffering from their drink, but I've hardly begun to celebrate."

The overseer took a pose that acknowledged the command and scampered
off, returning immediately with his gathered light. Adrah and his father sat at
a long stone table. Dark tapestries hung from the wall, red and orange and
gold. When the doors were safely closed behind them, Idaan pulled out one of
the stools and sat on it. Her gaze moved from the father's face to the son's. She
took a pose of query.

"You seem distressed," she said. "The whole city is loud with my brother's
glory, and you two are skulking in here like criminals."

"We have reason to be distressed," Daaya Vaunyogi said. She wondered
whether Adrah would age into the same loose jowls and watery eyes. "I've finally reached the Galts. They've cooled. Killing Oshai's made them nervous,
and now with Danat back . . . we expected to have the fighting between your
brothers to cover our . . . our work. There's no hope of that now. And that poet
hasn't stopped hunting around, even with the holes Oshai poked in him."

"The more reason you have to be distressed," Idaan said, "the more important that you should not seem it. Besides, I still have two living brothers."

"Ah, and you have some way to make Danat die at Otah's hand?" the old
man said. There was mockery in his voice, but there was also hope. And fear.
He had seen what she had done, and perhaps now he thought her capable of
anything. She supposed that would be something worthy of his hope and
fear.

"I don't have the details. But, yes. The longer we wait, the more suspicious
it will look when Danat and the poet die."

"You still want Maati Vaupathai dead?" Daaya asked.

"Otah is locked away, and the poet's digging. Maati Vaupathai isn't satisfied to blame the upstart for everything, even if the whole city besides him is. There are three breathing men between Adrah and my father's chair. Danat, Otah, and the poet. I'll need armsmen, though, to do what I intend. How many could you put together? They would have to be men you trust."

Daaya looked at his son, as if expecting to find some answer there, but Adrah neither spoke nor moved. He might very nearly not have been there at all. Idaan swallowed her impatience and leaned forward, her palms spread on the cool stone of the table. One of the candles sputtered and spat.

"I know a man. A mercenary lord. He's done work for me before and kept quiet," Daaya said at last. He didn't seem certain.

"We'll free the upstart and slit the poet's throat," Idaan said. "There won't be any question who's actually done the thing. No sane person would doubt that it was Otah's hand. And when Danat rides out to find him, our men will be ready to ride with him. That will be the dangerous part. You'll have to find a way to get him apart from anyone else who goes."

"And the upstart?" Daaya asked.

"He'll go where we tell him to go. We'll just have saved him, after all. There will be no reason to think we mean him harm. They'll all be dead in time for the wedding, and if we do it well, the joy that is our bonding will put us as the clear favorites to take the chair. That should be enough to push the Galts into action. Adrah will be Khai before the harvest."

Idaan leaned back, smiling in grim satisfaction. It was Adrah who broke the silence, his voice calm and sure and unlike him.

"It won't work."

Idaan began to take a pose of challenge, but she hesitated when she saw his eyes. Adrah had gone cold as winter. It wasn't fear that drove him, whatever his father's weakness. There was something else in him, and Idaan felt a stirring of unease.

"I can't see why not," Idaan said, her voice still strong and sure.

"Killing the poet and freeing Otah would be simple enough to manage. But the other. No. It supposes that Danat would lead the hunt himself. He wouldn't. And if he doesn't, the whole thing falls apart. It won't work."

"I say that he would," Idaan said.

"And I say that your history planning these schemes isn't one that inspires confidence," Adrah said and stood. The candlelight caught his face at an angle, casting shadows across his eyes. Idaan rose, feeling the blood rushing into her face.

"I was the one who saved us when Oshai fell," she said. "You two were mewling like kittens, and crying despair—"

"That's enough," Adrah said.

"I don't recall you being in a position to order me when to speak and when to be silent."

Daaya coughed, looking from one to the other of them like a lamb caught between wolf and lion. The smile that touched Adrah's mouth was thin and unamused.

"Idaan-kya," Adrah said, "I am to be your husband and the Khai of this city. Sit with that. Your plan to free Oshai failed. Do you understand that? It *failed*. It lost us the support of our backers, it killed the man most effective in carrying out these unfortunate duties we've taken on, and it exposed me and my father to risk. You failed before, and this scheme you've put before us now would also fail if we did as you propose."

Adrah began to pace slowly, one hand brushing the hanging tapestries. Idaan shook her head, remembering some epic she'd seen when she was young. A performer in the role of Black Chaos had moved as Adrah moved now. Idaan felt her heart grow tight.

"It isn't that it's without merit—the shape of it generally is useful, but the specifics are wrong. If Danat is to grab what men he can find and rush out into the night, it can't be because he's off to avenge a poet. He would have to be possessed by some greater passion. And it would help if he were drunk, but I don't know that we can arrange that."

"So if not the Maati Vaupathai . . ." she began, and her throat closed.

Cehmai, she thought. He means to kill Cehmai and free the andat. Her hands balled into fists, her heart thudded as if she'd been sprinting. Adrah turned to face her, his arms folded, his expression calm as a butcher in the slaughterhouse.

"You said there were three breaths blocking us. There's a fourth. Your father."

No one spoke. When Idaan laughed, it sounded shrill and panicked in her own ears. She took a pose that rejected the suggestion.

"You've gone mad, Adrah-kya. You've lost all sense. My father is dying. He's dying, there's no call to . . ."

"What else would enrage Danat enough to let his caution slip? The upstart escapes. Your father is murdered. In the confusion, we come to him, a hunting party in hand, ready to ride with him. We can put it out today that we're planning to ride out before the end of the week. Fresh meat for the wedding feast, we'll say."

"It won't work," Idaan said, raising her chin.

"And why not?" Adrah replied.

"Because I won't let you!"

She spun and grabbed for the door. As she hauled it open, Adrah was around her, his arms pressing it shut again. Daaya was there too, his wide hands patting at her in placating gestures that filled her with rage. Her mind left her, and she shrieked and howled and wept. She clawed at them both and kicked and tried to bite her way free, but Adrah's arms locked around her, lifted her, tightened until she lost her breath and the room spun and grew darker.

She found herself sitting again without knowing when she'd been set down. Adrah was raising a cup to her lips. Strong, unwatered wine. She sipped it, then pushed it away.

"Have you calmed yourself yet?" Adrah asked. There was warmth in his voice again, as if she'd been sick and was only just recovering.

"You can't do it, Adrah-kya. He's an old man, and . . ."

Adrah let the silence stretch before he leaned toward her and wiped her lips with a soft cloth. She was trembling, and it annoyed her. Her body was supposed to be stronger than that.

"It will cost him a few days," Adrah said. "A few weeks at most. Idaan-kya, his murder is the thing that will draw your brother out if anything will. You said it to me, love. If we falter, we fail."

He smiled and caressed her cheek with back of his hand. Daaya was at the table, drinking wine of his own. Idaan looked into Adrah's dark eyes, and despite the smiles, despite the caresses, she saw the hardness there. I should have said no, she thought. When he asked if I had taken another lover, I shouldn't have danced around it. I should have said no.

She nodded.

"We can make it quick. Painless," Adrah said. "It will be a mercy, really. His life as it is now can hardly be worth living. Sick, weak. That's no way for a proud man to live."

She nodded again. Her father. The simple pleasure in his eyes.

"He wanted so much to see us wed," she murmured. "He wanted so much for me to be happy."

Adrah took a pose that offered sympathy, but she wasn't such a fool as to believe it. She rose shakily to her feet. They did not stop her.

"I should go," she said. "I'll be expected at the palaces. I expect there will be food and song until the sun comes up."

Daaya looked up. His smile was sickly, but Adrah took a pose of reassurance and the old man looked away again.

"I'm trusting you, Idaan-kya," Adrah said. "To let you go. It's because I trust you."

"It's because you can't lock me away without attracting attention. If I vanish, people will wonder why, and my brother not the least. We can't have that, can we? Everything must seem perfectly normal."

"It still might be wise, locking you away," Adrah said. He pretended to be joking, but she could see the debate going on behind his eyes. For a moment, her life spread out before her. The first wife of the Khai Machi, looking into these eyes. She had loved him once. She had to remember that. Idaan smiled, leaned forward, kissed his lips.

"I'm only sad," she said. "It will pass. I'll come and meet you tomorrow. We can plan what needs to be done."

Outside, the revelry had spread. Garlands arched above the streets. Choirs had assembled and their voices made the city chime like a struck bell. Joy and relief were everywhere, except in her. For most of the afternoon, she moved from feast to feast, celebration to celebration—always careful not to be touched or bumped, afraid she might break like a girl made from spun sugar. As the sun hovered three hands' widths above the mountains to the west, she found the face she had been longing for.

Cehmai and Stone-Made-Soft were in a glade, sitting with a dozen children of the utkhaiem. The little boys and girls were sitting on the grass, grinding green into their silk robes with knees and elbows, while three slaves performed with puppets and dolls. The players squealed and whistled and sang, the puppets hopped and tumbled, beat one another, and fled. The children laughed. Cehmai himself was stretched out like a child, and two adventurous girls were sitting in Stone-Made-Soft's wide lap, their arms around each other. The andat seemed mildly amused.

When Cehmai caught sight of her, he came over immediately. She smiled as she had been doing all day, took a greeting pose that her hands had shaped a hundred times since morning. He was the first one, she thought, to see through pose and smile both.

"What's happened?" he asked, stepping close. His eyes were as dark as Adrah's, but they were soft. They were young. There wasn't any hatred there yet, or any pain. Or perhaps she only wished that was true. Her smile faltered.

"Nothing," she said, and he took her hand. Here where they might be seen—where the children at least were sure to see them—he took her hand and she let him.

"What's happened?" he repeated, his voice lower and closer. She shook her head.

"My father is going to die," she said, her voice breaking on the words, her lips growing weak. "My father's going to die, and there's nothing I can do to help it. No way for me to stop it. And the only time crying makes me feel better is when I can do it with you. Isn't that strange?"

>+< Cehmai rode up the wide track, switchbacking up the side of the mountain. The ore chute ran straight from the mine halfway up the mountain's face to the carter's base at its foot. When the path turned toward it, Cehmai considered the broad beams and pillars that held the chute smooth and even down the rough mountainside. When they turned away, he looked south to where the towers of Machi stood like reeds in the noonday sun. His head ached.

"We do appreciate your coming, Cehmai-cha," the mine's engineer said again. "With the new Khai come home, we thought everyone would put business off for a few days."

Cehmai didn't bother taking a pose accepting the thanks as he had the first few times. Repetition had made it clear that the gratitude was less than wholly sincere. He only nodded and angled his horse around the next bend, swinging around to a view of the ore chute.

There were six of them; Cehmai and Stone-Made-Soft, the mine's engineer, the overseer with the diagrams and contracts in a leather satchel on his hip, and two servants to carry the water and food. Normally there would have been twice as many people. Cehmai wondered how many miners would be in the tunnels, then found he didn't particularly care, and returned to contemplating the ore chute and his headache.

They had left before dawn, trekking to the Raadani mines. It had been arranged weeks before, and business and money carried a momentum that even stone didn't. A landslide might overrun a city, but it only went down. Something had to have tremendous power to propel something as tired and heavy as he felt *up* the mountainside. Something in the back of his mind twitched at the thought—attention shifting of its own accord like an extra limb moving without his willing it.

"Stop," Cehmai snapped.

The overseer and engineer hesitated for a moment before Cehmai understood their confusion.

"Not you," he said and gestured to Stone-Made-Soft. "Him. He was judging what it would take to start a landslide."

"Only as an exercise," the andat said, its low voice sounding both hurt and insincere. "I wasn't going to do it."

The engineer looked up the slope with an expression that suggested Cehmai might not hear any more false thanks. Cehmai felt a spark of vindictive pleasure at the man's unease and saw Stone-Made-Soft's lips thin so slightly that no other man alive would have recognized the smile.

Idaan had spent the first night of the festival with him, weeping and laughing, taking comfort and coupling until they had both fallen asleep in the middle of their pillow talk. The night candle had hardly burned down a full quarter mark when the servant had come, tapping on his door to wake him. He'd risen for the trek to the mines, and Idaan—alone in his bed—had turned, wrapping his bedclothes about her naked body, and watched him as if afraid he would tell her to leave. By the time he had found fresh robes, her eyelids had closed again and her breath was deep and slow. He'd paused for a moment, considering her sleeping face. With the paint worn off and the calm of sleep, she looked younger. Her lips, barely parted, looked too soft to bruise his own, and her skin glowed like honey in sunlight.

But instead of slipping back into bed and sending out a servant for new apples, old cheese, and sugared almonds, he'd strapped on his boots and gone out to meet his obligations. His horse plodded along, flies buzzed about his face, and the path turned away from the ore chute and looked back toward the city.

There would be celebrations from now until Idaan's wedding to Adrah Vaunyogi. Between those two joys—the finished succession and the marriage of the high families—there would also be the preparations for the Khai Machi's final ceremony. And, despite everything Maati-kvo had done, likely the execution of Otah Machi in there as well. With as many rituals and ceremonies as the city faced, they'd be lucky to get any real work done before winter.

The yipping of the mine dogs brought him back to himself, and he realized he'd been half-dozing for the last few switchbacks. He rubbed his eyes with the heel of his palm. He would have to pull himself together when they began working in earnest. It would help, he told himself, to have some particular problem to set his mind to instead of the tedium of travel. Thankfully, Stone-Made-Soft wasn't resisting him today. The effort it would have taken to force the unwilling andat to do as it was told could have pushed the day from merely unpleasant to awful.

They reached the mouth of the mine and were greeted by several workers and minor functionaries. Cehmai dismounted and walked unsteadily to the wide table that had been set up for their consultations. His legs and back and head ached. When the drawings and notes were laid out before him, it took effort to turn his attention to them. His mind wandered off to Idaan or his own discomfort or the mental windstorm that was the andat.

"We would like to join these two passages," the overseer was saying, his fingers tracing lines on the maps. Cehmai had seen hundreds of sets of plans like this, and his mind picked up the markings and translated them into holes dug through the living rock of the mountain only slightly less easily than usual. "The vein seems richest here and then here. Our concern is—"

"My concern," the engineer broke in, "is not bringing half the mountain down on us while we do it."

The structure of tunnels that honeycombed the mountain wasn't the most complicated Cehmai had ever seen, but neither was it simple. The mines around Machi were capable of a complexity difficult in the rest of the world, mostly because he himself was not in the rest of the world, and mines in the Westlands and Galt weren't interested in paying the Khai Machi for his services. The engineer made his case—where the stone would support the tunnels and where it would not. The overseer made his counter-case—pointing out where the ores seemed richest. The decision was left to him.

The servants gave them bowls of honeyed beef and sausages that tasted of smoke and black pepper; a tart, sweet paste made from last year's berries; and salted flatbread. Cehmai ate and drank and looked at the maps and drawings. He kept remembering the curve of Idaan's mouth, the feeling of her hips against his own. He remembered her tears, her reticence. He would have sacrificed a good deal to better understand her sorrow.

It was more, he thought, than the struggle to face her father's mortality. Perhaps he should talk to Maati about it. He was older and had greater experience with women. Cehmai shook his head and forced himself to concentrate. It was half a hand before he saw a path through the stone that would yield a fair return and not collapse the works. Stone-Made-Soft neither approved nor dissented. It never did.

The overseer took a pose of gratitude and approval, then folded up the maps. The engineer sucked his teeth, craning his neck as the diagrams and notes vanished into the overseer's satchel, as if hoping to see one last objection, but then he too took an approving pose. They lit the lanterns and turned to the wide, black wound in the mountain's side.

The tunnels were cool, and darker than night. The smell of rock dust made the air thick. As he'd guessed, there were few men working, and the sounds of their songs and the barking of their dogs only made the darkness seem more isolating. They talked very little as they wound their way through the maze. Usually Cehmai made a practice of keeping a mental map, tracking their progress through the dark passages. After the second unexpected intersection, he gave up and was content to let the overseer lead them.

Unlike the mines on the plain, even the deepest tunnels here were dry. When they reached the point Cehmai had chosen, they took out the maps one last time, consulting them in the narrow section of the passageway that the lanterns lit. Above them, the mountain felt bigger than the sky.

"Don't make it too soft," the engineer said.

"It doesn't bear any load," the overseer said. "Gods! Who's been telling you ghost stories? You're nervous as a puppy first time down the hole."

Cehmai ignored them, looked up, considering the stone above him as if he could see through it. He wanted a path wide as two men walking with their arms outstretched. And it would need to go forward from here and then tilt to the left and then up. Cehmai pictured the distances as if he would walk them. It was about as far from where he was now to the turning point as from the rose pavilion to the library. And then, the shorter leg would be no longer than the walk from the library to Maati's apartments. He turned his mind to it, pressed the whirlwind, applied it to the stone before him, slowly, carefully loosening the stone in the path he had imagined. Stone-Made-Soft resisted—not in the body that scowled now looking at the tunnel's blank side, but in their shared mind. The andat shifted and writhed and pushed, though not so badly as it might have. Cehmai reached the turning point, shifted his attention and began the shorter, upward movement.

The storm's energy turned and leapt ahead, spreading like spilled water, pushing its influence out of the channel Cehmai's intention had prepared. Cehmai gritted his teeth with the effort of pulling it back in before the structure above them weakened and failed. The andat pressed again, trying to pull the mountain down on top of them. Cehmai felt a rivulet of sweat run down past his ear. The overseer and the engineer were speaking someplace a long way off, but he couldn't be bothered by them. They were idiots to distract him. He paused and gathered the storm, concentrated on the ideas and grammars that had tied the andat to him in the first place, that had held it for generations. And when it had been brought to heel, he took it the rest of the way through his pathway and then slowly, carefully, brought his mind, and its, back to where they stood.

"Cehmai-cha?" the overseer asked again. The engineer was eyeing the walls as if they might start speaking with him.

"I'm done," he said. "It's fine. I only have a headache."

Stone-Made-Soft smiled placidly. Neither of them would tell the men how near they had all just come to dying: Cehmai, because he wished to keep it from them, Stone-Made-Soft, because it would never occur to it to care.

The overseer took a hand pick from his satchel and struck the wall. The metal head chimed and a white mark appeared on the stone. Cehmai waved his hand.

"To your left," he said. "There."

The overseer struck again, and the pick sank deep into the stone with a sound like a footstep on gravel.

"Excellent," the overseer said. "Perfect."

Even the engineer seemed grudgingly pleased. Cehmai only wanted to get out, into the light and back to the city and his own bed. Even if they left now, they wouldn't reach Machi before nightfall. Probably not before the night candle hit its half mark.

On the way back up, the engineer started telling jokes. Cehmai allowed himself to smile. There was no call to make things unpleasant even if the pain in his head and spine were echoing his heartbeats.

When they reached the light and fresh air, the servants had laid out a more satisfying meal—rice, fresh chickens killed here at the mine, roasted nuts with lemon, cheeses melted until they could be spread over their bread with a blade. Cehmai lowered himself into a chair of strung cloth and sighed with relief. To the south, they could see the smoke of the forges rising from Machi and blowing off to the east. A city perpetually afire.

"When we get there," Cehmai said to the andat, "we'll be playing several games of stones. You'll be the one losing."

The andat shrugged almost imperceptibly.

"It's what I am," it said. "You may as well blame water for being wet."

"And when it soaks my robes, I do," Cehmai said. The andat chuckled and then was silent. Its wide face turned to him with something like concern. Its brow was furrowed.

"The girl," it said.

"What about her?"

"It seems to me the next time she asks if you love her, you could say yes."

Cehmai felt his heart jump in his chest, startled as a bird. The andat's expression didn't change; it might have been carved from stone. Idaan wept in his memory, and she laughed, and she curled herself in his bedclothes and asked silently not to be sent away. Love, he discovered, could feel very much like sorrow.

"I suppose you're right," he said, and the andat smiled in what looked like sympathy.

Maati laid his notes out on the wide table at the back of the library's main chamber. The distant throbbing of trumpet and drum wasn't so distracting here as in his rooms. Three times on the walk here, his sleeves heavy with paper and books, he'd been grabbed by some masked reveler and kissed. Twice, bowls of sweet wine had been forced into his hand. The palaces were a riot of dancing and song, and despite his best intentions, the memory of those three kisses drew his attention. It would be sweet to go out, to lose himself in that crowd, to find some woman willing to dance with him, and to take comfort in her body and her breath. It had been years since he had let himself be so young as that.

He turned himself to his puzzle. Danat, the man destined to be Khai Machi, had seemed the most likely to have engineered the rumors of Otah's return. Certainly he had gained the most. Kaiin Machi, whose death had already given Maati three kisses, was the other possibility. Until he dug in. He had asked the servants and the slaves of each household every question he could think of. No, none of them recalled any consultations with a man who matched the assassin's description. No, neither man had sent word or instruction since Maati's own arrival. He'd asked their social enemies what they knew or guessed or speculated on.

Kaiin Machi had been a weak-lunged man, pale of face and watery of eye. He'd had a penchant for sleeping with servant girls, but hadn't even gotten a child on one—likely because he was infertile. Danat was a bully and a sneak, a man whose oaths meant nothing to him—and the killing of noble, scholarly Kaiin showed that. Danat's triumph was the best of all possible outcomes or else the worst.

Searching for conspiracy in court gossip was like looking for raindrops in a thunderstorm. Everyone he spoke to seemed to have four or five suggestions of what might have happened, and of those, each half contradicted the other. By far, the most common assumption was that Otah had been the essential villain in all of it.

Maati had diagrammed the relationships of Danat and Kaiin with each of the high families—Kamau, Daikani, Radaani and a dozen more. Then with the great trading houses, with mistresses and rumored mistresses and the teahouses they liked best. At one point he'd even listed which horses each preferred to ride. The sad truth was that despite all these facts, all these words scribbled onto papers, referenced and checked, nothing pointed to either man as the author of Biitrah's death, the attempt on Maati's own life, or the slaughter of the assassin. He was either too dimwitted to see the pattern before him, it was too well hidden, or he was looking in the wrong place. Clearly neither man had been present in the city to direct the last two attacks, and there seemed to be no supporters in Machi who had managed the plans for them.

Nor was there any reason to attack *him*. Maati had been on the verge of exposing Otah-kvo. That was in everyone's best interest, barring Otah's. Maati closed his eyes, sighed, then opened them again, gathered up the pages of his notes and laid them out again, as if seeing them in a different pattern might spark something.

Drunken song burst from the side room to his left, and Baarath, librarian of Machi, stumbled in, grinning. His face was flushed, and he smelled of wine and something stronger. He threw open his arms and strode unevenly to Maati, embracing him like a brother.

"No one has ever loved these books as you and I have, Maati-kya," Baarath said. "The most glorious party of a generation. Wine flowing in the gutters, and food and dancing, and I'll jump off a tower if we don't see a crop of babes next spring that look nothing like their fathers. And where do we go, you and I? Here."

Baarath turned and made a sweeping gesture that took in the books and scrolls and codices, the shelves and alcoves and chests. He shook his head and seemed for a moment on the verge of tears. Maati patted him on the back and led him to a wooden bench at the side of the room. Baarath sat back, his head against the stone, and smiled like a baby.

"I'm not as drunk as I look," Baarath said.

"I'm sure you aren't," Maati agreed.

Baarath pounded the board beside him and gestured for Maati to sit. There was no graceful way to refuse, and at the moment, he could think of no reason. Going back to stand, frustrated, over the table had no appeal. He sat.

"What is bothering you, Maati-kya? You're still searching for some way to keep the upstart alive?"

"Is that an option? I don't see Danat-cha letting him walk free. No, I suppose I'm just hoping to see him killed for the right reasons. Except . . . I don't know. I can't find anyone else with reason to do the things that have been done."

"Perhaps there's more than one thing going on then?" Baarath suggested.

Maati took a pose of surrender.

"I can't comprehend one. The gods will have to lead me by the hand if there's two. Can you think of any other reason to kill Biitrah? The man seems to have moved through the world without making an enemy."

"He was the best of us," Baarath agreed and wiped his eyes with the end of his sleeve. "He was a good man."

"So it had to be one of his brothers. Gods, I wish the assassin hadn't been killed. He could have told us if there was a connection between Biitrah and what happened to me. Then at least I'd know if I were solving one puzzle or two."

"Doesn't have to," Baarath said.

Maati took a pose that asked for clarification. Baarath rolled his eyes and took on an expression of superiority that Maati had seen beneath his politeness for weeks now.

"It doesn't *have* to be one of his brothers," Baarath said. "You say it's not the upstart. Fine, that's what you choose. But then you say you can't find anything that Danat or Kaiin's done that makes you think they've done it. And why would they hide it, anyway? It's not shameful for them to kill their brother."

"But no one else has a reason," Maati said.

"No one? Or only no one you've found?"

"If it isn't about the succession, I can't find any call to kill Biitrah. If it isn't about my search for Otah, I can't think of any reason to want me dead. The only killing that makes sense at all was poking the assassin full of holes, and that only because he might have answered my questions."

"Why couldn't it have been the succession?"

Maati snorted. It was difficult being friendly with Baarath when he was sober. Now, with him half-maudlin, half-contemptuous, and reeking of wine, it was worse. Maati's frustration peaked, and his voice, when he spoke, was louder and angrier than he'd intended.

"Because Otah *didn't*, and Kaiin *didn't*, and Danat *didn't*, and there's no one else who's looking to sit on the chair. Is there some fifth brother I haven't been told about?"

Baarath raised his hands in a pose of a tutor posing an instructive question to a pupil. The effect was undercut by the slight weaving of his hands.

"What would happen if all three brothers died?"

"Otah would be Khai."

"Four. I meant four. What if they all die? What if none of them takes the chair?"

"The utkhaiem would fight over it like very polite pit dogs, and whichever one ended with the most blood on its muzzle would be elevated as the new Khai."

"So someone else might benefit from this yet, you see? They would have to hide it because having slaughtered the whole family of the previous Khai wouldn't help their family prestige, seeing as all their heads would be hanging from poles. But it would be about your precious succession, and there would be someone besides the three . . . four brothers with reason to do the thing."

"Except that Danat's alive and about to be named Khai Machi, it's a pretty story."

Baarath sneered and made a grand gesture at the world in general.

"What is there but pretty stories? What is history but the accumulation of plausible speculation and successful lies? You're a scholar, Maati-kya, you should enjoy them more."

Baarath chuckled drunkenly, and Maati rose to his feet. Outside, something cracked with a report like a stone slab broken or a roof tile dropped from a great height. A moment later, laughter followed it. Maati leaned against the table, his arms folded and each hand tucked into the opposite sleeve. Baarath shifted, lay back on the bench, and sighed.

"You don't think it's true," Maati said. "You don't think it's one of the high families plotting to be Khai."

"Of course not," Baarath said. "It's an idiot plan. If you were to start something like that, you'd need to be certain you'd win it, and that would take more money and influence than any one family could gather. Even the Radaani don't have that much gold, and they've got more than the Khai."

"Then you think I'm chasing mist," Maati said.

"I think the upstart is behind all of it, and that you're too much in awe of him to see it. Everyone knows he was your teacher when you were a boy. You still think he's twice what you are. Who knows, maybe he is."

His anger gave Maati the illusion of calm, and a steadiness to his voice. He took a pose of correction.

"That was rude, Baarath-cha. I'd thank you not to say it again."

"Oh, don't be ashamed of it," Baarath said. "There are any number of boys who have those sorts of little infatuations with—"

Maati's body lifted itself, sliding with an elegance and grace he didn't know he posessed. His palm moved out by its own accord and slapped Baarath's jaw hard enough to snap the man's head to the side. He put a hand on Baarath's chest, pinning him firmly to the bench. Baarath yelped in surprise and Maati saw the shock and fear in his face. Maati kept his voice calm.

"We aren't friends. Let's not be enemies. It would distract me, and you may have perfect faith that it would destroy you. I am here on the Dai-kvo's work, and no matter who becomes Khai Machi, he'll have need of the poets. Standing beside that, one too-clever librarian can't count for much."

Outrage shone in Baarath's eyes as he pushed Maati's hand away. Maati stepped back, allowing him to rise. The librarian pulled his disarrayed robes back into place, his features darkening. Maati's rage began to falter, but he kept his chin held high.

"You're a bully, Maati-cha," Baarath said, then he took a pose of farewell and marched proudly out of the library. His library. Maati heard the door slam closed and felt himself deflate.

It galled him, but he knew he would have to apologize later. He should never have struck the man. If he had borne the insults and insinuations, he could have forced contrition from Baarath, but he hadn't.

He looked at his scattered notes. Perhaps he was a bully. Perhaps there was nothing to be found in all this. After all, Otah would die regardless. Danat would take his father's place, and Maati would go back to the Dai-kvo. He would even be able to claim a measure of success. Otah was starving to death in the high air above Machi thanks to him, after all. And what was that if not victory? One small mystery left unsolved could hardly matter in the end.

He pulled his papers together, stacking them, folding them, tucking the packet away into his sleeve. There was nothing to be done here. He was tired and frustrated, ashamed of himself and in despair. There was a city of wine and distraction that would welcome him with open arms and delighted smiles.

He remembered Heshai-kvo—the poet of Saraykeht, the controller of Removing-The-Part-That-Continues who they'd called Seedless. He remembered his teacher's pilgrimages to the soft quarter with its drugs and gambling, its wine and whores. Heshai had felt this, or something like it; Maati knew he had.

He pulled the brown leather-bound book from his sleeve, where it always waited. He opened it and read Heshai's careful, beautiful handwriting. The chronicle and examination of his errors in binding the andat. He recalled Seedless' last words. *He's forgiven you.*

Maati turned back, his limbs heavy with exhaustion and dread. He put the book back into his sleeve and pulled out his notes. He rearranged them on the table. He began again, and the night stretched out endlessly before him.

THE PALACES WERE DRUNKEN AND DIZZY AND LOST IN THE RELIEF THAT COMES when a people believe that the worst is over. It was a celebration of fratricide, but of all the dancers, the drinkers, the declaimers of small verse, only Idaan seemed to remember that fact. She played her part, of course. She appeared in all the circles of which she had been part back before she'd entered this darkness. She drank wine and tea, she accepted the congratulations of the high families on her joining with the house of Vaunyogi. She blushed at the ribald comments made about her and Adrah, or else replied with lewder quips.

She played the part. The only sign was that she was more elaborate when she painted her face. Even if people noticed, what would they think but that the colors on her eyelids and the plum-dark rouge on her lips were a part of her celebration. Only she knew how badly she needed the mask.

The night candle was just past its middle mark when they broke away, she and Adrah with their arms around each other as if they were lovers. No one they saw had any question what they were planning, and no one would object. Half of the city had paired off already and slunk away to find an empty bed. It was the night for it. They laughed and stumbled toward the high palaces—her father's.

Once, when they were hidden behind a high row of hedges and it wasn't a performance for anyone, Adrah kissed her. He smelled of wine and the warm, musky scent of a young man's skin. Idaan kissed him back, and for that moment—that long silent, sensual moment—she meant it. Then he pulled away and smiled, and she hated him again.

The celebrations in the halls and galleries of the Khai's palace were the nearest to exhaustion—everyone from the highest family of the utkhaiem to the lowest firekeeper had dressed in their finest robes and set out to stain them with something. The days of revelry had taken their toll, and with the night half-passed, the wildest celebrations were over. Music and song still played, people still danced and talked, drew one another away into alcoves and corners. Old men talked gravely of who would benefit from Danat's survival and promotion. But the sense was growing that the time was drawing near when the city would catch its breath and rest a while.

She and Adrah made their way through to the private wings of the palace, where only servants and slaves and the wives of the Khai moved freely. They made no secret of their presence. There was no need. Idaan led the way up a series of wide, sweeping staircases to apartments on the south side of the palace. A servant—an old man with gray hair, a limp, and a rosy smile—greeted them, and Idaan instructed him that they were not to be disturbed for any reason. The old man took a solemn expression and a pose of acknowledgment, but there was merriment in his eyes. Idaan let him believe what she, after all, intended him to. Adrah opened the great wooden doors, and he also closed them behind her.

"They aren't the best rooms, are they?" Adrah said.

"They'll do," Idaan said, and went to the windows. She pulled open the shutters. The great tower, Otah Machi's prison, stood like a dark line inked in the air. Adrah moved to stand beside her.

"One of us should have gone with them," she said. "If the upstart's found safely in his cell come morning . . ."

"He won't be," Adrah said. "Father's mercenaries are competent men. He wouldn't have hired them for this if he hadn't been sure of them."

"I don't like using hired men," Idaan said. "If we can buy them, so can any-one."

"They're armsmen, not whores," Adrah said. "They've taken a contract, and they'll see it through. It's how they survive."

There were five lanterns, from small glass candleboxes to an oil lamp with a wick as wide as her thumb and heavy enough to require both of them to move it. They pulled them all as near the open window as they could, and Adrah lit them while Idaan pulled the thin silks from under her robes. The richest dyes in the world had given these their color—one blue, the other red. Idaan hung the blue over the window's frame, and then peered out, squinting into the night for the signal. And there, perhaps half a hand from the top of the tower, shone the answering light. Idaan turned away.

With all the light gathered at the window, the rooms were cast into dark-ness. Adrah had pulled a hooded cloak over his robes. Idaan remembered again the feeling of hanging over the void, feeling the wind tugging at her. This wasn't so different, except that the prospect of her own death had seemed somehow cleaner.

"He would want it," Idaan said. "If he knew that we'd planned this, he would allow it. You know that."

"Yes, Idaan-kya. I know."

"To live so weak. It disgraces him. It makes him seem less before the court. It's not a fit ending for a Khai."

Adrah drew a thin, blackened blade. It looked no wider than a finger, and not much longer. Adrah sighed and squared his shoulders. Idaan felt her stom-ach rise to her throat.

"I want to go with you," she said.

"We discussed this, Idaan-kya. You stay in case someone comes. You have to convince them that I'm still in here with you."

"They won't come. They've no reason to. And he's my father."

"More reason that you should stay."

Idaan moved to him, touching his arm like a beggar asking alms. She felt herself shaking and loathed the weakness, but she could not stop it. Adrah's eyes were as still and empty as pebbles. She remembered Danat, how he had looked when he arrived from the south. She had thought he was ill, but it had been this. He had become a killer, a murderer of the people he had once respected and loved. That he still respected and loved. Adrah had those eyes now, the look of near-nausea. He smiled, and she saw the determination. There were no words that would stop him now. The stone had been dropped, and not all the wishing in the world could call it back into her hand.

"I love you, Idaan-kya," Adrah said, his voice as cool as a gravestone. "I have always loved you. From the first time I kissed you. Even when you have hurt me, and you have hurt me worse than anyone alive, I have only ever loved you."

He was lying. He was saying it as she'd said that her father would welcome death, because he needed it to be true. And she found that she needed that as well. She stepped back and took a pose of gratitude. Adrah walked to the door, turned, nodded to her, and was gone. Idaan sat in the darkness and looked at nothing, her arms wrapped around herself. The night seemed unreal: absurd and undeniable at the same time, a terrible dream from which she might wake to find herself whole again. The weight of it was like a hand pressing down on her head.

There was time. She could call for armsmen. She could call for Danat. She could go and stop the blade with her own body. She sat silent, trying not to breathe. She remembered the ceremony of her tenth summer, the year after her mother's death. Her father had taken her to sit at his side during all that day's ritual. She had hated it, bored by the petitions and formality until tears ran down her cheeks. She remembered a meal with a representative from some Westlands warden where her father had forced her to sit on a hard wooden chair and swallow a cold bean soup that made her gag rather than seem ungracious to the Westlander for his food.

She fought to remember a smile, an embrace. She wanted a moment in the long years of her childhood to which she could point and say *here is how I know he loved me*. The blue silk stirred in the breeze. The lantern flames flickered, dimmed, and rose again. It must have happened. For him to be so desperate for her happiness now, there must have been some sign, some indication.

She found herself rocking rapidly back and forth. When a sound came from the door, she jumped up, panicked, looking around for some excuse to explain Adrah's absence. When he himself came in, she could see in his eyes that it was over.

Adrah pulled off the cloak, letting it pool around his ankles. His bright robes seemed incongruous as a butterfly in a butcher's shop. His face was stone.

"You've done it," Idaan said, and two full breaths later, he nodded. Something as much release as despair sank into her. She could feel her body made heavy by it.

She walked to him, pulled the blade and its soft black leather sheath from his belt, and let them drop to the floor. Adrah didn't try to stop her.

"Nothing we ever do will be so bad as this," she said. "This now is the worst it will ever be. Everything will be better than this."

"He never woke," Adrah said. "The drugs that let him sleep . . . He never woke."

"That's good."

A slow, mad grin bloomed on his face, stretching until the blood left his lips. There was a hardness in his eyes and a heat. It looked like fury or possession. He took her shoulders in his hands and pulled her near him. Their kiss was a gentle violence. For a moment, she thought he meant to open her robes, to drag her back to the bed in a sad parody of what they were expected to be doing. She pressed a palm to his sex and was surprised to find that he was not aroused. Slowly, with perfect control and a grip that bruised her, Adrah brought her away from him.

"I did this thing for you," he said. "I did this for *you*. Do you understand that?"

"I do."

"Never ask me for anything again," he said and released her, turning away. "From now until you die, you are in debt to me, and I owe you nothing."

"For the favor of killing my father?" she asked, unable to keep the edge from her voice.

"For what I have sacrificed to you," he said without looking back. Idaan felt her face flush, her hands ball into fists. She heard him groan from the next room, heard his robes shushing against the stone floor. The bed creaked.

A lifetime, married to him. There wouldn't be a moment in the years that followed that would not be poisoned. He would never forgive her, and she would never fail to hate him. They would go to their graves, each with teeth sunk in the other's neck.

They were perfect for each other.

Idaan walked silently to the window, took down the blue silk and put up the red.

THE ARMSMEN GAVE HIM ENOUGH WATER TO LIVE, THOUGH NOT SO MUCH AS TO slake his thirst. Almost enough food to live as well, though not quite. He had no clothing but the rags he'd worn when he'd come back to Machi and the cloak that Maati had brought. When dawn was coming near and the previous day's heat had gone from the tower, he would be huddling in that cloth. Through the day, sun heated the great tower, and that heat rose. And as it rose, it grew. In his stone cage, Otah lay sweating as if he'd been working at hard labor, his throat dry and his head pounding.

The towers of Machi, Otah had decided, were the stupidest buildings in the world. Too cold in winter, too hot in summer, unpleasant to use, exhausting to climb. They existed only to show that they could exist.

More and more of the time, his mind was in disarray; hunger and boredom, the stifling heat and the growing presentiment of his own death conspired to change the nature of time. Otah felt outside it all, apart from the world and adrift. He had always been in this room; the memories from before were like stories he'd heard told. He would always be in this room unless he wriggled out the window and into the cool, open air. Twice already he had dreamed that he'd leapt from the tower. Both times, he woke in a panic. It was that as much as anything that kept him from taking the one control left to him. When despair washed through him, he remembered the dream of falling, with its shrill regret. He didn't want to die. His ribs were showing, he was almost nauseated with thirst, his mind would not slow down or be quiet. He was going to be put to death, and he did not want to die.

The thought that his suffering saved Kiyan had ceased to comfort him. Part of him was glad that he had not known how wretched his father's treatment of him would be. He might have faltered. At least now he could not run. He would lose—he had lost, and badly—but he could not run. Maj sat on her chair—the tall, thin one with legs of woven cane that she'd had in their island hut. When she spoke, it was in the soft liquid sounds of her native language and too fast for Otah to follow. He struggled, but when he croaked out that he couldn't understand her, his own voice woke him until he drifted away again into nothing, troubled only by the conviction that he could hear rats chewing through the stone.

The shriek woke him completely. He sat upright, his arms trembling. The room was real again, unoccupied by visions. Outside the great door, he heard someone shout, and then something heavy pounded once against the door, shaking it visibly. Otah rose. There were voices—new ones. After so many days, he knew the armsmen by their rhythms and the timbre of their murmurs. The throats that made the sounds he heard now were unfamiliar. He walked to the door and leaned against it, pressing his ear to the hairline crack between the wood and its stone frame. One voice rose above the others, its tone commanding. Otah made out the word "chains."

The voices went away again for so long Otah began to suspect he'd imagined it all. The scrape of the bar being lifted from the door startled him. He stepped back, fear and relief coming together in his heart. This might be the end. He knew his brother had returned; this could be his death come for him. But at least it was an end to his time in this cell. He tried to hold himself with some dignity as the door swung open. The torches were so bright that Otah could hardly see.

"Good evening, Otah-cha," a man's voice said. "I hope you're well enough to move. I'm afraid we're in a bit of a hurry."

"Who are you?" Otah asked. His own voice sounded rough. Squinting, he could make out perhaps ten men in black leather armor. They had blades drawn. The armsmen lay in a pile against the far wall, stacked like goods in a warehouse, a black pool of blood surrounding them. The smell of them wasn't rotten, not yet, but it was disturbing—coppery and intimate. They had only been dead for minutes. If all of them were dead.

"We're the men who've come to take you out of here," the commander said. He was the one actually standing in the doorway. He had the long face of a man of the winter cities, but a westlander's flowing hair. Otah moved forward and took a pose of gratitude that seemed to amuse him.

"Can you walk?" he asked as Otah came out into the larger room. The signs of struggle were everywhere—spilled wine, overturned chairs, blood on the walls. The armsmen had been taken by surprise. Otah put a hand against the wall to steady himself. The stone felt warm as flesh.

"I'll do what I have to," Otah said.

"That's admirable," the commander said, "but I'm more curious about what you *can* do. I've suffered long confinement myself a time or two, and I know what it does. We can't take the easy way down. We've got to walk. If you can do this, that's all to the good. If you can't, we're prepared to carry you, but I need to have you out of the city quickly."

"I don't understand. Did Maati send you?"

"There's better places to discuss this, Otah-cha. We can't go down by the chains. Even if there weren't more armsmen waiting there, we've just broken them. Can you walk down the tower?"

A memory of the endlessly turning stairs and the ghost of pain in his knees and legs. Otah felt a stab of shame, but pulled himself up and shook his head.

"I don't believe I can," he said. The commander nodded and two of his men pulled lengths of wood from their backs and fitted them together in a cripple's litter. There was a small seat for Otah, canted against the slope of the stairway, and the poles were set one longer than the other to fit the tight curve. It would have been useless in any other situation, but for this task it was perfect. As one of the men helped Otah take his place on it, he wondered if the device had been built for this moment, or if things like it existed in service of these towers. The largest of the men spat on his hands and gripped the carrying poles that would start down the stairs and bear most of Otah's weight. One of his fellows took the other end, and Otah lurched up.

They began their descent, Otah with his back to the center of the spiral staircase. He watched the stone of the wall curl up from below. The men grunted and cursed, but they moved quickly. The man on the higher poles stumbled once, and the one below shouted angrily back at him.

The journey seemed to last forever—stone and darkness, the smell of sweat and lantern oil. Otah's knees bumped against the wall before him, his head against the wall behind. When they reached the halfway point, another huge man was waiting to take over the worst of the carrying. Otah felt his shame return. He tried to protest, but the commander put a strong, hard hand on his shoulder and kept him in the chair.

"You chose right the first time," the commander said.

The second half of the journey down was less terrible. Otah's mind was beginning to clear, and a savage hope was lifting him. He was being saved. He couldn't think who or why, but he was delivered from his cell. He thought of the armsmen new-slaughtered at the tower's height, and recalled Kiyan's words. *How do you expect to protect me and my house?* They could all be killed, his jailers and his rescuers alike. All in the name of tradition.

He could tell when they reached the level of the street—the walls had grown so thick there was almost no room for them to walk, but thin windows showed glimmers of light, and drunken, disjointed music filled the air. At the base of the stair, his carriers lowered Otah to the ground and took his arms over their shoulders as if he were drunk or sick. The commander squeezed to the front of the party. Despite his frown, Otah sensed the man was enjoying himself immensely.

They moved quickly and quietly through maze-like passages and out at last into an alley at the foot of the tower. A covered cart was waiting, two horses whickering restlessly. The commander made a sign, and the two bearers lifted Otah into the back of the cart. The commander and two of the men climbed in after, and the driver started the horses. Shod hooves rapped the stone, and the cart lurched and bumped. The commander pulled the back cloth closed and tied it, but loose enough he could peer out the seam. The lantern was extinguished, and the scent of its dying smoke filled the cart for a moment and was gone.

"What's happening out there?" Otah asked.

"Nothing," the commander said. "And best we keep it that way. No talking."

In silence and darkness, they continued. Otah felt lightheaded. The cart turned twice to the left and then again to the right. The driver was hailed and replied, but they never stopped. A breeze fluttered the thick cloth of the cover, and when it paused, Otah heard the sound of water; they were on the bridge heading south. He was free. He grinned, and then as the implications of his freedom unfolded themselves in his mind, his relief faltered.

"Forgive me. I don't know your name. I'm sorry. I can't do this."

The commander shifted. It was nearly black in the cart, so Otah couldn't see the man's face, but he imagined incredulity on the long features.

"I went to Machi to protect someone—a woman. If I vanish, they'll still have reason to suspect her. My brother might kill her on the chance that she's involved with this. I can't let that happen. I'm sorry, but we have to turn back."

"You love her that much?" the commander asked.

"This isn't her fault. It's mine."

"All this is your fault, eh? You have a lot to answer for." There was amusement in the man's voice. Otah felt himself smile.

"Well, perhaps not all my fault. But I can't let her be hurt. This is the price of it, and I'll pay it if I have to."

They were all silent for a long moment, then the commander sighed.

"You're an honorable man, Otah Machi. I want you to know I respect that. Boys. Chain him and gag him. I don't want him calling out."

They were on him in an instant, pushing him hard onto the rough wood of the cart. Someone's knee drove in between his shoulder blades; invisible hands bent his arms backwards. When he opened his mouth to scream, a wad of heavy cloth was shoved in so deeply he gagged. A leather strap followed, keeping it in place. He didn't know when his legs were bound, but in fewer than twenty breaths, he was immobile—his arms chained painfully behind him at his wrists and elbows, his mouth stuffed until it was hard to breathe. The knee moved to the small of his back, digging into his spine with every shift of the cart. He tried once to move, and the pressure from above increased. He tried again, and the man cursed him and rapped his head with something hard.

"I said no talking," the commander murmured, and returned to peering out the opening in the back cloth. Otah shifted, snarling in impotent rage that none of these men seemed to see or recognize. The cart moved off through the night. He could feel it when they moved from the paving of the main road to a dirt track; he could hear the high grass hushing against the wheels. They were taking him nowhere, and he couldn't think why.

He guessed it was almost three hands before the first light started to come. Dawn was still nothing more than a lighter kind of darkness, the commander's feet—the only part of the man Otah could see without lifting his head—were a dim form of shadow within shadow. It was something. Otah heard the trill of a daymartin, and then a rough rattling and the sound of water. A bridge over some small river. When the cart lurched back to ground, the commander turned.

"Have him stop," he said, and then a moment later, "I said stop the cart. Do it."

One of the other two—the one who wasn't kneeling on Otah—shifted and spoke to the driver. The jouncing slowed and stopped.

"I thought I heard something out there. In the trees on the left. Baat. Go check. If you see anything at all get back fast."

The pressure on Otah's back eased and one of the men clambered out. Otah turned over and no one tried to stop him. There was more light now. He could make out the grim set of the commander's features, the unease in the one remaining armsman.

"Well, this is interesting," the commander said.

"What's out there," the other man asked, his blade drawn. The commander looked out the slit of cloth and motioned for the armsman to pass over his sword. He did, and the commander took it, holding it with the ease of long familiarity.

"It may be nothing," he said. "Were you with me when I was working for the Warden of Elleais?"

"I'd just signed on then," the armsman said.

"You've always been a good fighter, Lachmi. I want you to know I respect that."

With the speed of a snake, the commander's wrist flickered, and the armsman fell back in the cart, blood flowing from his opened neck. Otah tried to push himself away as the commander turned and drove the sword into the armsman's chest. He dropped the blade then, letting it fall to the cart's floor, and took a pose of regret to the dying man.

"But," the commander said, "you should never have cheated me at tiles. *That* was stupid."

The commander stepped over the body and spoke to the driver. He spoke clearly enough for Otah to hear.

"Is it done?"

The driver said something.

"Good," the commander replied, and came back. He flipped Otah onto his belly with casual disregard, and Otah felt his bonds begin to loosen.

"All apologies, Otah-cha," the commander said. "But there's a lesson you can take from all this: just because someone's bought a mercenary captain, it doesn't mean his commanders aren't still for sale. Now I will need your robes, such as they are."

Otah pulled the leather strap from around his head and spat out the cloth, retching as he did so. Before he could speak, the commander had climbed out of the cart, and Otah was left to follow.

They had stopped at a clearing by a river, surrounded by white oaks. The bridge was old wood and looked almost too decrepit to cross. Six men with gray robes and hunting bows were walking toward them from the trees, two of them dragging the arrow-riddled body of the armsman the commander had sent out. Two others carried a litter with what was clearly another dead man— thin and naked. The commander took a pose of welcome, and the first archer returned it. Otah stumbled forward, rubbing his wrists. The archers were all smiling, pleased with themselves. When he came close enough, Otah saw the second corpse was on its back, and a wide swath of intricate black ink stained its breast. The first half of an east island marriage mark. A tattoo like his own.

"That's why we'll need your robes, Otah-cha," the commander said. "This poor bastard will have been in the water for a while before he reaches the main channel of the river. But the closer he seems to you, the less people will bother looking at him. I'll see whether I can find something for you to wear after, but you might consider sponging off in the brook there first. No offense, but you've been a while without a bath."

"Who is he?" Otah asked.

The commander shrugged.

"Nobody, now."

He clapped Otah on the shoulder and turned back toward the cart. The archers were pitching the corpses of the two armsmen into the water. Otah saw arrows rising from the river like reeds. The driver was coming forward now, his thumbs stuck in his belt. He was a hairy man, his full beard streaked with gray. He smiled at Otah and took a pose of welcome.

"I don't understand," Otah said. "What's happening?"

"We don't understand either, Itani-cha. Not precisely. We're only sure that it's something terrible," the carter said, and Otah's mouth dropped open. He spoke with the voice of Amiit Foss, his overseer in House Siyanti. Amiit grinned beneath his beard. "And we're sure that it isn't happening to you."

9

>+< The first few breaths after she woke were like rising new born. She didn't know who or where she was, she had no thought of the night before or the day ahead. There was only sensation—the warmth of the body beside her, the crisp softness of the bedclothes, the netting above the bed glowing in the captured light of dawn, the scent of black tea brought in by a servant with cat-quiet footsteps. She sat up, almost smiling until memory rushed in on her like a flood of black water. Idaan rose and pulled on her robes. Adrah stirred and moaned.

"You should go," she said, lifting the black iron teapot. "You're expected to go on a hunt today."

Adrah sat up, scratching his back and yawning. His hair stuck out in all directions. He looked older than he had the day before, or perhaps it was only how she felt. She poured a bowl of tea for him as well.

"Have they found him?" Adrah asked.

"I haven't heard the screams or lamentations yet, so I'd assume not."

She held out the porcelain bowl. It was thin enough to see through and hot enough to burn her fingertips, but Idaan didn't try to reduce the pain. When

Adrah took it from her, he drank from it straight, though she knew it must have scalded. Perhaps what they'd done had numbed them.

"And you, Idaan-kya?"

"I'm going to the baths. I'll join you after."

Adrah drank the last of the tea, grimaced as if it was distilled wine, and took a pose of leave-taking which Idaan returned. When he was gone, she took herself to the women's quarters and the baths. She hardly had time to wash her hair before the cry went up. The Khai Machi was dead. Killed horribly in his chambers. Idaan dried herself with a cloth and strode out to meet her brother. She was halfway there before she realized her face was bare; she hadn't put on her paints. She was surprised that she felt no need for them now.

Danat was pacing the great hall. The high marble archways echoed with the sound of his boots. There was blood on his sleeve, and his face was empty. When Idaan caught sight of him, she raised her chin but took no formal pose. Danat stopped. The room was silent.

"You've heard," he said. There was no question to it.

"Tell me anyway."

"Otah has killed our father," Danat said.

"Then yes. I've heard."

Danat resumed his pacing. His hands worried each other, as if he were trying to pluck honey off them. Idaan didn't move.

"I don't know how he did it, sister. There must be people backing him within the palaces. The armsmen in the tower were slaughtered."

"How did he find our father?" Idaan asked, uninterested in the answer. "He must have found a secret way into the palaces. Someone would have seen him."

Danat shook his head. There was rage in him, and pain. She could see them, could feel them resonate in her own breast. But more than that, there was an almost superstitious fear in him. The upstart had slipped his bonds, had struck in the very heart of the city, and her brother feared him like Black Chaos.

"We have to secure the city," he said. "I've called for more guards. You should stay here. We can't know how far he will take his vendetta."

"You're going to let him escape?" Idaan demanded. "You aren't going to hunt him down?"

"He has resources I can't guess at. Look! Look what he's done. Until I know what I'm walking towards, I don't dare follow."

The plan was failing. Danat was staying safe in his walls with his armsmen around him like a blanket. Idaan sighed. It was up to her, of course, to save it.

"Adrah Vaunyogi has a hunt prepared. It was to be for fresh meat for my wedding feast. You stay here, Danat-kya. I'll bring you Otah's head."

She turned and walked away. She couldn't hesitate, couldn't invite him to follow her. He would see it in her gait if she were anything less than totally committed. For a moment, she even believed herself that she was going out to find her father's killer and bring him down—riding with her hunt into the low towns and the fields to track down the evil Otah Machi, her fallen brother. Danat's voice stopped her.

"I forbid you, Idaan. You can't do this."

She paused and looked back at him. He was thicker than her father had been. Already his jaw line ran toward jowls. She took a pose that disagreed.

"I'm actually quite good with a bow," she said. "I'll find him. And I will see him dead."

"You're my child sister," Danat said. "You can't do this."

Something flared in her, dark and hot. She stepped back toward Danat, feeling the rage lift her up like a leaf in the wind.

"Ah, and if I do this thing, you'll be shamed. Because I have breasts and you've a prick, I'm supposed to muzzle myself and be glad. Is that it? Well I won't. You hear me? I will not be controlled, I will not be owned, and I will not step back from anything to protect your petty pride. It's gone too far for that, brother. If a woman shrinks meekly back into the shadows, then you be the woman. See how it feels to you!"

By the end she was shrieking. Her fists were balled so tight they hurt. Danat's expression was hard as stone and as gray.

"You shame me," he said.

"Live with it," she said and spat.

"Send my body servant," he said. "I'll want my own bow. And then go to Adrah. The hunt won't leave without me."

She was on the edge of refusing, of telling him that this wasn't courage. He was only more afraid of losing the respect of the utkhaiem than of dying, and that made him not only a coward but a stupid one. *She* was the one with courage. *She* was the one who had the will to act. What was he after all but a mewling kitten lost in the world, while she . . . she was Otah Machi. She was the upstart who had earned the Khai's chair. She had killed her father for it; it was more than Danat would have done.

But, of course, truth would destroy everything. That was its nature. So she swallowed it down deep where it could go on destroying her and took an acquiescing pose. She'd won. He'd know that soon enough.

Once Danat's body servant had been sent scampering for his bow, Idaan returned to her apartments, shrugged out of her robes and put on the wide, loose trousers and red leather shirt of a hunter. She paused by her table of paints, her mirror. She sat for a moment and looked at her bare face. Her eyes seemed small and flat without the kohl. Her lips seemed pale and wide as a fish's, her cheeks pallid and low. She could be a peasant girl, plowing fields outside some low town. Her beauty had been in paint. Perhaps it would be again, someday. This was a poor day for beauty.

The huntsmen were waiting impatiently outside the palaces of the Vaunyogi, their mounts' hooves clattering against the dark stones of the courtyard. Adrah took a pose of query when he saw her clothes. Idaan didn't answer it, but went to one of the horsemen, ordered him down, took his blade and his bow and mounted in his place. Adrah cantered over to her side. His mount was the larger, and he looked down at her as if he were standing on a step.

"My brother is coming," she said. "I'll ride with him."

"You think that wise?" he asked coolly.

"I have asked too much of you already, Adrah-kya."

His expression was cold, but he didn't object further. Danat Machi rode in wearing pale robes of mourning and seated on a great hunting stallion, the very picture of vigor and manly prowess. Five riders were with him: his friends, members of the utkhaiem unfortunate enough to have heard of this hunt and marry themselves to the effort. They would have to be dealt with. Adrah took a pose of obeisance before Danat.

"We've had word that a cart left by the south gate last night," Adrah said. "It was seen coming from an alley beside the tower."

"Then let us follow it," Danat said. He turned and rode. Idaan followed, the wind whipping her hair, the smell of the beast under her rich and sweet. There was no keeping up the gallop, of course. But this was theater—the last remaining sons of the Khai Machi, one the assassin and servant of chaos slipping away in darkness, one the righteous avenger riding forth in the name of justice. Danat knew the part he was to act, and Idaan gave him credit for playing it, now that she had goaded him into action. Those who saw them in the streets would tell others, and the word would spread. It was a sight songs were made from.

Once they had crossed the bridge over the Tidat, they slowed, looking for people who had heard or seen the cart go by. Idaan knew where it had really gone—the ruins of an old stone wayhouse a half-hand's walk from the nearest low town west of the city. The morning hadn't half passed before the hunt had taken a wrong scent, turned north and headed into the foothills. The false trail took them to a crossroad—a mining track led east and west, the thin road from the city winding north up the side of a mountain. Danat looked frustrated and tired. When Adrah spoke—his voice loud enough for everyone in the party to hear—Idaan's belly tightened.

"We should fan out, Danat-cha. Eight east, eight west, eight north, and two to stay here. If one group finds sign of the upstart, they can send back a runner, and the two waiting here will retrieve the rest."

Danat weighed the thought, then agreed. Danat claimed the north road for himself, and the members of the utkhaiem, smelling the chance of glory, divided themselves among the bands heading east and west.

Adrah took the east, his eyes locked on hers as he turned to go. She saw the meaning in his expression, daring her to do this thing. Idaan made no reply to him at all. She, six huntsmen of the Vaunyogi loyal to their house and master, and Danat rode into the mountains.

When the sun had reached the highest point in the day's arc, they stopped at small lake. The huntsmen rode out in their wide-ranging search as they had done at every pause before this. Danat dismounted, stretched, and paced. His eyes were dark. Idaan waited until the others disappeared into the trees, unslung her bow, and went to stand near her brother. He looked at her, then away.

"He didn't come this way," Danat said. "He's tricked us again."

"Perhaps. But he won't survive. Even if he killed you, he could never become Khai Machi. The utkhaiem and the poets wouldn't support him."

"It's hatred now," Danat said. "He's doing it from hatred."

"Perhaps," Idaan said. Out on the lake, a bird skimmed the shining surface of the water, then shrieked and plunged in, rising moments later with a flash of living silver in its claws. A quarter moon was in the sky—white crescent showing through the blue. The lake smelled colder than it was, and the wind tugged at her hair and the reeds alike. Danat sighed.

"Was it hard killing Kaiin?" Idaan asked.

Danat looked at her, as if shocked that she had asked. She met his gaze, her eyes fixed on his until he turned away.

"Yes," he said. "Yes it was. I loved him. I miss them both."

"But you did the thing anyway."

He nodded. Idaan stepped forward and kissed him on the cheek. His stubble tickled her lips, and she wiped her mouth with the back of her hand as she walked away, trying to stop the sensation. At ten paces she put an arrow to her bow, drew back the string. Danat was still looking out over the water. Passionlessly, she judged the wind, the distance.

The arrow struck the back of his head with a sound like an axe splitting wood. Danat seemed at first not to notice, and then slowly sank to the ground. Blood soaked the collar of his robes, the pale cloth looking like cut meat by the time she walked back to him. She knelt by him, took his hand in her own, and looked out over the lake.

She was singing before she knew she intended to sing. In her imagination, she had screamed and shrieked, her cries calling the hunters back to her, but instead she sang. It was an old song, a lamentation she'd heard in the darkness of the tunnels and the cold of winter. The words were from the Empire, and she hardly knew what they all meant. The rising and falling melody, aching and sorrowful, seemed to fill her and the world.

Two hunters approached her at last, unsure of themselves. She had not seen them emerge from the trees, and she didn't look at them now as she spoke.

"My brother has been murdered by Otah or one of his agents," she said. "While we were waiting for you."

The hunters looked at one another. For a long, sick moment, she thought they might not believe her. She wondered if they would be loyal enough to the Vaunyogi to overlook the crime. And then the elder of them spoke.

"We will find him, Idaan-cha," the man said, his voice trembling with rage. "We'll send for the others and turn every stone on this mountain until we find him."

"It won't bring back my father. Or Danat. There won't be anyone to stand at my wedding."

She broke off, half surprised to find her sobs unfeigned. Gently, she cradled the corpse of her brother to her, feeling the blood soak her robes.

"I'll gather his horse," another of the hunters said. "We can strap him to it—"

"No," Idaan said. "You can give him to me. I'll carry him home."

"It's a long ride back to the city. Are you sure that—"

"I'll carry him home. He'd have done the same if our places were reversed," she said. "It is the way of our family."

In the end, they draped him over her mount's haunches. The scent of the blood made him skittish, but Idaan held control firmly, cooing in the animal's ears, coaxing and demanding. When she could think of nothing else, she sang to the beast, and the dirges possessed her. She felt no sorrow, no regret. She felt no triumph. It was as if she was in the moment of grace between the blow and the pain. In her mind were only the sounds of the songs and of an arrow splitting bone.

THE FARMSTEAD WAS SET BACK A SHORT WALK FROM THE ROAD. A CREEK RAN BESIDE it, feeding, no doubt, into the river that was even now carrying dead men down to the main channel. The walls were as thick as a man's outstretched arm with a set of doors on both the inside and outside faces. On the second story, snow doors had been opened, letting in the summer air. Trees stood in close, making the house seem a part of the landscape. The horses were kept in the stables on the ground floor, hidden from casual observers.

Amiit led Otah up the stairs and into a bright, simple room with a table, a few rough wooden chairs, an unlit lantern and a wide, low cabinet. Roast chicken, fresh cheese, and apples just on the edge of ripeness had been laid out for them. Sharpened by Otah's hunger and relief and wonder, the smell of them was wonderful. Amiit gestured toward the table, then opened the cabinet and took out two earthenware mugs and flasks of wine and water. Otah took a leg from the chicken and bit into it—the flesh tasted of tarragon and black pepper. He closed his eyes and grinned. Nothing had ever in his life tasted so good.

Amiit chuckled.

"You've grown thinner, old friend," Amiit said as he poured himself wine and Otah a mixture of wine and water. "You'd think accommodations in Machi would be better."

"What's going on, Amiit-cha?" Otah asked, taking the proffered drink. "Last I heard, I was going to be either executed as a criminal or honorably killed in the succession. This . . ." he gestured at the room with his mug. "This wasn't suggested as an option."

"It wasn't approved by the Khaiem, that's truth," Amiit said. He sat across from Otah and picked up one of the apples, turning it over slowly as he spoke, inspecting it for worm holes. "The fact is, I only know half of what's going on in Machi, if that. After our last talk—when you were first coming up here—I thought it might be best to put some plans in motion. In case an opportunity arose, you understand. It would be very convenient for House Siyanti if one of their junior couriers became the Khai Machi. It didn't seem likely at the time. But . . ."

He shrugged and bit into the apple. Otah finished the chicken and took one of the fruits himself. Even watered, the wine was nearly too strong to drink.

"We put out men and women to listen," Amiit went on. "To gather what information we could find. We weren't looking for anything in particular, you understand. Just an opportunity."

"You were looking to sell information of me to the Khai in return for a foothold in Machi," Otah said.

"Only as a last resort," Amiit agreed. "It's business. You understand."

"But they found me instead," Otah said. The apple was sweet and chalky and just slightly bitter. Amiit pushed a platter of cheese toward him.

"That looked bleak. It's truth. And that you'd been in our pay seemed to seal it. House Siyanti wasn't going to be welcome, whichever of your brothers took the title."

"And taking me out of their tower was intended to win back their favor?"

Amiit's expression clouded. He shook his head.

"That wasn't our plan. Someone hired a mercenary company to take you from the city to a low town and hold you there. We don't know who it was; they only met with the captain, and he's not on our side. But I'm fairly certain it wasn't your brother or your father."

"But you got word of it?"

"I had word of it. Mercenaries . . . well, they aren't always the most reliable of companions. Sinja-cha knew I was in the city, and would be interested in your situation. He was ready to make a break with his old cohort for other reasons, and offered me the opportunity to . . . what? Outbid his captain for his services in the matter?"

"Sinja-cha is the commander?"

"Yes. Or, was. He's in my employ now. With luck, his old captain thinks him dead along with you and the other armsmen involved."

"And what will you do now? Ransom me back to the Khai?"

"No," Amiit said. "I've already made a bargain that won't allow that. Besides, I really did enjoy working with you. And . . . and you may yet be in a position to help me more as an ally than a commodity, ne?"

"It's a bad bet," Otah said and smiled.

Amiit grinned again.

"Ah, but the stakes are high. Would you rather just have water? I wasn't thinking."

"No, I'll keep this."

"Whatever you like. So. Yes, something's happening in Machi. I expect they're out scouring the world for you even now. And in a day, perhaps two, they'll find you floating down the river or caught on a sandbar."

"And then?"

"I don't know," Amiit said. "And then we'll know what's happened in the meantime. Things are moving quickly, and there's more going on than I can fathom. For instance, I don't know what the Galts have to do with it."

Otah put down his cup. Even under the blanket of whiskers, he could see the half-smile twitch at Amiit's mouth. The overseer's eyes sparkled.

"But perhaps you do?" Amiit suggested.

"No, but . . . no. I've dealt with something else once. Something happened. The Galts were behind it. What are they doing here? How do they figure in?"

"They're making contracts with half the houses in Machi. Large contracts at disadvantageous terms. They've been running roughshod over the Westlands so long they're sure to be good for it—they have almost as much money as the Khaiem. It may just be they've a new man acting as the overseer for the Machi contracts, and he's no good. But I doubt it. I think they're buying influence."

"Influence to do what?"

"I haven't the first clue," Amiit said. "I was hoping you might know."

Otah shook his head. He took another piece of chicken, but his mind was elsewhere. The Galts in Machi. He tried to make Biitrah's death, the attack on Maati, and his own improbable freedom into some pattern, but no two things seemed to fit. He drank his wine, feeling the warmth spread through his throat and belly.

"I need your word on something, Amiit-cha. That if I tell you what I know, you won't act on it lightly. There are lives at stake."

"Galtic lives?"

"Innocent ones."

Amiit considered silently. His face was closed. Otah poured more water into his cup. Amiit silently took a pose that accepted the offered terms. Otah looked at his hands, searching for the words he needed to say.

"Saraykeht. When Seedless acted against Heshai-kvo there, the Galts were involved. They were allied with the andat. I believe they hoped to find the andat willing allies in their own freedom, only Seedless was . . . unreliable. They hurt Heshai badly, even though their plan failed. They aren't the ones who murdered him, but Heshai-kvo let himself be killed rather than expose them."

"Why would he do an idiot thing like that?"

"He knew what would happen. He knew what the Khai Saraykeht would do."

Otah felt himself on the edge of confession, but he stopped before admitting that the poet had died at his hands. There was no need, and that, at least, was one secret that he chose to keep to himself. Instead, he looked up and met Amiit's gaze. When the overseer spoke, his voice was calm, measured, careful.

"He would have slaughtered Galt," Amiit said.

"Innocent lives."

"And some guilty ones."

"A few."

Amiit leaned back in his chair, his fingers steepled before his lips. Otah could almost see the calculations taking place behind those calm, dark eyes.

"So you think this is about the poets?"

"It was last time," Otah said. "Let me send a letter to Maati. Let me warn him—"

"We can't. You're dead, and half the safety we can give you depends on your staying dead until we know more than this. But . . . but I can tell a few well-placed people to be on alert. And give them some idea what to be alert for. Another Saraykeht would be devastating." Amiit sighed deeply. "And here I thought only the succession, your life, and my house were in play. Poets now, too."

Amiit's smile was thoughtful.

"I'll give you this. You make the world more interesting, Itani-cha. Or . . . ?"

He took a pose that asked for correction.

"Otah. Much as I've fought against it, my name is Otah Machi. We might as well both get used to saying it."

"Otah-cha, then," Amiit said. He seemed pleased, as if he'd won some small victory.

Voices came up through the window. The commander's was already familiar even after so short a time. Otah couldn't make out the words, but he sounded pleased. Another voice answered him that Otah didn't know, but the woman's laughter that pealed out after it was familiar as water.

Otah felt the air go thin. He stood and walked slowly to the open shutters. There in the yard behind the farmhouse Sinja and one of the archers were standing beside a lovely woman in loose cotton robes the blue of the sky at twilight. Her fox-thin face was smiling, one eyebrow arched as she said something to the commander, who chuckled in his turn. Her hair was dark and shot with individual strands of white that she had had since birth.

He saw the change in Kiyan's stance when she noticed him—a release and relaxation. She walked away from the two men and toward the open window. Otah's heart beat fast as if he'd been running. She stopped and put out her hands, palms up and open. It wasn't a formal pose, and seemed to mean *here I am* and *here you are* and *who would have guessed this* all at once.

"She came to me not long after you left," Amiit said from where he sat. "I'm half-partner in her wayhouse down in Udun. We've been keeping it a quiet arrangement, though. There's something to be said for having a whole wayhouse of one's own without the couriers of other houses knowing it's yours."

Otah wanted to look back at the man, but his gaze seemed fastened on Kiyan. He thought he caught a faint blush rising in her cheeks. She shook her head as if clearing away some unwanted thought and walked in toward the house and out of his view. She was smiling, though. Sinja had also caught sight of Otah in the window and took a pose of congratulation.

"She's changed her mind, then. About me?"

"Apparently."

Otah turned back and leaned against the wall. Its coolness surprised him. After so many days in the cell at the tower's height, he'd come to think of stone as warm. Amiit poured himself another cup of wine. Otah swallowed to loosen his throat. The question didn't want to be asked.

"Why? What changed it?"

"I have known Kiyan-cha well for almost a quarter of this year. Not even that. You've been her lover for what? Three summers? And you want me to explain her mind to you? You've become an optimist."

Otah sat because his knees felt too weak to hold him. Amiit chuckled again and rose.

"You'll need rest for a few days. And some food and space enough to move again. We'll have you strong enough to do whatever it is needs doing, I hope. This place is better watched than it looks. We'll have warning if anyone comes near. Don't let any of this trouble you for now; you can trust us to watch over things."

"I want to see her," Otah said.

"I know," Amiit said, clapping him on the shoulder. "And she wants to see you. It's why I'm leaving. Just remember you haven't eaten to speak of in days, you're weak from the cell, you've hardly slept, and you were abducted last night. Don't expect too much from yourself. There really is no hurry."

Otah blushed now, and Amiit grabbed one last apple and made for the door. Kiyan reached it just as he did, and he stepped back to let her through. He closed the door gently behind him. Otah rose to his feet, suddenly tongue-tied. Kiyan also didn't speak, but her gaze traveled over him. He could see the distress in it even though she tried to keep it hidden.

"'Tani," she said, "you . . . you look terrible."

"It's the beard," Otah said. "I'll shave it."

She didn't take up the humor, only walked across the room and folded him into her arms. The scent of her skin flooded him with a hundred jumbled memories of her. He put his arm around her, embarrassed to notice that his hand was unsteady.

"I didn't think I'd be seeing you again," he murmured. "I never meant to put you at risk."

"What did they do to you? Gods, what have they done?"

"Not so much. They only didn't feed me well for a time and locked me away. It wasn't so bad."

She kissed his cheek and pulled back from him until each could see the other's face. There were tears in her eyes, but she was angry.

"They were going to kill you," she said.

"Well, yes. I mean, I thought that was assumed."

"I'll kill them all with my bare hands if you'd like," she said with a smile that meant she was only half joking.

"That might be more than the situation calls for. But . . . why are you here? I thought . . . I thought I was too much a risk to you."

"That didn't change. Other things . . . other things did. Come. Sit with me."

Kiyan took a bite of the cheese and poured herself water. Her hands were thin and strong and as lovely as a sculpture. Otah rubbed his temples with the palms of his hands, hoping that this was all as real as it seemed, that he wouldn't wake again in the cell above the city.

"Sinja-cha told me you wanted to turn back. He said it was because of me. That your being there kept them from searching me out."

"Knowing me shouldn't have that kind of price on it," Otah said. "It was . . . it was what I could do. That's all."

"Thank you," she said, her voice solemn.

Kiyan looked out the window. There was a dread in the lines of her mouth, a fear that confused him. He reached out, thinking to take her hand in his own, but the movement brought her back and a smile flitted over her and was gone.

"I don't know if you want to hear this. But I've been waiting to say it for longer than I can stand, and so I'm going to be selfish. And I don't know how to. Not well."

"Is it something I'll want to hear?"

"I don't know. I hope . . . I . . . Gods. Here. When you left, I missed you worse than I'd expected. I was sick with it. Physically ill. I thought I should be patient. I thought it would pass. And then I noticed that I seemed to miss you most in the early mornings. You understand?"

She looked Otah deep in the eye, and he frowned, trying to find some deeper significance in the words. And then he did, and he felt the world drop away from under him. He took a pose of query, and she replied with a confirmation.

"Ah," he said and then sat, utterly at a loss. After ten or twenty breaths, Kiyan spoke again.

"The midwife thinks sometime around Candles Night. Maybe a little after. So you see, I knew there was no avoiding the issue, not as long as I was carrying a baby with your blood in it. I went to Amiit-cha and we . . . he, really . . . put things in motion."

"There are blood teas," Otah said.

"I know. The midwife offered them to me. Would you . . . I mean, is that what you would have wanted?"

"No! Only I . . . I'd thought you wouldn't give up what you had. Your father's wayhouse. I don't know that I have much of a life to give you. I was a dead man until a little before dawn today. But if you want . . ."

"I wouldn't have left the wayhouse for you, 'Tani. It's where I grew up. It's my home, and I wouldn't give it up for a man. Not even a good man. I made that decision the night you told me who your father was. But for the both of you. Or really, even just for her. That's a harder question."

"Her?"

"Or him," Kiyan said. "Whichever. But I suppose that puts the decision in your hands now. The last time I saw you, I turned you out of my house. I won't use this as a means of forcing you into something you'd rather not. I've made my choice, not yours."

Perhaps it was the fatigue or the wine, but it took Otah the space of two or three breaths to understand what she was saying. He felt the grin draw back the corners of his mouth until they nearly ached.

"I want you to be with me, Kiyan-kya. I want you to always be with me. And the baby too. If I have to flee to the Westlands and herd sheep, I want you both with me."

Kiyan breathed in deeply, and let the breath out with a rough stutter. He hadn't seen how unsure she'd been until now, when the relief relaxed her face. She took his hand and squeezed it until he thought both of their bones were creaking.

"That's good. That's very good. I would have been . . ." laughter entered her voice ". . . very disappointed."

A knock at the door startled them both. The commander opened the door and then glanced from one of the laughing pair to the other. His face took a stern expression.

"You told him," Sinja said. "You should at least let the man rest before you tell him things like that. He's had a hard day."

"He's been up to the task," Kiyan said.

"Well, I've come to make things worse. We've just had a runner from the city, Otah-cha. It appears you've murdered your father in his sleep. Your brother Danat led a hunting party bent on bringing back your head on a stick, but apparently you've killed him too. You're running out of family, Otah-cha."

"Ah," Otah said, and then a moment later. "I think perhaps I should lie down now."

10

>+< They burned the Khai Machi and his son together in the yard outside the temple. The head priest wore his pale robes, the hood pulled low over his eyes in respect, and tended the flames. Thick, black smoke rose from the pyre and vanished into the air high above the city. Machi had woken from its revels to find the world worse than when they'd begun, and Cehmai saw it in every face he passed. A thousand of them at least stood in the afternoon sun. Shock and sorrow, confusion and fear.

And excitement. In a few eyes among the utkhaiem, he saw the bright eyes and sharp ears of men who smelled opportunity. He walked among them, Stone-Made-Soft at his side, peering through the funereal throng for the one familiar face. Idaan had to be there, but he could not find her.

The lower priests also passed through the crowds, singing dirges and beating the dry notes of drums. Slaves in ceremonially torn robes passed out tin cups of bittered water. Cehmai ignored them. The burning would go on through the night until the ashes of the men and the ashes of the coal were indistinguishable. And then a week's mourning. And then these men weeping or staring, grim or secretly pleased, would meet and decide which of their number would have the honor of sitting on the dead family's chair and leading the hunt for the man who had murdered his own father. Cehmai found himself unable to care particularly who won or lost, whether the upstart was caught or escaped. Somewhere among all these mourners was the woman he'd come to love, in more pain than she had ever been in since he'd known her. And he—he who could topple towers at a whim and make mountains flow like floodwater—couldn't find her.

Instead, he found Maati in brown poet's robes standing on a raised walkway that overlooked the mourning throng. Though they were on the edge of the ceremony, Cehmai saw the pyre light reflecting in Maati's fixed eyes. Cehmai almost didn't approach him, almost didn't speak. There was a darkness wrapped around the poet. But it was possible he had been there from the ceremony's beginning. He might know where Idaan was. Cehmai took a pose of greeting which Maati did not return.

"Maati-kvo?"

Maati looked over first at Cehmai, then Stone-Made-Soft, and then back again at the fire. After a moment's pause, his face twisted in disgust.

"Not *kvo*. Never *kvo*. I haven't taught you anything, so don't address me as a teacher. I was wrong. From the beginning, I was wrong."

"Otah was very convincing," Cehmai said. "No one thought he would—"

"Not about that. He didn't do this. Baarath . . . Gods, why did it have to be Baarath that saw it? Prancing, self-important, smug . . ."

Maati fumbled with a sewn-leather wineskin and took a long deep, joyless drink from it. He wiped his mouth with the back of a hand, then held the skin out in offering. Cehmai declined. Maati offered it to the andat, but Stone-Made-Soft only smiled as if amused.

"I thought it was someone in the family. One of his brothers. It had to be. Who else would benefit? I was stupid."

"Forgive me, Maati-kvo. But no one did benefit."

"One of *them* did," he said, gesturing out at the mourners. "One of them is going to be the new Khai. He'll tell you what to do, and you'll do it. He'll live in the high palaces, and everyone else in the city will lick his ass if he tells them to. That's what it's all about. Who has to lick whose ass. And there's blood enough to fill a river answering that." He took another long pull from the wineskin, then dropped it idly to the ground at his feet. "I hate all of them."

"So do I," Stone-Made-Soft said, his tone light and conversational.

"You're drunk, Maati-kvo."

"Not half enough. Here, look at this. You know what this is?"

Cehmai glanced at the object Maati had pulled from his sleeve.

"A book."

"This is my teacher's masterwork. Heshai-kvo, poet of Saraykeht. The Dai-kvo sent me to him when I was hardly younger than you are now. I was going to study under him, take control of Seedless. Removing-The-Part-That-Continues. We called him Seedless. This is Heshai-kvo's examination of everything he'd done wrong. Every improvement he could have made to his binding, if he'd had it to do over again. It's brilliant."

"But it can't work, can it?" Cehmai said. "It would be too close. . . ."

"Of course not, it's a refinement of his work, not how to bind Seedless again. It's a record of his failure. Do you understand what I'm saying?"

Cehmai grasped for a right answer to the question and ended with honesty.

"No," he said.

"Heshai-kvo was a drunkard. He was a failure. He was haunted his whole life by the woman he loved and the child he lost, and every measure of the hatred he had for himself was in his binding. He imagined the andat as the perfect man and implicit in that was the disdain he imagined such a man would feel looking at him. But Heshai was strong enough to look his mistake in the face. He was strong enough to sit with it and catalog it and *understand*. And the Dai-kvo sent me to him. Because he thought we could be the same. He thought I would understand him well enough to stand in his place."

"Maati-kvo, I'm sorry. Have you seen Idaan?"

"Well," Maati said, ignoring the question as he swayed slightly and frowned at the crowd. "I can face my stupidities just as well as he did. The Dai-kvo wants to know who killed Biitrah? I'll find out. He can tell me it's too late and he can tell me to come home, but he can't make me stop looking. Whoever gets that chair . . . whoever gets it . . ."

Maati frowned, confused for a moment, and a sudden racking sob shook him. He leaned forward. Cehmai moved to him, certain for a moment that Maati was about to pitch off the walkway and down to the distant ground, but instead the older poet gathered himself and took a pose of apology.

"I'm . . . making an ass of myself," he said. "You were saying something."

Cehmai was torn for a moment. He could see the red that lined Maati's eyes, could smell the sick reek of distilled wine on his breath and something deeper—some drug mixed with the wine. Someone needed to see Maati back to his apartments, needed to see that he was cared for. On another night, Cehmai would have done it.

"Idaan," he said. "She must have been here. They're burning her brother and her father. She had to attend the ceremony."

"She did." Maati agreed. "I saw her."

"Where's she gone?"

"With her man, I think. He was there beside her," Maati said. "I don't know where they went."

"Are you going to be all right, Maati-kvo?"

Maati seemed to think about this, then nodded once and turned back to watch the pyre burning. The brown leather book had fallen to the ground by the wineskin, and the andat retrieved it and put it back in Maati's sleeve. As they walked away, Cehmai took a pose of query.

"I didn't think he'd want to lose it," the andat said.

"So that was a favor to him?" Cehmai said. Stone-Made-Soft didn't reply. They walked toward the women's quarters and Idaan's apartments. If she was not there, he would go to the Vaunyogi's palace. He would say he was there to offer condolences to Idaan-cha. That it was his duty as poet and representative of the Dai-kvo to offer condolences to Idaan Machi on this most sorrowful of days. It was his duty. Gods. And the Vaunyogi would be chewing their own livers out. They'd contracted to marry their son to the Khai Machi's sister. Now she was no one's family.

"Maybe they'll cancel the arrangement," Stone-Made-Soft said. "It isn't as if anyone would blame them. She could come live with us."

"You can be quiet now," Cehmai said.

At Idaan's quarters, the servant boy reported that Idaan-cha had been there, but had gone. Yes, Adrah-cha had been there as well, but he had also gone. The unease in the boy's manner made Cehmai wonder. Part of him hoped that they had been fighting, those two. It was despicable, but it was there: the desire that he and not Adrah Vaunyogi be the one to comfort her.

He stopped next at the palace of the Vaunyogi. A servant led him to a waiting chamber that had been dressed in pale mourning cloth fragrant from the cedar chests in which it had been stored. The chairs and statuary, windows and floors were all swathed in white rags that candlelight made gold. The andat stood at the window, peering out at the courtyard while Cehmai sat on the front handspan of a seat. Every breath he took here made him wonder if coming had been a mistake.

The door to the main hall swung open. Adrah Vaunyogi stepped in. His shoulders rode high and tight, his lips thin as a line drawn on paper. Cehmai stood and took a pose of greeting which Adrah mirrored before he closed the door.

"I'm surprised to see you, Cehmai-cha," Adrah said, walking forward slowly, as if unsure what precisely he was approaching. Cehmai smiled to keep his unease from showing. "My father is occupied. But perhaps I might be able to help you?"

"You're most kind. I came to offer my sympathies to Idaan-cha. I had heard she was with you, and so . . ."

"No. She was, but she's left. Perhaps she went back to the ceremony." Adrah's voice was distant, as if only half his attention was on the conversation. His eyes, however, were fixed on Cehmai like a snake on a mouse, only Cehmai wasn't sure which of them would be the mouse, which the serpent.

"I will look there," Cehmai said. "I didn't mean to disturb you."

"We are always pleased by an audience with the poet of Machi. Wait. Don't . . . don't go. Sit with me a moment."

Stone-Made-Soft didn't shift, but Cehmai could feel its interest and amusement in the back of his mind. Cehmai sat in a rag-covered chair. Adrah pulled a stool near to him, nearer than custom required. It was as if Adrah wanted to make him feel they were in a smaller room together. Cehmai kept his face as placid as the andat's.

"The city is in terrible trouble, Cehmai-cha. You know how bad these things can get. When it's only the three sons of the Khai, it's bad enough. But with all the utkhaiem scheming and fighting and betraying one another, the damage to the city . . ."

"I'd thought about that," Cehmai said, though in truth he cared more about

Idaan than the political struggles that the coming weeks would bring. "And there's still the problem of Otah. He has a claim . . ."

"He's murdered his own father."

"Have we proven that?"

"You doubt that he did the thing?"

"No," Cehmai said after a moment's pause. "No, I don't." *But Maati-kvo still does.*

"It would be best to end this quickly. To name the new Khai before things can get out of control. You are a man of tremendous power. I know the Dai-kvo takes no sides in matters of succession. But if you were to let it be known that you favored some particular house, without taking any formal position, it would make things easier."

"Only if I backed a house that was prepared to win," Cehmai said. "If I chose poorly, I'd throw some poor unprepared family in with the pit hounds."

"My family is ready. We are well respected, we have partners in all the great trading houses, and the silversmiths and ironworkers are closer to us than to any other family. Idaan is the only blood of the old Khai remaining in the city. Her brothers will never be Khai Machi, but someday, her son might."

Cehmai considered. Here was a man asking his help, asking for political backing, unaware that Cehmai knew the shape and taste of his lover's body as well as he did. It likely was in his power to elevate Adrah Vaunyogi to the ranks of the Khaiem. He wondered if it was what Idaan would want.

"That may be wise," Cehmai said. "I would need to think about it, of course, before I could act."

Adrah put his hand on Cehmai's knee, familiar as if they were brothers. The andat moved first, ambling toward the door, and then Cehmai stood and adopted a pose appropriate to parting. The amusement coming from Stone-Made-Soft was like constant laughter that only Cehmai could hear.

When they had made their farewells, Cehmai started east again, toward the burning bodies and the priests. His mind was a jumble—concern for Idaan, frustration at not finding her, unease with Adrah's proposal, and at the back, stirring like something half asleep, a dread that seemed wrapped up with Maati Vaupathai staring drunk into the fire.

One of *them*, Maati had said, meaning the high families of the utkhaiem. One of them would benefit. Unless Cehmai took a hand and put his own lover's husband in the chair. That wasn't the sort of thing that could have been planned for. No scheme for power could include the supposition that Cehmai would fall in love with Idaan, or that her husband would ask his aid, or that his guilt and affection would drive him to give it. It was the kind of thing that could come from nowhere and upset the perfect plan.

If it wasn't Otah Machi who had engineered all this bloodletting, then some other viper was in the city, and the prospect of Adrah Vaunyogi taking the prize away by marrying Idaan and wooing the poets would drive the killer mad. And even if it *was* Otah Machi, he might still hope to take his father's place. Adrah's rise would threaten *that* claim as well.

"You're thinking too hard," the andat said.

"Thinking never hurt anyone."

"So you've all said," the andat sighed.

She wasn't at the ceremony. She wasn't at her quarters. Cehmai and Stone-Made-Soft walked together through the gardens and pavilions, the courtyards and halls and passages. Mourning didn't fill the streets and towers the way celebration had. The dry music of the funeral drums wasn't taken up in the teahouses or gardens. Only the pillar of smoke blotting out the stars stood testament to the ceremony. Twice, Cehmai took them past his own quarters, hoping that Idaan might be there waiting for him, but without effect. She had vanished from the city like a bird flying up into darkness.

His old notes were gone, left in a packet in his rooms. Kaiin and Danat were forgotten, and instead, Maati had fresh papers spread over the library table. Lists of the houses of the utkhaiem that might possibly succeed in a bid to become the next Khai. Beside them, a fresh ink brick, a pen with a new bronze nib, and a pot of tea that smelled rich, fresh cut, and green. Summer tea in the winter cities. Maati poured himself a bowl, then blew across the pale surface, his eyes going over the names again.

According to Baarath, who had accepted his second apology with a grace that had surprised him, the most likely was Kamau—a family that traced its bloodline back to the Second Empire. They had the wealth and the prestige. And, most important, an unmarried son in his twenties who was well-respected and active in the court. Then the Vaunani, less wealthy, less prestigious, but more ruthless. Or possibly the Radaani, who had spent generations putting their hands into the import and export trade until almost every transaction in the city fed their coffers. They were the richest of the utkhaiem, but apparently unable to father males. There were seventeen daughters, and the only candidates for the Khai's chair were the head of the house, his son presently overseeing a trading venture in Yalakeht, and a six-year-old grandson.

And then there were the Vaunyogi. Adrah Vaunyogi was a decent candidate, largely because he was young and virile, and about to be married to Idaan Machi. But the rumors held that the family was underfunded and not as well connected in court. Maati sipped his tea and considered whether to leave them on his list. One of these houses—most likely one of these, though there were certainly other possibilities—had engineered the murder of the Khai Machi. They had placed the blame on Otah. They had spirited him away, and once the mourning was finished with . . .

Once the mourning was finished, the city would attend the wedding of

Adrah Vaunyogi to Idaan. No, no, he would keep the Vaunyogi on his list. It was such a convenient match, and the timing so apt.

Others, of course, put the crimes down to Otah-kvo. A dozen hunting packs had gone out in the four days since the bloody morning that killed the Khai and Danat both. The utkhaiem were searching the low towns for Otah and those who had aided his escape, but so far no one had succeeded. It was Maati's task now to solve the puzzle before they found him. He wondered how many of them had guessed that he alone in the city was working to destroy all their chances. If someone else had done these things . . . if he could show it . . . Otah would still be able to take his father's place. He would become Khai Machi.

And what, Maati wondered, would Liat think of that, once she heard of it? He imagined her cursing her ill judgment in losing the ruler of a city and gaining half a poet who hadn't proved worth keeping.

"Maati," Baarath said.

Maati jumped, startled, and spilled a few drops of tea over his papers. Ink swirled into the pale green as he blotted them with a cloth. Baarath clicked his teeth and hurried over to help.

"My fault," the librarian said. "I thought you had noticed me. You were scowling, after all."

Maati didn't know whether to laugh at that, so he only took a pose of gratitude as Baarath blew across the still damp pages. The damage was minor. Even where the ink had smudged, he knew what he had meant. Baarath fumbled in his sleeve and drew out a letter, its edges sewn in green silk.

"It's just come for you," he said. "The Dai-kvo, I think?"

Maati took it. The last he had reported, Otah had been found and turned over to the Khai Machi. It was a faster response than he had expected. He turned the letter over, looking at the familiar handwriting that formed his name. Baarath sat across the table from him, smiling as if he were, of course, welcome, and waiting to see what the message said. It was one of the little rudenesses to which the librarian seemed to feel himself entitled since Maati's apology. Maati had the uncomfortable feeling Baarath thought they were becoming friends.

He tore the paper at the sewn seams, pulled the thread free, and unfolded it. The chop was clearly the Dai-kvo's own. It began with the traditional forms and etiquette. Only at the end of the first page did the matter become specific to the situation at hand.

With Otah discovered and given over to the Khai, your work in Machi is completed. Your suggestion that he be accepted again as a poet is, of course, impossible but the sentiment is commendable. I am quite pleased with you, and trust that this will mark a change in your work. There are many tasks that a man in

your position might take on to the benefit of all—we shall discuss these oppor-
tunities upon your return.

The critical issue now is that you withdraw from Machi. We have per-
formed our service to the Khai, and your continued presence would only serve
to draw attention to the fact that he and whichever of his sons eventually takes
his place were unable to discover the plot without aid. It is dangerous for the
poets to involve themselves with the politics of the courts.

For this reason, I now recall you to my side. You are to announce that you
have found the citations in the library that I had desired, and must now return
them to me. I will expect you within five weeks. . . .

It continued, though Maati did not. Baarath smiled and leaned forward in
obvious interest as Maati tucked the letter into his own sleeve. After a moment's silence, Baarath frowned.

"Fine," he said. "If it's the sort of thing you have to keep to yourself, I can
certainly respect that."

"I knew you could, Baarath-cha. You're a man of great discretion."

"You needn't flatter me. I know my proper place. I only thought you might
want someone to speak with. In case there were questions that someone with
my knowledge of the court could answer for you."

"No," Maati said, taking a pose that offered thanks. "It's on another matter
entirely."

Maati sat with a pleasant, empty expression until Baarath huffed, stood,
took a pose of leave-taking, and walked deeper into the galleries of the library.
Maati turned back to his notes, but his mind would not stay focused on them.
After half a hand of frustration and distress, he packed them quietly into his
sleeve and took himself away.

The sun shone bright and clear, but to the west, huge clouds rose white and
proud into the highest reaches of the sky. There would be storms later—if not
today, in the summer weeks to come. Maati imagined he could smell the rain in
the air. He walked toward his rooms, and then past them and into a walled garden. The cherry trees had lost their flowers, the fruits forming and swelling toward ripeness. Netting covered the wide branches like a bed, keeping the birds
from stealing the harvest. Maati walked in the dappled shade. The pangs from
his belly were fewer now and farther between. The wounds were nearly healed.

It would be easiest, of course, to do as he was told. The Dai-kvo had taken
him back into his good graces, and the fact that things had gone awry since his
last report could in no way be considered his responsibility. He had discovered
Otah, and if it was through no skill of his own, that didn't change the result.
He had given Otah over to the Khai. Everything past that was court politics;
even the murder of the Khai was nothing the Dai-kvo would want to become
involved with.

Maati could leave now with honor and let the utkhaiem follow his investigations or ignore them. The worst that would happen was that Otah would be found and slaughtered for something he had not done and an evil man would become the Khai Machi. It wouldn't be the first time in the world that an innocent had suffered or that murder had been rewarded. The sun would still rise, winter would still become spring. And Maati would be restored to something like his right place among the poets. He might even be set over the school, set to teach boys like himself the lessons that he and Otah-kvo and Heshai-kvo and Cehmai had all learned. It would be something worth taking pride in.

So why was it, he wondered, that he would not do as he was told? Why was the prospect of leaving and accepting the rewards he had dreamed of less appealing than staying, risking the Dai-kvo's displeasure, and discovering what had truly happened to the Khai Machi? It wasn't love of justice. It was more personal than that.

Maati paused, closed his eyes, and considered the roiling anger in his breast. It was a familiar feeling, like an old companion or an illness so protracted it has become indistinguishable from health. He couldn't say who he was angry with or why the banked rage demanded that he follow his own judgment over anyone else's. He couldn't even say what he hoped he would find.

He plucked the Dai-kvo's letter from his sleeve, read it again slowly from start to finish, and began to mentally compose his reply.

Most high Dai-kvo, I hope you will forgive me, but the situation in Machi is such that . . .

Most high Dai-kvo, I am sure that, had you known the turns of event since my last report . . .

Most high, I must respectfully . . .

Most high Dai-kvo, what have you ever done for me that I should do anything you say? Why do I agree to be your creature when that agreement has only ever caused me pain and loss, and you still instruct me to turn my back on the people I care for most?

Most high Dai-kvo, I have fed your last letter to pigs. . . .

"Maati-kvo!"

Maati opened his eyes and turned. Cehmai, who had been running toward him, stopped short. Maati thought he saw fear in the boy's expression and wondered for a moment what Cehmai had seen in his face to inspire it. Maati took a pose that invited him to speak.

"Otah," Cehmai said. "They've found him."

Too late, then, Maati thought. I've been too slow and come too late.

"Where?" he asked.

"In the river. There's a bend down near one of the low towns. They found his body, and a man in leather armor. One of the men who helped him escape, or that's what they've guessed. The Master of Tides is having them brought to the Khai's physicians. I told him that you had seen Otah most recently. You would be able to confirm it's really him."

Maati sighed and watched a sparrow try to land on the branch of a cherry tree. The netting confused it, and the bird pecked at the lines that barred it from the fruit just growing sweet. Maati smiled in sympathy.

"Let's go, then," he said.

There was a crowd in the courtyard outside the physician's apartments. Armsmen wearing mourning robes barred most of the onlookers but parted when Maati and Cehmai arrived. The physician's workroom was wide as a kitchen, huge slate tables in the center of the room and thick incense billowing from a copper brazier. The bodies were laid out naked on their bellies—one thick and well-muscled with a heaped pile of black leather on the table beside it, the other thinner with what might have been the robes of a prisoner or cleaning rags clinging to its back. The Master of Tides—a thin man named Saani Vaanga—and the Khai's chief physician were talking passionately, but stopped when they saw the poets.

The Master of Tides took a pose that offered service.

"I have come on behalf of the Dai-kvo," Maati said. "I wished to confirm the reports that Otah Machi is dead."

"Well, he isn't going dancing," the physician said, pointing to the thinner corpse with his chin.

"We're pleased by the Dai-kvo's interest," the Master of Tides said, ignoring the comment. "Cehmai-cha suggested that you might be able to confirm for us that this is indeed the upstart."

Maati took a pose of compliance and stepped forward. The reek was terrible—rotting flesh and something deeper, more disturbing. Cehmai hung back as Maati circled the table.

Maati gestured at the body, his hand moving in a circle to suggest turning it over that he might better see the dead man's face. The physician sighed, came to Maati's side, and took a long iron hook. He slid the hook under the body's shoulder and heaved. There was a wet sound as it lifted and fell. The physician put away the hook and arranged the limbs as Maati considered the bare flesh before him. Clearly the body had spent its journey face down. The features were bloated and fish-eaten—it might have been Otah-kvo. It might have been anyone.

On the pale, water-swollen flesh of the corpse's breast, the dark ink was still visible. The tattoo. Maati had his hand halfway out to touch it before he realized what he was doing and pulled his fingers back. The ink was so dark, though, the line where the tattoo began and ended so sharp. A stirring of the air brought the scent fully to his nose, and Maati gagged, but didn't look away.

"Will this satisfy the Dai-kvo?" the Master of Tides asked.

Maati nodded and took a pose of thanks, then turned and gestured to Cehmai that he should follow. The younger poet was stone-faced. Maati wondered if he had seen many dead men before, much less smelled them. Out in the fresh air again, they navigated the crowd, ignoring the questions asked them. Cehmai was silent until they were well away from any curious ear.

"I'm sorry, Maati-kvo. I know you and he were—"

"It's not him," Maati said.

Cehmai paused, his hands moved up into a pose that spoke of his confusion. Maati stopped, looking around.

"It isn't him," Maati said. "It's close enough to be mistaken, but it isn't him. Someone wants us to think him dead—someone willing to go to elaborate lengths. But that's no more Otah Machi than I am."

"I don't understand," Cehmai said.

"Neither do I. But I can say this, someone wants the rumor of his death but not the actual thing. They're buying time. Possibly time they can use to find who's really done these things, then—"

"We have to go back! You have to tell the Master of Tides!"

Maati blinked. Cehmai's face had gone red and he was pointing back toward the physician's apartments. The boy was outraged.

"If we do that," Maati said, "we spoil all the advantage. It can't get out that—"

"Are you blind? Gods! It *is* him. All the time it's *been* him. This as much as proves it! Otah Machi came here to slaughter his family. To slaughter you. He has backers who could free him from the tower, and he has done everything that he's been accused of. Buying time? He's buying safety! Once everyone thinks him dead, they'll stop looking. He'll be free. You have to tell them the truth!"

"Otah didn't kill his father. Or his brothers. It's someone else."

Cehmai was breathing hard and fast as a runner at the race's end, but his voice was lower now, more controlled.

"How do you know that?" he asked.

"I know Otah-kvo. I know what he would do, and—"

"Is he innocent because he's innocent, or because you love him?" Cehmai demanded.

"This isn't the place to—"

"Tell me! Say you have proof and not just that you wish the sky was red instead of blue, because otherwise you're blinded and you're letting him escape because of it. There were times I more than half believed you, Maati-kvo. But when I look at this I see nothing to suggest any conspiracy but his."

Maati rubbed the point between his eyes with his thumb, pressing hard to keep his annoyance at bay. He shouldn't have spoken to the boy, but now that he had, there was nothing for it.

"Your anger—" he began, but Cehmai cut him off.

"You're risking people's lives, Maati-kvo. You're hanging them on the thought that you can't be wrong about the upstart."

"Whose lives?"

"The lives of people he would kill."

"There is no risk from Otah-kvo. You don't understand."

"Then teach me." It was as much an insult as a challenge. Maati felt the blood rising to his cheeks even as his mind dissected Cehmai's reaction. There was something to it, some reason for the violence and frustration of it, that didn't make sense. The boy was reacting to something more than Maati knew. Maati swallowed his rage.

"I'll ask five days. Trust me for five days, and I will show you proof. Will that do?"

He saw the struggle in Cehmai's face. The impulse to refuse, to fight, to spread the news across the city that Otah Machi lived. And then the respect for his elders that had been ground into him from his first day in the school and for all the years since he'd taken the brown robes they shared. Maati waited, forcing himself to patience. And in the end, Cehmai nodded once, turned, and stalked away.

Five days, Maati thought, shaking his head. I wonder what I thought to manage in that time. I should have asked for ten.

THE RAINS CAME IN THE EARLY EVENING: LIGHTNING AND THE BLUE-GRAY BELLIES of cloudbank. The first few drops sounded like stones, and then the clouds broke with a sudden pounding—thousands of small drums rolling. Otah sat in the window and looked out at the courtyard as puddles appeared and danced white and clear. The trees twisted and shifted under gusts of wind and the weight of water. The little storms rarely lasted more than a hand and a half, but in that time, they seemed like doomsday, and they reminded Otah of being young, when everything had been full and torrential and brief. He wished now that he had the skill to draw this brief landscape before the clouds passed and it was gone. There was something beautiful in it, something worth preserving.

"You're looking better."

Otah shifted, glancing back into the room. Sinja was there, his long hair slicked down by the rain, his robes sodden. Otah took a welcoming pose as the commander strode across the room toward him, dripping as he came.

"Brighter about the eyes, blood in your skin again. One would think you'd been eating, perhaps even walking around a bit."

"I feel better," Otah said. "That's truth."

"I didn't doubt you would. I've seen men far worse off than you pull through just fine. They've found your corpse, by the way. Identified it as you, just as we'd hoped. There are already half a hundred stories about how that came to be, and none of them near the truth. Amiit-cha is quite pleased, I think."

"I suppose it's worth being pleased over," Otah said.

"You don't seem overjoyed."

"Someone killed my father and my brothers and placed the blame on me. It just seems an odd time to celebrate."

Sinja didn't answer this, and for a moment, the two men sat in silence broken only by the rain. Then Otah spoke again. "Who was he? The man with my tattoo? Where did you find him?"

"He wasn't the sort of man the world will miss," Sinja said. "Amiit found him in a low town, and we arranged to purchase his indenture from the low magistrate before they hung him."

"What had he done?"

"I don't know. Killed someone. Raped a puppy. Whatever soothes your conscience, he did that."

"You really don't care."

"No," Sinja agreed. "And perhaps that makes me a bad person, but since I don't care about that, either . . ."

He took a pose of completion, as if he had finished a demonstration. Otah nodded, then looked away.

"Too many people die over this," Otah said. "Too many lives wasted. It's an idiot system."

"This is nothing. You should see a real war. There is no bigger waste than that."

"You have? Seen war, I mean?"

"Yes. I fought in the Westlands. Sometimes when the Wardens took issue with each other. Sometimes against the nomad bands when they got big enough to pose a real threat. And then when the Galts decide to come take another bite out of them. There's more than enough opportunity there."

A distant flash of lightning lit the trees, and then a breath later, a growl of thunder. Otah reached his hand out, letting the cool drops wet his palm.

"What's it like?" he asked.

"War? Violent. Brutish, stupid. Unnecessary, as often as not. But I like the part where we win."

Otah chuckled.

"You seem . . . don't mind my prying at you, but for a man pulled from certain death, you don't seem to be as happy as I'd expected," Sinja said. "Something weighing on you?"

"Have you even been to Yalakeht?"

"No, too far east for me."

"They have tall gates on the mouths of their side streets that they close and lock every night. And there's a tower in the harbor with a permanent fire that guides ships in the darkness. In Chaburi-Tan, the street children play a game I've never seen anywhere else. They get just within shouting distance, strung out all through the streets, and then one will start singing, and the next will call the song on to the next after him, until it loops around to the first singer with all the mistakes and misunderstandings that make it something new. They can go on for hours. I stayed in a low town halfway between Lachi and Shosheyn-Tan where they served a stew of smoked sausage and pepper rice that was the best meal I've ever had. And the eastern islands."

"I was a fisherman out there for a few years. A very bad one, but . . . but I spent my time out on the water, listening to the waves against my little boat. I saw the way the water changed color with the day and the weather. The salt cracked my palms, and the woman I was with made me sleep with greased cloth on my hands. I think I'll miss that the most."

"Cracked palms?"

"The sea. I think that will be the worst of it."

Sinja shifted. The rain intensified and then slackened as suddenly as it had come. The trees stood straighter. The pools of water danced less.

"The sea hasn't gone anywhere," Sinja said.

"No, but I have. I've gone to the mountains. And I don't expect I'll ever leave them again. I knew it was the danger when I became a courier. I was warned. But I hadn't understood it until now. It's the problem in seeing too much of the world. In loving too much of it. You can only live in one place at a time. And eventually, you pick your spot, and the memories of all the others just become ghosts."

Sinja nodded, taking a pose that expressed his understanding. Otah smiled, and wondered what memories the commander carried with him. From the distance in his eyes, it couldn't all have been blood and terror. Something of it must have been worth keeping.

"You've decided, then," Sinja said. "Amiit-cha was thinking he'd need to speak with you about the issue soon. Things will be moving in Machi as soon as the mourning's done."

"I know. And yes, I've decided."

"Would you mind if I asked why you chose to stay?"

Otah turned and let himself down into the room. He took two bowls from the cabinet and poured the deep red wine into both before he answered. Sinja took the one he was offered and drank half at a swig. Otah sat on the table, his feet on the seat of the bench and swirled the red of the wine against the bone white of the bowl.

"Someone killed my father and my brothers."

"You didn't know them," Sinja said. "Don't tell me this is love."

"They killed my old family. Do you think they'd hesitate to kill my new one?"

"Spoken like a man," Sinja said, raising his bowl in salute. "The gods all know it won't be easy. As long as the utkhaiem think you've done everything you're accused of, they'll kill you first and crown you after. You'll have to find who did the thing and feed them to the crowds, and even then half of them will think you're guilty and clever. But if you don't do the thing . . . No, I think you're right. The options are live in fear or take the world by the balls. You can be the Khai Machi, or you can be the Khai Machi's victim. I don't see a third way."

"I'll take the first. And I'll be glad about it. It's only . . ."

"You mourn that other life, I know. It comes with leaving your boyhood behind."

"I wouldn't have thought I was still just a boy."

"It doesn't matter what you've done or seen. Every man's a child until he's a father. It's the way the world's made."

Otah raised his brows and took a pose of query only slightly hampered by the bowl of wine.

"Oh yes, several," Sinja said. "So far the mothers haven't met one another, so that's all for the best. But your woman? Kiyan-cha?"

Otah nodded.

"I traveled with her for a time," Sinja said. "I've never met another like her, and I've known more than my share of women. You're lucky to have her, even if it means freezing your prick off for half the year up here in the north."

"Are you telling me you're in love with my lover?" Otah asked, half joking, half serious.

"I'm saying she's worth giving up the sea for," Sinja said. He finished the last of his wine, spun the bowl on the table, and then clapped Otah's shoulder. Otah met his gaze for a moment before Sinja turned and strode out. Otah looked into the wine bowl again, smelled the memory of grapes hot from the sun, and drank it down. Outside, the sun broke through, and the green of the trees and blue of the sky where it peeked past the gray and white and yellow clouds showed vibrant as something newly washed.

Their quarters were down a short corridor, and then through a thin wooden door on leather hinges halfway to wearing through. Kiyan lay on the cot, the netting pulled around her to keep the gnats and mosquitoes off. Otah slipped through and lay gently beside her, watching her eyes flutter and her lips take up a smile as she recognized him.

"I heard you talking," she said, sleep slurring the words.

"Sinja-cha came up."

"What was the matter?"

"Nothing," he said, and kissed her temple. "We were only talking about the sea."

CEHMAI CLOSED THE DOOR OF THE POET'S HOUSE AGAIN AND STARTED PACING THE length of the room. The storm in the back of his mind was hardly a match for the one at the front. Stone-Made-Soft, sitting at the empty, cold brazier, looked up. Its face showed a mild interest.

"Trees still there?" the andat asked.

"Yes."

"And the sky?"

"And the sky."

"But still no girl."

Cehmai dropped onto the couch, his hands worrying each other, restless. The andat sighed and went back to its contemplation of the ashes and fire-black metal. Cehmai smelled smoke in the air. It was likely just the forges, but his mind made the scent into Idaan's father and brother burning. He stood up again, walked to the door, turned back and sat down again.

"You could go out and look for her," the andat said.

"And why should I find her now? The mourning week's almost done. You think if she wanted me, there wouldn't have been word? I just . . . I don't understand it."

"She's a woman. You're a man."

"Your point being?"

The andat didn't reply. It might as well have been a statue. Cehmai probed at the connection between them, at the part of him that was the binding of the andat, but Stone-Made-Soft was in retreat. It had never been so passive in all the years Cehmai had held it. The quiet was a blessing, though he didn't understand it. He had enough to work through, and he was glad not to have his burden made any heavier.

"I shouldn't have been angry with Maati-kvo," Cehmai said. "I shouldn't have confronted him like that."

"No?"

"No. I should have gone back to the Master of Tides and told him what Maati-kvo had said. Instead, I promised him five days, and now three of them have passed and I can't do anything but chew at the grass."

"You can break promises," the andat said. "It's the definition, really. A promise is something that can be broken. If it can't, it's something else."

"You're singularly unhelpful," Cehmai said. The andat nodded as if remembering something, and then was still again. Cehmai stood, went to the shutters, and opened them. The trees were still lush with summer—the green so deep and rich he could almost see the autumn starting to creep in at the edge. In winter, he could see the towers rising up to the sky through the bare branches. Now he only knew they were there. He turned to look at the path that led back to the palaces, then went to the door, opened it, and looked down it, willing someone to be there. Willing Idaan's dark eyes to greet his own.

"I don't know what to do about Adrah Vaunyogi. I don't know if I should back him or not."

"For something you consider singularly unhelpful, I seem to receive more than my share of your troubles."

"You aren't real," Cehmai said. "You're like talking to myself."

The andat seemed to weigh that for a moment, then took a pose that conceded the point. Cehmai looked out again, then closed the door.

"I'm going to lose my mind if I stay here. I have to do something," he said. Stone-Made-Soft didn't respond, so Cehmai tightened the straps of his boots, stood, and pulled his robes into place. "Stay here."

"All right."

Cehmai paused at the door, one foot already outside, and turned back.

"Does nothing bother you?" he asked the andat.

"Being," Stone-Made-Soft suggested.

The palaces were still draped with rags of mourning cloth, the dry, steady beat of the funeral drum and the low wailing dirges still the only music. Cehmai took poses of greeting to the utkhaiem whom he passed. At the burning, they had all worn pale mourning cloth. Now, as the week wore on, there were more colors in the robes—here a mix of pale cloth and yellow or blue, there a delicate red robe with a wide sash of mourning cloth. No one went without, but few followed the full custom. It reminded Cehmai of a snow lily, green under the white and budding, swelling, preparing to burst out into new life and growth, new conflict and struggle. The sense of sorrow was slipping from Machi, and the sense of opportunity was coming forth.

He found he could not say whether that reassured or disgusted him. Perhaps both.

Idaan was, of course, not at her chambers. The servants assured him that she had been by—she was in the city, she hadn't truly vanished. Cehmai thanked them and continued on his way to the palace of the Vaunyogi. He didn't allow himself to think too deeply about what he was going to do or say. It would happen soon enough anyway.

A servant brought him to one of the inner courtyards to wait. An apple tree stood open to the air, its fruits unpecked by birds. Still unripe. Cehmai sat on a low stone bench and watched the branches bob as sparrows landed and took wing. His mind was deeply unquiet. On the one hand, he had to see Idaan, had to speak with her at least if not hold her against him. On the other, he could not bring himself to love Adrah Vaunyogi only because she loved him. And the secret he held twisted in his breast. Otah Machi lived. . . .

"Cehmai-cha."

Adrah was dressed in full mourning robes. His eyes were sunken and bloodshot, his movements sluggish. He looked like a man haunted. Cehmai wondered how much sleep Adrah had managed in these last days. He wondered how many of those late hours had been spent comforting Idaan. The image of Idaan, her body entwined with Adrah's, flashed in his mind and was pressed away. Cehmai took a pose of greeting.

"I'm pleased you've come," Adrah said. "You've considered what I said?"

"Yes, Adrah-cha. I have. But I'm concerned for Idaan-cha. I'm told she's been by her apartments, but I haven't been able to find her. And now, with the mourning week almost gone . . ."

"You've been looking for her, then?"

"I wished to offer my condolences. And then, after our conversation, I thought it would be wise to consult her on the matter as well. If it were not her will to go on living in the palaces after all that's happened, I would feel uncomfortable lending my support to a cause that would require it."

Adrah's eyes narrowed, and Cehmai felt a touch of heat in his cheeks. He coughed, looked down, and then, composed once again, raised his eyes to Adrah. He half expected to see rage there, but Adrah seemed pleased. Perhaps he was not so obvious as he felt. Adrah sat on the bench beside him, leaning in toward him as if they were intimate friends.

"But if you could satisfy yourself that this is what she would wish, you're willing? You would back me for her sake?"

"It's what would be best for the city," Cehmai said, trying to make it sound more like agreement than denial. "The sooner the question is resolved, the better we all are. And Idaan-cha would provide a sense of continuity, don't you think?"

"Yes," Adrah said. "I think she would."

They sat silent for a moment. The sense that Adrah knew or suspected something crept into Cehmai's throat, drawing it tight. He tried to calm himself; there was ultimately nothing Adrah could do to him. He was the poet of Machi, and the city itself rode on his shoulders and on Stone-Made-Soft. But Adrah was about to marry Idaan, and she loved him. There was quite a bit Adrah might yet do to hurt her.

"We're allies, then," Adrah said at last. "You and I. We've become allies."

"I suppose we have. Provided Idaan-cha . . ."

"She's here," Adrah said. "I'll take you to her. She's been here since her brother died. We thought it would be best if she were able to grieve in private. But if we need to break into her solitude now in order to assure her future for the rest of her life, I don't think there's any question what the right thing is to do."

"I don't . . . I don't mean to intrude."

Adrah grinned and slapped him on the back. He rose as he spoke.

"Never concern yourself with that, Cehmai-kya. You've come to our aid on an uncertain day. Think of us as your family now."

"That's very kind," Cehmai said, but Adrah was already striding away, and he had to hurry to keep pace.

He had never been so far into the halls and chambers that belonged to the Vaunyogi before. The dark stone passageways down which Cehmai was led seemed simpler than he had expected. The halls, more sparely furnished. Only the statuary—bronze likenesses of emperors and of the heads of the Vaunyogi—spoke of the wealth of a high family of the utkhaiem, and these were displayed in the halls and courtyards with such pride that they seemed more to point out the relative spareness of their surroundings than to distract from it. Diamonds set in brass.

Adrah spoke little, but when he did, his voice and demeanor were pleasant enough. Cehmai felt himself watched, evaluated. There was some reason that Adrah was showing him these signs of a struggling family—the worn tapestry, the great ironwork candleholders filled with half a hundred candles of tallow instead of wax, the empty incense burners, the long stairway leading up to the higher floors that still showed the marks where cloth runners had once softened the stone corners and no longer did—but Cehmai couldn't quite fathom it. In another man, at another time, it would have been a humbling thing to show a poet through a compound like this, but Adrah seemed anything but humble. It might have been a challenge or a play for Cehmai's sympathy. Or it might have been a boast. *My house has little, and still Idaan chose me.*

They stopped at last at a wide door—dark wood inlaid with bone and black stone. Adrah knocked, and when a servant girl opened the door a fraction, he pressed his way in, gesturing Cehmai to follow. They were summer quarters with wide arched windows, the shutters open to the air. Silk banners with the yellow and gray of the Vaunyogi bellied and fluttered in the breeze, as graceful as dancers. A desk stood at one wall, a brick of ink and a metal pen sitting on it, ready should anyone wish to use them. This room smelled of cedar and sandalwood. And sitting in one of the sills, her feet out over the void, Idaan. Cehmai breathed in deep, and let the air slide out slowly, taking with it a tension he'd only half known he carried. She turned, looking at them over her shoulder. Her face was unpainted, but she was just as lovely as she had ever been. The bare, unadorned skin reminded Cehmai of the soft curve of her mouth when she slept and the slow, languorous way she stretched when she was on the verge of waking.

He took a pose of formal greeting. There was perhaps a moment's surprise, and then she pulled her legs back into the room. Her expression asked the question.

"Cehmai-kya wished to speak with you, love," Adrah said.

"I am always pleased to meet with the servant of the Dai-kvo," Idaan said. Her smile was formal and calm, and gave away nothing. Cehmai hoped that he had not been wrong to come, but feared that her pleasant words might cover anger.

"Forgive me," he said. "I hadn't meant to intrude. Only I had hoped to find you at your own quarters, and these last few days . . ."

Something in her demeanor softened slightly, as if she had heard the deeper layer of his apology—*I had to see you, and there was no other way*—and accepted it. Idaan returned his formal greeting, then sauntered to the desk and sat, her hands folded on her knees, her gaze cast down in what would have been proper form for a girl of the utkhaiem before a poet. From her, it was a bitter joke. Adrah coughed. Cehmai glanced at him and realized the man thought she was being rude.

"I had hoped to offer my sympathies before this, Idaan-cha," Cehmai said.

"Your congratulations, too, I hope," Idaan said. "I am to be married once the mourning week has passed."

Cehmai felt his heart go tighter, but only smiled and nodded.

"Congratulations as well," he said.

"Cehmai-kya and I have been talking," Adrah said. "About the city and the succession."

Idaan seemed almost to wake at the words. Her body didn't move, but her attention sharpened. When she spoke, her voice had lost a slowness Cehmai had hardly known was there.

"Is that so? And what conclusions have you fine gentlemen reached?"

"Cehmai-kya agrees with me that the longer the struggle among the ut-khaiem, the worse for the city. It would be better if it were done quickly. That's the most important thing."

"I see," Idaan said. Her gaze, dark as skies at midnight, shifted to Cehmai. She moved to brush her hair back from her brow, though Cehmai saw no stray lock there. "Then I suppose he would be wise to back whichever house has the strongest claim. If he has decided to back anyone. The Dai-kvo has been scrupulous about removing himself from these things."

"A man may voice an opinion," Adrah said, an edge in his voice, "without shouting on street corners."

"And what opinion would you voice, Cehmai-cha?"

Cehmai stood silent, his breath deep and fast. With every impotent thread of his will, he wished Adrah away. His hands were drawn toward Idaan, and he felt himself lean toward her like a reed in the wind. And yet her lover's eyes were on him, holding him back as effectively as chains.

"Whatever opinion you should choose," he said.

Idaan smiled, but there was more in her face than pleasure. Her jaw shifted forward, her eyes brightened. There was rage beneath her calm, and Cehmai felt it in his belly like an illness. The silence stretched out for three long breaths, four, five. . . .

"Love," Adrah said in a voice without affection. "I know our good fortune at this unexpected ally is overwhelming, but—"

"I didn't want to take any action until I spoke to you," Cehmai said. "That's why I had Adrah-cha bring me here. I hope I haven't given offense."

"Of course not, Cehmai-cha," she said. "But if you can't take my husband's word for my mind, whose could you trust? Who could know me better than he?"

"I would still prefer to discuss it with you," Cehmai said, packing as much meaning into the words as he could without sounding forced. "It will have some influence over the shape your life takes, and I wouldn't wish to guess wrong."

A spark of amusement flashed in her eyes, and she took a pose of gratitude before turning to Adrah.

"Leave us, then."

"Leave you . . ."

"Certainly he can't expect a woman to speak her mind openly with her husband floating above her like a hunting hawk. If Cehmai-cha is to trust what I say, he must see that I'm free to do my own will, ne?"

"It might be best," Cehmai agreed, trying to make his voice conciliatory. "If it wouldn't disturb you, Adrah-kya?"

Adrah smiled without even the echo of pleasure.

"Of course," he said. "I've arrangements to see to. The wedding is almost upon us, you know. There's so much to do, and with the mourning week . . . I do regret that the Khai did not live long enough to see this day come."

Adrah shook his head, then took a pose of farewell and retreated, closing the door behind him. When they were alone, Idaan's face shifted, naked venom in her stare.

"I'm sorry," Cehmai began, but Idaan cut him off.

"Not here. Gods only know how many servants he's set to listening. Come with me."

Idaan took him by the arm and led him through the door Adrah had used, then down a long corridor, and up a flight of winding stairs. Cehmai felt the warmth of her hand on his arm, and it felt like relief. She was here, she was well, she was with him. The world could be falling to pieces, and her presence would make it bearable.

She led him through a high hall and out to an open garden that looked down over the city. There were six or seven floors between them and the streets below. Idaan leaned against the rail and looked down, then back at him.

"So he's gotten to you, has he?" she asked, her voice gray as ashes.

"No one's gotten to me. If Adrah had wanted me to bray like a mule and paint my face like a whore's before he'd take me to you, I'd have been a stranger sight than this."

And, almost as if it was against her will, Idaan laughed. Not long, and not deep, hardly more than a faint smile and a fast exhalation, but it was there. Cehmai stepped in and pulled her body to his. He felt her start to push him back, hesitate, and then her cheek was pressed to his, her hair filling his breath with its scent. He couldn't say if the tears between them were hers or his or both.

"Why?" he whispered. "Why did you go? Why didn't you come to me?"

"I couldn't," she said. "There was . . . there's too much."

"I love you, Idaan. I didn't say it before because it wasn't true, but it is now. I love you. Please let me help."

Now she did push him away, holding one arm out before her to keep him at a distance and wiping her eyes with the sleeve of the other.

"Don't," she said. "Don't say that. You . . . you don't love me, Cehmai. You don't love me, and I do not love you."

"Then why are we weeping?" he asked, not moving to dry his own cheek.

"Because we're young and stupid," she said, her voice catching. "Because we think we can forget what happens to things that I care for."

"And what's that?"

"I kill them," she said, her voice soft and choking. "I cut them or I poison them or I turn them into something wrong. I won't do that to you. You can't be part of this, because I won't do that to you."

Cehmai didn't step toward her. Instead, he pulled back, walked to the edge of the garden and looked out over the city. The scent of flowers and forge-smoke mixed. "You're right, Idaan-kya. You won't do that. Not to me. You couldn't if you tried."

"Please," she said, and her voice was near him. She had followed. "You have to forget me. Forget what happened. It was . . ."

"Wrong?"

For a breath, he waited.

"No," she said. "Not wrong. But it was dangerous. I'm being married in a few days time. Because I choose to be. And it won't be you on the other end of the cord."

"Do you want me to support Adrah for the Khai's chair?"

"No. I want you to have nothing to do with any of this. Go home. Find someone else. Find someone better."

"I can love you from whatever distance you wish—"

"Oh shut up," Idaan snapped. "Just stop. Stop being the noble little boy who's going to suffer in silence. Stop pretending that your love of me started in anything more gallant than opening my robes. I don't need you. And if I want you . . . well, there are a hundred other things I want and I can't have them either. So just go."

He turned, surprised, but her face was stony, the tears and tenderness gone as if they'd never been.

"What are you trying to protect me from?" he asked.

"The answer to that question, among other things," she said. "I want you away from me, Cehmai. I want you elsewhere. If you love me as much as you claim, you'll respect that."

"But—"

"You'll respect it."

Cehmai had to think, had to pick the words as if they were stuck in mud. The confusion and distress rang in his mind, but he could see what any protests would bring. He had walked away from her, and she had followed. Perhaps she would again. That was the only comfort here.

"I'll leave you," he said. "If it's what you want."

"It is. And remember this: Adrah Vaunyogi isn't your friend. Whatever he says, whatever he does, you watch him. He will destroy you if he can."

"He can't," Cehmai said. "I'm the poet of Machi. The worst he can do to me is take you, and that's already done."

That seemed to stop her. She softened again, but didn't move to him, or away.

"Just be careful, Cehmai-kya. And *go*."

Cehmai's leaden hands took a pose of acceptance, but he did not move. Idaan crossed her arms.

"You also have to be careful. Especially if Adrah wants to become Khai Machi," Cehmai said. "It's the other thing I came for. The body they found was false. Your brother Otah is alive."

He might have told her that the plague had come. Her face went pale and empty. It was a moment before she seemed able to draw a breath.

"What . . . ?" she said, then coughed and began again. "How do you know that?"

"If I tell you, will you still send me away?"

Something washed through Idaan's expression—disappointment or depair or sorrow. She took a pose that accepted a contract.

"Tell me everything," Idaan said.

Cehmai did.

11

>+< Idaan walked through the halls, her hands clenched in fists. Her body felt as if a storm were running through it, as if flood waters were washing out her veins. She trembled with the need to do something, but there was nothing to be done. She remembered seeing the superstitious dread with which others had treated the name Otah Machi. She had found it amusing, but she no longer knew why.

She had made Cehmai repeat himself until she was certain that she'd understood what he was saying. It had taken all the pain and sorrow of seeing him again and put it aside. Cehmai had meant to save her by it.

Adrah was in the kitchens, talking with his father's house master. She took a pose of apology and extracted him, leading him to a private chamber, pulling closed the shutters, and sliding home the door before she spoke. Adrah sat in a low chair of pale wood and red velvet as she paced. The words spilled out of her, one upon another as she repeated the story Cehmai had told her. Even she could hear the tones of panic in her voice.

"Tell me," she said as the news came to its end. "Tell me it's not true. Tell me you're sure he's dead."

"He's dead. It's a mistake. It has to be. No one knew when he'd be leaving the city. No one could have rescued him."

"Tell me that you *know*!"

Adrah scowled.

"How would I do that? We hired men to free him, take him away, and kill him. They took him away, and his body floated back down the river. But I wasn't there, I didn't strangle him myself. I can't keep these men from knowing who's paid their fee and also be there to hold their hands, Idaan. You know that."

Idaan put her hands to her mouth. Her fingers were shaking. It was a dream. It was a sick dream, and she would wake from it. She would wake up, and none of it would have been true.

"He's used us," she said. "Otah's used us to do his work."

"What?"

"Look at it! We've done everything for him. We've killed them all. Even . . . even my father. We've done everything he would have needed to do. He *knew*. He knew from the start. He's planned for everything we've done."

Adrah made an impatient sound at the back of his throat.

"You're imagining things," he said. "He can't have known what we were doing, or how we would do it. He isn't a god, and he isn't a ghost."

"You're sure of that, are you? We've fallen into his trap, Adrah! It's a trap!"

"It is a rumor started by Cehmai Tyan. Or maybe it's Maati Vaupathai who's set you a trap. He could suspect us and say these things to make us panic. Or Cehmai could."

"He wouldn't do that," Idaan said. "Cehmai wouldn't do that to—to us."

"To you, you mean," Adrah said, pulling the words out slow and bitter.

Idaan stopped her pacing and took a pose of query, her gaze locked on Adrah's. As much challenge as question. Adrah leaned back in his chair, the wood creaking under his weight.

"He's your lover, isn't he?" Adrah said. "This limp story about wanting to offer condolences and being willing to back my claim only if he could see you, could speak with you. And you sending me away like I was a puppy you'd finished playing with. Do you think I'm dim, Idaan?"

Her throat closed, and she coughed to loosen it, only the cough didn't end. It became laughter, and it shook her the way a dog might shake a rat. It was nothing about mirth, everything about violence. Adrah's face went red, and then white.

"This?" Idaan finally managed to stammer. "This is what we're going to argue about?"

"Is there something else you'd prefer?"

"You're about to live a life filled with women who aren't me. You and your father must have a list drawn up of allies we can make by taking their daughters for wives. You have no right to accuse me of anything."

"That was your choice," he said. "We agreed when we started this . . . this landslide. It would be the two of us, together, no matter if we won this or lost."

"And how long would that have lasted after you took my father's place?" she asked. "Who would I appeal to when you broke your word?"

Adrah rose to his feet, stepping toward her. His hand open flat, pointed toward her like a knife.

"That isn't fair to me. You never gave me the chance to fail you. You assumed it and went on to punish me as though it had happened."

"I'm not wrong, Adrah. You know I'm not wrong."

"There's a price for doing what you say, do you know that? I loved you more than I loved anything. My father, my mother, my sisters, anything or anyone. I did all of this because it was what you wanted."

"And not for any gain of your own? How selfless. Becoming Khai Machi must be such a chore for you."

"You wouldn't have *had* me if my ambition didn't match yours," Adrah said. "What I've become, I've become for you."

"That isn't fair," Idaan said.

Adrah whooped and turned in a wide circle, like a child playing before an invisible audience.

"Fair! When did this become about fair? When someone finally asked you to take some responsibility? You made the plans, love. This is yours, Idaan! All of it's yours, and you won't blame me that you've got to live with it!"

He was breathing fast now, as if he'd been running, but she could see in his shoulders and the corners of his mouth that the rage was failing. He dropped his arms and looked at her. His breath slowed. His face relaxed. They stood in silence, considering each other for what felt like half a hand. There was no anger now and no sorrow. He only looked tired and lost, very young and very old at once. He looked the way she felt. It was as if the air they both breathed had changed. He was the one to look away and break the silence.

"You know, love, you never said Cehmai wasn't your lover."

"He is," Idaan said, then shrugged. The battle was over. They were both too thin now for any more damage to matter. "He has been for a few weeks."

"Why?"

"I don't know. Because he wasn't part of all this. Because he was clean."

"Because he is power, and you're drawn to that more than anything?"

Idaan bit back her first response and let the accusation sit. Then she nodded.

"Perhaps a bit of that, yes," she said.

Adrah sighed and leaned against the wall. Slowly, he slid down until he was sitting on the floor, his arms resting on his knees.

"There is a list of houses and their women," he said. "There was before you and Cehmai took up with each other. I argued against it, but my father said it was just as an exercise. Just in case it was needed later. Only tell me . . . today, when he came . . . you didn't . . . the two of you didn't . . ."

Idaan laughed again, but this was a lower sound, gentler.

"No, I haven't lain down for another man in your house, Adrah-kya. I can't say why I think that would be worse than what I have done, but I do."

Adrah nodded. She could see another question in the way he shifted his eyes, the way he moved his hands. They had been lovers and conspirators for years. She knew him as if he were her family, or a distant part of herself. It didn't make her love him, but she remembered when she had.

"The first time I kissed you, you looked so frightened," she said. "Do you remember that? It was the middle of winter, and we'd all gone skating. There must have been twenty of us. We all raced, and you won."

"And you kissed me for the prize," he said. "Noichi Vausadar was chewing his own tongue, he was so jealous of me."

"Poor Noichi. I half did it to annoy him, you know."

"And the other half?"

"Because I wanted to," she said. "And then it was weeks before you came back for another."

"I was afraid you'd laugh at me. I went to sleep every night thinking about you, and woke up every morning just as possessed. Can you imagine only being afraid that someone would laugh at you?"

"Now? No."

"Do you remember the night we both went to the inn. With the little dog out front?"

"The one that danced when the keep played flute? Yes."

Idaan smiled. It had been a tiny animal with gray hair and soft, dark eyes. It had seemed so delighted, rearing up on its hind legs and capering, small paws waving for balance. It had seemed happy. She wiped away the tear before it could mar her kohl, then remembered that her eyes were only her eyes now. In her mind, the tiny dog leapt and looked at her. It had been so happy and so innocent. She pushed her own heart out toward that memory, pleading with the cold world that the pup was somewhere out there, still safe and well, trusting and loved as it had been that day. She didn't bother wiping the tears away now.

"We were other people then," she said.

They were silent again. After a moment, Idaan went to sit on the floor beside Adrah. He put his arm across her shoulder, and she leaned into him, weeping silently for too many things for one mind to hold. He didn't speak until the worst of the tears had passed.

"Do they bother you?" he asked at last, his voice low and hoarse.

"Who?"

"Them," he said, and she knew. She heard the sound of the arrow again, and shivered.

"Yes," she said.

"Do you know what's funny? It isn't your father who haunts me. It should be, I know. He was helpless, and I went there knowing what I was going to do. But he isn't the one."

Idaan frowned, trying to think who else there had been. Adrah saw her confusion and smiled, as if confirming something for himself. Perhaps only that she hadn't known some part of him, that his life was something different from her own.

"When we went in for the assassin, Oshai. There was a guard. I hit him. With a blade. It split his jaw. I can still see it. Have you ever swung a thin bar of iron into hard snow? It felt just like that. A hard, fast arc and then something that both gave way and didn't. I remember how it sounded. And afterward, you wouldn't touch me."

"Adrah . . ."

He raised his hands, stopping anything that might have been sympathy. Idaan swallowed it. She had no right to pardon him.

"Men do this," Adrah said. "All over the world, in every land, men do this. They slaughter each other over money or sex or power. The Khaiem do it to their own families. I never wondered how. Even now, I can't imagine it. I can't imagine doing the things I've done, even after I've done them. Can you?"

"There's a price they pay," Idaan said. "The soldiers and the armsmen. Even the thugs and drunkards who carve each other up outside comfort houses. They pay a price, and we're paying it too. That's all."

She felt him sigh.

"I suppose you're right," he said.

"So what do we do from here? What about Otah?"

Adrah shrugged, as if the answer were obvious.

"If Maati Vaupathai's set himself to be Otah's champion, Otah will eventually come to him. And Cehmai's already shown that there's one person in the world he'll break his silence for."

"I want Cehmai kept out of this."

"It's too late for that," Adrah said. His voice should have been cold or angry or cruel, and perhaps those were in him. Mostly, he sounded exhausted. "He's the only one who can lead us to Otah Machi. And you're the only one he'll tell."

PORSHA RADAANI GESTURED TOWARD MAATI'S BOWL, AND A SERVANT BOY MOVED forward, graceful as a dancer, to refill it. Maati took a pose of gratitude toward the man. There were times and places that he would have thanked the servant, but this was not one of them. Maati lifted the bowl and blew across the surface. The pale green-yellow tea smelled richly of rice and fresh, unsmoked leaves. Radaani laced thick fingers over his wide belly and smiled. His eyes, sunk deep in their sockets and padded by generous fat, glittered like wet stones in a brook.

"I confess, Maati-cha, that I hadn't expected a visit from the Dai-kvo's envoy. I've had men from every major house in the city here to talk with me these last few days, but the most high Dai-kvo usually keeps clear of these messy little affairs."

Maati sipped his tea though it was still too hot. He had to be careful how he answered this. It was a fine line between letting it be assumed that he had the Dai-kvo's backing and actually saying as much, but that difference was critical. He had so far kept away from anything that might reach back to the Dai-kvo's village, but Radaani was an older man than Ghiah Vaunani or Adaut Kamau. And he seemed more at home with the bullying attitude of wealth than the subtleties of court. Maati put down his bowl.

"The Dai-kvo isn't taking a hand in it," Maati said, "but that hardly means he should embrace ignorance. The better he knows the world, the better he can direct the poets to everyone's benefit, ne?"

"Spoken like a man of the court," Radaani said, and despite the smile in his voice, Maati didn't think it had been a compliment.

"I have heard that the Radaani might have designs on the Khai's chair," Maati said, dropping the oblique path he had intended. It would have done no good here. "Is that the case?"

Radaani smiled and pointed for the servant boy to go. The boy dropped into a formal pose and retreated, sliding the door closed behind him. Maati sat, smiling pleasantly, but not filling the silence. It was a small room, richly appointed—wood varnished until it seemed to glow and ornaments of worked gold and carved stone. The windows were adorned with shutters of carved cedar so fine that they let the breeze in and kept the birds and insects out even as they scented the air. Radaani tilted his head, distant eyes narrowing. Maati felt like a gem being valued by a merchant.

"I have one son in Yalakeht, overseeing our business interests. I have a grandson who has recently learned how to sing and jump sticks at the same time. I can't see that either of them would be well suited to the Khai's chair. I would have to either abandon my family's business or put a child in power over the city."

"Certainly there must be some financial advantages to being the Khai Machi," Maati said. "I can't think it would hurt your family to exchange your work in Yalakeht to join the Khaiem."

"Then you haven't spoken to my overseers," Radaani laughed. "We are pulling in more gold from the ships in Yalakeht and Chaburi-Tan than the Khai Machi can pull out of the ground, even with the andat. No. If I want power, I can purchase it and not have to compromise anything. Besides, I have six or eight daughters I'd be happy for the new Khai to marry. He could have one for every day of the week."

"You could take the chair for yourself," Maati said. "You're not so old. . . ."

"And I'm not so young as to be that stupid. Here, Vaupathai, let me lay this out for you. I am old, gouty as often as not, and rich. I have what I want from life, and being the Khai Machi would mean that if I were lucky, my grandsons would be slitting each other's throats. I don't want that for them, and I don't want the trouble of running a city for myself. Other men want it, and they can have it. None of them will cross me, and I will support whoever takes the name."

"So you have no preference," Maati said.

"Now I didn't go so far as to say that, did I? Why does the Dai-kvo care which of us becomes the Khai?"

"He doesn't. But that doesn't mean he's uninterested."

"Then let him wait two weeks, and he can have the name. It doesn't figure.

Either he has a favorite or . . . or is this about your belly getting opened for you?" Radaani pursed his lips, his eyes darting back and forth over Maati's face. "The upstart's dead, so it isn't that. You think someone was working with Otah Machi? That one of the houses was backing him?"

"I didn't go so far as to say that, did I? And even if they were, it's no concern of the Dai-kvo's," Maati said.

"True, but no one tried to fish-gut the Dai-kvo. Could it be, Maati-cha, that you're here on your own interest?"

"You give me too much credit," Maati said. "I'm only a simple man trying to make sense of complex times."

"Yes, aren't we all," Radaani said with an expression of distaste.

Maati kept the rest of the interview to empty niceties and social forms, and left with the distinct feeling that he'd given out more information than he'd gathered. Chewing absently at his inner lip, he turned west, away from the palaces and out into the streets of the city. The pale mourning cloth was coming down already, and the festival colors were going back up for the marriage of Adrah Vaunyogi and Idaan Machi. Maati watched as a young boy, skin brown as a nut, sat atop a lantern pole with pale mourning rags in one hand and a garland of flowers in the other. Maati wondered if a city had ever gone from celebration to sorrow and back again so quickly.

Tomorrow ended the mourning week, marked the wedding of the dead Khai's last daughter, and began the open struggle to find the city's new master. The quiet struggle had, of course, been going on for the week. Adaut Kamau had denied any interest in the Khai's chair, but had spent enough time intimating that support from the Dai-kvo might sway his opinion that Maati felt sure the Kamau hadn't abandoned their ambitions. Ghiah Vaunani had been perfectly pleasant, friendly, open, and had managed in the course of their conversation to say nothing at all. Even now, Maati saw messengers moving through the streets and alleyways. The grand conversation of power might put on the clothes of sorrow, but the chatter only changed form.

Maati walked more often these days. The wound in his belly was still pink, but the twinges of pain were few and widely spaced. While he walked the streets, his robes marked him as a man of importance, and not someone to interrupt. He was less likely to be disturbed here than in the library or his own rooms. And moving seemed to help him think.

He had to speak to Daaya Vaunyogi, the soon-to-be father of Idaan Machi. He'd been putting off that moment, dreading the awkwardness of condolence and congratulations mixed. He wasn't sure whether to be long-faced and formal or jolly and pleasant, and he felt a deep certainty that whatever he chose would be the wrong thing. But it had to be done, and it wasn't the worst of the errands he'd set himself for the day.

There wasn't a soft quarter set aside for the comfort houses in Machi as there had been in Saraykeht. Here the whores and gambling, drug-laced wine and private rooms were distributed throughout the city. Maati was sorry for that. For all its subterranean entertainments, the soft quarter of Saraykeht had been safe—protected by an armed watch paid by all the houses. He'd never heard of another place like it. In most cities of the Khaiem, a particular house might guard the street outside its own door, but little more than that. In low towns, it was often wise to travel in groups or with a guard after dark.

Maati paused at a waterseller's cart and paid a length of copper for a cup of cool water with a hint of peach to it. As he drank, he looked up at the sun. He'd spent almost a full hand's time reminiscing about Saraykeht and avoiding any real consideration of the Vaunyogi. He should have been thinking his way through the puzzles of who had killed the Khai and his son, who had spirited Otah-kvo away, and then falsified his death, and why.

The sad truth was, he didn't know and wasn't sure that anything he'd done since he'd come had brought him much closer. He understood more of the court politics, he knew the names of the great houses and trivia about them: Kamau was supported by the breeders who raised mine dogs and the copper workers, the Vaunani by the goldsmiths, tanners and leatherworkers, Vaunyogi had business ties to Eddensea, Galt and the Westlands and little money to show for it when compared to the Radaani. But none of that brought him close to understanding the simple facts as he knew them. Someone had killed these men and meant the world to put the blame on Otah-kvo. And Otah-kvo had not done the thing.

Still, there had to be someone backing Otah-kvo. Someone who had freed him and staged his false death. He ran through his conversation with Radaani again, seeing if perhaps the man's lack of ambition masked support for Otah-kvo, but there was nothing.

He gave back the waterseller's cup and let his steps wander through the streets, his hands tucked inside his sleeves, until his hip and knee started to complain. The sun was shifting down toward the western mountains. Winter days here would be brief and bitter, the swift winter sun ducking behind stone before it even reached the horizon. It hardly seemed fair.

By the time he regained the palaces, the prospect of walking all the way to the Vaunyogi failed to appeal. They would be busy with preparations for the wedding anyway. There was no point intruding now. Better to speak to Daaya Vaunyogi afterwards, when things had calmed. Though, of course, by then the utkhaiem would be in council, and the gods only knew whether he'd be able to get through then, or if he'd be in time.

He might only find who'd done the thing by seeing who became the next Khai.

There was still the one other thing to do. He wasn't sure how he would accomplish it either, but it had to be tried. And at least the poet's house was nearer than the Vaunyogi. He angled down the path through the oaks, the gravel of the pathway scraping under his weight. The mourning cloth had already been taken from the tree branches and the lamp posts and benches, but no bright banners or flowers had taken their places.

When he stepped out from the trees, he saw Stone-Made-Soft sitting on the steps before the open doorway, its wide face considering him with a calm half-smile. Maati had the impression that had he been a sparrow or an assassin with a flaming sword, the andat's reaction would have been the same. He saw the large form lean back, turning to face into the house, and heard the deep, rough voice if not the words themselves. Cehmai was at the door in an instant, his eyes wide and bright, and then bleak with disappointment before becoming merely polite.

With an almost physical sensation, it fit together—Cehmai's rage at holding back news of Otah's survival, the lack of wedding decoration, and the disappointment that Maati was only himself and not some other, more desired guest. The poor bastard was in love with Idaan Machi.

Well, that was one secret discovered. It wasn't much, but the gods all knew he'd take anything these days. He took a pose of greeting and Cehmai returned it.

"I was wondering if you had a moment," Maati said.

"Of course, Maati-kvo. Come in."

The house was in a neat sort of disarray. Tables hadn't been overturned or scrolls set in the brazier, but things were out of place, and the air seemed close and stifling. Memories rose in his mind. He recalled the moments in his own life when a woman had left him. The scent was very much the same. He suppressed the impulse to put his hand on the boy's shoulder and say something comforting. Better to pretend he hadn't guessed. At least he could spare Cehmai that indignity. He lowered himself into a chair, groaning with relief as the weight left his legs and feet.

"I've gotten old. When I was your age I could walk all day and never feel it."

"Perhaps if you made it more a habit," Cehmai said. "I have some tea. It's a little tepid now, but if you'd like . . ."

Maati raised a hand, refusing politely. Cehmai, seeming to notice the state of the house now there were someone else's eyes on it, opened the shutters wide before he came to sit at Maati's side.

"I've come to ask for more time," Maati said. "I can make excuses first if you like, or tell you that as your elder and an envoy of the Dai-kvo it's something you owe me. Any of that theater you'd like. But it comes to this: I don't know yet what's happening, and it's important to me that if something does go wrong for Otah-kvo it not have been my doing."

Cehmai seemed to weigh this.

"Baarath tells me you had a message from the Dai-kvo," Cehmai said.

"Yes. After he heard I'd turned Otah-kvo over to his father, he called me back."

"And you're disobeying that call."

"I'm exercising my own judgment."

"Will the Dai-kvo make that distinction?"

"I don't know," Maati said. "If he agrees with me, I suppose he'll agree with me. If not, then not. I can only guess what he would have said if he'd known everything I know, and move from there."

"And you think he'd want Otah's secret kept?"

Maati laughed and rubbed his hands together. His legs were twitching pleasantly, relaxing from their work. He stretched and his shoulder cracked.

"Probably not," he said. "He'd more likely say that it isn't our place to take an active role in the succession. That he'd sent me here with that story about rooting through the library so that it wouldn't be clear to everyone over three summers old what I was really here for. He might also mention that the questions I've been asking have been bad enough without lying to the utkhaiem while I'm at it."

"You haven't lied," Cehmai said, and then a moment later. "Well, actually, I suppose you have. You aren't really doing what you believe the Dai-kvo would want."

"No."

"And you want my complicity?"

"Yes. Or, that is, I have to ask it of you. And I have to persuade you if I can, though in truth I'd be as happy if you could talk me out of it."

"I don't understand. Why *are* you doing this? And don't only say that you want to sleep well after you've seen another twenty summers. You've done more than anyone could have asked of you. What is it about Otah Machi that's driving you to this?"

Oh, Maati thought, you shouldn't have asked that question, my boy. Because *that* one I know how to answer, and it'll sting you as much as me.

He steepled his fingers and spoke.

"He and I loved the same woman once, when we were younger men. If I do him harm or let him come to harm that I could have avoided, I couldn't look at her again and say it wasn't my anger that drove me. My anger at her love for him. I haven't seen her in years, but I will someday. And when I do, I need it to be with a clear conscience. The Dai-kvo may not need it. The poets may not. But despite our reputations, we're men under these robes, and as a man . . . as a man to a man, it's something I would ask of you. Another week. Just until we can see who's likely to be the new Khai."

There was a shifting sound behind him. The andat had come in silently at some point and was standing at the doorway with the same simple, placid smile. Cehmai leaned forward and ran his hands through his hair three times in fast succession, as if he were washing himself without water.

"Another week," Cehmai said. "I'll keep quiet another week."

Maati blinked. He had expected at least an appeal to the danger he was putting Idaan in by keeping silent. Some form of *at least let me warn her* . . . Maati frowned, and then understood.

He'd already done it. Cehmai had already told Idaan Machi that Otah was alive. Annoyance and anger flared brief as a firefly, and then faded, replaced by something deeper and more humane. Amusement, pleasure, and even a kind of pride in the young poet. We are men beneath these robes, he thought, and we do what we must.

SINJA SPUN, THE THICK WOODEN CUDGEL HISSING THROUGH THE AIR. OTAH stepped inside the blow, striking at the man's wrist. He missed, his own rough wooden stick hitting Sinja's with a clack and a shock that ran up his arm. Sinja snarled, pushed him back, and then ruefully considered his weapon.

"That was decent," Sinja said. "Amateur, granted, but not hopeless."

Otah set his stick down, then sat—head between his knees—as he fought to get his breath back. His ribs felt as though he'd rolled down a rocky hill, and his fingers were half numb from the shocks they'd absorbed. And he felt good—exhausted, bruised, dirty, and profoundly back in control of his own body again, free in the open air. His eyes stung with sweat, his spit tasted of blood, and when he looked up at Sinja, they were both grinning. Otah held out his hand and Sinja hefted him to his feet.

"Again?" Sinja said.

"I wouldn't . . . want to . . . take advantage . . . when you're . . . so tired."

Sinja's face folded into a caricature of helplessness as he took a pose of gratitude. They turned back toward the farmhouse. The high summer afternoon was thick with gnats and the scent of pine resin. The thick gray walls of the farmhouse, the wide low trees around it, looked like a painting of modest tranquility. Nothing about it suggested court intrigue or violence or death. That, Otah supposed, was why Amiit had chosen it.

They had gone out after a late breakfast. Otah had felt well enough, he thought, to spar a bit. And there was the chance that this would all come to blades before it was over, whether he chose it or not. He'd never been trained as a fighter, and Sinja was happy to offer a day's instruction. There was an easy camaraderie that Otah had enjoyed on the way out. The work itself reminded him that Sinja had slaughtered his last comrades, and the walk back was somehow much longer than the one out had been.

"A little practice, and you'd be a decent soldier," Sinja said as they walked. "You're too cautious. You'll lose a good strike in order to protect yourself, and that's a vice. You'll need to be careful of it."

"I'm actually hoping for a life that doesn't require much blade work of me."

"I wasn't only talking about fighting."

When they reached the farmhouse, the stables had four unfamiliar horses in them, hot from the road. An armsman of House Siyanti—one Otah recognized, but whose name he'd never learned—was caring for them. Sinja traded a knowing look with the man, then strode up the stairs to the main rooms. Otah followed, his aches half-forgotten in the mingled curiosity and dread.

Amiit Foss and Kiyan were sitting at the main table with two other men. One—an older man with heavy, beetled brows and a hooked nose—wore robes embroidered with the sun and stars of House Siyanti. The other, a young man with round cheeks and a generous belly, wore a simple blue robe of inexpensive cloth, but enough rings on his fingers to pay for a small house. Their conversation stopped as Otah and Sinja entered the room. Amiit smiled and gestured toward the benches.

"Well timed," Amiit said. "We've just been discussing the next step in our little dance."

"What's the issue?" Sinja asked.

"The mourning's ending. Tomorrow, the heads of all the houses of the utkhaiem meet. I expect it will take them a few days before the assassinations start, but within the month it'll be decided who the new Khai is to be."

"We'll have to act before that," Otah said.

"True enough, but that doesn't mean we'd be wise to act now," Amiit said. "We know, or guess well enough, what power is behind all this—the Galts. But we don't know the mechanism. Who are they backing? Why? I don't like the idea of moving forward without that in hand. And yet, time's short."

Amiit held out his open hands, and Otah understood this choice was being laid at his door. It was his life most at risk, and Amiit wasn't going to demand anything of Otah that he wasn't prepared to do. Otah sat, laced his fingers together, and frowned. It was Kiyan's voice that interrupted his uncertainty.

"Either we stay here or we go to Machi. If we stay here, we're unlikely to be discovered, but it takes half a day for us to get news, and half a day at least to respond to it. Amiit-cha thinks the safety might be worth it, but Lamara-cha," she gestured to the hook-nosed man, "has been arguing that we'll want the speed we can only have by being present. He's arranged a place for us to stay—in the tunnels below the palaces."

"I have an armsman of the Saya family in my employ," the hook-nosed Lamara said. His voice was a rough whisper, and Otah noticed for the first time a long, deep, old scar across the man's throat. "The Saya are a minor family, but they will be at the council. We can keep clear on what's said and by whom."

"And if you're discovered, we'll all be killed," Sinja said. "As far as the world's concerned, you've murdered a Khai. It's not a precedent anyone wants set. Especially not the other Khaiem. Bad enough they have to watch their brothers. If it's their sons, too. . . ."

"I understand that," Otah said. Then, to Amiit, "Are we any closer to knowing who the Galts are backing?"

"We don't know for certain that they're backing anyone," Amiit said. "That's an assumption we've made. We can make some educated guesses, but that's all. It may be that their schemes are about the poets, the way you suggested, and not the succession at all."

"But you don't believe that," Otah said.

"And the poets don't either," the round-cheeked man said. "At least not the new one."

"Shojen-cha is the man we set to follow Maati Vaupathai," Amiit said.

"He's been digging at all the major houses of the utkhaiem," Shojen said, leaning forward, his rings glittering in the light. "In the last week, he's had audiences with all the highest families and half the low ones. And he's been asking questions about court politics and money and power. He hasn't been looking to the Galts in particular, but it's clear enough he thinks some family or families of the utkhaiem are involved in the killings."

"What's he found out?" Otah asked,

"We don't know. I can't say what he's looking for or what he's found, but there's no question he's conducting an investigation."

"He's the one who gave you over to the Khai in the first place, isn't he, Otah-cha?" Lamara said in his ruined voice.

"He's also the one who took a knife in the gut," Sinja said.

"Can we say why he's looking?" Otah asked. "What would he do if he discovered the truth? Report it to the utkhaiem? Or only the Dai-kvo?"

"I can't say," Shojen said. "I know what he's doing, not what he's thinking."

"We *can* say this," Amiit said, his expression dour and serious. "As it stands, there's no one in the city who'll think you innocent, Otah-cha. If you're found in Machi, you'll be killed. And whoever sticks the first knife in will use it as grounds that he should be Khai. The only protection you'll have is obscurity."

"No armsmen?" Otah asked.

"Not enough," Amiit said. "First, they'd only draw attention to you, and second, there aren't enough guards in the city to protect you if the utkhaiem get your scent in their noses."

"But that's true wherever he is," Lamara said. "If they find out he's alive on a desolate rock in the middle of the sea, they'll send men to kill him. He's murdered the Khai!"

"Then best to keep him where he won't be found," Amiit said. There was an impatience in his tone that told Otah this debate had been going on long before he'd come in the room. Tempers were fraying, and even Amiit Foss' deep patience was wearing thin. He felt Kiyan's eyes on him, and looked up to meet her gaze. Her half-smile carried more meaning than half a hand's debate.

They will never agree and *you may as well practice giving orders now—if it goes well, you'll be doing it for the rest of your life* and *I'm sorry, love.*

Otah felt a warmth in his chest, felt the panic and distress relax like a stiff muscle rubbed in hot oils. Lamara and Amiit were talking over each other, each making points and suggestions it was clear they'd made before. Otah coughed, but they paid him no attention. He looked from one, flushed, grim face to the other, sighed, and slapped his palm on the table hard enough to make the wine bowls rattle. The room went silent, surprised eyes turning to him.

"I believe, gentlemen, that I understand the issues at hand," Otah said. "I appreciate Amiit-cha's concern for my safety, but the time for caution has passed."

"It's a vice," Sinja agreed, grinning.

"Next time, you can give me your advice without cracking my ribs," Otah said. "Lamara-cha, I thank you for the offer of the tunnels to work from, and I accept it. We'll leave tonight."

"Otah-cha, I don't think you've . . ." Amiit began, his hands held out in an appeal, but Otah only shook his head. Amiit frowned deeply, and then, to Otah's surprise, smiled and took a pose of acceptance.

"Shojen-cha," Otah said. "I need to know what Maati is thinking. What he's found, what he intends, whether he's hoping to save me or destroy me. Both are possible, and everything we do will be different depending on his stance."

"I appreciate that," Shojen said, "but I don't know how I'd discover it. It isn't as though he confides in me. Or in anyone else that I can tell."

Otah rubbed his fingertips across the rough wood of the table, considering that. He felt their eyes on him, pressing him for a decision. This one, at least, was simple enough. He knew what had to be done.

"Bring him to me," he said. "Once we've set ourselves up and we're sure of the place, bring him there. I'll speak with him."

"That's a mistake," Sinja said.

"Then it's the mistake I'm making," Otah said. "How long before we can be ready to leave?"

"We can have all the things we need on a cart by sundown," Amiit said. "That would put us in Machi just after the half-candle. We could be in the tunnels and tucked as safely away as we're likely to manage by dawn. But there are going to be some people in the streets, even then."

"Get flowers. Decorate the cart as if we're preparing for the wedding," Otah said. "Then even if they think it odd to see us, they'll have a story to tell themselves."

"I'll collect the poet whenever you like," Shojen said, his confident voice undermined by the nervous way he fingered his rings.

"Also tomorrow. And Lamara-cha, I'll want reports from your man at the council as soon as there's word to be had."

"As you say," Lamara said.

Otah moved his hands into a pose of thanks, then stood.

"Unless there's more to be said, I'm going to sleep now. I'm not sure when I'll have the chance again. Any of you who aren't involved in preparations for the move might consider doing the same."

They murmured their agreement, and the meeting ended, but when later Otah lay in the cot, one arm thrown over his eyes to blot out the light, he was certain he could no more sleep than fly. He was wrong. Sleep came easily, and he didn't hear the old leather hinges creak when Kiyan entered the room. It was her voice that pulled him into awareness.

"*It's a mistake I'm making?* That's quite the way to lead men."

He stretched. His ribs still hurt, and worse, they'd stiffened.

"Was it too harsh, do you think?"

Kiyan pushed the netting aside and sat next to him, her hand seeking his.

"If Sinja-cha's that delicate, he's in the wrong line of work," she said. "He may think you're wrong, but if you'd turned back because he told you to, you'd have lost part of his respect. You did fine, love. Better than fine. I think you've made Amiit a very happy man."

"How so?"

"You've become the Khai Machi. Oh, I know, it's not done yet, but out there just then? You weren't speaking like a junior courier or an east islands fisherman."

Otah sighed. Her face was calm and smooth. He brought her hand to his lips and kissed her wrist.

"I suppose not," he said. "I didn't want this, you know. The wayhouse would have been enough."

"I'm sure the gods will take that into consideration," she said. "They're usually so good about giving us the lives we expect."

Otah chuckled. Kiyan let herself be pulled down slowly, until she lay beside him, her body against his own. Otah's hand strayed to her belly, caressing the tiny life growing inside her. Kiyan raised her eyebrows and tilted her head.

"You look sad," she said. "Are you sad, 'Tani?"

"No, love," Otah said. "Not sad. Only frightened."

"About going back to the city?"

"About being discovered," he said. And a moment later, "About what I'm going to have to say to Maati."

12

>+< Cehmai sat back on a cushion, his back aching and his mind askew. Stone-Made-Soft sat beside him, its stillness unbroken even by breath. At the front of the temple, on a dais where the witnesses could see her, sat Idaan. Her eyes were cast down, her robe the vibrant rose and blue of a new bride. The distance between them seemed longer than the space within the walls, as if a year's journey had been fit into the empty air.

The crowd was not as great as the occasion deserved: women and the second sons of the utkhaiem. Elsewhere, the council was meeting, and those who had a place in it were there. Given the choice of spectacle, many others would choose the men, their speeches and arguments, the debates and politics and subtle drama, to the simple marrying off of an orphan girl of the best lineage and the least influence to the son of a good, solid family.

Cehmai stared at her, willing the kohl-dark eyes to look up, the painted lips to smile at him. Cymbals chimed, and the priests dressed in gold and silver robes with the symbols of order and chaos embroidered in black began their chanting procession. Their voices blended and rose until the temple walls themselves seemed to ring with the melody. Cehmai plucked at the cushion. He couldn't watch, and he couldn't look away. One priest—an old man with a bare head and a thin white beard—stopped behind Idaan in the place that her father or brother should have taken. The high priest stood at the back of the dais, lifted his hands slowly, palms out to the temple, and, with an embracing gesture, seemed to encompass them all. When he spoke, it was in the language of the Old Empire, syllables known to no one on the cushions besides himself.

Eyan ta nyot baa, dan salaa khai dan umsalaa.

The will of the gods has always been that woman shall act as servant to man.

An old tongue for an old thought. Cehmai let the words that followed it—the ancient ritual known more by its rhythm than its significance—wash over him. He closed his eyes and told himself he was not drowning. He focused on his breath, smoothing its ragged edges until he regained the appearance of calm. He watched the sorrow and the anger and the jealousy writhe inside him as if they were afflicting someone else.

When he opened his eyes, the andat had shifted, its gaze on him and expressionless. Cehmai felt the storm on the back of his mind shift, as if taking stock of the confusion in his heart, testing him for weakness. Cehmai waited, prepared for Stone-Made-Soft to press, for the struggle to engulf him. He almost longed for it.

But the andat seemed to feel that anticipation, because it pulled back. The pressure lessened, and Stone-Made-Soft smiled its idiot, empty smile, and turned back to the ceremony. Adrah was standing now, a long cord looped in his hand. The priest asked him the ritual questions, and Adrah spoke the ritual answers. His face seemed drawn, his shoulders too square, his movements too careful. Cehmai thought he seemed exhausted.

The priest who stood behind Idaan spoke for her family in their absence, and the end of the cord, cut and knotted, passed from Adrah to the priest and then to Idaan's hand. The rituals would continue for some time, Cehmai knew, but as soon as the cord was accepted, the binding was done. Idaan Machi had entered the house of the Vaunyogi and only Adrah's death would cast her back into the ghost arms of her dead family. Those two were wed, and he had no right to the pain the thought caused him. He had no right to it.

He rose and walked silently to the wide stone archway and out of the temple. If Idaan looked up at his departure, he didn't notice.

The sun wasn't halfway through its arc, and a fresh wind from the north was blowing the forge smoke away. High, thin clouds scudded past, giving the illusion that the great stone towers were slowly, endlessly toppling. Cehmai walked the temple grounds, Stone-Made-Soft a pace behind him. There were few others there—a woman in rich robes sitting alone by a fountain, her face a mask of grief; a round-faced man with rings glittering on his fingers reading a scroll; an apprentice priest raking the gravel paths smooth with a long metal rake. And at the edge of the grounds, where temple became palace, a familiar shape in brown poet's robes. Cehmai hesitated, then slowly walked to him, the andat close by and trailing him like a shadow.

"I hadn't expected to see you here, Maati-kvo."

"No, but I expected you," the older poet said. "I've been at the council all morning. I needed some time away. May I walk with you?"

"If you like. I don't know that I'm going anywhere in particular."

"Not marching with the wedding party? I thought it was traditional for the celebrants to make an appearance in the city with the new couple. Let the city look over the pair and see who's allied themselves with the families. I assume that's what all the flowers and decorations out there are for."

"There will be enough without me."

Cehmai turned north, the wind blowing gently into his face, drawing his robes out behind him as if he were walking through water. A slave girl was standing beside the path singing an old love song, her high, sweet voice carrying like a flute's. Cehmai felt Maati-kvo's attention, but wasn't sure what to make of it. He felt as examined as the corpse on the physician's table. At length, he spoke to break the silence.

"How is it?"

"The council? Like a very long, very awkward dinner party. I imagine it will deteriorate. The only interesting thing is that a number of houses are calling for Vaunyogi to take the chair."

"Interesting," Cehmai said. "I knew Adrah-cha was thinking of it, but I wouldn't have thought his father had the money to sway many people."

"I wouldn't have either. But there are powers besides money."

The comment seemed to hang in the air.

"I'm not sure what you mean, Maati-kvo."

"Symbols have weight. The wedding coming as it does might sway the sentimental. Or perhaps Vaunyogi has advocates we aren't aware of."

"Such as?"

Maati stopped. They had reached a wide courtyard, rich with the scent of cropped summer grass. The andat halted as well, its broad head tilted in an attitude of polite interest. Cehmai felt a brief flare of hatred toward it, and saw its lips twitch slightly toward a smile.

"If you've spoken for the Vaunyogi, I need to know it," Matti said.

"We're not to take sides in these things. Not without direction from the Dai-kvo."

"I'm aware of that, and I don't mean to accuse you or pry into what's not mine, but on this one thing, I have to know. They did ask you to speak for them, didn't they?"

"I suppose," Cehmai said.

"And did you speak for them?"

"No. Why should I?"

"Because Idaan Machi is your lover," Maati said, his voice soft and full of pity.

Cehmai felt the blood come into his face, his neck. The anger at everything that he had seen and heard pressed at him, and he let himself borrow certainty from the rage.

"Idaan Machi is Adrah's wife. No, I did not speak for Vaunyogi. Despite your experience, not everyone falls in love with the man who's taken his lover."

Maati leaned back. The words had struck home, and Cehmai pressed on, following the one attack with another.

"And, forgive me, Maati-cha, but you seem in an odd position to take me to task for following my private affairs where they don't have a place. You are still doing all this without the Dai-kvo's knowledge?"

"He might have a few of my letters," Maati-kvo said. "If not yet, then soon."

"But since you're a man under those robes, on you go. I am doing as the

Dai-kvo set me to do. I am carrying this great bastard around; I am keeping myself apart from the politics of the court; I'm not willing to stand accused of lighting candles while you're busy burning the city down!"

"Calling me a bastard seems harsh," Stone-Made-Soft said. "*I* haven't told you how to behave."

"Be quiet!"

"If you think it will help," the andat said, its voice amused, and Cehmai turned the fury inward, pressing at the space where he and Stone-Made-Soft were one thing, pushing the storm into a smaller and smaller thing. He felt his hands in fists, felt his teeth ache with the pressure of his clenched jaw. And the andat, shifted, bent to his fire-bright will, knelt and cast down its gaze. He forced its hands into a pose of apology.

"Cehmai-cha."

He turned on Maati. The wind was picking up, whipping their robes. The fluttering of cloth sounded like a sail.

"I'm sorry," Maati-kvo said. "I truly am very sorry. I know what it must mean to have these things questioned, but I have to know."

"Why? Why is my heart suddenly your business?"

"Let me ask this another way," Maati said. "If you aren't backing Vaunyogi, who is?"

Cehmai blinked. His rage whirled, lost its coherence, and left him feeling weaker and confused. On the ground beside them, Stone-Made-Soft sighed and rose to its feet. Shaking its great head, it gestured to the green streaks on its robe.

"The launderers won't be pleased by that," it said.

"What do you mean?" Cehmai said, not to the andat, but to Maati-kvo. And yet, it was Stone-Made-Soft's deep rough voice that answered him.

"He's asking you how badly Adrah Vaunyogi wants that chair. And he's suggesting that Idaan-cha may have just married her father's killer, all unaware. It seems a simple enough proposition to me. They aren't going to blame *you* for these stains, you know. They never do."

Maati stood silently, peering at him, waiting. Cehmai held his hands together to stop their shaking.

"You think that?" he asked. "You think that Adrah might have arranged the wedding because he knew what was going to happen? You think *Adrah* killed them?"

"I think it worth considering," Maati said.

Cehmai looked down and pressed his lips together until they ached. If he didn't—if he looked up, if he relaxed—he knew that he would smile. He knew what that would say about himself and his small, petty soul, so he swallowed and kept his head low until he could speak. Unbidden, he imagined himself exposing Adrah's crime, rejoining Idaan with her sole remaining family. He imagined her eyes looking into his as he told her what Maati knew.

"Tell me how I can help," he said.

MAATI SAT IN THE FIRST GALLERY, LOOKING DOWN INTO THE GREAT HALL AND waiting for the council to go on. It was a rare event, all the houses of the ut-khaiem meeting without a Khai to whom they all answered, and they seemed both uncertain what the proper rituals were and unwilling to let the thing move quickly. It was nearly dark now, and candles were being set out on the dozen long tables below him and the speaker's pulpit beyond them. The small flames were reflected in the parquet floor and the silvered glass on the walls below him. A second gallery rose above him, where women and children of the lower families and representatives of the trading houses could sit and observe. The architect had been brilliant—a man standing as speaker need hardly raise his voice and the stone walls would carry his words through the air without need of whisperers. Even over the murmurs of the tables below and the galleries above, the prepared, elaborate, ornate, deathly dull speeches of the ut-khaiem reached every ear. The morning session had been interesting at least—the novelty of the situation had held his attention. But apart from his conversation with Cehmai, Maati had filled the hours of his day with little more than the voices of men practiced at saying little with many words. Praise of the utkhaiem generally and of their own families in particular, horror at the crimes and misfortunes that had brought them here, and the best wishes of the speaker and his father or his son or his cousin for the city as a whole, and on and on and on.

Maati had pictured the struggle for power as a thing of blood and fire, betrayal and intrigue and danger. And, when he listened for the matter beneath the droning words, yes, all that was there. That even this could be made dull impressed him.

The talk with Cehmai had gone better than he had hoped. He felt guilty using Idaan Machi against him that way, but perhaps the boy had been ready to be used. And there was very little time.

He was relying now on the competence of his enemies. There would be only a brief window between the time when it became clear who would take the prize and the actual naming of the Khai Machi. In that moment, Maati would know who had engineered all this, who had used Otah-kvo as a cover, who had attempted his own slaughter. And if he were wise and lucky and well-positioned, he might be able to take action. Enlisting Cehmai in his service was only a way to improve the chances of setting a lever in the right place.

"The concern our kind brother of Saya brings up is a wise one to consider," a sallow-faced scion of the Daikani said. "The days are indeed growing shorter, and the time for preparation is well upon us. There are roofs that must be made ready to hold their burden of snow. There are granaries to be filled and stocks to be prepared. There are crops to be harvested, for men and beasts both."

"I didn't know the Khai did all that," a familiar voice whispered. "He must have been a very busy man. I don't suppose there's anyone could take up the slack for him?"

Baarath shifted down and sat beside Maati. He smelled of wine, his cheeks were rosy, his eyes too bright. But he had an oilcloth cone filled with strips of fried trout that he offered to Maati, and the distraction was almost welcome. Maati took a bit of the fish.

"What have I missed?" Baarath said.

"The Vaunyogi appear to be a surprise contender," Maati said. "They've been mentioned by four families, and praised in particular by two others. I think the Vaunani and Kamau are feeling upset by it, but they seem to hate each other too much to do anything about it."

"That's truth," Baraath said. "Ijan Vaunani came to blows with old Kamau's grandson this afternoon at a teahouse in the jeweler's quarter. Broke his nose for him, I heard."

"Really?"

Baarath nodded. The sallow man droned on half forgotten now as Baarath spoke close to Maati's ear.

"There are rumors of reprisal, but old Kamau's made it clear that anyone doing anything will be sent to tar ships in the Westlands. They say he doesn't want people thinking ill of the house, but I think it's his last effort to keep an alliance open against Adrah Vaunyogi. It's clear enough that someone's bought little Adrah a great deal more influence than just sleeping with a dead man's daughter would earn."

Baarath grinned, then coughed and looked concerned.

"Don't repeat that to anyone, though," he said. "Or if you do, don't say it was me. It's terribly rude, and I'm rather drunk. I only came up here to sober up a bit."

"Yes, well, I came up to keep an eye on the process, and I think it's more likely to put your head on a pillow than clear it."

Baarath chuckled.

"You're an idiot if you came here to see what's happening. It's all out in the piss troughs where a man can actually speak. Didn't you know that? Honestly, Maati-kya, if you went to a comfort house, you'd spend all your time watching the girls in the front dance and wondering when the fucking was supposed to start."

Maati's jaw went tight. When Baarath offered the fish again, Maati refused it. The sallow man finished, and an old, thick-faced man rose, took the pulpit, announced himself to be Cielah Pahdri, and began listing the various achievements of his house dating back to the fall of the Empire. Maati listened to the recitation and Baraath's overloud chewing with equal displeasure.

He was right before, Maati told himself. Baarath was the worst kind of ass, but he wasn't wrong.

"I assume," Maati said, "that 'piss troughs' is a euphemism."

"Only half. Most of the interesting news comes to a few teahouses at the south edge of the palaces. They're near the moneylenders, and that always leads to lively conversations. Going to try your luck there?"

"I thought I might," Maati said as he rose.

"Look for the places with too many rich people yelling at each other. You'll be fine," Baarath said and went back to chewing his trout.

Maati took the steps two at a time, and slipped out the rear of the gallery into a long, dark corridor. Lanterns were lit at each end, and Maati strode through the darkness with the slow burning runout of annoyance that the librarian always seemed to inspire. He didn't see the woman at the hallway's end until he had almost reached her. She was thin, fox-faced, and dressed in a simple green robe. She smiled when she caught his eye and took a pose of greeting.

"Maati-cha?"

Maati hesitated, then answered her greeting.

"I'm sorry," he said. "I seem to have forgotten your name."

"We haven't met. My name is Kiyan. Itani's told me all about you."

It took the space of a breath for him to truly understand what she'd said and all it meant. The woman nodded confirmation, and Maati stepped close to her, looking back over his shoulder and then down the corridor behind her to be sure they were alone.

"We were going to send you an escort," the woman said, "but no one could think of how to approach you without seeming like we were assassins. I thought an unarmed woman coming to you alone might suffice."

"You were right," he said, and then a moment later, "That's likely naïve of me, isn't it?"

"A bit."

"Please. Take me to him."

Twilight had soaked the sky in indigo. In the east, stars were peeking over the mountain tops, and the towers rose up into the air as if they led up to the clouds themselves. Maati and the woman walked quickly; she didn't speak, and he didn't press her to. His mind was busy enough already. They walked side by side along darkening paths. Kiyan smiled and nodded to those who took notice of them. Maati wondered how many people would be reporting that he had left the council with a woman. He looked back often for pursuers. No one *seemed* to be tracking them, but even at the edge of the palaces, there were enough people to prevent him from being sure.

They reached a teahouse, its windows blazing with light and its air rich with the scent of lemon candles to keep off the insects. The woman strode up the wide steps and into the warmth and light. The keep seemed to expect her, because they were led without a word into a back room where red wine was waiting along with a plate of rich cheese, black bread, and the first of the summer grapes. Kiyan sat at the table and gestured to the bench across from her. Maati sat as she plucked two of the small bright green grapes, bit into them and made a face.

"Too early?" he asked.

"Another week and they'll be decent. Here, pass me the cheese and bread."

Kiyan chewed these and Maati poured himself a bowl of wine. It was good—rich and deep and clean. He lifted the bottle but she shook her head.

"He'll be joining us, then?"

"No. We're just waiting a moment to be sure we're not leading anyone to him."

"Very professional," he said.

"Actually I'm new to all this. But I take advice well."

She had a good smile. Maati felt sure that this was the woman Otah had told him about that day in the gardens when Otah had left in chains. The woman he loved and whom he'd asked Maati to help protect. He tried to see Liat in her—the shape of her eyes, the curve of her cheek. There was nothing. Or perhaps there was something the two women shared that was simply beyond his ability to see.

As if feeling the weight of his attention, Kiyan took a querying pose. Maati shook his head.

"Reflecting on ages past," he said. "That's all."

She seemed about to ask something when a soft knock came at the door and the keep appeared, carrying a bundle of cloth. Kiyan stood, accepted the bundle, and took a pose that expressed her gratitude only slightly hampered by her burden. The keep left without speaking, and Kiyan pulled the cloth apart—two thin gray hooded cloaks that would cover their robes and hide their faces. She handed one to Maati and pulled the other on.

When they were both ready, Kiyan dug awkwardly in her doubled sleeve for a moment before coming out with four lengths of silver that she left on the table. Seeing Maati's surprise, she smiled.

"We didn't ask for the food and wine," she said. "It's rude to underpay."

"The grapes were sour," Maati said.

Kiyan considered this for a moment and scooped one silver length back into her sleeve. They didn't leave through the front door or out to the alley, but descended a narrow stairway into the tunnels beneath the city. Someone—the keep or one of Kiyan's conspirators—had left a lit lantern for them. Kiyan took it in hand and strode into the black tunnels as assured as a woman who had walked this maze her whole life. Maati kept close to her, dread pricking at him for the first time.

The descent seemed as deep as the mines in the plain. The stairs were worn smooth by generations of footsteps, the path they traveled inhabited by the memory of men and women long dead. At length the stairs gave way to a wide, tiled hallway shrouded in darkness. Kiyan's small lantern lit only part way up the deep blue and worked gold of the walls, the darkness above them more profound than a moonless sky.

The mouths of galleries and halls seemed to gape and close as they passed. Maati could see the scorch marks rising up the walls where torches had been set during some past winter, the smoke staining the tiles. A breath seemed to move through the dim air, like the earth exhaling.

The tunnels seemed empty except for them. No glimmer of light came from the doors and passages they passed, no voices however distant competed with the rustle of their robes. At a branching of the great hallway, Kiyan hesitated, then bore left. A pair of great brass gates opened onto a space like a garden, the plants all designed from silk, the birds perched on the branches dead and dust-covered.

"Unreal, isn't it?" Kiyan said as she picked her way across the sterile terrain. "I think they must go a little mad in the winters down here. All those months without seeing the sunlight."

"I suppose," Maati said.

After the garden, they went down a series of corridors so narrow that Maati could place his palms on both walls without stretching. She came to a high wooden doorway with brass fittings that was barred from within. Kiyan passed the lantern to Maati and knocked a complex pattern. A scraping sound spoke of the bar being lifted, and then the door swung in. Three men with blades in their hands stood. The center one smiled, stepped back and silently gestured them through.

Lanterns filled the stone-walled passage with warm, buttery light and the scent of burnt oil. There was no door at the end, only an archway that opened out into a wide, tall space that smelled of sweat and damp wool and torch smoke. A storehouse, then, with the door frames stuffed with rope to keep out even a glimmer of light.

Half a dozen men stopped their conversations as Kiyan led him across the empty space to the overseer's office—a shack within the structure that glowed from within.

Kiyan opened the office door and stood aside, smiling encouragement to Maati as he stepped past her and into the small room. A desk. Four chairs. A stand for scrolls. A map of the winter cities nailed to the wall. Three lanterns. And Otah-kvo rising now from his seat.

He was still thin, but there was an energy about him—in the way he held his shoulders and his hands. In the way he moved.

"You're looking well for a dead man," Maati said.

"Feeling better than expected, too," Otah said, and a smile spread across his long, northern face. "Thank you for coming."

"How could I not?" Maati drew one of the chairs close to him and sat, his fingers laced around one knee. "So you've chosen to take the city after all?"

Otah hesitated a moment, then sat. He rubbed the desktop with his open palm—a dry sound—and his brow furrowed.

"I don't see my option," he said at last. "That sounds convenient, I know. But . . . you said before that you'd realized I had nothing to do with Biitrah's death and your assault. I didn't have a part in Danat's murder either. Or my father's. Or even my own rescue from the tower, come to that. It's all simply *happened* up to now. And I didn't know whether you still believed me innocent."

Maati smiled ruefully. There was something in Otah's voice that sounded like hope. Maati didn't know his own heart—the resentment, the anger, the love of Otah-kvo and of Liat and the child she'd borne. He couldn't say even what they all had to do with this man sitting across his appropriated desk.

"I do," Maati said at last. "I've been looking into the matter, but I suppose you know that if you've had me watched."

"Yes. That's one reason I wanted to speak to you."

"There are others?"

"I have a confession to make. I'd likely be wiser to keep quiet until this whole round is finished, but . . . I've lied to you, Maati. I told you that I'd been with a woman in the east islands and failed to father a child on her. She . . . she wasn't real. That never happened."

Maati considered this, waiting for his heart to rise in anger or shrivel, but it only beat in its customary rhythm. He wondered when it had stopped mattering to him, the father of the boy he'd lost. Since the last time he had spoken with Otah in the high stone cell, certainly, but looking back, he couldn't put a moment to it. If the boy was his get or Otah's, neither would bring him back. Neither would undo the years gone by. And there were other things that he had that he might still lose, or else save.

"I thought I was going to die," Otah said. "I thought it wouldn't matter to me, and if it gave you some comfort, then . . ."

"Let it go," Maati said. "If there's anything to be said about it, we can say it later. There are other matters at hand."

"Have you found something, then?"

"I have a family name, I think. Certainly there's someone putting money and influence behind the Vaunyogi."

"Likely the Galts," Otah said. "They've been making contracts bad enough to look like bribes. We didn't know what influence they were buying."

"It could be this," Maati said. "Do you know why they'd do it?"

"No," Otah said. "But if you've proof that the Vaunyogi are behind the murderers—"

"I don't," Maati said. "I have a suspicion, but nothing more than that. Not yet. And if we don't uncover them quickly, they'll likely have Adrah named Khai Machi and have the resources of the whole city to find you and kill you for crimes that everyone outside this warehouse assumes you guilty of."

They sat in silence for the space of three breaths.

"Well," Otah-kvo said, "it appears we have some work to do then. But at least we've an idea where to look."

IN HER DREAM, IDAAN WAS AT A CELEBRATION. FIRE BURNED IN A RING ALL AROUND the pavilion, and she knew with the logic of dreams that the flames were going to close, that the circle was growing smaller. They were all going to burn. She tried to shout, tried to warn the dancers, but she could only croak; no one heard her. There was someone there who could stop the thing from happening—a single man who was Cehmai and Otah and her father all at once. She beat her way through the bodies, trying to find him, but there were dogs in with the people. The flames were too close already, and to keep themselves alive, the women were throwing the animals into the fire. She woke to the screams and howls in her mind and the silence in her chamber.

The night candle had failed. The chamber was dim, silvered by moonlight beyond the dark web of the netting. The shutters along the wall were all open, but no breath of air stirred. Idaan swallowed and shook her head, willing the last wisps of nightmare into forgetfulness. She waited, listening to her breath, until her mind was her own again. Even then she was reluctant to sleep for fear of falling into the same dream. She turned to Adrah, but the bed at her side was empty. He was gone.

"Adrah?"

There was no answer.

Idaan wrapped herself with a thin blanket, pushed aside the netting and stepped out of her bed—her new bed. Her marriage bed. The smooth stone of the floor was cool against her bare feet. She walked through the chambers of their apartments—hers and her husband's—silently. She found him sitting on a low couch, a bottle beside him. A thick earthenware bowl on the floor stank of distilled wine. Or perhaps it was his breath.

"You aren't sleeping?" she asked.

"Neither are you," he said. The slurred words were half accusation.

"I had a dream," she said. "It woke me."

Adrah lifted the bottle, drinking from its neck. She watched the delicate shifting mechanism of his throat, the planes of his cheeks, his eyes closed and as smooth as a man asleep. Her fingers twitched toward him, moving to caress that familiar skin without consulting him on her wishes. Coughing, he put down the wine, and the eyes opened. Whatever beauty had been in him, however briefly, was gone now.

"You should go to him," Adrah said. Perversely, he sounded less drunk now. Idaan took a pose of query. Adrah waved it away with the sloshing bottle. "The poet boy. Cehmai. You should go to him. See if you can get more information."

"You don't want me here?"

"No," Adrah said, pressing the bottle into her hand. As he rose and staggered past her, Idaan felt the insult and the rejection and a certain relief that she hadn't had to find an excuse to slip away.

The palaces were deserted, the empty paths dreamlike in their own way. Idaan let herself imagine that she had woken into a new, different world. As she slept, everyone had vanished, and she was walking now alone through an empty city. Or she had died in her sleep and the gods had put her here, into a world with nothing but herself and darkness. If they had meant it for punishment, they had misjudged.

The bottle was below a quarter when she stepped under the canopy of sculpted oaks. She had expected the poet's house to be dark as well, but as she advanced, she caught glimpses of candle glow, more light than a single night candle could account for. Something like hope surged in her, and she slowly walked forward. The shutters and door were open, the lanterns within all lit. But the wide, still figure on the steps wasn't him. Idaan hesitated. The andat raised its hand in greeting and motioned her closer.

"I was starting to think you wouldn't come," Stone-Made-Soft said in its distant, rumbling voice.

"I hadn't intended to," Idaan said. "You had no call to expect me."

"If you say so," it agreed, amiably. "Come inside. He's been waiting to see you for days."

Going up the steps felt like walking downhill, the pull to be there and see him was more powerful than weight. The andat stood and followed her in, closing the door behind her and then proceeding around the room, fastening the shutters and snuffing the flames. Idaan looked around the room, but there were only the two of them.

"It's late. He's in the back," the andat said and pinched out another small light. "You should go to him."

"I don't want to disturb him."

"He'd want you to."

She didn't move. The spirit tilted its broad head and smiled.

"He said he loves me," Idaan said. "When I saw him last, he said that he loved me."

"I know."

"Is it true?"

The smile broadened. Its teeth were white as marble and perfectly regular. She noticed for the first time that it had no canines—every tooth was even and square as the one beside it. For a moment, the inhuman mouth disturbed her.

"Why are you asking me?"

"You know him," she said. "You are him."

"True on both counts," Stone-Made-Soft said. "But I'm not credited as being the most honest source. I'm his creature, after all. And all dogs hate the leash, however well they pretend otherwise."

"You've never lied to me."

The andat looked startled, then chuckled with a sound like a boulder rolling downhill.

"No," it said. "I haven't, have I? And I won't start now. Yes, Cehmai-kya has fallen in love with you. He's young. His passions are still a large part of what he is. In forty years, he won't burn so hot. It's the way it's been with all of them."

"I don't want him hurt," she said.

"Then stay."

"I'm not sure that would save him pain. Not in the long term."

The andat went still a moment, then shrugged.

"Then go," it said. "But when he finds you've gone, he'll chew his own guts out over it. There's been nothing he's wanted more than for you to come here, to him. Coming this close, talking to me, and leaving? It'd hardly make him feel better about things."

Idaan looked at her feet. The sandals weren't laced well. She'd done the thing in darkness, and the wine had, perhaps, had more effect on her than she'd thought. She shook her head as she had when shaking off the dreams.

"He doesn't have to know I came."

"Late for that," the andat said and put out another candle. "He woke up as soon as we started talking."

"Idaan-kya?" his voice came from behind her.

Cehmai stood in the corridor that led back to his bedchamber. His hair was tousled by sleep. His feet were bare. Idaan caught her breath, seeing him here in the dim light of candles. He was beautiful. He was innocent and powerful, and she loved him more than anyone in the world.

"Cehmai."

"Only Cehmai?" he asked, stepping into the room. He looked hurt and hopeful both. She had no right to feel this young. She had no right to feel afraid or thrilled.

"Cehmai-kya," she whispered. "I had to see you."

"I'm glad of it. But . . . but you aren't, are you? Glad to see me, I mean."

"It wasn't supposed to be like this," she said, and the sorrow rose up in her like a flood. "It's my wedding night, Cehmai-kya. I was married today, and I couldn't go a whole night in that bed."

Her voice broke. She closed her eyes against the tears, but they simply came, rolling down her cheeks as fast as raindrops. She heard him move toward her, and between wanting to step into his arms and wanting to run, she stood unmoving, feeling herself tremble.

He didn't speak. She was standing alone and apart, the sorrow and guilt beating her like storm waves, and then his arms folded her into him. His skin smelled dark and musky and male. He didn't kiss her, he didn't try to open her robes. He only held her there as if he had never wanted anything more. She put her arms around him and held on as though he was a branch hanging over a precipice. She heard herself sob, and it sounded like violence.

"I'm sorry," she said. "I'm so sorry. I'm so sorry. I want it back. I want it all back. I'm so sorry."

"What, love? What do you want back?"

"All of it," she wailed, and the blackness and despair and rage and sorrow rose up, taking her in its teeth and shaking her. Cehmai held her close, murmured soft words to her, stroked her hair and her face. When she sank to the ground, he sank with her.

She couldn't say how long it was before the crying passed. She only knew that the night around them was perfectly dark, that she was curled in on herself with her head in his lap, and that her body was tired to the bone. She felt as if she'd swum for a day. She found Cehmai's hand and laced her fingers with his, wondering where dawn was. It seemed the night had already lasted for years. Surely there would be light soon.

"You feel better?" he asked, and she nodded her reply, trusting him to feel the movement against his flesh.

"Do you want to tell me what it is?" he asked.

Idaan felt her throat go tighter for a moment. He must have felt some change in her body, because he raised her hand to his lips. His mouth was so soft and so warm.

"I do," she said. "I want to. But I'm afraid."

"Of me?"

"Of what I would say."

There was something in his expression. Not a hardening, not a pulling away, but a change. It was as if she'd confirmed something.

"There's nothing you can say that will hurt me," Cehmai said. "Not if it's true. It's the Vaunyogi, isn't it? It's Adrah."

"I can't, love. Please don't talk about it."

But he only ran his free hand over her arm, the sound of skin against skin loud in the night's silence. When he spoke again, Cehmai's voice was gentle, but urgent.

"It's about your father and your brothers, isn't it?"

Idaan swallowed, trying to loosen her throat. She didn't answer, not even with a movement, but Cehmai's soft, beautiful voice pressed on.

"Otah Machi didn't kill them, did he?"

The air went thin as a mountaintop's. Idaan couldn't catch her breath. Cehmai's fingers pressed hers gently. He leaned forward and kissed her temple.

"It's all right," he said. "Tell me."

"I can't," she said.

"I love you, Idaan-kya. And I will protect you, whatever happens."

Idaan closed her eyes, even in the darkness. Her heart seemed on the edge of bursting she wanted it so badly to be true. She wanted so badly to lay her sins before him and be forgiven. And he knew already. He knew the truth or else guessed it, and he hadn't denounced her.

"I love you," he repeated, his voice softer than the sound of his hand stroking her skin. "How did it start?"

"I don't know," she said. And then, a moment later, "When I was young, I think."

Quietly, she told him everything, even the things she had never told Adrah. Seeing her brothers sent to the school and being told that she could not go herself because of her sex. Watching her mother brood and suffer and know that one day she would be sent away or else die there, in the women's quarters and be remembered only as something that had borne a Khai's babies.

She told him about listening to songs about the sons of the Khaiem battling for the succession and how, as a girl, she'd pretend to be one of them and force her playmates to take on the roles of her rivals. And the sense of injustice that her older brothers would pick their own wives and command their own fates, while she would be sold at convenience.

At some point, Cehmai stopped stroking her, and only listened, but that open, receptive silence was all she needed of him. She poured out everything. The wild, impossible plans she'd woven with Adrah. The intimation, one night when a Galtic dignitary had come to Machi, that the schemes might not be impossible after all. The bargain they had struck—access to a library's depth of old books and scrolls traded for power and freedom. And from there, the progression, inevitable as water flowing toward the sea, that led Adrah to her father's sleeping chambers and her to the still moment by the lake, the terrible sound of the arrow striking home.

With every phrase, she felt the horror of it ease. It lost none of the sorrow, none of the regret, but the bleak, soul-eating despair began to fade from black to merely the darkest gray. By the time she came to the end of one sentence and found nothing following it, the birds outside had begun to trill and sing. It would be light soon. Dawn would come after all. She sighed.

"That was a longer answer than you hoped for, maybe," she said.

"It was enough," he said.

Idaan shifted and sat up, pulling her hair back from her face. Cehmai didn't move.

"Hiami told me once," she said, "just before she left, that to become Khai you had to forget how to love. I see why she believed that. But it isn't what's happened. Not to me. Thank you, Cehmai-kya."

"For what?"

"For loving me. For protecting me," she said. "I didn't guess how much I needed to tell you all that. It was . . . it was too much. You see that."

"I do," Cehmai said.

"Are you angry with me now?"

"Of course not," he said.

"Are you horrified by me?"

She heard him shift his weight. The pause stretched, her heart sickening with every beat.

"I love you, Idaan," he said at last, and she felt the tears come again, but this time with a very different pressure behind them. It wasn't joy, but it was perhaps relief.

She shifted forward in the darkness, found his body there waiting, and held him for a time. She was the one who kissed him this time. She was the one who moved their conversation from the intimacy of confession to the intimacy of sex. Cehmai seemed almost reluctant, as if afraid that taking her body now would betray some deeper moment that they had shared. But Idaan led him to his bed in the darkness, opened her own robes and his, and coaxed his flesh until whatever objection he'd fostered was forgotten. She found herself at ease, lighter, almost as if she was half in dream.

Afterwards, she lay nestled in his arms, warm, safe, and calm as she had never been in years. Sunlight pressed at the closed shutters as she drifted down to sleep.

13

The tunnels beneath Machi were a city unto themselves. Otah found himself drawn out into them more and more often as the days crept forward. Sinja and Amiit had tried to keep him from leaving the storehouse beneath the underground palaces of the Saya, but Otah had overruled them.

The risk of a few quiet hours walking abandoned corridors was less, he judged, than the risk of going quietly mad waiting in the same sunless room day after day. Sinja had convinced him to take an armsman as guard when he went.

Otah had expected the darkness and the quiet—wide halls empty, water troughs dry—but the beauty he stumbled on took him by surprise. Here a wide square of stone smooth as beach sand, delicate pillars spiraling up from it like bolts of twisting silk made from stone. And down another corridor, a bath-house left dry for the winter but rich with the scent of cedar and pine resin.

Even when he returned to the storehouse and the voices and faces he knew, he found his mind lingering in the dark corridors and galleries, unsure whether the images of the spaces lit with the white shadowless light of a thousand candles were imagination or memory.

A sharp rapping brought him back to himself, and the door of his private office swung open. Amiit and Sinja walked in, already half into a conversation. Sinja's expression was mildly annoyed. Amiit, Otah thought, seemed worried.

"It would only make things worse," Amiit said.

"We'd earn more time. And it isn't as if they'd accuse Otah-cha here of it. They think he's dead."

"Then they'll accuse him of it once they find he's alive," Amiit said and turned to Otah. "Sinja wants to assassinate the head of a high family in order to slow the work of the council."

"We won't do that," Otah said. "My hands aren't particularly bloodied yet, and I'd like to keep it that way—"

"It isn't as though people are going to believe it," Sinja said. "If you're going to carry the blame you may as well get the advantages from doing the thing."

"It'll be easier to convince them of my innocence later if I'm actually innocent of something," Otah said, "but there may be other roads that come to the same place. Is there something else that would slow the council and doesn't involve putting holes in someone?"

Sinja frowned, his eyes shifting as if he were reading text written in the air. He half-smiled.

"Perhaps. Let me look into that."

With a pose that ended his conversation, Sinja left. Amiit sighed and lowered himself into one of the chairs.

"What news?" Amiit asked.

"Kamau and Vaunani are talking about merging their forces," Otah said. "Most of the talks seem to involve someone hitting someone or throwing a knife. The Loiya, Bentani, and Coirah have all been quietly, and so far as I can tell, independently, backing the Vaunyogi."

"And they all have contracts with Galt," Amiit said. "What about the others?"

"Of the families we know? None have come out against them. And none for, or at least not openly."

"There should be more fighting," Amiit said. "There should be struggles and coalitions. Alliances should be forming and breaking by the moment. It's too steady."

"Only if there was a real struggle going on. If the decision was already made, it would look exactly like this."

"Yes. There are times I hate being right. Any word from the poet?"

Otah shook his head and sat, then stood again. Maati had gone from their first meeting, and he'd seemed convinced. Otah had been sure at the time that he wouldn't betray them. He was sure in his bones. He only wished he'd had his thoughts more in order at the time. He'd been swept up in the moment, more concerned with his lies about Liat's son than anything else. He'd had time since to reflect, and the other worries had swarmed out. Otah had sat up until the night candle was at its halfway mark, listing the things he needed to consider. It hadn't lent him peace.

"It's hard, waiting," Amiit said. "You must feel like you're back up in that tower."

"That was easier. Then at least I knew what was going to happen. I wish I could go *out*. If I could be up there listening to the people themselves . . . If I spent half an evening in the right teahouse, I'd know more than I'll learn skulking down here for days. Yes, I know. You've the best minds of the house out watching for us. But listening to reports isn't the same as putting my hands to something."

"I know it. More than half my work has been trying to guess the truth out of a dozen different reports of a thing. There's a knack to it. You'll have your practice with it."

"If this ends well," Otah said.

"Yes," Amiit agreed. "If that."

Otah filled a tin cup with water from a stone jar and sat back down. It was warm, and a thin grit swam at the cup's bottom. He wished it were wine and pushed the thought away. If there was any time in his life to be sober as stone, this was it, but his unease shifted and tightened. He looked up from his water to see Amiit's gaze on him, his expression quizzical.

"We have to make a plan for if we lose," Otah said. "If the Vaunyogi are to blame and the council gives them power, they'll be able to wash away any number of crimes. And all those families that supported them will be invested in keeping things quiet. If it comes out that Daaya Vaunyogi killed the Khai in order to raise up his son and half the families of the utkhaiem took money to support it, they'll all share in the guilt. Being in the right won't mean much then."

"There's time yet," Amiit said, but he was looking away when he said it.

"And what happens if we fail?"

"That all depends on how we fail. If we're discovered before we're ready to move, we'll all be killed. If Adrah is named Khai, we'll at least have a chance to slip away quietly."

"You'll take care of Kiyan?"

Amiit smiled. "I hope to see to it that you can perform that duty."

"But if not?"

"Then of course," Amiit said. "Provided I live."

The rapping came again, and the door opened on a young man. Otah recognized him from the meetings in House Siyanti, but he couldn't recall his name.

"The poet's come," the young man said.

Amiit rose, took a pose appropriate to the parting of friends, and left. The young man went with him, and for a moment the door swung free, half closing. Otah drank the last of his water, the grit rough in his throat. Maati came in slowly, a diffidence in his body and his face, like a man called in to hear news that might bring him good or ill or some unimagined change that folded both inextricably together. Otah gestured to the door, and Maati closed it.

"You sent for me?" Maati asked. "That's a dangerous habit, Otah-kvo."

"I know it, but . . . Please. Sit. I've been thinking. About what we do if things go poorly."

"If we fail?"

"I want to be ready for it, and when Kiyan and I were talking last night, something occurred to me. Nayiit? That's his name, isn't it? The child that you and Liat had?"

Maati's expression was cool and distant and misleading. Otah could see the pain in it, however still the eyes.

"What of him?"

"He mustn't be my son. Whatever happens, he has to be yours."

"If you fail, you don't take your father's title—"

"If I don't take his title, and someone besides you decides he's mine, they'll kill him to remove all doubt of the succession. And if I succeed, Kiyan may have a son," Otah said. "And then they would someday have to kill each other. Nayiit is *your* son. He has to be."

"I see," Maati said.

"I've written a letter. It looks like something I'd have sent Kiyan before, when I was in Chaburi-Tan. It talks about the night I left Saraykeht. It says that on the night I came back to the city, I found the two of you together. That I walked into her cell, and you and she were in her cot. It makes it clear that I didn't touch her, that I couldn't have fathered a child on her. Kiyan's put it in her things. If we have to flee, we'll take it with us and find a way for it to come to light—we can hide it at her wayhouse, perhaps. If we're found and killed here, it will be found with us. You have to back that story."

Maati steepled his fingers and leaned back in the chair.

"You've put it with Kiyan-cha's things to be found in case she's slaughtered?" he asked.

"Yes," Otah said. "I don't think about it when I can help it, but I know she could die here. There's no reason that your son should die with us."

Maati nodded slowly. He was struggling with something, Otah could see that much, but whether it was sorrow or anger or joy, he had no way to know. When the question came, though, it was the one he had been dreading for years.

"What did happen?" Maati asked at last, his voice low and hushed. "The night Heshai-kvo died. What happened? Did you just leave? Did you take Maj with you? Did . . . did you kill him?"

Otah remembered the cord cutting into his hands, remembered the way Maj had balked and he had taken the task himself. For years, those few minutes had haunted him.

"He knew what was coming," Otah said. "He knew it was necessary. The consequences if he had lived would have been worse. Heshai was right when he warned you to let the thing drop. The Khai Saraykeht would have turned the andat against Galt. There would have been thousands of innocent lives ruined. And when it was over, you would still have been yoked to Seedless. Trapped in the torture box just the way Heshai had been all those years. Heshai knew that, and he waited for me to do the thing."

"And you did it."

"I did."

Maati was silent. Otah sat. His knees seemed less solid than he would have liked, but he didn't let the weakness stop him.

"It was the worst thing I have ever done," Otah said. "I never stopped dreaming about it. Even now, I see it sometimes. Heshai was a good man, but what he'd created in Seedless . . ."

"Seedless was only part of him. They all are. They couldn't be anything else. Heshai-kvo hated himself, and Seedless was that."

"Everyone hates themselves sometimes. There isn't often a price in blood," Otah said. "You know what would happen if that were proven. Killing a Khai would pale beside murdering a poet."

Maati nodded slowly, and still nodding, spoke.

"I didn't ask on the Dai-kvo's behalf. I asked for myself. When Heshai-kvo died, Seedless . . . vanished. I was with him. I was there. He was asking me whether I would have forgiven you. If you'd committed some terrible crime, like what he had done to Maj, if I would forgive you. And I told him I would. I would forgive you, and not him. Because . . ."

They were silent. Maati's eyes were dark as coal.

"Because?" Otah asked.

"Because I loved you, and I didn't love him. He said it was a pity to think that love and justice weren't the same. The last thing he said was that you had forgiven me."

"Forgiven you?"

"For Liat. For taking your lover."

"I suppose it's true," Otah said. "I was angry with you. But there was a part of me that was . . . relieved, I suppose."

"Why?"

"Because I didn't love her. I thought I did. I wanted to, and I enjoyed her company and her bed. I liked her and respected her. Sometimes, I wanted her as badly as I've ever wanted anyone. And that was enough to let me mistake it for love. But I don't remember it hurting that deeply or for that long. Sometimes I was even glad. You had each other to take care of, and so it wasn't mine to do."

"You said, that last time we spoke before you left . . . before Heshai-kvo died, that you didn't trust me."

"That's true," Otah said. "I do remember that."

"But you've come to me now, and you've told me this. You've told me all of it. Even after I gave you over to the Khai. You've brought me in here, shown me where you've hidden. You know there are half a hundred people I could say a word to, and you and all these other people would be dead before the sun set. So it seems you trust me now."

"I do," Otah said without hesitating.

"Why?"

Otah sat with the question. His mind had been consumed for days with a thousand different things that all nipped and shrieked and robbed him of his rest. To reach out to Maati had seemed natural and obvious, and even though when he looked at it coldly it was true that each had in some way betrayed the other, his heart had never been in doubt. He could feel the heaviness in the air, and he knew that *I don't know* wouldn't be answer enough. He looked for words to give his feelings shape.

"Because," he said at last, "in all the time I knew you, you never once did the wrong thing. Even when what you did hurt me, it was never wrong."

To his surprise, there were tears on Maati's cheeks.

"Thank you, Otah-kvo," he said.

A shout went up in the tunnels outside the storehouse and the sound of running feet. Maati wiped his eyes with the sleeve of his robes, and Otah stood, his heart beating fast. The murmur of voices grew, but there were no sounds of blade against blade. It sounded like a busy corner more than a battle. Otah walked to the door and, Maati close behind him, stepped out into the main space. A knot of men were talking and gesturing one to the other by the mouth of the stairs. Otah caught a glimpse of Kiyan in their midst, frowning deeply and speaking fast. Amiit detached himself from the throng and strode to Otah.

"What's happened?"

"Bad news, Otah-cha. Daaya Vaunyogi has called for a decision, and enough of the families have backed the call to push it through."

Otah felt his heart sink.

"They're bound to decide by morning," Amiit went on, "and if all the houses that backed him for the call side with him in the decision, Adrah Vaunyogi will be the Khai Machi by the time the sun comes up."

"And then what?" Maati asked.

"And then we run," Otah said, "as far and fast and quiet as we can, and we hope he never finds us."

THE SUN HAD PASSED ITS HIGHEST POINT AND STARTED THE LONG, SLOW SLIDE toward darkness. Idaan had chosen robes the blue-gray of twilight and bound her hair back with clasps of silver and moonstone. Around her, the gallery was nearly full, the air thick with heat and the mingled scents of bodies and perfumes. She stood at the rail, looking down into the press of bodies below her. The parquet of the floor was scuffed with the marks of boots. There were no empty places at the tables or against the stone walls, no quiet negotiations going on in hallways or teahouses. That time had passed, and in its wake, they were all brought here. Voices washed together like the hushing of wind, and she could feel the weight of the eyes upon her—the men below her sneaking glances up, the representatives of the merchant houses at her side considering her, and the lower orders in the gallery above staring down at her and the men over whom she loomed. She was a woman, and not welcome to speak or sit at the tables below. But still, she would make her presence felt.

"How is it that we accept the word of these men that they are the wisest?" Ghiah Vaunani pounded the speaker's pulpit before him with each word, a dry, shallow sound. Idaan almost thought she could see flecks of foam at the corners of his mouth. "How is it that the houses of the utkhaiem are so much like sheep that they would consent to be led by this shepherd boy of Vaunyogi?"

It was meant, Idaan knew, to be a speech to sway the others from their confidence, but all she heard in the words was the confusion and pain of a boy whose plans have fallen through. He could pound and rail and screech his questions as long as his voice held out. Idaan, standing above the proceedings like a protective ghost, knew the answers to every one, and she would never tell them to him.

Below her, Adrah Vaunyogi looked up, his expression calm and certain. It had been late in the morning that she'd woken in the poet's house, later still when she'd returned to the rooms she shared now with her husband. He had been there, waiting for her. The night's excesses had weighed heavy on him. They hadn't spoken—she had only called for a bath and clean robes. When she'd cleaned herself and washed her hair, she sat at her mirror and painted her face with all her old skill and delicacy. The woman who looked out at her when she put down her brushes might have been the loveliest in Machi.

Adrah had left without a word. It had been almost half a hand before she learned that her new father, Daaya Vaunyogi, had called for the decision, and that the houses had agreed. No one had told her to come here, no one had asked her to lend the sight of her silent presence to the cause. She had done it, perhaps, *because* Adrah had not demanded it of her.

"We must not hurry! We must not allow sentiment to push us into a decision that will change our city forever!"

Idaan allowed herself a smile. It would seem to most people that the force of the story had won the day. The last daughter of the old line would be the first mother of the new, and if a quiet structure of money and obligation supported it, if she were really the lover of the poet a hundred times more than the Khai, it hardly mattered. It was what the city would see, and that was enough.

Ghiah's energy was beginning to flag. She heard his words lose their crispness and the pounding on his table fall out of rhythm. The anger in his voice became merely petulance, and the objections to Adrah in particular and the Vaunyogi in general lost their force. It would have been better, she thought, if he'd ended half a hand earlier. Still insufficient, but less so.

The Master of Tides stood when Ghiah at last surrendered the floor. He was an old man with a long, northern face and a deep, sonorous voice. Idaan saw his eyes flicker up to her and then away.

"Adaut Kamau has also asked to address the council," he said, "before the houses speak on the decision to accept Adrah Vaunyogi as the Khai Machi. . . ."

A chorus of jeers rose from the galleries and even the council tables. Idaan held herself still and quiet. Her feet were starting to ache, but she didn't shift her weight. The effect she desired wouldn't be served by showing her pleasure. Adaut Kamau rose, his face gray and pinched. He opened his arms, but before he could speak, a bundle of rough cloth arced from the highest gallery. A long tail of brown fluttered behind it like a banner as it fell, and in the instant that it struck the floor, the screaming began.

Idaan's composure broke, and she leaned forward. The men at the tables nearest the thing waved their arms and fled, shrieking and pounding at the air. Voices buzzed and a cloud of pale, moving smoke rose toward the galleries.

No. The buzzing was not voices, the cloud was not smoke. These were wasps. The bundle on the council floor had been a nest wrapped in cloth and wax. The first of the insects buzzed past her, a glimpse of black and yellow. She turned and ran.

Bodies filled the corridors, panic pressing them together until there was no air, no space. People screamed and cursed—men, women, children. Their shrill voices mixed with the angry buzz. She was pushed from all sides. An elbow dug into her back. The surge of the crowd pressed the breath from her. She was suffocating, and insects filled the air above her. Idaan felt something bite the flesh at the back of her neck like a hot iron burning her. She screamed and tried to reach back to bat the thing away, but there was no room to move her arm, no air. She lashed out at whoever, whatever, was near. The crowd was a single, huge, biting beast and Idaan flailed and shrieked, her mind lost to fear and pain and confusion.

Stepping into the open air of the street was like waking from a nightmare. The bodies around her thinned, becoming only themselves again. The fierce buzz of tiny wings was gone, the cries of pain and terror replaced by the groans of the stung. People were still streaming out of the palace, arms flapping, but others were sitting on benches or else the ground. Servants and slaves were rushing about, tending to the hurt and the humiliated. Idaan felt the back of her neck—three angry bumps were already forming.

"It's a poor omen," a man in the red robes of the needle wrights said. "Something more's going on than meets the eye if someone's willing to attack the council to keep old Kamau from talking."

"What could he have said?" the man's companion asked.

"I don't know, but you can be sure whatever it was, he'll be saying something else tomorrow. Someone wanted him stopped. Unless this is about Adrah Vaunyogi. It could be that someone wants him closed down."

"Then why loose the things when his critics were about to speak?"

"Good point. Perhaps . . ."

Idaan moved on down the street. It was like the aftermath of some gentle, bloodless battle. People bound bruised limbs. Slaves brought plasters to suck out the wasps' venom. But already, all down the wide street, the talk had turned back to the business of the council.

Her neck was burning now, but she pushed the pain aside. There would be no decision made today. That was clear. Kamau or Vaunani had disrupted the proceedings to get more time. It had to be that. It couldn't be more, except that of course it could. The fear was different now, deeper and more complex. Almost like nausea.

Adrah was leaning against the wall at the mouth of an alleyway. His father was sitting beside him, a serving girl dabbing white paste on the angry welts that covered his arms and face. Idaan went to her husband. His eyes were hard and shallow as stones.

"May I speak with you, Adrah-kya?" she said softly.

Adrah looked at her as if seeing her for the first time, then at his father. He nodded toward the shadows of the alley behind him, and Idaan followed him until the noises of the street were vague and distant.

"It was Otah," she said. "He did this. He knows."

"Are you about to tell me that he's planned it all from the start again? It was a cheap, desperate trick. It won't matter, except that anyone who doesn't like us will say we did it, and anyone who has a grudge against our enemies will put it to them. Nothing changes."

"Who would do it?"

Adrah shook his head, impatient, and turned to walk back out into the street and noise and light. "Anyone might have. There's no point trying to solve every puzzle in the world."

"Don't be stupid, Adrah. Someone's acted against—"

The violence and suddenness of his movement was shocking. He was walking away, his back to her, and then a heartbeat later, there was no more room between them than the width of a leaf. His face was twisted, flushed, possessed by anger.

"Don't be *stupid*? Is that what you said?"

Idaan took a step back, her feet unsteady beneath her.

"How do you mean, stupid, Idaan? Stupid like calling out my lover's name in a crowd?"

"What?"

"Cehmai. The poet boy. When you were running, you called his name."

"I did?"

"Everyone heard it," Adrah said. "Everybody knows. At least you could keep it between us and not parade it all over the city!"

"I didn't mean to," she said. "I swear it, Adrah. I didn't know I had."

He stepped back and spat, the spittle striking the wall beside him and dripping down toward the ground. His gaze locked on her, daring her to push him, to meet his anger with defiance or submission. Either would be devastating. Idaan felt herself go hard. It wasn't unlike the feeling of seeing her father dying breath by breath, his belly rotting out and taking him with it.

"It won't get better, will it?" she asked. "It will go on. It will change. But it will never get better than it is right now."

The dread in Adrah's eyes told her she'd struck home. When he turned and stalked away, she didn't try to stop him.

TELL ME, HE'D SAID.

I can't, she'd replied.

And now Cehmai sat on a chair, staring at the bare wall and wished that he'd left it there. The hours since morning had been filled with a kind of anguish he'd never known. He'd told her he loved her. He did love her. But . . . Gods! She'd murdered her own family. She'd engineered her own father's death and as much as sold the Khai's library to the Galts. And the only thing that had saved her was that she loved him and he'd sworn he'd protect her. He'd sworn it.

"What did you expect?" Stone-Made-Soft asked.

"That it was Adrah. That I'd be protecting her from the Vaunyogi," Cehmai said.

"Well. Perhaps you should have been more specific."

The sun had passed behind the mountains, but the daylight hadn't yet taken on the ruddy hues of sunset. This was not night but shadow. The andat stood at the window, looking out. A servant had come from the palaces earlier bearing a meal of roast chicken and rich, dark bread. The smell of it filled the house, though the platter had been set outside to be taken away. He hadn't been able to eat.

Cehmai could barely feel where the struggle in the back of his mind met the confusion at the front. Idaan. It had been Idaan all along.

"You couldn't have known," the andat said, its tone conciliatory. "And it isn't as if she asked you to be part of the thing."

"You think she was using me."

"Yes. But since I'm a creature of your mind, it seems to follow that you'd think the same. She did extract a promise from you. You're sworn to protect her."

"I love her."

"You'd better. If you don't, then she told you all that under a false impression that you led her to believe. If she hadn't truly thought she could trust you, she'd have kept her secrets to herself."

"I do love her."

"And that's good," Stone-Made-Soft said. "Since all that blood she spilled is part yours now."

Cehmai leaned forward. His foot knocked over the thin porcelain bowl at his feet. The last dregs of the wine spilled to the floor, but he didn't bother with it. Stained carpet was beneath his notice now. His head was stuffed with wool, and none of his thoughts seemed to connect. He thought of Idaan's smile and the way she turned toward him, nestling into him as she slept. Her voice had been so soft, so quiet. And then, when she had asked him if he was horrified by her, there had been so much fear in her.

He hadn't been able to say yes. It had been there, waiting in his throat, and he'd swallowed it. He'd told her he loved her, and he hadn't lied. But he hadn't slept either. The andat's wide hand turned the bowl upright and pressed a cloth onto the spill. Cehmai watched the red wick up into the white cloth.

"Thank you," he said.

Stone-Made-Soft took a brief, dismissive pose and lumbered away. Cehmai heard it pouring water into a basin to rinse the cloth, and felt a pang of shame. He was falling apart. The andat itself was taking care of him now. He was pathetic. Cehmai rose and stalked to the window. He felt as much as heard the andat come up behind him.

"So," the andat said. "What are you going to do?"

"I don't know."

"Do you think she's got her legs around him now? Just at the moment, I mean," the andat said, its voice as calm and placid and distantly amused as always. "He is her husband. He must get her knees apart now and again. And she must enjoy him on some level. She did slaughter her family to elevate Adrah. It's not something most girls would do."

"You're not helping," Cehmai said.

"It could be you're just a part of her plan. She did fall into your bed awfully easily. Do you think they talk about it, the two of them? About what she can do to you or for you to win your support? Having the poet's oath protecting you would be a powerful thing. And if you protect her, you protect them. You can't suggest anything evil of the Vaunyogi now without drawing her into it."

"She isn't like that!"

Cehmai gathered his will, but before he could turn it on the andat, before he pushed the rage and the anger and the hurt into a force that would make the beast be quiet, Stone-Made-Soft smiled, leaned forward, and gently kissed Cehmai's forehead. In all the years he'd held it, Cehmai had never seen the andat do anything of the sort.

"No," it said. "She isn't. She's in terrible trouble, and she needs you to save her if you can. If she can be saved. And she trusts you. Standing with her is the only thing you could do and still be a decent man."

Cehmai glared at the wide face, the slow, calm eyes, searching for a shred of sarcasm. There was none.

"Why are you trying to confuse me?" he asked.

The andat turned to look out the window and stood as still as a statue. Cehmai waited, but it didn't shift, even to look at him. The rooms darkened and Cehmai lit lemon candles to keep the insects away. His mind was divided into a hundred different thoughts, each of them powerful and convincing and no two fitting together.

When at last he went up to his bed, he couldn't sleep. The blankets still smelled of her, of the two of them. Of love and sleep. Cehmai wrapped the sheets around himself and willed his mind to quiet, but the whirl of thoughts didn't allow rest. Idaan loved him. She had had her own father killed. Maati had been right, all this time. It was his duty to tell what he knew, but he couldn't. It was possible—she might have tricked him all along. He felt as cracked as river ice when a stone had been dropped through it, jagged fissures cut through him in all directions. There was no center of peace within him.

And yet he must have drifted off, because the storm pulled him awake. Cehmai stumbled out of bed, pulling down half his netting with a soft ripping sound. He crawled to the corridor almost before he understood that the pitching and moaning, the shrieking and the nausea were all in the private space behind his eyes. It had never been so powerful.

He fell as he went to the front of the house, barking his knee against the wall. The thick carpets were sickening to touch, the fibers seeming to writhe under his fingers like dry worms. Stone-Made-Soft sat at the gaming table. The white marble, the black basalt. A single white stone was shifted out of its beginning line.

"Not now," Cehmai croaked.

"Now," the andat said, its voice loud and low and undeniable.

The room pitched and spun. Cehmai dragged himself to the table and tried to focus on the pieces. The game was simple enough. He'd played it a thousand times. He shifted a black stone forward. He felt he was still half dreaming. The stone he'd moved was Idaan. Stone-Made-Soft's reply moved a token that was both its fourth column and also Otah Machi. Groggy with sleep and distress and annoyance and the angry pressure of the andat struggling against him, he didn't understand how far things had gone until twelve moves later when he shifted a black stone one place to the left, and Stone-Made-Soft smiled.

"Maybe she'll still love you afterwards," the andat said. "Do you think she'll care as much about your love when you're just a man in a brown robe?"

Cehmai looked at the stones, the shifting line of them, flowing and sinuous as a river, and he saw his mistake. Stone-Made-Soft pushed a white stone forward and the storm in Cehmai's mind redoubled. He could hear his own breath rattling. He was sticky with the rancid sweat of effort and fear. He was losing. He couldn't make himself think, controlling his own mind was like wrestling a beast—something large and angry and stronger than he was. In his confusion, Idaan and Adrah and the death of the Khai all seemed connected to the tokens glowing on the board. Each was enmeshed with the others, and all of them were lost. He could feel the andat pressing toward freedom and oblivion. All the generations of carrying it, gone because of him.

"It's your move," the andat said.

"I can't," Cehmai said. His own voice sounded distant.

"I can wait as long as you care to," it said. "Just tell me when you think it'll get easier."

"You knew this would happen," Cehmai said. "You knew."

"Chaos has a smell to it," the andat agreed. "Move."

Cehmai tried to study the board, but every line he could see led to failure. He closed his eyes and rubbed them until ghosts bloomed in the darkness, but when he reopened them, it was no better. The sickness grew in his belly. He felt he was falling. The knock on the door behind him was something of a different world, a memory from some other life, until the voice came.

"I know you're in there! You won't believe what's happened. Half the ut-khaiem are spotty with welts. Open the door!"

"Baarath!"

Cehmai didn't know how loud he'd called—it might have been a whisper or a scream. But it was enough. The librarian appeared beside him. The stout man's eyes were wide, his lips thin.

"What's wrong?" Baarath asked. "Are you sick? Gods, Cehmai. . . . Stay here. Don't move. I'll have a physician—"

"Paper. Bring me paper. And ink."

"It's your *move*!" the andat shouted, and Baarath seemed about to bolt.

"Hurry," Cehmai said.

It was a week, a month, a year of struggle before the paper and ink brick appeared at his side. He could no longer tell whether the andat was shouting to him in the real world or only within their shared mind. The game pulled at him, sucking like a whirlpool. The stones shifted with significance beyond their own, and confusion built on confusion in waves so that Cehmai grasped his one thought until it was a certainty.

There was too much. There was more than he could survive. The only choice was to simplify the panoply of conflicts warring within him; there wasn't room for them all. He had to fix things, and if he couldn't make them right, he could at least make them end.

He didn't let himself feel the sorrow or the horror or the guilt as he scratched out a note—brief and clear as he could manage. The letters were shaky, the grammar poor. Idaan and the Vaunyogi and the Galts. Everything he knew written in short, unadorned phrases. He dropped the pen to the floor and pressed the paper into Baarath's hand.

"Maati," Cehmai said. "Take it to Maati. Now."

Baarath read the letter, and whatever blood had remained in his face drained from it now.

"This . . . this isn't . . ."

"Run!" Cehmai screamed, and Baarath was off, faster than Cehmai could have gone if he'd tried, Idaan's doom in his hands. Cehmai closed his eyes. That was over, then. That was decided, and for good or ill, he was committed. The stones now could be only stones.

He pulled himself back to the game board. Stone-Made-Soft had gone silent again. The storm was as fierce as it had ever been, but Cehmai found he also had some greater degree of strength against it. He forced himself along every line he could imagine, shifting the stones in his mind until at last he pushed one black token forward. Stone-Made-Soft didn't pause. It shifted a white stone behind the black that had just moved, trapping it. Cehmai took a long deep breath and shifted a black stone on the far end of the board back one space.

The andat stretched out its wide fingers, then paused. The storm shifted, lessened. Stone-Made-Soft smiled ruefully and pulled back its hand. The wide brow furrowed.

"Good sacrifice," it said.

Cehmai leaned back. His body was shuddering with exhaustion and effort and perhaps something else more to do with Baarath running through the night. The andat moved a piece forward. It was the obvious move, but it was doomed. They had to play it out, but the game was as good as finished. Cehmai moved a black token.

"I think she does love you," the andat said. "And you did swear you'd protect her."

"She killed two men and plotted her own father's slaughter," Cehmai said.

"You love her. I know you do."

"I know it too," Cehmai said, and then a long moment later. "It's your move."

14

Rain came in from the south. By midmorning tall clouds of billowing white and yellow and gray had filled the wide sky of the valley. When the sun, had it been visible, would have reached the top of its arc, the rain poured down on the city like an upended bucket. The black cobbled streets were brooks, every slant roof a little waterfall. Maati sat in the side room of the teahouse and watched. The water seemed lighter than the sky or the stone—alive and hopeful. It chilled the air, making the warmth of the earthenware bowl in his hands more present. Across the smooth wooden table, Otah-kvo's chief armsman scratched at the angry red weals on his wrists.

"If you keep doing that, they'll never heal," Maati said.

"Thank you, grandmother," Sinja said. "I had an arrow through my arm once that hurt less than this."

"It's no worse than what half the people in that hall suffered," Maati said.

"It's a thousand times worse. Those stings are on them. These are on me. I'd have thought the difference obvious."

Maati smiled. It had taken three days to get all the insects out of the great hall, and the argument about whether to simply choose a new venue or wait for the last nervous slave to find and crush the last dying wasp would easily have gone on longer than the problem itself. The time had been precious. Sinja scratched again, winced, and pressed his hands flat against the table, as if he could pin them there and not rely on his own will to control himself.

"I hear you've had another letter from the Dai-kvo," Sinja said.

Maati pursed his lips. The pages were in his sleeve even now. They'd arrived in the night by a special courier who was waiting in apartments Maati had bullied out of the servants of the dead Khai. The message included an order to respond at once and commit his reply to the courier. He hadn't picked up a pen yet. He wasn't sure what he wanted to say.

"He ordered you back?" Sinja asked.

"Among other things," Maati agreed. "Apparently he's been getting information from someone in the city besides myself."

"The other one? The boy?"

"Cehmai you mean? No. One of the houses that the Galts bought, I'd guess. But I don't know which. It doesn't matter. He'll know the truth soon enough."

"If you say so."

A bolt of lightning flashed and a half breath later, thunder rolled through the thick air. Maati raised the bowl to his lips. The tea was smoky and sweet, and it did nothing to unknot his guts. Sinja leaned toward the window, his eyes suddenly bright. Maati followed his gaze. Three figures leaned into the slanting rain—one a thick man with a slight limp, the others clearly servants holding a canopy over the first in a vain attempt to keep their master from being soaked to the skin. All wore cloaks with deep hoods that hid their faces.

"Is that him?" Sinja asked.

"I think so," Maati said. "Go. Get ready."

Sinja vanished and Maati refilled his bowl of tea. It was only moments before the door to the private room opened again and Porsha Radaani came into the room. His hair was plastered back against his skull, and his rich, ornately embroidered robes were dark and heavy with water. Maati rose and took a pose of welcome. Radaani ignored it, pulled out the chair Sinja had only recently left, and sat in it with a grunt.

"I'm sorry for the foul weather," Maati said. "I'd thought you'd take the tunnels."

Radaani made an impatient sound.

"They're half flooded. The city was designed with snow in mind, not water. The first thaw's always like a little slice of hell in the spring. But tell me you didn't bring me here to talk about rain, Maati-cha. I'm a busy man. The council's just about pulled itself back together, and I'd like to see an end to this nonsense."

"That's what I wanted to speak to you about, Porsha-cha. I'd like you to call for the council to disband. You're well respected. If you were to adopt the position, the lower families would take interest. And the Vaunani and Kamau can both work with you without having to work with each other."

"I'm a powerful enough man to do that," Radaani agreed, his tone matter-of-fact. "But I can't think why I would."

"There's no reason for the council to be called."

"No reason? We're short a Khai, Maati-cha."

"The last one left a son to take his place," Maati said. "No one in that hall has a legitimate claim to the name Khai Machi."

Radaani laced his thick fingers over his belly and narrowed his eyes. A smile touched his lips that might have meant anything.

"I think you have some things to tell me," he said.

Maati began not with his own investigation, but with the story as it had unfolded. Idaan Machi and Adrah Vaunyogi, the backing of the Galts, the murder of Biitrah Machi. He told it like a tale, and found it was easier than he'd expected. Radaani chuckled when he reached the night of Otah's escape and grew somber when he drew the connection between the murder of Danat Machi and the hunting party that had gone with him. It was all true, but it was not all of the truth. In the long conversations that had followed Baarath's delivery of Cehmai's letter, Otah and Maati, Kiyan and Amiit had all agreed that the Galts' interest in the library was something that could be safely neglected. It added nothing to their story, and knowing more than they seemed to might yet prove an advantage. Watching Porsha Radaani's eyes, Maati thought it had been the right decision.

He outlined what he wanted of the Radaani—the timing of the proposal to disband, the manner in which it would be best approached, the support they would need on the council. Radaani listened like a cat watching a pigeon until the whole proposal was laid out before him. He coughed and loosened the belt of his robe.

"It's a pretty story," Radaani said. "It'll play well to a crowd. But you'll need more than this to convince the utkhaiem that your friend's hem isn't red. We're all quite pleased to have a Khai who's walked through his brothers' blood, but fathers are a different thing."

"I'm not the only one to tell it," Maati said. "I have one of the hunting party who watched Danat die to swear there was no sign of an ambush. I have the commander who collected Otah from the tower to say what he was bought to do and by whom. I have Cehmai Tyan and Stone-Made-Soft. And I have them in the next room if you'd like to speak with them."

"Really?" Radaani leaned forward. The chair groaned under his weight.

"And if it's needed, I have a list of all the houses and families who've supported Vaunyogi. If it's a question what their relationships are with Galt, all we have to do is open those contracts and judge the terms. Though there may be some of them who would rather that didn't happen. So perhaps it won't be necessary."

Radaani chuckled again, a deep, wet sound. He rubbed his fingers against his thumbs, pinching the air.

"You've been busy since last we spoke," he said.

"It isn't hard finding confirmation once you know what the truth is. Would you like to speak to the men? You can ask them whatever you like. They'll back what I've said."

"Is he here himself?"

"Otah thought it might be better not to attend. Until he knew whether you intended to help him or have him killed."

"He's wise. Just the poet, then," Radaani said. "The others don't matter."

Maati nodded and left the room. The teahouse proper was a wide, low room with fires burning low in two corners. Radaani's servants were drinking something that Maati doubted was only tea and talking with one of the couriers of House Siyanti. There would be more information from that, he guessed, than from the more formal meeting. At the door to the back room, Sinja leaned back in a chair looking bored but commanding a view of every approach.

"Well?" Sinja asked.

"He'd like to speak with Cehmai-cha."

"But not the others?"

"Apparently not."

"He doesn't care if it's true, then. Just whether the poets are backing our man," Sinja let his chair down and stood, stretching. "The forms of power are fascinating stuff. Reminds me why I started fighting for a living."

Maati opened the door. The back room was quieter, though the rush of rain was everywhere. Cehmai and the andat were sitting by the fire. The huntsman Sinja-cha had tracked down was at a small table, half drunk. It was best, perhaps, that Radaani hadn't wanted him. And three armsmen in the colors of House Siyanti also lounged about. Cehmai looked up, meeting Maati's gaze. Maati nodded.

Radaadni's expression when Cehmai and Stone-Made-Soft entered the room was profoundly satisfied. It was as if the young poet's presence answered all the questions that were important to ask. Still, Maati watched Cehmai take a pose of greeting and Radaani return it.

"You wished to speak with me," Cehmai asked. His voice was low and tired. Maati could see how much this moment was costing him.

"Your fellow poet here's told me quite a tale," Radaani said. "He says that Otah Machi's not dead, and that Idaan Machi's the one who arranged her family's death."

"That's so," Cehmai agreed.

"I see. And you were the one who brought that to light?"

"That's so."

Radaani paused, his lips pursed, his fingers knotted around each other.

"Does the Dai-kvo back the upstart, then?"

"No," Maati said before Cehmai could speak. "We take no side in this. We support the council's decision, but that doesn't mean we withhold the truth from the utkhaiem."

"As Maati-kvo says," Cehmai agreed. "We are servants here."

"Servants with the world by its balls," Radaani said. "It's easy, Cehmai-cha, to support a position in a side room with no one much around to hear you. It's a harder thing to say the same words in front of the gods and the court and the world in general. If I take this to the council and you decide that perhaps it wasn't all quite what you've said it was, it will go badly for me."

"I'll tell what I know," Cehmai said. "Whoever asks."

"Well," Radaani said, then more than half to himself, "Well well well."

In the pause that followed, another roll of thunder rattled the shutters. But Porsha Radaani's smile had faded into something less amused, more serious. We have him, Maati thought. Radaani clapped his hands on his thighs and stood.

"I have some conversations I'll have to conduct, Maati-cha," he said. "You understand that I'm taking a great personal risk doing this? Me and my family both."

"And I know that Otah-kvo will appreciate that," Maati said. "In my experience, he has always been good to his friends."

"That's best," Radaani said. "After this, I expect he'll have about two of them. Just so long as he remembers what he owes me."

"He will. And so will the Kamau and the Vaunani. And I imagine a fair number of your rival families will be getting less favorable terms from the Galts in the future."

"Yes. That had occurred to me too."

Radaani smiled broadly and took a formal pose of leavetaking that included the room and all three of them in it—the two poets, the one spirit. When he was gone, Maati went to the window again. Radaani was walking fast down the street, his servants half-skipping to keep the canopy over him. His limp was almost gone.

Maati closed the shutters.

"He's agreed?" Cehmai asked.

"As near as we can expect. He smells profit in it for himself and disappointment for his rivals. That's the best we can offer, but I think he's pleased enough to do the thing."

"That's good."

Maati sat in the chair Radaani had used, sighing. Cehmai leaned against the table, his arms folded. His mouth was thin, his eyes dark. He looked more than half ill. The andat pulled out the chair beside him and sat with a mild, companionable expression.

"What did the Dai-kvo say?" Cehmai asked. "In the letter?"

"He said I was under no circumstances to take sides in the succession. He repeated that I was to return to his village as soon as possible. He seems to think that by involving myself in all this court intrigue, I may be upsetting the utkhaiem. And then he went into a long commentary about the andat being used in political struggle as the reason that the Empire ate itself."

"He's not wrong," Cehmai said.

"Well, perhaps not. But it's late to undo it."

"You can blame me if you'd like," Cehmai said.

"I think not. I chose what I'd do, and I don't think I chose poorly. If the Dai-kvo disagrees, we can have a conversation about it."

"He'll throw you out," Cehmai said.

Maati thought for a moment of his little cell at the village, of the years spent in minor tasks at the will of the Dai-kvo and the poets senior to himself. Liat had asked him to leave it all a hundred times, and he'd refused. The prospect of failure and disgrace faced him now, and he heard her words, saw her face, and wondered why it had all seemed so wrong when she'd said it and so clear now. Age perhaps. Experience. Some tiny sliver of wisdom that told him that in the balance between the world and a woman, either answer could be right.

"I'm sorry for all this, Cehmai. About Idaan. I know how hard this is for you."

"She picked it. No one made her plot against her family."

"But you love her."

The young poet frowned now, then shrugged.

"Less now than I did two days ago," he said. "Ask again in a month. I'm a poet, after all. There's only so much room in my life. Yes, I loved her. I'll love someone else later. Likely someone that hasn't set herself to kill off her relations."

"It's always like this," Stone-Made-Soft said. "Every one of them. The first love always comes closest. I had hopes for this one. I really did."

"You'll live with the disappointment," Cehmai said.

"Yes," the andat said amiably. "There's always another first girl."

Maati laughed once, amused though it was also unbearably sad. The andat shifted to look at him quizzically. Cehmai's hands took a pose of query. Maati tried to find words to fit his thoughts, surprised by the sense of peace that the prospect of his own failure brought him.

"You're who I was supposed to be, Cehmai-kvo, and you're much better at it. I never did very well."

IDAAN LEANED FORWARD, HER HANDS ON THE RAIL. THE GALLERY BEHIND HER WAS full but restless, the air thick with the scent of their bodies and perfumes.

People shifted in their seats and spoke in low tones, prepared for some new attack, and Idaan had noticed a great fashion for veils that covered the heads and necks of men and women alike that tucked into their robes like netting on a bed. The wasps had done their work, and even if they were gone now, the feeling of uncertainty remained. She took another deep breath and tried to play her role. She was the last blood of her murdered father. She was the bride of Adrah Vaunyogi. Looking down over the council, her part was to remind them of how Adrah's marriage connected him to the old line of the Khaiem.

And yet she felt like nothing so much as an actor, put out to sing a part on stage that she didn't have the range to voice. It had been so recently that she'd stood here, inhabiting this space, owning the air and the hall around her. To-day, everything was the same—the families of the utkhaiem arrayed at their tables, the leaves-in-wind whispering from the galleries, the feeling of eyes turned toward her. But it wasn't working. The air itself seemed different, and she couldn't begin to say why.

"The attack leveled against this council must not weaken us," Daaya, her father now, half-shouted. His voice was hoarse and scratched. "We will not be bullied! We will not be turned aside! When these vandals tried to make mock-ery of the powers of the utkhaiem, we were preparing to consider my son, the honorable Adrah Vaunyogi, as the proper man to take the place of our la-mented Khai. And to that matter we must return."

Applause filled the air, and Idaan smiled sweetly. She wondered how many of the people now present had heard her cry out Cehmai's name in her panic. Those that hadn't had no doubt heard it from other lips. She had kept clear of the poet's house since then, but there hadn't been a moment her heart hadn't longed toward it. He would understand, she told herself. He would forgive her absence once this was all finished. All would be well.

And yet, when Adrah looked up to her, when their gaze met, it was like looking at a stranger. He was beautiful: his hair fresh cut, his robes of jeweled silk. He was her husband, and she no longer knew him.

Daaya stepped down, glittering, and Adaut Kamau rose. If, as the gossip-mongers had told, the wasps had been meant to keep old Kamau silent that day, this would be the moment when something more should follow. The gal-leries became suddenly quiet as the old man stepped to the stage. Even from across the hall, Idaan could see the red weal on his face where the sting had marked him.

"I had intended," he said, "to speak in support of Ghiah Vaunani in his urg-ing of caution and against hasty decision. Since that time, however, my posi-tion has changed, and I would like to invite my old, dear friend Porsha Radaani to address the council."

With nothing more than that, old Kamau stepped down. Idaan leaned for-ward, looking for the green and gray robes of the Radaani. And there, moving between the tables, was the man striding toward the speaker's dais. Adrah and his father were bent together, speaking swiftly and softly. Idaan strained to hear something of what they said. She didn't notice how tight she was holding the rail until her fingers started to ache with it.

Radaani rose up in the speaker's pulpit, looking over the council and the galleries for the space of a half-dozen breaths. His expression was considering, like a man at a fish market judging the freshest catch. Idaan felt her belly tighten. Below her and across the hall, Radaani lifted his arms to the crowd.

"Brothers, we have come here in these solemn times to take the fate of our city into our hands," he intoned, and his voice was rich as cream. "We have suffered tragedy and in the spirit of our ancestors, we rise to overcome it. No one can doubt the nobility of our intentions. And yet the time has come to dissolve this council. There is no call to choose a new Khai Machi when a man with legitimate claim to the chair still lives."

The noise was like a storm. Voices rose and feet stamped. On the council floor, half the families were on their feet, the others sitting with stunned expressions. And yet it was as if it were happening in some other place. Idaan felt the unreality of the moment wash over her. It was a dream. A nightmare.

"I have not stood down!" Radaani shouted. "I have not finished! Yes, an heir lives! And he has the support of my family and my house! Who among you will refuse the son of the Khai Machi his place? Who will side with the traitors and killers that slaughtered his father?"

"Porsha-cha!" one of the men of the council said, loud enough to carry over the clamor. "Explain yourself or step down! You've lost your mind!"

"I'll better that! Brothers, I give my place before you to the son of the Khai and his one surviving heir!"

Had she thought the hall loud before? It was deafening. No one was left seated. Bodies pressed at her back, jostling her against the railing as they craned and stretched for a glimpse of the man entering the chamber. He stood tall and straight, his dark robes with their high collar looking almost priestly. Otah Machi, the upstart, strode into the hall, with the grace and calm of a man who owned it and every man and woman who breathed air.

He's mad, she thought. He's gone mad to come here. They'll tear him apart with their hands. And then she saw behind him the brown robes of a poet— Maati Vaupathai, the envoy of the Dai-kvo. And behind him . . .

Her mouth went dry and her body began to tremble. She shrieked, she screamed, but no one could hear her over the crowd. She couldn't even hear herself. And yet, walking at Maati's side, Cehmai looked up. His face was grim and calm and distant. The poets strode together behind the upstart. And then the armsmen of Radaani and Vaunani, Kamau and Daikani and Saya. Hardly a tenth of the families of the utkhaiem, but still a show of power. The poets alone would have been enough.

She didn't think, couldn't recall pushing back the people around her, she only knew her own intentions when she was over the rail and falling. It wasn't so far to the ground—no more than the height of two men, and yet in the roar and chaos, the drop seemed to last forever. When she struck the floor at last, it jarred her to the bone. Her ankle bloomed with pain. She put it aside and ran as best she could through the stunned men of the utkhaiem. Men all about her, unable to act, unable to move. They were like statues, frozen by their uncertainty and confusion. She knew that she was screaming—she could feel it in her throat, could hear it in her ears. She sounded crazed, but that was unimportant. Her attention was single, focused. The rage that possessed her, that lifted her up and sped her steps by its power alone, was only for the upstart, Otah Machi, who had taken her lover from her.

She saw Adrah and Daaya already on the floor, an armsman kneeling on each back. There was a blade still in Adrah's hand. And then there before her like a fish rising to the surface of a pond was Otah Machi, her brother. She launched herself at him, her hands reaching for him like claws. She didn't see how the andat moved between them; perhaps it had been waiting for her. Its wide, cold body appeared, and she collided with it. Huge hands wrapped her own, and the wide, inhuman face bent close to hers.

"Stop this," it said. "It won't help."

"This isn't right!" she shouted, aware now that the pandemonium had quieted, that her voice could be heard, but she could no more stop herself now than learn to fly. "He swore he'd protect me. He swore it. It's not right!"

"Nothing is," the andat agreed, as it pulled her aside, lifted her as if she was still a child, and pressed her against the wall. She felt herself sinking into it, the stone giving way to her like mud. She fought, but the wide hands were implacable. She shrieked and kicked, sure that the stone would close over her like water, and then she stopped fighting. Let it kill her, let her die.

Let it end.

The hands went away, and Idaan found herself immobile, trapped in stone that had found its solidity again. She could breathe, she could see, she could hear. She opened her mouth to scream, to call for Cehmai. To beg. Stone-Made-Soft put a single finger to her lips.

"It won't help," the andat said again, then turned and lumbered up beside the speaker's pulpit where Cehmai stood waiting for it. She didn't look at her brother as he took the pulpit, only Cehmai. He didn't look back at her. When Otah spoke, his words cut through the air, clean and strong as wine.

"I am Otah Machi, sixth son of the Khai Machi. I have never renounced my claim to this place; I have never killed or plotted to kill my brothers or my father. But I know who has, and I have come here before this council to show you what has been done, and by whom, and to claim what is mine by right."

Idaan closed her eyes and wept, surprised to find her desolation complicated by relief.

"I NOTICE YOU NEVER MENTIONED THE GALTS," AMIIT SAID.

The waiting area to which the protocol servant had led them was open and light, looking out over a garden of flowering vines. A silver bowl with water cooling fresh peaches sat on a low table. Amiit leaned against the railing. He looked calm, but Otah could see the white at the corners of his mouth and the small movements of his hands; Amiit's belly was as much in knots as his own.

"There was no call," Otah said. "The families that were involved know that they were being used, and if they only suspect that I know it, that's almost as good as being sure. How long are we going to have to wait?"

"Until they've finished deciding whether to kill you as a murderer or raise you up as the Khai Machi," Amiit said. "It shouldn't take long. You were very good out there."

"You could sound more sure of all this."

"We'll be fine," Amiit said. "We have backing. We have the poets."

"And yet?"

Amiit forced a chuckle.

"This is why I don't play tiles. Just before the tiles man turns the last chit, I convince myself that there's something I've overlooked."

"I hope you aren't right this time."

"If I am, I won't have to worry about next. They'll kill me as dead as you."

Otah picked up a peach and bit into it. The fuzz made his lips itch, but the taste was sweet and rich and complex. He sighed and looked out. Above the garden wall rose the towers, and beyond them the blue of the sky.

"If we win, you will have to have them killed, you know," Amiit said. "Adrah and his father. Your sister, Idaan."

"Not her."

"Otah-cha, this is going to be hard enough as it stands. The utkhaiem are going to accept you because they have to. But you won't be hailed as a savior. And Kiyan-cha's a common woman from no family. She kept a wayhouse. Showing mercy to the girl who killed your father isn't going to win you anyone's support."

"I am the Khai Machi," Otah said. "I'll make my way."

"You don't understand how complex this is likely to be."

Otah shrugged.

"I trust your advice, Amiit-cha," Otah said. "You'll have to trust my judgment."

The overseer's expression soured for a moment, and then he laughed. They lapsed into silence. It was true. It was early in his career to appear weak, and the Vaunyogi had killed two of his brothers and his father, and had tried to kill Maati as well. And behind them, the Galts. And the library. There had been something in there, some book or scroll or codex worth all those lives, all that money, and the risk. By the time the sun fled behind the mountains in the west, he would know whether he'd have the power to crush their nation, reduce their houses to slag, their cities to ruins. A word to Cehmai would put it in motion. All it would require of him would be to forget that they also had children and lovers, that the people of Galt were as likely as anyone in the cities of the Khaiem to love and betray, lie and dream. And he was having pangs over executing his own father's killer. He took another bite of the peach.

"You've gone quiet," Amiit said softly.

"Thinking about how complex this is likely to be," Otah said.

He finished the last of the peach flesh and threw the stone out into the garden before he washed his hands clean in the water bowl it had come from. A company of armsmen in ceremonial mail appeared at the door with a grim-faced servant in simple black robes.

"Your presence is requested in the council chamber," the servant said.

"I'll see you once it's over," Amiit said.

Otah straightened his robes, took and released a deep breath, and adopted a pose of thanks. The servant turned silently, and Otah followed with armsmen on either side of him and behind. Their pace was solemn.

The halls with their high, arched ceilings and silvered glass, adornments of gold and silver and iron, were empty except for the jingle of mail and the tread of boots. Slowly the murmur of voices and the smells of bodies and lamp oil filled the air. The black-robed servant turned a corner, and a pair of double doors swung open to the council hall. The Master of Tides stood on the speaker's pulpit.

The black lacquer chair reserved for the Khai Machi had been brought, and stood empty on a dais of its own. Otah held himself straight and tall. He strode into the chamber as if his mind were not racing, his heart not conflicted.

He walked to the base of the pulpit and looked up. The Master of Tides was a smaller man than he'd thought, but his voice was strong enough.

"Otah Machi. In recognition of your blood and claim, we of the high families of Machi have chosen to dissolve our council, and cede to you the chair that was your father's."

Otah took a pose of thanks that he realized as he took it was a thousand times too casual for the moment, dropped it, and walked up the dais. Someone in the second gallery high above him began to applaud, and within moments, the air was thick with the sound. Otah sat on the black and uncomfortable chair and looked out. There were thousands of faces, all of them fixed upon him. Old men, young men, children. The highest families of the city and the palace servants. Some were exultant, some stunned. A few, he thought, were dark with anger. He picked out Maati and Cehmai. Even the andat had joined in. The tables at which the Kamau and Vaunani, Radaani and Saya and Daikani all sat were surrounded by cheering men. The table of the Vaunyogi was empty.

They would never all truly believe him innocent. They would never all give him their loyalty. He looked out into their faces and he saw years of his life laid out before him, constrained by necessity and petty expedience. He guessed at the mockery he would endure behind his back while he struggled to learn his new-acquired place. He tried to appear gracious and grave at once, certain he was failing at both.

For this, he thought, I have given up the world.

And then, at the far back of the hall, he caught sight of Kiyan. She, perhaps alone, wasn't applauding him. She only smiled as if amused and perhaps pleased. He felt himself soften. Amid all the meaningless celebration, all the empty delight, she was the single point of stillness. Kiyan was safe, and she was his, and their child would be born into safety and love.

If all the rest was the price for those few things, it was one he would pay.

EPILOG

It was winter when Maati Vaupathai returned to Machi. The days were brief and bitter, the sky often white with a scrim of cloud that faded seamlessly into the horizon. Roads were forgotten; the snow covered road and river and empty field. The sledge dogs ran on the thick glaze of ice wherever the teamsman aimed them. Maati sat on the skidding waxed wood, his arms pulled inside his clothes, the hood of his cloak pulled low and tight to warm the air before he breathed it. He'd been told that he must above all else be careful not to sweat. If his robes got wet, they would freeze, and that would be little better than running naked through the drifts. He had chosen not to make the experiment.

His guide seemed to stop at every wayhouse and low town. Maati learned that the towns had been planned by local farmers and merchants so that no place was more than a day's fast travel from shelter, even on the short days around Candles Night when the darkness was three times as long as the light. When Maati walked up the shallow ramps and through the snow doors, he appreciated their wisdom. A night in the open during a northern winter might not kill someone who had been born and bred there. A northerner would know the secrets of carving snow into shelter and warming the air without drenching himself. He, on the other hand, would simply have died, and so he made certain that his guide and the dogs were well housed and fed. Even so, when the time came to sleep in a bed piled high with blankets and dogs, he often found himself as exhausted from the cold as from a full day's work.

What in summer would have been the journey of weeks took him from just before Candles Night almost halfway to the thaw. The days began to blend together—blazing bright white and then warm, close darkness—until he felt he was traveling through a dream and might wake at any moment.

When at last the dark stone towers of Machi appeared in the distance—lines of ink on a pale parchment—it was difficult to believe. He had lost track of the days. He felt as if he had been traveling forever, or perhaps that he had only just begun. As they drew nearer, he opened his hood despite the stinging air and watched the towers thicken and take form.

He didn't know when they passed over the river. The bridge would have been no more than a rise in the snow, indistinguishable from a random drift.

Still, they must have passed it, because they entered into the city itself. The high snow made the houses seemed shorter. Other dog teams yipped and called, pulled wide sledges filled with boxes or ore or the goods of trade; even the teeth of winter would not stop Machi. Maati even saw men with wide, leather-laced nets on their shoes and goods for sale strapped to their backs tramping down worn paths that led from one house to the next. He heard voices lifted in loud conversation and the barking of dogs and the murmur of the platform chains that rose up with the towers and shifted, scraping against the stone.

The city seemed to have nothing in common with the one he had known, and still there was a beauty to it. It was stark and terrible, and the wide sky forgave it nothing, but he could imagine how someone might boast they lived here in the midst of the desolation and carved out a life worth living. Only the verdigris domes over the forges were free from snow, the fires never slackening enough to bow before the winter.

On the way to the palace of the Khai Machi, his guide passed what had once been the palaces of the Vaunyogi. The broken walls jutted from the snow. He thought he could still make out scorch marks on the stones. There were no bodies now. The Vaunyogi were broken, and those who were not dead had scattered into the world where they would be wise never to mention their true names again. The bones of their house made Maati shiver in a way that had little to do with the biting air. Otah-kvo had done this, or ordered it done. It had been necessary, or so Maati told himself. He couldn't think of another path, and still the ruins disturbed him.

He entered the offices of the Master of Tides through the snow door, tramping up the slick painted wood of the ramp and into rooms he'd known in summer. When he had taken off his outer cloaks and let himself be led to the chamber where the servants of the Khai set schedules, Piyun See, the assistant to the Master of Tides, fell at once into a pose of welcome.

"It's a pleasure to have you back," he said. "The Khai mentioned that we should expect you. But he had thought you might be here earlier."

Though the air in the offices felt warm, the man's breath was still visible. Maati's ideas of cold had changed during his journey.

"The way was slower than I'd hoped," Maati said.

"The most high is in meetings and cannot be disturbed, but he has left us with instructions for your accommodation. . . ."

Maati felt a pang of disappointment. It was naïve of him to expect Otah-kvo to be there to greet him, and yet he had to admit that he had harbored hopes.

"Whatever is most convenient will, I'm sure, suffice," Maati said.

"Don't bother yourself Piyun-cha," a woman's voice said from behind them. "I can see to this."

The changes of the previous months had left Kiyan untransformed. Her hair—black with its lacing of white—was tied back in a simple knot that seemed out of place above the ornate robes of a Khai's wife. Her smile didn't have the chill formal distance or false pleasure of a player at court intrigue. When she embraced him, her hair smelled of lavender oil. For all her position and the incarcerating power of being her husband's wife she would, Maati thought, still look at home at a wayhouse watching over guests or haggling with the farmers, bakers and butchers at the at the market.

But perhaps that was only his own wish that things could change and still be the same.

"You look tired," she said, leading him down a long flight of smooth-worn granite stairs. "How long have you been traveling?"

"I left the Dai-kvo before Candles Night," he said.

"You still dress like a poet," she said, gently. So she knew.

"The Dai-kvo agreed to Otah-kvo's proposal. I'm not formally removed so long as I don't appear in public ceremony in my poet's robes. I'm not permitted to live in a poet's house or present myself in any way as carrying the authority of the Dai-kvo."

"And Cehmai?"

"Cehmai's had some admonishing letters, I think. But I took the worst of it. It was easier that way, and I don't mind so much as I might have when I was younger."

The doors at the stairway's end stood open. They had descended below the level of the street, even under its burden of snow, and the candlelit tunnel before them seemed almost hot. His breath had stopped ghosting.

"I'm sorry for that," Kiyan said, leading the way. "It seems wrong that you should suffer for doing the right thing."

"I'm not suffering," Maati said. "Not as badly as I did when I was in the Dai-kvo's good graces, at least. The more I see of the honors I was offered, the better I feel about having lost them."

She chuckled.

The passageway glowed gold. A high, vaulted arch above them was covered with tiles that reflected the light back into the air where it hung like pollen. An echo of song came from a great distance, the words blurred by the tunnels. And then the melody was joined and the whispering voices of the gods seemed to touch the air. Maati's steps faltered, and Kiyan turned to look at him and then followed his gaze into the air.

"The winter choir," she said. Her voice was suddenly smaller, sharing his awe. "There are a lot of idle hands in the colder seasons. Music becomes more important, I think, when things are cold and dark."

"It's beautiful," Maati said. "I knew there were tunnels, but . . ."

"It's another city," Kiyan said. "Think how I feel. I didn't know half the depth of it until I was supposed to help rule it."

They began walking again, their words rising above the song.

"How is he?"

"Not idle," she said with both amusement and melancholy in her tone. "He's been working until he's half exhausted every day and then getting up early. There's a thousand critical things that he's called on to do, and a thousand more that are nothing more than ceremony that only swallow his time. It makes him cranky. He'll be angry that he wasn't free to meet you, but it will help that I could. That's the best I can do these days. Make sure that the things most important to him are seen to while he's off making sure the city doesn't fall into chaos."

"I'd think it would be able to grind on without him for a time just from habit," Maati said.

"Politics takes all the time you can give it," Kiyan said with distaste.

They walked through a wide gate and into a great subterranean hall. A thousand lanterns glowed, their white light filling the air. Men and women and children passed on their various errands, the gabble of voices like a brook over stones. A beggar sang, his lacquered begging box on the stone floor before him. Maati saw a waterseller's cart, and another vendor selling waxpaper cones of rice and fish. It was almost like a street, almost like a wide pavilion with a canopy of stone.

"Your rooms?" Kiyan asked. "Or would you rather have something to eat first? There's not much fresh this deep into winter, but I've found a woman who makes a hot barley soup that's simply lovely."

"Actually . . . could I meet the child?"

Kiyan's smile seemed to have a light of its own.

"Can you imagine a world where I said no?" she asked.

She nodded to a branching in the wide hall, and led him west, deeper into the underground. The change was subtle, moving from the public space of the street to the private tunnels beneath the palaces. There were gates, it was true, but they were open. There were armsmen here and there, but only a few of them. And yet soon all the people they passed wore the robes of servants or slaves of the Khai, and they had entered the Khai's private domain. Kiyan stopped at a thin oak door, pulled it open and gestured him to follow her up the staircase it revealed.

The nursery was high above the tunnel-world. The air was kept warm by a roaring fire in a stone grate, but the light was from the sun. The nurse, a young girl, no more than sixteen summers, sat dozing in her chair while the baby cooed and gurgled to itself. Maati stepped to the edge of the crib, and the child quieted, staring up at him with distrustful eyes, and then breaking into a wide toothless grin.

"She's only just started sleeping through the night," Kiyan said, speaking softly to keep from waking her servant. "And there were two weeks of colic that were close to hell. I don't know what we'd have done with her if it hadn't been for the nurses. She's been doing better now. We've named her Eiah."

She reached down, scooped up her daughter, and settled her in her arms. It was a movement so natural as to seem inevitable. Maati remembered having done it himself, many years ago, in a very different place. Kiyan seemed almost to know his mind.

"'Tani-kya said that if things went as you'd expected with the Dai-kvo you were thinking of seeking out your son. Nayiit?"

"Nayiit," Maati agreed. "I sent letters to the places I knew to send them, but I haven't heard back yet. I may not. But I'll be here, in one place. If he and his mother want to find me, it won't be difficult."

"I'm sorry," Kiyan said. "Not that it will be easy for them, only that . . ."

Maati only shook his head. In Kiyan's arms, the tiny girl with deep brown eyes grasped at air and gurgled, unaware, he knew, of all the blood and pain and betrayal that had gone into bringing her here.

"She's beautiful," he said.

"BE REASONABLE!"

Cehmai lay back in his bath. Beside him, Stone-Made-Soft had put its feet into the warm water and was gazing placidly out into the thick salt-scented steam that rose from the water and filled the bathhouse. Against the far wall, a group of young women was rising from the pool and walking back toward the dressing rooms, leaving a servant to fish the floating trays with their teapots and bowls from the small, bobbing waves. Baarath slapped the water impatiently.

"You can look at naked girls later," he said. "This is important. If Maati-cha's come back to help me catalog the library . . ."

"He might quibble on 'help you,'" Cehmai said, and might as well have kept silent.

". . . then it's clearly of critical importance to the Dai-kvo. I've heard the rumors. I know the Vaunyogi were looking to sell the library to some Westlands warden. That's why Maati was sent here in the first place."

Cehmai closed his eyes. Rumors and speculation had run wild, and perhaps it would have been a kindness to correct Baarath. But Otah had asked him to keep silent, and the letters from the Dai-kvo had encouraged this strategy. If it were known what the Galts had done, what they had intended to do, it would mean the destruction of their nation: cities drowned, innocent men and women and children starved when a quiet word heavy with threat might suffice instead. There was always recourse to destruction. So long as one poet held one andat, they could find a path to ruin. So instead of slaughtering countless innocents, Cehmai put up with the excited, inaccurate speculation of his old friend and waited for the days to grow longer and warmer.

"If the collection is split," Baraath went on, his voice dropping to a rough whisper, "we might overlook the very thing that made the library so important. You have to move your collection over to the library, or terrible things might happen."

"Terrible things like what?"

"I don't know," Baraath said, his whisper turning peevish. "That's what Maati-cha and I are trying to find out."

"Well, once you've gone through your collection and found nothing, the two of you can come to the poet's house and look through mine."

"That would take years!"

"I'll make sure they're well kept until then," Cehmai said. "Have you spoken with the Khai about his private collection?"

"Who'd want that? It's all copies of contracts and agreements from five generations ago. Unless it's the most obscure etiquette ever to see sunlight. Anyone who wants that, let them have it. You've got all the *good* books. The philosophy, the grammars, the studies of the andat."

"It's a hard life you lead," Cehmai said. "So close and still, no."

"You are an arrogant prig," Baraath said. "Everyone knows it, but I'm the only man in the city with the courage to say it to your face. Arrogant and selfish and small-souled."

"Well, perhaps it's not too much to go over to the library. It isn't as if it was that long a walk."

Baraath's face brightened for a moment, then, as the insincerity of the comment came clear, squeezed as if he'd taken a bite of fresh lemon. With a sound like an angry duck, he rose up and stalked from the baths and into the fog.

"He's a terrible person," the andat said.

"I know. But he's a friend of mine."

"And terrible people need friends as much as good ones do," the andat said, its tone an agreement. "More, perhaps."

"Which of us are you thinking of?"

Stone-Made-Soft didn't speak. Cehmai let the warmth of the water slip into his flesh for a moment longer. Then he too rose, the water sluicing from him, and walked to the dressing rooms. He dried himself with a fresh cloth and found his robes, newly cleaned and dry. The other men in the room spoke among themselves, joked, laughed. Cehmai was more aware than usual of the formal poses with which they greeted him. In this quiet season, there was little work for him, and the days were filled with music and singing, gatherings organized by the young men and women of the utkhaiem. But all the cakes tasted slightly of ashes, and the brightest songs seemed tinny and false. Somewhere in the city, under her brother's watchful eye, the woman he'd sworn to protect was locked away. He adjusted his robes in the mirror, smiled as if trying the expression like a party mask, and for the thousandth time noticed the weight of his decision.

He left the bathhouse, following a broad, low tunnel to the east where it would join a larger passage, one of the midwinter roads, which in turn ran beneath the trees outside the poet's house before it broke into a thousand maze-like corridors running under the old city. Along the length of the passage, men and women stood or sat, some talking, some singing. An old man, his dog lying at his feet, sold bread and sausages from a hand cart. The girls he'd seen in the bathhouse had been joined by young men, joking and posing in the timeless rituals of courtship. Stone-Made-Soft was kneeling by the wall, looking out over all of it, silently judging what it would take to bring the roof down and bury them all. Cehmai reached out with his will and tugged at the andat. Still smiling, Stone-Made-Soft rose and ambled over.

"I think the one on the far left was hoping to meet you," it said, gesturing to the knot of young men and women as it drew near. "She was watching you all the time we were in the baths."

"Perhaps it was Baraath she was looking at," Cehmai said.

"You think so?" the andat said. "I suppose he's a decent looking man. And many women are overcome by the romance of the librarian. No doubt you're right."

"Don't," Cehmai said. "I don't want to play that game again."

Something like real sympathy showed in the andat's wide face. The struggle at the back of Cehmai's mind neither worsened nor diminished as Stone-Made-Soft's broad hand reached out to rest on his shoulder.

"Enough," it said. "You did what you had to do, and whipping yourself now won't help you or her. Let's go meet that girl. Talk to her. We can find someone selling sweetcakes. Otherwise we'll only go back to the rooms and sulk away another night."

Cehmai looked over, and indeed, the girl farthest to the left—her long, dark hair unbound, her robes well cut and the green of jade—caught his eyes, and blushing, looked away. He had seen her before, he realized. She was beautiful, and he did not know her name.

"Perhaps another day," he said.

"There are only so many other days," the andat said, its voice low and gentle. "I may go on for generations, but you little men rise and fall with the seasons. Stop biting yourself. It's been months."

"One more day. I'll bite myself for one more day at least," Cehmai said. "Come on."

The andat sighed and dropped its hand to its side. Cehmai turned east, walking into the dim tunnels. He felt the temptation to look back, to see whether the girl was watching his departure and if she was, what expression she wore. He kept his eyes on the path before him and the moment passed.

THE KHAI MACHI HAD NO OTHER NAME NOW THAT HE HAD TAKEN HIS FATHER'S office. It had been stripped from him in formal ceremony. He had renounced

it and sworn before the gods and the Emperor that he would be nothing beyond this trust with which he had been charged. Otah had forced his way
through the ceremony, bristling at both the waste of time and the institutional
requirement that he lie in order to preserve etiquette. Of Itani Noygu, Otah
Machi, and the Khai Machi, the last was the one least in his heart. But he was
willing to pretend to have no other self and the utkhaiem and the priests and
the people of the city were all willing to pretend to believe him. It was all like
some incredibly long, awkward, tedious game. And so when the rare occasion
arose when he could do something real, something with consequences, he
found himself enjoying it more perhaps than it deserved.

The emissary from Galt looked as if he were trying to convince himself
he'd misunderstood.

"Most high," he said, "I came here as soon as our ambassadors sent word
that they'd been expelled. It was a long journey, and winter travel's difficult in
the north. I had hoped that we could address your concerns and . . ."

Otah took a pose that commanded silence, then sat back on the black lacquer chair that had grown no more comfortable in the months since he'd first
taken it. He switched from speaking in the Khaiate tongue to Galtic. It
seemed, if anything, to make the man more uncomfortable.

"I appreciate that the generals and lords of Galt are so interested in . . .
what? Addressing my concerns? And I thank you for coming so quickly, even
when I'd made it clear that you were not particularly welcome."

"I apologize, most high, if I've given offense."

"Not at all," Otah said, smiling. "Since you've come, you can do me the favor of explaining *again* to the High Council how precarious their position is
with me. The Dai-kvo has been alerted to all I've learned, and he shares my
opinion and my policy."

"But I—"

"I know the role your people played in the succession. And more than that,
I know what happened in Saraykeht. Your nation survives now on my suffer-
ance. If word reaches me of one more intervention in the matters of the cities
of the Khaiem or the poets or the andat, I will wipe your people from the
memory of the world."

The emissary opened his mouth and closed it again, his eyes darting about
as if there was a word written somewhere on the walls that would open the
floodgates of his diplomacy. Otah let the silence press at him.

"I don't understand, most high," he managed at last.

"Then go home," Otah said, "and repeat what I've told you to your overseer
and then to his, and keep doing so until you find someone who does. If you
reach the High Council, you'll have gone far enough."

"I'm sure if you'll just tell me what's happened to upset you, most high,
there must be something I can do to make it right."

Otah pressed his steepled fingers to his lips. For a moment, he remembered Saraykeht—the feel of the poet's death struggles under his own hand. He remembered the fires that had consumed the compound of the Vaunyogi and the screams and cries of his sister as her husband and his father met their ends.

"You can't make this right," he said, letting his weariness show in his voice. "I wish that you could."

"But the contracts . . . I can't go back without some agreement made, most high. If you want me to take your message back, you have to leave me enough credibility that anyone will hear it."

"I can't help you," Otah said. "Take the letter I've given you and go home. Now."

As he turned and left the room, the letter in his hand sewn shut and sealed, the Galt moved like a man newly awakened. At Otah's gesture, the servants followed the emissary and pulled the great bronze doors closed behind them, leaving him alone in the audience chamber. The pale silk banners shifted in the slight breath of air. The charcoal in the iron braziers glowed, orange within white. He pressed his hands to his eyes. He was tired, terribly tired. And there was so much more to be done.

He heard the scrape of the servant's door behind him, heard the soft, careful footsteps and the faintest jingling of mail. He rose and turned, his robes shifting with a sound like sand on stone. Sinja took a pose of greeting.

"You sent for me, most high?"

"I've just sent the Galts packing again," Otah said.

"I heard the last of it. Do you think they'll keep sending men to bow and scrape at your feet? I was thinking how gratifying it must be, being able to bully a whole nation of people you've never met."

"Actually, it isn't. I imagine news of it will have spread through the city by nightfall. More stories of the Mad Khai."

"You aren't called that. Upstart's still the most common. After the wedding, there was a week or so of calling you the shopkeeper's wife, but I think it was too long. An insult can only sustain a certain number of syllables."

"Thank you," Otah said. "I feel much better now."

"You are going to have to start caring what they think, you know. These are people you're going to be living with for the rest of your life. Starting off by proving how disrespectful and independent you can be is only going to make things harder. And the Galts carry quite a few contracts," Sinja said. "Are you sure you want me away just now? It's traditional to have a guard close at hand when you're cultivating new enemies."

"Yes, I want you to go. If the utkhaiem are talking about the Galts, they may talk less about Idaan."

"You know they won't forget her. It doesn't matter what other issues you wave at them, they'll come back to her."

"I know. But it's the best I can do for now. Are you ready?"

"I have everything I need prepared. We can do it now if you'd like."

"I would."

THREE ROOMS HAD BEEN HER WORLD. A NARROW BED, A CHEAP IRON BRAZIER, A night pot taken away every second day. The armsmen brought her bits of candle—stubs left over from around the palaces. Once, someone had slipped a book in with her meal—a cheap translation of Westland court poems. Still, she'd read them all and even started composing some of her own. It galled her to be grateful for such small kindnesses, especially when she knew they would not have been extended to her had she been a man.

The only breaks came when she was taken out to walk down empty tunnels, deep under the palaces. Armsmen paced behind her and before her, as if she were dangerous. And her mind slowly folded in on itself, the days passing into weeks, the ankle she'd cracked in her fall mending. Some days she felt lost in dreams, struggling to wake only to wish herself back asleep when her mind came clear. She sang to herself. She spoke to Adrah as if he were still there, still alive. As if he still loved her. She raged at Cehmai or bedded him or begged his forgiveness. All on her narrow bed, by the light of candle stubs.

She woke to the sound of the bolt sliding open. She didn't think it was time to be fed or walked, but time had become a strange thing lately. When the door opened and the man in the black and silver robes of the Khai stepped in she told herself she was dreaming, half fearing he had come to kill her at last, and half hoping for it.

The Khai Machi looked around the cell. His smile seemed forced.

"You might not think it, but I've lived in worse," he said.

"Is that supposed to comfort me?"

"No," he said.

A second man entered the room, a thick bundle under his arm. A soldier, by his stance and by the mail that he wore under his robes. Idaan sat up, gathering herself, preparing for whatever came and desperate that the men not turn and close the door again behind them. The Khai Machi hitched up his robes and squatted, his back against the stone wall as if he was a laborer at rest between tasks. His long face was very much like Biitrah's, she saw. It was in the corners of his eyes and the shape of his jaw.

"Sister," he said.

"Most high," she replied.

He shook his head. The soldier shifted. She had the feeling that the two movements were the continuation of some conversation they had had, a subtle commentary to which she was not privileged.

"This is Sinja-cha," the Khai said. "You'll do as he says. If you fight him, he'll kill you. If you try to leave him before he gives you permission, he'll kill you."

"Are you whoring me to your pet thug then?" she asked, fighting to keep the quaver from her voice.

"What? No. Gods," Otah said. "No, I'm sending you into exile. He's to take you as far as Cetani. He'll leave you there with a good robe and a few lengths of silver. You can write. You have numbers. You'll be able to find some work, I expect."

"I am a daughter of the Khaiem," she said bitterly. "I'm not permitted to work."

"So lie," Otah said. "Pick a new name. Noygu always worked fairly well for me. You could be Sian Noygu. Your mother and father were merchants in . . . well, call it Udun. You don't want people thinking about Machi if you can help it. They died in a plague. Or a fire. Or bandits killed them. It isn't as if you don't know how to lie. Invent something."

Idaan stood, something like hope in her heart. To leave this hole. To leave this city and this life. To become someone else. She hadn't understood how weary and exhausted she had become until this moment. She had thought the cell was her prison.

The soldier looked at her with perfectly empty eyes. She might have been a cow or a large stone he'd been set to move. Otah levered himself back to standing.

"You can't mean this," Idaan said, her voice hardly a whisper. "I killed Danat. I as much as killed our father,"

"I didn't know them," her brother said. "I certainly didn't love them."

"I did."

"All the worse for you, then."

She looked into his eyes for the first time. There was a pain in them that she couldn't fathom.

"I tried to kill you."

"You won't do it again. I've killed and lived with it. I've been given mercy I didn't deserve. Sometimes that I didn't want. So you see, we may not be all that different, sister." He went silent for a moment, then, "Of course if you come back, or I find you conspiring against me—"

"I wouldn't come back here if they begged me," she said. "This city is ashes to me."

Her brother smiled and nodded as much to himself as to her.

"Sinja?" he said.

The soldier tossed the bundle to her. It was a leather traveler's cloak lined with wool and thick silk robes and leggings wrapped around heavy boots. She was appalled at how heavy they were, at how weak she'd become. Her brother ducked out of the room, leaving only the two of them. The soldier nodded to the robes in her arms.

"Best change into those quickly, Idaan-cha," he said. "I've got a sledge and team waiting, but it's an unpleasant winter out there, and I want to make the first low town before dark."

"This is madness," she said.

The soldier took a pose of agreement.

"He's making quite a few bad decisions," he said. "He's new at this, though. He'll get better."

Idaan stripped under the soldier's impassive gaze and pulled on the robes and the leggings, the cloak, the boots. She stepped out of her cell with the feeling of having shed her skin. She didn't understand how much those walls had become everything to her until she stepped out the last door and into the blasting cold and limitless white. For a moment, it was too much. The world was too huge and too open, and she was too small to survive even the sight of it. She wasn't conscious of shrinking back from it until the soldier touched her arm.

"The sledge is this way," he said.

Idaan stumbled, her boots new and awkward, her legs unaccustomed to the slick ice on the snow. But she followed.

THE CHAINS WERE FROZEN TO THE TOWER, THE LIFTING MECHANISM BRITTLE WITH cold. The only way was to walk, but Otah found he was much stronger than he had been when they'd marched him up the tower before, and the effort of it kept him warm. The air was bitterly cold; there weren't enough braziers in the city to keep the towers heated in winter. The floors he passed were filled with crates of food, bins of grains and dried fruits, smoked fish and meats. Supplies for the months until summer came again, and the city could forget for a while what the winter had been.

Back in the palaces, Kiyan was waiting for him. And Maati. They were to meet and talk over the strategies for searching the library. And other things, he supposed. And there was a petition from the silversmiths to reduce the tax paid to the city on work that was sold in the nearby low towns. And the head of the Saya wanted to discuss a proper match for his daughter, with the strong and awkward implication that the Khai Machi might want to consider who his second wife might be. But for now, all the voices were gone, even the ones he loved, and the solitude was sweet.

He stopped a little under two-thirds of the way to the top, his legs aching but his face warm. He wrestled open the inner sky doors and then unlatched and pushed open the outer. The city was splayed out beneath him, dark stone peeking out from under the snow, plumes of smoke rising as always from the forges. To the south, a hundred crows rose from the branches of dead trees, circled briefly, and took their perches again.

And beyond that, to the east, he saw the distant forms he'd come to see: a sledge with a small team and two figures on it, speeding out across the snow-fields. He sat, letting his feet dangle out over the rooftops, and watched until they were only a tiny black mark in the distance. And then as they vanished into the white.

ABOUT THE AUTHOR

Daniel Abraham is the author of the Long Price Quartet: *A Shadow in Summer*, *A Betrayal in Winter*, *An Autumn War*, and *The Price of Spring*. His most recent novel is *The Dragon's Path*. His short fiction has been published in the anthologies *Vanishing Acts*, *Bones of the World*, *The Dark*, and *Logorrhea*, and included in Gardner Dozois's *The Year's Best Science Fiction* and *The Year's Best Fantasy and Horror*, edited by Ellen Datlow, Kelly Link, and Gavin J. Grant as well. His story "Flat Diane" won the International Horror Guild Award for best short story. His novelette "The Cambist and Lord Iron" was runner-up for the Hugo Award. He is also the coauthor of *Hunter's Run* with Gardner Dozois and George R. R. Martin. He lives in New Mexico with his family.